BEFORE THE DEVIL BREAKS YOU

a DIVINERS novel

LIBBA BRAY

ATOM

First published in Great Britain in 2017 by Atom

3 5 7 9 10 8 6 4

Copyright © 2017 by Martha E. Bray

Title page image copyright © Burton Pritzker/Getty Images

"Let America Be America Again" from *The Collected Poems of Langston Hughes* by Langston Hughes, edited by Arnold Rampersad with David Roessel, Associate Editor, copyright © 1994 by the Estate of Langston Hughes. Used by permission of Alfred A. Knopf, an imprint of the Knopf Doubleday Publishing Group, a division of Penguin Random House LLC. All rights reserved.

"Harvest Song" from Cane by Jean Toomer. Copyright 1923 by Boni & Liveright, renewed 1951 by Jean Toomer. Used by permission of Liveright Publishing Corporation.

A CIP catalogue record for this book
is available from the British Library.

ISBN 978-1-9074-1044-4

Printed and bound in Great Britain by Clays Ltd, Elcograf S.p.A.

Papers used by Atom are from well-managed forests
and other responsible sources.

Atom
An imprint of
Little, Brown Book Group
Carmelite House
50 Victoria Embankment
London EC4Y 0DZ
An Hachette UK Company

www.hachette.co.uk
www.atombooks.co.uk

For the truth-tellers

For all the dreams we've dreamed
And all the songs we've sung
And all the hopes we've held
And all the flags we've hung,
The millions who have nothing for our pay—
Except the dream that's almost dead today.

O, let America be America again—
The land that never has been yet—
And yet must be—the land where *every*
    man is free.

—"Let America Be America Again,"
Langston Hughes

PART ONE

PART ONE

ASYLUM

Thick evening fog clung to the forlorn banks of Ward's Island, turning it into a ghost of itself. Across the dark calm of the East River, the glorious neon whirl of Manhattan was in full jazz-age bloom—glamorous clubs, basement speakeasies, illegal booze, all of it enjoyed by live-fast-forget-tomorrow flappers and Dapper Dons eager to throw off their cares and Charleston their way into tomorrow's hangover. On Ward's, it was quiet and dark, just a fat fist of neglected land housing the poor, the addicts, and the mentally ill, all of the city's great unwanted, kept well out of sight, the rivers separating the two worlds—the living and the dead.

Inside the gothic expanse of the Manhattan State Hospital for the Insane, in the common parlor on the third floor of ward A, Conor Flynn sat with his frail arms wrapped around his knobby knees listening to a radio program. It was called the Pears Soap Hour featuring the Sweetheart Seer, and it starred one of those Diviners, a young gifted girl who claimed she could read the secret histories of objects through her touch: *"Now, don't tell me anything about this watch, Mrs. Hempstead. I'll divine its very soul tonight. Just you wait!"*

On Ward's Island, that was called insanity. On the radio, it was called entertainment.

At the piano with the two missing keys, Mr. Potts, a cheery soul who'd murdered his mother at the breakfast table with a hunting knife, now plunked out a tuneless old beer hall song. Sad Mr. Roland worked his jigsaw puzzle with shaking hands. His shirt cuffs slid up, revealing the puckered scars running the width of each wrist. The squeak of a wheelchair announced an arrival to the parlor. Conor looked up to see a nurse wheeling in a newer resident, one of those shell-shocked veterans of the Great War. There were lots of broken men like that in the asylum—fellas who'd gone off to fight but hadn't fully come back. A wool blanket covered the soldier's lower half to disguise the fact that his legs ended at the knees, though Conor didn't know why they should hide it.

"Here we are, Luther. Nice view from here," the nurse said, patting his shoulder. "Bit of fog, but you can still see the river."

Conor glanced toward the barred windows at the bruising sky and the distant steel arch of the Hell Gate Bridge. It would be night soon. Night was when they came.

The thought gave Conor the shivers, so he counted.

"One, two, t'ree, four, five, seven. One, two, t'ree, four..."

Mr. Roland squinted in his direction. It startled Conor and he lost his place. Now he had to start over. He flexed his fingers exactly three times and tapped the tips of his fingers to his forehead and lips, up and down three times, each in rapid succession. Then he counted to seven until it felt right, until the uneasy sentinels on watch inside his mind gave the signal that it was okay to stop. Counting kept him safe. There were rules: Seven was the best number. Threes were good, too, but counting a six was bad. He didn't know why these were the rules, just that they were, and he followed them and had ever since he could remember.

"Evenin', gentlemen!" The night attendant, "Big Mike" Flanagan, strolled into the common parlor, all loose gait and sharp smile. Mike had been a guard at the penitentiary on Welfare Island. He looked at all the patients as if they were guilty of some crime, and he had a habit of doling out his own sentences in secret slaps, trips, and pinches.

"What's the matter, Mr. Roland? You're jumpy tonight."

Mr. Roland glanced over his shoulder toward the windows and the night pressing its ominous thoughts against the barred glass.

"What's out there, then? You expecting something?"

"G-ghosts," Mr. Roland said.

"There's no such thing as ghosts, Mr. Roland."

Mr. Roland reached for a new puzzle piece. "Tell that to Mr. Green."

Big Mike gripped Mr. Roland's shoulder in what might've seemed like a brotherly hold. Mr. Roland's pinched face said it clearly was not. "Whaddaya know about Mr. Green, boyo? Eh? D'ya see what happened? Do you know how he got that razor? Tell me!"

"Told you: ghosts."

Big Mike let go of Mr. Roland's arm. "Aaah, what am I even listening for? You didn't see nuttin'. I'll be as loony as you if I keep it up. You oughta be careful, boyo. Faye talked about the ghosts coming through. Wouldn't shut up about it. So Dr. Simpson took that thought right out of her head." Big Mike tapped the tip of his index finger just above Mr. Roland's left eye. With a meaty paw, he crumbled apart Mr. Roland's hard-won progress on the puzzle. "Lunatic," he huffed, and walked away.

In his head, where dark imaginings often spread their bladed wings, Conor imagined Big Mike's blue eyes widening with surprise, the blood bubbling up at his throat where Conor had taken a razor to it. That was a bad thought, Conor knew. It scared him, and so he counted to seven several times, a penance of numbers, until he could feel safe inside his skin again.

Outside, the wind howled mournfully. By the window, the soldier with the haunted eyes moaned softly and kept his gaze trained on the ceiling. Conor often got feelings about people—who could be trusted, like Mr. Roland, and who was rotten, like Big Mike or Father Hanlon, who was dead now and Conor was glad of it. Conor had a bad feeling about the soldier, too. There were unsettling secrets swirling around him. Someone or something was chasing Luther Clayton.

"The natives are restless," Big Mike joked to one of the nurses. He was standing just outside the common parlor in the long hallway lined with doorways that hid the patients' cramped rooms.

"Oh, you!" the nurse, whose name was Mary, flirted back.

A razor. Blood at Big Mike's throat. An animal eating him down to the bones while he screamed. *One, two, t're, four, five, seven. One, two, t're, four, five, seven.*

"D'you hear old Mrs. Liggett nattering on about ghosts now? Claims they're all over the island, with more coming. 'Course, she also thinks she's a bride and every day's her wedding. Still. Awfully dark out," Big Mike said. "Better let me walk you to your dormitory tonight."

"I might do," Mary said coyly. Her smile disappeared. "Why do you think they've been talking so much about ghosts?"

Big Mike shrugged. "We're in a madhouse, whaddaya expect? Ooh. Stuffy in here, idn't it?"

Big Mike stepped back into the common parlor and cracked open a window.

"D-don't!" Conor yelled. Under the table, his legs shook.

Big Mike scowled. "What's that, boyo?"

"D-don't open it."

"And why not? Stifling in here."

"They can get in," Conor said.

Mary looked worried. "Maybe we shouldn't...."

"Aww, go back to your countin', why don'tcha, Conor?" Big Mike said. "Now, Mary, don't let it bother you...." He took the opportunity to put his arm around the pretty nurse's shoulders.

At the piano, Mr. Potts's fingers stilled for a moment on the sickly keys. Then his quavery voice sang a new song. *"Pack up your troubles in your old kit bag, and smile, smile, smile!"* In his chair, the war vet twitched and whimpered in a way that made the hair on the back of Conor's neck stand at attention.

"What's the use of worrying? It never was worthwhile," Mr. Potts sang, really getting into it now. *"So pack up your troubles in your old kit bag, and smile, smile, smile!"*

Luther Clayton's head whipped in Conor's direction, eyes wide, haunted. "Don't let them in. They belong to *him*!"

And suddenly, Conor understood what had made him so uneasy about the soldier: He *knew*.

Big Mike hurried over to the veteran's chair, Mary following. "Now, now, what's the racket for, eh, Luther?"

"The time is now," Mr. Potts said, resting his hands flat on the tops of his thighs. He stared out the barred windows, one open just a crack, open just enough. And now Conor could see it, too: the odd bluish fog rolling across the dark lawn like a magician's best trick.

They were coming.

"The time is now, the time is now, the time is now," Luther said, his voice escalating.

The door slammed shut. Mary tugged at the handle. "It won't budge!"

"Ring the alarm!" Big Mike called.

The nurse pulled the string. "It isn't working!"

The fog pushed in around the window cracks.

"What in the name of—" Big Mike's voice cut off with a gasp.

The nurse screamed and Conor wanted to cry, wanted to wish it all away, but he didn't dare turn around to look. He was waiting for the lady in his head to tell him what to do.

"*Onetwot'reefourfivesevenonetwot'reefourfiveseven!*"

A curtain came down over Conor's fear. His muscles relaxed. In his head, the lady's voice guided him. *Bear witness.* He picked up the pencil. Behind him, there was the crack of overturned chairs and Big Mike crying, "No! Please, no!" and Mr. Potts screeching like a frightened monkey and Mr. Roland making sounds no human should make. There were the nurse's terrified, pleading screams dying to a gurgle and Luther Clayton shouting, "The time is now!" till his vocal cords strained into hoarseness. Down the long hallway, running footsteps approached, though it was already too late. The tang of fresh blood fouled the air.

"*Onetwot'reefourfiveseven,*" Conor murmured over and over, like a prayer, as he kept drawing.

The fog slipped back through the windows and stretched its arms around the edges of Ward's Island, the lights of the asylum barely visible in the murk. There were terrible things waiting in that fog, Conor knew. And just before the door to the common parlor creaked open of its own accord—*Strange*, they'd say later, as if it had never been locked to begin with—before the alarms and shouting and cries rent the night—*"Oh, sweet Jesus! Oh, dear god!"*—Conor heard the whispers traveling through the fog like current along a telephone line no one uses much:

"*We are the Forgotten, forgotten no more....*"

THE COMING STORM

At five o'clock on a cold February afternoon, Memphis Campbell and his little brother, Isaiah, mounted the steps of the ramshackle Museum of American Folklore, Superstition, and the Occult on West Sixty-eighth Street.

Isaiah peeked into the museum's dusk-dark front windows. "Looks closed. Says it's closed."

Memphis pulled on his brother's arm. "Quit it, now. You'll get arrested for being a Peeping Tom."

"Won't, either. Say, what's a Peeping Tom?"

"Something that gets you arrested," Memphis said, opening the front door.

"You're squawking at me for looking in the windows, and you're just opening the front door and walking in!" Isaiah said, running to catch up.

"It's okay. They're expecting us."

As they traveled the long hallway, Isaiah gawked at the museum's many collections—the poppet dolls, the haunted ventriloquist's dummy, the spirit photographs, and a slate used by mediums in their trances. He stopped in front of a painting of a root worker communing with a trio of wispy ancestors. Spooked, he ran to catch up to his brother.

"I thought we were gonna play ball." Isaiah punched his fist into his catcher's mitt. "You told Aunt Octavia—"

"*Never mind* what I told Octavia. Isaiah, I mean that—don't tell her about this."

Memphis slid open a pair of impressive pocket doors, and he and his brother caught their breath at the majesty of the museum's library. Dark wood shelves stuffed higgledy-piggledy with leather-bound books lined the walls on both the first and second floors. A grand spiral staircase connected the two. High above, a mural stretched across the long expanse of ceiling: houngans, shamans, and witches stood side by side with gray-wigged Founding Fathers against a backdrop of mountains, rivers, forests, and wildlife. America the Supernatural.

"Salutations, Campbell brothers!" a petite blond flapper called from a plump chair where she lay sprawled with her legs dangling over its rolled arm. Evie O'Neill. The radio's famous object reader, the Sweetheart Seer. Evie spread her arms wide to acknowledge the others in the room. "Welcome to our merry festival of freaks."

Memphis smiled nervously at everyone in turn. The museum's faithful assistant, Jericho Jones, nodded from his spot at one of the long oak tables, where he sat with an open book. His large, well-muscled frame dwarfed the chair. Pickpocket Sam Lloyd warmed his hands at the limestone fireplace. "Hiya, fellas!" he called good-naturedly. On the tufted brown sofa, dream walker and spirit conjurer Ling Chan wore a wary expression. She sat very straight, her hands tugging at the hem of her skirt as if she could hide her metal leg braces. Beside Ling, freckled and friendly Henry DuBois IV seemed to be writing a new piece of music in his head, his fingers playing imaginary arpeggios across Ling's crutches, which he cradled against his shoulder. Mabel Rose sat at the same table as Jericho, occasionally stealing glances at him. She had what Memphis's aunt Octavia would call a "wholesome face," which wasn't a comfort to the girls on the receiving end of that euphemism. Mabel wasn't a Diviner. She was the daughter of union organizers, and she spent a lot of her organizing skills on trying to keep her best friend, Evie, out of trouble.

That left only one other person in the room. Theta Knight smiled at Memphis, and his breath caught. "Hey, Poet," she said in her deep purr of a voice. Her sleek black bob gleamed in the warm glow cast by the library's Victorian chandelier. And suddenly, Memphis wasn't thinking about the reason they were all gathered in a musty museum of the occult. He was only thinking about Theta and how much he wanted to be alone with her.

"Evenin', everybody," Memphis said, but his smile, radiant and hopeful, was for Theta.

"Memphis," Isaiah said, nestling closer to his brother.

"This is my brother, Isaiah. Isaiah, meet everybody. Meet the Diviners."

Ling cleared her throat. She nodded toward the mantel clock ticking toward quarter past five. "I thought this meeting was called for five o'clock. They're late."

As if in answer, the library doors slid open, and the museum's director,

Professor William Fitzgerald, entered, trailed by his partner in the paranormal, Dr. Margaret "Sister" Walker.

Will tossed his hat and hung his umbrella on the stuffed grizzly's stiff paw. "I see you're all here. Good," Will said, patting his pockets for his cigarette case.

"Some of us were even on time," Ling muttered under her breath.

"Don't bite yet, *cher*," Henry whispered. "Save it for the finale."

"Good evening, everyone," Sister Walker said, drawing all eyes as she perched on the edge of a leather wingback chair. She sat as still as a queen surveying her subjects and waiting to hand down judgment. Seeing Isaiah, Sister Walker smiled. She had a broad smile, gap-toothed and welcoming. "Hello, Isaiah. My, I think you've grown a foot since I saw you last."

"Two whole inches. Auntie marked it on the wall. Gonna be taller than Memphis soon!" The brightness drained from Isaiah's face. He turned to Memphis in a worried whisper. "I thought Aunt Octavia said we couldn't have nothing to do with Sister."

"Anything to do with," Memphis corrected quietly. "And that's why we have to keep this secret for now, Ice Man."

Sam cleared his throat. "All right, Professor. We've waited long enough to hear this. What in the Sam Hill is going on? And what does it have to do with us?"

Rain spattered against the dusk-painted panes in a steady beat as Will lit a cigarette and pocketed his silver lighter. At last, he turned to the waiting assembly. "Evil has entered our world. A force from beyond. It is spreading across the country, getting worse by the day." Will paused to exhale. "And we are the only means of stopping it."

"Gee. And I was afraid this would be bad news," Henry said after a moment of stunned silence.

"You're talking about the ghosts," Memphis said when he found his voice again.

"Like John Hobbes," Jericho said.

"And Wai-Mae," Ling added quietly.

"And whatever those monsters were down in the subways," Sam said, leaning against the fireplace, arms folded at his chest. "Those things that wanted to eat us."

"They had teeth. Very sharp, very unfortunate teeth. You never think about ghosts having teeth." Evie shuddered. "I never want to think about it again."

"Unfortunately, you will all have to." Will's deep voice filled the space as he paced the same few feet of Persian carpet, his cigarette dropping ash onto the rug. "This museum was built by the railroad tycoon Cornelius T. Rathbone. Cornelius was my benefactor for a time, and also my friend, for a time," Will said with a note of sadness. "He was obsessed with the supernatural and he sank much of his fortune into investigating the mysterious and unexplained. He was particularly interested in Diviners. You see, his own sister, Liberty Anne, was a Diviner."

Evie sagged further into her chair. "Must we have a spooky history lesson, Uncle Will? We already *know* about Liberty Anne."

"Not everyone here knows the story, Evie," Sister Walker chided.

"When Liberty Anne was a little girl, she wandered into the woods and was lost," Will continued. "Two days later, she emerged from that same wood. Her hair had gone snow white. She spoke of meeting a funny man—a man in a tall black hat whose coat opened to show the wonders and frights of the world. She fell into a feverish state between waking and sleeping, speaking prophecy, which Cornelius dutifully recorded in his diary. Some of her future visions were thrilling; others were quite dark." Will pulled hard on his cigarette and exhaled a cloud of smoke. "Just before she died, Liberty Anne warned of a great storm to come—a battle between good and evil, of a time when the Diviners would be needed. That time is now. We believe there is a tear in the world, a crack between our world and another dimension beyond this one," Will said slowly, deliberately. "Our aim is to find out what we can about the man in the hat and the ghosts invading our world so that we can reestablish the balance between natural and supernatural, between the living and the dead—and to do it without causing a public panic."

"Swell!" Sam clapped his hands together. "So, uh, how do we do that?"

"That's what we hope to discover," Will said.

"For a couple of folks who run a museum of the supernatural, you sure don't know much," Theta said.

"We believe by working on strengthening your gifts, individually and as a team, we'll find the answer," Sister Walker added.

"I've spoken to the dead plenty during my dream walks," Ling said. "They ask me to deliver messages to the living. No one has said anything about a coming storm."

"My mother did," Memphis said rather suddenly.

Sister Walker's brow furrowed. "She did? When?"

"It was around the time of the Pentacle Murders, when my power started coming back to me," Memphis explained to the group. "I would sometimes see my mother while I was under a healing trance."

Memphis stopped for a second to catch his breath. He still missed his mother greatly, and he'd never quite forgiven himself for not being able to heal her as she lay dying, riddled with cancer. She'd begged him not to try to heal her—*Let me go, Memphis. You can't bring back what's gone.* It was then that the man in the hat had appeared to Memphis and offered him a bargain if he wanted to see his mother again. Memphis cleared his throat and stared down at his shoes for a second. "Anyway. She, uh, she came to me in a vision and told me that a storm was coming, that we had to be ready for it. Another time, she told me to heal the breach." Memphis shrugged. "I didn't know what she meant by any of it."

Memphis cast a glance Theta's way. She nodded at him, gave him a little smile that he knew meant, *It's okay. I'm here.*

"But Unc—Will. We got rid of Naughty John and Wai-Mae and those things in the subway."

Will took three long strides to the table and grabbed a sheaf of newspaper clippings, holding them aloft. "These are mentions of ghost sightings from newspapers all across the country. These are not isolated incidents. There are hundreds of sightings."

"So how come nobody's talking about it?" Sam asked.

"It's a big country. And not everyone is paying attention as closely as we are," Sister Walker said. "These stories are on the back pages of small-town newspapers. When you talk about seeing ghosts, most people assume you're either crazy or drunk or both. You don't have to disprove someone's claim if you can discredit the person saying it."

Will stubbed his cigarette into an ashtray. "We should be glad that most people aren't paying as close attention as we have been. It gives us time to work, to try to figure out what we're up against before..."

"Before what?" Theta said.

"The last thing we need is a panic. Panic breeds danger."

"How did these ghosts get here?" Isaiah asked, wide-eyed.

"Wait! Let me guess—*you don't know*," Evie said.

"We believe that somehow a door between this world and the next has been wedged open, allowing this new, more powerful ghostly energy to come into our world more freely," Sister Walker explained.

"But there have always been ghosts," Ling said again. "I've spoken to—"

"Not like this," Sister Walker interrupted. "This is a new breed."

"So what's keeping this door open? How did it get left open? And why are these ghosts so powerful?" Ling pressed.

"*We don't know!*" Evie, Sam, and Henry said as one.

"But those are all good questions, Ling," Sister Walker said.

"Say, I've got a question. How about you finally tell us everything about Project Buffalo." Sam fixed his gaze on Will and Sister Walker.

Will sighed and rubbed the bridge of his nose under his glasses. "We've told you," he said wearily. "Project Buffalo was a program of the United States Department of Paranormal aimed at the study, registry, and possible recruitment of Diviners in the event we'd need their help in times of crisis. That's all there is to tell." Will lit another cigarette.

Sam's anger rose. "I can't help wondering why you're both still here but my mother isn't."

"Your mother died of influenza, Sam," Sister Walker said gently. "I'm sorry, but that's the truth."

Then how come I got a postcard from her eight years after her supposed "death"? Sam thought. "Well, if it's the truth, it's the truth." Sam fought to keep the edge out of his voice. He watched Will and Sister Walker carefully, but their expressions gave nothing away.

"There's nothing else to tell about our days in the department," Will said.

"You sure about that?" Sam challenged. "'Cause if we found out you were lying to us for some reason…"

"I'm sure," Will answered with an air of finality. "The important thing is to get to work as soon as possible."

"I have a question," Mabel said. "Where do Jericho, Theta, and I fit into all of this? We're not Diviners."

"Everyone can be helpful in some fashion," Will said. "You three will be our research team. And we might need controls for our experiments from time to time."

Theta's cigarette stopped halfway to her lips. "Controls?"

"Yes. When testing certain powers, for instance. We need people who aren't Diviners," Sister Walker explained. "To gauge the effects."

"Gee, I don't know about that," Theta said.

"You can look through the books and files for stories or histories that might prove helpful," Will said.

"Like Liberty Anne's unholy correspondence?" Jericho suggested.

Ling turned to Henry. "What is that? That doesn't sound good."

"In a letter Cornelius wrote to Will just before he died, he claimed that Liberty Anne's last vision had been too grim to share," Jericho said. "Cornelius called it the unholy correspondence. Whatever it was frightened him so much that he never spoke of it until it was too late."

"Jericho and I tried to find it, but we had no luck," Mabel said, glancing shyly at him.

"Even Sam looked. And he's usually good at finding trouble," Jericho said.

"Haha. The giant made a joke. Hysterical!" Sam's exaggerated, silent laugh ended in an eye roll. "So, that's it? This is our plan? Strengthen our powers for some big ghost fight? Look for this unholy correspondence of Liberty Anne's that might not even exist? Close up this supernatural tear and keep the world from ending. Is that everything?"

"You forgot that these new ghosts might want to kill us," Ling said quietly.

"And that they have teeth," Henry said. "I don't think we can over-emphasize that point."

Isaiah had sidled up to Memphis's side. Memphis put his arm around his brother's shoulders. "It's okay, Ice Man. I won't let anything get you."

Sister Walker left her chair. She bent down to bring her face to Isaiah's, cupping his chin with her fingers. "Are you frightened, Isaiah?"

Isaiah didn't want the others to think he was a baby. But he *was* frightened. He'd seen what that monster had done to their friend Gabriel. He'd had visions and dreams about it before it happened. As much as he wanted to use his powers again—the ones his religious aunt had forbidden him even to think about—he was scared, too, of what he might see. Isaiah gave one quick nod.

Sister Walker put a hand on his shoulder. "You'll be safe, I promise. I know it's not right for us to ask you to keep this from your aunt. I'm sorry about that. But it's very important, Isaiah. It's only for a little while. Can you do that for me? For us?"

Isaiah looked to Memphis.

"That's your decision, Ice Man. I won't make it for you. But if you're coming here with me, we gotta keep it a secret between us. That means not telling nobody. Not Octavia or Uncle Bill."

"Anybody," Isaiah said, thrilled to correct his brother. He bit his lower lip, thinking it over. "Okay."

"Good." Sister Walker rubbed the top of Isaiah's head affectionately. She stood to address the room, towering above Isaiah. She was a tall woman, and in her heels, she was even taller. "We'll meet here at the museum every night at closing time, five o'clock."

The room erupted in protest.

"That's impossible. I have to work in my parents' restaurant," Ling said. "What can I tell them? How can I get to Sixty-eighth Street from Chinatown every day?"

"I'll have to think of some story for Isaiah to get past my aunt," Memphis said. "And I've got two jobs." *And a notebook full of poems to write.*

"The Follies are in rehearsal for a new show," Theta said. "Looking through creepy files won't pay my rent."

"And I've got an aversion to boredom," Sam said.

"This is important. We need all of you here," Will said. "We can't just hope this will all go away—it won't. That's quite clear now. And no one is going to swoop in and save us, either. It's up to us. All of us. We have to figure this out together."

"Fine. But I'll have to work around my radio show," Evie said, reaching for her cloche. "As it is, I'm late to WGI right now."

"Evangeline, I don't think you should continue to do the show," Will said. "We don't understand the forces at work here. You could be drawing evil into our world with each object you read."

"Didn't you just ask me to use my gifts in your merry jazz band of ghost-hunting Diviners?" Evie sputtered.

"That's different."

"*Ohhh, I seeee.* It's perfectly swell for me to read objects and dance with the Devil if it helps you and the museum, but not if it makes me happy. And famous."

"What if your uncle's right?" Ling asked.

"Sure. Why don't you just give up dream walking?" Evie shot back. Anger pooled in her gut. "Will never lets himself think he might be wrong. It's a swell magic trick if you can manage it. Oh, don't worry—I'll help you. But I'm not giving up my show. Nothin' doing. Same old Uncle Will. Only looking out for himself."

"You're one to talk, kid," Sam snapped.

"Says the thief," Jericho said.

Sam smirked. "Pal, I've never pretended I wasn't looking out for myself. And anyway, you should be happy now that the coast is clear." He jerked his head in Evie's direction. Too late, he caught Mabel's pained expression. *Nice going, Lloyd. Great work.* "Applesauce," he muttered, feeling like a real heel.

Everyone began talking at once until Sister Walker's strong voice rose above the squabbling. "'The skies alight with strange fire. The eternal door is opened,'" she read aloud from Liberty Anne's prophecies. "'The Diviners must stand, or all shall fall.'" She shut the book. "Tomorrow. Five o'clock. I'll see you then."

Henry whistled. "And that, in the theater, is what we call an exit line."

Evie bounded up to Mabel, hoping she wasn't too upset by Sam's thoughtless remark. "Hiya, Pie Face," she said with extra *please don't hate me* brightness. "Say, do you want to come to the show with me tonight? There's a pos-i-tute-ly darb party I know about on Beekman Place afterward, and I have the *most scandalous* story to tell you!"

"I can't. I have a meeting," Mabel said, fighting with her coat. She was still smarting from Sam's comment. It wasn't so much that he'd said it as that he was right: Jericho liked Evie, not Mabel. Everyone knew it. It wasn't anybody's fault—people got disappointed all the time. Mabel only wished she could stop liking him.

"Mabesie…" Evie started.

"Please, Evie." Mabel sighed and blinked up at the ceiling. "I forgive you. All right? Honestly, I *do* have a meeting. I'll phone you later."

As the others gathered their coats, Memphis followed Theta into an anteroom off the library. He shut the door, and Theta ran over and wrapped her arms around his neck, kissing him until they both had to break for a breath.

"Pretty spooky stuff in there, huh, Poet?" Theta said, laying her head in the crook of his neck. Memphis could smell her perfume.

"Mm-hmm. Fortunately, I got a cure for that."

Theta raised her face to his, and his breath caught anew at how much space one person could take up inside him. When he looked into her eyes, he saw home. He saw hope. "Yeah?" Theta teased. "Is that a power you're gonna work on with them?"

"Nah. Just you." Memphis kissed Theta then, and for a minute, there were no ghosts or bad prophecies. There was only the world of them.

"Meet me at the Hotsy Totsy after the show tonight?" Memphis asked, touching his forehead to hers.

Theta kissed him once more, long and sweet. "Try and keep me away."

Memphis let Theta leave first. He counted to fifty, and then he walked out, too. Sister Walker was waiting for him when he came into the library again. "Thank you for coming, Memphis. I wasn't sure you would."

"To tell the truth, Sister, I wasn't sure I would, either. But if you can help Isaiah…" Memphis trailed off.

"What do you mean?"

Memphis glanced over at Isaiah, who was happily measuring himself against the giant stuffed grizzly bear whose paws served as a furred coatrack most of the time. "He's still having seizures."

"How often?" Sister Walker asked, concern in her voice.

"Once, sometimes twice a week. It wears him out. Octavia's had her whole prayer circle on it. It's just that…" Memphis cleared his throat and looked down at his hands. "I've been healing him up each time. I didn't know what else to do."

Besides Theta, Isaiah was Memphis's world. He needed Isaiah to get better.

Sister Walker placed a hand on Memphis's shoulder. "You did good. I'm confident that if we can strengthen Isaiah's powers, the seizures will stop."

Memphis wanted to believe she was right.

SECRETS

Sam was waiting for Evie on the front steps. He leaned against the railing, arms crossed, that familiar smirk in place. "Well, if it isn't the *former* future Mrs. Sam Lloyd."

"Don't start with me, Sam," Evie said tersely. "Oh, and I see the *Herald* ran with your story last week." With one gloved hand, Evie blocked out an imaginary headline in the air. "'Wedding Not in the Cards for Sweetheart Seer and Hero-Diviner Sam Lloyd.' Hero-Diviner." Evie rolled her eyes. "And how come *you* got a first and a last name?"

Sam spread his arms in what was supposed to be an apology but most definitely was not. "What can I say? I lead a charmed life. Look, that's all water under the bridge. We've got bigger fish to fry. Bigger than you and me. Can we agree on that?"

"That depends," Evie said, striding toward the sidewalk, Sam on her heels. "Will you be speaking in clichés on the primrose path of our glorious future?"

"Evie."

"Yes. Fine," she answered with a sigh. "Say, why didn't you needle Uncle Will and Sister Walker for more answers about Project Buffalo? They know more than they're telling us."

"Exactly! You play much poker?"

"Not really."

"I can tell. We got us a poker game here. You see how they dodged the question? Like career politicians. They keep playing coy, *we* don't volunteer what we know."

Evie thought it over. "I hate to say it, Sam, but you're making sense. I still think it's odd that I couldn't read those coded punch cards we found. It's almost as if somebody wanted to make sure a Diviner couldn't do it. I know that sounds funny, but that was the feeling I got. Have you had any luck finding that card-reading machine?"

"Not yet. I keep throwing chum on the water, but everybody's spooked. Remember my informant on Project Buffalo?"

"Your creepy man?"

"The same. Fella named Ben Arnold. This was sent to me at the museum, no return address."

Sam handed Evie a small, back-pages newspaper mention of a mysterious death. "He was found dead on an ash heap in Queens. He'd been strangled with piano wire."

Exasperated, Evie handed the article back. "There's no need for me to read it if you're just going to *narrate* the whole thing, Sam."

Evie shoved her hands into her coat pockets and charged down Sixty-eighth Street toward Broadway. Sam kept pace beside her.

"Okay. We gonna have this fight now?" he asked.

Evie kept her eyes straight ahead. "What fight? *I'm* not fighting."

"You're the one who wanted that meshuga phony romance for publicity," Sam reminded her. "I'm just the fella who had the decency to end it."

Evie stopped so fast Sam had to back up.

"Decency? Decency! Says the fella out every night with a different girl! 'Jilted Sam Lloyd Finds Comfort with Chorus Girls! Hard-Hearted Hannah Evie O'Neill Breaks Hero's Heart.' What a lot of hooey!"

Sam leaned against the light post like he owned it. "What do you care? It's not like you want me, right?"

Evie drew in a sharp breath. "I-I...don't care!" she said with a toss of her head. "But it's embarrassing. And you get to be 'poor Sam' while I'm 'fickle Evie.'"

"Give the papers another few weeks, and they'll flip the story to 'Poor Evie, Cad Sam.' What am I supposed to do, sit at home and fog up the bathroom mirror with lonely sighs?"

"Gee, can you do that? That's a swell trick," Evie said sarcastically. "What is it? Why are you making that face?"

"Incredible. You actually worked up a little angry spit in the corner of your mouth *right there*...."

Evie batted Sam's finger away. "Good. It'll make it easier for me to digest you."

They squared off under the street lamp. Over Sam's shoulder, Evie saw Jericho part the drapes at the front window and look down the street to find the source of the commotion. With the light behind him, he was nothing but a shadow, but even his shadow had a pull Evie found hard to ignore.

She tugged at Sam's sleeve. She didn't want Jericho to see them fighting. "Let's keep walking."

When they'd reached the corner of Columbus and Sixty-eighth, Sam stopped, his tone conciliatory. "Listen, doll, we don't have to be best friends. But can we call a truce until we solve the mystery of Project Buffalo? I got a feeling we're getting closer, and the closer we get, the more dangerous it gets. I'd rather have you on my side than against me. Truce?"

He stuck out his hand. Evie had a visceral memory of that hand on her back as they kissed, just the two of them against the world. What had started out as a phony romance had turned far too real before coming painfully apart, leaving wounds on both sides.

"Truce," Evie said on a sigh, and gave Sam's hand a quick shake. "Should we tell the others that we're still looking into Project Buffalo?"

"Not till we find out what's on those cards. For now, it's our secret."

"And Woody's," Evie said apologetically.

Sam's laugh was bitter. "T. S. Woodhouse. How could I forget you told that rat reporter about Project Buffalo? Fine. Let the bum see what he can find. But that's on you. I'm not paying him."

Evie shrugged. "Fine."

There it was: the old battle stations resumed. How long had it taken since the truce—ten seconds? They stood awkwardly on the corner, their breaths coming out in soft wisps. Sam clapped his woolly mitten–clad hands together, his infamous smirk in place.

"Well, this has been fun. I'm headed that way." He pointed toward Central Park. "Plenty of pockets to pick this time of evening."

"Then I'm going the other way. Toward *civilization*."

"Always a *pleasure*, Lamb Chop." Sam saluted angrily and marched toward the park.

"Just remember, Sam Lubovitch Lloyd!" Evie shouted after him.

"What?" Sam called, barely glancing over his shoulder.

Evie's voice rang down the street: "You still owe me twenty bucks!"

On her way to the New Amsterdam Theatre, Theta relived her stolen kiss with Memphis. She knew their love was trouble. All she had to do was keep it a secret long enough to make it from Broadway to the pictures. There was money to be made in pictures. Louise Brooks, Colleen Moore, Clara Bow—they were raking it in. Once Theta made a bundle, it would be Theta and Memphis and Isaiah in a little Hollywood bungalow with a lemon tree in the yard and a dog yipping at their heels. Memphis would be a famous poet, and Theta would be a mysterious movie star. Henry could live right next door. Together, they'd make their own rules. And then they'd go about changing the rules. Was that too much to hope for?

It would be the family she'd always wanted, the family she'd never had. She could finally bury the horrors of her past once and for all. Theta held out her gloved hands. They were fine. Perfectly normal. It was going to be okay.

At the corner of Forty-ninth Street and Broadway, Theta passed a hysterical woman holding tightly to a policeman's arms. "I'm telling you, it was a ghost! I saw it!"

"Now, Miss, it was probably just your eyes playing tricks on you in the dark."

"*It was a ghost! There was a ghost in my bedroom!*" the woman insisted. "Oh, I can't go back in that room now. Never, never!"

Theta clutched her coat collar to her neck and walked faster.

Backstage, the theater was in its usual state of preshow chaos. Costumers ran past with gigantic beaded headdresses needing last-minute touch-ups. A few of the young actors flirted with one another in the wings, where they thought no one could see or judge. Two chorus girls passed a bottle of Listerine back and forth. They gargled the pungent mouthwash and spat it into cups.

"Theta! Where's Theta?"

"In here, Wally," Theta shouted, and the burly stage manager poked his head into the dressing room.

"Congratulations, kid. You've got yourself a screen test with Vitagraph Studios."

Theta whirled around. "Are you pulling my leg, Wally?"

"On the level. Two weeks from tomorrow in Brooklyn. If this goes well, kid, they might send you out to Hollywood to make pictures with the likes of Charlie Chaplin and Eddie Cantor. Then you can go away and stop being such a pain in my neck."

Theta grinned. She kissed Wally's cheek. "I love you, too, Wally."

Wally blushed. "Ten minutes. Get a wiggle on. Flo wants to run through the 'Stardust' number before the show."

At her makeup table, Theta peered into the lighted mirror and applied a swipe of Dorin of Paris rouge to each cheek as she imagined herself on the silver screen, performing stunts alongside Buster Keaton or playing the poor, dying consumptive opposite John Barrymore. The house. The lemon tree. The little dog. Theta and Memphis. It was that much closer. She could feel it.

She just had to get her awful power under control.

Theta lifted the lid on her box of face powder and screamed. A dead mouse lay inside. A note covered the top of its small, lifeless body. With shaking fingers, Theta lifted the note and read.

> *Dear Betty: Violets are blue. Red is the rose.*
> *You left him for dead. But somebody knows.*

Somebody knows.

Quickly, Theta grabbed the box and ran for the stage door and out into the back alley. Already, smoke was rising from the sides of the box where her hands gripped it. Heat rushed up her arms. As the box caught fire between her palms, she dropped it into the trash can, where it fizzled. Her hands were bright red still. For a moment, she was back in Kansas. She could see the flames crackling up the walls, smell the smoke filling the tiny room. She could hear Roy's screams.

Her mind went blank then, as it always did.

But somebody else remembered. Somebody who wanted Theta to know, too. The past had found her at last, and it threatened to burn down everything she'd built.

☀

The entire walk home, Isaiah had talked a mile a minute. "So I get to use my powers again, Memphis? Do I? And I can make 'em as strong as I want? Memphis, hey, Memphis!"

"Yes, yes, Isaiah!" Memphis laughed. "But remember: You can't say nothing to Octavia about it."

Isaiah grinned. "You mean I can't say *anything* to Octavia."

"Oh, yeah? Put 'em up." Memphis dropped into a crouch, dukes up, and he and Isaiah pretend-boxed their way down the sidewalk past folks hurrying home to their suppers. Isaiah stopped suddenly. They were in front of Madame Seraphina's brownstone. A sign hung from a hook: MADAME SERAPHINA, PRIESTESS. A crow flitted above Memphis's head and came to rest on the hand railing.

"There's that bird again," Isaiah said.

"Why, hello, Berenice," Memphis said, greeting the bird with a grand flourish of a bow that made Isaiah laugh, which was Memphis's second-favorite sound. The first was Theta whispering his name followed by *I love you*.

"How come that bird's always chasing after you?"

"All the ladies chase after me!" Memphis said with mock-umbrage. "Even the birds!"

The crow squawked three times and cocked its small, shiny head toward the partially closed drapes of the basement. Through them, Memphis could see Seraphina's altar with its offerings to the spirits and ancestors. Seraphina's face appeared at the window.

"Bet I can beat you home," Memphis said, and took off running, slowing down at the end to let Isaiah beat him into their aunt Octavia's apartment. It wasn't Octavia, but her boarder, Blind Bill Johnson, who greeted them. He sat on Octavia's prized settee with his guitar on his lap and his cane at his side.

"Well, well, well. Is that the Campbell brothers I hear?" Bill called in his raspy voice.

"Evenin', Uncle Bill," Isaiah said. "Where's Auntie?"

"At church. She left you some pork and plantains in the icebox, though. What you boys get up to this evenin' that kept you out past suppertime?"

Isaiah looked to Memphis, who shook his head. "Just went to play ball with Shrimpy here," Memphis said.

"That so? How'd you do, little man?"

Isaiah was uncharacteristically quiet. "I, uh, I threw real good," he said after a moment's pause.

The pause told the old man all he needed to know: The Campbell boys had a secret. Bill could just make out the dim shapes of them moving through the endless gray cloud of his vision. But even that tiny slice of sight would fade soon unless he did something about it.

"Well," Bill said at last. "Good. Good."

Later, after the boys had eaten their fill of Octavia's spicy pork scooped up with buttery corn bread, Memphis left for the Hotsy Totsy, to work for Papa Charles and meet up with that girl he was seeing, the girl he didn't bring 'round to the house. "Don't you worry. I'll look after little man," Bill assured Memphis on his way out. "I got the spoon handy in case he has one of his fits."

"That happens, you send Brother Julius upstairs over to the club for me."

"Of course," Bill said, smiling.

Now Blind Bill sat on the settee with Isaiah listening to a radio show. The show was funny. Two bumbling men chasing after a goat they couldn't seem to tie up. Isaiah laughed and laughed.

"Say, little man, you really go play ball this afternoon?" Bill asked when the announcer came on to praise the sponsor, the Parker Dental System— *Don't your teeth deserve the very best?*

"Mm-hmm," Isaiah said, but he sounded nervous. Memphis had surely warned his little brother not to say anything about where they'd been.

"I know you're lying, Isaiah."

Isaiah's voice was small. "Memphis told me not to tell."

"That so? Well, that ain't fair he done that to you. Run off and made you be the liar to your old pal Bill. Ain't right."

"I'm not a liar," Isaiah grumbled. There was guilt in it, though.

"Sure do hope Memphis ain't gettin' you mixed up in something bad." Bill let that land. Then he shook his head slowly, like a disappointed father. "And here I thought we was friends. *Good* friends, too. But I guess if you don't trust your uncle Bill, well..." Bill took his arm away. There was no greater bartering tool with a child than love or the threat of its absence.

"We saw Sister Walker!" Isaiah blurted.

There it was. The Walker woman. And if she was involved, it meant one thing: Diviners. Powers. She was working with them again.

"Don't tell Auntie. Please."

"No. I won't. 'Course I won't! Who's your best friend in this world?"

"Memphis. And you."

"Mm-hmm. It's just…What that woman want with you?"

Another pause. Being blind had taught Bill to read silences. This one was big.

"Gonna work on my powers."

Confirmation.

"Didn't old Bill tell you the same thing? Wasn't I working with you good?"

"Yes, sir. But…"

"But what?"

"She says it's not just about me. We gotta keep the country safe."

"Safe from what?"

"A big storm that's coming."

"Hmph. That what she said?"

"Uncle Bill, how come you don't like Sister Walker?"

"I got my reasons," Bill said. "Listen, don't you worry none. You keep telling old Bill everything that happens with Sister Walker, and I promise I won't let nothing bad happen to you. We got us a deal?"

"Deal."

"And you don't hafta tell Memphis one word 'bout our deal, neither. He don't need to know."

The boy leaned into Bill as if he were his father. Bill wrapped his long arm around the boy and held him tight like the son he might've had, the son he never would have thanks to people like Margaret Andrews Walker. This time he'd beat her at whatever game she was playing.

Bill let the power trickle down from his shoulder to his fingers and into Isaiah, connecting them. The warm coin taste was strong on the back of Bill's tongue as he sucked energy from the boy. Just enough to bring on one of the boy's fits. Already, he could feel the faint traces of Memphis's week-old healing power flowing into him and thinning the gray cloud of his vision as Isaiah convulsed on the family sofa. To see a little better for a day or three was worth it. Wasn't it? And anyway, it wasn't Bill's fault. This was Memphis's doing. The boy had lied to him all this time, said he still couldn't heal when Bill knew for a fact he'd gone and healed that old, no-good drunk. And if he could do that, there was no reason he couldn't heal Bill's blindness.

What a man couldn't get through asking, he would take in whatever fashion he needed.

"There, there," Bill said, turning Isaiah on his side as the boy's fit subsided. "It's all gonna be all right."

Bill shuffled to the door, which he could see as a faint outline now that the fumes of Memphis's healing flowed through him. He stuck his head out and shouted up the stairs, "Brother Julius! Brother Julius! Come quick! The boy had another one a' his fits! You better run for Memphis now. Hurry!"

Then Bill sat on the couch, the fallen Isaiah in his arms, and waited.

※

Jericho opened a desk drawer and shoved in the stacks of letters from the tax office informing Will that the Museum of American Folklore, Superstition, and the Occult needed to pay its back taxes or the entire place would be shut down for good in a little over two months, and a brand-new apartment building put up in its place. Jericho looked around with affection at the odd collections of occult ephemera. There would be so much to pack up when the taxman came for the place. Ever since the day Will Fitzgerald had marched into the hospital and adopted Jericho as his ward, making him an assistant curator, the museum had been Jericho's only true home.

He hadn't always believed in ghosts, of course. Not until the Pentacle Murders. Not until the night he and Evie had been trapped in John Hobbes's haunted house and barely survived. Now he knew the truth: Everything in this museum was real. Evil was not an abstract idea; it was real, too. And no matter what Will and Sister Walker thought, Jericho knew that they were all just ordinary people when it came down to it, the Diviners included. How could ordinary people possibly stop such a threat? He hoped Will and Sister Walker knew what they were doing.

From his coat pocket, Jericho retrieved a small leather pouch. MARLOWE INDUSTRIES was stamped across the front. Inside was a vial of blue serum. That serum, developed by the great Jake Marlowe himself, kept the tubes and wires connected to Jericho's damaged heart and lungs functioning. It kept him alive. For that, Jericho should've been grateful to Marlowe.

But now Marlowe had issued an ultimatum: Jericho should leave the museum—his home—and go to stay with Marlowe so that the great man could parade Jericho at his Future of America Exhibition. After all, Jericho was Marlowe's greatest invention, and no one knew. No doubt that galled Marlowe. He liked all of his victories out in front. So far, Jericho had resisted. But what choice did he have? And why now, just when it seemed that Jericho might finally have a chance with Evie?

Jericho held one of the vials up to the light. Marlowe's secret compound. Would Marlowe really cut Jericho off from his supply of lifesaving serum?

It was possible that Marlowe was bluffing and Jericho didn't need his "vitamin tonic" at all. Still. That was a big chance to take. He'd seen what had happened to all the others in the Daedalus program. Jericho was the only one who'd survived. But why?

That, apparently, was what Marlowe wanted to know so desperately.

Jericho curled his fingers into a fist. Piece of cake. He was fine.

But without Marlowe, for how much longer?

※

Henry left the taxi idling by the curb outside the Tea House on Doyers Street. Steam clouded the front windows of the Chan family's popular restaurant. Delicious smells wafted into the street, making Henry's stomach gurgle.

"You could come in. My mother would *plotz* to feed you," Ling said.

Henry laughed. "*Plotz*—did Sam teach you that word?"

"No. Mr. Gerstein up the block. Sam isn't the only person who knows Yiddish."

"Don't tell Sam that," Henry joked. "Another time. I'm late for the show."

"You're always late."

"Well, at least I'm consistent." Henry handed over his watch. "Don't lose it."

Ling shot him an annoyed look. "I can go by myself tonight."

"No, ma'am. We're a team. More fun that way," Henry said, and Ling fought her smile.

"Around one thirty, then?" Henry said, sliding back into the taxi.

"One thirty," Ling agreed.

Twenty minutes later, Henry raced into the Shubert Theatre on Forty-fourth Street, nearly toppling an easel boasting a hand-lettered sign for THE GREENWICH FOLLIES REVUE! ALL NEW! In a corner by the coat check, Henry's writing partner, David Cohn, paced, checking his watch.

"I'm here, I'm here," Henry announced.

"Cutting it a bit close," David said, helping Henry out of his coat. The audience was already piling into their seats. The trills of performers vocalizing scales wafted out from backstage.

"Sorry. Couldn't be helped." Henry smiled. "Spiffy suit, old boy."

"Got it for my nephew's bar mitzvah. Where *were* you?"

"A meeting at the Creepy Crawly."

"Anything I should know?" David asked.

"The world is ending and evil is loose in the world?"

"Sounds like Friday night."

Henry grinned, trying to put aside his misgivings. He'd told David about his and Ling's dream walking, but the scary rest of it he'd kept to himself. He kept a lot to himself. It was called survival.

"You sure clean up nice," Henry drawled, giving David an appreciative once-over. He was tall and slender, with a strong profile like a *New Yorker* cartoon, and soulful brown eyes that sometimes took Henry's breath away. David nodded to the coatroom and Henry followed. There, in the deep recesses of mink, raccoon, and camel hair, David pulled Henry to him and kissed him, slipping his tongue between Henry's lips.

"Missed you," David whispered, smiling. He reached up to take off Henry's boater hat.

Henry held fast to it with both hands. "You know I never play a show without this. It's my lucky charm."

David's smile vanished. "When are you gonna let Louis go and give us a chance?"

"Aww, now, *cher*—"

"You only call me *cher* when you want to sweet-talk your way out of something—"

"Honey," Henry said, batting his peepers. "Sugar? Sweet Man o' Mine?"

David sighed and hung up Henry's coat.

Henry tried to ignore the feeling in his gut that said he was being disloyal to the memory of his first love, Louis. It had only been a few weeks since Henry had spent his nights with Louis inside the dreamscape only to discover the tragic truth: Louis was dead and had been for some time. Maybe it wasn't fair for Henry to let David love him when his heart wasn't fully healed.

"We've got a great new song to play tonight, darlin'. Everybody loves it," Henry said, a peace offering. "Between my music and your lyrics, we'll be the next Rodgers and Hart."

David shook his head and pecked Henry on the cheek. "It's *my* heart I'm worried about. Come on. Curtain up."

Inside the theater, Henry took his seat at the piano in the orchestra pit. The house lights dimmed. There was a storm coming. Henry and his friends had to meet it head-on. And he was still a little in love with a ghost named Louis.

David smiled at Henry from the wings, where the actors milled about, ready for their cues. The conductor raised his baton. The show had to go on.

※

Adelaide Proctor waited for her teakettle to come to a boil. The steam heat whistled through the radiator of her parlor in the Bennington Apartments, but she could not feel warm. One of her many cats, an orange tabby, threaded through her legs, and she bent to pick him up. "Come, Archibald, you old cuss. Give us a cuddle." But the cat wouldn't be contained. He leaped from her arms as if he knew. The dead were coming stronger now. The proof was everywhere. And with them came the man in the hat.

With management watching her, she would have to be very clever about her rituals. She'd tried to explain to the stupid men about the salt and herbs. About the necessary protections. They'd smiled as if she were a wayward child. Addie was not a child. She was a witch, had been for most of her eighty-one years. And she knew a great evil loomed.

While she waited for her tea, Addie reached for one of her spell books from the back of her bookshelf. The book was quite old, handwritten by the good cunning folk of Salem. It had been preserved and passed down through the Proctor family line over the generations, coming to rest with Addie and her sister. The pages crackled as she turned them.

Something fluttered onto the floor.

Addie cried out as if bitten. She stumbled into her bedroom and yanked open the top of her music box. Beneath the plush red velvet, the secret compartment was empty, the iron box gone. A terrible memory came to her: A few weeks before, Addie had dreamed of the man in the hat. In the dream, he'd been sitting *right there* in the Morris chair—oh, merciful heaven; it was all coming back to her. The trickster had spoken to her in her sleep. She'd carried the iron box to the garbage chute. She'd untied the binding string and thrown it all—Elijah's finger bone, the tooth, the lock of his golden hair, and his photograph—down into the incinerator.

She'd undone the spell!

"Addie! What's the matter? What has happened?" her sister, Lillian, called as Adelaide staggered back into the parlor and slumped against the wall. Her heart beat frantically.

Lillian raced to her side and placed a nitroglycerin tablet under Adelaide's tongue to settle her sister's heart.

In the kitchen, the teakettle screamed.

"Addie! You're frightening me! What is it?"

A trembling Addie pointed to the floor, to the desiccated daisy petals that had slipped from the book, a gift for her.

Elijah had come home at last.

WELCOME TO THE UNDERGROUND

Mabel was late. Being late made her anxious, and she was already anxious about this evening. As she raced along Carmine Street, she wondered why she had wasted her time at the museum. "You're not even a Diviner," she muttered to herself, drawing strange looks from a man selling handmade cigars from a wooden stall. The minute Mabel had set foot inside the museum, she'd known it was a mistake. She'd felt small and out of place and ill-equipped among all those Diviners. Even non-Diviner Theta was on her way to becoming a movie star. Being surrounded by so much special was hard to take—and Sam's comment about Jericho and Evie had been the icing.

Mabel wanted to make a difference in the world. But she couldn't read objects or heal people or see the future. What power did she have? When would it be her moment to shine?

A throng of boisterous children ran around either side of Mabel like a river, their coats flapping open in the February wind. A woman sweeping the sidewalk yelled to them in Italian, and the children's faces sobered as they buttoned their coats to the neck and carried on. The same woman eyed Mabel suspiciously.

No need to worry, Mabel thought. *Haven't you heard? I'm nobody.*

"Pardon me," Mabel said. "I'm looking for Maria Provenza?"

With a sharp nod, the woman indicated the building next door. Mabel knocked and read over the note in her hands as she waited: *Miss Rose, I meet you in Union Square last October. My sister Anna missing still. Please come? Sixty-one Carmine Street.*

At least she might be able to help someone. But when Maria Provenza opened the door, she glanced anxiously up and down the street. "Quickly, quickly," she said, leading the way up steep, narrow flights of stairs, and once again, Mabel wondered what she was doing.

The tenement was cold and dark. It smelled of kerosene and rancid oil. Mabel followed Maria down a skinny, dim corridor past the one bathroom shared by all the tenants of the floor to a tiny apartment with a sink and a coal stove. An old woman and three young children crowded around a small, newsprint-covered table, where they assembled paper roses they could sell on the street. They'd have to sell a lot of paper roses to make ends meet, Mabel knew. Maria said something to the others in Italian, and the children gave up a chair for their guest, making Mabel feel humbled and a little guilty.

"Thank you for coming," Maria said.

"To be perfectly honest, Miss Provenza, I don't see how I can help. You're better off going to the authorities if your sister is still missing."

Maria shook her head vehemently. "No. You. It must be you. Ever since we are young, my sister sees visions. Who will marry or die or journey far. But then she sees something and she is afraid. That night, she made this."

Maria removed a loose brick from the wall behind the stove, inching out a scroll hidden inside the cubby. She unrolled it for Mabel. The charcoal had smeared a bit, and Anna's talent was not art, but it was disturbing nonetheless: Lightning in the sky. Terrifying creatures looking out from between trees. And some strange metal contraption like a diving bell. Mabel had never seen anything like it.

"You will help us find my sister?"

"I'll see what I can do," Mabel said. "May I take this drawing?"

Maria nodded. Mabel noted that the drawing had been made on the back of a pamphlet for the Fitter Families for Future Firesides, one of those eugenics tents they set up at state fairs and carnivals. They usually subjected visitors to a physical examination plus a lengthy questionnaire about heredity. Mabel's parents had said that it was bigotry dressed up to look like science.

"There is something else," Maria said. "My sister, she sees you in a vision."

"Me? What did she see?"

"She sees that you help many people."

"Oh," Mabel said, deflated. "That's me. Good old Mabel, the helper."

"No. She was worried for you. For the trouble to come."

"What sort of trouble?"

Maria shook her head apologetically. "The one who knows is my sister, and the men took her away from the factory."

"Who were these men? Management?"

Maria shook her head. "There are two. Dark suits. *I falsi sorrisi*, eh—false . . . *smiles*."

"That's not much help, I'm afraid," Mabel said.

"Wait! They wear a pin like—" Maria struggled for the word in English. She grabbed the pencil, and in a corner of her sister's sketch, she drew an eye with a lightning bolt coming down.

Mabel swallowed hard. A few weeks earlier, she had spied two men in a brown sedan across the street from the museum, just keeping watch. A lifetime working with radicals and labor organizers had taught Mabel how to ferret out Pinkerton Detectives, Bureau of Investigation agents, and plainclothes cops, and the men in the sedan had that air about them. When she'd taken a closer look, she noticed that they both wore that same odd lapel pin. Maybe it was time for Mabel to find out more about those men and whomever it was they were working for. So she couldn't read an object and glean its history, but she could be nosy and ask around.

The bells of a distant church tolled the hour. "Jeepers! I'm later than I thought!" Mabel rolled up the drawing and shoved it into her handbag. It was too big and poked out of the open top.

"Miss . . ." Maria looked embarrassed.

"What is it?"

"I am ashamed to ask. Could you spare some money? For the children?"

"Oh. Um. Of course." Mabel fished in her coin purse and handed over the quarter she'd planned to use for a *Photoplay* magazine and a pastry. She'd really wanted both, but it was better that the money go to feed Maria's children.

"Bless you, bless you," Maria said, taking Mabel's hands in hers. "Please: Be careful, Miss Rose. Those men, I feel they are out there, watching us."

❃

The bell over the door of the Bohemian Reader jingled as Mabel blew in. Behind the counter, the bookshop's owner, Mr. Jenkins, was busy chatting with a customer. Seeing Mabel, he jerked his head toward the back of the shop. Mabel nodded and walked past the shelves and tables stacked high with books she longed to stop and read, and slipped behind the heavy velvet drapes, trotting up the set of rickety wooden steps to Arthur Brown's attic garret. She gave the secret knock, and a moment later, Arthur opened up.

"Sorry I'm late," Mabel said, bustling inside the tiny vestibule, shedding her coat, hat, and gloves as she did.

Arthur winked. "Don't worry. You've only missed a lot of hot air. Wait right here. I'll introduce you."

Mabel peeked around the corner. Cigarette smoke filled the cramped, nearly barren garret. It wasn't much: Two dormer windows faced the streets. The low roof leaked into a bucket set up in a tiny kitchenette, which housed a bathtub. There was a water closet, a steamer trunk that doubled as seating, an easel in a corner, and, off to one side, an unmade bed peeking out behind a sheet rigged to a clothesline. The sight of the bed, messy and intimate, brought a blush to Mabel's cheeks. Sketches had been cellophaned to the walls. They were very good: still lifes and street scenes and some figure drawings of nude women, which only intensified the heat in Mabel's face. If they were Arthur's, he had real talent.

Two men and a woman sat at a chipped table, arguing. "Marlowe doesn't care about his workers. He just wants his exhibition to go up on time," a heavyset young man with a mustache and goatee was saying. His cheeks were a mottled pink, and his thick, round glasses made his blue eyes seem enormous. "The workers want to strike!"

"But they've signed yellow-dog contracts," the other fella said in a soft, Spanish-accented voice. A Lenin-style cap topped his shaggy dark hair.

"Yellow-dog contracts are criminal! You sign away all your rights," the young woman said. She wore a beret over her thick reddish-brown hair. Her face was delicate and pretty, and as much as Mabel wanted to be above jealousy, she felt its sharp sting anyway.

"Hey!" Arthur said sharply, and the small room quieted. He gestured toward the doorway. "Everyone, I'd like to introduce you to our newest member. Miss Mabel Rose."

Mabel gave a small wave. Her cheeks went hot. "Hello," she said, her voice cracking on the word.

The others eyed her suspiciously, except for the girl, who leaned back, appraising Mabel. "Virginia Rose's daughter?"

"Yes," Mabel said, irritated. She didn't want to be known as her mother's daughter here. She wanted to be enough on her own. "And it's Mabel. Just Mabel."

The larger boy with the glasses folded his arms across his chest. "You should have talked to us first, Arthur. We make decisions together. We are not an oligarchy."

"Sorry, Aron. But Mabel is a real asset. We could use her." Everyone was silent. "Come on. Where are your manners?"

"Manners are bourgeois," the pink-cheeked boy said.

"Enough, Aron," the dark-eyed boy in the cap said. He bowed his head. "Luis Miguel Hernandez. Pleased to meet you, Mabel."

"Gloria Cowan," the girl said, shaking Mabel's hand.

The pink-cheeked boy only nodded. "Aron Minsky."

Arthur offered Mabel a ratty chair. It was one of only two. Gloria sat in the other while Aron and Luis occupied the steamer trunk. "It's not much. But as you can see, I'm not living in the Waldorf."

"I've never even seen the Waldorf," Mabel said, smiling back at Arthur.

"I'll bet your grandmother has," Gloria said coolly. "After all, she's old New York money."

"So, you're the infamous Secret Six? The 'anarchist agitators' the police are looking for," Mabel said, changing the subject quickly. She didn't want to talk about that side of her family. "But there are only four of you."

"There was trouble at a rally in October. One of us was deported, the other arrested," Luis explained.

"We were lucky they didn't catch all of us," Gloria said.

Mabel had a vague memory of her parents telling her about some explosions at a Sacco and Vanzetti rally that had been blamed on anarchists. They seemed to think Arthur had been involved, which didn't make them happy.

"The newspapers sure don't like you," Mabel said.

"Ach! The newspapers are the tool of the capitalist oppressors," Aron said, stabbing the air with his fist. "You cannot find real news there. Take this business with Jake Marlowe, for instance."

"What business?" Mabel asked.

"The strike at his mine out in New Jersey," Luis said.

Arthur perched on the edge of the bathtub close to Mabel. "Three days ago, Jake Marlowe's miners went on strike to protest conditions at his uranium mine," he explained. "They've been putting in very long hours. And many of them are sick from the work. When they complained and talked union, management fired them, turned them out of company housing, and hired scabs. Now the miners and their families are living in a tent city in a field across from the mine. They're cold and hungry and scared."

"The press only wants to talk about Marlowe's Future of America Exhibition going up in April. To them, it's the biggest thrill to hit New York in ages. It's going to make a lot of money, too. Why write about poor, striking workers when you can write about the capitalist circus coming to town?" Luis added.

"Because these industrialists own the newspapers! You think a man like Hearst cares about workers? He wants to keep the unions far from his own business," Aron sniped.

"I could get my father to write about it," Mabel offered.

"No offense, Mabel," Arthur said, "but anybody reading *The Proletariat* already sympathizes with the workers. We need to get Mom and Pop in their comfortable living rooms to care about these people, to see them as fellow human beings, not rabble-rousers the way they've been painted by powerful people with money to lose."

"What's this?" Gloria asked. She'd pulled the drawing from Mabel's bag and was examining it closely. "It's terrifying."

"It was given to me by a woman on Carmine Street. She wrote to me that some men had taken her sister away from the garment factory where she worked. This was months ago, and she's still missing. The girl had some clairvoyant abilities. A Diviner, I guess you'd call her."

Aron scoffed. "If anything embodies the dangers of capitalism, it's those so-called Diviners, claiming to have powers that elevate them above the rest of us. And now they're making money from it and spending their nights in hotel parties being photographed by reporters on the payroll—like that Sweetheart Seer."

Mabel knew she should stick up for Evie, but she had just met these people. Besides, she was irritated with Evie. "They're not all like that," she said with a shrug.

"If this woman was a Diviner, why couldn't she see the men coming to take her away?" Luis asked.

Gloria was looking at Mabel as if she were on the witness stand and failing. "Why did this woman come to *you* for help?"

"She said her sister had seen in a vision that I should help her."

Gloria stared for a minute. And then she laughed. "You *fell* for that line? Oh, Arthur. *Honestly*. You found us a real Girl Scout."

Mabel's face went hot again. She wished she could unsay everything.

Arthur's eyes flashed. "Gloria. Try not to be a barracuda, will you?"

"Probably she wanted money. She tells you that there's something threatening you, and then she offers to take away the curse if you pay her. It's an old trick," Luis said sympathetically.

"She seemed genuinely frightened," Mabel insisted. But now she wondered if she had been naive. What did she know about Maria Provenza? Nothing, really. And she *had* asked for money, hadn't she? Maybe Maria Provenza could tell that Mabel was an easy mark, a girl desperate to be seen.

Aron pushed his glasses up on his nose. "I'm not concerned about a bunch of hocus-pocus types. We've got real troubles to solve."

"Perhaps Mabel could get her Diviner friend to solve it for us!" Gloria cooed.

Mabel had had enough. Arthur could keep his stuck-up, phony friends. Angry tears stung her eyes. "Well. I'll leave you to it, then," she said, marching over to the vestibule and retrieving her coat and hat from the hook. She hoped she could get out of Arthur's flat before she started to cry and *really* embarrassed herself. "I've got to conduct a *séance* for workers' rights."

The wind whipped across the wet cobblestones of Bleecker Street and eddied about Mabel's legs, cutting right through her woolen hosiery, but Mabel's anger kept her warm. Those Secret Six phonies acted as if she had never even been to a strike, when Mabel was practically born on a picket line! She almost didn't hear Arthur shouting after her. He was jogging down the street in the rain without a coat. "Mabel! Mabel, stop!" he shouted, and she let him catch up to her. "Please don't be angry."

"I'm not angry," Mabel said.

"You're a terrible liar."

"Add it to my list of faults."

"No. I like that about you. You are exactly who you seem to be. That's ... rare."

"Oh," was all Mabel could manage. She still felt the fool and she was afraid anything else she said would only add to her embarrassment.

"Look, don't pay any attention to Aron and Gloria. They want to change the world, to make it better, and sometimes they can be a little rough around the edges—and blunt."

"You forgot rude and insufferable," Mabel grumbled, forgetting her earlier promise to herself to keep quiet.

"That, too." Arthur's smile was sheepish. "So. Will I see you again, Mabel Rose?"

"I'm not sure I'm welcome here."

"I said, will *I* see you again?" Arthur slipped two fingers beneath her chin, lifting her face back up to his. His eyes were a mix of brown and gold, two different reads depending on the light. "Give them a chance. Show 'em what you're capable of. You'd be a good influence on them—you've been inside the labor movement forever. And those workers out in the tent city sure could use all the help they can get."

She'd wanted to make a difference, hadn't she?

"All right," Mabel said, feeling a little breathless.

"All right?"

"I'll do it."

"That's swell. Because I'm gonna need somebody to help me, kid."

"I'm not a kid," Mabel groused. "Besides, how old are *you*?"

"Does it matter?"

"I suppose not. Wait! Yes. It does."

"I'm twenty." He spread his arms wide. "I'm allowed to make all my own decisions. I even cut my own steak. Well, when I can get steak."

He gave his lopsided grin again, and Mabel found herself softening. He offered his hand for a shake. "Welcome to the messy underground, Mabel Rose."

Mabel shook Arthur's hand. Across the street, she noticed a man standing under a street lamp. He was reading a newspaper. Or pretending to. Mostly, he seemed to be watching the two of them.

"Arthur, don't look now, but I think somebody's keeping tabs on us."

Arthur stopped smiling. "What? Where?"

"Over there. Under the lamp. Man in the brown hat. Don't make it obvious," Mabel said, training her eyes on the ground now.

Arthur pretended to tie his shoe, looking over his shoulder. He stood up, shrugged. "Nobody there now. Unless you mean old Sal from the pizzeria. I suspect he keeps an eye on me to make sure I come in for his pizza."

Mabel looked up again. The space under the street lamp was empty. But the man had been there, and he hadn't seemed like a casual bystander. She thought about Maria's words: *They are out there, watching us.*

✵

At the end of the night, the Tea House emptied; the CLOSED sign was hung. Ling's mother counted up the day's receipts while humming a song from her native Ireland. From the kitchen came the clanging of dishes, laughter, and Cantonese as her father worked alongside the cooks. After the last pot had been washed and put away, Ling and her family returned to their apartment. Ling removed her leg braces, letting the air cool the chafed skin above and below her knees.

"How was your science club meeting?" Mrs. Chan asked, placing Ling's crutches within reach for the morning.

"Good," Ling said, feeling a little guilty for the lie.

"And how was our dear Henry?"

"Also good." Ling was pretty sure her mother had already married them off in her mind.

"Good night, my girl," her mother said, kissing her forehead. "Sweet dreams."

Ling lay in bed staring at the ceiling. Just before one thirty, she took Henry's watch in her hands, letting its steady tick lull her into a trance, her green eyes growing heavier, until she fell deeply asleep. She woke inside a dream, aware of everything around her. A large house loomed in the distance like a many-roomed castle of the sort she'd seen in library books about English manors.

"You jake?" Henry said, making her jump.

"I've told you not to sneak up on me," she said.

"Just keeping you on your toes. Wouldn't want our dream walks to become boring."

The laughter of happy children echoed through the dreamscape.

"Do you hear that?" Ling asked.

Henry nodded.

"Come on," Ling said, running over the pine-needle carpet beneath their feet. Here in the dream world, she could run and walk and jump, and for the first few minutes, she reveled in the ease of movement. Ever since she and Henry had begun to dream walk together, the dreamscapes had become much more vivid. At first, Ling had chalked it up to the enchantment wrought by the supernatural sleeping sickness that had terrorized New York only a few weeks earlier. But it seemed that the new power Ling and Henry had sparked during that time hadn't completely waned. Even now, she could smell the spicy pine and feel the suggestion of a cool breeze coming from the forest to their right.

"We're inside Evie's dream," Henry said. "I've been here before."

"Me, too. Once," Ling said.

"James? Where are you?" Evie called, moving through the trees, her hands out in front of her as if she were feeling her way through fog.

"That's her brother she's calling for?" Ling asked.

Henry nodded. "She's never really gotten over his death during the war. They were very close. She dreams about him a lot."

"James!" Evie called again, and it sounded as if her heart would break. She disappeared into the forest. The trees fell away like a painted sheet tugged quickly from a line. Henry and Ling stood on the lawn of the great house now. The joyful laughter of children echoed across dream time, and then, one by one, the children winked into existence on the lawn, where they hunted for brightly colored eggs, dropping them into their baskets as they went.

"Easter?" Henry said with a smile. "I love Easter! Actually, I love ham, and since ham is the food of Easter, by definition, I love Easter."

"You should come for Easter at my house, then," Ling said. "It's all pig. Chinese pork and Irish ham. You'll be trapped watching my cousins, Seamus and Liam, eat, though. They're barbarians. You can actually hear them chewing. It sounds like a gravel truck filled with spit."

"You're really selling me on Easter at your house," Henry deadpanned, but Ling was frowning.

"Henry, look at the children."

They were lined up on the lawn, their heads cocked toward the sky as if they were waiting for a message. But around the edges, they shimmered.

"Are they...?" Henry started.

Ling nodded. "They're all dead."

The Easter eggs cracked open. Snakes slithered out into the browning, curling grass.

"They never should have done it," the children said.

A giant hand pushed the skies apart. It was made of thousands of dark, screaming birds. The hand reached toward the children as if to scoop them up.

"What is that?" Ling said.

"We're not waiting to find out. Run," Henry said. He had just grazed Ling's fingers with his own when the scene shifted like machinery, sending them toppling through layers of dream time. When everything settled, Henry was alone in a room he didn't recognize. It reminded him of a hospital except that there were bars over the windows. There was a piano in the corner.

"At least there's a piano," Henry said, sitting to play. "*Ling Chan, Ling Chan, oh, where can you be? I'm lost here without you and it's mighty...spook...y....*"

"You should go."

Henry nearly jumped off the piano bench. There was a boy in the room. He was skinny, with dark hair and eyebrows. He wasn't fully awake like Henry. But he was aware of Henry's presence somehow. And in the corner was a man in a wheelchair, his back turned toward Henry. The man in the wheelchair was dreaming, Henry knew. And he talked in his sleep: "The time is now. The time is now. We are the one forty-four!"

"He'll be looking for you," the boy said, drawing Henry's attention again. "He's looking for all of us. You should go now. Before he sees you. Before he finds you."

"Who?" Henry asked.

The boy held out his palm. In the center was the faint outline of a symbol Henry had seen many times in his dreams: an eye with a jagged lightning bolt underneath.

"The man in the hat," the boy said. "The King of Crows."

RISING STARS

As Evie entered the radio station the following day, a group of whispering secretaries scattered to their typewriters, leaving one unlucky girl to take the lead.

"Mr. Phillips wants to see you, Miss O'Neill," the secretary said, averting her eyes.

With a knot in her stomach, Evie approached Mr. Phillips's imposing office. Usually, she loved coming in here. She thrilled at being up so high—there were no buildings this tall in Zenith, Ohio—and looking through the corner windows at the city spread out like a modern kingdom.

"Eevvieeee!" Mr. Phillips said. "Come in and take a seat."

Evie perched on the edge of a chair as Mr. Phillips laced his fingers together and looked her straight in the eye. "Evie. You know I think you're strictly top-drawer, don't you? And your show has been a terrific asset for WGI."

"Gee. That's swell, then," Evie managed. Listening to Mr. Phillips's speech was like watching storm clouds rolling in and knowing she'd forgotten her umbrella.

"But it seems that not everybody feels as I do. Pears soap may be switching their advertising sponsorship to Miss Snow's program."

"*Sarah Snow?* But why?"

Mr. Phillips pushed forward the day's paper, open to the gossip pages. There'd been more and more of them cropping up these days, scandal mongers intent on making and breaking Broadway, radio, and motion picture stars. With a little ink and insinuation, they could plant a story—*We hear so-and-so is the top choice for Charlie Chaplin's leading lady in his latest picture*—or ruin a reputation. The worst of them was Harriet Henderson and her column, "Rumor Has It." Harriet had her favorites, whom she protected and promoted. Sarah Snow was one of those favorites. Evie was not. The picture of Evie had landed squarely in Harriet's column, and it was a shot of a post-party Evie sprawled across the giant planter in front of her hotel, her legs up in the air. The headline read, SWEETHEART SEER GETS POTTED. Evie felt a little queasy. She *had* been pretty drunk. After the meeting at the museum, she'd wanted nothing more than to forget for a while about everything Will had told them. So once her radio show came to an end and all the autographs had been signed, she'd set out to do just that. It had been a wonderful party; there'd been a lavish buffet, a ballet troupe twirling on the tables, and loads of fascinating people she never would've met back in Ohio. She had a vague memory of taking off her shoes and jumping through a wreath of fire on a dare after her fourth glass of champagne. But she could barely remember getting back to her suite at the Winthrop Hotel, and now there was photographic evidence of her wild night. Harriet Henderson and Sarah Snow were taking all the fun out of Evie's nightlife.

"Well, I admit, it's not my best side," Evie said, trying to save face, though she was mortified.

"Our advertisers are afraid that your antics may reflect badly on them. After all, who buys soap? Mothers. Mothers with unruly daughters they'd like to keep in line."

"I thought Pears wanted to be the 'modern soap for the modern girl': 'Keep your complexion *flapper fresh*!'"

"That thinking has changed. They want to associate their product with someone of Sarah Snow's reputation—good, pure, likable, a paean to real womanhood."

For months, they'd all said they loved Evie. In fact, the *more* they loved her. She'd acted out what they couldn't—or wouldn't dare. And now they were throwing her under the car wheels for it like a bunch of cowards. "I see." Evie bristled. "Is there anything else? Would they like me to turn gin into Ovaltine or start a home for feral kittens?"

"Evie..." Mr. Phillips warned.

Evie cast her eyes downward. "Sorry."

"It's this whole Diviner business these days. It's begun to *unsettle* people."

Evie's head popped back up. "You said you loved my show!"

"Yes, I did."

"Did?" she asked, heart sinking.

"I do. But people are nervous, what with first those Pentacle Murders and then that sleeping sickness. And now this talk of some people seeing ghosts in the city! Sarah takes away that nervousness. She reassures our citizens, makes them feel that a higher power is looking out for them."

"Well, maybe people *should* be nervous about the ghosts. Maybe Sarah's not doing them any favors at all!"

Mr. Phillips frowned. "Now, Evie. That's unbecoming."

Evie's cheeks burned with everything she wanted to say back to Mr. Phillips but knew she couldn't. Not if she wanted to keep her radio show.

"Frankly, Pears soap got spooked when you read that fella's comb and…started screaming at him, asking where he got it. It was a frightening display."

Bob Bateman. He'd lied to her about that comb. But she couldn't tell Mr. Phillips what she'd seen or why it was so upsetting to her.

"I reported exactly what I saw," Evie said, and wished she didn't sound so defensive.

"Oh, say, now, Evie. People have short memories. This nonsense can be forgotten. Why don't you start getting yourself in good with Harriet and her readers?"

Evie would rather eat glass.

"Listen here: Why don't you clean yourself up a bit, eh? Show Pears and the people of New York what a good girl you are," Mr. Phillips said, as if he were delivering a pep speech to a losing football team heading into their last quarter. "When you read objects, keep it all on the happy side—tell them more about what they want to hear and nothing too alarming. Keep it entertaining! Do a bit of charity work! Make yourself a little more like, well, like Sarah."

Evie imagined pummeling her boss with a basket full of Pears soap.

Still clutching the newspaper, a thoroughly unhappy Evie left Mr. Phillips's office. Around her, WGI's Art Deco hallways buzzed with activity and ambition. Evie passed two comics honing their patter, a jazz orchestra tuning up, and a soprano decked out in a velvet evening gown practicing rollercoaster vocal scales just outside the ladies' lounge. Everybody wanted to be heard on the radio these days. Everybody wanted to become famous.

Staying famous was harder.

Earsplitting screams drew Evie back to WGI's golden doors. Sarah Snow had arrived and was shaking hands with the many fans crowding around her, desperate for her to notice them. With her hair set in a fresh permanent wave and an orchid corsage pinned to her white dress—her signature look—Sarah gleamed like a modern angel, a saint with jazz-age flair. A month ago, she'd been a struggling radio evangelist. Now she was WGI's rising star. And if the crowds outside were any sign, she was rising right past Evie.

A newsman's camera flashed. It bounced off the glass and hurt Evie's eyes.

"You seem to be awfully chummy with Jake Marlowe, Miss Snow. Any truth to the rumor that you might become Mrs. Marlowe?" a woman in a turban asked. Harriet Henderson, the scandal-sheet snake herself.

"Mr. Marlowe is a wonderful man. I'm pleased to be his friend," Sarah said, smiling for the cameras.

But you didn't deny it, you crafty little crusader, Evie thought, not without admiration.

With a last wave of her white-gloved hand and a bright smile, Sarah walked toward WGI's golden doors, and Evie tried to sneak away.

"Good evening, Miss O'Neill," Sarah called, catching Evie mid-tiptoe.

Evie turned around with a pasted-on smile. "Good evening, Miss Snow. My, you sure do have a lot of fans!"

"I'm simply the Lord's vessel," Sarah said, opening her arms wide.

"Like the *Titanic*?" Evie muttered under her breath.

"I beg your pardon?"

"I said, it's *terrific*!"

"Why, thank you." Sarah's expression was all wincing sympathy. "I was sorry to hear about your broken engagement."

I'll bet.

"Must be especially hard after the way Sam so gallantly saved your life from that poor man who tried to shoot you. What was his name?"

"Luther Clayton," Evie said.

"Oh, yes. I heard they've put him in the asylum. Poor thing."

"That *poor thing* tried to kill me," Evie reminded her.

"Jesus asks us to forgive our trespassers. Anyway, I'm terribly sorry about your broken engagement," Sarah said again in case anyone in the hallway missed it the first time. "You must be devastated by the loss."

Evie's lips stretched into a smile as phony as Sarah's sympathy. "Yes, I've put teacups all around my room to catch the overflow of my tears. Somehow I muddle through without Sam. Though I do have to go out if I want tea."

Sarah appraised Evie for an uncomfortably long time. "You're not really as jaded as you make yourself out to be, Miss O'Neill."

"Says you."

"Well, I will keep you in my prayers, Miss O'Neill," Sarah said, and walked away.

"Why'd she have to go and say something human," Evie muttered as she closed herself off in one of WGI's telephone booths to sulk. She watched the enthusiastic secretary pool gather around Sarah, eager for her attention. Months before, it was Evie they'd been gathering around. The picture of her toppling into the hotel's giant potted plant blared up from the newspaper. "At least my gams look good," Evie said. She leafed through the pages, stopping when she came to a small mention of some grisly murders out at the Manhattan State Hospital for the Insane, the very place where they were holding Luther Clayton. Quickly, Evie grabbed the telephone, asking the operator for the number of the *Daily News*.

T. S. Woodhouse's oily voice slithered over the line. "Well, if it isn't the Sweetheart Seer herself! To what do I owe this honor?"

"Listen, Woody, I've got a hot tip for you: The Sweetheart Seer is going out to the asylum at Ward's Island to meet with Luther Clayton."

"The fella who tried to shoot you?"

"Yes. I'm…I'm going to forgive him! Poor…fellow," she said, making it up as she went along. "I thought you might like to write a story about it."

There was a pause, followed by a laugh. "This is about Sarah Snow, isn't it?"

Evie poked her head out the telephone booth's glass door. At the end of the long hall, Sarah posed with Mr. Phillips as Harriet Henderson looked on and a photographer captured it all. Evie felt the jealousy down to her toenails. "I don't have the foggiest notion what you mean, Mr. Woodhouse."

"Don't you? I got news for you, Sheba: You will never be able to best Miss Pure-as-Snow at the good-girl game."

Evie snapped the door shut again. "Come on, Woody. Help a girl out."

"All right. I want to sniff around about the murders out there anyway, but, understandably, they don't want any press. You get me in, and I promise to write up your Luther Clayton story in a way that makes your halo shine brighter than ten Sarah Snows."

Evie grinned in relief. "It's a deal."

As she hung up, the photographer's blinding flash went off, and Evie blinked against Sarah's refracted glory.

TESTED

Ling arrived at the museum at precisely five o'clock. It had taken her two buses, a trolley, and a full hour to get there. Her hands burned from the constant pressure of her crutches, and even though it was brisk outside, under her wool coat, she was covered in a sheen of sweat. She removed her damp coat and dropped into a chair, flexing her aching fingers. "I can't stay long. I told my mother I was attending an evening Mass with Henry and Evie at St. Patrick's Cathedral."

Henry put a hand to his chest in faux shock. "You used the Lord to lie to them? I'll just stand over here in case you're struck by lightning."

"We'll need to figure out a better way to get me here if you want me to continue," Ling said. "It took a long time. And I can't keep lying to my parents. I feel too guilty."

"Fair enough. Dr. Fitzgerald and I will come up with a solution, Ling," Sister Walker promised.

"Thank you," Ling said. The others were there, scattered around the library's first floor looking like the aftermath of a party no one had wanted to attend. "So what do we do now?"

"Let's begin with a few questions," Sister Walker said, settling herself beside a credenza hosting an array of strange-looking instruments. "Tell me what you know about your powers thus far—when did they start? What happens while you are engaged? Are there any aftereffects that you've noticed, illness or dizziness, anything like that? What are your limits or weaknesses?"

"Henry and I can dream walk," Ling said. "And during the sleeping sickness, we discovered that we can dream walk together. I can also speak to the dead inside dreams if I have an object that belonged to the deceased."

"I can sometimes influence a person inside a dream," Henry added. "For instance, if someone were having a nightmare, I might say, 'Why don't you dream about clowns instead?'"

"*Clowns* are your cure for a nightmare?" Evie said from the couch, where she lay half-sprawled again, legs crossed, one leg kicking out and back. "Never, *ever* say that to me inside one of my dreams, Henry. Promise me." She shivered. "Clowns."

"Henry can't move after a dream walk," Theta volunteered. She sat at the long table with her chair close beside Memphis's. "Sometimes it's as long as five minutes. I get really worried about him."

"Ling? Any of those same troubles for you?" Sister Walker asked.

"No. I'm fine afterward," Ling said with a note of stoic pride.

Sister Walker took this down, too. "What else? Anyone?"

"After an object reading, I get the granddaddy of skull-bangers," Evie said.

Sam stroked his chin. "You know, Miss Walker, it's the darnedest thing, but I seem to be getting more irresistible every day. Golly, is *that* a side effect of my gift?"

"I believe it's a side effect of your ego," Evie said, punctuating it with a generous eye roll.

Jericho laughed out loud at that, something he rarely did. It pleased Evie.

"Wasn't that funny," Sam grumbled.

"Yes, it was." Jericho gave Evie a sly glance. She returned it with a raised brow, enjoying the guilty pleasure of this small, secret exchange.

Memphis cleared his throat before charging into the fray. "During the Pentacle Murders, Isaiah had some bad nightmares. He'd wake up in the night shaking with visions. He even predicted Gabe's death," Memphis said, his heart sinking at the memory of his murdered best friend.

"I don't remember it so much, though," Isaiah said. "Don't remember what happens during my fits, either."

"Well. We'll see if we can get you stronger so that you can remember more and not be bothered by those seizures any longer. Sound fair?" Sister Walker said gently. "In fact, I hope that by working on your powers daily and in new ways, we'll strengthen all of you and eliminate any troubles you might be experiencing. We'll work with you alone, in pairs, and as teams to see how your gifts interact, whether you increase each other's powers or perhaps affect one another negatively."

"Like *atoms* with the potential to attract or repel," Ling said. "To create energy."

At the word *attract*, Evie glanced sidelong at Jericho where he leaned against the wall, arms folded across his broad chest, head tilted slightly back so that he could look down at everything from under those somewhat sleepy eyelids, remote, like a god from on high. The curve of his throat was inviting. She wondered what it would be like to kiss him there.

"Do you like science, Ling?" Sister Walker asked, mercifully pulling Evie's attention back to the group.

"Science is what she lives for," Henry said.

A smile lit up Sister Walker's face. "Then you'll have to let me know your thoughts as we proceed. Here. Take this for making notes." She handed Ling a small leather-bound book and a pencil.

"Thank you," Ling said, blushing.

"Don't thank me yet. I'll expect things from you," Sister Walker said.

"Ooh. Teacher's pet," Henry whispered.

"Not all of us get expelled from prep school," she shot back.

Henry nodded appreciatively. "Touché."

Ling cracked open the notebook, inhaling the scent of good leather and of the possibilities lurking in all those blank pages. She was embarrassingly proud of the attention from Sister Walker. Back on Mott Street, everyone knew that Ling could walk in dreams and speak to the dead, but no one really understood her love of science or how those worlds could coexist when to Ling they were simply different sides of the same coin, the exploration of equal mysteries. Sister Walker had the same two passions. Ling sensed in her a kindred spirit. The notebook was acknowledgment: *I see you. I know you.*

Isaiah was bored. Sister Walker said they'd test powers, but so far it was just a bunch of talking. He'd never been in a place as fascinating as the museum, and he wanted to explore everything in it. While Sister Walker and Will asked the others a series of questions, Isaiah wandered over to the fat chest between the windows so he could get a closer look at the instrument sitting on top of it: a small wooden box with a hand crank on the side and, on its face, a needle that measured in tens from zero to eighty. It looked as if someone had tried to make a cuckoo clock with a speedometer. Isaiah ran a finger across the dark filament of the bulb in the instrument's center. Then he turned the crank, and it flared briefly, the needle tipping up the scale to thirty with an electric scratching sound. Isaiah jumped back, and the machine calmed.

Isaiah put up his hands. "I didn't do anything!"

"Careful," Will said, marching toward Isaiah.

Now that Isaiah knew he wasn't in trouble, his curiosity took over. "What is it?"

"It's called a Metaphysickometer," Will said.

Isaiah shrugged, unimpressed. "Doesn't seem like much."

"Just wait till we start working, and you generate energy. Then that needle will bounce around like an excited puppy. It's one of Jake Marlowe's finest early inventions," Will said.

"Jake Marlowe built this?" Ling said, drawing closer.

"Yes. When we worked together. In the United States Department of Paranormal," Sister Walker explained.

"Ling's his greatest admirer. She met him at his Future of America Exhibition announcement. He's promised her tickets to the exhibit's opening day," Henry explained.

"Jake Marlowe." Mabel practically spat his name like a curse word. "Did you know his miners are striking?"

"Now you've done it," Evie said under her breath.

"They're living in tents with their families. They're cold and hungry. But the newspapers refuse to report it," Mabel continued.

"Then they should show up for work and not complain," Ling said.

Mabel's voice grew even more heated. "The conditions at his mine are terrible! They've been mining uranium twelve, thirteen hours a day, and getting awfully sick from it."

"Why does Jake Marlowe need so much uranium?" Ling wondered aloud.

"I don't know," Mabel said. She'd never really stopped to think about it before.

Ling scoffed. "We all have to work hard," she said, returning to the argument. "I know people in Chinatown who work *seventeen* hours a day. My parents never take a day off. I feel like a bad daughter being here and not there, helping them. As for your unions, I don't see them sticking up for Chinese workers."

Henry managed a strained smile. "I love this play. I can't wait till it comes to Broadway next month," he said, trying to smooth things over.

Ling knew Henry was kidding and she knew it was because he hated to see people fight. But it bothered her anyway, the way he slid around anything too uncomfortable. Ling didn't have that luxury. She was an outsider among outsiders—a half-Chinese, half-Irish, partially paralyzed girl living in Chinatown. She could not escape the looks of pity and discomfort she garnered when she struggled into a room on her crutches. All those eyes on her, then all those eyes looking away out of a fear that they could catch the bad luck of her. It had taught her to be blunt, to lash out first. Better to frighten people a little and keep them at a distance than to suffer the eventual disappointment of them. Better to wound a little than to hurt a lot. Even Ling's gift made people uncomfortable. The messages she carried back from the ancestor spirits she spoke to during her dream walks weren't always what the relatives who'd hired her wanted to hear. When that happened, they often took it out on the messenger: Ling. Only in the scientific world, among the beauty of theories and observations, equations and atoms, did Ling feel she truly belonged. And in dreams, where she could do anything, even walk. Even run.

Ling turned her attention to the Metaphysickometer. It was cruder than Marlowe's sleeker, newer inventions, and it encouraged her to know that everyone, even Jake Marlowe, had to start somewhere.

"What does it do?" she asked, examining its many dials.

"It measures electromagnetic radiation. Both ghosts and Diviners seem to emit much more of it than the rest of the population. In theory, Diviners together can disrupt or create energy fields." Will flipped a switch on the box's side and turned the crank a few times until a pleasant hum warmed the machine. The needle tipped up and down like a conductor's baton. "Quite a bit of it in this room right now." Will switched it off and the needle dropped like a fainting ingenue. "Mr. Marlowe was quite interested in what could be made from that energy—whole industries might be powered from it."

"I thought Jake Marlowe hated Diviners," Theta said. "He's always running 'em down."

"How come he does that if he used to be one of you, Sister?" Isaiah said, flipping the switch on the Metaphysickometer on and off until Sister Walker stopped him.

"Yes, what happened? Did one of the Diviners pick out the wrong Christmas present for him?" Evie said.

"Socks," Sam agreed. "It's always socks."

"It's a long story," Sister Walker said. "And not important at the moment."

"That Metaphys—needle thing—is all fine and dandy. But what about weapons? What do you have that gets rid of ghosts? Is there a Jake Marlowe ghost container lying around somewhere?" Evie asked.

"Ghosts were once people," Will said. "People *want* things. Even dead people. You have to figure out what that thing is. John Hobbes believed he was the anti-Christ and that he could only be banished by luring his essence into a holy relic and destroying that relic. Wai-Mae could not rest until she could face the trauma of her death, until her bones had been given a proper burial. There isn't one solution. You have to see them ghost by ghost."

Theta reached into her pocketbook for a stick of gum. "No offense, Professor, but if I run into a ghost, I'm not asking it to dinner so we can talk things over."

"Why don't we begin?" Sister Walker led the group to the rug and the circle of chairs she'd put out.

"Say, how come Memphis and Isaiah call you Sister?" Sam asked, settling into his seat.

"We know her. She was friends with our mama. She lives near us," Isaiah said.

Sam tried out his most charming smile on Sister Walker. "So can I call you Sister, too?"

"You may call me Miss Walker," she answered, turning her attention to the Metaphysickometer's dials.

"Was she ever a nun or a cop?" Sam whispered to Memphis.

"No. But I *was* a government agent," Sister Walker said with a hint of a grin.

※

For the next few days, the Diviners reported to the museum when they could, in varying configurations, while Sister Walker and Will worked with them, pushing the boundaries of what they'd been able to do. There'd been small gains: By keeping a hand on Henry's arm, Memphis could lessen the duration and intensity of Henry's post-dream paralysis. If Evie read an object when Sam was near, she was somehow able to reach much deeper into the object's past. "It's almost as if your *don't see me* routine has the opposite effect on my reading, Sam."

"I'll send you a bill," he joked.

"I'll deduct twenty clams," Evie shot back.

But nothing so far had made a truly significant or lasting change in any of the Diviners' powers. Sister Walker reassured them that this was all a normal part of the process, but it still felt like failure.

"We'll just try again tomorrow," Sister Walker said gently each time, but everyone knew that she and Will were concerned, and the Diviners themselves were growing frustrated. Whatever storm Liberty Anne had prophesied was still on the horizon, and they were no closer to knowing what it was or how to stop it.

It wasn't just that the testing of the Diviners' skills was going poorly that had everyone on edge. Ghost sightings had increased in the city. Every day, there was new, worrying gossip—disturbances heard in apartment hallways late at night. Rooms that went so cold that condensation formed on every surface. Objects gone missing only to be found later far from where they belonged. A diner cook had come in early one morning to find a towering stack of cans in the middle of the kitchen. All the windows and doors had been locked from the inside. A honeymooning couple at the Plaza Hotel left in the middle of the night, insisting that something shook their bed and whispered terrible things as they tried to sleep.

Ghosts, they all insisted. *Ghosts*, the people repeated.

The fear caught like a spark in wind and spread across the city. It was laughed at in speakeasies. Discussed down at the fish market and in the stands of Yankee Stadium, where the locals stopped to watch Babe Ruth and Lou Gehrig practice. It was whispered about behind the perfume counters at Macy's and Wanamaker's and among the pushcart peddlers of the Lower East Side. Numbers were played for it in Harlem. At Webster Hall, a phantom-themed drag ball was planned. And in the noisy rooms of Tin Pan Alley, songwriters capitalized on the spooky phenomena with danceable ditties— "Goo-Goo-Googly-Eyed Ghosts!" "The Revenant Rag!"—because, after all, a buck was a buck. Switchboard operators' fingers ached from patching in frightened callers to the police stations. Most reported pale faces spotted in mirrors or wispy movements glimpsed on the other side of fogged windows.

Ghosts.

The reporters followed up—it made for good morning copy:

—*What were they doing?* they asked.

—*Watching us*, the people said.

—*Just watching?*

—*Just watching. Closely, though. Like they were studying us.*

Sometimes there were more frightening sightings that made the back pages of the tabloids: A night watchman making his rounds in Brooklyn followed noises to the weedy lot behind the factory. When he lifted his lantern, its weak glow fell upon a pack of glowing things, hairless and deformed, their wan bodies covered in sores, their sharp mouths smeared in blood as they feasted on squirming rats. Before he ran for his life, he thought he heard them whisper, *More*. Late on a chilly night, the caretaker of Prospect Cemetery heard an animal's cries. He stepped onto the path in time to see the ghost of a woman in Puritan gray floating between the tombstones, the hangman's noose still tight about her neck, a mewling cat tucked beneath her incandescent arm. The hanged woman stopped suddenly, turning her head completely around on her broken neck until it faced backward. And then she hissed at the caretaker, and he saw that her eyes were clay-pale and soulless in her pallid, peeling face.

On his way into the 21 Club with yet another starlet on his arm, Mayor Jimmy Walker tried to soothe the city's fears. "Seems like most of these so-called ghost sightings can be traced back to poisoned bathtub gin. If you see ghosts, you might want to call your bootlegger instead of the mayor's office," he joked.

There were reassurances: The honeymoon couple at the hotel didn't want to pay for the room. The diner cook was angry with his boss and had likely stacked the cans himself for attention. The poor night watchman hadn't slept in two days. The caretaker's wife had left him for another and he was not himself. That was good enough for most New Yorkers. People who hadn't felt the air go cold as death's hand as they passed the flophouse where several forgotten men had died. People who didn't hear the faint whinny of horses followed by the momentary vision, camera-flash quick, of a funeral carriage driver whipping down the cobblestones along the seaport. Who hadn't had disquieting dreams, visitations from dead relatives warning that a storm was coming.

"Why aren't we out there making a name for ourselves fighting these ghosts?" Sam asked after yet another disappointing effort at combining their abilities had resulted in nothing but headaches, nosebleeds, and exhaustion.

"I've told you—we don't want to panic the populace," Will said.

"But the *populace* is already panicked," Sam said.

"No," Will said gravely. "True panic is ugly. You'll know it when you see it."

That afternoon, Ling and Sister Walker worked side by side, comparing notes on the Metaphysickometer's readings.

"You don't like Mr. Marlowe much, do you?" Ling said at last.

"I admire his genius and I deplore his methods."

"How could you work by his side if you hated him—"

"I didn't *hate* Jake—"

"Disliked him, then."

"In this life, you have to work with people you dislike. You find compromises. But sometimes you find that a person's beliefs are so harmful that you must speak against them. You can't let such harmful statements stand without challenge. They have a tendency to grow into tumors." Sister Walker paused.

"Is that why you went to prison?" Isaiah asked, and Ling's mouth opened in surprise.

Memphis nudged Isaiah hard with his elbow. "Isaiah! Apologize."

"What? Ever'body knows Sister went to jail. She knows it most of all!"

"Isaiah," Memphis warned.

Isaiah stared down at his shoes. "Sorry, Miss Walker."

"That's all right, Isaiah. You didn't mean any harm."

"Is that true?" Ling asked.

"Yes."

"So did you steal something?" Isaiah asked, unable to help himself. "Did you kill somebody, Sister?"

"No. And no."

"Then what?"

Sister Walker took in a deep breath. "Sedition."

"What's that?" Isaiah asked.

"It's when you rile people up and disobey authority."

"When I acted up, my mama just got the switch. Who'd you make mad?" Isaiah asked.

"The United States government," Sister Walker said. "I spoke out against something I thought was wrong. I tried to stop it."

"And they threw you in the slammer for that?" Sam said.

"We were at war, and I worked for the Department of Paranormal, a government agency." Sister Walker took a sip of her tea, then continued. "They said what I did wasn't patriotic."

"Weren't they right?"

"I suppose it's all in how you define patriotism. Some say that's only saying good things about your country. Others say that it's speaking against what you feel is wrong with your country and trying to make a change."

"I don't understand. Isn't freedom of speech guaranteed by the First Amendment?" Memphis asked.

"Guarantees. You mean, like the Fourteenth Amendment?" Sister Walker said pointedly. "All right. Now you know about that secret, too. Will there be any more bloodletting required, or may we get back to your training?"

Memphis leaned down and whispered to Isaiah. "You're gonna hear about this on the way home."

"It's all right to ask questions, Memphis," Sister Walker said. "That's how we learn."

"Sister, I think you might be a Diviner with that hearing," Memphis said, shaking his head.

"Sam, I'd like to try testing your powers again," Sister Walker announced. So far, they'd had little luck in boosting his gifts. He tried not to let it bother him, passing it off with jokes—*Can't improve on perfection!*—but it made him feel small and lacking, like when he was a kid in Chicago running from the bullies who tormented him with fists and taunts of *Jew!* When he realized he could make those bullies go blank in his presence, Sam had, for the first time in his life, experienced what it was to be powerful. That power had gotten him from Chicago to New York. It had helped him survive on the streets. He'd come to rely on it. In fact, he'd been down-right cocky about it. But now, surrounded by everyone else, what he felt was competitive.

"Let's try a control. Theta? Would you mind?" Sister Walker asked.

Theta blanched. "Me? Oh, I don't know, Sister…."

"Aw, Theta's too smart to fall for my hooey," Sam said, trying to save her. "Besides, she knows all about my powers."

"So does most of New York City by now. The question is, will your powers work now that they are known? Does that knowledge affect people's suggestibility?"

"Oh. I hadn't thought about that," Sam said.

"Theta, could you, please?" Sister Walker extended a hand to her.

Theta put out her cigarette and, feeling nervous, took a seat opposite Sam.

"Okay?" Sam asked.

"Okay," she said.

"Evie, since Sam seems to affect your reading ability, let's see if you have any sway over his powers. Come sit close to him, if you would, please," Sister Walker said.

With a pained sigh, Evie left the comfort of her chair and came to sit beside Sam. She liked the way he smelled, like spicy aftershave and something else, something she could only describe as Sam.

Sam squinted at her. "You jake? You look funny."

"I'm fine. Just…don't steal anything from me," Evie warned.

"Here goes." Sam thrust his left hand toward Theta. "Don't see me."

Theta blinked and Sam's shoulders sagged. She could see him losing confidence.

"Try again," she urged. "Go all out."

"You sure?" Sam said quietly.

"Yeah. Think about putting me right to sleep."

"Sam's good at that," Evie grumbled.

"Okaaay," Sam said, breathing deeply.

Theta took hold of Sam's other arm, and he looked into her eyes, think-ing of every time he'd been doubted. A memory swam into his head. The night his mother kissed him good-bye. *I must do this, Little Fox. Our country needs me. But I will be home soon enough.* He never saw his mother again. He would find her. He would get stronger and he would find her.

"Don't. See. Me," Sam growled.

Static charged the air, raising the hair on Evie's arms and the back of her neck. She blinked, a bit dazed. Sam was no longer beside her. Had she gone under?

"Sam? Sam!" Evie called as she turned in her chair, searching.

"You already tried that little stunt, Evie."

She could hear Sam's voice, but she couldn't see him. At his desk, Will had gone slack and glassy-eyed, as had Mabel and Jericho. Theta stared straight ahead. Even Henry, Ling, and Isaiah looked dazed. Other than Evie herself, only Memphis and Sister Walker were alert.

"I'm not pulling your leg, Sam. Honest!" Evie put out a hand and yelped when she touched something solid. *He was right next to her.* "Sam. You're… *invisible!*"

"I am?"

"Yes, you're—aaah!" Evie shrieked, and leaped from her chair. "Stop tickling me!"

"This is the best day of my life!" Sam's laughter rippled the air where he sat, and then he began to reappear like a ghost image on film until he was fully restored.

"Twenty-two seconds," Sister Walker said, clearly excited. "That's how long you were invisible."

"Five seconds. That's how long it's gonna take me to give you a black eye," Evie said.

Ling blinked, coming fully around. "Wh-what happened?"

"Sam went invisible. Unfortunately, he came back," Evie told her.

Ling opened her notebook, excited. "Where—where did you go when you disappeared? Do you feel strange in any way?"

"Sam is strange in every way," Jericho said, shaking his head and getting his bearings. Mabel and Will were still under, Evie noticed.

"I didn't go anywhere. I was right here. But it's funny. I felt really alive—like I was hitting on all sixes!" Sam scratched at his arms. "Jeepers, that smarts. Aaah! Feels like ants!"

"That could be an aftereffect of the invisibility," Sister Walker said.

60

Sam left his chair to rub his back against the grizzly bear's stiff hide. "Wait—my swell new power gives me a rash? Aww, that ain't fair at all!"

Theta snorted, drawing Sister Walker's eyes. Too late, Theta realized that she should have faked going under for longer. The Metaphysickometer hummed loudly as the needle shot to the other side for a second, then settled.

Sister Walker eyed her suspiciously. "Theta, have you ever experienced any abilities?"

Theta tucked her hands under her thighs in case they got the idea to heat up. "No."

"Were either of your parents gifted?"

"I wouldn't know. They left me on a doorstep when I was a baby."

"Oh. I'm sorry," Sister Walker said.

"Why doesn't Sam's power affect you, Miss Walker?" Evie asked. The others were starting to come around now, and Ling was filling them in on the breakthrough.

"Training," Sister Walker said. "I suspect Memphis's healing powers make him immune. As for you, Evie, it would appear that you and Sam share a special bond."

Evie looked over at Sam, who was still scratching himself against the bear. "Swell," she said.

Sister Walker still scrutinized Theta. "It's possible that you have some latent power you're only now coming into, Theta. If you could let us test you—"

"The only test I'm doing is a screen test for Vitagraph. And then it's on to Hollywood, to one of those pretty bungalows with a lemon tree out back. They say the sun shines out there all the time, Miss Walker. I like the sun. So, please, just look after my pals and leave me out of it," Theta said, grabbing her pocketbook. "'Scuse me. I need to powder my nose."

Theta sneaked out to the small scrap of garden behind the museum. She unfolded the note that had been left on her makeup table back at the theater. *Somebody knows.*

"You ever gonna tell 'em?" Sam said from behind her.

Theta quickly stuffed the note deep into her purse. "You might warn a girl before sneaking up on her."

"Defeats the purpose of sneaking up." Sam folded his arms and leaned against the cold brick. "Asked you a question."

Theta squished a mealy acorn under her shoe. "Tell 'em what?"

"About what happened down in those tunnels, how you set fire to one of those wraiths with your bare hands." When Theta didn't answer, Sam pleaded with her. "Theta, you got a big power. Bigger than mine. We might need it?"

"Shhh!" Theta hurried over to Sam and lowered her voice. "Whatever this disease is inside me, I just want it gone."

"Maybe they can help you with it," Sam tried.

"Nothing doing."

"Why?"

"Because I'm the only one of us whose powers are bad!" Theta blurted. "Makes me feel like I'm dirty or something. Like a killer." Theta looked Sam in the eyes. She hated feeling so vulnerable. "You gonna snitch on me?"

Sam let out a long exhale. "Nah. I'm no snitch. But I really wish you'd tell the professor and Miss Walker about what you can do."

"Yeah. Well," Theta said sadly. "We all wish for something, don't we?"

CHASING GHOSTS

Before heading out, Evie paused at Will's office door. The light from his lamp bled under the crack, along with the sound of his old Victrola playing a classical record, and Evie could imagine Will staying up half the night, reading spooky ghost reports in the deepening gloom while a Chopin nocturne kept him company.

Evie knocked and poked her head in. "Mind if I come in?"

"Make yourself at home."

"Same old Creepy Crawly," Evie said, taking in the mess of papers and books and odd supernatural knickknacks. She picked up a book from the edge of Will's desk and was surprised to discover it wasn't some macabre ghost tome but Dickens. "*A Tale of Two Cities*?"

Will managed a fond smile. "That happens to be my favorite book."

Evie made a face. "It's *no one's* favorite book."

"It's mine," Will said on a laugh. "It reminds us that even in the midst of chaos and terror, there is the capacity for change. For a new and better society. For selflessness. I admire Sydney Carton tremendously."

"Because you fancy yourself a hero?" Evie said. She hadn't meant it to sound so sneering.

Will's smile vanished. "Because I know that I'm not."

Already, the conversation was making Evie uncomfortable. She lifted the book's cover. The first page was inscribed, *To Will with love from Rotke, Christmas 1916.*

Will cleared his throat. "Do you mind?"

Evie snapped the book shut and returned it to its spot before resuming her slow circle of the room. "I wanted to talk to you about something. Do you remember a few weeks ago I had an incident on my radio show?"

"I don't listen to the radio much," Will said.

Evie stared in disbelief. "How can you *not* listen to the radio, Uncle Will? It's 1927! *Everyone* listens to the radio. It's how we live."

Will fought another smile. "I'm as much of an artifact as everything in here. But I'm guessing you had something else to tell me."

For the past few months, Evie had gotten used to thinking of Will as the enemy. But he was family, too. And Will knew things. Things that could be helpful. She was just going to have to risk trusting him a little bit.

"A curious thing happened," Evie said, finally coming to rest in a button-back leather club chair that she wished she could steal for her own room at the Winthrop. "A fellow named Bob Bateman came on the show and asked me to read his friend's comb. He said his friend had died in the war. While I was under, I *did* see soldiers. They were on a train. I saw the soldier who tried to shoot me—Luther Clayton? He wasn't much older than I am now. He still had his legs and his mind was unbroken. And then I saw James on that train. Will, that comb belonged to James."

"You're sure?" Will asked, his face grave.

"Positive."

Her uncle reached for his ever-present cigarette case, selecting one from inside its sardine-like hold and tamping the end against the top of his desk till the loose tobacco conformed. "How did this Bateman fellow get James's comb?"

"Here's where it gets stranger. I chased Bob Bateman down the street and demanded to know where he'd gotten the comb. He told me he'd been paid to say that by some men in dark suits."

"That's not particularly helpful. You might as well say, 'I was paid by a man with a mustache,'" Will said, reaching for his lighter.

"I know." Evie pushed the words out on a heavy sigh. She snapped her fingers. "Adams! That was the man's name."

Will fumbled with his cigarette lighter. He raked his thumb against the little wheel until the flame caught.

"Does that name mean something to you? Do you know who that is?" Evie asked.

"No." Will drew on his cigarette.

Evie leaned into the chair, letting its comfort cradle her. "The comb showed me the soldiers playing a guessing game with cards. James knew the card one of the soldiers held. He knew it was the Ace of Spades without even seeing it."

Will blew out a thick cloud of smoke. "Could've been a lucky guess. Or he could've seen the card beforehand and not told."

"I suppose so. Except…"

"Except?"

"When he guessed it, one of the other soldiers said, 'Right again.' That suggests James had done it before. Doesn't it?"

"Evie, where are you leading with this?"

Evie sat forward. "Do you think it's possible that James had special powers, too? I was so young when he died, I can't remember him doing anything, well, Diviners-like. Do you?"

"Mostly, I remember that he loved baseball, especially the Chicago White Sox. I don't think that makes him exceptional. I think that made him an American kid," Will said, tapping ash into an overflowing brass tray.

Evie liked hearing stories about her brother. Why had they never talked about James before? "What else?"

Will pulled on his cigarette again, smiling at some private memory. "He once stole a pie your neighbor had baked from off her kitchen windowsill, where she'd set it to cool. He took it into the woods and ate the entire thing with his hands."

"His hands?"

"Indeed. And then he vomited all night. Your mother told him it served him right."

"She would." Evie laughed. "I can't believe he didn't share any with me."

"You were only two or three, if memory serves."

The record spun out. It wasn't jazz, but it was pretty. She wondered what James would think of the Hotsy Totsy, how fun it would be to take him there. How she wished he could've seen the girl she'd grown up to be. Would he be proud of her? Disappointed?

"I dream about him all the time," Evie said, her smile fading.

"I understand."

Almost automatically, it seemed to Evie, Will looked over at the framed photograph of his dead fiancée that he kept on his desk. Evie had caught glimpses of Rotke when reading over Sam's mother's mementos, so she'd picked up bits here and there—Rotke seemed warm and happy. "What was she like?"

"She was clever," Will said after a long pause. "So very smart. And a Diviner."

"She was?"

"Her powers weren't as strong as all of yours. But she could read people. She could read me. And I suppose I needed reading. I didn't even understand myself. Not as well as Rotke did."

"You never really said. How did she die?"

Will drew slowly on his cigarette, letting his answer out with the smoke. "It was an accident. In the lab. There was nothing that could be done."

Evie wanted to know more, but she also didn't want to pry into her uncle's private pain. "About Bob Bateman's comb," she said, bringing the conversation around again. "I've been thinking: What if James is trying to send me a message from beyond?"

"Oh, Evie…" Will started.

"But what if he is? I dream of soldiers all the time—"

"That doesn't mean anything—"

"The same dream. Over and over—"

"Evangeline. Don't *do* this to yourself—"

"They're in a forest. And James is trying to tell me something important. He's trying to warn me and—"

"*James is dead*, Evangeline!" Will thundered, bringing his fist down on the desk, rattling his papers. "He is dead! And the dead. Must. Rest. Let him go and move on."

Will's words hit like a fist. Tears pricked at Evie's eyes.

Will raked his fingers through his hair, his nervous habit, and took in a settling breath. "I'm…I'm sorry, Evie. I shouldn't have shouted. I know what it is to lose someone. But when they're gone, they're gone," he said quietly. "We learn to live without them. To let go. To move forward."

Evie swallowed. Her throat ached. "Sure. Once it's gone, it's gone. I guess that's why we're chasing ghosts."

Will rose and came to stand awkwardly beside Evie's chair, his hands in his pockets. He reached out and patted Evie's shoulder as if he'd read it in a manual on how to be a human. No wonder he'd needed Rotke.

"I'm sorry, Evie. Truly, I am."

Evie shirked away. This whole conversation had been a mistake.

"Why? It's not like *you* killed anybody," Evie said, and closed the door behind her harder than was necessary.

On Friday evening, after the week of experiments had left the Diviners tired and grumpy, Sister Walker brought out a plate of cookies. "Not to worry, I didn't bake these. My neighbor did. So they are perfectly edible," she said with a wink to Memphis and Isaiah.

"What did you do with Diviners before, when you worked with the Department of Paranormal?" Sam asked between slurps of steaming tea.

"Oh. We talked to people like you. We wrote down your stories. Asked questions." Will dunked a cookie half into his cup while Evie watched in fascinated revulsion.

She wrinkled her nose. "Honestly, Unc," she said, accidentally using the affectionate nickname she'd given him ages ago. He smiled at her, and she was immediately angry at herself for the slip. After the argument they'd had earlier in the week about James, she'd determined to be aloof with Will. As usual, she was an utter failure at holding a grudge.

"I suppose you got to know those Diviners pretty well, then," Ling said.

Will brushed his hands of crumbs and took out his silver case, wedging a Lucky Strike between his lips. "We got to know what they could do."

Ling frowned. "That's not the same thing at all."

"Did you test them like you're testing us?" Isaiah asked.

"Yes, we did. Some people had a small amount of ability and some had quite a bit more," Sister Walker said.

"What about me? How much do I have?"

"A great deal. And there's more in there we haven't even explored yet," Sister Walker said, and Isaiah broke into a huge grin. "That goes for all of you."

"You, uh, ever experiment on those Diviners?" Sam asked cagily. "You know, did you look under the hood, see what made 'em tick? Did you take blood samples or anything like that?"

He avoided eye contact with Evie, but he could sense her leaning forward. Sister Walker put down her cup. "From time to time."

"Why'd you do that?" Isaiah asked. He shuddered. "I don't like needles."

Will exhaled. The smoke floated in front of his face like a veil. "We wanted to know if there was an hereditary difference in Diviners that caused their powers. Was this evidence of an evolutionary leap? What if Diviners, with their connection to the supernatural, were the key to unlocking untapped human potential?"

"So, these Diviners you tested," Sam asked. "Can we talk to any of 'em? I mean, if we're all needed to fight off this spooky showdown…"

"Spooky *showdown*?" Evie repeated, eyebrow raised.

"Just seems odd we're not reaching out to them is all."

"We can't," Sister Walker said. "Our files were destroyed when the department was shut down. We have no way of reaching them. I'm afraid it's down to the six of you."

"Any runner in Harlem would tell you those aren't great odds," Memphis said.

"*Why* did they shut you down?" Ling asked. "If you were doing important work."

"The war ended us." Will spoke as if each word cost him dearly. "The war and its horrors. It was no longer an age for mystery and miracles. It was an age of industry and weapons and the industry of weapons."

"So," Theta said after a moment of uncomfortable silence, "in all this *investigating* you two did, you ever meet a bad Diviner?"

Sister Walker warmed her hands against her china cup. "There is always the capacity to abuse power," she said evenly.

"Must be pretty rotten if you won't even talk about it." Theta's palms prickled.

Sister Walker sipped her tea, then set her cup down. "There was a Diviner once who could pull the life out of things."

"Holy smokes!" Sam said on a gasp.

"He could *kill people*?" Isaiah blurted.

"That's some power—"

"Who'd he kill? How many?"

"He didn't kill anyone that I know of," Sister Walker said. "But he could ease an animal's passing or wilt a rose in a vase."

"Can we meet him?" Isaiah asked. "Or do they keep him in a special jail somewhere?"

"I don't know where he is," Sister Walker said with a note of sadness. "He left us one day. We never saw him again."

A hush fell over the table. The wind thundered across the roof like a ghostly herd, drawing everyone's eyes for a moment to the painted expanse of ceiling—bewigged Founding Fathers surrounded by spirits and magic and mysteries.

"Kinda funny when you think about it," Sam said around a mouthful of cookie.

"What's that?" Will asked. He'd abandoned his cookie in favor of a cigarette.

"Me and Isaiah. Evie. Memphis. Ling. Henry. And—" Sam quickly stopped himself from saying Theta. "Us. We got a Jew, two Negroes, a half-Chinese-half-Irish girl. Coupla Catholics. Sounds like the start of some really awful joke the stuffed shirts would tell behind closed doors."

"What's your point?" Ling said.

"Well, people like to say we're not true Americans, whatever that means. But we're the ones with these powers." Sam shrugged. "It's just kinda funny is all."

He caught Sister Walker throwing a meaningful glance Will's way. It was quick but noticeable. But then Sister Walker was putting aside her tea and standing to her full height, smoothing down the front of her dress as if to announce that no wrinkle, no flaw could find purchase in her. "Time to get back to work. Sam, Henry, and Ling, let's see what you can do together."

Henry slurped down the rest of his milky tea and wiped his mouth. He winked at Evie. "We who are about to die salute you."

Evie put a hand over her heart. "I'll remember you fondly on your birthday," she said with mock-solemnity. She was suddenly aware of Jericho beside her.

"Meet me in the collections room," he whispered in her ear, making the skin along her neck buzz. And just like that, everything about him that she'd tried to put away came flooding back.

☀

Evie waited until a new test was under way, and then she slipped out of the library. Her stomach had begun to flutter. *Don't you dare*, she scolded, but her stomach wouldn't listen.

"Hi," Jericho said with a shy smile as Evie entered the collections room.

"Hi," she said back. *Steady*, she thought.

"You, ah, looked like you might need a rescue."

"Thanks." Evie laughed, relieved that she didn't have to pretend otherwise. It was one of the things she liked about Jericho. Around him, she didn't feel the need to pretend. There was a certain loneliness in Jericho that she recognized, a twin to her own. The way he looked at her from time to time, like a searchlight that had found what it sought, made her go a little dizzy.

Evie hopped up on the sideboard. "Gee, I love what you've done with the place. How smart you are to put the spectral barometer beside the... um"—Evie gestured vaguely to a group of shriveled potato-like cuttings on a table beside Jericho—"dead vegetables."

Jericho smiled and lifted one eyebrow. "It's a mandrake root."

"So it is! *I'm* certainly rooting for it."

"Evie, I need to tell you something. You're the only person I can tell, actually," he added.

"All right," she said. It made her feel special that he trusted her.

From his pocket, Jericho brought out a leather pouch. He unrolled it and took out a stoppered glass vial with a small portion of blue liquid inside. "It's all I've got left. Marlowe gave me an ultimatum: Be part of his Future of America Exhibition, let him test me, parade me onstage as his shining victory—or he'll cut me off for good."

Evie knew that Marlowe's serum was lifesaving. It kept the tubes and wires inside Jericho working. "He wouldn't really do that, would he? Why, that's blackmail!"

"No. It's Marlowe," Jericho said. He hopped up beside her on the sideboard. "If I agree, I'd need to live with Marlowe upstate until the exhibition. I'd have to leave the museum and Will and you just when you need me most."

"Oh," Evie said, deflating a bit at the thought of Jericho being gone. "We'll manage. Don't worry about us."

"I do worry, though. Feels like something big is happening. I don't want you to get hurt." Jericho reached out and tucked one of Evie's loose curls behind her ear, and she caught her breath. "As terrible as it was, that night with John Hobbes made me start to come alive again. I saw that I had just been existing before. I want more than that. You made me see that, Evie. I'm forever grateful to your uncle. But I don't want to shelve books for the rest of my life. I want to make my mark." He took hold of her hand. "It never would've worked for Mabel and me, you know."

"I see that now. But does Mabel?"

"I think so. What about you and Sam?"

What about Sam? It was probably for the best that he had ended things. They were combustible together—perfection one minute and at each other's throats the next. Still, it hurt her pride to be the "jilted woman," with the papers reporting on all of Sam's flings. And she'd be lying if she said she didn't still carry a torch for him. Was it normal to have a crush on two boys at the same time?

Jericho was looking right at her. His eyes were the blue of a summer sky.

"Just a publicity stunt," she said, hoping it didn't sound bitter.

"Seems like, for the first time since we met, there's nothing standing in our way," Jericho said. Very gently, Jericho took her hand and brought it to his shirt, above his heart. It had been months since their kiss on the roof of the Bennington, but she knew that the feeling hadn't gone away. She'd only pushed it aside again and again. Evie spread her fingers against Jericho's broad chest, and he moaned softly. It made her dizzy; it made her feel powerful.

"Evie, I don't want to waste any more time." Jericho leaned in to kiss her.

There was a loud knock. Theta popped her head around the door. She looked from Evie to Jericho, her eyebrows rising. Quickly, Evie yanked her hand away from Jericho's chest and shoved both hands under her armpits.

"Hi, Theta! We were just talking!" she said.

"Yeah. I didn't ask. Sister Walker's looking for you, Evil. She wants you to come read some objects. So when you're finished *talking*, we're in the library." Before Theta shut the door, she shot Evie a *We will talk about this later oh yes we will* look, to which Evie responded with her own: *Okay. Fine. Yes. Go!*

"I'd better report for duty," Evie said with a mock-salute. Her cheeks were warm. She let her hand rest on a poppet doll, and its secrets licked at her palm before she snapped her fingers away again.

"Say, Evie?"

"Mm-hmm?" Evie said, chasing the object's thoughts from her mind.

"Maybe you'd like to go to the pictures sometime? Or for a walk. Or anything, really."

"Maybe," she said. "Sure."

"Sure?" Jericho smiled.

Evie bit her lip and nodded. "Sure," she said.

"Say, I was just looking for you. Are you okay?" Mabel asked as Evie breezed back into the library and took a seat.

"Of course! Why wouldn't I be?"

"I don't know. You're all flushed. And your voice is really high. Are you sick?"

"I . . . I think it's just been too much excitement," Evie managed.

Mabel laughed. "You? Too much excitement? I never thought I'd hear those words come out of your mouth!"

The pocket doors slid open again, and Jericho let himself in silently. He looked over at Evie, smiling shyly, guiltily. Evie did her best not to return the glance but failed.

Mabel saw it all.

RABBLE-ROUSERS

Why?

That was the question on Mabel's mind as she crossed Sixth Avenue, her bones rattling as the elevated train rumbled far above her head.

Why did Jericho like Evie and not her? (It was painfully obvious and had been for some time. Mabel just couldn't seem to let go.)

Why did some people have special powers but not her?

Why did she let it bother her so?

Oh, Mabel knew that she and Jericho weren't a good match. Not really. But it stung that he hadn't wanted her. Just once in her life, Mabel had wanted to come first. She'd wanted to be the chosen one instead of the chosen one's reliable, unexciting best friend. A kid tried to sell her a newspaper. "No, *thank* you!" Mabel barked. Then she felt guilty for it and tossed him a nickel at the last minute, taking the newspaper she hadn't even wanted in the first place.

Why had she done that? *Why* did she feel like she had to be so good all the time?

As Mabel turned the corner onto Bleecker Street, she noticed the man in the brown fedora at the bottom of the train steps. He was just standing there, watching her. Her stomach fluttered. Quickly, she tucked her purse and the newspaper under her arm, walking up Bleecker Street. She glanced behind her. The man followed. She couldn't lead him to Arthur's place. Mabel took a sharp left onto Macdougal Street and stopped in front of a bakery window, pretending to admire a pastry display. Out of the corner of her eye, she saw the man stop a few windows down, pretending to check his watch. That was all the confirmation Mabel needed. Heart beating fast, she walked briskly toward Washington Square Park, trying to lose herself among the throngs of people. She let the newspaper fly. Its pages scattered on the wind, a distraction Mabel used to duck into a drugstore and sneak out the back door into an alley, practically running to the Bohemian Reader and up the back stairs to Arthur's garret. The others were already there, gathered around the small, scuffed wooden table, smoking cigarettes and knocking back coffee.

Mabel fought to get her breathing under control. She didn't want to come off half-cocked.

"Ah. Mabel. How is your little Italian friend? Any more visions?" Aron joked, and everything about Mabel's rotten day came crashing down inside her.

"Maybe you should ask the man who's been following me," Mabel blurted.

"What do you mean? What did this man look like?" Arthur asked, coming toward her.

"Like a Pinkerton trying not to be seen. I have spent my whole life on the lookout for just that sort of thing, you know, and I can spot it."

"Did he follow you here?" Luis asked.

Mabel shook her head. "I did my best to lose him. It's why I was late." Mabel told them everything that had happened. "And then I managed to lose him," she said, sinking into a chair, all the earlier adrenaline washing away, leaving her feeling loose and sleepy.

Gloria rushed to the window, yanking up the blinds.

"Hey!" Arthur said. He lowered the blinds again. "We've gotta be careful now. If any of you think you're being followed, take another route, like Mabel did, or buy a book from Mr. Jenkins downstairs for our 'book club.' You all remember the Palmer Raids. If we're caught with radical publications, we could all be arrested. Aron could be deported to the Soviet Union, and Luis to Mexico."

Arthur peeked out through two of the slats. "No one there now."

He squatted at Mabel's side, looking up at her. "You sure you're all right?"

"Fine," Mabel said, but she liked that Arthur had asked. Most people didn't.

Satisfied, Arthur took a seat on the edge of the battered steamer trunk. "On to business, then. No one's paying attention to the striking workers. The press has lost interest. They only want to talk about Marlowe's Future of America Exhibition."

Luis untied a handkerchief full of roasted nuts, offering them to all. "I

74

hear management has hired local thugs as militiamen. They beat one of the miners last night and sent him to the hospital. Word is those militiamen are driving around the camp in trucks with Gatling guns mounted in the back to intimidate them."

"And the radium and uranium they're mining is making the men sick. They can scarcely breathe," Gloria said.

"Why do you suppose Marlowe needs so much uranium?" Mabel asked, echoing Ling's earlier question.

"He probably sells it," Gloria said. "It's just pure, old-fashioned greed."

"Well, if everybody could see what's happening in the camp, surely they'd be horrified; they'd have to do something to stop it," Mabel said.

"People choose not to see," Arthur said in his gentle way.

Mabel thought for a moment. "What if we made a newsreel? Marlowe makes them all the time to tout how great he is. But we could show people how sick his miners are and how bad the conditions are in the tent camp. If people could see it for themselves, they couldn't ignore what's really happening."

Aron snorted. "Where are we going to get a movie camera? Who's gonna pay for that? Vitagraph Studios? They have pictures to make with Clara Bow. They're not going to bring trouble on themselves making newsreels for socialists about immigrant workers they don't see as Americans— or even as people."

"I don't see you coming up with any bright ideas," Mabel snapped.

Aron chuckled and put up his hands. "Now, don't get mad—"

"Too late. I'm already there," Mabel said.

Gloria put out her cigarette and linked her arm through Mabel's. "Hear, hear, Mabel. You boys act like you run the revolution. If you think we're going to iron your shirts while you spout slogans, you're all wet."

"You're putting words in my mouth," Aron grumbled.

Mabel ignored him. "What if I *could* get us a camera?"

Gloria arched an eyebrow. "You have an uncle at Vitagraph?"

Mabel smiled. "Let's just say that I know someone who has a talent for borrowing."

"We need guns, not film," Aron grumbled.

"Just like them?" Mabel shot back. She'd seen this argument unfold at countless meetings. There was always one organizer eager to escalate the fight. "My mother says the minute we pick up guns we become the enemy we're fighting."

Aron scoffed. "Your mother, your mother. Do you have your own thoughts?"

Mabel's cheeks burned. "Yes. I'm having a thought about you just now."

"Nobody's picking up a gun. And we're not here to fight with one another," Arthur said, staring at Aron until he looked away.

"Sorry, Mabel," Aron mumbled.

"Thank you," Mabel said.

Arthur smiled at Mabel. "All right, then. Mabel Rose, you are officially the director of the Secret Six motion picture division. Now, let's talk about the rally for Sacco and Vanzetti downtown tomorrow...."

They talked well past suppertime, and Mabel found herself growing more excited by the hour. It was so different from the museum. There, she felt out of place. She had no special powers like Evie and the others. Her place was firmly rooted in fighting the evils of *this* world, and there were plenty of them to fight. That's what the Secret Six was about—changing the world for good. For fairness. For justice. That, she was realizing, was something she could do, something she *had* to do.

As the others trickled out, Mabel stayed behind. She was alive with a sense of purpose, and she didn't want to put that excitement away just yet. She began gathering plates.

"You don't have to clear the dishes, you know," Arthur said as Mabel loaded the tiny, chipped sink with sudsy water.

"I know," Mabel said, smiling. She removed her gold watch and laid it on the drainboard.

Arthur whistled. "That doesn't look like a socialist's watch."

"It was a gift from my grandmother," Mabel said, somewhat apologetically.

"Ah, yes. The famous Newells of the Social Register, one of New York's oldest and wealthiest families." Arthur shook his head and dried the clean plate Mabel had handed him. "Must be strange. Do you ever see your mother's family?"

"At Christmas. And on my grandmother's birthday."

"I've always wondered: What's it like with the very rich?"

What was it like? When Mabel visited Nana Newell, white-aproned servants moved in and out of the rooms silently with tiered plates of finger sandwiches and hot coffee in china cups. Everyone in the house called her Miss Mabel. Her confident mother seemed to shrink in that huge house. Often, the visits ended with Mabel's grandmother silent, offended, and Mabel's mother in angry tears. Mabel did love the house, though. She couldn't help running a finger across the shining, monogrammed silver or admiring the well-polished grand piano. Mabel had always wanted to take lessons, but there hadn't been money for it, and Mabel's mother felt that such pastimes were too closely aligned with the idle rich. It was better, in her mother's mind, for Mabel to have a solid education.

"She always serves petits fours," Mabel said after a pause.

Arthur grinned. "Well, I suppose that's something. Do you love your grandmother?"

"Well, I really love her petits fours."

Arthur barked out a laugh, which made Mabel laugh, too.

"What about your family?" she asked.

For the first time, Arthur seemed sad. "I grew up poor." He gestured to the cramped, leaky garret. "Now I live in luxury. Petits fours all the time." He reached into the soapy water for a cup and his fingers brushed Mabel's.

Mabel's cheeks flushed. She kept her eyes on her task.

"My mother died when I was five. My father when I was eight. My older brother, Paul, raised me after that. I went to school till I was eleven, and then I left school and worked in the textiles factory with him. Twelve hours a day. It was Paulie who started the Secret Six."

Mabel passed Arthur a cup. "He did?"

Arthur nodded.

"Where is your brother now?"

"In prison." Arthur wiped the towel across the coffee cup with care. "He was tired of seeing friends living in two-room shacks with their families while management fat cats lived well. The Bureau was after him for every little thing—he couldn't walk to the corner store for bread without being followed. He got fed up. So he sent a bomb to a congressman. The congressman's secretary opened the package, though. It blew off her hands."

Mabel grimaced, imagining the poor secretary. It was all coming back to her now. "I remember. It was in all the papers. My parents were very upset. They said violence like that gives radicals a bad name. Oh, I'm sorry. I shouldn't have..."

"It's okay." Arthur pulled the plug from the sink and watched the dirty water swirl down.

"Isn't he to be executed?" Mabel asked gingerly.

"By firing squad," Arthur said, gently drying Mabel's soapy hands with a rag. "Unless his appeal goes through."

"Is there anything I can do to help?"

Arthur smiled. "You can come back tomorrow."

Mabel's stomach did a flip-flop. "Of course. I'm sure there's all manner of, um, plans to make. With the Six. Of course."

Arthur still smiled. "Mm-hmm."

Mabel was so nervous she backed up and bumped into the table. "Sorry." She reached for her gloves. Blueprints peeked out from underneath a workers' newspaper. "What's this?"

Quickly, Arthur grabbed the blueprints away, rolling them into a tight paper club. "It's nothing."

And suddenly, Mabel felt dumb again. After they'd opened up to each other, she'd assumed a closeness; she'd overstepped. "Gee, it's late. I-I'd better go," she said, walking briskly to the door.

"Mabel, wait! I'm sorry. I'm just...not accustomed to trusting people." Arthur took hold of Mabel's hand, and a tingle traveled up her arm and made her neck buzzy. "With my brother's situation, you can understand. See, I want to stage a protest. At the Future of America Exhibition. Jake Marlowe is a symbol of everything that's wrong with American capitalism. That exhibition is a wicked lie—it's amoral—when good men are dying in his mine with no hope of participating in the pretty future he's building."

Mabel liked how passionate Arthur was. He wasn't the most handsome man she'd ever seen, not like Jericho. But Arthur had principles and courage. That was attractive. "I could help you spread the word about the protest."

"Not just yet," Arthur said, locking the blueprints in a trunk. "Let's get you home. Wouldn't want your parents to have another reason to hate me."

"You don't have to see me home," Mabel said.

Arthur raised an eyebrow. "You said there was a fella following you."

"Maybe I was wrong. I don't know." Mabel felt a bit silly now. Perhaps he'd only been walking the same direction she had.

"Well," Arthur said, reaching for his coat, "I'm not taking any chances."

❋

"Extra! Extra! Two Men Drowned in Hell Gate Waters Off Ward's Island!" a newsie called as they neared the Sixth Avenue train. "Ghosts in the Asylum, Patients Say! Haunted Hospital! Monsters in the Madhouse!" Eager readers swarmed the boy, tossing their nickels and grabbing the hot sheets.

Arthur jerked a thumb at them. "*That's* what sells newspapers these days," he said, and shook his head as they climbed the steps to the train. "Do you know why people make up ghost stories?"

There were many things Mabel could say to that, but she didn't want Arthur to know about her work at the museum and think her foolish. She settled on, "Why?"

"Because it's easier than believing that ordinary people can be cruel and downright evil," Arthur said.

❋

The minute she got home to the Bennington, Mabel knocked on Will Fitzgerald's door.

"Mabel!" Sam said. "Say, this is a nice surprise."

"Sam, could you steal me a movie camera?"

Sam's eyebrows went up. "That is, without a doubt, the most interesting question I've been asked today. And considering the day involved talk about ghosts and the end of the world, that's saying something."

Jericho came up behind Sam, and Mabel caught her breath. She wished she could just stop liking him. It would be so much easier. "Why do you need a movie camera?" he asked.

"I can assure you, it's for a good cause."

"You wouldn't take on a cause if it weren't good," Jericho said, and Mabel wasn't entirely sure it was meant as a compliment.

"You don't really have to steal it, but I figured you might know somebody," Mabel said. "You always know somebody, Sam."

Sam stroked his chin. "That's true. Come to think of it, I *do* know a fella owes me a favor. If he's not in jail or hasn't been shot by a jealous girlfriend, I can get it for you."

"Thanks, Sam. I owe you." Mabel kissed Sam on the cheek, stealing a glance at Jericho as she did. *Take that, Jericho.*

On her way back to her apartment, Mabel reflected on Arthur's comment about the human capacity for evil. She wasn't naive; she'd seen plenty of bad. What Jake Marlowe and his management were doing to the workers in the name of profit was certainly cruel, if not evil. But sometimes evil was made up of small acts: cheating someone out of their due or ignoring a wrong, like during the Palmer Raids, when agents had pulled people from their homes to deport them and their neighbors had looked the other way. The longer those smaller acts of wrong went unchallenged, the more they compounded into a monster. But there had to be a counterbalance to that, and it was the human capacity for good. For kindness and self-sacrifice and justice. Toward helping your neighbor because, after all, weren't we all in this world together? Those, too, were often small acts. Like Arthur leaving his garret to travel uptown—far out of his way—just to make sure that Mabel got home all right. That was good. That was unselfish. It made Mabel like Arthur all the more. It made her want to be an even better person. And those small acts of good carried forward with a breathtaking momentum. Over time, they could change the world for the better. Mabel believed that, perhaps more fervently than any prayer.

Before she'd even reached her apartment, Mabel could hear her father's typewriter keys clacking away.

"Hello, Papa," she said, breezing through the door, stopping to kiss his cheek.

Smiling, her father cupped her chin in one hand. *"Shayna Punim."* Her father's Yiddish came out when he was feeling sentimental or whenever he couldn't quite find the words he was looking for in English.

Mabel rolled her eyes at her father's sentimentality. "I do not have a beautiful face, Papa. I have a serviceable face."

She didn't say, *Mama's the beautiful one. I take after you.*

"I know *shayna* when I see it," her father said, as if that settled the matter. He pecked out another sentence on the typewriter using just his index fingers and returned the carriage with a cheery *ting!*

"Papa…" Mabel began.

"Yes, dear heart," he said without looking up.

"Nothing." She sat to remove her shoes, letting her toes breathe.

The typing stopped. "That's a heavy sigh for such a nothing."

"Have you heard anything about workers disappearing?"

Her father's thick brows came together in concentration. "Do you mean walking off the job or being held by the police without being charged?"

"No, I mean *disappearing.* Being taken away by strange men. Government men. Or maybe not government men. I don't know." She wasn't making sense. The whole thing seemed unreal the more she thought about it. "You heard anything about some men wearing a lapel pin—an eye with a lightning bolt?"

Her father shook his head. "Never. What's all this about, *Maideleh*?"

"Nothing, Papa. Just…nothing," she said, and he resumed his typing.

"Why don't you like Arthur Brown?" she blurted out at last. "He seems like a very smart fellow."

Her father's fingers paused above the Underwood's keys. "Smart, yes. And very…ambitious," her father said. *Ambitious* wasn't a compliment from her father. It usually meant "reckless" or "arrogant." "So, who's asking about Arthur Brown?"

"Oh. I ran into him on Bleecker Street the other day."

"That's all?"

"That's *all*, Papa," Mabel said, stepping into the cramped bathroom to check her reflection.

"Good," her father said under his breath. Mabel could hear him cranking a fresh sheet of paper around the typewriter's cylinder and thwacking the metal bar back to hold it in place. "How is your friend, the student? Reads all the time? Jacob?"

"Jericho," Mabel corrected. She dabbed on a bit of the lipstick Evie had given her. It didn't look bad, but it didn't turn her into Gloria Swanson, either. "He's more interested in Diviners than me."

"Ach, Diviners."

"What do you have against Diviners?"

"Nothing, it's only that I don't understand why people will put their faith in soothsayers but not reformers. They will go out of their way to believe what they can't see rather than change what's right before their eyes!" As she came out of the bathroom, her father looked up at her, squinting. "Lipstick?"

"I like it," Mabel said defiantly.

"You don't need it. You're already beautiful."

"You're just saying that because you're my father," Mabel said, rolling her eyes.

"I'm saying that because it's true," her father said above the din of his typing, and even though the compliment had come from her father, which rendered it mostly moot, Mabel still appreciated it.

Mabel took a big bite of her father's uneaten hamantasch. It was poppy seed, her favorite. "Wha ahr you wridding abouw?"

"A textile strike in New Jersey. A few nights ago, someone sabotaged the machinery at the factory so they couldn't hire any more scabs."

"Who did it? The workers?"

"No one knows. Possibly the Secret Six, that group of anarchists trying to make a name for themselves in the worst possible way. They're causing us no end of headaches."

Mabel swallowed the hard lump of pastry. "They would never do that."

Her father stopped typing. "And you would know this how?"

Mabel looked down at the plate to hide her face from him. "I mean, it just doesn't seem like something they would do. Is that all they did? Sabotage the works?"

"Yes. For now. But this sort of destruction breaks down talks and makes it hard for the rest of us trying to help the workers. And it can lead to greater violence. I've seen it." Mabel's father frowned. "You know the Secret Six was the name of the six men who subsidized the raids of John

Brown, the abolitionist, just before the Civil War. These anarchists must think mighty highly of themselves to take that name."

Mabel pretended to be very interested in the pastry. "You want the same things the Six do, though."

"We share the same goals, yes, but violence is never the answer. An eye for an eye is supposed to be a deterrent, not a prescription, *shayna*. You want to help your mother and me paint picket signs tomorrow?"

Mabel sighed. That was all she was good for here. Serving coffee to socialist leaders. Handing out pamphlets. Painting signs. Boring. "I can't. I'm meeting Evie," she lied.

"Tell the troublemaker I said hello," her father said, using his pet nickname for Evie.

"Maybe *I'm* the troublemaker," Mabel said.

"You? My *Maideleh Mabeleh*? Never!" her father said, getting back to his typing.

Oh, Papa, Mabel thought. *If you only knew.*

※

After Arthur saw Mabel to the Bennington, he rode the subway back downtown and returned to his apartment. He opened the steamer trunk and examined the blueprints, making notes. Then he locked them up again. He lifted the blinds on his dormer window and peeked out. In the upstairs room of a brownstone across the way, an artist in a paint-splattered undershirt worked on a large canvas, and Arthur looked at his own, abandoned sketches with both longing and regret. Down on the noisy sidewalk, the barber, Mr. D'Agostino, stepped out of his shop to smoke. A trio of short-haired women dressed in tuxedos walked toward Macdougal Street, presumably to the famous nightclub that catered to an all-female clientele. Just another Friday night in Greenwich Village.

The man in the brown fedora was easy to miss at first. Just a man standing under a street lamp smoking a cigarette. But then he looked straight up at the bookstore's attic, right at Arthur, and Arthur drew quickly away from the window, out of sight.

Evie read the late-edition article about the reports of HAUNTED HOSPITAL! and realized that she still hadn't heard from Woody about a trip out to see Luther Clayton at the asylum. She rang the *Daily News*. "Woody? Evie O'Neill. Say, have you had any luck getting us in to see Luther Clayton?"

"Not so far, Sheba. What with the murder out there, they're leery of newsboys like me trying to…"

As Woody talked, Evie flipped through the newspaper, stopping when she came to a picture of Sarah Snow serving porridge at the Salvation Army: SAINTLY SARAH DISHES UP A BOWL OF KINDNESS.

"You've just got to make it happen, Woody!"

"I got other stories to chase down, Sheba. There's a murder every day on *this* island. Why don't you decide to forgive Lucky Luciano or Legs Diamond instead?"

"Haha*ha*. They didn't try to shoot me."

"Give 'em time."

"Woody, are you going to help me with this or not?"

"I'll try again with the warden over there, but it may be a lost cause, Sheba. I'm telling you, they're not letting anybody over to Ward's except crazy people. Say, on second thought…"

"Good-*bye*, Woody," Evie said, and hung up.

A CRAZY DREAM

1916
Department of Paranormal
Hopeful Harbor, NY

"Will, hurry! They're waiting!"

Margaret "Sister" Walker paced impatiently at the door to the office of her friend and colleague, Will Fitzgerald. At his desk, Will laid down his pen and closed his notebook. He yanked up his suspenders, slipped on his suit jacket, and slicked a hand through his unruly hair, and then he and Margaret were moving quickly down the maroon-carpeted staircase and through a ballroom aglow in sparkling prisms of chandelier light.

"It's transmitting, Will. Do you realize what this means?"

"I...I didn't hope to imagine," Will said as they bustled into the estate's wood-paneled library. "I thought it was just a crazy dream."

"Not anymore."

Will rushed to the middle bookcase and pulled down two books in the center of the third shelf, and the bookcase swung open, revealing a private elevator. Margaret pushed a button marked *S*, and the lift rattled upward. With a shake of her head and a laugh, she reached over and adjusted Will's off-kilter glasses. "I have never met anyone whose spectacles simply refused to stay put. It's a wonder you can see at all."

"That's why I'm lucky to have you as a friend."

"And don't you forget it."

The elevator stopped and the door opened. Sunlight poured in from a glass panel in the roof. It glinted off every shiny surface of the top secret laboratory. A metallic hum filled the room and, under that, the steady scratching of some instrument at work.

"There you are!" Rotke called. She hurried over, grabbing Will by the hands. "This way."

"Don't mind me," Margaret muttered, and followed, head held high.

"Will! Come quickly! You must see this," Jake called to his best friend, grinning. He was talking without punctuation, as if his mouth were a harried stenographer racing to keep up with the dictation of his busy thoughts. "Electromagnetic…boosted the signal…necessary energy field…recalibrated the gyrometer and *bam!* There it was."

"There what was?" Will asked, pushing up his wayward glasses once more.

"This."

Jake positioned Will in front of one of the many machines he'd been toying with over the past few months. It was a cube with a whirring gyrometer on top and, in the center of the cube, a large glass tube alive with an erratic, pulsing light. Coming out from the bottom of the cube was a stylus. Its mechanical arm scratched excitedly over a roll of paper that had spooled inches thick on the floor.

"It's been going all morning," Jake said. He looked as if he hadn't slept all night, but his smile was ecstatic.

"And you're sure?" Will asked.

"Positive," Jake answered. "Go on."

Will lifted the flowing paper, reading it as it slipped across his palms. There were equations, numbers, words in various languages, and several occult symbols.

"It appears to be some sort of…schematic," Will said. He could scarcely keep from shouting with excitement.

"Can you and Rotke decipher it?"

"I can't wait to try."

Jake leaned in close to Will with a reproachful grin. "You remember what you told me?"

"That you'd never reach the speeds necessary for it," Will repeated, taking the hit in stride. "But honestly, Bohr and Einstein haven't even figured that out yet."

"And I said that I was going to be bigger than Einstein and Bohr put together!" Marlowe's grin spread even wider. "Because I'm American."

Will noted the same number and symbol repeating: *144* and a hieroglyph of an eye surrounded by the rays of the sun with a lightning strike underneath at a diagonal. "I've seen that symbol before," Will said. "I have it in my notes. It's associated with Diviners."

"Yes, many of them have seen it in their visions or dreams," Rotke confirmed.

"What about you, my darling? Have you…?" Jake asked.

Rotke shook her head. "Sadly, no."

Margaret peered over Will's shoulder. "Yes. I remember. They seemed rather wary of it, though, Will. Something about the man in the stovepipe hat."

"None of your gloom and doom, Margaret. This is a happy day! What do you think of your fiancé now, darling?" Jake said, pulling Rotke to him and dancing her gracefully around the room. Will watched the two of them, the paper sliding through his fingers.

Margaret whispered low in his ear. "You shouldn't stare. You'll only make it obvious how much you care for her."

Red-faced, Will concentrated instead on the exciting parade of sigils coming over Jake's wireless, a history-making transmission from an unknown dimension. It was incredible. Unthinkable.

Will stared in awe. "You've done it, Jake. You've really done it."

"*We've* done it," Margaret corrected quietly.

"This is the beginning. Of everything. A new Manifest Destiny." Marlowe wrapped his arm around Will's shoulders like a brother. "Congratulations. We are now communicating with the world of the dead."

CONOR FLYNN

Conor Flynn was a son of Hell's Kitchen. He'd been born too early and half-sick and laid in a cradle of squalor that was rarely rocked. The streets had raised Conor. From them he learned which corners to avoid, when to back down, and when to hit somebody hard and fast without warning. By the time he was seven, he was picking pockets for the West Side Boys. By the time he was ten, he'd landed in the New York House of Refuge for juvenile delinquents, which wasn't much different from the streets he'd left behind. Conor was only supposed to stay six months. But then he'd killed Father Hanlon, and the refuge people found out about the ghosts Conor saw and the voices in his head telling him secrets. That was when they moved him to the asylum.

Conor didn't mind the hospital. He got to draw, and sometimes they brought in special guests like the opera singer they'd had last month. She was real good, with a voice that rose up behind her like a beautiful dragon, though Conor knew not to say that out loud. The doctors and nurses were pretty nice. Most of them. Conor didn't like Dr. Simpson. He'd heard things. Whispers. Sometimes the lady patients went in for operations. He'd overheard one of the nurses talking, something about "sterilizing them so they couldn't breed more trouble." Still other patients went into Dr. Simpson's office and came out changed. Like Frances. Once, she'd stuck a fork in a guard's leg because he touched her the wrong way one too many times. Conor understood all about the wrong touching. He was glad when Frances forked the jackass in the leg. When they carried her off, Frances had kicked and screamed like a banshee. But after her visit to Dr. Simpson, she'd come back emptied, a ribbon of drool strung across her chin. Dr. Simpson had cut the fight out of Frances along with everything else.

Conor had been scared of the voices and the ghosts at first. The pictures that showed up in his head when he didn't want them and made him feel panicked. But he was more afraid of the things regular people could do to one another. He'd run with the West Side Boys. He'd lived in the refuge. He'd seen the way a mess of angry, lost boys could ramp it up for one another. If one cried *knuckles* another cried *sticks* and then somebody else had to top that with cries of *knives!* He'd seen it turn quick as a flash fire. One minute, they were a group; the next, they were a mob. And that was what scared him about the dead things inside the fog: They were the blood-fever of those wild nights on the streets of Hell's Kitchen. They were the dark corners of the refuge where the priests didn't bother looking.

The lights dimmed down to slivers, plunging the room into shadow. Conor held his breath until they brightened again. He counted until he felt safe. The lady told him to be careful. He heard her talking inside his head as if she were a voice on the radio. Like the Sweetheart Seer. The lady in his head told him there were others like him in the world. Sometimes, when he closed himself off and dove deep into his mind, he could sense them. He could feel their power as if it were connected to his own. It was the lady in his head who told Conor to be afraid of the things in the fog. The things that belonged to the man in the hat.

Conor stole a glance at Luther Clayton. Right now, he was in his chair staring at the wall and living through whatever terrible memories wouldn't leave him alone. Conor knew about bad memories.

In the corner, Mr. Boschert stared at the checkers board. His memories were leaving him, and as peaceful as that forgetting sounded to Conor, he could see that it wasn't. Sometimes Mr. Boschert didn't know where he was. It frightened the old man something awful, and Conor would pretend to be the person Mr. Boschert imagined he was, somebody from long ago. There were ghosts and then there were ghosts.

Outside the room two attendants sat at the desk talking baseball. The season was starting up soon, and Babe Ruth and Lou Gehrig were promising to make it a season to remember. Conor sure missed baseball.

"*Pssst.* Luther," Conor hissed.

Luther rolled his head toward Conor.

"You seen 'em, right?" Conor patted his lips with his fingertips in quick, rhythmic bursts until it felt safe to keep talking. "You seen them things in the fog?"

Luther's eyes were fixed on Conor's, but Conor couldn't be sure Luther was really seeing him. But then he said, "The d-door, d-d-door is open. Open. Open your eyes, eye, the Eye...d-draws them. D-draw them."

"Who are they?"

Luther didn't answer.

"Say, why'd you try to shoot da Sweetheart Seer?" Conor asked.

"They n-never should have d-done it." Luther shut his eyes tight. He whispered in his broken voice, "We are the one, four, four. We are the one, four, four. We are..."

"Good evening, Terrence, Joseph," Dr. Simpson greeted the attendants at the desk, and Conor whipped his attention back to his drawings. Why was Dr. Simpson here so late? "Mind if I have a word with one of your patients?"

"Of course, Dr. Simpson."

Dr. Simpson made a slow turn of the room. His coat collar was turned up sharply against the threat of rain and wind outside. "Evening, gentlemen."

From the corner of his eye, Conor could see Dr. Simpson staring at Luther, the doc's mouth turned down at the corners in disapproval. Dr. Simpson left Luther's side and stood next to Conor. "And how are you this evening, Conor?"

"Good." Conor kept his pencil scratching on the paper.

Dr. Simpson sat across from him at the table. He smiled. It was not a warm smile. He wore spectacles that magnified his pupils like an insect's. Conor began to sweat. He wanted to count. Counting was safety. But he was too frightened to do it in front of Dr. Simpson. What if the doc took him away and he came back like Frances?

"Now, Conor, I'd like to ask you some questions. Would that be all right?"

Conor gave a terse nod.

"It's about what happened with Mr. Flanagan and Miss Cleary. What Mr. Roland did to them. I understand you saw the whole thing." Dr. Simpson waited. He was good at that. Waiting. Conor didn't give him anything, though, so he said, "Is that true?"

"Wadn't Mr. Roland done that," Conor mumbled.

"Who was it, then?"

Conor clammed up.

"Now, now, Conor. We all know that Mr. Roland did it. Can you tell me what you saw?" Dr. Simpson barely blinked his big eyes.

Conor wanted to count so badly he thought he could explode from the need. Under the table, he moved his fingers in the same rhythmic rotation, pinkie to thumb. "It was him but not him. Somethin' got inside 'im."

"I don't understand."

Conor's voice was soft as dandelion fluff. "Ghosts. They can get inside ya. Make ya do things. That's why I hafta count. To keep 'em out."

"Do you see these ghosts often?"

The lady's voice flitted through Conor's head, very faint: *Don't tell him anything. He will hurt you if you do.* Conor's eyes widened.

Dr. Simpson's thin lips turned down again. "Are the ghosts speaking to you now, Conor?"

Keep still, the lady commanded.

Conor's breathing shallowed. He shook his head slowly. Under the table, his fingers worked quickly through their rotations.

"All right. Just one more question," Dr. Simpson said, and leaned in so that Conor felt as if the doc's eyes were everywhere, inescapable, like the voices in his head. "Have you ever seen a man with a tall hat and a feathered coat? Does *he* ever speak to you, Conor?"

And that was when Conor felt the world fall away.

"I want to help you. You know that, don't you, Conor?"

Dr. Simpson's gaze pressed into him like the hot end of a match. Conor tried to swallow. He nearly choked. And then the numbers exploded from his throat: "Onetwot'reefourfivesevenonetwot'reefourfivesevenonetwot'ree-fourfiveseven!"

"Well," Dr. Simpson said, as if Conor had disappointed him greatly. He picked up Conor's drawing and frowned at the broken soldiers flying through the air and a giant sun with an eye in the center. "We'll speak when I return from my trip. I'm to deliver a speech at a eugenics conference. Do you know what eugenics is, Conor?"

Conor shook his head.

"It's the future. The promise of a great and unsullied America." Dr. Simpson rose from the table. "Do let me know if you see the fellow I mentioned, Conor. It's very important."

Conor listened to the even *click, clack* of the doc's heels receding in the hallway—left, right, left, right, one, two, one, two, steady as a clock, no variation—until there was nothing. He sat at the table for another half hour or so, and then a terrible feeling came over Conor all of a sudden, like an army of ghosts walking across his grave. His skin tingled. The vision was coming down.

"There's a window open," Conor said calmly in his other voice, the one he used when he was his other self, the one who saw things. "You hafta shut all the windows so they can't get in."

"What's that?" Terrence asked, walking over.

"They come in wit' the fog."

Terrence checked all the windows. "Everything's locked tight, Conor." He looked out through the bars. "A little hazy but no fog to speak of. Not tonight."

"They c-come in w-with the f-fog," Luther echoed. "He t-tells them t-to c-c-come."

"Swell." Terrence sighed. "Now we got two of them. Before we know it, they'll all be talking about it." He put on the radio. The parlor filled with the sounds of a tenor's aria.

"They're gonna die," Conor said, and picked up his pencil.

※

Deep in the bowels of the hospital, two night nurses made their rounds, a lantern in hand just in case the lights cut out again.

"Thank you for going with me, Mrs. Bennett. I don't want to go down there on my own," the younger nurse said.

"You mustn't allow the patients' talk to rattle you, Miss Headley," Mrs. Bennett, the head nurse, reprimanded. She was older and had been at the hospital for many years. "You have to remain strong."

"Yes, Mrs. Bennett."

After what had happened to Big Mike and poor Mary, the young nurse had been jumpy. It didn't help that many of the patients kept talking about ghosts on Ward's Island. In the music room. At breakfast. While exercising in the yard. The same whisperings: The island was haunted. No one was safe. Just that afternoon, as she'd given dear Mrs. Pruett a sponge bath, the poor woman had muttered about seeing figures out on the lawn—*Winking in the mist like fearsome diamonds. Oh, Miss. I fear they mean us harm!*

The fog. Each night, it seemed to get worse and worse, till it was hard to see anything at all. It was like being stuck inside a dark cloud, cut off from the rest of the world.

It was just fog, Miss Headley told herself. The nights were cold and they were smack-dab in the middle of the river—nothing supernatural about it. Mrs. Bennett was right: She was letting the patients' fears and that terrible murder get to her. There were no ghosts. She was here to do a job. To be a beacon to others. This thought made her feel better.

As they neared the hydrotherapy room, freezing air greeted them. There was a window open at the back of the room.

"Now, who left that window open?" the head nurse tutted, marching into the hydrotherapy room. Mist curled in the corners, thick as vines, making it look as though they were walking into an active steam room instead of a frigid bathhouse. The fog lent a sinister quality to the shadowy tubs and pipes of the room. Like they'd entered a ghost world.

"The lights, if you please, Miss Headley."

Miss Headley did as she was told, toggling the buttons on the wall. "It's no good, I'm afraid, Mrs. Bennett."

"That infernal Hell Gate blasting," Mrs. Bennett muttered. "Keep the lantern held high, please."

Though the lantern's glow was weak, the young nurse was still grateful for it. As she lifted it, the beam fell across the silent claw-foot tubs and the gooseneck pipes that fed them. On nearby hooks hung heavy canvas tarps that could be placed over patients sitting in those tubs to keep them calm. Sometimes, the young nurse thought about the memories those tarps held. The asylum was far better now in its treatment of the patients than it had been when journalist Nellie Bly had gone undercover on Blackwell's Island in 1887. She'd lasted slightly more than a week in the hellish asylum there before she begged her editor to get her out. And then she'd written her famous exposé of the treatment of the mentally ill, "Ten Days in a Mad-House."

That had been the start of reform, but reform, the young nurse knew, was slow. You could feel it in the place, the horrors that had come before. Patients restrained against their will. Dunked into ice-cold baths. Sweated in fever boxes to rid them of syphilis. Beaten, starved, experimented upon, neglected, and abused, and horrors far worse than she dared think of at present. The mind was mysterious, and when those minds didn't conform to society's standards, it was hard going for the afflicted. That was why Miss Headley studied psychiatry: She and others like her wanted to bring hope and change to the field. She wanted to make a difference in the care of her patients.

But the head nurse belonged to a different generation. She scoffed at the notion of music and art therapy, of talking daily with the patients to see if, together, they could heal the trauma of their fractured minds and work toward making them whole. Mrs. Bennett didn't see the patients as people feeling sad or hurting. She didn't see them as people needing care. She saw them as less than human, as problems to be solved or disappointments to be shut away out of sight. Miss Headley had overheard the head nurse telling Mrs. Washington, who lay in bed with severe depression, that she should *Cheer up—come now, things aren't as bad as all that, are they, hmm?* She'd witnessed Mrs. Bennett escorting a female patient to that awful Dr. Simpson for sterilization. *Sarah is a loose woman. Best to take care of that now*, Mrs. Bennett had said, even though poor Sarah could neither read nor write and had the mind of a child.

Power over others. That was what motivated some of these people. They didn't want to heal so much as they wanted to win. Miss Headley would be glad when the last of their kind was gone, and the new ideas could come in. There was hope, even in a place like this. Even on Ward's Island, spring eventually forced its way up from the frostbitten ground.

The head nurse struggled with the window. "Why, it's stuck as stuck can be. See if you can shut this, won't you please, Miss Headley?"

"Yes, Mrs. Bennett." Miss Headley put down the lantern. With a grunt and a few hops, she snugged the sash down inch by inch, then stopped to catch her breath. On the other side of the glass, a thick block of mist blotted out any view of the bridge or river. When had that fog come up? It hadn't been there when they'd started their rounds. She could just barely make out the skeletons of winter-stripped trees. It gave her a shiver.

The door to the hydrotherapy room slammed shut, and Miss Headley yelped.

"Mrs. Bennett?" she called. The fog inside the room had also thickened. But she could still make out Mrs. Bennett at the door, turning the lock. Where the head nurse had been standing, the lantern lay on its side. There was a sound in the room. An insect-like keening. Miss Headley was a nurse. She recognized that her pulse, normally rock-steady, was very fast.

"Mrs. Bennett?" she called again, frightened.

"I know you want me gone," Mrs. Bennett said, taking a step forward. Mist curled at her fingertips, as if she were made of ice. "You think I'm old and should retire."

The young nurse took a step back. "No, Mrs. B-Bennett, I never—"

"Liar! I can hear inside your head. I always knew, but they've shown me I was right."

"Who?"

"The Forgotten."

The moment the word left the head nurse's lips, Miss Headley saw spectral figures taking shape in the mist: pale, dead flesh, formless as specimens floating in jars of formaldehyde solution, a great mob of spirits. Some wore clothes that seemed to stretch back centuries. Others looked as if they had only been buried last week. She could feel their need and their anger as if it, too, were a physical presence, could feel it shifting toward hate as their voices slithered around the room, overwhelming her:

> You forgot about us.
> Forgot us, forgotten, oh why?
> > *Eat you down to the bones, you bitch!*
> Left to rot in the cold, dark ground…
> > *He will lift us up to our rightful place!*
> > *We will suck the dreams from your marrow.*
> > *Fear us, fear us, fear is us is fear all fear!*
> We are the Forgotten…
>
> > *Forgotten no more!*

The fog curled up behind Mrs. Bennett and puffed from her mouth like a long, murky snake. "Oh, everything is so clear to me now."

They'd gotten inside Mrs. Bennett somehow. Miss Headley took a step back. She shook her head. Her voice was weak. "No. No. They're lying to you, Mrs. Bennett."

"You're the liar!" the head nurse screeched, matching the force of the mob.

Hanging on the wall was a long, hooked pole that could be used to secure the tarps. Miss Headley ran for it, only to see the pole fly from its perch with supernatural strength and into Mrs. Bennett's waiting hand. One by one, the taps squeaked on, filling the baths with scalding water. Steam billowed up, joining the fog. The pole scraped across the tile floor as the head nurse advanced along with the ghostly mob.

Miss Headley put up her hands. "Please, Mrs. Bennett."

Mrs. Bennett pushed Miss Headley into the tub. She screamed, "Help! Help! Oh, please, someone help!" Faster than her eyes could register, the tarp whipped across the tub, fastening at the sides like a canvas seal, trapping her inside. In horror, the young nurse watched as the tap to her tub prison began its slow turn.

"No. Please," she cried, drawing her feet close, then screaming and thrashing as the blistering water reached her. Hundreds of whispers filled the room, speaking all at once until the maddening din formed one unearthly voice that burst from Mrs. Bennett's mouth: "Oh, King of Crows. Show us the way. For we are the Forgotten, forgotten no more."

The water rose. Under the tarp, Miss Headley's body twitched and blistered in the hot water. Her eyes rolled up as her body finally stilled. Mrs. Bennett raised the hook high above her own head, bringing it down again and again.

Upstairs, Conor Flynn already knew.

He drew it all.

RUNNING

The world is black and white, gray and red.

White snow. Thin gray smoke. Its acrid smell hurts your nose.

The black: A scorched world. Crisped trees. Smoldering cabins. Charred horses. Bodies.

And red snow, like strange flowers blooming.

The man sinks to his knees. Cries. A great animal howl above the scream of wind.

Red snow shifts, transforms into redbrick church.

The man's sad face looms above yours.

Feel the warm scratch of wool tucked snugly around you.

He speaks but you cannot hear.

There is loud knocking against the church doors. Light spills out, hard and yellow. Arms reach for you—not the man's. He is gone. Angels in black and white lift you into light.

You shift in your sleep and the dream shifts with you.

Now it is the room.

The room in the house.

The room in the house near the railroad tracks.

To your left, the open window. Hot wind sucks cheap nylon curtains against the peeling paint of a wood frame. To your right, a chest of drawers: an overturned lamp, lampshade gone, naked bulb exposed. A pink wildflower droops in a small blue vase.

Watch the vase. The wildflower. Don't look up. Don't look up. Don't…

He grabs your chin, roughs your face toward his. His hard, beautiful face.

He is shouting, wet mouth spilling out hateful words on a tide of boozy breath.

Shouting. Purplish veins strain against the anger-red skin of his neck.

Shouting. *You ever try to leave me, I'll kill you first!*

Shouting's over, and the first slap comes stinging across your cheek. It shouldn't be a surprise to you by now, but it always is. In your ears, a crack like a gunshot and the room goes wavy. Another blow follows. And another. Blood in your mouth like warm, liquid iron. One hand presses against your neck, holds you in place. You cannot see the other. But you hear it working.

The clinking of the belt buckle giving way. The angry rustle of trousers.

And it's worse than the shouting and the slapping. Your eyes slide toward the rattling chest of drawers bumped by the bed again and again. The flower shakes in the vase. With each thump, petals fall off, drift to the warped floorboards. You drift down with them. You are not here. You are gone. Floating up and away as you've taught yourself to do.

The hand at your neck tightens. You cannot speak. Cannot breathe.

No longer floating, you are trapped in your body.

That's when it starts, deep in your belly.

The world goes black and white, gray and red. Terror. Desperation. Survival. Rage. A twisting, whirring universe of emotion exploding into heat. It rushes through your veins like a brush fire through rain-starved grass. His eyes widen in horror, such horror you want to stop it for yourself as much as for him. You put up a hand, press it to his cheek to anchor yourself, and he screams and screams. The pressure of his palm leaves your neck.

A sound reaches your ears. A voice on the wind. "Theta."

The vase cracks open on the floor. He falls beside it, hands to his face, still screaming. Inside, the universe keeps exploding. Flames crawl up the wall behind the headboard. The bedsheets are blackened, like the horses, the trees, the cabins, the bodies.

The voice again: "Time to leave, Theta. You don't want to stay here."

You look over. He's standing in the doorway. Henry is talking to you here inside your dream. "Theta, darlin'. You don't have to stay here."

"Yes. I do. It's my fault."

"No. It's not. You can leave, Theta. Why don't you get out?"

"I can't. Fire. Fire will get me."

"There's a door." He nods to something you can't see, just over your shoulder. You look, and there it is, shining through the flames, a door. "Go on, darlin'. No reason to stick around here."

You walk through the door. And then you are running.

Running from the burning house and the beating man.

Running from the broken vase and the broken screams.

Running onto the bright stage, where applause greets you like wild-flowers scattered on the wind. But you can never outrun the coiled fever hiding inside you, and the fear that it will return and burn through everything you love.

Theta woke from her dream drenched in sweat and gasping for breath. She threw off her damp sleep mask and looked around wildly, relieved to see that she was in her bedroom in the Bennington and not that other place. Her pajamas were soaked through, but she was burning up inside, so she stumbled to the bathroom and splashed her face and hands with water until her skin cooled. It wasn't until she returned to her bedroom that she noticed the faint, scorched outlines of her hands imprinted on the sheets: black and white.

Sleep would be impossible now, so Theta made a cup of coffee, lit a cigarette, and sat by the window overlooking the rain-ravaged street. Henry was with David downtown. How she wished he were home so that she could crawl into bed with him, rest her head on his chest, and hear him say, "It's just a dream, darlin'." It was like a monster lived inside her, and with each night, it was getting closer to breaking through her skin. Theta couldn't shut down the worry buzzing around her brain:

What if the monster came out when she was onstage or talking to reporters?

What if it came out during her screen test at Vitagraph in a few hours?

What if her friends knew about the destructive power coiled inside her? Would they feel safe around her anymore?

Would Memphis? *What if she hurt Memphis?*

Theta pressed her cheek to the window. It was cold from the rain and felt good. It was those threatening notes that had made things so much worse. There was nothing familiar about the handwriting. After the first one, Theta had paid a visit to the florist's shop, but no one remembered who had bought the flowers. "It was a telephone order," the florist recalled. "That's all I know."

Whoever it was remembered Theta from her days on the Orpheum

Circuit, when she played the vaudeville theaters all across the country as Little Betty Sue Bowers, "The Ringleted Rascal." Betty Sue Bowers wore a pinafore dress, tap shoes, and sweet, girlish curls. Betty Sue Bowers had a stage mother from hell and, later, a handsome husband named Roy who took out his anger at the world on his young wife with his fists. And one night, Betty Sue Bowers had killed him with a power she didn't know she had: a dangerous ability to start fires with her emotions. As far as anyone else knew, Betty Sue Bowers had also died in the inferno that night. They didn't know that Theta had hopped a freight car out of Kansas, bound for the bright lights of Broadway. In New York City, Theta had met Henry, cut her hair, traded in Kansas homespun charm for sleek glamour, and become a reinvention: Theta Knight, Ziegfeld Follies girl.

Someone did, though. And now they were in her city, leaving her cryptic notes. Was it Mrs. Bowers? It would be just like her adoptive mother to try for a payday through blackmail. Could it be one of Roy's former pals at the soda shop? What about the neighbors—would any of them have seen Theta running for her life toward the railroad tracks? (Not that any of the neighbors had ever bothered to come upstairs during the shouting and screaming; not one had ever asked about the bruises and black eyes.) Could one of the hoboes she'd shared the freight car with have told others? All it would take was one of them to see her face in the newspaper, so different but still a ghost of the old Betty left there—*Say, doesn't that look a little like…?* It wouldn't matter that Theta hadn't meant to kill Roy and that she had very little memory of that night. The world would see a cold-blooded murderess. They'd call Roy a good fella who got involved with the wrong girl. She'd seen such things play out before. She knew the world was stacked against girls like her.

Theta finished her cigarette. She took a bath. Combed out her sleek bob and short bangs. She drew on her pencil-thin eyebrows and painted a Cupid's bow mouth in crimson. As the dawn inched up along the Manhattan skyline, Theta chose her outfit—a deep blue silk dress, a long strand of knotted pearls, and a gray velvet cocoon coat with a fat fur-trimmed collar that she'd "borrowed" from the Follies costume shop for the day. She stuck out her hand for an imaginary shake. "How do you do?" she said in her smoky purr of a voice. "I am Miss Theta Knight."

Yes. She was Theta Knight. Not Betty Sue Bowers. Nobody could threaten her back into being that girl. That girl was dead and buried. *Theta Knight* had a screen test today at Vitagraph. *Theta Knight* would get that contract and run all the way to Hollywood with Memphis if she had to. She took the elevator down to the lobby.

"Sure look nice today, Miss Knight," the elevator operator commented.

"Thanks, Tom."

"You going somewhere special?"

"Vitagraph," Theta said, enjoying the feel of the word on her tongue.

"Oh, well, good luck. You might say a wish to Mr. Bennington on your way out, then."

"Come again?"

"That picture of Mr. Bennington that hangs there in the hallway? I heard he looks after the Bennington guests if you ask him to." Tom shrugged. "Can't hurt. Here's the lobby now."

Theta stopped before the large framed photograph of a somber Reginald Bennington seated at a table in the dining room back when it had been a showplace and not just a shabby spot that served weak coffee. She'd passed the photograph daily, but never really thought to look at it. Reginald Bennington looked to be about sixty, with dark curly hair going to gray, and a salt-and-pepper beard and mustache. Put a cap on his head, and Theta could imagine him as the captain of a grand ship. There were all sorts of stories about him: He was a magician involved with the occult. He performed pagan ceremonies in the basement. He ran naked through Central Park. It was said that he'd had the Bennington constructed according to magical specifications, as both a beacon to the otherworldly and as a protection against evil. Theta glanced up and down the hall. Empty. Feeling the fool, she stepped forward. "Hiya, Mr. Bennington," she said very softly. "Listen, I, uh, don't know if you're really in the wish-granting business, but if you are, I sure could use some luck today. Okay. Thanks. I'm Theta, by the way."

Theta shifted from one foot to the other, waiting—for what, she couldn't say. From his chair in the Victorian-appointed dining room, Mr. Bennington stared back, a lost relic from another generation.

"Yeah," Theta said on a sigh. "It's okay. I'm embarrassed for myself. You don't have to say a word, pal."

On her way out of the Bennington lobby—*I am Theta Knight, I am Theta Knight, I am Theta Knight*—Theta bumped into Miss Addie. The old woman looked terrible. Dark shadows ringed her bright eyes, and her frizzy white hair was more of a mess than usual.

"Oh, my dear, can't you feel it?" Miss Addie said.

"Feel what?"

"*Him.* He's coming. He's coming for *us.* I fear we shall have to stage quite the battle to beat him this time, for he grows more powerful by the day," Miss Addie said, her pitch rising in concert with her sparse eyebrows.

Theta fumbled nervously with her handbag. "Sorry. I-I've gotta ankle, Miss Addie."

"Yes. Of course. You know there's a ghost after you, my dear, don't you?" Addie blurted.

"A ghost?" Theta said, her voice barely a whisper.

Miss Addie nodded. "It means you harm, I'm afraid. Be careful, my dear girl."

I am Theta Knight.

Theta shook her head as she pushed angrily through the Bennington's revolving door. "Terrific. This day just gets better and better."

A BORN STAR

By eleven o'clock, Theta, Ling, Evie, and Mabel were huddled together in their seats on the elevated Brighton Beach line out to Brooklyn and Vitagraph Studios, hands clapped over giggling mouths as Evie kept everyone entertained with a risqué story about a secretary at WGI who'd been caught petting with an auditioning act.

"Well, she didn't realize the man had a parrot who'd seen the whole thing—Polly wanted more than just a cracker, and how!" she said to scandalized laughter from Mabel and Ling.

The story was rude, and it was clearly shocking the Blue Noses within earshot, which, with Evie, was the point. Evie loved scandalizing the hypocrites, of course, but more than that, Theta knew, Evie was telling her naughty stories to distract Theta from the butterflies in her stomach. And after her strange morning asking the spirit of Reginald Bennington for luck and then getting a creepy warning from Adelaide Proctor, Theta needed it.

"Brooklyn. Huh. It's like being in Kansas," she said, peering out the window at the borough's low, sleepy houses flying past. Up ahead, she could see a tall smokestack at the corner of Avenue M and Fourteenth Street with black letters down the side spelling out VITAGRAPH.

The girls crowded together at the window to get a good look. The train pulled into the station, and they stepped out onto the platform. "Hold on," Evie said, fluffing the fur collar to frame Theta's face. "There. You look like a proper film star now."

Theta put a hand to her fluttering stomach. "Well. Here goes nothing."

"Sure is impressive," Mabel said as they approached the giant brick studio, which took up an entire block. "You think we'll see any movie stars? Like Harold Lloyd. Oh, I love him!"

"Harold Lloyd!" Evie and Theta complained together before bursting into giggles.

Mabel grinned. "I like his big round glasses! Fine. Who do *you* like?"

"Gary Cooper, of course," Evie said, swooning. "Or Ramon Novarro."

The girls all sighed except for Ling.

"You don't find him handsome?" Mabel prodded.

Ling made a face. "He's hammy. I like Anna May Wong."

Mabel laughed. "No. I mean who do you *like*?" She waggled her eyebrows as if Ling hadn't understood the first time.

Anna May Wong, Ling thought, the movie star's beautiful face swimming up so strongly in Ling's mind that she hoped the embarrassment couldn't be read on her face.

"Albert Einstein," Ling said, and pushed forward on her crutches.

"I don't think he counts," Mabel said, following after.

"He does in my book."

Outside, a swarm of Erasmus Hall High School girls milled in front of the studio gate. They were doing their best posing, but trying not to look too obvious about it.

"Look at that," Evie said, and Theta knew whatever came next would be a little catty and probably true. "They all hope if they pose and sigh and bat their peepers, they'll be picked out of the crowd to become the next Norma Talmadge. I've got news for them: Not everybody is Norma Talmadge. Excuse us, please," Evie announced with a circus barker's flair as she parted the girl-throng. "Miss Theta Knight of the Follies coming through for her screen test. Excuse us, please, thank you, thank you."

A guard waited at the front gate. He frowned. "Only Miss Knight is expected."

"Oh, but I'm her sister and her *chaperone*," Evie bluffed, putting a hand to her chest as if the idea of Theta going into the Hollywood viper pit unaccompanied was unthinkable. "And this lovely lady is her secretary, Miss Ling Chan, and this is her personal seamstress, Miss Mabel Rose."

"I've made all of Miss Knight's costumes for the Follies," Mabel said, falling right in. "I love to sew."

The guard eyed Ling suspiciously. "And I love to . . . secretary."

"Fine. Go in," the weary guard said, ushering them inside the gates of Brooklyn's famous film lot.

"I love to secretary?" Mabel whispered to Ling.

"We're in, aren't we?" Ling groused.

Theta gawked at the many painted sets and the tall, bright lights, the movie cameras perched like giant birds around the lot. They passed a shop where carpenters hammered away at sets and a costume shop where the sewing machines revved. Actors milled about, drinking coffee, smoking, and going over their lines. A tall, somber-looking man walked past.

"Oh, jeepers! That's Boris Karloff!" Mabel said excitedly. "I loved him in *Flaming Fury!*"

"For a socialist, you sure do know a lot about movie stars," Ling said. She'd stopped to examine a recording machine of some sort. She couldn't help but fiddle with the gears to see how it worked. A man in a pair of plus fours came racing toward her, his ridiculous puffy trouser legs waffling like a bellows. "Say, what are you doing? Now, come on, sweetheart, come away from there!"

"I like machines," Ling said quietly.

"She's very good with machines," Mabel confirmed.

"That's no place for ladies," the man said. "We have a wonderful costume shop if you'd like to visit."

Ling narrowed her eyes. "Perhaps you could see them about a pair of proper pants, then."

"I think you might've made him angry," Mabel said with a glance over her shoulder as they walked away.

"Good. Do you know why I like machines?" Ling said.

"Why?"

"They're not nearly as annoying as people."

They caught up to Evie and Theta.

"I'm sorry," a cameraman told them. "But you ladies will have to wait out by the gate until the screen test is over."

"Good luck, Theta!" Evie called. The girls waved as the cameraman showed Theta onto a stage decorated like a living room, where a camera and several lights had been positioned.

"Doesn't she look just like a star?" Mabel said wistfully.

※

"Have a seat right here, sweetheart," the director said, ushering Theta to a chair beside a table displaying a photograph of a handsome soldier. "You know Warner Brothers owns this whole kit and caboodle now. Do well here, and you'll be out in Hollywood in no time, kid."

"Swell," Theta said, swallowing down her nerves.

"You know what's coming next, don'tcha?" the makeup man said, touching up Theta's powder. "Talkies. Warner Brothers—they've got us experimenting with sound out here. I hear Al Jolson is gonna sing in a picture!"

"Is that a fact?" Theta said, though she couldn't imagine anybody talking in a movie. People would probably laugh it out of the theater.

"You ready, sweetheart?" the director asked from behind the camera.

"Sure."

The director barked out orders, and Theta followed every command.

"Not quite so much, sweetheart. This isn't like the stage. The camera does some of the work for you," he said.

"Oh. Got it," Theta said, even though she didn't. She was acting, just like she'd been doing her whole life. But she'd figure it out. Theta was a great performer; she knew that. So many performers needed the audience's love and approval. Theta didn't need it, and that seemed to be the very thing that drove audiences wild: They wanted what they felt they couldn't have. When her stage mother, Mrs. Bowers, had forced Theta to smile and curtsy for all the managers and vaudevillians on the Orpheum Circuit, she'd told her again and again, *You're nobody without them and me. You belong to us.* Then Roy had come along and told Theta she belonged to him. But when Theta was onstage, she was hers alone. There, no one could have Theta Knight without her permission.

"Okay, sweetheart! Give me those sad peepers!" the director shouted from behind his camera.

Theta gave a deep sigh, letting her shoulders sag as she pressed the back of her hand to her forehead.

"That's it! Now I want you to show me your bear cat, but not *too* hot. You still want the Sunday school crowd thinking you're pure. That's the trick: Make 'em want you, make 'em think they've got a chance at making whoopee; then show 'em you're strictly the marrying kind. Think you can do that?"

Theta resisted the urge to roll her eyes. "Can I do that? Pal, that's what every girl learns along with her ABCs," she mumbled. "Just keep that contraption pointed at my face."

Theta lowered her head and looked up longingly at the camera with her soulful brown eyes. Lips parted slightly, she stared back at the camera as if it were her lover while she crept a hand up her neck in a desperate caress. She closed her eyes and shuddered. Then, just when she was on the brink of wanton, she clutched the picture of her soldier boy to her chest, kissed his face gently, put it down, and clasped her hands in prayer, beseeching the heavens for his safe return.

"You and your lover have been separated by cruel fate! You fear you will never see him again!" the director yelled.

She kept her eyes trained upward and thought of Memphis. His sweet, slow grin. The way he looked at her sideways from under cover of those long lashes, his head slightly bowed, like he was almost embarrassed by how much he liked her. When Theta was with Memphis, she felt as safe and happy as she could allow herself to be. She could be not just herself but all her selves. So why was she so afraid to tell him about the fire that burned inside her? About Roy and Kansas and the menacing notes that had been left for her? It was like being in a dream and reaching for something that was always just beyond your grasp. Would she always be reaching for a happiness she couldn't hold?

A single tear coursed down Theta's cheek, and then she was crying openly.

"That's incredible," the cameraman said. "Oh, baby. Keep it coming."

"And cut!" the director shouted. He applauded enthusiastically. "Astounding."

"Big word. Was I good or bad?" Theta said, wiping her eyes. They didn't need to know how real it had all been.

"Good. Very, very good."

Theta sniffed up the last of her tears and took out a cigarette. "Swell. Anybody got a light?"

"Miss Knight. How'd you like a contract at one hundred and fifty per week?" the director said.

Theta's mouth hung open. "Are you pulling my leg?"

"Huh-uh."

"Forget the light. Got a pen?"

The cameraman finally offered Theta a match. "Honey, you should see yourself through that thing. Why, it's like you're lit from the inside."

"Oh, um. Is *that* good, too?" Theta's hands trembled on her cigarette, but at least they didn't feel warm. Yet.

"You kidding me? It's better than good. You're a born star."

A born star, Theta thought on her way out of Vitagraph Studios, past the revving sewing machines and hammering carpenters engaged in the world of make-believe.

A born star.

For no reason she could name, she stopped and said a silent thank-you to Mr. Bennington. "Just in case," she told herself.

"Well?" Evie said when Theta exited the gate again onto Avenue M.

The girls rushed forward, eager for news. Theta decided to keep them in suspense. She sighed heavily. "Oh, well…"

The girls glanced nervously at one another.

"Oh, gee. Oh, Theta, why, you're the darlingest girl in the world! If they don't want you, why, why, they're *chumps*!" Evie declared.

Mabel and Ling nodded decisively.

Theta burst into a grin. She struck a pose like a proper motion picture vamp. "Oh, well…it looks like somebody's making pictures with Vitagraph!"

With a collective, delighted clamor, Mabel and Evie crowded Theta, hugging and congratulating, while Ling stood at a comfortable distance.

"Congratulations. You should be very proud," Ling said evenly.

Mabel laughed. "I believe that's the Ling Chan Hip, Hip, Hooray."

"One hundred and fifty clams per week!" Theta crowed to her friends. They had spread out in the mostly empty street as if, for just a while, they owned it. "We'll be living like sheiks! I'm gonna get me a mink! And I'm gonna buy Henry that piano, finally."

"A mink-lined piano!" Evie said, looping her arm through Theta's, and Theta knew that this was a day she'd remember forever.

Mabel giggled. "Every single key!"

Evie mimed a phone receiver at her ear. "Yes, sir, I'd like to report trouble with this Steinway. I'm afraid the sound is a bit…fuzzy." And they collapsed into one another, laughing.

"Come on. Let's grab some cherry phosphates and a chipped beef sandwich at Schrafft's—my treat!" Theta insisted, and no one argued otherwise.

Theta spotted a small bookshop. "Wait! Hold on a minute." She disappeared into the shop and came out a few minutes later cradling a paper-wrapped bundle.

"What's that?" Ling asked.

Theta peeled back a corner of the brown paper and showed them the leather-bound copy of *Leaves of Grass*. "Walt Whitman," she said. "For Memphis."

✷

When Theta returned to the Bennington, she stopped and blew a kiss to the portrait of Mr. Bennington. "Thanks, Mr. B. You really came through today," she said. Upstairs in her kitchen, Theta lit the stove, letting the flame catch on the corner of the first note. She watched it burn. Then she did the same with the other card until the threats were nothing but smoke. If she didn't have them, they didn't exist. There was a coating of smudgy soot on her fingertips. Theta went into the bathroom to wash it off. She faced her reflection in the mirror.

"I am Theta Knight," she said.

And watched her past swirl down the drain.

ALL THE WAY

By Friday, Sam had delivered a small movie camera as promised. "It's a Filmo by Bell and Howell. Like the little brother to the cameras they use for motion pictures. All you gotta do is pop the film in, thread it into the sprockets, close it up, wind this key here on the side, and you're in business. I could only get you one roll of film, though."

"It's more than enough! Oh, Sam, you're swell!" Mabel threw her arms around his neck and squeezed.

"Shucks. What gives? You planning to be the next Chaplin?"

Mabel gave a Cheshire cat smile. "Sorry. It's top secret information. Oh, and, Sam? Please don't tell Evie about this."

"Now you've really got my curiosity up," Sam said. But he mimed locking his lips with a key. "Good luck, Mabel."

Luis knew a friend with a truck, and now the Secret Six were crowded into it on the way to Marlowe's mine in New Jersey. As they drove out of the city, they passed plenty of billboards advertising the good life: "Wilson Brothers Suits for the Man on the Way Up." "I'm a Lucky Strike Girl!" "Marlowe Industries: The Good Life Is the American Life."

"That's what they do, you know," Luis said over the wind and the hum of the engine. "They want you to believe you must have all of it. Otherwise, you're not keeping up with the Joneses."

"And all of it built on the backs of labor!" Aron shouted above the din.

Mabel smiled and patted the camera. "Let's see if we can change that."

Eventually, the billboards and congestion gave way to farmland, a filling station here and there, and even a log cabin tucked into the hills as if modernity were just a passing phase it hoped to ride out. Mabel could hear the mine before she saw it: The gunfire retort of the drills and the rumble of a mine train carrying its load on the tracks were loud even from this distance. As the truck rounded a corner, the mine at last came into view. Three smokestacks belched sooty black plumes into the blue sky. Rocks chugged along on a conveyor belt. Behind it lay a group of modest shotgun-style houses, a school for the workers' children, and a company store. Mabel knew from her parents that the miners were paid in company scrip, which would buy them goods only at the company store, where the prices were often high. It was a vicious cycle that made it nearly impossible for the workers to ever get ahead.

In front of the mine itself was a gate that was patrolled by armed guards.

About a hundred feet from the mine across a muddy field lay the tent city where the striking workers lived. Some of the wives cooked over meager fires while trying to corral their children. Mabel could only imagine how hard it was.

"There are the machine guns," Luis said, nodding toward the trucks with Gatling guns mounted on the back.

"And those look like militiamen," Gloria said, pointing through the dusty windshield at a group of men drinking coffee and smoking cigarettes, their rifles slung across their shoulders.

They parked the truck in the tent city. Arthur looked around. "Let's film the tents to show the conditions here."

Mabel noticed a woman huddling in the cold with her children. "That's what you should film, if you really want to arouse sympathy."

Luis spoke with the mothers and returned with their blessing. Mabel experimented with the camera until the mechanics were second nature to her. Then she peered through the lens, adjusting until one mother's worried face came into focus, the camera capturing the desperation and worry in her eyes. Mabel had observed people most of her life. She'd learned to be invisible. And right now, that was an advantage. She was the ghost behind the all-seeing camera, shaping pictures into a story. That part was surprisingly instinctual.

Despite the conditions in the camp, the children ran around, playing with sticks and a doll they shared, and Mabel marveled at how resilient they were. She made sure to show them. Surely, people had to feel for the hungry children. But there was something more. Something ephemeral she hoped to catch. She raised the camera again, and this time, she captured the workers coming over the land in a collective joyful spirit—men hoisting children on their shoulders, women in their aprons marching side by side, sons standing with their fathers, girls Mabel's age holding hands and singing a labor song of solidarity. She wished the camera could record the sound of their singing, but at least it captured their pride, their hope. Her camera found one young girl of perhaps nine or ten. The girl's hair gleamed in the sunlight. Her eyes were bright. Mabel kept the camera on the child's smiling face. This, Mabel's gut told her, was what the country needed to see—a future of possibility shining out from a new, young American. Hope. Wasn't that American?

Wasn't that *America*?

At last, Mabel lowered the camera. Her arms were exhausted, but she'd never been more certain of her purpose. Across the field, a new crew of scabs reported for work. Aron spat into the field. "Traitors."

"They're afraid," Mabel said. "They're worried they won't be able to feed their children, that they'll be deported. You can't blame them for being afraid. Come on. Let's do some good."

Mabel and the rest of the Six moved among the workers. With each tin of beans or blanket they handed out, they heard the miners' stories.

"At night, the men with guns drive circles around the camp. They fire rifles into the sky to frighten us. It makes the children cry," a man with a thick Polish accent said. "Inside our tents, we dig tunnels to hide our wives and children in case."

"In case?" Arthur said.

"In case they decide to no longer shoot at only the sky."

"Sometimes, they give us tests," the man's son said. He looked to be about Mabel's age.

"What sorts of tests?" Mabel asked.

"There is a doctor, thin, with glasses. We call him Dr. Scarecrow. No one likes him. He asks us about gifts—can we read cards or see into the future, do we have the healing gift?"

Mabel immediately thought of Maria Provenza's story, but before she could follow up with more questions, everyone's attention was drawn to the sight of a beautiful Stutz Bearcat bobbling over the rutted road, followed by a small fleet of other, less expensive cars.

"Well, I'll be. It's the great man himself," Arthur said, yanking his cap down tight on his head. "It's Marlowe."

Everyone crowded to the limit of the camp line to watch as America's prince stepped out of his luxurious automobile and shook hands with the guards and militiamen. Several reporters filed out of the other cars. Marlowe had cider doughnuts brought out to them, which the reporters dug into heartily.

"That snake!" Mabel grumbled. "He's buying them!"

Marlowe posed for pictures with the smiling guards. "Apparently, some of my miners don't like the idea of an honest day's work for honest pay," Marlowe announced with a paternal shake of his bright head. "I pay a fair wage for fair work. Ask anybody. Then these union rabble-rousers come in and upend things. Why, they're holding American industry hostage, like a bunch of thugs and bullies! By golly, I say, if you come here looking for a better life and the opportunities this great country offers, you have to work for it the American way, and the American way is not union. But as you boys can see, there are always people ready to work."

The newsboys ate Marlowe's doughnuts and took down his every word. Not one of them bothered to talk to the workers themselves.

"He's treating this like some nuisance he wants to scrape off his shoe when there are kids with hungry bellies right here!" Mabel said, furious.

She hopped up onto a tree stump. Her voice soared on the March wind. "Do you remember the Triangle Shirtwaist Fire? Do you remember the bodies of those girls lying on Greene Street?" Beside Mabel, the miners removed their caps. The mothers held their children tight. "Those girls came here looking for a better way of life, too. *They* had families. *They* were loved. *They* had dreams, too! But the men who ran the factory didn't think of them that way. They thought those girls would try to steal scraps of cloth from them. Those men cared more about their profits than they did about the workers making them rich. So they locked them inside for twelve hours a day. When the fire broke out, those poor girls were trapped with no way out. Many jumped to their deaths. The others screamed as they burned. And what happened to the owners, to the men who had sealed their fate?" Mabel paused. She had the reporters' attention now. "Nothing!"

A clamor went up among the workers. They were cheering Mabel on.

"Is that the American way? It would be wonderful if we could depend upon the kindness and fairness of men, Mr. Marlowe, but we can't. Without unions, there is no protection." Mabel raised her fist high in the air and shouted, "Union!"

The workers answered in kind. Shouts of "Union!" echoed across the muddy New Jersey field, drowning out Marlowe altogether.

"Who is that? Find out," Jake Marlowe asked the mine foreman.

The word went 'round and came back: "That's Mabel Rose, sir. Virginia Rose's daughter."

❋

"I think you might've gotten some of your mother's spirit after all, Mabel," Luis said later as they shared a loaf of bread he'd brought. They each took a piece and passed the loaf around to others in the tent camp.

"Yeah, you're a chip off the old block," Gloria said.

"No, she's not," Arthur said. "Mabel's even braver than her mother—smarter, too. The newsreel was a swell idea. You'll pardon me, but Mabel's parents are the old guard. We are the new. The future. This is ours."

Ours. Mabel liked the sound of that. She liked that Arthur believed in her so strongly.

"Do you think we can win?" Mabel asked.

"We're certainly gonna try, Mabel Rose," Arthur said, and she loved the way he said her name, like a mantra. With the sun behind him, he looked like a bold new American hero, someone who would shape the future. Arthur wiped his hands on his trouser legs and pulled Mabel to her feet. His hands were warm and strong like hers, and she liked the feel of them. "Let's find somebody to print that newsreel and get it out there for people to see."

A woman who'd been standing nearby beckoned Mabel. The woman spoke little English, so she relied on her nephew to relay the message. He listened, nodding.

"What is it?" Mabel asked.

"My aunt Ekadie says that bad is coming,"

"Fortune-tellers again," Aron scoffed. "Bad is coming for Marlowe once the people see this newsreel."

"Go on," Mabel said, shooing Aron toward the truck. "I'll be there in just a minute."

The woman spoke to her nephew with rising urgency. Worry was etched into her face.

"It is your aura," he translated. "She says she can see it all around you, the danger. The ghosts are warning her. There is betrayal. Fire. Death."

Hadn't Maria Provenza said much the same?

"What does she mean? What sort of betrayal?"

The young man spoke with his aunt once more. He shook his head. "She doesn't know. But she says you must be careful."

Gloria honked the horn. The others were in the truck waving to her, impatient, so Mabel thanked both the woman and her nephew and tried to shake off the warning.

❈

"We've only got one shot at this," Luis said, handing over the canister with the edited newsreel inside. "The projectionist is sympathetic. I paid him a few bucks to take a walk tonight during the premiere of this new Fritz Lang picture, *Metropolis*."

"We'll sneak in and put on the newsreel before the picture starts," Aron said.

Through the square of a window, Mabel could watch the well-heeled audience flow in and take their seats while an organist played a boisterous tune on the theater's Mighty Wurlitzer. Mabel's stomach was all butterflies as the lights dimmed, the tuxedo-clad manager announced the picture, and the gilt-edged, red velvet curtains parted to the audience's excited applause.

"Here we go," Luis said. He set the newsreel in motion and left their calling card—THE SECRET SIX—next to the projector so that everyone would know. Then they ran quickly to the upper balcony to watch from behind the safety of the dark.

A title card appeared: THE FUTURE OF AMERICA? NO FUTURE FOR JAKE MARLOWE'S STRIKING MINERS! The newsreel's first images spooled across the screen: The hungry children. The worried mothers. The militia men driving around in their trucks with their guns. A second title card read: UNION! It was followed by the long shot Mabel had gotten of the workers coming across the field, arms linked in solidarity, that then became the close-ups of those shining eyes in hopeful faces. That scene made her heart swell more than anything she'd ever seen in a Hollywood picture. She'd shot that footage *herself.* She was making a difference.

The audience grew restless—*"What's going on here? Is this part of the picture? Is it a joke? Start the picture!"* Some booed, but there were others who cheered when the words A FAIR AMERICA FOR ALL! appeared on-screen. "Hear! Hear!" they called, applauding, and Mabel thought it might be the best sound she'd ever heard.

Down below, the manager hurried up the aisle, scowling up at the projection booth.

"That's our cue. Time to go," Arthur said, snugging his cap down low on his head, and they slunk down the stairs and through the front doors, disappearing into the crowds of Forty-second Street. Mabel looked up at the night sky, wanting to memorize every star. It didn't matter that the newsreel was most likely being destroyed now. They'd done it. They'd made their mark.

But the following morning, only two newspapers carried a mention of the movie premiere's disruption-by-newsreel, and it was hardly complimentary.

"'Anarchist Thugs the Secret Six Take Over Movie Palace with Seditious Propaganda Newsreel,'" Gloria read aloud to the group as they huddled around a table at Chumley's, a speakeasy. "'We will keep these lying, outside agitators from disrupting our American way of life, promises mayor.'" She slapped the paper down on the table. "They're calling *us* thugs when those militiamen are shooting up the camp? The very nerve!"

"But people saw it," Mabel reminded them. "Once they've seen the truth, it's harder to ignore. Small acts of resistance matter!" She found herself looking to Arthur, who stared back at her as if he were just seeing her for the first time, as if she were the only girl in the world. The blush burned all the way to Mabel's toes.

A shaken Luis arrived late. "Management heard about the newsreel," he said. "They had the militiamen tear up the camp. They beat some of the miners pretty badly. And they've threatened worse."

Mabel's misery compounded. Hadn't the newsreel been her idea? The night before, Mabel had been electric with the joy of accomplishment. Now she couldn't remember a time when she'd felt more powerless.

"It was still a good idea," Arthur said, trying to comfort her as the two of them sat in a basement Romanian tavern on Christopher Street, a plate of untouched cabbage rolls between them.

"It was a lousy idea. It didn't help the miners at all. It just made things worse for them," Mabel said. How naive she'd been to think that people would be swayed by ideas of right and wrong, by images of hardworking miners and their families trying to survive against the machinery of business. "We're losing this fight. Jake Marlowe is so powerful. How do you fight back against that kind of power? We're only five rebels and some striking workers."

"Today. By tomorrow, who knows how many of us there'll be?"

"We couldn't even get people on our side when they could see the conditions for themselves! If they could deny that, then..." Mabel trailed off, her fists clenched on the scarred wooden table.

Arthur lifted her chin with his fingers. As their eyes met, Mabel's stomach did its flip-flop. How had she not noticed that handsome square jaw before? "Don't give up hope, Mabel Rose. You anchor me. If you lose hope, well, I might, too."

A new hope did perch inside Mabel, but it had nothing to do with unions and workers.

By the time Mabel returned home, it was getting late, the lights in the windows of Manhattan blinking on, millions of glowing eyes in the jagged beast of the city. She'd promised Arthur she'd get a good night's sleep, and the next day, they'd start planning a new resistance.

"Tomorrow," he'd said, and he made it sound like a battle cry and a love song at the same time.

"Tomorrow," Mabel had echoed.

When Mabel opened the door to her apartment, her parents were seated on the sofa. They looked worried.

"What is it? Did someone die? Is it Aunt Ruth?"

"No one is dead," her father assured her. "Your mother and I want to talk to you. I heard from Micah from the IWW. He says that you have been going to the strike at Jake Marlowe's mine."

"Doesn't Micah have better things to do than act like an old gossip?" Mabel grumbled as she perched at one end of the sofa.

"Mabel. Is this true?" her father pressed.

"Yes," Mabel said, her stomach sinking.

"It's that riffraff, Arthur Brown. It's his fault," Mrs. Rose said, the ghost of her former aristocratic life creeping into her tone. Mabel wished she could tell her mother how much she sounded like Nana Newell just now.

Mabel folded her arms across her chest. "You don't know him."

"I know *of* him. He's got more passion than sense," Mabel's mother snapped. "The last thing we need is Arthur and his hotheaded friends in there making a mess of our efforts."

"Why? Because they're not your acolytes? Because it wasn't your idea to go out to Marlowe's mine?"

"Mabel Rebecca. Apologize to your mother," her father warned with rare sternness.

Mabel looked down at her hands in her lap. "Sorry, Mama. But you don't know the whole story."

"Mabel, darling." Mrs. Rose moved closer to Mabel. With both hands, she swept Mabel's hair back and cradled her daughter's face with her palms, like she'd done when Mabel was a little girl. Mabel had spent her life running to catch up in the hope that her mother would notice her. But not anymore. She wasn't living in her mother's shadow. She'd moved past her. Mabel was the future, and the future was with Arthur and the Six.

"Darling, rules exist for a reason. Even within disobedience, we need order," her mother said.

"Do we? It seems like all you ever do is fight at these meetings, and change is too slow. Meanwhile, people are starving and freezing in tents! They're being beaten up by bullies hired by the rich!"

"I appreciate your passion, my *shayna*, but you must marry passion to purpose and purpose to reason. Change takes time."

"That's what you always say, and it feels like we never get anywhere. Papa, Arthur got those people food. And he helped to set up a small school for the children. He even found a doctor to see to some of the pregnant wives. He's making—*we* are making a difference."

"We?" Mrs. Rose scoffed. "I see. Did you know he'd been in prison?"

"You mean his brother," Mabel said.

"No. I mean Arthur."

It was as if her mother's words had cut off the oxygen in the room. Why hadn't Arthur told her? Above all, she didn't want her mother to suspect that she hadn't known. "You and Papa know plenty of people who've gone to jail!"

"For peaceful protest. Arthur and his brother blew up a factory! A foreman died in that explosion. A man with a family." Mrs. Rose's eyes glinted. "This is what comes of reform without rules: chaos. And children without their fathers."

Mabel's stomach hurt. Arthur wouldn't do that. He was so very kind. He'd been looking out for her, protecting her. From the start, he'd taken her seriously, brought her in, respected her ideas. She was sure he'd been waiting for the right moment to tell her about his time in prison. No doubt it was embarrassing for him—why wouldn't he want to keep it hidden? Mabel would let him know that she was his true friend, that he could trust her. If her parents had meant to dissuade her by blurting out this bit of gossip, they'd miscalculated. If anything, she was even more committed to Arthur and their mission. They were treating her like a child.

"I forbid you from seeing Arthur Brown," her mother said, as if Mabel had absolutely no say over her own life.

"Isn't that what your mother said to you when you wanted to marry Papa?" Mabel shot back.

"Mabel!"

"*Shayna*, we don't want to see you get hurt," her father said, the peacemaker again. "If you want to work the picket line, you can volunteer with the IWW or the AFL. They always need help."

"They'll have me making coffee. Not on the front lines."

"The front lines. Do you hear yourself?" her mother said. "As if this were a war!"

"Isn't it?" Mabel asked.

"Sweetheart—" her father started, but Mabel had had enough.

"You don't understand! You don't know me! You only see me the way you want to see me—as another part of you. Well, I'm not you and I am not a child! I am my own person. And I wish you could see me, the true me."

Mabel stormed from the apartment with no clear idea of where she was headed. She walked to Fifty-seventh Street and boarded the train, and before she knew it, she was running up the back stairs of the Bohemian Reader and pounding at Arthur's door.

He opened up, rubbing his eyes. "Heya, Mabel. Sorry. I was asleep. What is it?"

"When were you going to tell me about the explosion at the factory? The foreman who died? About the time you spent in jail?"

Arthur chewed at his lip, then opened the door wide. "I suppose you'd better come in."

Mabel took a seat at the table. Arthur lowered the blinds halfway, then poured Mabel a cup of lukewarm coffee from the percolator and sat across from her.

"I didn't tell you because I didn't know what you'd think of me. I was afraid you'd stop coming around."

"I…" Mabel didn't know what to say. The inside of her was at war: He wanted her around; he'd killed a man. There should be no balance between the things weighed in those two scales, but she liked Arthur. She liked him a lot.

"You killed a man," she said quietly.

"I know. Not a day goes by that I don't regret that choice. Not a day goes by that I don't wish that man were still alive. Not one, Mabel."

His eyes were pained. She believed him. Mabel got up and moved across the room to the safety of the window. "You should have told me," she said, turning to face him.

"I know. I'm sorry."

"What you did, that was terrorism."

Arthur's eyes flashed. "What do you call it when they shoot up our camp with machine guns and terrify the workers? Why does no one hold them accountable? Where are the prisons for them, huh?"

Mabel wanted to say something, but she had no easy answer. It was all so confusing.

Arthur came toward her with his loping boxer's stride. "You want the truth, then here it is: The time for placards and peace and newsreels is gone. We have a plan. We're going to sabotage the works at Marlowe's mine."

Mabel's head was light, as if it had come loose from her neck. "What… what do you mean, sabotage?"

"We're going to blow up the mine and the company store so they can't keep hiring scabs. We're sending a message to Marlowe." Arthur cupped Mabel's face in both hands. "More than anything, I want to share this with you, Mabel Rose. But it's all or nothing from now on. No half measures. So I need to know: Are you in? Or are you out?"

Mabel broke from Arthur's caress, but already she wanted him back. On the windowsill, a pigeon pecked for what it could get. Mabel watched it hopping around and thought about something Jericho had asked her once. He'd asked her if she'd ever faced a true moral dilemma, and she'd had to admit that she never had. And now, here she was, trying to figure out what was right—or the least wrong. If there was one lesson Mabel's parents had drilled, it was this: Never stoop to violence. But how did you fight an enemy who never fought fair? Didn't you have to break the rules to win against the Devil? Mabel's head was spinning. They were trying to keep Jake Marlowe from hurting the workers. That was good, wasn't it? They were destroying property. That was bad. Wasn't it? If you did the wrong things for the right reasons, did that make the wrong things right? Or did that just mean you had turned your back on finding a more right way? And once you justified violence, did that make it easier the next time and the next, until you'd become the villain of your own story?

What was good?

She thought she'd known once, but now she wasn't so sure.

Arthur was waiting for her answer.

"And no one will get hurt? You promise?" Mabel said.

Arthur put one hand on his heart. "I promise."

With a great fluttering of wings, the pigeon pushed away from the windowsill and disappeared. "Okay," Mabel said.

"Okay?"

"Okay," Mabel said. "I'm in. All the way."

GUILLAUME JOHNSON

When the Diviners weren't testing their abilities, they were reading through Will's notes from his time with the Department of Paranormal and searching through the library's thousands of books for any hint of Liberty Anne Rathbone's unholy correspondence. So far, they'd found nothing. But Memphis enjoyed squirreling away on the second-floor gallery in a patch of sunlight behind bookcases brimming with dusty volumes whose musty smell and crackling pages were a comfort. He wondered if someday someone like him or Isaiah would be sitting in a library reading a Memphis Campbell book.

From Jericho, he'd gotten Cornelius Rathbone's diary. Memphis turned the yellowed pages with care, hunting for clues to Liberty Anne's final prophecy. There were riveting revelations—future steam engines and automobiles and assassinations seen from well before they occurred. But to Memphis, nothing was more compelling than young Cornelius's confessions of his dreams and doubts. People didn't lie in their diaries. They wrote their true hearts there:

> Today is the darkest day of my life. Liberty Anne has left us. Pastor Poole tries to comfort Mother, but she is inconsolable. The light has gone from our family. We will never be the same. Godspeed, dear sister.

An ache pressed against Memphis's throat. He remembered how unreal the days after his mother's death had seemed. The procession of neighbors bringing food to the house, patting his back as they cried into handkerchiefs while Memphis appeared numb; there had been a great hole at the center of him waiting to suck him down with pain and grief, and he fought to keep it at bay. Even the sunlight had felt wrong somehow, as if it were trying to shine through a gauze bandage. Sometime during the long visiting hours after the funeral, Memphis had stolen away into his parents' bedroom. He'd stretched out across the narrow indentation his mother's body had left in the mattress where she had lain those last weeks, hollowed by the cancer, her cloudy gaze fixed to a spot on the ceiling, as if she were searching for something no one else could see, some link to the next world—a god the mourners crying in the other room believed in so fervently. A god Memphis felt had betrayed and abandoned him.

It wasn't until his mother was gone that Memphis realized just how much she had been the glue holding them all together. Without her, they were their own familial diaspora, flung apart and into a new land where grief had arrived first and tilled the soil with sorrow. The painful memory of that loss still had a fierce grip. It would drag him under now if he lingered too long with it. Memphis put his own thoughts aside. The diary's pages were disordered, and he was trying to piece together a history out of time.

> Father has forbidden us to allow the slate to Liberty Anne during her fits. I argued that the messages she received from beyond could come from the Almighty himself, for haven't angels with trumpets appeared to simple shepherds?
>
> "What she draws is unholy. I will suffer no more of it," Father told us, and he broke the slate into pieces.

Fits and drawings made Memphis think of Isaiah. He read on, growing more excited.

> I dare not tell Father about the events of last night.
>
> I had been up late reading by lantern on the porch. Father had traveled to town to deliver the widow Jenkins of a new son. Mother slept deeply, having taken a tincture of laudanum for a painful tooth, though I suspect it was more for the deep ache in her heart. The night was sharp of the sort that turns your thoughts

into friendly companions. Looking at the sky stretching out across the tall prairie grass, the stars flung into constellations above me, I felt at one with nature and myself. When suddenly, from inside our cabin, I heard a stirring.

Inside, I found Liberty Anne up from her sickbed and crouched upon the braided rug with Mother's stationery and pen and ink. She drew as if possessed and had, by my count, finished four drawings, each more terrifying than the one before. These were things far beyond my ken, dark birds filling the skies, strange explosions, clouds torn apart, and men flying through the air like broken angels. Around the edges, fearsome specters haunted the land, and always, there is the man in the hat, watching it all. I could only surmise that these events were yet to be and, should that be true, may God help us all. I fear if Father should find these, he will destroy them and commit Liberty Anne to a sanitarium. For this reason, I have hidden her unholy visions within the pages of my Bible, where they will not be seen—

Memphis sat straight up.

Unholy visions. *Unholy.* What if Liberty Anne's lost prophecy wasn't a letter or diary entry? What if they had been looking for the wrong thing all along?

"Hey, Sam, Jericho. Take a look at this," Memphis said, bounding down the spiral staircase to the library's ground floor. He showed them the passage and put forth his theory.

"So they're drawings?" Sam said.

"It makes sense to me. Just like Liberty Anne, Isaiah's been drawing his visions. During the sleeping sickness, he had a premonition about Ling and

Henry down in the subway with all those wraiths. He drew it in my book and I got sore at him for it," Memphis said. He felt guilty about that now. "Cornelius says he hid them in his Bible. We need to find that Bible."

Sam looked at the two full floors of bookcases. "You gotta be kidding me."

"At least we know what to look for now," Memphis offered.

"Spooky spirit sketches," Sam grumbled.

"Nice alliteration," Memphis said.

"Nice what?"

"Alliteration. It's when you repeat the same consonant in a phrase," Memphis explained.

"Huh. I was hoping it was something dirty."

"Ignore him, Memphis," Jericho said with a roll of his eyes. "We all do. Come on. We might as well get started."

As the first hour stretched into two and they'd still found no sign of Liberty Anne's possibly prophetic drawings, Sam groaned and tossed aside another book. "If I have to look through one more of these, I'm throwing myself off that balcony," he moaned.

"Let me know if you need help," Jericho said as he calmly restored Sam's discarded book to its rightful place on the shelves.

Memphis laughed. Those two. They were like squabbling brothers. Their arguments were better than going to the pictures.

"Maybe it's not even here. Maybe it's in a collection somewhere. I could always ask Mrs. Andrews for help," Memphis said, closing another heavy book with a thump of dust.

"Who's Mrs. Andrews?" Jericho asked.

"She's my favorite librarian at the One Hundred Thirty-fifth Street library. If she can't find it, it can't be found."

Sam smirked. "You have a favorite *librarian*?"

"*You've* got a favorite speakeasy, don'tcha?" Memphis shot back. He raised his voice like a sidewalk preacher: "As for me, 'I am large, I contain multitudes!'"

"Who said that? Calvin Coolidge?"

"Walt Whitman." Memphis's grin spread slowly, sweetly. "You'd know that if you had a favorite librarian."

"I like having you around, Memphis," Jericho said. He stood and stretched his cramped muscles. "Come on. Let's try the cellar."

Sam cocked his head, squinting. "You've got a funny idea of fun, Freddy. Ha!" He pointed at Memphis. "Alliteration! Besides, we already hauled up all the crates that were down there."

"Maybe there's something we're missing. Let's look again."

Jericho kicked the Persian rug back and lifted the trapdoor set into the floor of the collections room. Memphis peered into the dark hole.

"It's just as charming as it seems. Dark. Damp. Tubercular. Possibly haunted," Sam said. "Come on! I'll give ya the grand tour!"

The three of them climbed down the rickety steps, dropping onto the dirt floor. Memphis coughed up a lungful of dust. He wiped his filthy hands against his trousers. The damp smell of the earth was close.

"Here," Sam said, handing over a lantern.

Memphis struck a match and turned up the flame, and the cellar flared with dancing light. They were in a large room whose bricks were covered in fading murals. Ahead, though, the cellar's brick gave way to the earthen walls of a tunnel that seemed to stretch for a mile. Memphis paused in front of a mural of a slave family reaching their hands toward the sun, the word *freedom* painted above it.

"Cornelius's house was also a stop on the Underground Railroad," Jericho said, coming up beside him.

"God bless Mr. Rathbone," Memphis whispered. He put a hand to the cool, painted stones bearing witness to so many names, so many histories. In the mural, there were painted lines for the Underground, like scars stretched across the skin of the infected nation. There were wounds and then there were *wounds*. Some were so great Memphis had no idea how they could ever be healed.

"Where does that tunnel open up?" Memphis asked.

"Don't know. And I can't say I'm too keen on tunnels after those things chased us through the subway," Sam said, coughing.

Memphis lifted the lantern. Its light could reach only so far. "I need to see. Just a little." He started down the narrow passageway, ducking his head as he came to a low beam. "Watch out there," he cautioned.

"Watch out for what?" Sam said.

"Your…" Memphis looked over his shoulder. There were a good couple of inches between Sam's head and the low ceiling. "Head," Memphis said, fighting a smile.

"Some of us have to duck," Jericho said, clearly happy to have a reason to needle Sam.

Sam folded his arms. "You're really enjoying yourself, aren't you?"

Jericho broke into a full grin. "More than you can imagine."

Memphis hoisted his lantern again and peered through its hazy glow into the earthen curve of the tunnel. "This thing looks like it goes on for a mile."

"I'm not up for a mile, pal. Sorry," Sam said. "It's been closed up for decades. For all we know, there's no way out."

There was a lot Memphis wanted to say to that. "So where's this storeroom?" he said instead.

"This way," Jericho said, opening up an easily overlooked door into a cold tomb of a room. "This is where I found all of Cornelius's letters to Will."

He snapped the chain for the overhead bulb. Its sick yellow light fell across another mural: a dark, macabre forest full of ghosts. There in the center was the man in the hat facing a young Negro man. Memphis frowned.

"Yeah, me, too, pal," Sam said, coming up beside him. "It's the creepiest thing I've ever seen—and I once saw my uncle Moishe naked at the Russian baths."

"Why would somebody put that here?" Memphis said. "It doesn't look like the others. The others are hopeful. This…" He shuddered. "This is a nightmare."

"Hey! Come see what I found," Jericho called.

Sam turned to Memphis. "See, when somebody says that to me in a dirty, creepy hole of a cellar, my first inclination is to run."

In the corner, Jericho held up a small canvas sack. Sam and Memphis coughed as they waved away the clouds of dust released into the stale air. "How come it doesn't bother you, Freddy?" Sam croaked out on a burst of coughing.

"Giant's blood," Jericho said, getting in one more jab. "I found this tucked behind some Christmas ornaments."

"The professor used to decorate for Christmas? That may be the most surprising thing I've learned today," Sam said, wiping his eyes.

They peered into the canvas sack. Inside were several moldy cardboard canisters. The paper labels, freckled with black mildew spots, read EDISON GOLD MOULDED RECORDS.

Sam wiggled off the top of a canister and pulled out what was inside. "What are these? Look like dusty, hollow candles."

Memphis turned one over carefully in his hand, then put it up to his eye, peering through the tube of it. "They're wax cylinders! My father recorded some of his music on these."

"How did we miss this last time?" Sam said.

"We weren't looking for them. We were looking for letters," Jericho reminded him. He examined the old canister. A faint stamp on the bottom, barely legible, read, U.S. DEPARTMENT OF PARANORMAL. "These could have valuable information on them."

"Or they could be recordings of somebody's eighty-year-old aunt singing patriotic songs," Sam said.

Memphis shrugged. "Worth a listen."

"Okay. But if I hear a quavery soprano, I'm outta here," Sam said.

"Where's the player?"

"What's it look like?"

"Like a phonograph player—wooden box with a big megaphone coming out of it."

"I've seen it. It's upstairs in Will's office," Jericho said.

They climbed back up, restored the rug to its rightful place over the cellar door, and crept into Will's darkened office. "Don't worry," Jericho said, turning on a desk lamp. "He's giving a lecture in Connecticut today. Still trying to pay off the tax bill so they don't close this place. Here. In the corner."

On a side table wedged into an alcove was something Jericho had always regarded as one of Will's many curious, slightly useless artifacts. Now, watching Memphis thread the wax cylinder into place and turn the side crank, he understood.

"These sure look old. Not even sure it'll play. But here goes," Memphis said, dropping the needle. The cylinder spun around, spilling out its tale in pops and hisses until, finally, an echoey, familiar voice came through the attached megaphone:

"Good afternoon, Mr. Johnson. How are you today?"

"Sister Walker?" Sam whispered.

Memphis nodded.

"Fine, thank you. And yourself, Miss Walker?"

"I'm very well, thank you. You know my colleagues, Mr. Marlowe, Miss Wasserman, and Mr. Fitzgerald."

"Yes'm. Afternoon, Sir, Miss. Uh, there gonna be more a them shots today, Miss Walker?" Mr. Johnson asked in a deep, melodic voice. He sounded shy, polite, and a little frightened.

"No, no. We don't need your blood today."

At the mention of blood, the boys' eyes widened.

"What were they—" Sam started, but Jericho shushed him.

"Could you state your name and age for me, please?"

"Yes, ma'am. Guillaume Johnson. I'm eighteen years old."

"It's him! The Diviner she mentioned," Jericho whispered.

"How come it's okay when you talk but not—"

"Shhh," Memphis pleaded. He leaned in to the megaphone, straining to hear.

"What is your height and weight? Oh, and please speak into the cone, if you will."

"I'm six foot two inches, and I weigh one hun'erd ninety pounds."

"Big man," Sam said under his breath. "Big as the giant over here."

"I heard you're strong enough to lift a wagon full of hay bales, Mr. Johnson," Sister Walker's voice prompted.

"Yes, ma'am. Picked the whole back end up clean off the road so's they could change out a cracked wheel. Held it a long time, too," Guillaume Johnson answered. He sounded very proud.

"Can you tell us a little more about your powers?"

"Yes, ma'am. Long as I can recall, I been able to ease the passing of animals."

"Just animals?"

Pause.

"Well, uh…just people on their way out, Miss. Like Old Gertie, all ate up with consumption and pain. I helped her sleep. The good lord done the rest."

"Are you telling me the full truth, Mr. Johnson?"

Pause.

"I been sorely tempted, Miss Walker. Like Jesus in the wilderness. It's hard working cotton. Very hard. Long days on a hungry belly. And the landlord, he…well, he wadn't no good man, Miss. No, he wadn't."

"Is that what happened, Mr. Johnson? Did you bring on that stroke?"

"I might done. I don't know, Miss Walker, and that is the gospel truth. I only know that after, I was sick in my guts and I got a touch'a gray in my hair."

"Can you go out to the chicken coop with us, Mr. Johnson? We need a demonstration of your powers. We'll eat that chicken for dinner, so it's a necessary death."

"Yes, ma'am. I could do."

The cylinder stopped. Memphis quickly removed it and searched through the other cylinders for more of the mysterious Mr. Guillaume Johnson, who could draw the life from things. There was only one other. Quickly, Memphis threaded it and dropped the needle. This one was quieter. Mr. Johnson's sweet, deep voice had gone rough around the edges, as if he'd been gargling with sawdust. They leaned forward to hear. "Miss Walker, them fellas in the suits, them Shadow Men…they been making me work for 'em."

Pause.

"They want me to…to do things I don't feel right 'bout doin'."

"What sorts of things?"

"I…I'd rather not say, Miss Walker."

"If you don't tell me, how can I help you?"

The cylinder was nothing but pop and hiss for a few seconds. Then: "They want me to use my powers to…to hurt people. To kill 'em. They told me them folks was our enemies, but…I'm sick all the time, Miss Walker. All the time. Just look at me, Miss Walker. Look what they done to me."

Footsteps. Muffled talk. A new voice.

"Miss Walker, if you've finished with Mr. Johnson's examination, we'll take him now."

"Hey, I know that voice," Sam whispered excitedly.

"Shhh," Jericho scolded again.

Sister Walker's words crackled through the speaker. "Oh, I think Mr. Johnson should stay here. He's…he's ill."

"We'll take good care of him, won't we, Mr. Adams?"

"Mr. Jefferson and I will take it from here."

"Wait! Mr. Johnson! Guillaume!"

Pop. Hiss. And then silence.

A chill passed over Memphis. "What did they do to Mr. Johnson?"

"Who? Miss Walker or the Shadow Men?"

"Both," Memphis said softly.

Sam paced in front of Will's desk. "Those creepy fellas are the ones Evie and I saw when we broke into the old Paranormal offices. I recognize that fella Adams's voice."

"What about Guillaume Johnson? You think he's still out there somewhere?" Jericho asked. "What if we could find him, talk to him?"

"I got the feeling this Mr. Johnson didn't live too long. Sounds like his powers were making him really sick, and those Shadow Men didn't care one bit. They're bad news."

Some unnameable dread tugged at Memphis's gut. There was something so familiar about this Guillaume Johnson, something in the cadence of the man's speech, though he couldn't put his finger on it. Besides, Sam was probably right: In all likelihood, poor Guillaume Johnson, the Diviner who could draw life from the living, had taken ill and died, killed by his own gifts.

"Memphis? You jake?" Jericho asked.

Memphis was hunched forward, his elbows on his knees and his chin resting on his clasped hands. "Yeah. I was just thinking. Death. That's an awfully strong power. The strongest of all, I suppose."

Sam stopped. "You don't get it, do you? *You* have the strongest power, Memphis."

Memphis rolled his head to one side. "Me?" *I'm too scared to even show my writing to people*, Memphis thought. *I can't even date my girl in the open.*

"Any fool can kill somebody. But healing people up? That's a whole 'nother ball of wax. You can save lives, Memphis! If I were those creepy Shadow Men, frankly, I'd be looking for you first!"

PROJECT BUFFALO

In her hotel suite, Evie gooped a Boncilla "invigorating" skin mask onto her face and opened the day's paper to the gossip pages.

RUMOR HAS IT

BY HARRIET HENDERSON

This reporter has it on exclusive authority that radio's true sweetheart, the saintly Sarah Snow, has been asked by none other than our brave national hero, Jake Marlowe, to appear at his eagerly awaited Future of America Exhibition next month. "I can think of no better person to represent the future of this great country than Miss Snow and her ministry. She is pure of heart and deed and a shining example of American exceptionalism." Rumor has it…that Mr. Marlowe admires more than Miss Snow's pure heart, and that the millionaire might be set on making Miss Snow into Mrs. Marlowe. As for the question of whether Diviners will be included in his exhibition, Mr. Marlowe remained firm that they are not jake with him. "I don't go for chicanery and flimflam. If you want to see a magic trick, why, you can walk over to Forty-second Street and watch those sidewalk boys taking nickels from the gullible. Even Harry Houdini himself, the greatest magician of all, worked to expose the fraud of spiritualism and mediums and all that hooey. A bunch of folks calling themselves magical? Why, that's un-American, if you ask me."

I did, Mr. Marlowe. Thanks for setting the record straight.

And that's today's Rumor Has It!

Evie crumpled the newspaper into a ball. Harriet Henderson was a snake, but she was a snake on Sarah's side, and that was a problem. *Radio's true sweetheart.* Harriet was gutting Evie in the papers without even showing her blade. No doubt Mr. Phillips and the Pears soap folks read that, too. She had to get in to see Luther Clayton!

It wasn't only about shoving Sarah off the front pages, though that would certainly be worth it. Deep down, Evie really wanted to know why Luther had tried to shoot her. It seemed too much of a coincidence the way the soldier kept colliding with her life. She remembered meeting him for the second time, how he'd grabbed her arm and cried, *I hear them screaming…!* as if he desperately wanted her to understand. But what? Why her?

If Woody couldn't manage to get her in, she'd just have to do it herself. Evie dashed off a letter to the hospital's warden using her special WGI letterhead, mentioning how much she hoped to *also shine a light on the stellar work of the dedicated staff,* and signed it, *With Pos-i-tute-ly the Utmost Sincerity, Evie O'Neill, WGI's Sweetheart Seer.* She spritzed it with her perfume and spritzed the envelope, too, for good measure. Then she raced into the hall and dropped the note into the hotel's letter chute for the next day's pickup, frightening a bellhop. The skin mask. She'd forgotten.

"Boo!" Evie said, and watched the young man hurry away.

When Evie returned to her room, the telephone was ringing. She dove for it, pressing the bell-shaped receiver against her ear as she lay back on her silk pillow. "Good afternoon," she said in her best radio voice.

"Miss O'Neill? Call for you from Mr. I. M. Hansom," the operator said.

Evie couldn't help but grin. She was grateful for the distraction of Sam just now. "You may patch Mr. *Hansom* through, thank you," she said around the tightening mask.

"Sheba! What are you doing tonight?"

"Entertaining heads of state. Just the heads, though. Saves on having a butler for their coats."

"So nothing, then. Swell. I'll pick you up at eight."

"Now, hold on a minute! As a matter of fact, I…I have a date. With a darling boy. From New Jersey," she lied.

"Nothing darling comes from New Jersey," Sam said. "Listen, can you break it?"

"That depends. What've you got in mind? And if you say the words *ghost* or *Creepy Crawly Museum*, I'm hanging up."

"How ya feel about rum runners?"

"Those are two words I pos-i-tute-ly adore!"

"Swell. See you at eight. Oh, and doll?"

"Yes?"

"Wear something you don't mind getting wet."

"What does that mean? Sam? Sam!" Evie shouted into the phone, but the line had gone dead.

＊

Now Sam and Evie drove along the quiet nighttime roads of Long Island's North Fork. Evie had been silent most of the way, her mood darkening as she stared out through the passenger window at the dotting of houses, lonely train stations, and occasional mansion giving way to long stretches of scrubby country watched over by a seemingly endless line of telephone poles, sentinels of human connection that only made Evie feel more alone.

"Okay. Let's have it. What's eating you, Sheba?" Sam said as they bumped along, past a shadowy Burma-Shave sign. Long Island Sound peeked up behind the rise of a dune, shimmering in the newborn moonlight.

"It's nothing," Evie said on a sigh.

"That's how I know it's something. You never say that."

It was everything. If Evie could've unbuttoned her skin to escape her own terrible restlessness, she would have. She angled herself toward Sam. "Do you think I'm selfish?"

Sam laughed. "Is that a trick question?"

"Forget I said anything." Evie's eyes pricked with tears. She lolled her head toward the window.

"Aww, Sheba. So you're working for Evie. Honestly, who isn't working for himself in this meshuga world? Some people just hide it better than others."

"People like Sarah Snow?"

"So you read today's 'Rumor Has It.' Okay, sure. Maybe. But honestly, name one person who isn't selfish."

Evie didn't have to think long. "Mabel."

Sam nodded. "Yeah. Mabel."

"I wish I could be more like that. Like Sarah or Mabel."

"Yeah? Between you and me, I don't think you'd make it very long. The real you would come popping out like a showgirl hiding inside a plain vanilla cake. Just my two cents' worth. Besides, you always come through for your friends in the clinch. So the Bible thumper does a lot of good. You think she coulda faced down a demon like John Hobbes all by herself? You think she'd'a been able to take on those beasties chasing us through the subway tunnels?"

Evie whirled toward Sam again. "But no one will ever know I did that, so what good is it?"

Sam kept his eyes on the dark road ahead. "Oh, I see. It only counts if everybody knows about it. Don't you get enough attention?"

"You asked," Evie said, staring out the window again.

"Aw, Sheba. I didn't mean anything by that. Look, I know I'm no egghead and I'm no saint. I can't heal like Memphis or play the piano like Henry. And I sure don't look like Freddy the Giant," he said, exposing his own soft wound. "But I got my own kind of smarts, from the streets, and when I go after something, well, just try'n shake me off. I'm an odd fella, but I *know* I'm an odd fella. What I can't figure out is why you gotta make yourself crackers trying to be somebody you can't ever be instead of just letting yourself be the one and only Evie O'Neill."

Because I'm not enough, she thought. That was the terrible echo shouting up at her: *Fraud, fraud, fraud*. She got drunk and talked too much and danced on tables. She had a temper and a sharp tongue, and she often blurted out things she instantly regretted. Worst of all, she suspected that was who she truly was—not so much a bright young thing as a messy young thing. There were a hundred fears Evie could list. She imagined palming every one of them into a big, ugly rock and watching that rock sink to the bottom of the Sound.

"Anyway. You can worry about new things, like being arrested by the Coast Guard, because we're here." Sam rolled to a stop behind an old shed. The car's headlamps cast an eerie glow on a sardine row of cars parked along the curve of the beach. "Loyal customers," he said.

They stumbled toward the shore, each trying to get there first. A narrow slipper of a motorboat was stashed up on the beach. "A little help?" Sam asked, and then he and Evie were pushing the boat toward the water. "By the way," he grunted, "what's that thing on your head?"

"It's called a tam, if you must know, and it came all the way from Scotland. It's very fashionable."

"Does the poor Scottish shepherd know you took his hat?" Sam said, easing the craft into the water.

"You should talk. You dress like Trotsky. So where is this mystery ship?" There was nothing in the bay that Evie could see.

"The *Kill Devil*? About a mile or so out that way, hidden in that cove over there," Sam said, pointing to a curved finger of high land jutting into the water on the other side of the Sound. "They're risking it for sure. There's a twelve-mile limit. Any boat caught inside that limit can be picked off by the Coast Guard—or pirates. I'm guessing the *Kill Devil*'s got some secret storage inside her to take that risk."

"Are you saying we could be arrested?"

Sam shrugged. "Or shot."

Sam helped Evie into the boat. It wobbled precariously as he hopped on board and took a seat himself.

"If this kills me, I'll never forgive you," Evie groused.

Sam leaned over with a pair of binoculars. "The list of things you'll never forgive me for is long, Sheba. Just keep your peepers peeled for the Coast Guard. Ow!"

"What?"

Sam rubbed his left eye. "Your funny hat just got me in the peeper."

"Well, you insulted it," Evie said, raising the binoculars and looking out at the open water for signs of trouble. "The Scots are not a forgiving people. Neither are their hats."

Sam leaned over the stern and looped the string around the outboard motor, pulling until it sputtered into noisy motion. Evie shivered as Sam steered them across the calm water, watching the darkened houses of Long Island growing smaller. From where she sat, they seemed content, tucked into the cove like sleeping children. She wanted to ask Sam if he ever felt frightened about the danger they'd face if Will and Miss Walker were right about the coming storm. She wanted to tell him how she still had awful nightmares about James. But it didn't seem like the sort of conversation to have while shouting over the hammering of a motorboat.

When they'd put enough sea behind them, Sam rounded the cove, and Evie saw the *Kill Devil*. It wasn't a schooner, low and fast like most rum runners. The *Kill Devil* was a yacht, easily more than one hundred feet long, and there was a party taking place on board. Two smaller boats were speeding away, their bellies presumably filled with crates of booze smuggled in from Canada. Sam cut the motor as they pulled up alongside the ship. Two crewmen peered down from the deck. They did not look friendly to Evie. Sam stood and waved his arms, rocking the boat as he called out, "Ahoy! Permission to board? Eloise sent me," Sam said, using the password he'd been given. "Said I should talk to Captain Moony himself."

A rope ladder tumbled down and thumped against the boat's flank.

Evie eyed the swaying ladder. "Every time I go somewhere with you, Sam, I'm sure it'll be the end of me. And my shoes," she sighed as she climbed.

On deck, a few gangsters and their molls laughed it up. A balding man played a banjo while two flappers in beaded dresses and furs, stockings rolled down to show off rouged knees, danced the Charleston, stopping to swig from unmarked brown bottles—the good stuff that hadn't been cut with water and cheap grain liquor yet. As she and Sam passed by, Evie raised her hands in the air like a holy roller. "Beware the dangers of demon rum! That way lies eeeevillll!" she thundered in her best Sarah Snow impression, making Sam laugh full out, and just like that, her mood lifted, and she was glad she'd come.

"Say, you folks don't know where a fella could find the lavatory, do you?" a drunken passenger asked.

"Sure. It's this way." Sam stuck out his arm and narrowed his eyes, concentrating. "Don't see me."

The man went slack. Sam reached into his pocket and took out a chunk of cash.

"Sam!" Evie said, looking over her shoulder. "What are you doing?"

"We might need extra money for information."

"That's terrible!"

"Yeah? Say, when did you develop a conscience?"

"About the time I started reading people's secrets for a living," Evie said, but she was laughing. "And I *hate* having a conscience. Very inconvenient."

Sam unfolded the man's money, lifted a twenty, and put the rest back in the man's pocket. "Happy now, Sheba?"

Evie pursed her lips and looked toward the ship's ceiling. "That depends. Are you sore about it, Sam?"

"Yes."

She looped her arm through his. "Then I'm happy."

Sam burst into laughter. "Okay, Lamb Chop. You win."

That was the thing about being with Evie—she was a high-wire act, exciting and dangerous and exhilarating. When Sam had run away from home to find his mother, he'd joined up with Barnes & Bellwether's Traveling Circus Pandemonium. They'd given him passage, and in return, he'd worked for them, first as a roustabout, then as a clown, and then, when it was discovered that he was quick on his feet, as a tumbler and acrobat. His most vivid memory was hanging by his knees from the trapeze bar, arms out, ready to catch the flier, his stomach somersaulting with high-stakes expectation. As they stole belowdeck in search of Moony Runyon, Sam felt that same fluttering excitement. Some of it was the hope that he would finally get some answers about Project Buffalo and the whereabouts of his missing mother. The other part was pure Evie, the two of them, an adventurous team, up for anything. Sure, Evie was selfish sometimes. She liked being the star. But she would do anything for her friends, Sam included. That was what he couldn't tell her—that the end of their fake romance was really about saving himself. He'd gone goofy for her, and if she broke his heart, that would be the end of the best friendship he'd ever had. He couldn't risk that.

"You think there are pirates on board?" Evie whispered, her eyes alight with puckish mischief.

"We can always hope," Sam said, feeling alive.

At the very back of the boat, they came to a door with a sign reading, CAPTAIN'S QUARTERS. KEEP OUT. YES, THAT MEANS YOU.

"Very welcoming," Evie said, and opened the door without knocking. The modest cabin was mostly dark, the only light coming from a desk lamp. A potbellied man glared at her from behind that desk. His hands were wrapped around a mug. A half-empty bottle of whiskey sat nearby. "What's the big idea? Can't you read?" he growled.

"Oh, I'm afraid not. Tragic accident in the convent. I stared too long at the rays of the sun coming through the stained-glass windows. The nuns are still praying for my recovery," Evie said breezily, taking in the whole of the close quarters, whose every inch of wall space was occupied by bleached sea creature bones. "My. What a lot of dead things you have in here. I can only imagine what your nursery was like."

"Moony Runyon?" Sam asked before the man could get up and throw them out.

"Who wants to know?" It was more command than question.

"A fella interested in knowing what happened to Ben Arnold," Sam answered.

Moony Runyon settled back against his chair. "Oh. It's you. Wasn't sure if you were coming. You have the money?"

Sam offered the fifty dollars he'd made lifting wallets in Central Park plus the twenty he'd just taken from the drunken party guest. Captain Moony gestured for them to sit. Sam dragged over two skinny chairs—one for himself and one for Evie—from a narrow table against the wall.

Captain Moony counted the money while he talked. "Heard old Ben ended up dead on an ash heap. He never was too careful. Me? I'm careful." He slapped a knife on the table and stuffed the money into his pocket. "So. What was it you wanted to know?"

"We're looking for the machine that reads these." Sam handed over one of the coded punch cards. "Know where we could find it?"

Moony examined it briefly before handing it back. "I smuggle booze. Not government documents."

Sam smirked. "Yeah? How'd you know it was a government document?"

"I seen one of those before. With Ben. Department of Paranormal, United States government. Project Buffalo."

Sam sat as still as he could. But inside, he was buzzing. For two years, he'd been doing nothing but hunting down leads on the secret government project that had taken his mother from him. He'd never been this close. Next to him, he could feel Evie holding her breath, too.

"You go first. Tell me what you know, and I'll fill in," Moony said.

"We know it had to do with the government's Department of Paranormal," Evie said. "And with Diviners. Testing them."

Moony poured whiskey into his mug and swallowed a third of it. "Testing them? Sure. That came later."

Evie started to ask another question, but Sam pressed his knee against hers in private warning: *Don't say more.*

"Project Buffalo was so top secret there was even a private outfit within the Bureau assigned to look after it," Moony continued. "The Shadow Men. Ben was one of 'em once. He told me the agents all had code names. Mr. Jefferson. Mr. Adams. Mr. Jackson. You get the idea. They were a rogue agency—they could work outside the law. Word was, the whole project got private money from the Founders Club."

"The Founders Club? What's that, some sort of rich folks' summer camp?" Sam asked.

"Not too far off. It's a social club, one of those eugenics things, made up of the richest men in America, the kind who want to stay rich. They pulled the strings on a lotta things. And they were bully on Diviners. Wanted to know everything about them: What could they do? Were there ways to make their gifts even stronger? Could you use Diviners to make America the greatest, most unstoppable country on earth?"

Nothing was making sense in Sam's head. "How were they gonna do that?"

"You still don't get it, do ya?" Moony Runyon leaned forward and put his fists on the desk. The dim lamp cast shadows across his unshaven face. "Project Buffalo wasn't just about testing and recruiting Diviners. It was about *making* them."

The cabin suddenly felt very small to Sam. It was all he could do not to run up to the deck and breathe in clean night air. "Making them?"

"Yes, indeed. Super Americans, engineered in the womb. Pump 'em up with some concoction Jake Marlowe and that woman, Miss Walker, made. They'd work with those kids over the years, run 'em through tests to strengthen their gifts. And then they'd recruit those same Diviner kids as secret weapons. Imagine it: a private army of gifted Americans who could use their powers to predict an attack by the enemy or crack secret codes. They could read the minds of kings and rulers signing treaties. They'd know if those leaders were on the level. They'd know at a glance if a fella was telling the truth or not. If he was loyal or a traitor or an anarchist." Moony Runyon swigged the last of his whiskey and examined the empty mug as if it might hold answers to questions he wasn't sharing. "But from what I heard, the experiment didn't take for most of the kids. It even made some kids come out wrong."

"Wrong how?" Evie asked.

Moony shrugged. "But then the war broke out and something happened along the way. Ben would never tell me. And after that, they shut it all down—the program and the department, everything."

"'Cept I heard they didn't," Sam said.

"Yeah? Who told you that?"

"Ben Arnold."

"And now he's dead."

"You think one of those Shadow Men murdered Ben Arnold?"

"I'd bet my bottom dollar on it."

"Why?"

Moony Runyon shrugged. "Ben talked too much. To fellas like you, for instance. That's what a gambling habit will do to a fella. Maybe I shouldn't even be talking to you. Go on. Get off my boat. Let me drink in peace."

Moony handed back the punch card and swigged straight from the bottle. At the cabin door, Evie turned back. "Just one more question, please, Mr. Runyon? The machine that reads these cards—we're desperate to find it, but we don't even know where to look. Please, can you help us?"

"If there's a machine to read it somewhere, the person who'd know would be Jake Marlowe. After all, he probably built it." Moony snickered. "But good luck trying to get into any of Marlowe's strongholds. You might as well try to get into Fort Knox."

※

Evie took the wheel on the way back to the city. She watched the rutted road appear like a surprise in the headlamps' glare. Everything looked sideways to her now. The car bounced as it hit a bump, and Sam grabbed hold of the door handle. "Holy moly! You always drive this fast?"

Evie hadn't realized how fast she was going. "Slow is for chumps."

"Well, I'd like to be a live chump. Take it easy, will ya?"

Evie eased her foot off the accelerator and the car settled into a healthy purr. "Sam, could all of that be true? Do you think we're . . . test subjects?"

"Pretty sure I am," Sam said. "That would explain why Rotke Wasserman kept coming around to see me."

"But that could have to do with your mother, too. Didn't you say she was a Diviner? They probably wanted to know if you'd inherited her talents."

"Maybe. Except that I can't remember any of that stuff. When you read my mother's photograph, that was the first time I knew of it."

Evie thought about what she'd seen then: A beautiful room full of paintings, books, and fancy chandeliers, like a museum or a palace. Will's fiancée, Rotke, asking Sam if he could read cards. But Sam couldn't. He didn't seem to have any powers. And then there were all those children on the front lawn crying about the sinking of the *Lusitania* seconds before it was known. What if those children had been part of Project Buffalo? If so, where were they now?

"What if they had a way of erasing my memories?" Sam said from the passenger seat, bringing Evie back. "Say, do you remember anything about *your* childhood, anybody testing you?"

"No. Never," Evie said. But just because she couldn't remember it, did that mean it had never happened? Unnatural. Created. The thought of it made Evie's skin crawl. And something else had been nagging at Evie for the entire drive back. "Sam, what Moony said, about strengthening Diviners' powers. What if . . ."

"What if Sister Walker and Will aren't on the level about this 'coming storm' business? What if they're using us for something else? Yeah. I thought about that, too. I think until we know more, we gotta keep pretending that everything's jake."

They'd reached the city's shiny edge, smears of neon sharpening into tall window blocks of light.

"What does any of this have to do with all these ghosts showing up?" Evie said.

"I don't know. My head feels like it's been twirled on a merry-go-round."

"Mine, too."

"First things first: We gotta find this card reader if we want answers. Doesn't Jake Marlowe have some kinda house upstate?"

"Yes. An estate. I heard Will say it belonged to his family."

"Seems like a good place to start." Sam let out a long, hard sigh. "Aww, how we gonna get into Marlowe's house anyhow?"

"I know somebody who could." She turned the car toward the Bennington.

※

"Coast is clear. The professor's room is empty," Sam said, letting Evie into the apartment.

Jericho stepped out of the bathroom, startling them all into shrieks. He was shirtless, with a towel wrapped around his waist. Evie pretended to be interested in Jericho's painted battle figurines on the kitchen table while stealing sideways glances at the impressive muscles of his broad back.

"I didn't know we had company," Jericho growled at Sam as he ducked back into the bathroom. A moment later, he emerged in trousers and an undershirt.

"I'm mostly decent," Jericho said. "What's got you both so excited?"

They sat at the table while Evie and Sam told Jericho all about their meeting with Moony Runyon.

"The samples," Jericho said when they'd finished their tale. "In all of Will's letters to Cornelius, Will mentioned collecting samples from the Diviners they were testing. Wait just a minute." Jericho disappeared into his room and returned with a cache of bound letters.

Sam snorted. "You kept those and *I'm* the bad guy?"

"Sam, you steal from people all the time."

"Just like Robin Hood."

"He gave to the poor."

"So...*I'm* poor."

"I'm not going to entertain this argument," Jericho said. "I'd meant to ask Will about it at some point. And they were a little damaged, so I kept them out of the damp basement."

Watching Jericho untie the string and sift through the letters made Evie antsy. She wanted to know what was in them and didn't at the same time.

"Here's one. 'Today we visited with Miss Maudie Lemieux, a Diviner in Poughkeepsie with the ability to commune with the spirit world through séance.' Et cetera, et cetera…"

"Et cetera, et cetera?" Sam said, incredulous. "You're skipping over the best parts, Freddy."

"You know how to read, don't you, Sam? You can go through them to your heart's content," Jericho said, exchanging a brief smile with Evie before returning his attention to the letter. "Here it is: 'She consented to allow Margaret the liberty of a sample or two.'"

"Diviner blood," Evie mused.

"The question is, what did they do with it?" Jericho asked.

"I got a feeling whatever it was, we're the end result," Sam said.

Evie examined the letter. She squinted at the return address, feeling a tingle. "'Hopeful Harbor, New York,'" she read aloud. "Where's that?"

"That's the name of Marlowe's family home upstate," Jericho said. "Why?"

"Sam, remember when I read your mother's photograph, I heard Will asking her to come to the Harbor? I thought it was an actual harbor somewhere. But what if he meant Hopeful Harbor? What if that's where all the Project Buffalo testing happened?"

"Doll, I think you were right that all of these things are connected. And don't say anything about Nietzsche and the eternal recurrence, Freddy."

Evie frowned. "What's the matter, Jericho? You do look very serious."

"He was born that way," Sam said. "Came out reading philosophy."

"It's these letters. The last one was from Will, dated 1917. It read, 'You were right. I was wrong. I'm sorry.' That's it. No explanation."

"Maybe he was sorry for being a chump."

"Maybe," Jericho said. "But what if it was something else?"

There was a creaking sound, and they all stilled, eyes on the door in case it was Will coming home. But it was only the wind making the Bennington's Victorian bones moan.

Evie bit her lip. "Jericho, I feel awful asking this—"

"But it's not going to stop her," Sam said.

"What if you said yes to Marlowe's offer? What if you went up to his estate after all?"

Sam sat up, looking from Evie to Jericho. "What are you talking about?"

Evie ignored him. "You could spy on him, report back to us."

"Spy on Jake Marlowe?" Jericho's eyebrows shot up. "That's a tall order."

"Wait, why are we spying? What are you talking about?" Sam pressed.

"Marlowe was part of the Paranormal Department. He knows what happened with Project Buffalo! And that card reader is probably at his house. You could find it for us." Evie took Jericho's hand. "Please. We have to know what happened."

"All right," Jericho said. He didn't want to let go of Evie's hand just yet.

"Really? You will?"

It was her smile that did it. Jericho would do anything for that smile. Hadn't he wanted to make his mark? This was a start. Instead of shelving books filled with adventures, he'd be living one. "I'm almost out of serum. I have to do something. At least if I'm spying on Marlowe and getting answers about Project Buffalo, I won't feel like he holds all the power over my choices."

Sam waved his hands. "Is no one gonna tell me what this is about?"

"Okay if I fill Sam in?" Evie said.

"You'll have to. Otherwise, he'll never shut up. You'll wander the streets hearing only his annoying voice in your head. I can think of no greater torture," Jericho deadpanned.

Sam clipped Jericho's arm playfully with his fist. Jericho didn't even flinch. Wincing, Sam shook out his hand. "Holy smokes, you are solid."

"You can see me out, Sam. I'll tell you on the way," Evie said, putting on her hat.

Sam nodded at Evie's hat. "It's called a tam," Sam whispered to Jericho. "Whatever you do, don't insult it."

"I don't know what to say to Will, though. He and Marlowe hate each other, and Marlowe hates Diviners. If Will hears I left to join up with Marlowe's exhibition, it'll feel like a betrayal," Jericho said, the thought weighing heavily on him.

"Will could never hate you. It's only for a few weeks, and then you

145

can let him know the truth," Evie promised. "Oh, thank you, Jericho!" She hugged Jericho, and Jericho didn't say what bothered him most about their plan: He'd be away from Evie.

Evie shrugged on her coat and made a beeline for the telephone.

"Thought we were leaving. What are you doing now?" Sam asked.

"I'm calling an emergency Diviners meeting."

"Now? Here?" Sam asked.

Evie made a face as she dialed Theta's number. "Don't be silly. At the Hotsy Totsy. I'm not having this discussion without jazz and gin."

THE HOTSY TOTSY

While Cal Cooper and the St. Nicholas Playboys pounded out a stomping jazz number onstage behind the shimmying Hotsy Totsy chorus girls, and Harlem's hottest nightclub swirled with dancers hopped up on bootleg booze served by waiters carrying silver trays high in the air, the Diviners, along with Mabel and Jericho, crowded around a corner table partially obscured by the splayed fronds of a potted palm.

"What did you want to talk to us about?" Memphis asked, keeping one eye on the floor. He wanted to make sure Papa Charles didn't see him camped at a table with his friends when he was supposed to be working.

"This," Sam said, unloading onto the table his secret cache of coded punch cards they'd found in the abandoned office of the Department of Paranormal.

Henry held one up, peering at the holes. "Is this your failed attempt at making Swiss cheese?"

"It's code, remember?" Evie said. "These are all files on subjects from Project Buffalo."

"I thought you only found one of these," Ling said, turning the card over, peering at it.

"We only showed you one before the professor and Sister Walker came in. I didn't want to tip our hand that we had a lot of 'em," Sam said. "These cards? They're proof."

"Proof of what?" Theta asked.

Evie nodded at Sam. "Tell 'em."

"We are not a fluke of nature. We Diviners were *made*. Engineered right in our mother's wombs through Project Buffalo," Sam said. "And Will and Sister Walker and Jake Marlowe all had something to do with it."

He and Evie told them everything then—about how they'd broken into an abandoned Department of Paranormal office a few weeks earlier and found the cards. How they'd had to hide under a desk from the two Shadow Men who'd come sniffing around for a prophecy. The map on the wall with thumbtacks stuck into different towns and the cryptic notations written beside each marked town: *Subject #7, Subject #59, Subject #122.* Finally, they told them everything Moony had just admitted to them on the *Kill Devil.* When they'd finished, there was a sick stillness around the table that was at odds with the nightclub's fizzy glamour.

"We were made?" Ling repeated, as if she were trying to convince herself.

"Yeah. Didn't you ever think it was funny that we're all the same age? There's a good chance every one of us is a test subject, and the secrets we need to know are on these cards," Sam said, tapping the tip of his index finger on the stack. "Trouble is, we need a special tabulating machine to read them, and we don't have it."

Ling examined one of the cards. "It's not at the museum somewhere?"

"No. We've searched that place from top to bottom," Jericho said.

"Can't any old code-reading machine work in a pinch?" Memphis asked.

Sam shook his head. "Huh-uh. The code is specific to the machine."

Ling nodded at Evie. "Why don't *you* just read the cards and get the information?"

Evie bristled. "Why don't *you* just dream walk and ask your dead relatives to tell you? Do you think I haven't tried? I haven't been able to get much from them. Maybe because they were meant to be read by a machine."

"How many of those cards are there?" Henry asked.

Sam held up one of the cards. "One hundred forty-four."

Memphis's head shot up. "There's that number again."

"What is it, Poet?"

"In Harlem, we're superstitious about numbers. A hymn at church or a street number that comes up twice in one day or you have a dream about something, well, there's a number for that, too. You can look it up in the policy book. One forty-four is the same number my aunt's boarder, Blind Bill, has been playing for a few weeks now. Calls it his lucky number even though it hasn't hit for him but once. But it's also the number Isaiah calls out sometimes when he's in a trance. That's an awful lot of coincidence."

"Makes me think about what that egghead fella Carl Jung said when we went to visit him," Theta added. "Something about coincidences being more than that. About them being related."

"The eternal recurrence," Jericho said.

"Not this again. Pal, can we let Nietzsche have the night off?" Sam protested. "Look around: We're in a nightclub. People are having fun here."

Theta frowned. "Come to think of it, when I dropped Dr. Jung's book, what page you think it was opened to?"

"If I say one forty-four, do I get a prize?" Evie asked.

"Yeah. You get to be right," Theta said, trying to ignore the itching in her palms. What she didn't say was that the book had been opened to a picture of a Phoenix rising from the flames. A mythological firebird.

"We're also superstitious about numbers in Chinatown," Ling said, frowning. "Fours are unlucky. The word for *four* sounds like the word for *death*."

Sam looked from Ling to Jericho and back. "You know what? I'm gonna call you two the spooky twins."

"What are we going to do about this?" Henry asked. "Clearly, Dr. Fitzgerald and Miss Walker have lied to us."

Ling didn't like knowing that Miss Walker had lied. She looked up to Miss Walker and had come to see her as a mentor. Now her heart wrestled with a problem: Could you still like someone who had done something so clearly wrong? Could you admire someone for their talents even if you condemned their methods? "Maybe they had reasons for doing what they did. We don't know everything about Project Buffalo. Why don't we just ask them about it?"

"Nothing doing!" Sam said. "Until we get the card reader and find out what's on these, we're gonna keep our traps shut."

"Memphis Campbell!"

Ling looked up to see a glamorous chorus girl in a skimpy beaded costume and a glittering headband sauntering toward their table, a red carnation tucked into her cleavage. Her smile was dazzling, and she walked with a rare confidence. The chorus girl threw her arms around Memphis's neck and kissed his cheek. Ling glanced over at Theta, but she didn't seem bothered.

"Where you been hiding yourself lately? And don't tell me you've been going back to that old African graveyard to write," the chorus girl said.

"Oh, you know how it is. Here and there," Memphis said, and Ling could see that they were friends. In fact, they almost seemed like siblings. "Everybody, this is my friend Alma. Alma, I think you know most everybody here."

"I surely do. Well…" Alma cocked her head and smiled at Ling. "Not everybody."

"Miss Alma LaVoy, may I present Miss Ling Chan."

Alma stuck out her hand and offered up her most winning smile. "Charmed. Why, I had no idea Memphis had such a sweet friend." She dragged over a chair, positioning it between Ling and Memphis. "Mind if I join you all?"

Memphis snorted. "Like I could stop you."

Alma stole a sip from Memphis's drink and made a face. "Ugh. What is that?"

"Coca-Cola."

Evie slid over her glass. "Bourbon."

Alma's mischievous grin returned. "I knew I liked you. Now. What are you all talking about over here with your heads bent together like pieces of the same dreary puzzle?"

"Ghosts. Demons. Murder. As one does at the city's best nightclubs," Henry said.

Alma choked on her sip of Evie's bourbon. "I would say don't stop on my account. But you can stop on my account." She shuddered, then turned toward Ling again. "Ling. My, that's a pretty name," she purred. "How come I haven't seen you before? Why has my very good friend Memphis not bothered to introduce us?"

"You better stop now," Memphis chided playfully under his breath.

"I already got one grandmother, Memphis. Don't need another," Alma answered in kind through smiling teeth.

"Alma!" one of the chorines shouted, waving wildly. "Get your crown! We're on!"

"You don't need to tell *me* when we're on—I *know* when we're on, Minnie!" Alma shooed Minnie away with a flick of her fingers. "Time to shake a leg." Alma took the red carnation from her dress and plopped it into Ling's empty cup, enjoying the matching blush that rose in Ling's cheeks. "Hope you enjoy the show." Alma winked, then raced up to the stage just as the band broke into a fast-paced number. Ling watched in awe as Alma danced, all arms and legs and joy. Freedom in motion. For a moment, Ling was envious. But then Alma executed a series of steps, tapping out a complex rhythm with toes and heels, and Ling knew that even if she had never had infantile paralysis, she'd never be able to own a stage like that. There was a word for Memphis's friend Alma: mesmerizing.

"She's good. She's *very* good," Ling said, eyes trained on Alma's shaking hips.

Henry looked from Ling to Alma and back again. His mouth slid into a sly smile. "Oh my."

Jericho accidentally brushed against Mabel. "Sorry."

"It's fine," Mabel said, and she realized, with sudden clarity, that it was. In fact, for the first time in years, being this close to Jericho didn't make her stomach quiver or her cheeks flush. It was liberating, like the breaking of a spell.

"How are you, Jericho?" she asked brightly.

"Fine, thank you. How are you?"

"I'm swell!"

"Well, that's good news." He was smiling at her, head cocked, as if he could tell she'd changed. *For the first time, she had the upper hand.* "I'm headed upstate tomorrow."

"Oh? Where?" Mabel was a little disappointed that she'd just developed her *not in love with Jericho anymore* muscle and wouldn't have a chance to flex it.

"Jake Marlowe's mansion. He's asked me to take part in his Future of America Exhibition. I leave tomorrow morning."

"You're going to be *living in the house of the enemy*?" Mabel blurted, her voice going high.

Jericho sighed in irritation. "He's not the enemy."

"Tell that to his workers."

Jericho glared. "It's more complicated than black and white, good and evil. Don't forget: Jake Marlowe saved my life once upon a time."

"And for that you owe him your blind loyalty?"

"Okay. You two crazy kids," Sam said, laughing nervously. "Tell me the truth: What have you both got against fun? Was it a childhood trauma? There is no prohibition against fun. Yet."

Jericho stood, pushing his chair back. "You're right. And since it's my last night here, I'd like to have some of that fun. Evie, would you care to dance?"

Evie glanced nervously at Mabel.

"You don't need my permission," Mabel said. "Oh, honestly. Go."

"Well, maybe just one dance," Evie said.

"On second thought, boo to fun. Really. Best to just stay in and read dead German philosophers," Sam said, watching them go. "Me and my big mouth."

Mabel sipped her soda water and gazed out at the dance floor. Evie and Jericho looked good together, the fancy Diviner and the golden god. For just a moment, the old hurts flared; Mabel tugged at her skirt, feeling plain and too earnest and out of place in this world because she *was* out of place in this world. But not in Arthur's garret in Greenwich Village. She had a sense of purpose there, and as much as she loved her friends, she couldn't help feeling angry that they could come up here and dance and drink while there were miners and their families living in tents. As for Jericho, well, he was no Arthur Brown.

Mabel gathered her belongings. "Sorry. I'm suddenly very tired. Tell Evie I said good-bye, will you?"

"Sure. I'll, uh, tell the giant you said good-bye, too," Sam said.

"Don't bother," Mabel said.

On her way out, Mabel passed Papa Charles. He strolled through the club looking dapper in his crisp white dinner jacket, a white rose in the buttonhole of his lapel and his hair slicked back, one of his ever-present cigars wedged between his thick fingers. He moved from table to table, welcoming his patrons, before stopping at Memphis's table.

"Evenin', Memphis. You enjoying the show?" Papa Charles said with a tight smile.

"Just saying hello to some friends of mine, sir."

"Evenin', everyone," Papa Charles said, all charm. "Memphis, we have some business to attend to. I'll expect you in my office. Five minutes."

"Uh-oh. Dad's sore," Sam said under his breath once Papa Charles had walked away.

"You don't know the half of it," Memphis said.

"Everything copacetic?" Theta asked, concerned.

"Guess I'll find out." Memphis looked longingly at Theta. He wanted to kiss her, but he couldn't do that here in the club with everyone looking on. The bright young things drinking away their night at the next table kept casting sidelong glances at him and his friends as it was.

Theta leaned in and whispered in his ear, "Meet me at our lighthouse later."

And Memphis didn't care about the people at the next table or what Papa Charles was going to ask him to do so long as Theta was with him.

THE COTTON CLUB

Papa Charles's chauffeured Chrysler Imperial rolled through Harlem's neon-drenched streets, past the swells in their tuxedos, the dames in their furs and pearls out for a night of jazz and dancing. After a few blocks, the car stopped in front of the Cotton Club, one of the crown jewels of Harlem nightlife, where Manhattan's elite came to hear the best of the best and buy overpriced, forbidden booze from the owner and premier bootlegger, Owney Madden. But the Cotton Club had a strict color line—most of the staff and entertainers were black; the clientele was white. Memphis had never been inside, but he'd heard the place was even decorated like a plantation.

So why the hell was Papa Charles bringing him here?

"You know Owney's boys won't let us come in. They got a color line," Memphis challenged.

"Not when it comes to healing, they don't."

Memphis couldn't believe what he was hearing. "You brought me here to heal? Who? What for? Why are—"

"Memphis, Memphis: Just follow my lead and everything'll be fine."

At the front door, the attendant held up a white-gloved hand and jerked his head toward the side entrance. *Told you*, Memphis wanted to say.

"Doesn't seem right," he said instead as they knocked at the service door.

"I decide what's right," Papa Charles said. "Listen here, Memphis, we make friends with these boys, show 'em we can work together, and they'll leave us alone, stick to their own territory. We make good with Owney, he'll back us against Dutch and his boys. One of his boys got himself shot up in a turf war with Dutch's gang. Owney's outfit can't take this fella to a hospital without too many questions that lead right back to Owney and the Cotton Club. This healing is a business deal. A peace treaty. You understand?"

Memphis understood, all right. He was being used. Just like when Papa Charles had had him heal Mrs. Carrington during the sleeping sickness.

Memphis had foolishly thought that would be a onetime deal. His pride made him want to refuse. But maybe this could work to his advantage. Hadn't Sister Walker wanted them all to work on strengthening their gifts? This was practice. At least that was what he was telling himself. Still, in Memphis's mind, healing somebody who was sick wasn't the same as healing some fool who'd gone and gotten himself shot up, probably while trying to kill somebody else.

A man wearing a holster let them in and showed them to a small room off the kitchen. "Wait here," he instructed. Through the walls, Memphis could hear Duke Ellington's band going to town. Memphis wasn't allowed to come and see the show, but he was allowed to come through a back door in order to heal? His anger burned bright. To hell with Owney Madden and his color line! And to hell with Papa Charles, too.

The gangster returned. "This way."

He led them to Owney Madden's office. It was twice as big as Papa Charles's, with expensive rugs and giant ferns and lamps that looked as if they belonged in a museum. For all Memphis knew, they'd been stolen from one. Owney's man lay on a cot, moaning. His leg was propped up on a stack of pillows soaked with blood. A bloody towel had been wrapped around the bullet wounds in his thigh. He was pale and sweating; his breathing was shallow.

"Gonna need to take that off," Memphis said, gesturing to the towel. The gangster nodded and Memphis carefully removed the blood-soaked towel. The man's leg was a mess, and he was losing blood fast. Memphis needed to act quickly. He was nervous, though. This wasn't a small healing, like after Isaiah's seizures. This was big, like when he'd healed Mrs. Carrington, and that had cost him dearly. This would take a lot of energy; it would exhaust him. He might even be too tired to meet up with Theta later, and that bitterness lodged in his heart.

But what if the healing didn't come on? If it didn't, he and Papa Charles were unprotected here in a back room in enemy territory with guns and gangsters all around. They might not get out alive if Memphis couldn't deliver. Memphis was angry with Papa Charles for putting him in this position. He was angry that he had to work on this man who, on a regular day, would probably spit at Memphis in the street. He had to put that aside to do the work, and he was angry that he had to put aside his anger, too.

"All right, then," he whispered, and placed his hands on the man's leg. The man moaned in sharp agony and the guns came out then.

Memphis raised his hands. "Can't do any work with those pointed at me."

"Gentlemen, it's all right," Papa Charles soothed. "Part of the healing. Trust us."

And in that, Memphis heard, *I'm trusting you, Memphis. Better not let me down.*

Memphis closed his eyes. *Come on, please,* he prayed silently. The electric itch traveled along the tips of his fingers, then caught, crawling up his arms, faster and faster, until his whole body hummed with energy and he felt as if he were floating. Pressure followed—the soft weight of many hands pressed against him, receiving him, holding him in the land of spirits. And then the hands were gone. Memphis stood in a dark wood of denuded, ashen trees whose twisted limbs reached up and around, a cage of brambles and spindly, multi-tiered branches. The cracked earth was dry; nothing could grow here. The air was unnaturally still. Above, the starless sky groaned in turmoil. A diseased moon leaked its sickly glow, streaking the edges of the roiling, dusky clouds with jaundice while strange blue threads of static pulsed here and there, disturbing the clouds into further discord. When Memphis traced the origin of the clouds, he saw that they were manufactured—curling plumes of choking smoke pumped from the open mouths atop a row of ghostly smokestacks in the distance.

Something moved deep in the trees. A voice swirled around his head: "Memphis. My son, my son."

The branches quivered and became the beating of wings. And then, his mother was walking toward him in her blue-black feathered cape. Her blinking eyes were all pupil, captured night; her movements were quick as a heartbeat.

"Mama?" Memphis tried to run toward her but found he couldn't move.

"Memphis. Son. I must be brief. It doesn't take him long to find me."

"Who?"

"The King of Crows. I belong to him now. You must stop him, Memphis! Heal the breach."

"*How* do we heal it?"

"More than this, I'm forbidden to tell you. He has a million eyes."

And then Memphis saw the phosphorescent, sharp-toothed things rising from the charred ground, their mouths open in hungry growls. They shrieked their insatiable need into the night. Memphis took a step back. His heel came down with a squish on a three-headed slug covered in ghastly tumors. "What is this place?"

"It's his place."

There were eyes in the trees. Watching. "I can't leave you here with those things—"

"I told you, I belong to him now. But I am also with you. Keeping close. Go, Memphis."

"I'm going to free you, Mama."

"You can't bring back what's gone, Memphis." His mother coughed violently, spitting out two slimy feathers. They dropped to the ground and slithered into snakes. Her skin rippled with change that was too fast for Memphis's eyes to register. He heard the flapping of wings and the echo of his mother's voice. "Go to Seraphina. The time is now. Wake, my son!"

The shrieking of the dead increased, a storm building, and then, like a fast-moving train, the sounds of the nightclub rushed him: jazz, dancing feet, people talking. Just like that, Memphis was back in Owney Madden's private room in the Cotton Club, everybody looking at him as he blinked and swallowed and tried to return to normal.

"What…how's the patient?" Memphis croaked.

"Sleeping. Without a scratch on him," the man with the matchstick in his mouth said, pointing to the gangster's healed leg. He clapped Memphis on the back. "Congratulations, kid. You get to live."

On the way out, Papa Charles handed Memphis a crisp twenty-dollar bill, pocketing the other one. "You earned it. And Owney's backing us against Dutch. We shouldn't have any more trouble with rabbits in our garden."

"Yes, sir," Memphis said, but he had the idea that trouble was just getting started.

Memphis was so tired he slept through most of his date with Theta at the lighthouse. "Come on, Poet. We better get you home," she said after he'd nodded off a third time, and even though Memphis protested that he was fine, not tired at all, Theta insisted on putting him in a taxi.

Blind Bill was waiting up in the living room when Memphis let himself in. The old man sat on the sofa, still and quiet, in the dark. Memphis turned on the lamp. He was bone-tired and his mouth tasted of hot metal. "Evenin', Mr. Johnson."

"Told you—it's Bill. You sound wore out."

Memphis suppressed a yawn. "Suppose I am. Everything good tonight? Isaiah all right?"

"Fine. Fine. Octavia made a cake. Even put a little rum in it."

"She did? What for?"

"For my birthday."

"Gee, I didn't know."

"Didn't make no announcement."

"Well, happy birthday. You make a wish?"

"Mm-hmm," Bill said without a hint of a smile.

"So, how old are you now, Mr. Johnson?"

Blind Bill's shoulders shook with a silent laugh. "Feel old as Methuselah till a pretty girl walk by. Then I'm young as any man. And 'fore you ask, yes, I can tell when a pretty girl pass by even without seeing her. Go on. Get yourself some cake."

Bill waited. He was good at waiting. When the boy returned, Bill listened to the scrape of his fork across the plate and sucked in a breath. "Been meaning t'ask you—you seen any more of that Walker woman?"

The fork stopped for a second. "No."

"That the truth?"

"Why you asking?"

"Well," Bill said with a heavy sigh, "little man been acting nervous. And then he said her name in his sleep. Had the feeling he mighta seen her, maybe she got him all upset again. I know we don't want him having more fits."

"We haven't seen her," Memphis said.

Bill could hear the guilt and worry lurking in the lie. Good. Let the boy chew on it along with his cake. He grunted as he pushed himself off the settee and reached for his cane. "Now I'm a whole year older, reckon I best turn in. You rest easy, now."

Bill tapped his way to his small room off the kitchen. He undressed down to his long underwear and felt his way over to the cot, easing his aching joints down onto it. He wondered what his face looked like now. Wrinkled, definitely. Bill could feel the veins popped up on the backs of his hands. Could feel the cold and damp in his bones. That was what happened over the long years of birthdays. For Bill, though, it had happened much quicker; with every life he'd taken for the Shadow Men, another year had been sucked away from him, stooping, bending, and, finally, blinding him. Margaret Walker had let those men take Bill away. And now she wanted to mess with the Campbell brothers? Not if he could help it. Bill had made his birthday wish: First, a healing. And then, revenge.

"Happy birthday, Guillaume," Bill whispered to himself.

He was thirty-seven years old.

※

In the back bedroom they shared, Memphis watched his sleeping brother's narrow chest rise and fall. Memphis was worried now: What if the testing was wearing his little brother out and making him worse instead of better? Isaiah had kicked his quilt to the bottom of the bed. Memphis tucked it neatly around Isaiah again. Then, unable to keep his eyes open another minute, he crawled into his own bed.

He fell into rough dreams. Dark storm clouds stampeded across the electric sky. The wind roared, rent leaves from the trees. Memphis needed to take shelter immediately, but Isaiah was nowhere to be found. The dread overflowed the dream, and Memphis whimpered in his sleep. A stroke of strange blue light cracked the roiling sky, and Memphis saw Isaiah standing at the top of a hill, lost.

"Isaiah!" Memphis shouted into the howling wind.

Lightning clawed at the clouds' rounded gray bellies with animal ferocity. The sky slashed open. The hungry dead spilled out from the rip, their ragged edges flickering with a radium glow—an army of the dead on the march.

And there was Isaiah on the hill, shivering like a lamb, unaware.

"Isaiah! Isaiah!" Memphis shouted, wild with fear. His feet would not move. It was as if he'd been nailed to the spot.

"Brother…"

The familiar voice whispered up Memphis's neck and made his skin crawl. He whipped his head to the right.

"Gabe," Memphis said, for his murdered best friend was beside him, glowing just like the things that had emerged from the ruptured sky. Gabe's eyes were gone. Flies collected in the empty sockets. The embalmer's thread still stretched across the brutal wound of Gabe's mouth where John Hobbes's knife had done its demonic work. Beetles pushed their shiny heads against the frayed crisscrossed hatching at his lips and crawled out from the darkness inside, down Gabe's gray neck.

Gabe's raspy whisper seeped between the Xs of thread. "We are coming for you, brother. For you—and your friends. He is here. His work has begun. We will never let you stop us."

The last of the funereal thread popped free. The ragged hole in Gabriel's face opened. Inside were two rows of serrated teeth. Gabe screamed into the storm.

The hungry dead answered in kind.

DEAD DAISIES

The next morning, Jericho woke before dawn. He packed a small suitcase—a few clothes, more than a few books, and his leather pouch—and left a note for Will on the kitchen table beside the war figurines Jericho had painted the past several years. The note read:

> DEAR WILL,
>   THANK YOU FOR EVERYTHING. I AM SORRY THAT I HAVE TO LEAVE. SOMEDAY I WILL EXPLAIN. NO MATTER WHAT YOU MAY HEAR, PLEASE KNOW THAT I WILL ALWAYS HOLD YOU IN THE HIGHEST ESTEEM.
>   REGARDS,
>   JERICHO JONES

He stood in the old Bennington flat with its grandmotherly furniture, the slightly leaky kitchen faucet, and the hat rack by the front door where Will hung his trusty umbrella, and tried to memorize every smudge on the walls, every play of light across the floor. This was the place he had lived ever since Will brought him home from the hospital and the failed Daedalus program under Jake's orders. Jericho had been abandoned. Now he was the one abandoning Will.

He left before he could change his mind.

＊

Theta also woke before dawn. It had been a bad dream that had stolen her sleep. She scarcely remembered it now, something about fire. She padded past Henry's empty room. He hadn't come home yet, and she remembered that he and David were staying up late to work on new music. An envelope addressed to Theta had been shoved under her door. She rarely got mail at home. When you were an orphan, there were no newsy letters or complaints from relatives. She tore open the envelope. Tucked inside was a photograph of Theta and Mrs. Bowers in front of the Novelty Vaudeville Theater in Topeka. On the back, someone had written, *The truth has found you out, Betty. Meet me Thursday. Midnight. Come alone.*

There was a Bowery address printed at the bottom.

The edges of the photograph smoked between her fingers, and Theta dropped it quickly. She felt dizzy with panic. Whoever was sending these threatening notes knew where she lived! And now they wanted to meet with her. Alone. Theta wished Henry were home. She needed to talk to somebody, but who? Evie would listen, but when Evie got blotto, she had a habit of blurting out secrets. No, not Evie. If she told Memphis, he'd surely want to go with her—Henry, too. She couldn't risk it. Besides, it was four thirty in the morning. She'd have to wait. Oh, she'd lose her mind before then. She had to get out, go for a walk. But now even that seemed nerve-racking. It wasn't just the gossip reporters paying doormen and neighbors to keep tabs on Theta and reveal her every, possibly scandalous, move. Clearly, somebody far more sinister was watching her, too. She wasn't even safe in her own home.

But they were all looking for Theta Knight, Follies star. What if she didn't look anything like that? After all, what good was being an actress if you couldn't play a character? Quickly, Theta went to Henry's closet, riffling through his clothes till she found what she was after. She slipped into a pair of his trousers and one of his pullover sweaters. Last, she snugged a hat down low on her head so she'd look less like prey. Less like a girl.

"Thanks for the loaner, Hen," she said to the empty room.

Out on the rain-slicked streets, Theta shoved her hands in her pockets, hunched her shoulders forward, and adjusted her gait. She slipped right past the hungry gossip jackals yawning in their parked cars with their cameras resting beside thermoses of coffee. They barely even glanced her way, and for a minute, she let herself enjoy the ease of that. It was like having a pocket full of money to spend any way she liked. Right now she could do things she never could as Theta, like walk confidently down a nighttime street, alone and unbothered. What freedom in that. Theta crossed the bumpy street and headed into the sheltering park to think.

There was a sharpness to this time of day, just before the city woke up and lurched into its frantic pace. Like the world was holding its breath. It helped her make a plan: She'd go meet her blackmailer and, hopefully, talk her way out of this mess. She'd pretend she didn't know what they were talking about. *Betty Sue Who? You must have me mistaken for someone else; I'm Theta Knight. I only came because I was curious! Honestly, I figured it was a prank played by one of my pals.* Yes. She'd talk—and act—her way out of it. She could do that. Theta Knight could do that.

Theta breathed in the early-morning air. The earthen footpath welcomed her. A couple of thin squirrels skittered across the grass, no doubt in search of whatever acorns they'd buried months before. She imagined that they welcomed her, too. She came to the old wooden bridge that spanned the lake. The bridge welcomed her. This was her park, her town. The lake, littered with new petals, welcomed her. The air welcomed her. The sky welcomed her.

The ghost welcomed her.

There it was, at the base of the bridge, a see-through figure in an old-fashioned suit; he was like the tail of a departing dream. Theta's breath caught in her throat. Carefully, she stepped backward. The bridge's old boards creaked. The ghost turned to her, and then, quick as a finger snap, *it was right in front of her*!

Theta cried out. She turned and ran across the bridge, back through the park. But at the curve of the path, the ghost was there, waiting for her. Theta skidded to a stop. Panicked, she whirled around to run back toward the bridge.

"Wait…" the ghost commanded. And then, very softly: "Please."

Slowly, Theta turned. She recognized the spirit. Dark, wavy hair. Graying beard and mustache. It was Reginald Bennington.

"Wh-what do you w-want?" Theta asked, trembling.

"Go…back. She needs"—the ghost of Mr. Bennington took a shuddering breath—"you."

"Who needs me?"

"The guardian of the Bennington. The old witch."

"I don't know what you mean."

"In...the basement." Already, Mr. Bennington was wearing thin at the edges, an erasure.

"Please. Please leave me alone."

"She is in...grave danger. Help her. Help..." Mr. Bennington said, his voice lingering for a few seconds on the wind, though he had gone.

＊

In the dark of the Bennington basement, Adelaide Proctor worked quickly. There was no time to waste. Her hands, bent by arthritis, were not as nimble as they once were. It was harder to wield the knife, but she managed a cut, hissing as the blood pooled in her palm. She let the cut drip into the bowl. Next she mixed in her herbs. She wrinkled her nose. There was a smell, sickly sweet. Not the herbs. More like a rotted bouquet left in stagnant water. Her weak heart thundered in her chest. She started her incantation, a spell for protection from evil. The smell grew stronger. Addie could not finish her spell for gagging. The lights cut out suddenly, plunging the basement into darkness. In the dark was a voice she had not heard in many years.

"Adelaide..."

A cry clawed at Addie's throat, but she didn't dare utter it. *Still. Remain perfectly still. Whatever you do, don't look.* Shafts of street light shone through the high basement windows. Behind her lay the elevator doors. Could she make it in time? And if she did, how long before salvation rattled down to her?

Addie gripped the knife in her shaking hand. *"What a friend we have in Je...sus..."* she sang in a voice fading to a whisper, her mouth too dry to furnish more sound as she moved carefully in the dark, sprinkling salt behind her as she did. He was somewhere in the room with her. *"All our sins and griefs to bear..."*

The elevator. She was close. Blood trickled down her arm and stained the fine lace cuffs of her nightgown. The salt stung in the wound. She'd made it to the elevator. With a shaking hand, she pressed the button and watched the golden arrow slowly ticking off the floors. Four. Three.

"Oh, please, please!" she whispered. Blood whooshed in Addie's ears. She was faint with fear. She would not turn around. *"Wh-what a f-f-friend..."*

The elevator had stopped at one.

"Adelaide…"

Miss Addie gasped. She tried to keep singing. *"Our s-sins and g-griefs to bear…"*

"You've freed me at last."

She pushed the button over and over.

"And now I've come for you, as I promised I would."

Through the frayed gray curtain of her hair, Addie stole a glance over her shoulder.

Elijah.

Once, he had been the handsomest boy she'd ever known, with hair that turned buttery gold in summer. The thing shuffling toward her had the mummified skin of the grave. It peeled back from his mouth; his yellowed teeth appeared monstrous. Two maggots wriggled from his ears and fell to the basement floor with sickening plops. That once-lustrous hair was nothing more than brittle straw sticking out in clumps. She could smell rot on his breath as he crept closer.

"You made me."

Adelaide Proctor backed against the wall. "No," she whispered. Elijah's feet scraped across the floor.

"Did you forget your promise, my love?"

His voice was cruel, taunting. Not at all as she had remembered.

"Every debt shall be paid now, for the King of Crows brings us through at last. Soon this world will belong to him. And you and I, Adelaide, will be together, forever and always.…"

"No!" Addie screamed, frantic as a child.

The elevator doors opened. With a great cry, Adelaide Proctor fell against Theta. "Go, quickly! Oh, please! Don't let him get me!"

"Who?" Theta asked, her eyes searching the empty basement. "Miss Addie, there's nothing there."

Miss Addie lifted her head from Theta's side. The lights had come back up. Her dead lover was nowhere to be seen.

But I saw him. He came back.

As the doors slowly closed, Adelaide spied a frayed break in the salt circle mere inches from where she'd stood moments earlier. Something had fallen there: the blackened petals of dead daisies.

A gift to her from Elijah.

A warning.

※

As the weak morning sun broke through the branches of Central Park, Theta sat in Miss Addie's Morris chair beneath an old quilt while a parade of curious cats meowed and rubbed their noses against her legs. One curled up in her lap, and she happily scratched under its chin while it closed its eyes in bliss.

"How did you know to come for me?" Miss Addie asked. Her hands had only just stopped shaking. Her sister, Lillian, brought out a silver tray with a tea service comprised of mismatched china cups.

"This is gonna sound crackers, but a ghost told me to come. Mr. Bennington's ghost. He said you were in trouble."

"Oh, dear Reginald!" Miss Addie said joyfully, as if she were speaking of a favorite old friend.

"He said something about how you were the guardian of the Bennington. The, uh, the old witch, he called you."

"I don't think the *old* was necessary," Lillian tutted.

"But we are, dear sister. We are," Miss Addie said.

"Nevertheless," Lillian sniffed. She poured the tea into three cups and handed one to Theta. "The Bennington was built for safety, you see. There has always been a Diviner in residence. Someone to be sure it would remain safe from evil spirits. Before Reginald died, he entrusted that duty to Addie."

"I think I woulda passed on that little gift," Theta said. "How come Mr. Bennington didn't seem scary?"

"Not all spirits mean harm, you know," Miss Lillian said. "Some want to help. Or they need help."

"I'm guessing this Elijah isn't one of those, though," Theta said. "Who is he?"

Miss Addie's face went sad. Her eyes seemed fixed on a point in time long passed. "He was my everything, my greatest love. And one day he was taken from me, cut down in the prime of his youth."

"Gee. I'm sorry," Theta said. She tried to imagine losing Memphis. It hurt so much she didn't want to even think about it. She grimaced as she sipped her tea. "What kind of tea is this?"

"Dandelion! It will ease your dreams. It will help you come into your power."

"I . . . I don't have any power," Theta said quickly.

"Yes, you do. I can always tell. I could tell about your friend who came to see me, the boy with the boater hat, and his green-eyed friend. And I could tell about your Miss O'Neill."

"My sister has always been gifted," Miss Lillian said. She squeezed Addie's hand. "And I have been her protector."

"You have *great* power," Addie said to Theta. "You mustn't be afraid of it, child."

Ha, Theta thought. *You don't know what I can do. Then you'd be afraid, too.*

"Tell me, do you have family near?" Miss Addie asked.

"I'm an orphan," Theta said.

"You're wrong." The old woman blinked up at the ceiling, her fingers waving in the air. "You do have family. I see it in your aura. They're . . . they're all around you."

"Sorry, Miss Addie. But if I got family, they've done a good job of hiding it for the past seventeen years."

Miss Addie picked up Theta's cup. She read the tea leaves, frowning.

Theta got nervous. "What is it now? You see something bad?"

"Some ghost does wait for you. This is a bad ghost. You must not let it win."

"Okay. Now you're scaring me."

"We'll read the signs. Come along, Archibald," Lillian said. She pushed herself out of the chair and grabbed one of the cats and a curved knife. The cat squirmed in her arms, meowing his displeasure.

Theta jumped up. "Wait! What are you gonna do with that cat?"

"He'll need to be sacrificed, of course. To read the signs."

"Nothing doing!" Theta ripped the cat from Miss Lillian's arms. She pressed him tightly to her chest. Archibald meowed loudly. "Nobody's killing any cats."

Miss Lillian glowered. "It's what we've always done."

"Yeah, well, I'm changing how things are done."

Miss Lillian started to protest, but Miss Addie cut her off. "Very well. We could stand to change." She smiled. "I do believe that Archibald likes you. You should take him home. He can be your familiar."

"My what?"

"Your witch friend."

Theta looked into the ginger cat's green eyes. He meowed again and licked her cheek, and Theta knew she was going home with a cat. "Swell. Just what I need."

"I've made mistakes," Addie said, fidgeting with her lace handkerchief. "And I have tried to make amends for that. I've tried to do good in my life. I want to help you. All of you." She pinned a brooch to Theta's dress, a silver filigree heart. Dead leaves rattled around in the chamber.

"What's in there?" Theta asked.

"Wolfsbane and rosemary, birch bark and sweet basil. It's for protection. And this"—Miss Addie removed her own silver locket and slipped it around Theta's neck—"this is a bloodstone. It is for courage."

"Miss Addie. I can't take this. It's yours."

"And now it's yours, my dear," Addie said, squeezing Theta's hand. "Bloodstone asks you to work for the good of others. It demands courage." Miss Addie swept an age-spotted hand across Theta's brow, and for a moment, Theta thought of her as the grandmother she'd always wanted but never had. "You've been very hurt, my dear. But you're safe with me. And it's high time to stop hiding from your power. It will find you out, you know, whether you accept it or not. Best to let it in, show it who's boss."

"I'll think about it," Theta said, cuddling the purring Archibald close. "But I'll be counting the cats when I come over. There better be the same number each time."

PUNISHMENT FOR THEIR SINS

The next day, the Diviners gathered as usual in the library. They were on edge, like the prophesied storm was already happening inside them.

"Good afternoon," Will said as he and Sister Walker swept into the room, where the Diviners were seated around the long table, silent and scowling. "What's the matter? Did the city run out of jazz?"

"Why did you breed Diviners as part of your Project Buffalo?" Ling blurted out.

Sam groaned and buried his head in his hands.

"Ling, what part of 'keep our traps shut' didn't you understand?" Henry said under his breath.

Ling appraised him coolly. "I understood fine. I simply didn't agree. It's silly to pretend we don't know when they have the answers we need." She turned to Will and Sister Walker. "How do you expect us to work for you when you've been lying? You owe us the answers. You owe us the truth."

Sam readied himself for further stonewalling, but to his surprise, Will nodded at Sister Walker.

"You're right," she said. "We do."

Will started a fresh fire, poking at the kindling and newspaper until it roared to life. Then he took up his pacing, as if he could outrun the truth, while Sister Walker stood beside the fireplace quite still, her hands clasped at her waist like a schoolmarm ferreting out trouble.

"We thought we were helping. That we would make our country safer with the help of Diviners," Will said at last.

"Yeah? By breeding Diviners?" Sam threw the punch cards on the table. "You made us out of some kind of crazy serum. You *made* us!"

"You made *me*," Evie said with barely controlled fury.

"Evangeline, I...Where did you get those?" Will asked, pointing at the cards.

"And now you're changing the subject!" Evie growled.

"It's important. Please."

"A room that used to belong to the Department of Paranormal down in the basement of the post office. Evie and I broke in," Sam said.

Will blanched. "Did anyone see you breaking in?"

"No," Sam said. "Why?"

Will let out a deep breath. "Because … because that was a government office and you could be arrested."

"Still waiting for that answer," Sam demanded.

"Yes, we all are," Evie chimed in.

"We thought we could create a generation of extraordinary Americans with extraordinary powers." Will sagged into one of the club chairs. "We thought we were doing something good for the country."

Sam was starting to piece together what he'd been trying to ignore. "My mother was sick with me on the boat over from Russia. Rotke singled her out at immigration. Is that how you picked your subjects? Did you camp out at Ellis Island waiting for all the immigrants coming through?"

"We did choose from immigrants, yes," Sister Walker said. The fireplace lent an otherworldly glow to her cheekbones.

"Would you tell them they couldn't come into the country if they said no to your little 'vitamin tonic'?" Sam spat.

"It wasn't just immigrants." Memphis's voice shimmered with anger. "You went after your own people."

Sister Walker glared. "Did you want to be left out of the new America? Or should those special powers belong only to white folks?"

Memphis had never felt so conflicted. He was appalled by Sister Walker's choices even as he understood them. "What about Isaiah? My mother wasn't in the program by the time he was born. How did he … ?"

"Sister?" Isaiah prompted.

For the first time since they'd arrived, Sister Walker seemed at a loss. She lifted the poker from its stand, and, though it needed no help at all, she stoked the fire, staring into the flames as she spoke. "It appears to stay in the cells. A mutation that can affect future children."

"What else does it do to the cells?" In Memphis's mind, he saw his mother's gaunt face and cracked lips as she stared up at the ceiling, the cancer eating her up. She had been only thirty-five.

Sister Walker returned the poker to its proper place. "We don't really know," she said softly.

Memphis balled his fists at his sides. "You shot our mothers up with this stuff, and you didn't even know what it would do?"

"We had to be willing to take certain risks—"

"Take 'em yourself. Leave us out of it!"

"Did they know?" Henry said with a rare flash of anger. "Did you tell our mothers what you were doing? Or did you lie to them?"

"We felt it best to keep it quiet," Will said. "We told them we were giving them vitamins to help with their pregnancies, which was true. Many of those women would've lost their babies without—"

"Stop defending it!" Evie said, leaving her seat and coming to stand beside Henry. "They're human beings, Will—women, not *things*! You experimented on them—on your own sister—*and you didn't tell them*!"

"Not intentionally."

"What does that mean?"

Will kept his eyes trained on the Persian rug.

Sister Walker's voice was church quiet. "Will."

"No," Will whispered.

"For the last time—*tell us the truth*!" Evie demanded.

"I administered the formula to James when he was a child!" Will admitted.

Evie sank into a chair again. "You what?"

"He was sick. Pneumonia. The doctors thought…he wasn't expected to live and Jake had developed the tonic…." Will raked a hand through his hair. "So I gave it to him. His recovery was miraculous. James was the proof Jake needed to move forward with Project Buffalo."

"Subject zero. Zenith, Ohio," Evie said numbly. The first thumbtack in the map they'd seen was her own brother. Evie's eyes stung. She narrowed them at Will. "What about me?"

"That was a mistake."

Evie flinched at the word *mistake*.

"The tonic. I'd left it behind. Your mother was already expecting you. She'd had several miscarriages after James. She figured if the tonic had made James strong and healthy, then…so she…" Will looked down at his shoes.

"I didn't know until she was well along with you. You said you wanted the truth, Evangeline. But truth is complicated."

Evie slapped a hand down on the table. "No. It isn't complicated. It's very simple. You experimented on human beings and we are the results. What's left of them, anyway. That board we saw had thumbtacks all over the country. One hundred and forty-four of them, to be exact. So, where are the rest?"

"Some of our subjects simply never developed any powers," Will said. "It turned out that it was actually very hard to make Diviners."

Theta narrowed her eyes. "You said *some* didn't develop powers."

"You don't seem to understand: Once they shut down the department, that was the end of it. We never saw the files or the subjects ever again. We were finished," Will said. "We don't know what happened to the others. For all we know, their powers didn't take and they're out there now, living perfectly ordinary lives without a lick of connection to the supernatural."

"Well, somebody didn't think it was finished," Sam said. "And I'm pretty sure that those somebodies have my mother. And now they're going around killing people who had anything to do with Project Buffalo. You remember a fella named Ben Arnold?"

"I have read my history books, Sam," Will snapped.

"Wrong Ben Arnold. This one was my informant. Except now he's dead, right after he told me a buncha stuff about Project Buffalo. And his death notice was slipped under our door at the Bennington."

Will paled. "Why didn't you tell me?"

Sam snorted. "Why didn't *I* tell *you*? Oh. That's rich. You're the ones who've been keeping secrets *about* us *from* us and telling us to trust you!"

"All right! Now you know." Sister Walker marched forward and planted herself in front of the Diviners. "We can't undo the past. But we are here now. If you truly want to help your country, you'll move past this. We have work to do to save—"

Memphis leaped up, voice thick with scorn. "Move past this?"

"You've got some nerve saying that—" Sam said, joining him.

"Don't yell at her," Ling snapped.

"How 'bout you don't tell me what to do!"

Will came forward now, hands up. "Now, wait just a minute—"

"Hang your ghosts!" Henry growled. He was out of his seat now. They all were. "You're liars!"

The Diviners had gathered, without realizing it, in a tight huddle, nearly nose-to-nose, arguing, their voices rising over one another:

"—What choice do we have?—"

"—I don't like being lied to—"

"—Easy for you to say—"

"—Who asked you?—"

The Metaphysickometer hummed loudly, its needle popping up and down. The radio came on with a sudden squawk and raced through stations in a jumbled jazz of speech, music, and static. A corner of the room seemed to wobble and bend.

"What just happened?" Theta asked when it quieted. The smell of electricity hung in the air.

"I think you just happened," Sister Walker said, breathless with new excitement.

Ling put her hand on the wall. It was warm. "We created some sort of energy field together."

"I think we should try again. Right away," Sister Walker said.

"Nothing doin'! Why should we do anything for you?" Sam said.

"What Sam said!" Evie chimed in.

"I know how angry you are. We made mistakes. We have a lot to answer for. But the threat we face is enormous. I'm asking…" Will looked to Sister Walker, who nodded. "*We're* asking, if you can put aside your misgivings long enough to continue the work."

For a moment, everyone was quiet. There was nothing but the crackling of the fire.

"Maybe we *should* see what we can do. Not for them," Ling said at last, nodding toward Will and Sister Walker. "But for us."

"If Ling's in, so am I," Henry said.

Isaiah came and stood beside Sam. "I'll do it."

"Isaiah, you don't know what you're promising," Memphis said.

"I do, too!"

"Sam?" Evie asked.

"Yeah, okay. I'm in. But for us," Sam said.

"Poet? Whaddaya think?" Theta asked.

Memphis let his arms hang at his sides. He took in a deep breath, then let it out. "For my mother," he said.

"We'll continue," Ling said to Will and Sister Walker. "But if you lie to us even once more…"

"We'll never, ever come back," Evie finished. She gave Will a hard look. "And I will never speak to you again."

Will nodded. "Understood."

"What do we do? Do we stand in a circle and hold hands?" Isaiah asked.

"If you ask us to sing camp songs, I refuse," Evie said.

"Gather here. On the rug." Will pushed back some chairs and the Diviners made a circle.

"Now what happens?" Memphis asked.

"I want you to shut your eyes and concentrate."

"Shouldn't it be something specific?" Ling asked. "Something we can all see in our minds?"

Evie looked at Henry. "Do not say clowns."

Henry sighed. "Well, now you've done it. Clowns are all I can see."

"Ling's right. I want you to concentrate on something concrete," Sister Walker said. "Think of creating an energy field…around this credenza." Sister Walker marched over to a long, beautifully carved chest. "Stare at the credenza. Concentrate. Be aware of your energy as well as the energy coming from your fellow Diviners."

It was very still. Beside him, Sam could hear Henry breathing, and soon, the rhythm of his breath matched the rhythm of Sam's breathing, and Evie's matched Sam's, all the way around the circle. Sitting on the sofa outside the circle, Theta could feel her own restless energy wanting to join the others, like a horse longing to run with the herd. She could feel Memphis's heartbeat strong inside her, lining up perfectly with hers. A great hum filled Evie's ears, like a strong wind carrying a million voices inside. An aura appeared around the credenza, the air dancing with pinpricks of light that stretched to the Diviners themselves. The hum became a roar. The chandelier directly above them flared bright and hot, shattering the bulbs and showering the carpet with broken glass. With a shriek, the Diviners dropped one another's hands.

"Aaah!" Sam said, putting his hands over his ears. "Did you feel that?"

"For a minute there, it was like falling—" Ling said, excited.

"Then floating—" Evie added.

"In a warm bath made of stars that you felt joined to?" Memphis finished.

Sam jerked a thumb at the others. "Uh, what they said."

"Yes," Theta said so quietly that no one heard.

Henry's eyes widened. "Is it just me or is the credenza rather…un-credenza-like?"

Across the room, the antique oak table bowed out in the middle, as if trying to give birth to some other form. And then it contracted and settled back to its proper table shape.

"Will…" Sister Walker whispered.

"I know," he answered. "Incredible."

Ling moved as swiftly as she could. She touched the credenza gingerly. It was still warm. "It's pos-i-tute-ly solid now."

"You're using the word!" Henry beamed. "I taught her that word, you know."

Ling's excitement bubbled out of her in a torrent of words. "Everything radiates. The radiation we emit isn't visible to the naked eye, but it's there. This is incredible. Our combined energy can disrupt electromagnetic fields or create one!" She burst out with a rare full grin. "We're an unimaginable source of energy!"

"Diviner Industries—powering the nation! Charleston, Charleston!" Evie sang, pulling Henry in to dance with her.

"People who could do that would be pretty valuable," Memphis said.

"Yeah. And dangerous," Sam said.

"What do you mean?" Evie had stopped dancing, but she still held Henry's hand.

"I mean, either everybody would want 'em around, or nobody would. We were created for national security, right?" He looked to Sister Walker, who nodded. "Well, what happens if somebody decides we aren't so secure? What happens if somebody decides that a bunch of people like us with Diviner powers are a threat to that new, special America they're trying to build?"

"Ice Man, you okay?" Memphis crouched down in front of his brother. Isaiah was breathing heavily. He seemed frightened. "What's the matter?"

"Anybody else see something scary while they were under?" Isaiah asked.

Will moved closer. "What did you see?"

"It was real dark. And then I could see there was a rip in the dark, like when I tore my shirt on a branch one time and Octavia fussed at me for it. I could feel that there was something inside the rip trying to get out. Something bad." Isaiah swallowed. "I heard a voice."

"What did it say?"

"It called me the clairvoyant," Isaiah said, sounding out the unfamiliar word. "It said, 'I see you, Clairvoyant.'"

"Something made contact with you," Sister Walker said. "We should go back in."

"No," Memphis said.

"I understand that you're concerned about your brother, Memphis. But something from the other side wants to talk with Isaiah. This may be our best chance to talk to that entity."

"What if that something…" With a glance at his brother, Memphis moved to Sister Walker, whispering, "What if that something wants to hurt him?"

"Do you trust me, Memphis?"

If they were on the street or in church, Memphis would back down from Sister Walker's imperious gaze with an *I didn't mean any disrespect, ma'am* smile. Smile. Nod. Look away. Get along. But Sister Walker had gone to jail for sedition. She and Will had lied to them about their origins, about what Project Buffalo really was. Hadn't Blind Bill and Aunt Octavia said that Sister Walker couldn't be trusted? And from what Memphis had heard on those recordings, Sister Walker, Will, and the others hadn't been able to look out for poor Guillaume, and he was a Diviner—a powerful one at that. But if Sister Walker was right, and this was a chance to find out how to heal the breach Memphis's mother had talked about, then they had to take it. For now, Memphis needed to believe that once they closed the door between worlds, things would be better. The ghosts would go away. Isaiah's seizures would stop.

"He's not going in without me," Memphis said finally.

"Fair enough." Sister Walker maneuvered around Memphis, making straight for Isaiah, and crouched before him. "Isaiah, you remember when you warned me about the chair?"

"Yes, Sister." It had been a few months ago. Isaiah had been at Sister Walker's house reading cards. He'd guessed most of them before they were turned over. On the way out, he'd taken hold of Sister Walker's hand and gotten a strong sense that something was wrong. He saw her standing on the chair to reach into a kitchen cupboard, and then he saw her fall.

"You were right. Not ten minutes after you left, I climbed up on that chair to get some sugar and the chair leg broke underneath me. Let's see what you can find out from this."

Isaiah was excited and a little scared. He wanted to show off what he could do in front of the bigger Diviners so they'd see him as one of them, less of a kid.

"Memphis, I want you to sit beside your brother. The rest of you gather 'round. Let's see if we can increase the strength of Isaiah's clairvoyance. Okay. Put your hands on Isaiah's shoulders . . . that's it."

"Feels as if we're posing for a family photograph. I refuse to put on a Shriner's hat or hold a monkey." Evie sighed.

Sam quirked an eyebrow. "What sort of family do you—"

"Shhh, please," Sister Walker chided. "Memphis, take hold of Isaiah's hands. Isaiah, I want you to relax as much as you can. When you're under, concentrate on your surroundings, look around, remember what you see. The rest of you, I want you to think about helping Isaiah."

Isaiah was nervous. For once, he was the special one. He wasn't just a kid. But it was scary, too. What if nothing happened? It was odd having everybody's hands on his shoulders, too.

But slowly, he relaxed. And then he was drifting off somewhere else, like floating down a river on his back, and all around him was the mist and roar of a waterfall. The roar sucked into complete silence. Isaiah found himself on a dusty road. To his left, he saw a farmhouse with a sagging porch. Fields full of corn rotting on their stalks. Crows circled above in a mesmerizing figure eight. And then, as if it were the most natural thing in the world, Isaiah entered the world he saw as simply as entering a new room. He could smell the wind, scented with coming rain. Beyond the farmhouse, out in an arid spot of land, an enormous tree, grayed with age, rose up from the earth like a multi-armed god Isaiah had seen in a storybook his mama got from the library one time. No leaves grew there; none looked as if they could.

It was a mighty ghost of a tree. From a fat bough hung a rope swing, and when Isaiah put out his hand toward it, he could tell that it had never been used. It had been tethered to the branch with hope, but sadness hung about it now. There was sadness hanging over the whole farm. Fear, too. Something didn't feel right. Why was he here? What had happened in this place? What was going to happen in the future?

Dust kicked up on the road ahead like a storm moving in. Isaiah thought he heard Memphis's voice carried faintly in the blowing dust, and then he saw his brother and another man he didn't know—a big, strong-looking man with broad shoulders and a face like an African prince. Memphis and this unknown man were whispers of bodies flickering in and out with the wind.

"Memphis? That you?" Isaiah called. But the voice and the vision had gone.

The squawking of crows drew his attention back to the porch. A barefoot girl in a nightgown stood on the warped steps. Her pale hair wanted brushing, and the peach satin bow she wore had slid halfway down, stuck in the rat's nest of it. She looked to be about the same age as Memphis. Just like the farm, there was something a little off about her. A crop turning bad.

"I know you," the girl whispered, and her whisper slipped inside him like a bad dream. A crow came to rest on each of her shoulders. A third settled atop her head. It blinked at Isaiah, and he gasped to see it had only one eye, right in the middle of its shiny forehead.

"Isaiah…" the girl said, as if tasting his name. "Isaiah Campbell. The one who sees. The clairvoyant."

"Where am I?" Isaiah asked.

"Bountiful," the girl answered. "Bountiful, Nebraska."

"Who are you?" he asked.

"*I* see, too. Something's coming. For you and your brother and your friends."

Her head jerked, crow-like, toward the horizon. Down the long dirt ribbon of road, the great ball of dust had grown bigger, and Isaiah caught glimpses of sharp white glinting in the filthy gloom. There was a demonic whine in the wind, like a choir singing thousands of clashing parts—keening moans and bird shrieks and a high-pitched, whirring hiss that reminded him of cicadas in tall grass. The sound crawled into Isaiah's chest. It made him want to run. But he wouldn't. He had to prove to Sister Walker, Will, and the others that he wasn't a baby. If he did good, they couldn't leave him behind anymore.

The crows' squawking startled Isaiah. He gasped and fell back: *The girl was on the road with him!* How had she gotten there so fast? He saw now that the left side of her face was like melted candle wax that had cooled into a scarred mound of flesh. She only had one good eye, too—the right—and it was so blue it was nearly silver. "They did this to us, you know. It's their fault. They deserve punishment for their sins. Don't tell them anything! But he wants to help us."

Isaiah stumbled backward, away from the silvery-eyed girl. He felt dizzy with her so close. He tried to right himself. *Look around*, Sister Walker had told him. *Remember what you see.* So Isaiah looked hard: At the farmhouse. The crows. The tree with its bare, twisted limbs. The crooked mailbox, number one, four, four.

One forty-four!

He opened his mouth in a gasp and tasted dust at the back of his throat. The whine grew louder; it reverberated through his blood, calling. The girl was so close he could feel her breath. She cocked her head, studying him. "Can you feel him calling to you, Isaiah Campbell?" she asked. Her teeth were as mottled as an old piling in a drought-low river.

Who? Isaiah thought, and he knew the girl heard his thoughts.

"The King of Crows. He loves us and our gifts. And if we help him, he will give us everything we want."

"What kind of help?"

"There's another seer. A boy who draws. We need him. He won't talk to us, though. But he'd talk to you."

The girl attempted a smile, and that frightened Isaiah more than anything. Isaiah didn't know if this was a dream or a vision of the future. He only knew that he didn't want to be here anymore with this girl and the farmhouse and whatever lurked down the road in that dust.

The girl turned her head toward the ball of dust. She smiled her rotted smile. "Ghosts on the road," she whispered.

"Isaiah!"

On the edge of the cornfield, Isaiah's mother shimmered in the blue-black feathered cape he'd seen her wear in dreams before. She didn't look sick and tired like she had at the end of her life. But she didn't look entirely human, either.

"Mama?" he said.

"Isaiah. Concentrate. Wake up."

"I'm too scared, Mama."

"You can do it." His mother's voice rasped as if she'd had a bad cough. "I want you to imagine a door that you can walk right through, and then you'll wake up."

Make a door. He could do that. Isaiah pictured the open pocket doors of the library a few feet away. The strange girl was back, though, and she was screeching like a flock of mad birds at his mother. "He will punish you! You will not glory in his future!"

"Hush up!" his mother snapped like the girl was acting up in church.

But behind his mama, the dark moved like a living thing, and Isaiah was afraid for her.

"Go now," his mother commanded in her strange, squawking voice. "Tell the others: Follow the Eye. Heal the breach. Protect Conor Flynn. Don't let—"

The girl screeched and the sky was filled with black birds. Her hair flew up around her face. Her eyes were wrong. "We will meet again."

The darkness swallowed his mama, the girl, the farm, everything.

"Mama!" Isaiah cried.

Isaiah came out of his trance thrashing and gasping. Memphis's concerned face hovered just above his. "Isaiah? Isaiah!"

"Memphis!"

Memphis let out his breath in a big whoosh. "You okay, Ice Man?"

Isaiah nodded, coming back to himself, and Memphis pulled him in tight for a long minute.

Will checked his watch. "He was under for three minutes."

"What did you see, Isaiah?" Sister Walker asked.

"It was a place, a farm, I think. The farm wasn't doing so well. The crops had turned bad. And…" Isaiah licked his lips, trying to work some moisture back into them. He could still taste the dust in his mouth. "I think I saw another Diviner. But she wasn't very nice. She was kinda scary."

"Do you know her name?" Will asked.

"Huh-uh." Isaiah hoped he hadn't failed the test. "But when I asked where she was, she told me Bountiful, Nebraska."

At Evie's gasp, Memphis asked, "What is it?"

"Bountiful, Nebraska, was one of the places with a thumbtack stuck into it on that map Sam and I found," she explained.

Isaiah looked to Memphis. "Mama was there, Memphis."

Memphis swallowed hard. "She say anything?"

Isaiah nodded. "Told us to follow the Eye and heal the breach. Or else we'd be lost. And she said we should protect Conor Flynn."

"Who or what is Conor Flynn?" Ling asked, but no one knew.

"Was there anything else you remember about that farm?" Sister Walker pressed.

Suddenly, Isaiah brightened. "The house had a number. Saw it on the mailbox!"

"What was it?" Sister Walker asked.

"One forty-four."

❋

"Evie!" Will called. Evie stopped on the steps of the museum and turned to him. "I'm sorry that I didn't tell you before."

"You should have."

"I know. I made a mistake. That formula absolutely saved James's life. But perhaps I shouldn't have been playing god."

Evie tried to imagine what her life would've been like if James had died of pneumonia before she was even born. She couldn't bear the thought of it. "No. No, I'm glad," she said on a long sigh. "If you hadn't saved him…I couldn't imagine not knowing James." Then: "I suppose that explains Bob Bateman's comb, then. Maybe James was just like me and he didn't come into his powers until he was older."

Will shifted his weight from one foot to the other. "Maybe," he said at last.

BEFORE THE DEVIL
BREAKS YOU

The first time Margaret Andrews Walker saw an actual Diviner at work, she was ten years old and helping her mother nurse the sick at the Frederick Douglass Memorial Hospital and Training School in Philadelphia. On Sundays after church, Margaret's mother had her come and read to the patients. An elderly woman named Lavinia Cooper had been brought in, weak and short of breath. In Mrs. Cooper's hometown, there had been no colored hospital, and the white hospitals wouldn't admit her. By the time she'd been brought to Frederick Douglass, her chest cold had progressed to pneumonia.

When Lavinia began to recover, word spread along the ward that she could talk to the spirits and deliver prophecy. Already, she'd saved the life of one of the young doctors. On a rainy night, she warned him not to take his usual route home—"I can see that road washed clean away." Sure enough, a flash flood swept up four people on the very road that doctor would've traveled. A day later, Lavinia had clasped the hands of a young nurse and, with her eyes staring straight up to the ceiling, announced that the nurse was pregnant days before it was confirmed. Whispers circulated: Lavinia Cooper had the sight. She was a spirit talker. One of the cunning folk. What the old-timers called a Diviner.

Margaret was not an impressionable child. As far as she was concerned, doctors and nurses couldn't afford to believe in that sort of superstitious nonsense. She found the Cooper woman highly suspicious and did her best to avoid her.

"You are not here to serve yourself, Margaret Andrews Walker," her mother had scolded, swatting her across the bottom even though Margaret was already ten. "You are here to serve the sick and the needy. Now, please make yourself useful and go read to Mrs. Cooper."

Scowling, Margaret had sat in the chair farthest from the woman's bed, nursing her wounded dignity as she read aloud from *Little Women*.

"Come close, child," Mrs. Cooper bade in a voice made scratchy from coughing.

Margaret dragged her chair nearer to the old woman's bedside.

"Your grandmother's here. She wants me to tell you something."

"My grandmother passed on last spring," Margaret said matter-of-factly.

"Uh-huh, I know. But she's here with us now, in this very room."

"My grandmother is *dead*, Mrs. Cooper."

"You don't believe in spirits? Don't believe in your ancestors, all your past kin?"

"No, ma'am, I don't," Margaret said.

"Mmmm. Well. They surely do believe in you." Mrs. Cooper looked up at the ceiling, and Margaret had the distinct impression that the old woman was speaking to someone else. "Yes. Yes, all right, then. Your grandmother and me having a chat. She says she got a special name for you. Now. What might that name be?"

Margaret decided to test Mrs. Cooper. "Lil Bit," she lied.

"Lil Bit? Lil Bit, is it? All right. *Lil Bit.*"

Margaret's anger spread at Lavinia Cooper's satisfied smile. Grandmother Walker had been young Margaret's favorite person in the whole world, and her passing had nearly broken Margaret's heart. How dare this woman, this stranger, trespass on that sacred memory!

The old woman managed a feathery laugh between wheezes. "Your gran says you best quit lying 'fore she has to reach out from the grave and give you a slap like she did that time you put your cousin Dee in the attic for tattling. A bat got in there, and Dee screamed so loud it made a vase fall off the end of your gran's sideboard. The vase had been a wedding present from your granddaddy Moses, and when your gran come in from putting the canning up in the basement, she let Dee out and gave you a proper whupping. Even made you break off your own switch. Your gran never called you no Lil Bit. She called you Sister on account of how you boss everybody 'round, just like you was in charge."

That night, Sister Walker had lain awake. Only she and her grandmother knew that story. It had been their secret. That moment with Lavinia Cooper had been the start of Sister Walker's conversion to belief in the supernatural world. She wanted to ask Mrs. Cooper all sorts of questions: What was this power? Where was her grandmother now? How many other Diviners were out there? But when she'd returned to Frederick Douglass two days later, *Little Women* in hand, the bed had been stripped. Mrs. Cooper was gone. The pneumonia had weakened her heart, and she'd died peacefully in her sleep.

Margaret "Sister" Walker read everything she could find about Diviners. It was an obsession that saw her through medical training at Howard University. It was noted by a professor who, in turn, recommended her for a job at the newly created U.S. Department of Paranormal, where she would meet the only other person who shared her devotion: Will Fitzgerald. They made a formidable team: Will was scholarly but impulsive, too trusting and given to romantic ideals; Margaret, whose life hadn't allowed her the privilege of romantic ideals as a birthright, was forthright and wary, organized and patient.

And when the eugenicists argued that her people were inferior by design, Margaret Walker meant to prove them wrong. After all, Lavinia Cooper was a Diviner, an exceptional person. And that exceptional person was black, like her. If she found more people like that, she could prove those eugenicists and their pseudoscience wrong. She would combat prejudice with real science. With fact and study and documentation. If there truly was a golden age coming in America, if the land of opportunity was at hand, she would make sure that her people weren't left out of it.

And when presented with the perfect chance to make sure of that, she took it. She even went to prison for it. What would she be willing to do now? Sister Walker tapped her fingers on top of the file she'd saved. It held everything about Memphis: The records of Viola's pregnancy. The monitoring. Dates. Addresses. Names of family. There were newspaper articles about the boy healer up in Harlem. It was foolish to keep them, she supposed. But it was a record. It was a witness to what they'd done. She'd seen how easy it was for her word to be dismissed. A person needed evidence. And sometimes even that wasn't enough. Sister Walker closed the files back up in the cubby and blocked it with the painting of Paris, a city she'd always longed to visit, the city where Josephine Baker and Ada "Bricktop" Smith had found themselves.

A racking cough rumbled through Sister Walker's lungs, a souvenir of the war and her time in that damp prison. She placed a lozenge under her tongue and waited for the spasm to subside.

There'd been one thing that Lavinia Cooper had said to Margaret that fateful night that had stuck with her for all these years. Margaret had thought that Lavinia was sleeping. But as she bent closer to the old woman, Lavinia took hold of Margaret's wrist. Lavinia's eyes were wide and frightened.

"I see you. You and your friends. You mustn't let him in, child!"

Margaret's wrist hurt. "Let who in?"

Lavinia shook with the force of her vision. "Before the Devil breaks you, first he will make you love him. Beware, little sister. Beware the King of Crows!"

Margaret hadn't understood then.

She understood now. And she was afraid.

INTO THE MADHOUSE

When Evie returned to the Winthrop, there was a letter waiting for her from the superintendent at the Manhattan State Hospital for the Insane. Evie ripped it open and read with mounting excitement—they had approved her visit and spelled out the rules: The warden would personally escort her around the grounds and the hospital itself. But under no circumstances could they allow her to speak with Luther Clayton, by order of the police. Evie had charmed her way around plenty of rules, though. This would be no different. She raced upstairs to call Woody and Sam. Then she got to work selecting just the right outfit, something that would look swell in the *Daily News* under the headline SAINTLY SWEETHEART SEER FORGIVES MAN WHO TRIED TO KILL HER.

The following afternoon, Evie, Sam, and T. S. Woodhouse boarded the steamer from Manhattan, traveling up the East River toward Ward's Island.

"Is that it? What a forsaken little spot," Evie said as the boat pulled up to the long wooden pier sticking out from the stone seawall. Ward's Island wasn't much—a dotting of barracks-style buildings that Evie had heard were for the nurses, a collection of simple white outbuildings, a few scrubby trees. At the island's far end, a train rattled across the Hell Gate's elevated tracks, though there was no stop on Ward's. The boat was the only way onto or off of the island. Everything about the place felt vulnerable and exposed—except for the asylum. Set back from the river a good five hundred feet or so, the enormous gothic masterpiece dominated the island like the witch's palace in a twisted fairy tale, all turrets and spires and barred windows.

"Looks like a big spooky bat made outta bricks," Sam said as they stepped onto the pier.

He was right, Evie thought. The main building sat out in front as a welcome to visitors, but the asylum's many three-story pavilions—the long brick rectangles that housed the patients—all connected to one another through a series of zigzagging right angles that swept out and around, like the giant wings of a bat.

"The island of the undesirables," Woody snarked. "That's what they call this place, you know. It's where they stick everybody the rest of the swells would rather not see. It used to house the drunks, the juvenile delinquents, the consumptives. Before Ellis Island, it's where they sent immigrants for processing."

Evie didn't need to hold an object to feel the sadness, the loneliness coming off the island. It made her feel unsettled. And they hadn't even gone inside yet.

The warden, a Mr. John Smith, trundled down the pier, waving. He was a jovial man with a well-trimmed mustache and a stiff collar that looked to be pinching his neck.

"How do you do, Miss O'Neill. What an honor to have you here at our hospital," he said, pumping Evie's hand. "And Mr. Woodhouse, I do so appreciate your writing a story about us out here in the middle of the river! We're overcrowded and underfunded. That story just might carry some weight with the governor and secure us the money we need."

Woody smirked. "Thank Miss O'Neill. It was her idea."

"Miss O'Neill. We are indebted to you. Well, there's much to see. This way, if you would."

"You told him you were writing about the hospital?" Sam whispered as they followed the warden up the stone pathway that wound through the marshy, windswept grass.

Woody shrugged. "I am. In a manner of speaking."

"We had to find a way out here," Evie explained.

Sam shook his head. "You two are something else."

Woody narrowed his eyes. "Yeah? And I'm sure you use that little skill of yours only for the benefit of others. Save the sermons for Sarah Snow."

A ferry trudged past the pier, heading toward the northern tip of the island. Several prisoners in black-and-white-striped uniforms stood on deck looking back at Evie, Sam, and Woody.

"We sometimes use prisoners from Welfare Island for labor," the warden said, following Evie's gaze.

"Yeah? You pay 'em for that labor?" Woody said, pen at the ready.

The warden's eyes narrowed. "They've done tremendous work building seawalls, repairing roofs," he said, ignoring the question. "Burials."

Sam craned his neck, scanning the flat landscape. "I don't see a cemetery."

"They're potter's fields," the warden explained. "Unmarked mass graves for the unwanted dead. It's unfortunate, but there are people who have no one to speak for them and nowhere to go."

Woody muttered as he continued jotting in his notebook. "Land of the insane is also home to the dead. That oughta sell a few papers in the morning."

Now that she looked, Evie could see several tightly swaddled bodies lying in a row on the ferry's broad back. Her stomach gave a little flip that sent needle-pricks of chill up her neck. "Mr. Smith, how many dead would you say are buried here?"

Mr. Smith blinked up at the dwindling sun. "Hard to say. But I'd put the figure at around fifty thousand, give or take."

"Fifty thousand?" Woody repeated.

"Give or take. Now, if I can direct your attention to our wonderful tinsmithing shop on your right, operated by the patients themselves..."

"The unwanted dead? I sure hope they stay put while we're here," Sam whispered to Evie.

"Gotta hand it to you, Sheba, you sure know how to have fun," Woody said, and popped his chewing gum.

They'd reached the columned portico of the main building; it jutted out from the asylum like the tongue in a great gothic skull, and Evie felt a strange sense of foreboding, as if the stones themselves wanted to confess their every secret. Surprisingly, the inside of the asylum was quite lovely and clean, with a coatroom, offices for bookkeeping and records, and nicely appointed waiting rooms for visitors. The warden led them past the surgeries and the examination and X-ray therapy rooms, past the dayrooms where some patients wove together straw mats. There were rooms dedicated to art and music therapy. The asylum even had its own bowling alley. On the crowded wards, nurses and attendants in crisp uniforms tended efficiently to patients. One nurse sat beside a female patient, holding her hand and listening attentively as the woman talked. Evie was warmed by the sight, and she felt guilty for having been so cavalier in lying to get into the asylum.

These were good people trying to help other people who were hurting and in need of help. She'd make sure that Woody's story gave them their due.

"How many patients live here?" Evie asked as the warden continued their tour.

"Nearly seven thousand," the warden said. "The asylum was built to house *far less than that.* And we've only a third of the staff we need. We've written to the governor countless times. It seems that no one cares about these poor people except us."

Woody edged ahead of Sam and Evie. He licked the end of his pencil and took out his notebook. "Caring doctors and nurses…ignored by callous state…" Woody said, writing.

"Precisely so. Thank you, Mr. Woodhouse."

"Don't mention it," Woody said, still scribbling away. "Say, that reminds me, Mr. Smith, how about this business with these murders? The *Daily News* hears the patient—a Mr. Roland, was it?—turned cannibal and ate an attendant and a nurse? The attendant, Mike Flanagan, was a big man, from what I hear. How did an old man like Mr. Roland have the strength to do that?"

"The asylum has no comment, sir." Mr. Smith bristled.

"Oh, sure, sure. I just figured you'd want to set the record straight about that, the men who drowned, and those nurses who died. So many stories out there and whatnot. See, I heard that some of the patients have been complaining about ghosts?"

"There's no such thing as ghosts, Mr. Woodhouse," Mr. Smith said emphatically. "Only the ghosts that haunt the mind. That is what we try to help with here at the hospital. Now, this is our art room…."

Evie was getting impatient to find Luther Clayton. In a waiting room, Evie spied a pamphlet on a table. AMERICA'S FUTURE DEPENDS ON EUGENICS. BETTERING OUR RACE THROUGH CAREFUL SELECTION AND PROPER RACIAL HYGIENE. WELL BORN IS WELL BRED. It was distributed by the Fitter Families of Future Firesides. Evie remembered seeing their tent at the fair up in Brethren. The pamphlet argued that the feebleminded, the promiscuous, the homosexual should be sterilized. And there should never be any mixing of races.

Evie had the urge to "accidentally" drop the pamphlet in the fire. A curious insert had been left inside the pamphlet:

Could you be an exceptional American? Do
you exhibit unusual gifts? Have you ever
had unexplained dreams of the future or
of the past? Have you or anyone in your
family had a visitation from spirits from
beyond? The Eugenics Society adminis-
ters tests to likely candidates free of
charge. Write to us care of this address
or visit a Fitter Families tent near you.

Why would eugenicists like Fitter Families be interested in Diviners?

"What's this?" Evie asked.

Mr. Smith peered at the paper in her hand. "Oh. That belongs to one of our doctors, Dr. Simpson," he said in a clipped, disapproving tone. "He's of the opinion that ailments of the mind can be prevented through better breeding and racial hygiene laws. He is an advocate for the sterilization of patients, inmates, and the poor."

"I'm guessing your Dr. Simpson isn't a fan of Jews," Sam said, his eyes narrowed.

"But what about this bit here? Seems they're looking for Diviners" Evie showed it to him.

"I don't have the foggiest idea. I don't believe in eugenics. And my dear wife is Jewish, Mr. Lloyd," Mr. Smith said. He took the pamphlet and shoved it in a drawer. "Come. Let me show you our music therapy room— the best in the state!"

"I've seen one of those pamphlets before," Woody whispered to Evie and Sam as Mr. Smith stopped to comfort a patient. "At Marlowe's ground-breaking ceremony. There was a Fitter Families tent there. A nurse was handing them out."

"Something's not on the level about it," Evie said.

"Yeah? You think there's something not right about a buncha people claiming they're a superior race? You don't say," Sam grumbled.

Mr. Smith led them through a spacious common room. An attendant played the piano while one of the patients bowed a violin. Some of the patients sang along. Others sat mute, staring. In one corner, four men had formed a circle, their chairs facing one another.

"We have a lot of shell-shocked men," the warden said gently, following Evie's line of sight.

"Oh," Evie said, thinking of all the boys like James who'd fought in the Great War—the ones like her brother, who never made it home, and the broken men in this room, trapped in their own private hells.

It was curious, though. The men were performing the same panto-mime motions with their hands. And then, suddenly, they began laughing all at once, as if they'd just been told a joke no one else could hear. There was something oddly familiar about the scene, and a shiver passed down Evie's back.

The lights dimmed down to nothing. In a few seconds, they revved back up.

"What was that?" Sam asked.

Mr. Smith smiled sympathetically. "Don't be alarmed. That happens quite a lot. They're blasting rock in the Hell Gate to make the passage deeper. Those explosions coupled with the violent currents affect us here in the hospital."

"Well, it is called the Hell Gate," Sam joked.

"From the Dutch *hellegat*," Woody said. "It means 'bright passage.' Except that it's not. It's the most dangerous water in New York City. Those currents are so bad the sailors renamed it: hellhole. Just in case you had any notions about swimming back to Manhattan."

"And when can I see Luther Clayton?" Evie said.

Mr. Smith's expression was pained. "Oh, dear. I thought it had been made clear. We can't allow it. By order of the police."

"But we've come all this way!" Evie said. "I'd only need a few minutes and—and think how much good it would do for Luther to know I for-give him."

"And it sure would be great for the story," Woody added. "Just the sort of thing that makes those state boys with the money take notice."

The warden remained unmoved. "I'm sorry, Miss O'Neill. I wish I could allow it. But rules are rules. Even for radio stars."

"I'll bet *Sarah Snow* could get in," Evie griped once they'd managed to ditch Mr. Smith under the pretense of Evie's "delicate Diviner sensibilities" needing a rest. She lay on a cot in a receiving room.

"Lamb Chop, you gotta let go of this Sarah Snow business," Sam said.

"Easy for you to say. You're not the one watching that Jesus viper take over your spot."

"Jesus . . . viper . . ." Woody said, writing.

"Woody, you print that and I will throw your body right into the Hell Gate." Evie sat up and tossed the compress she'd been given to the end of the cot. "Applesauce! How are we gonna get to Luther Clayton?"

"Won't be easy. Look here," Sam said, walking over to the wall, which boasted a proud, framed photograph of the asylum on its opening day. "This is where we are now." Sam pointed to the main building out front. "And according to the chatty Mr. Smith, this is where they hold the most disturbed patients." Sam pointed to a three-story rectangular ward all the way in the back. "This pavilion. Top floor. That's where Luther Clayton is. Where they don't allow visitors. *Not even radio stars,*" Sam said in perfect imitation.

"I am not leaving without seeing him," Evie swore.

"Baby Vamp, with your moxie and my good looks . . ." Sam spread his arms wide.

"So we're half-doomed is what you're telling me. Well. I suppose you can always just . . ." Evie wiggled her fingers.

"What, dry my nail varnish? Pretend I'm a bird? Play an imaginary piano?" Sam said.

"No! Do your *don't see me* trick."

"How come yours is a 'gift' and mine is a 'trick'? I'm insulted."

"Just make yourself useful, Sam."

Woody laughed. "Shame you two called off your engagement. You're a perfect couple. Why don't you former lovebirds wait here. I'll step out and see if the coast is clear," Woody said. He slipped into the hall, leaving Sam and Evie alone together.

"How's Will taking Jericho's leaving?" Evie asked, breaking the awkward silence.

"Oh, you know how it is with your uncle—impossible to tell what he's thinking. He has the same expression whether it's figuring out what to eat for lunch or facing the possible end of the world. You, ah, hear from the big fella?"

Evie shook her head.

Woody sneaked back in. "I think I found a way. Let's ankle while we can."

The three of them set off down the labyrinthine halls of the asylum. For the first time, Evie realized that the work they'd been doing with Sister Walker had opened her gifts up further. The very walls seemed to want to whisper their long-held secrets to her:

"…I wasn't crazy. My husband put me here so he could marry another…."

"…Dirty Robert…does things to us when the warden's away…."

"I only want the pain to stop, don't you see? Just end it…."

"There's evil in this world…."

Sam looked concerned. "You okay?"

Evie nodded. "Too many secrets here," she said, and kept straight down the middle.

At the entrance to Luther Clayton's ward, an attendant was on duty at his desk.

"Afternoon, sir." Woody tipped his hat briefly as he approached the guard. "The name's T. S. Woodhouse of the *Daily News*. And this lovely lady is the Sweetheart Seer."

The guard stood and smoothed a hand over his hair. "Well, Miss, it's an honor. A real honor. I sure do love your show!"

"Aren't you just the berries!" Evie said, smiling flirtatiously and fluttering her lashes just a bit.

"Don't cause a windstorm with that peepers-batting," Sam whispered.

Evie stepped lightly on his foot with the heel of her Mary Janes.

The attendant frowned. "Gee, you're not supposed to be back here, though, Miss. Not without permission."

"I've come to see the man who tried to kill me, Luther Clayton," Evie said quickly, managing to work up a few perfect tears. "I want to forgive the poor tortured soul."

"Golly, Miss O'Neill, I sure wish I could let you see Luther, but he can't receive visitors. Orders of the police. You'd need permission. Should I call up to the warden…?"

"No! That is, I wouldn't want to bother him. I'm sure the warden wouldn't mind if I just popped my little head in and—"

The attendant crossed his arms. "Sorry, Miss. Orders are orders."

"Well, I suppose it's time to dry that nail varnish, then, isn't it, Sam? Woody, could you turn around and cover your ears, please?"

"What? Ohhh. Sure."

"Sam, do you mind?"

"For you, Lamb Chop? Anything." Sam stretched out an arm. "Don't see me," he said. The attendant's eyes went blank. His arms dangled loosely at his sides. Evie tapped Woody's shoulder. He took in the sight of the mesmerized man and shook his head, whistling.

"That is a neat trick, kid. Wish I could use it on my bookie next time I run into him and he wants his money."

"How much time do we have, Sam?" Evie asked.

"Three, maybe four minutes, tops?"

Evie bit her bottom lip. "It's not much. But it'll have to do."

"See, why you gotta say that? Three minutes—do you know how hard that is? How much skill that takes? Look at these hands. These are gifted hands. I should insure 'em."

"Whaddaya wanna see Luther for?" The question came from a slight, dark-haired boy drawing feverishly at a corner table. It was hard to know his true age. The freckles made him seem young, but his eyes were wary, and much, much older than they should be.

"Luther is an old friend of mine," Evie said.

"You're lying."

Evie started to protest, but something about this fragile-looking boy made her want to tell the truth. "Yes. I'm lying. He tried to shoot me."

"You're the Sweetheart Seer," the boy said. "I recognize your voice. From the radio."

"Seems you've got fans everywhere, Sheba," Woodhouse said.

The boy seemed very nervous to her. Like someone whose mind wouldn't allow him to rest. Sam tugged gently on Evie's arm. "Come on, doll—we gotta ankle before that guard wakes up."

"You gotta leave before nightfall! That's when they come. Wit' the night and the fog."

"Who?" Evie asked the nervous boy.

He flicked his gaze toward the window. "The Forgotten. They can get inside you. Make you do things. Awful things. They belong to—" His eyes were as large as a fish's. "Just don't be here when it's dark," he said, and ran back the way he'd come, disappearing down another hallway.

"Evie!" Sam pleaded.

"Not in this room," Woody said, closing the door to one of the many rooms along the ward's long hallway. "One minute gone."

"Thanks. That's a big help," Sam said.

Evie peeked through the inset window of room number seven. There was a young man in a wheelchair. "Found him!" she whisper-shouted, and opened the door.

"Don't…even…lock…the doors." Woody scribbled quickly on his pad. "Sweetheart Seer put aside concerns for her own safety…gained entry to the cell of violent madman…"

"Luther? Luther Clayton?" Evie said softly into the dim room. It was very still and sparse: only a bed and a bedside table with an unopened Bible on top. Luther Clayton sat in his wheelchair, staring at the wall.

Evie drew closer. "Mr. Clayton?"

"Hold still. I want to get a picture. Evie, lean in, will ya?" Woody urged, taking a long-snouted accordion camera from his reporter's bag.

"To the man who tried to kill her?" Sam said. "Nothing doing."

"It's okay, Sam," Evie said. "Just make sure you get my good side, Woody."

Evie moved closer to Luther. He smelled of old sweat. There were bruises on his neck, sores on his chapped lips. War and pain had aged him, but underneath, Luther was delicately handsome, with a face that seemed familiar, as if he might have been a bit actor in a cowboy picture. Evie was jealous of Memphis's Diviner power; if she could, she would try to heal this man's broken heart.

This close, she could feel his clothes wanting to whisper to her.

"Hurry," she said to Woody.

The flash cut the gloom. "Got it," Woody said.

Evie took a step back. "Do you remember me, Mr. Clayton?" she said softly. "I'm Evie O'Neill."

He inclined his head toward her. His eyes were still distant.

"I want you to know that I forgive you for trying to shoot me. I only wish I understood why you did it."

Luther blinked several times, as if trying to wake up from a dream. Evie kept talking: "You once took hold of my hand on the street. Do you remember? I put a dollar in your tin cup and you grabbed my hand. You were trying to tell me something back then. Something about following the Eye. I'm sorry I ran away then. I was frightened. Were you mad at me about that? Is that why you tried to shoot me?"

Luther Clayton's voice was so soft Evie had to lean forward to hear.

"They...m-made m-me."

"Who made you do it, Luther?"

Luther's sad brown eyes were bloodshot. It looked as if he hadn't slept in weeks. His whisper gained power. "The Shadow M-men. They said it... would s-stop the sc-c-screaming. I hear them...sc-screaming."

"I don't understand—who's screaming?"

Spit bubbled up on Luther's bottom lip as if he were trying to birth his words. But nothing came.

"Kid, you got what you came for. Let's ankle," Woody said.

"They never should've done it! Follow the Eye! He is coming—don't let him find me!" Luther cried out suddenly, his back arching with tension. His palm came up and pounded the side of his head. "Stop screaming! Stop screaming!"

"Mr. Clayton! Please! You'll hurt yourself!" Evie reached for Luther's arm. With surprising quickness and strength, he grabbed hold of her wrist. Evie's fingers grazed the leather strap of his radium-dial watch.

"Let go!" Sam said. He raced forward and then fell back as if he'd been shoved by a giant's hand. "What the...?"

Luther Clayton's eyes locked on Evie's. Whispers from Luther's watch crawled up her arm and settled in her head. Her mind flashed with gunfire-quick glimpses of the terrible secrets he carried. She saw a train transporting soldiers through mountains and trees. She saw those same soldiers in a forest clearing. A Victrola playing "Pack Up Your Troubles." It was a scene

Evie knew all too well from her own dreams. Her body shook from the force of Luther's revelations. She could smell blood and fear and a presence so sinister it made her want to run as far as she could get from the asylum and the demons inside Luther Clayton's mind.

"Help them," Luther pleaded. "Please. Help. Him."

Evie struggled to speak over the whispers inside her head. "Who?"

"Help *James*."

Sam and Woody tore Evie loose from Luther's grip. The whispers floated away.

"Doll," Sam said, concerned. He dabbed his handkerchief against her nose and it came away bloody. She was still trembling.

"H-how...how do you know James?" Silence. "How do you know my brother? Where is he?"

"We should get outta here." Sam put an arm around Evie's shoulder.

She shrugged it off. "Tell me! Tell me!"

Luther Clayton's eyes were again fixed on the wall. "The Eye has him."

A thin stream of tears trickled down his cheek. He tapped his head gently against the back of his chair: "The land is old, the land is vast, he has no future, he has no past, his coat is sewn with many woes, he'll bring the dead, the King of Crows....He'll bring the dead, the King of Crows, King of Crows, King of Cr—"

The door flew open. The guard was still a little woozy from Sam's touch, but that was no match for his fury. "Out," he said. "Now."

※

"I can't believe we actually got thrown out of an asylum," Sam said.

"I prefer 'firmly escorted from the premises,'" Evie said, holding Woody's wet handkerchief to her aching head, his parting gift to her before he'd decamped for the newsroom. It didn't help that she and Sam were winding through Times Square, their ears assaulted by the discordant symphony of car horns, clattering trolleys, and the rumble-and-clang of a steam shovel and pile driver pumping away at a nearby construction dig, where men in coveralls busied themselves making way for more skyscrapers in the city that never stopped reaching higher. "Where *are* we going, Sam?"

"Somewhere safe."

On Eleventh Avenue, Sam knocked on the basement door of a building that looked to be falling down.

"This is your idea of safe?" Evie said. "It's probably crawling with thieves and ne'er-do-wells."

Sam grinned. "Yeah. I'm in my element."

"As long as they have gin."

A panel in the door slid open. "All for one, and one for all," Sam said.

The door swung open, and Sam escorted Evie through the dank basement speakeasy, past a rough crowd to a dark-paneled booth in the very back. It smelled like dust and stale booze wiped up by a stinky rag.

"Okay. Spill. What did you see?" Sam pressed.

"It all happened so fast. But it felt familiar, too. I've seen those very images in my dreams, Sam. And he knows James! You heard him—he told me to help James."

"Doll, you don't know that he meant your brother. That coulda been anybody named James."

"No. Sam, I can't explain it. It was a feeling. Just like you knew about your mother, I know he was talking about my brother." Evie sipped her gin, grateful for the familiar warm sting of it as it burned down to her stomach. "What did he mean, the Eye has him?"

"Evie, he's not right in the head."

"Something terrible happened to Luther," Evie said, staring into her cup. "I saw things in his mind that I've only seen inside my own dreams: The soldiers. The Victrola. The forest. It went by very quickly, but it was there. When Bob Bateman brought me James's comb to read, he said somebody had paid him to do it. Men in dark suits. Luther said Shadow Men told him to shoot me. We saw two men in dark suits when we broke into the abandoned offices of the Department of Paranormal. Somehow, this is all connected to Project Buffalo and us. I just know it is. And Luther Clayton is the key that unlocks these mysteries, Sam. I've simply got to talk to him again."

"Well, good luck, doll. You just got us thrown out of there. That warden was not happy. How you gonna get back in?"

"I'll think of something," Evie said.

"Yes, you will. And that's what I'm afraid of."

The minute Evie returned to her hotel, she asked the operator to dial the number for the *Daily News*.

"Woody? It's Evie."

"Tell me something I don't know."

"Listen: That story on me forgiving Luther Clayton?"

"Yeah, yeah. I'm working on it right now."

"Well, forget it. I've got a better story."

There was a pause. "Okay. I'm all ears."

When Evie had finished enlisting Woody's help, she called Theta. "Theta, who's your dearest friend?"

"Henry," Theta replied.

"After Henry."

"Memphis."

"After Memphis," Evie said, annoyed.

"I'm pretty fond of my doorman."

"Theta!"

"I'm just pulling your leg, Evil. What plan is cooking up in that feverish noggin of yours? I can hear the diabolical wheels turning from here."

"I need an acting job. How'd you like to come on my show tomorrow night?"

There was a pause followed by a heavy sigh. "Why do I know I'll regret this?"

BEFORE IT'S TOO LATE

The next morning's headline was a beauty:

EXTRA! EXTRA! SWEETHEART SEER SEES GHOSTS AT ASYLUM

Exclusive to *The Daily News* by T. S. Woodhouse

> Just yesterday, New York's beloved Sweetheart Seer, the irrepressible Evie O'Neill, made the arduous trek to the Manhattan State Hospital for the Insane on desolate Ward's Island.

"Arduous trek? You took a ferry ride!" Mabel interrupted. She was sitting at Evie's vanity table painting on a fresh coat of her best nail varnish.

"Ahem. You are interrupting my dramatic reading," Evie said.

> Her mission? To forgive the man who so recently attempted to murder her, Luther Clayton. While there, Miss O'Neill became aware of a far greater danger to the inhabitants of the asylum, for it seems that ghosts haunt the halls and moors of Ward's Island, or so claim the patients. Some folks might say that believing in ghosts is enough to put one into an asylum. Yet, in light of the recent, unfortunate murders there, it's hard to doubt them outright, especially now that they've got a Diviner on their side.

> "There is pos-i-tute-ly a ghostly presence at the asylum," Miss O'Neill insisted to this reporter after her brief visit. "Why, with my Diviner sensibilities, I detected it right away! I know how deeply

the doctors and nurses care for their patients, and that is why I urge them to have my uncle Will Fitzgerald and his team of Diviners out to investigate and rid the island of any spiritual trouble right away!"

The brave and kind Miss O'Neill did not worry at all about her own safety but was only concerned with the well-being of Luther Clayton and the nearly seven thousand patients housed at the asylum. "I fear they are in great danger!" Miss O'Neill insisted.

This newspaper eagerly awaits the response of the hospital administration.

Mabel gave Evie a hard squint. "You're using those poor people so you can get back to the asylum and Luther Clayton."

Evie started to protest, but there was no conning Mabel. "Maybe I am. But they *did* talk about ghosts, Mabesie. And Luther knows something about James. We keep getting these messages—'Follow the Eye'—and Luther said, 'The Eye has him.'"

"What do you think that means?"

"I don't know. That's why I pos-i-tute-ly have to see him again!"

Mabel considered this. "And you talked Theta into doing your show tonight?"

"I didn't talk her into it," Evie said with a bit of umbrage. "She *wanted* to do it."

That afternoon, Theta had pretended to be a secretary from WGI, calling up the press to announce that the Sweetheart Seer would have a very special guest that evening, Miss Theta Knight of the Ziegfeld Follies.

"If the luck of the spirits is on her side tonight, Miss O'Neill will uncover the mystery of Miss Knight's past in Russia," the "secretary" had promised in a nasal voice. "It'll be a swell show. You don't want to miss it for the world."

"I hope you know what you're doing," Mabel said. "That Harriet Henderson doesn't like you."

"Gee, thanks, Mabesie."

"It's the truth. Ignore it at your peril!" Mabel said in her best Nana Newell voice, making Evie laugh. Mabel's smile faded. "It *is* the truth. And you *do* ignore it at your peril. She can twist the story any way she likes. And once she writes it in her paper, people believe every word as fact, whether it is or not."

Evie waved away the comment. "Let me worry about the Harriet Hendersons of the world."

"I do worry about them," Mabel said.

"Will you come to the show tonight? Theta and I are going to the Hotsy Totsy afterward. It'll be the berries!"

Mabel blew on her nails. "Sorry. I've got a meeting."

"All these secret meetings. When will I get to meet the mysterious Arthur Brown?"

"Oh, sometime."

Never, Mabel thought.

※

By the time Evie and Theta arrived at the radio station, a crowd had gathered outside along with the press. As expected, Harriet Henderson was front and center.

"Oh, Miss Knight! Miss O'Neill!" Harriet called, waving her lace handkerchief, a gift, she'd proudly reported, from Jake Marlowe himself. It was no wonder to Evie that Harriet only wrote glowing articles about Jake.

Evie winked at Theta. "Like clockwork."

Harriet sidled up to the girls. She was short and solid as a barber's pole and wore a ridiculous hat festooned in enough netting and flowers to look like a wedding cake. Around her neck was a fox stole. The fox's button eyes stared straight ahead while its mouth bit into its tail. *A biter, just like its owner*, Evie thought.

"Miss Knight. Don't you look lovely," Harriet cooed. Her voice was nasal and flat, straight out of Buffalo.

"Thank you, Mrs. Henderson. I love your…" Theta pointed to the fox. "Animal."

"Hello, Mrs. Henderson," Evie said brightly.

Harriet gave her a tight smile. "Miss O'Neill."

Evie imagined Harriet taking a cream pie to her overly powdered face.

"My goodness, Miss Knight, I didn't realize you went in for Diviners," Harriet said. It sounded innocent enough, but the girls knew that nothing Harriet said was innocent. Even her grocery list was probably a trap.

"If Miss O'Neill's powers can help me find out who I really am, I'm all for it. Hip, hip, hooray for Diviners, I say."

"Hmm." Harriet's eyes glinted with something hard as she pivoted to Evie. "Miss O'Neill, is it *really* true that you think there are ghosts on Ward's Island?"

"It *is*, Mrs. Henderson," Evie said, using every bit of those elocution lessons the radio station had forced her to take. "Why, the patients are scared to death! I do hope the warden will allow me back before it's too late."

"Too late for what?"

"Indeed," Evie said as ominously as possible. She could feel Theta about to break into giggles.

"Why do you think that man tried to shoot you, Miss O'Neill?"

"I suppose that's a question for Miss Snow to ask the Lord."

"Evil, don't push it," Theta muttered under her breath.

But Evie wanted to push it. She'd grown up in a small town of small minds. She knew a Blue Nose like Harriet when she saw one—the types to smile and feign concern, then tear you apart behind your back. People like Harriet Henderson only rose by climbing up the misery steps of someone else's misfortune.

"Perhaps that man—"

"Luther Clayton." *He has a name*, Evie wanted to shout.

"Yes. He's a war hero, is he not?"

"Yes."

Harriet smiled, and Evie's stomach flipped as if registering an alarm a second too late. "You see, I heard that fellow, the war hero, wanted to shoot you because you were a Diviner, and he believed that Diviners can't be trusted. That they are a plague upon the nation. Must be awful to be doubted by one of our finest, our boys back from the noble fight. What do you say to that, Miss O'Neill? Should we be more afraid of Diviners, perhaps, than we are of any supposed ghosts?"

"Golly, look at the time! I'm afraid Miss O'Neill has a show to do!" Theta pulled Evie toward the door before she could lose her temper and say something she'd regret come the morning papers. "Don't take the bait, Evil."

But Harriet Henderson wasn't finished. "Miss Knight!" she called after the girls. "Is it true that you spend a great deal of your time up in Harlem with Negroes? My spies have seen you there quite a lot. I do wonder, what's so interesting uptown?"

The fear hit Theta like a lightning strike. All she could do was stare back at the cold light of Harriet Henderson's eyes.

"You keep on wondering, Mrs. Henderson—it's swell for the mind!" Evie said with forced jollity. And this time, it was Evie pulling Theta to safety.

"That reptile! That pinched-face, stupid-hat-wearing reptile!" Evie groused as she and Theta powdered their noses in the ladies' lounge.

"Well, that reptile has a lot of power." Theta's eyes met Evie's in the mirror. "Say, I'm having second thoughts about letting you use that scrap of baby blanket for the reading tonight. I know we wanted to make it look authentic, but…"

Evie lowered her voice. "Don't worry. I've got it all figured out. When we're up there, I won't be able to feel a thing. Promise."

Every seat in the audience was filled tonight. Sarah Snow slipped into the audience at the back, along with Harriet Henderson. Mr. Forman, the announcer, welcomed Evie to the stage and they shilled for the sponsor: "Pears is American pure," Evie said, reading from her script, trying to give the line extra enthusiasm so they'd be happy with her. So far, they were still boosting her show rather than Sarah's, and she meant to hold on to their support. At last, Mr. Forman called Theta to the stage to much applause. She greeted Evie warmly, whispering in her ear, "I hope you know what you're doing, kid."

"Just follow my lead," Evie whispered back. "Welcome to the Pears Soap Hour, Miss Knight. I understand you have no memory of your former life in Russia?"

"I only have this scrap of blanket. It was with me when I was found at the orphanage. If you could find something about my lost family, why, I'd be awfully grateful, Miss O'Neill," Theta said, like the great actress she was, and Evie had to bite her lip to keep from giggling.

"Leave it to me. And to the spirits, of course." Evie took hold of the scrap of blanket Theta had brought. The wool was old and scratchy and rich with memory. Evie could sense its power, but, as promised, she'd taken precautions: Backstage, she'd glued small squares of paper to her palms in the hope that it would dull the signals from beyond. She closed her eyes and pretended to go under. "I see a sweet little boy...perhaps your brother?"

"Oh, gee, I hope so!" Theta said, playing along.

Evie drew in a sharp, sudden breath. The audience gasped, too, on the edge of their seats. "Oh. Oh, no."

"Miss O'Neill? Are you all right?"

Evie staggered. "Why, this has never happened to me before...I'm...I'm receiving a message from beyond...."

Evie peeked through her lashes. The audience was eating it up. *Here goes*, she thought.

"We...are the ghosts of Ward's Island," Evie intoned as if in a deep trance. "Help our spirits rest or face..." Face what? What would get her back to the asylum? "Our vengeance!"

Evie swayed softly, meaning to faint for pure drama—why not?—but something wouldn't let her. Some very real memory was fighting its way through to her, paper shields be damned. The whispers of Theta's past curled inside Evie's mind like smoke. She saw white. A blanket of fresh snow. Blood dotted the snow. A trail of it led to a tiny village thick with black smoke from burning houses. Bodies lay facedown in the bloodied snow like discarded dolls. There were men moving through with rifles. Evie's muscles tensed. She'd seen those men before—the gray suits. A frightened woman clutching a baby to her chest waited until the men had turned the other way, and then she ran frantically from the burning village up the hill toward the cover of trees. Her moccasins sank into the heavy snow with each step, and her long black braid thumped against her back. The memory of this mother's terror was strong; it wormed its way inside Evie's own chest. Just as the woman reached the tree line, the rifle shot found its mark in the woman's back. Gravely wounded, she dragged herself toward an ancient oak, secreting the bundled baby inside a hollow there. And then she lay back, her lifeless eyes staring toward the unforgiving sky. The eyes were deep and brown. Just like Theta's. As the men pulled away from the village on their horses, a trapper emerged from the woods. He fell to his knees in that same snow and wiped tears from his bearded cheeks as he retrieved the bundle of fussing baby, warming it against his chest under a fur pelt. This golden-bearded man was the baby's father. Evie could feel his fear and great sorrow as he grappled with a heartrending choice. Next, Evie saw the church steps, saw the light spill out from inside the church as the nuns approached the wriggling baby swaddled in its only inheritance, a blanket.

Evie stumbled out of the memory to see Theta's face, so like the faces in the snow.

In the back row, Sarah watched closely.

Harriet took notes.

※

"What did you see?" Theta asked later at their favorite booth in the Hotsy Totsy. Theta kept looking nervously over her shoulder for anyone who might be one of Harriet's spies.

"Theta, do you have any memory of a village on fire?"

Theta's eyes widened. "It's a dream I have sometimes. There's all this snow. And then I can smell smoke and see blood on the snow."

"I'm not sure that's just a dream."

"What do you mean?"

"Theta, I saw those fellas in the gray suits. They were shooting up a village and then they set it on fire. I think it was an Indian village. And I saw your mother. She tried to run away with you, but they shot her. And then, a trapper came along and found you—your father. He was the one who left you on the church steps. I could feel that he didn't want to, but he felt he *had* to; you weren't safe with him."

Theta took in a shuddering breath. She'd had a mother who had loved her enough to spend her very last breath protecting her, and a father who'd tried to do the same. Theta blinked back tears thinking about what her life could have been with parents who loved her so. "Where was this? Could you tell?"

Evie shook her head. "Out west somewhere. There were mountains and trees and snow. It was really pretty. Like a postcard."

Theta's chest was tight and achy. She'd never known so much about her past before. "Feels like there's this hole in the center of me, and I keep trying to fill it but I don't know how," she said, drawing on her cigarette. "Like there's part of me that's just been erased."

"But you're not erased! You're here. Right now."

"That's not it. You know where you come from. Your parents. Your brother. Your house. Your town. You got a story. Me? I got no story. I'm making it up as I go along."

"Aren't we all?"

"It's not the same thing." Theta's eyes welled up with both sadness over her emptiness and frustration at not being able to make Evie understand.

Evie covered Theta's hand with her own. "I'm glad I'm part of your story."

"Me, too, Evil. Even when I wanna kill you for acting dumb."

Evie frowned. "Was that nice?"

"No. But it was honest. That's how much I love you."

"Could you love me a little less?" Evie grumbled.

"You wanna be real friends or pretend friends?"

Evie sipped her drink. "Fine. I love you, too. And I wish you'd trust me more."

"I trust you."

"Now who's lying?"

Theta had spent her whole life pretending to be other people, both onstage and off. It was her armor. Her adoptive mother, Mrs. Bowers, had never wanted to hear about what Theta was feeling. "Betty Sue, no one likes a complainer. Now get out there and smile like you mean it." Smile. Dance. Entertain. It was what she'd been taught. And then Roy had come along. At first, Theta had mistaken his interest for love. Everything she ever said to him became a weapon to be used against her. So she just stopped saying anything. It had taken a lot to trust Henry. She wanted to open herself up to Evie and Memphis and the others, but it was scary. What if she got hurt as she had been hurt before?

"Why would those gray suits burn down the village? Doesn't make sense," Theta said, changing the subject.

"I don't know. But I'm starting to be very afraid of those men."

Theta was afraid, too. The whole world suddenly felt like too much, as threatening as Roy in one of his slow drunks, when she could see his rage and disappointment rolling in like a destructive storm.

"Well, well, the party's all here," Henry said as he scooted in next to Evie along with Sam, Mabel, Memphis, and Ling. "Congratulations, by the way, you two."

"Thanks. For what?" Evie asked.

"Seems Will got a call after your show tonight from the warden out at the asylum. We're going out tomorrow to investigate 'the ghostly menace.'" Henry wiggled his fingers and made a face.

"It worked!" Evie said.

"Yeah. And our reward is to spend a day at an asylum. Hip, hip, hooray," Theta sniped.

"All we have to do is walk around with the Metaphysickometer, talk to a few people, and get me in to see Luther Clayton."

"Just promise me we'll be out of there before it gets dark," Theta said.

"I promise," Evie said.

"Meet me downstairs?" Memphis whispered to Theta. She waited a few careful minutes, then slipped backstage and downstairs, joining Memphis in the small room where they'd had their first encounter six months before. She locked the door behind her and sat on his lap.

"Missed you," Memphis said.

"Yeah?" Theta grinned. "How much?"

"I could show you, but I'm not real sure how good the lock is on that door." He kissed her, slow and sweet. It made Theta dizzy with wanting.

"I was thinking about something the other day," Memphis said between kisses.

"Don't make that a habit," Theta joked. Once she and Memphis started kissing, she never wanted to stop.

"When we first met, and you saw the drawing I'd done of that eye symbol, you said you'd dreamed of it, too."

"Yeah?" Theta said, suddenly nervous.

"Well, just seems funny. You're not even a Diviner."

I'm not a Diviner. I'm a murderer.

"Maybe it's from being around Henry so much," Theta said, feeling rotten for the lie.

"Reckon that could be it."

Theta snuggled in to Memphis, resting her head against his chest. She didn't want to think about Diviners or eye symbols or notes from mysterious strangers. She only wanted to have this moment together. Memphis kissed the top of her head and wrapped his arms around her. "Papa Charles still making you heal for him?" she asked.

"Mm-hmm. There hasn't been any trouble for a few days. But I never know when he'll come for me. Makes me a little sick afterward, though. The first time, when I healed a fella who'd been shot, I had these little sores on my hands. They're gone now, but…"

"Gee, Poet. Maybe you better stop."

Memphis's eyebrows shot up. "Say no to Papa Charles? No, thank you. Besides…" Memphis bent his head to Theta's and sucked gently at her lower lip, then kissed her fully, like a thirsty man drinking from a well. "I don't wanna talk about that just now. You wanna get out of here for a while?"

"I can't."

"You got another date?"

"Need my beauty sleep."

"You get any more beautiful and I'll have to start washing my eyes every night. I won't be able to take it." He put one hand over his heart and shook, making Theta laugh. She kissed him harder. Memphis moaned softly, running a hand up her back until Theta felt warm and tingly.

"I gotta go, Poet," she said between kisses.

Memphis was flushed. Sweat beaded around his freshly shaved hairline. "You're cruel, woman."

Theta laughed. "We all got our talents." She fixed her dress and reached for her coat.

"Hey…" Memphis took hold of Theta's hand, drawing her back for one more kiss. "I love you, you know."

"Yeah," Theta said, pressing herself against him until she thought she might lose her mind. "I know."

Upstairs again, Theta passed through the club like a phantom. Around her, people stomped and danced. The band played on. Trumpets wailed against the night. The chorus girls glittered and winked. In that corner booth, her friends were huddled together, happy. Sam was telling some story using his hands. Henry wiped away tears of laughter. Ling kept stealing glances at Alma up onstage, and anybody with any kind of sense could see that she was smitten. Theta tried to imagine cantankerous Ling lovestruck, and it was almost enough to chase away her fear. Out on the street, Theta checked the time. Eleven thirty. She read over the note one more time. *Midnight. Come alone.*

The doorman hailed Theta a taxi. "Where to?" the cabbie asked.

"The Bowery," she said. "And step on it."

REUNION

"Thanks. Keep the change," Theta said, and set off down the Bowery. Steam pulsed up around the edges of the manhole covers, lending the streets a grainy wash. Just past the darkened windows of a hosiery shop, Theta found the building—a skinny door nestled between a bakery and a tailor's shop. Theta climbed up two steep flights, listening to a baby's hungry wail drifting down the stairwell. At the end of a dim hallway with a chipped floor, she saw it: 3C. There was a note with her name on it taped there: *Door's open*, it read.

Heart thumping, Theta turned the knob. The apartment was dark. Only the lights from the Bowery leaking in through the windows gave the room any shape at all. She wanted to run, but if she did, the threats would never stop. She had to know who was sending those notes. Theta shut the door behind her.

A lamp clicked on, and Theta blinked against the sudden bright. Her surprise turned slowly to disbelief, then horror at the figure on the bed sitting half in shadow. Her knees wobbled as she was seized by a fear so overwhelming it had a smell and taste. Bile inched into her throat. She fought to swallow it down.

"Roy?" she managed at last.

"Hello, Betty. D'ya miss me, baby?"

The wildflower in the vase. The hand at her throat. The slap across the cheek.

She was having a hard time staying in the room, staying in her body.

Her hands shook as she stood in the middle of the room like a guilty child.

The bed creaked as Roy stood up. He'd filled out the past two years. His arms and shoulders were thickly muscled, making him look even more of a menace. Slowly, he circled the room, prowling like a panther.

"You look good. Never used to wear all that face paint, but…" Roy added quickly, "Golly. You sure are pretty, Betty."

He was talking to her the way he used to when he was a handsome soda jerk in Kansas and she was a gawky-legged girl on the vaudeville circuit. Theta felt like a small, cornered rabbit. She kept her eyes on the scarred floorboards.

"I suppose those New York fellas like all that face paint you wear, huh? Yes, sir, must be lined up for you."

"No," Theta said too fast. "I mean, I, uh, I work all the time."

"Yeah? Who's that fella you're living with?"

That Roy knew about Henry terrified Theta. "Just a fella works at the show. Piano player."

Roy laughed. "Oh. A theater type. A sissy, then?"

Theta's cheeks burned at the insult. The less she said, the better. For once, her palms were stone cold. It was as if her fear were a breath blowing out the flame.

"Well, well. This is a nice reunion, ain't it? Took me a long time to find you. Nobody knew where you'd got to. And then I was doing a job in Brooklyn and I happened to see that newspaper article on Theta Knight, the Russian princess turned showgirl," Roy said, giving the last bit a showman's flair. From the corner of her eye, she saw him wagging a finger at her, grinning. "You looked different in the picture, but I knew, I knew that Theta was my long-lost wife, Betty Sue. And that Russian baloney was made up by those showbiz people." He took a deep breath. "I missed you, Betty Sue."

Her mind could only absorb snatches of thought: *Memphis. Flo. Scandal. All gone. All gone.*

"See, I figured after that night and the fire, you musta had, whatchamacallit—amnesia or something. Walking around without a clue who you were or where you come from."

Theta had spent her life not knowing that. All she could do was move forward. Roy was like falling back. He was studying her the way he used to, waiting to catch her for some invisible wrongdoing. But Theta had learned a lot the past two years.

"I don't remember much at all," she said, acting the part.

"You remember doing this? Look at me, Betty. *Look.*"

Slowly, Theta turned toward him. Roy moved into the light and Theta gasped. Half of his face was burned all the way up to the hairline. She could just see the faint outline of her handprint on his left cheek, a bumpy scar.

"You did that. I don't know how, but you did."

She was fighting to stay in her body. Her mind wanted to flee.

"I-I don't remember," she heard herself say.

"Well, don't you worry, Betty. I'm here now," Roy said, and Theta's gut screamed at her like a scared child. *Run. Go. Hide.* She remembered how his threat used to lay coiled under caring words, like a venomous snake hidden deep inside a pretty velvet bag.

"Tomorrow we can go back to Kansas."

"I got a contract," Theta said, again too quickly. "At the Follies."

"Yeah? You make good money? I'll bet you make good money. Okay. We'll wait till your contract is up. Tell the sissy you're moving out." He patted the bed. "After all, I'm still your husband in the eyes of the law." Roy's smile changed. "Or did you get yourself another sucker?"

Theta could only imagine Memphis's fate if Roy found out.

"I told you, I work all the time," Theta said.

"Work is good. Keeps a girl outta trouble," Roy said meaningfully. And then, like a wind, his glowering face changed. He smiled. "You know, now I think about it, why go back to that lousy two-flea circus in Kansas? This town's gonna be good for us. I could be your agent. Look after your career."

He would own her. "People don't know me as married."

"So now they will."

"It ain't that simple, Roy." Her voice had gotten so tiny.

A familiar shadow passed over Roy's face. He didn't like *no*. "Gee, if I go to the newspapers, this sure would look bad on you. I mean, lotsa people remember you was my wife. Lotsa people remember that fire. How suspicious it was. The whole place goin' up like that? Police back home might wanna ask you questions."

There it was, the snake in the bag. She had to stall him until she could figure this whole mess out. "I just have to find a way to tell Flo without him getting sore. He's worked so hard on this Russian princess angle. If he got mad, I could be out of a job. Out of *money*."

Roy searched her face. Theta spent every ounce of energy maintaining a look of pure truth. "Okay. You figure it out. I'll give you till next week, but then I want a meeting."

Theta's heart sank. A week was no time at all. "Sure, Roy. Sure."

Theta inched toward the door. "I better get some rest before tomorrow's rehears—"

Roy crossed the floor in three quick strides and pulled Theta to him. Gripping the back of her head, he forced his kiss on her. When he pulled away, he was smiling. "Now I found you, Betty, things'll be like they was again. Just the two of us." He stroked her hair, wrapping a section tightly between his fingers. He put his mouth to her ear, and even his whisper felt like a violation. "If I find out you been lying to me about another fella, well, I wouldn't want to be that fella, Betty Sue. Nod if you understand me."

Theta nodded.

The baby's wailing was loud in Theta's ears as she raced down the steps of Roy's seedy building and out onto the Bowery. The Third Avenue El rumbled overhead, drowning out her choked sobs. What was she going to tell Flo? If the papers, if somebody like Harriet Henderson, got wind of this story, she'd be ruined. She was trapped. And if Roy found out about Memphis, he'd kill him. She knew that. Theta could still feel Roy's foul kiss on her mouth as she stumbled down the streets of Chinatown. Feverishly, she wiped at her lips. She cried until she had no tears left, until she was numb and hollowed. Theta wandered the city until dawn. As the day's first gray stirrings sniffed between the skyscrapers, she knew what she had to do.

HOPEFUL HARBOR

The Marlowe estate was nestled deep in the Adirondacks, nearly a day's drive from the city. The clouds sat low on the mountaintops and blew out across the valley below. It was colder up here; snow still dotted the ground and the roads were muddy. Weak sunlight peeked between the towering firs. Marlowe's chauffeur rounded a corner, and the sprawling gray estate came into view, stretched out across the hillside like a huge stone animal in repose.

A gray-haired butler met Jericho at the door. He seemed as if he'd come with the house as much as the furniture and trees. "I'll tell Mr. Marlowe you've arrived, Mr. Jones," he said, disappearing up the massive, red-carpeted staircase, which was backlit by the most impressive set of stained-glass windows Jericho had ever seen outside a church. Moments later, a shiny, pressed Marlowe bounded down those stairs with the energy of a boy.

"Jericho! Welcome to Hopeful Harbor! Leave your suitcase here. Ames'll see to it. Let me show you around."

Marlowe led a wide-eyed Jericho down a long, chandelier-lit hallway whose walls boasted Chinese vases on pedestals, expensive-looking paintings of somber ancestors, and a wooden, gold-leafed coat of arms with a crowned, upright lion at its center under the motto VICTORIA SINE TERMINO: Victory without end. In the billiards room, a bust of Caesar stared down from a long marble mantel while another of Hannibal topped a tall stack of books, all of them about conquerors. There was a dining room the size of a football field where two maids vigorously buffed the silver laid out in a neat line across the gleaming table fit for a king's court. Jericho had thought that the museum was the most impressive place he'd ever seen. But it was no match for Hopeful Harbor. As they passed from room to room, Jericho kept his eyes open for a possible card reader, but so far, he'd seen nothing.

Back on the first floor, Jericho stopped outside a long room that held a dozen iron beds. "What's this?"

"We opened the estate to some soldiers during the war. There wasn't adequate housing. It was the patriotic thing to do. You know, I don't believe anyone's stayed in this room since." Marlowe barked out a hearty laugh. "Jericho, there are just too many rooms in this house—I've forgotten half of them!"

Marlowe showed Jericho a dizzying number of other rooms before ending the tour in a tasteful library.

"What do you think?" Marlowe asked.

"Nice castle," Jericho said.

Marlowe laughed. "Well, every man's home *is* his castle, they say. But I saved the best for last."

Marlowe tipped down two books on the third shelf of a bookcase, and it opened, revealing a secret lift. A grinning Marlowe ushered Jericho inside.

"This is my crowning glory," he said, his fingers trailing over the golden panel of buttons—B, 1, 2, 3, and S—before selecting the B. The lift descended, and the doors opened again onto a long, shadowy corridor with steel doors lining each side.

Why steel? Jericho wondered.

"This is where the magic happens," Marlowe said, leading Jericho to the first door on the right. Inside was a shining, white-tiled laboratory that seemed as if it had sprung forth from the pages of Jules Verne. Elaborate contraptions and strange equipment filled the cavernous space. One half of the room had been set up as an operating theater. A sheet-covered hydraulic table sat in the center of the room beneath a spiderlike array of strong lights. Beside it, a smaller metal table held a collection of syringes and vials on a tray, as well as a glass-fronted cabinet that Jericho thought might be an autoclave for sterilizing equipment. The whole arrangement made him very nervous.

"This is the birthplace of the future," Marlowe said, barely able to contain his pride. "It's also where you'll be spending most of your time over the next few weeks as we ready you for your victory lap at the Future of America Exhibition. But there's time for this later. Come. You must be famished."

Back in the lift, Jericho pointed to the buttons. "What is the *S* for?"

"Solarium. There's one on the roof."

When Jericho had lived with Will at the Bennington, he'd often escape to the roof to think and to read and to feed the pigeons. From there, he could see the great steel backbone of the city and feel that he was joined to it. He wondered what he could see from the top of Marlowe's estate.

"Could we see it?" Jericho said.

"I'm afraid the solarium is off-limits," Marlowe said in a tone that did not invite further questioning.

Jericho and Marlowe sat in the heated sunroom eating their ham sandwiches with tall glasses of cold milk. The sandwiches, smeared with mayonnaise and sweet pickle relish, were delicious, and Jericho ate two.

"Good appetite." Marlowe grinned. "That's good. Healthy." He trained his blue-eyed gaze on Jericho. "What do you remember about the Daedalus program?"

"It cured me. It cured a lot of us. Made us all stronger, faster. And then it reversed. Drove most of the men mad. Made them violent or catatonic. It killed many of them." Jericho paused. "Or it drove them to kill themselves."

Jericho slugged back some of his milk. He kept his eyes on Marlowe.

"Like your friend Sergeant Leonard." Marlowe nodded. He looked sad. "It was one of the darkest moments of my life. All those men. I wanted so much to save them. To make them whole. When it reversed, I was devastated. I felt personally responsible."

"Perhaps because you were personally responsible."

Marlowe winced. "Still want to punish me?"

"No. I just want you to take accountability."

"It was my fault," Marlowe said. "And I've never stopped regretting it. I've spent the past decade trying to fix my mistakes."

Jericho softened. "And *have* you fixed them?"

Marlowe's eyes gleamed. "I think so. I'm much closer to a cure. Which is why I wanted your help, Jericho. You are the lone survivor of the Daedalus program. You can be the key to a cure for so many diseases."

"You blackmailed me into it."

"Yes. And I'm sorry. I want you to know now that it's your choice. You can leave at any time. I am not telling you what to do. I'm asking for your help—not just for me and Marlowe Industries, of course, but for the country. You'd be helping everyone." Marlowe leaned forward, his eyes glowing with some inner light. "You're some sort of evolutionary jump! You are, quite literally, the Übermensch. That gunshot wound you took to your chest, it should've killed you. Instead, the wound healed in record time. Imagine: Superior strength and mental fitness. No illness! You'll age more slowly. When your friends are suffering the aches and pains of forty-five, you'll still look and feel like a man in his prime."

"That sounds lonely," Jericho said.

"Well. If I can isolate the cause, that serum will be available to more than just you."

"What do I have to do?"

"First, there's the new and improved serum. I've been perfecting it for years. All it needs to be perfect is a few drops of your blood mixed in and put through my patented purification system."

Jericho winced. "How much of my blood?"

Marlowe pushed the concern away with a wave of his hand. "Oh, not much at all. A few vials should suffice until I figure out how to duplicate it. Then there'll be physical endurance tests, of course. And mental tests as well, to see if we can push past normal human limits into superhuman strengths, into areas of the mind where we've never been able to reach before. It's a new frontier! And you and I are the pioneers staking our claim. In a few weeks' time, everyone will know your name, Jericho."

Jericho drank his milk. "What if people find out about…" He pounded his chest.

Marlowe looked around. He lowered his voice. "They won't if you don't say anything. The machinery inside you saved your life, Jericho. It didn't change who you are."

And that, more than anything, was what Jericho needed to hear.

"Is there anything you need to make your life here more comfortable? Anything at all. Name it," Marlowe said, and Jericho had to smile. Everything Marlowe did was big. Even his promises. Especially his promises.

"I'd like to be able to write to Evie."

"The Diviner niece of my long-lost enemy," Marlowe said coolly as he cut a second sandwich in two with an engraved silver butter knife that mostly mangled the job of it. "All right, then. I'll have Ames bring around stationery and a typewriter. But the testing that happens here is strictly confidential, Jericho. I'm afraid all of your correspondence must be reviewed first. Part of Marlowe Industries policy."

Jericho hadn't counted on that. His letters to Evie and the others would need to be coded in some way.

"For the next few weeks, this"—Marlowe gestured to the room with the butter knife—"the house, the grounds, the woods—is your whole world. You'll not be permitted to leave. You are our prize, and we have to keep you pure." Marlowe beamed and bit into his sandwich.

※

Jericho settled into his room. It was grand, with a four-poster bed worthy of a king. He spread his long body out on it diagonally, taking up as much of the bed as possible. He scissored his arms and legs, laughing. So much space!

Do not stay....

Startled, Jericho jolted upright and leaped to his feet.

"Hello?" he called to the empty room. It had been a woman's voice, whispery and urgent. He opened the door and stuck his head out, peering left and right down the wing's long, deserted hallway.

"Hello?" he said again, but there was no answer. He was alone.

Shaking it off, Jericho drew himself a bath, luxuriating in the deep tub, which he filled with fresh hot water twice just because he could and because there was no one—not Will or Sam or Evie—waiting for their turn. When he returned to his room, a bit pruny from his long soak, a new-model Underwood typewriter and a fresh stack of stationery sat atop the desk. Jericho dressed quickly and threaded a sheet of the fine paper around the typewriter's cylinder and began a note.

```
Dear Evie,
     I hope this letter finds you well. How
is everything at the museum? I imagine
Will is still pacing the floor and
cataloging his ghost objects. Just as I'm
certain Sam is still short.
```

That part didn't require code. *Take that, Sam.*

> I've just arrived at Hopeful Harbor
> and am settling in fine. Mr. Marlowe
> informs me that all correspondence is
> reviewed to make certain I'm not giving
> away important Marlowe Industries
> secrets. You might keep that in mind
> when writing unless you want the details
> of your wild parties to end up in the
> newspapers. Please give my regards to
> everyone. I'll write as soon as I have
> anything worth reporting.
>
>   Fondly,
>   Jericho

Jericho placed his elbows on the desk and brought his fists together, resting his chin across the little trough created by his knuckles as he considered his thoroughly ordinary letter. He wished he had Memphis's skill with words or a fraction of Sam's charm. He wished for much more these days, and had ever since Evie had shown up, bursting with ambition. Her appetite for life had unearthed the dreamy boy he'd been before he'd taken sick and nearly died. Before he'd been cast off to the state by his family. After that betrayal—first by his body, then by his mother and father—he hadn't allowed himself to wish for much.

No, Jericho realized quite suddenly as he watched the weak sun trying to make its presence felt behind the thin cover of clouds on the other side of the leaded-glass window. For most of his eighteen years, he'd been guarding against the brutality of disappointment. This time at Hopeful Harbor was a new start, then. A chance to become the hero of his own life. Perhaps this experiment of Marlowe's would free him at last from the secret fear that he didn't deserve happiness.

He'd start tomorrow by working at improving his letter writing, because, ye gods, another one like this, and he'd put Evie straight to sleep. Chuckling over that, Jericho tucked the note into an envelope, addressed it, and left it for the morning's mail.

Most of the gloom had burned away, leaving a blue sky patched with gray above the rounded backs of the distant mountains. It was a fine afternoon for a walk, and so Jericho wandered into the velvety woods surrounding the property. A hawk circled far above, flying higher until it was an outline against the sun-drenched clouds. Down in the cover of trees, it was dim and quiet except for the rustlings of animals. The heels of Jericho's boots sank into the leafy thatch with a satisfying *thwick*, and for a moment, with the smell of pine and earth so close, he was reminded of his childhood on the farm. Were the men tilling the soil for spring planting now? Was his mother letting the lambs out to pasture? Did she and his brothers ever think of Jericho, or had time erased him from their lives the way a river recuts the shape of the bank till its original contours are forgotten?

He looked back to see the faint line of his footprints in the soft earth, a small marker of his quiet presence. "I will not be erased," he said to the silence of the forest. His words echoed back to him: "*not be erased, be erased, rased, rase.*"

Farther in, the woods thinned. There were smaller, newer trees here, and some spots where the pine and birch had burned down to nothing more than blackened sticks. Curious, Jericho pressed on, coming to a large clearing that bordered a lake. The area was charred and flattened, as if a great fire had roared through once upon a time.

Soft voices carried on the wind. Jericho whirled around, searching for the source.

"Hello?" he called. "Is someone there?"

Silence. Maybe he wasn't supposed to be here. What if this part was restricted? The feathery-distant conversations returned with the wind. Laughter. Muffled talking. And just underneath, a faint thread of music: "*Pack up your troubles in your old kit bag, and smile, smile, smile!*"

"Hello?" Jericho called again.

Whispers whipped through the forest with the force of a wind gust, everywhere at once, Jericho at the eye of a sound storm. From the corner of his eye, Jericho caught movement in the trees. He whirled around—"Who's there!" he demanded, and all at once, the whispering din, the fluttering movement, was gone, as if it had been sucked from the world and contained in a jar. He hadn't been able to make out what the whispers said, but deep in his gut, he had the same foreboding he'd felt when trapped inside John Hobbes's murder house: Some memory of bad death lingered here. A silent scream seeking release. And then, very faintly, he heard a last, soft echo on the wind: *"The time is now!"*

Jericho ran back the way he came and didn't stop until he was safely inside the mansion.

That night, Jericho lay in the kingly bed in the room Marlowe had arranged for him and reflected on his strange encounter in the clearing. It had felt as if he'd trespassed on holy ground and was being asked to bear witness, though to what, he couldn't say. He wished that Evie were down the hall so that he could knock at her door with a *You won't believe what happened to me today...*. Jericho rolled onto his stomach, only then realizing how utterly exhausted he was. It had been a long day of travel. Most likely, that accounted for what had happened in the woods. Just before he fell deeply asleep, Jericho heard a woman's soft crying, but he was so tired even that was suspect.

He dreamed he stood in the charred ruins of the forest. The song he'd heard that afternoon came to him: *"Pack up your troubles in your old kit bag, and smile, smile, smile!"* Staticky light lit the sky, splitting the dark clouds like a serrated knife. The wind picked up, blowing dirt into Jericho's face. He spat and swatted at his face, recoiling as his fingers came away streaked with blood. Blood seeped up from the ground in thick, oozy puddles. It streamed down the hillside and eddied at his feet. Hands reached up from the blood and clutched at his trouser cuffs. Jericho tried to run away from the horror, but the hands' grip was strong. With a cry, he broke free and ran. The blood flowed past like a river. The music was everywhere. *"While you've a lucifer to light your... light your... you've a lucifer... a lucifer... lucifer... lucifer..."*

The sky was tearing apart. Flocks of screeching birds poured out in a wave. And from inside the tear, Jericho heard an insect drone that made his very soul quake. And underneath it all was a machinelike sound, like an automated heartbeat fueled by screams of pain and terror. *What was that?*

In front of him was the faint impression of a girl with a long braid. Her brown eyes were huge with some unnameable dread. Her voice was like a memory that had taken years to reach him: *"Help... please..."*

And then Sergeant Leonard stepped out from inside the blighted hollow of a decomposing tree crawling with flies. His face was white as a grease-painted actor's in a motion picture; dark shadows circled his black eyes. "Hey, kid. Remember me? Your old friend?"

Jericho moaned in his sleep.

Behind his thin lips, Sergeant Leonard's teeth were rotten. "You're behind enemy lines, soldier. Abort your mission. Before it's too late."

※

The following morning, Ames brought Jericho his breakfast on a silver tray. Jericho didn't fully remember his dreams, only that he'd had them and they'd been disturbing.

"Good morning, sir. I trust you slept well."

"Yes," Jericho said, because that was what he was supposed to say.

"Mr. Marlowe will call for you in an hour. Shall I draw you a bath?"

"Thank you."

Jericho ate his breakfast, took his bath, dressed, and read from *Walden*: *I went to the woods because I wished to live deliberately . . . and see if I could not learn what it had to teach, and not, when I came to die, discover that I had not lived.* In an hour, as promised, Marlowe knocked at his door.

"Are you ready to make history?"

And there was something about the way Marlowe said it, with the full confidence of his optimism, that buoyed Jericho's spirits. He recalled the promise he'd made to himself the day before. This was his chance to banish the banal fear that lurked in his depths and prove himself heroic. To live deliberately.

Jericho closed the book. "Yes. I'm ready."

Marlowe smiled. "Then follow me."

※

"Roll up your sleeve, please, and lie down on the table," Marlowe instructed.

Jericho did as he was told, but his earlier enthusiasm dimmed. The laboratory's hydraulic table had wrist and ankle restraints. He had a visceral memory of all that had come before—the paralysis, the iron lung, the

223

Daedalus program—which made his heart thud hard and fast. *Be your own hero*, he thought. Jericho lay perfectly still, blinking up at the surgery lights as Marlowe plunged in the needle, pulling out three vials of blood. To this, he added a milky liquid, which curlicued through the red like the weak tendrils of a young plant trying to take root. Marlowe pressed rubber sealings into the glass tubes and secured them in holes anchored inside a small brass box of a machine. A tiny glass door allowed Jericho to view the proceedings from where he lay.

"Here we go," Marlowe said. He flipped a series of switches along the front panel, and an accordion pump attached to the side whooshed up and down, faster and faster, squealing with the effort. The machine glowed with increasing warmth. Staticky filaments of blue electricity flickered behind the glass, mesmerizing Jericho. At last, Marlowe shut it down; the machine whined into silence again. Smoke poured out as Marlowe opened the door with a rag. The serum had become an inky blue, a night sky captured in glass.

"What is that stuff?" Jericho asked. He hoped he didn't sound as nervous as he felt.

Marlowe beamed. "The Future of America." He came around and buckled the heavy restraints tightly across Jericho's wrists and ankles. "Just a precaution. The serum could make you a bit rowdy at first. Not to worry."

Marlowe leaned over Jericho, his face blocking the bright light, and Jericho had a vivid memory of seeing him for the first time. Jericho had been a young, frightened boy lying inside Jake's iron lung prototype after the infantile paralysis, and the great man had promised to make him walk again. At the time, Jake Marlowe had seemed like an all-powerful god.

"Jericho?"

"Yes?"

The light behind Marlowe threw shadows across his handsome face. "Let's make history, shall we?"

With that, Marlowe plunged the hypodermic into Jericho's arm.

Serum rushed through Jericho's veins, cold at first, but then warm and warmer still. Sweat dotted his forehead and upper lip.

"What do you feel?"

Fear. Confusion. A need to run. "I…uh…Fight or flight," Jericho said, panting. "I-I want up. Can you let me up?" Jericho's muscles tensed. The table rattled.

Marlowe's voice was reassuring. "It's okay. It'll pass. Give it a minute."

A minute? He wouldn't last five more seconds. It was too warm. It made his heart race. Jericho thought he would crawl out of his skin. He yanked at the restraints, nearly coming off the table.

"Jericho! Fight through it. Come on!" Marlowe shouted.

Fight it *how*? *Be your own hero be your own…* But the intensity clawed at his insides, challenging him. He was as restless as that blue electricity inside the machine. He needed to remove the fear. Unclench his thoughts. Calm. What would calm him?

Evie. He thought of Evie. The two of them soaring above the fairgrounds up in Brethren on the Ferris wheel. The late-afternoon autumn light catching the halo of her loose hair as she laughed and leaned forward, never back, as if she could catch the wind in her arms and hold it. *Evie. Evie. Evie.* The tension in his muscles eased. His fingers flattened. He was a passenger floating down the river of his own body.

"Jericho?"

"Calm. I'm calm."

"Good. Good."

The calm edged into exhilaration and euphoria, like the first swoop of that Ferris wheel. He suddenly felt as if he could do anything—chop down forests, build a cabin or three, hunt deer and wear their skins, conquer new worlds, live as a god; all of it felt like a birthright promised him. The exhilaration told him he could pursue this happiness forever and ever, amen. Jericho liked this new sensation. He liked it very much.

"I'm going to loosen the restraints now, Jericho. All right?"

Yes, yes! Let me loose on the world! "Fine," Jericho said.

Marlowe unbuckled the leather and helped Jericho to a sitting position and bandaged his arm.

"How do you feel?" Marlowe asked, regarding Jericho quizzically.

How did he feel? Like sunshine lighting the tips of summer grass on a June morning. Like a barn dance in full swing or the morning he'd kissed Evie on the roof of the Bennington as dawn clawed its way up the sides of Manhattan's ambitious skyline. He felt gloriously, completely, marvelously alive.

"Good," he said, a little breathless.

Marlowe's brows came together. "Just good?"

Jericho laughed. "Great. I feel great! Fantastic, in fact."

"Attaboy!" Marlowe's grin was a match for the new, expansive joy inside Jericho. If this was the future Marlowe envisioned, Jericho could get used to it. He stumbled off the table and Marlowe caught him.

"Ho! Careful there. You might be a bit woozy at first. That'll get better with time and more serum. Come on. Let's start seeing what you can do."

Marlowe put Jericho through his paces. Jericho pressed a heavy set of iron barbells above his head forty times, holding them up on the last go for a solid five minutes. Push-ups were no trouble. Jericho performed five hundred of them; it seemed like nothing. He wasn't even winded. While Marlowe drove his protégé through a battery of endurance tests, he'd ask Jericho what he felt:

"Now?"

"Awake. Alive. God, so alive!"

Marlowe beamed. "Keep going."

At last, they'd finished their routine for the day, three hours of intensive physical training. But Jericho's blood still called to him: *More.*

"I think I need to run," he said, chest heaving with pent-up excitement.

"All right, Übermensch. There are miles of grounds. Go run off some of that incredible energy," Marlowe said, patting Jericho on the back.

Jericho stood on the front lawn of Hopeful Harbor. Which way to go? Another hawk circled overhead, flying toward the long line of forest. Jericho grinned. He'd give that bird a race. Jericho faced the forest and set off at a clip. Dodging trees was effortless. It was almost as if he could sense them before seeing them, and his sharpened reflexes took over, allowing him to avoid collisions easily. He chased the hawk's path. The shrubs blurred to blobs of green as Jericho picked up more speed. Wind whined in his ears. Ahead, a towering bank of jagged rocks poked up, demanding caution. Jericho did not slow. In the next second, he was airborne. He'd leaped them without breaking stride. It felt as if this was what he was born for. His body had never been more alive. The hawk. For one glorious still moment,

Jericho and the hawk occupied the same space in the air. Their eyes locked. Bird. Man. No. Not man. Übermensch. Jericho stretched out his arms and lay back, letting himself fall back to earth. His feet disturbed the ground as he landed. Jericho stopped to admire the deep impressions of footprints. "Thus spoke Zarathustra."

Jericho made a fist, not out of fear but of defiance. It was strong and good. Clean, pine-scented air filled his lungs. The hawk settled nearby. It cocked its head, regarding him not as a man but as an equal. Jericho could feel this. He could feel it! Sun broke through the clouds. It fuzzed the brush-stroke tops of the tall pines with gold. Laughing, Jericho tipped his face toward the sky, drinking in the sun till he felt drunk on its promise.

*

Every day, Jericho ate breakfast and reported to the underground laboratory. They took his blood, and a little while later, they returned with an injection of the mysterious blue serum. They covered his eyes and placed him under a sunlamp and gave him radiation therapy with an X-ray machine. Then there were the endurance tests: push-ups, boxing, running, swimming. They tested him against heat and cold. Gave him complex puzzles to solve. Every day, Jericho noticed significant improvement. He'd come to look forward to it all, waiting for that exhilarating rush as the serum grabbed hold and shook him from the inside, told him who and what he could be if he was willing.

Whenever Jericho had a free moment, he made his way through the house carefully, searching for the card reader, crossing each room off his mental list. He felt a little guilty doing so. Marlowe had been nothing but nice to him; more than nice—he'd seen to Jericho's every need. Even though he wasn't really doing anything except looking, he couldn't help feeling that it was a betrayal somehow. But he'd promised Evie, and Jericho kept his promises. So far, he'd explored ten of the mansion's many rooms but had had no luck. Still, he knew the machine was there somewhere. He couldn't explain why he knew, just that he did. It was strange, but since the experiments, Jericho's senses had all been heightened, along with his strength and his appetite. His vision was phenomenal. He could see a spot on the road nearly a quarter mile away and make out the model of the car from up on the hill. When a squirrel or rabbit scuttled through the grass, Jericho sensed the animal by its musk before it ever made an appearance. Even his hearing had become more acute. Lying on his bed, he'd once heard the slightly muffled voices of the servants in the kitchen and could pick out whole phrases (an Irish maid named Kathleen had a bit of a crush on Jake, and the housekeeper, Mrs. Billings, upbraided her for being "a foolish girl with foolish notions" who should "remember her place." "But anything can happen here; it's not like back home," Kathleen had answered. Mrs. Billings had scoffed, "Fairy tales, my girl.")

Jericho had gotten in the habit of taking breakfast with Marlowe first thing in the morning before his physical regimen and the testing began. During these morning meetings, Marlowe was usually upbeat and friendly. Jericho had begun to look forward to their time together, talking about books and history. As much as Jericho cared about Will, he'd found him remote. Jericho and Will were both quiet and scholarly, and that made it harder for them to really talk. Their conversations were often filled with awkward silences or sentences that hung in the air. Jericho hadn't realized till now how lonely it had made him feel. In that way, it was a relief to be with Jake, who was never short on conversation. He'd dig into his eggs with a chipper "So, Jericho, what did you think of that book I lent you?" "Jericho, who do you like better: Charlie Chaplin or Buster Keaton?" "Jericho, I've got the most brilliant idea—let's take the Duesenberg out for a spin." "Jericho, have you taken a gander at the art in the ballroom? There's a Renoir I think you'd like."

Against his better judgment, Jericho was coming to like Marlowe.

One morning, as they sat laughing over a story Jake told about meeting a bear in the woods—"The same bear Will uses to hang his hat on now?" "The very same one!"—Jericho grew bolder.

"What do you know about Project Buffalo?" he asked, biting into a square of toast.

Marlowe's fork halted in midair. All mirth was gone. "Where did you hear that?"

"Some old letters of Will's at the museum."

"Project Buffalo was a mistake," Marlowe said, and scooped up a forkful of egg.

Jericho swallowed down his toast. "I heard you invented some swell machines during that time, though," Jericho said, still fishing. "Ghost measuring equipment. Diviner testing machines—that Metaphysickometer? Even punch code card readers."

Marlowe's easy demeanor shifted to something hard and cold. "I don't talk about Project Buffalo. Is that understood?" Jericho nodded. Marlowe's easy smile returned. "Now. Eat up. You'll need your strength for today."

In the afternoon, Marlowe knocked at Jericho's door. "I'm heading to town for a few hours. Anything I can bring you?"

"No, thank you. I think I'll take a nap, if it's all the same," Jericho said. He forced a yawn to back up his lie.

"Of course. Well, then. See you at dinner. We'll resume our testing this evening."

Jericho listened for the crunch of automobile wheels on the gravel outside, and then he slipped through the sprawling mansion, trying doors and peeking through keyholes. There were plenty of unoccupied bedrooms and old parlors, a billiards room, and a servants' wing. The house had a lonely air to it, as if it had been emptied of joy long ago, and all that remained were the ghosts of happiness. If Evie were here, she'd most likely want to read everything. He could just imagine her mischievously grabbing some priceless object from a shelf as if it were nothing and diving right into its mysteries without fear. Now, Evie lived full out. Was that part of what attracted him to her? That she had qualities he lacked? Thinking about Evie stirred lust in Jericho. Since the serum, he'd been having more fantasies about her. He imagined taking her in his arms, slipping down her dress, his mouth moving across the curve of her neck and...

He was in an embarrassing state now. He took several steadying breaths and decided he'd better go back to his room and take care of the situation. But he took a wrong turn and found himself wandering into a part of the estate Marlowe hadn't shown him, where all the furniture was still covered by white sheets like a summer lodge closed for the off-season. He heard a commotion and followed the sound to a large bathroom where two men in gray suits had hold of a haunted-looking woman in a nightgown who struggled weakly against their hold.

"Say, what's going on here?" Jericho said.

One of the men looked up, glaring at Jericho for just a second before correcting it with a pained smile. "A mental patient Mr. Marlowe's trying to help. Tough case."

The woman's dark hair was half out of its braid. She reminded him a little of the woman he'd seen in his strange dream. "Help me, please!" she pleaded.

"Go on, now. Give the poor girl her dignity," one of the men said. His voice was full of sympathy, but he had a firm grip on the woman's arm, and Jericho's brain tried to make sense of those two inconsistencies. His gut told him something wasn't quite right, but he had no reason not to believe what the men were telling him. He backed away and let them pass by.

"Tell my sister I am here!" the woman called to Jericho over her shoulder.

"Now, now, Anna. You're only hurting yourself," one of the dark-suited men tutted. They were outright dragging her now, her heels thudding a protest against the wooden floors.

"I say my name! Anna!" the woman cried, her voice strained to breaking. "Anna Provenza, Anna Provenza, Anna Provenza!"

A BETTER AMERICA

1917
Department of Paranormal
Hopeful Harbor, NY

Rotke and Will walked through the estate's lush gardens. It was coming up on spring. Early pink flowers pushed through the green caul of their buds. But Rotke was worried. "You haven't told him yet, have you?"

Will stopped to watch a sparrow building a nest on the limb of an oak. "It'll be the end of our friendship. Jake is not accustomed to losing."

Rotke peered up at him, and Will lost himself in her deep brown eyes. He had never known anyone who could make him feel like both a useless schoolboy and a lion at the same time.

"Don't wait too long and let him find some other way, my love." She kissed him gently and smiled. "Mrs. William Fitzgerald. I like the sound of that."

The Founders Club fellows were leaving Jake's library as Will entered. He nodded curtly as they passed by.

Seeing Will, Jake grinned and waved him over. "Ah! Here's my favorite ghost explorer now. You're just in time. Ames has brought around some delicious lemonade."

"What was that about?" Will asked, taking a seat. He put up a hand to the lemonade and rolled a cigarette instead.

"I thought you didn't like to think too much about where our money comes from." Jake poured himself a glass of lemonade from a crystal decanter. "They wanted a report on Project Buffalo. That's their right, since they funded it."

"I don't like them," Will grumbled, striking a match.

"Eugenics, Will. The scientific eradication of inferior traits for a better America. That's the future."

"That's not science, Jake. You know that. Or you used to know it."

"I've changed my mind. All these foreigners coming into the country, polluting our ideals. This war with Germany." He shook his head. "Fix the bloodline and you fix our troubles. We'll build a superior race of Americans."

"What about Margaret? What about Rotke?" Will challenged. His heart was beating fast. He had to tell Jake. He would tell Jake. He—

"Margaret is a pot stirrer. Always seeing trouble." Jake sighed as if exasperated by a tantruming child. "But I've already begun working on Rotke."

A chill passed through Will. "You've...wait. What do you mean?"

From his pocket, Jake fished out a vial of blue serum. "I've isolated the Diviner strain. And I've cleansed her blood of Jewishness."

"What the hell are you talking about, Jake?"

"I've been injecting her with the purification serum for weeks now."

Will was reeling. "You said you were giving her iron. For her anemia!"

"I was. But I was also correcting."

Will leaped up, pacing the same square of carpet. "For Chrissakes, Jake, she doesn't need *correcting*! She's a human being!" The terrifying image of Rotke's frequent nosebleeds swam in Will's head. He whirled toward Jake, pointing an accusing finger. "I swear, if you've hurt her..."

Marlowe glowered. "I would never hurt Rotke. She's my fiancée, Will!" He stared into his lemonade. "Or she will be again soon enough, when this whole war business is over and she comes back to me. It's her Diviner nature. She's too sensitive. I'll help her with that, too."

"My god. Your ego."

"I'm changing the future, Will! I'm making our nation great. The power and envy of the world. That was always the aim of Project Buffalo!"

Anger uncoiled inside Will and reared its head, eager to bite. "She's not coming back to you, Jake. She's never coming back."

Marlowe chuckled. "Attaboy! There's that Fitzgerald optimism! Thanks for your belief in me, old sport."

"She's not coming back to you because...because she's marrying me."

This time, Marlowe's laugh exploded out of him. "Oh, Will. You and Rotke?"

"Ask her."

"Come now, Will. You're being ridiculous."

Will balled his fists at his sides. "Ask. Her."

Jake's mouth parted in shock. "My god. You're serious."

The punch had landed. Marlowe, the golden boy, sagged against the mantel, vulnerable at last. The anger Will had felt earlier left him, taking his bravery with it. In its place was a sick emptiness. He adjusted his spectacles. "I'm sorry. I...we wanted to tell you, but..."

"You were my best friend, Will."

"I'm still your fr—"

"No. No more. Never again."

"Jake—"

Jake drained his lemonade and tossed the glass into the fireplace. It shattered into pieces. Will flinched. There were tears in Jake's eyes. "You should be very happy, William. You've finally become what you love most: From this day forward, you are a ghost to me. I don't even see you."

THE FORGOTTEN

On the steamer ride to Ward's Island, the sky was the color of slate, the threat of rain sewn into every cloud. Mist curled off the water in great tufts as the boat bounced mercilessly over the choppy East River. Memphis gripped the railing and kept his eyes on the distant serpentine curve of the Hell Gate Bridge and prayed for his stomach's contents to stay put.

Beside him, a relaxed Henry pulled the briny air deep into his lungs. "Mmmm. Love that smell. Reminds me of my time playing piano on the steamboats that went up and down the Mississippi."

They hit a swell. Memphis moaned.

Henry chuckled. "Kind of funny that a healer gets seasick."

Memphis spat into the water. "Hilarious."

"It's miserable to be seasick," Evie said, leaning against the ferry railing. "Why, once, I got splifficated on a boat and upchucked all over the deck. And I'd just had a good steak, too."

"Please," Memphis begged, putting a hand to his roiling stomach.

"Golly. Sorry," Evie said. "Here."

She removed her glove and put a cold hand at the base of his neck, and after the shock of it, Memphis began to feel slightly better. Some of what he felt was seasickness. The rest was fear. There had been a small flock of reporters to see them off, all of them shouting questions as the Diviners boarded the boat:

"How do you plan to get rid of the ghosts?"

"Whaddaya say to folks who think you're all wet to believe in ghosts— that there are no ghosts?"

"Should we be afraid that those ghosts could cross the river and come to Manhattan?"

"How come you're going, Miss Knight?" one of the reporters asked Theta.

"Couldn't let my best pals go without me. Especially after what happened on Evie's show," she answered.

"Say, where's your uncle Will, Evie? How come he's not here?"

"Poor Unc has a terrible cold. I'd hate for him to catch his death of pneumonia. Who'd dust all of the spooky knickknacks then?" Evie lied, getting a few laughs from the newsboys.

In truth, Evie and Will had fought bitterly about the trip. "But why don't you want us to go?" Evie kept saying. "Will, Luther Clayton knows things!"

"Leave that poor man alone!" Will had barked.

And Evie had spat back, "That *poor man* tried to kill me, I'll remind you. I'd like to know why."

"You should stay and continue with your training. That's what's most important."

Evie remained defiant. "We're going."

"Then you're going without me," Will had said with the same defiance, like the two of them had been cut from the same stubborn cloth.

Memphis had purposely kept himself and Isaiah hidden during the reporters' questions. He didn't want their names and faces in the papers, where Papa Charles or Owney Madden might see. Evie had been out front, of course, lapping up the attention. Memphis wasn't always sure what to make of her. One minute, she was self-absorbed and an attention hog, and the next, she was trying to cure his seasickness or looking after Isaiah. When Gabe had been murdered, it was Evie who had wanted to help find Gabe's murderer. In some ways, she was like all those smart set girls who came into the Hotsy Totsy, and at the same time, she was nothing like them.

"Any better?" she asked him now.

His stomach had calmed a bit. "Yeah. Thanks."

"Is that it?" Henry asked, leaning over the ferry railing slightly to get a better look.

Behind the thickening haze, the imposing asylum emerged brick by brick, ward by ward, like some mythological beast willing itself into existence. Rows of windows bled yellow against the murk like infected eyes.

Evie gripped her coat collar tight against her throat. "That's the joint."

The warden waited on the pier, hands clasped tightly at his stomach. Mr. Smith's demeanor wasn't jovial, as it had been the first time he'd met with Sam and Evie. He seemed jumpy and his eyes were bloodshot. "Thank you for coming. I didn't know where else to turn," he said as they disembarked.

"I've arranged for you to speak with several of the patients who claim to have experienced the ghosts, as well as some of our staff. Luther Clayton will not be one of them. I hope you will abide by the rules of decency this time, Miss O'Neill," the warden said, frowning. "We should move quickly, however. They say there's a storm moving in. This way, please."

"Applesauce!" Evie muttered as they fell in behind the warden. "I've simply got to get to Luther!"

"Yeah, and before that storm moves in. I don't like the sound of that," Theta said as they trudged across the swell of land toward the hospital. The air was chilled and damp with no breeze; it clung to their necks and weighted their clothes. The gauzy haze sitting over the island gave everything the appearance of a dream. Clusters of skeletal trees appeared here and there like a memory that would not fully come.

"This place feels bad," Ling said, and struggled forward with her crutches on the mucky path.

Henry frowned up at the forbidding asylum pushing itself into view. "I'll be glad when this is over," he agreed.

Nearby, several prisoners piled quarried stone for a new seawall while two guards with guns watched. The prisoners paused in their work for a moment to watch the spectacle of the Diviners moving past: Memphis and Sam carrying the bulky Metaphysickometer by its iron handles, Evie and Theta dressed to the nines like proper stars, Ling navigating the tricky ground with her crutches, Henry in his straw boater even though it was barely spring, and Isaiah, bringing up the rear, his head swiveling left and right as he tried to take in everything.

Isaiah ran to catch up with his brother and tugged at his sleeve. "We're gonna be gone by nighttime, right?"

"Don't worry, Ice Man. We are leaving here before the sun sets. Even if we gotta swim back."

"If you tried, the cold would kill you," Ling said. "If the cold didn't kill you, the current would. These are some of the most treacherous waters in New York City."

Memphis shook his head. "Well. That's a comfort."

"I read a lot."

"Me, too. One Hundred and Thirty-fifth Street Library," Memphis said, a little cocky.

"Seward Park Library," Ling answered in kind.

"It's like you're picking baseball teams for books," Sam said. The Metaphysickometer was heavy and the chill cut right through Sam's coat. He was eager to get inside. He couldn't help noticing that the island felt different from the last time they'd been there. Something was off.

"There's no birds!" he said at last. "When we were here last time, they were all over the place, chirping like a jazz band. Look around—there's not a one anywhere."

Theta glowered. "Are you saying that to give me the heebie-jeebies? Because if you are, it's working."

"We're almost there." Mr. Smith's voice echoed through the soupy air. Up ahead, he was a ghostly silhouette.

By the time they'd reached the asylum and settled into a gracious visiting room near the back of the main building, the rain, which had started gently, had become a fierce pounding that danced off the roof in angry syncopation. Henry watched it soaking the ground into puddles. "We're certainly stuck here until that lets up," Memphis said.

"Swell. I can't wait to try the tapioca," Sam said.

"Say, it's not so bad," Theta said, shaking the damp from her cloche as she took in the room's homey decor—several fat chairs, a thick carpet, and a coatrack. Two hissing radiators kept the cold at bay. An upright piano occupied the far wall. "I expected worse."

"'Expect the worst' is my motto," Evie said, hanging her coat on the rack. "Saves on disappointment."

"When did you become a cynic?" Sam asked.

Evie smiled. "When I found out I was a little girl."

Sam and Memphis set up the Metaphysickometer on a side table. Sam flipped the switch and thumped at the dials with a flick of his finger, but nothing happened. "Terrific. It doesn't seem to be working. I think the damp got to it."

Henry sat at the piano, plinking out a tune on the tinny keys. "*There's things in the night, out of infernal dreaming,"* he sang. *"Can you hear it now—my internal screaming?"*

Isaiah made a face. "What song is that?"

Henry kept his fingers tripping along the keys. "It's from a new show I'm working on, called *I've Been Eaten by Ghosts with Big Teeth and I'm Very Upset About It.*"

"Nobody's getting eaten by ghosts," Sam promised Isaiah, because he looked worried.

"I told you, all we have to do is interview a few of the patients and poke around a bit, make it look on the level. Once we've talked to Luther, we can leave," Evie assured everyone.

"Well, let's get this show on the road, then," Theta said, peering out at the gloomy, wet skies. "The sooner we can get outta here, the better."

***

They started with the patients first.

"What is your name, please?" Sam asked a nervous woman about his mother's age. She had graying hair done up in braids across the top of her head.

"Mrs. Evelyn Langford," she said. "I'm only here because my husband wanted to be with another woman. He didn't want me anymore. So I stopped eating. And then I couldn't start. It frightened me to eat. The doctors say I have to eat or I won't get any better. I'm trying."

Sam flashed Evie a *what do I do* look over his shoulder.

"Just talk to her," Evie urged.

"You, uh, seen any ghosts, Mrs. Langford?" Sam asked.

"Oh, yes!" She leaned forward. "It was eight nights ago. I was playing Spite and Malice—that's a card game, dear—with Mrs. Lowell, who cheats at cards, but beggars can't be choosers. The lights winked on and off. And I saw a host of spirits standing outside the room, watching us. It got very cold. There were things that happened on this land. Savage, sinister things," she said in ominous tones. "Murder and worse. The land runs with blood. Its heart beats with violence. I can feel it. The spirits rise up from that land. They want us to know! They don't want us to forget!"

"I'll be sure to send a card at Christmas," Sam joked.

Mrs. Langford's face went stony with wounded dignity. "Everybody needs a little help now and then, young man."

"You shouldn't've been so mean," Isaiah said after the nurse had escorted Mrs. Langford back to her room.

"Aw, come on. I was just making a little joke," Sam scoffed. The others stared at him.

"It wasn't funny," Henry said.

"Gee, this is fun," Sam grumbled. "Anybody else having a swell time here at the old asylum?"

"Just call in the next person," Theta said. "I want to get out of here as soon as we can."

They interviewed a nurse named Molly next.

"I was here the night Mrs. Bennett…" Molly looked away. "The night she killed Miss Headley and herself."

"Gee, I'm sorry. That musta been awful," Theta said, patting Molly's hand.

"That's how you behave like a human," Evie whispered to Sam. "Take notes so you can remember."

"Did you know the nurses very well?" Theta asked.

"Oh, yes. Neither one of them would've hurt a fly! We're all terrified now. We won't go anywhere alone. That fog comes around most nights— you can't even see your own hand in front of your face. The patients say there's ghosts inside it. I've heard noises late at night when I'm trying to sleep. The lights blink on and off and the warden says it's the blasting, but who can say?"

"Have the patients said or done anything out of the ordinary?" Ling asked.

"The drawings," Molly said. "They all draw the same thing."

"Could we see those drawings?"

Molly led the Diviners to the art therapy room and opened a drawer, taking out a batch of patients' sketches. The scenes were eerily similar: They all showed the man in the stovepipe hat leading an army of the dead. Above him, the sky crackled with lightning.

"Okay. Now I'm really scared," Theta said.

"There is one patient…" Molly stopped. "Oh. I don't know if I should say."

"Oh, you should say! You should pos-i-tute-ly say," Sam cooed. "I mean, a girl as pretty as you? If I can do anything to keep worry from your door." He grinned and took Molly's hand.

"Charming," Ling muttered.

Molly blushed. "There's a patient. A very disturbed young man, but he's quite a talented artist. Conor Flynn."

"Conor Flynn," Isaiah said. At Memphis's silent urging, he lowered his voice. "Memphis, that's who Mama said we had to protect."

"Tell us about Conor," Evie said to Molly.

"Conor was there in the room when Mr. Roland killed Big Mike and Mary—drew the whole thing even though he said he never turned around once. And he drew what happened with Mrs. Bennett and Miss Headley, too, even though he was upstairs when the murders took place. He's always drawing frightening things. I put some of them away for the doctors to see," the nurse whispered.

"We'd better take a look at those," Evie said.

From deep inside a locked cabinet, Molly retrieved a shirt box. Inside were an array of drawings. Conor was indeed quite talented. He'd drawn a detailed view of the Hell Gate Bridge as seen from a barred window and a study of a chair where the wood grain was so finely rendered it practically leaped from the page. But there were other, more disturbing pictures. In one, a great cloud with the face of an angry skull bore down on the island. In another, he'd captured the ghoulish moment with the two nurses. One of the nurses held a hook, and it seemed as if several bodies fought inside her at once. Evie paused at a drawing of the all-seeing eye symbol. It loomed in the sky like the eye of a god, and all around, floating in its beams, were the bodies of soldiers. There were also several drawings of Luther, and Evie had to wonder: Why was Conor Flynn so interested in Luther Clayton?

"Memphis!" Isaiah said, picking up one of the drawings, a sketch of an old farmhouse with a sagging porch. "I've seen this before. In a vision."

"Excuse me, but could we speak to Conor Flynn?" Evie asked.

Molly shook her head. "I wouldn't recommend it, Miss O'Neill."

"Why not?"

"Conor is a very troubled young man. Before he came to us, he'd been in the boy's refuge from the age of twelve. He lies. He hears voices. He even tried to take his own life."

"Poor kid," Theta said.

"Don't let him fool you, Miss Knight. There's a reason he's in the violent ward."

"What did he do?" Ling asked.

"He killed Father Hanlon."

Memphis's eyebrows went up. "He murdered a *priest*?"

"Father Hanlon worked at the refuge from time to time. One day, he tried to take one of the younger boys for an ice cream. Conor was jealous of the attention shown the boy. He attacked Father with a slice of broken bottle he'd hidden up his sleeve. Sliced clean through his throat. Make no mistake: Conor Flynn is quite dangerous."

"Why would Mama want us to protect a murderer?" Isaiah asked, and Memphis shook his head.

"Still. We'd like to speak with him, please," Evie said.

"Very well. I'll see to it."

An attendant brought Conor to the interview room, and Evie immediately recognized him as the boy who'd spoken to her when she'd come to see Luther. The one who'd tried to warn her about the fog. He was skittish, Evie thought. Like a fawn catching the first acrid warning of an approaching forest fire.

"Hello, Conor," Evie said. "We met once before. Do you remember?"

Conor nodded. "You talked to Luther."

"That's right. Conor, when we were here last time, you said, 'They come in with the fog.'"

"The Forgotten," Conor said.

"Who are the Forgotten? Are they ghosts?"

Conor frowned. "Yeah. But not regular. They can hurt you. They *want* to hurt you." Conor twirled and tugged at his hair. "When the fog comes in, they comes in wit' it. Late at night, after all the boats're gone and we're alone out here. When it's dark. When he tells 'em to come. They crawl in t'rough your mouth like spiders. Spiders laying eggs in your brains. Can't shake 'em out. And then the whisperin' starts. They'll make you do things. Terrible things. They made Mr. Roland kill Big Mike and Nurse Mary and Mr. Potts."

"Why did the Forgotten want to do that?"

Conor shoved his hands beneath his armpits, hugging himself. "*He* makes 'em do it," he said in a paper-thin voice.

"He? Who is he?"

Conor shook his head. "Won't say his name."

"Why not? Does he live on your floor?"

Conor shook his head harder.

"Is it Luther Clayton?" Evie tried.

"What happened to those nurses?" Theta said, redirecting. "Was that the Forgotten, too?"

"Yeah," Conor whispered, fidgeting in his seat, one hand tapping against his thigh in an almost hypnotic rhythm.

"Gee, sport, how do you know that if you weren't there?" Sam said.

"I can hear the dead. In here." He tapped the side of his head. "I hear the dead and I hear the lady's voice, telling me what to do."

"The lady's voice," Sam repeated, glaring at Evie. He motioned to the others to huddle up away from Conor, who was performing some sort of ritual, counting objects over and over. "The lady's voice tells him things? The dead talk to him? Buncha hooey."

Ling frowned. "Don't forget, Sam—I can hear the dead, too."

"That's different."

"Is it?" Ling challenged.

"You think he could be a Diviner, like us?" Memphis asked.

"It's possible," Evie said.

Sam shook his head. "I don't think we should get off the trolley. We came here to find out what we could about Luther. That's all."

"But what if Conor is onto something?" Evie said.

"Or what if Conor is just plain crazy?"

"Just because he's sick doesn't mean he isn't telling us the truth, or his version of it, anyway," Henry said, his voice tight.

"Okay, okay. Don't get hot."

"Then don't tell me what to feel," Henry said through his teeth.

"Why're you so keen on believing this fella, huh?"

"I've got my reasons," Henry said, stepping up to Sam. "Why are you being such a jackass?"

"I wasn't being...say, what's eating you, Henry?" Sam growled.

"I happen to think the people in here are very brave," Henry said, full of fire. "Imagine living each day and not being able to trust your own mind. Imagine having it lie to you, trick you, tell you you're worthless or that the world would be better off without you in it. It would be like...like always hearing an awful radio playing inside your head, one that you can't seem to turn off." He glared at Sam. "Or maybe I'm just 'crazy' for feeling sympathy for them."

"Gee, Hen, I'm sorry—"

But something had come loose inside Henry. He backed away from the others, hands up. "I need to calm down. Going for a walk."

"Hen!" Theta called as Henry stormed out, slamming the door behind him.

Memphis put a hand on her arm. "Might want to let him cool off a bit. At least, I know when I'm sore I need time to myself."

"I really am sorry," Sam said.

"I told you to take notes," Evie chided. "You can make it up to Henry later. Let's get back to Conor." Evie left the huddle. "Conor, can you tell me more about the lady in your head?"

"She's the one tol' me to draw the pictures. Sometimes I can hear her. Other times, I can't. Like something's keeping her from talking to me. She tol' me about keeping him out."

"Is the lady's name Viola?" Isaiah said hopefully.

Conor shook his head, and Isaiah's heart sank.

"Is she talking to you right now?" Ling asked.

"Maybe. Maybe." Conor's demeanor changed like a sudden wind. "What'd they tell you about me? Did they tell you I was a liar? No. I don't care. I don't care, I don't care! I ain't sorry I cut up Father Hanlon. I know I'm s'posed to be, but I ain't. I watched the blood pour over his collar, and I wished him dead a hundred times."

The air felt charged. Dangerous.

"Told you this was a bad idea," Sam said to the others in what he thought was a soft voice. "He doesn't know anything."

"I ain't no liar!" Conor's eyes flashed. And then, quick as a panther, he was up and rushing Sam, pummeling him with fists until Memphis could

243

pull him off and hold him in the chair. Conor's breathing slowed. A glazed look came over his face.

"I'll get the attendant," Theta said, throwing wide the door.

"Conor?" Memphis said, but it was as if the boy had turned the lights out inside himself and was refusing to answer the door.

"Conor?" Isaiah tried, but he wasn't answering. Isaiah took his pencil from his pocket and tucked it into Conor's pocket. "For later. When you need it."

The attendant, a big, burly man, had arrived. "All right, now, Conor. Time to go," he said gently. He helped Conor from the chair, but Conor resisted, balling his fists.

"He'll come tonight—they'll all come! You'll be trapped here and he'll come for you one by one! One by one. All seven. One, two, t'ree, four, five, seven!"

"Let's go, Conor. I know you don't want the restraints." The attendant led Conor by the arm, but he locked his feet and splayed a hand against the doorjamb, refusing to move. He was like a boy all of a sudden, wide-eyed and beseeching.

"Miriam!" he said.

"What did you say?" Sam said, stepping into the hall as the attendant hauled Conor away.

"The lady in my head! Her name is Miriam."

*

"You think it could be my mother?" Sam asked Evie.

"We might've had a chance to ask if *somebody* hadn't been so eager to get rid of him," Evie said.

"I object!"

"On what grounds?"

"On the grounds that I hate to be wrong," Sam said. "But you're right."

Evie smiled. "Music to my ears, Sam Lloyd."

"So the ghosts can possess people, make them do things," Memphis said, mulling over Conor's story. "Why? What do they want? And why are they haunting this place?"

"Pretty sure it's not for the beef stew," Sam said, patting his stomach and wincing.

Memphis made a face. "You ate that?"

Sam shrugged. "I was hungry." He raked a hand through his hair. "Now I gotta figure out a way to talk to Conor."

"Well, you can figure it out after *I* talk to Luther Clayton. That's the whole reason we came here, don't forget," Evie said, pacing.

"Well, thanks to you, they're not gonna let us back in that ward. Could you stop with that back-and-forth? You're making me dizzy. And you remind me of your uncle."

Evie glared. "That's a terrible thing to say."

"So: Don't. Pace." Sam held up his arms in a shrug.

"I can't help it. It's being cooped up in here." Through the barred windows, Evie looked out at the dismal weather. She could see the tinsmithing shop and the barn where some of the male patients tended peacefully to the animals. But that hadn't always been the case here on Ward's Island. Evie could sense it in the walls, like a stifled scream waiting to explode.

Down the hall, singing drifted out of the music therapy room, and Evie was grateful for the distraction of it to drown out the asylum's secret confessions. She wandered down and stood just outside the room, observing. The shell-shocked patients were there. Once again, they faced one another, holding up their hands and staring into their empty palms. As Evie watched, fascinated, one of the men placed an imaginary object on the table. Without pause, another of the patients put his hand on the "object," and after examining it, he transferred it to his left hand. Evie watched for another minute until she realized exactly where she'd seen this scenario before: It reminded her of those soldiers playing cards in her dreams. And then, as one, the men turned their heads toward Evie.

"They never should have done it," they said in unison. They fell to the ground, screaming and writhing as if in great distress. Nurses rushed in to help the men back into their chairs. The men still reached their hands toward Evie. "Help us. Help us. Help us."

Evie staggered down the hall, desperately in need of air. She stumbled outdoors and sucked in a lungful of cold mist. The rain was a solid wall. Evie couldn't even see the pier through it. "Miss O'Neill. Are you all right?"

One of the nurses had followed her outside.

"When is the next ferry back to Manhattan?" Evie asked.

"I'm afraid no one's leaving." The nurse nodded toward the heavy rain. "The storm's getting worse. They've canceled ferry service until tomorrow. You're all stuck here for the night."

☀

Theta sat in the window seat, staring out at the incessant rain. "What's the one thing I made you promise me?" she said on an angry plume of cigarette smoke.

"How was I to know there'd be a storm?" Evie asked. She'd taken up pacing again.

"I don't know, Evil. But I'm blaming you anyway."

"My aunt Octavia's gonna kill me for being out all night with Isaiah," Memphis said from the small table where he played peanut poker with Isaiah, who kept winning. "And whatever's left of me, Papa Charles is gonna take care of when I don't show up for work tonight. I can't even call because the telephone lines are down in this storm."

"There's nobody to feed Archibald," Theta fretted. "He'll be so hungry."

"Who's Archibald?" Sam asked.

"My cat."

"You got a cat?" Isaiah said, excited.

"Yeah. One of the Proctor sisters' brood. I saved him from an untimely death."

"Those old ladies in your building? They're creepy," Ling said.

"They're not," Theta said, and left it. She wanted to tell the others about what had happened with Miss Addie and the ghost. In fact, she'd meant to before, but she suddenly felt protective of the old woman—and of herself. Evie was always chiding Theta for holding on so tightly to her secrets, but secrets had kept Theta safe for years. Ever since she'd left Kansas. She wouldn't know how to stop swallowing down her story if she tried. Besides, most people just wanted to talk about themselves, and if you held your breath, they'd rush in to fill the emptiness.

"Do you think some places just hold on to evil? That you can't paint or wash it away? It lives on, no matter what you build on top," Evie mused, rushing in, just as Theta figured she would.

Isaiah threw his hands in the air. "Are you *trying* to scare the living daylights outta me?"

"Sorry, Isaiah," Evie said. "It's just that ever since we started doing experiments together, I'm a raw nerve. I can barely touch something, and its history starts to whisper to me."

As if to test or torture herself, Evie let her fingers drift from object to object, catching glimpses of their secrets:

"...I only wanted the pain to stop. That's why I swallowed the lye...."

"...There's a great big hole in the middle of me, and no matter how hard I try, I can't fill it. I try to keep the awful, empty sadness out, but it keeps coming back in...."

"...I'm to be committed? On what cause? Because I'm a suffragette? Is it mad to believe that women deserve the same rights as men? To fight against such injustice is bravery, not insanity, sir...."

"...I killed them all. And then I had my supper...."

"Feels like a living tomb. So much sadness and confusion, horror and fear." Evie's fingers skipped lightly along the buckles of a restraining jacket. The hair on her arm prickled as the metal began its whisper-call to her, eager to tell its stories. She yanked her hand away. She did not want to be the confessor to this place's sins.

Lightning flashed at the windows. Thunder ricocheted through the halls, making everybody jumpy. It was nearly half past four, the iron sky deepening toward dusk.

"Those men in the music room were acting out a scene from my dreams. It's always the same: The soldiers. The card game. The Victrola. And then something dreadful happens. They're all killed."

"If that was supposed to make me feel better, it didn't," Theta said.

"Every time I've talked to Luther, he's said the same thing: 'They never should've done it.' In my dreams, James has said it, too. Never should've done what? Who is they?"

"Sheba!" Sam waved to Evie from a doorway. He held up a key. "Who wants to say hi to Luther Clayton?"

"Where did you get that?" Theta asked.

"Stole it off Molly," Sam said. "It's the key to his room."

"So that's why you were cozying up to her," Evie said.

"That, and she's a real tomato."

"Once again, Sam, I don't know if I want to kiss or kill you."

"Better kiss me, then, to make sure," Sam said, and winked.

"Come on, Romeo," Evie said, tugging on Sam's sleeve. "Let's ankle while we can."

"I don't think Isaiah should go," Memphis said, and Isaiah started in with his protests.

"You never let me do anything!"

"I'm the one who has to look out for you," Memphis said.

"I'll stay here with him," Theta said. "I wanna be here for when Henry comes back. He won't know where we are."

"Don't wanna stay here with *her*," Isaiah said.

"Isaiah!" Memphis pointed a finger at his brother. "Apologize."

Isaiah pressed his lips tightly together and stared at the braided rug.

"Isaiah..." Memphis warned.

"It's jake," Theta said, even though it had hurt her feelings. "Go on and talk to Luther."

Memphis narrowed his eyes at Isaiah. "We're gonna talk about this later."

"There's a lot of ground to cover. Luther's ward is all the way in the back," Sam said, looking toward Ling. "You can stay here if you want."

Ling bristled. There had been a lot of walking already. A throbbing ache burned along Ling's muscles and burrowed deep into her spine, but she was afraid of being left behind, afraid of being seen as less than, or not seen at all.

"I'm fine," she said, hoisting herself up on her crutches.

And the four of them set off through the asylum's zigzagging wards toward its farthermost, forgotten realm and Luther Clayton.

☀

Luther was resting in his room.

"Hello, Luther," Evie said. "Remember me? Evie O'Neill?" She took a breath. "James's sister?"

Luther stirred. He inclined his head toward Evie. "You sh-shouldn't have c-c-come. It's n-not s-safe."

"I had to see you again."

"They never should've d-done it."

"I think he's on some kind of medicine," Memphis said. "It might make the reading harder. Maybe I'd better stay close?"

"Okay."

"I'm sorry for this, Luther. But I have to know what happened to you, and to my brother." Evie closed her hand around the watch at his wrist. The whispers started.

And then she was falling deeply into Luther's memory.

WITNESS

There was snow on the ground. A sugary, fairy-tale frost that glittered in the sun. On the frozen lawn of the great house, a dozen soldiers gathered around one of their own as he stood in front of a fat, round searchlight, eyes tightly closed, one hand stretched toward its bulk as if he could grab hold of its incandescence.

"Concentrate," Rotke Wasserman encouraged. She was a slim woman with a heart-shaped face and kind, dark eyes made watery by the cold.

"Yes, Miss." The young soldier recommitted, grimacing with the effort, and in the next second, the bulbs of the searchlight hummed, rising in pitch to a scream before exploding in sparks of light.

"That's extraordinary!" Jake Marlowe cried, clapping the young man on the back. "Extraordinary!"

"Thank you, sir." The soldier looked happy but exhausted. His nose bled. Someone else handed him a handkerchief.

"Thanks, O'Neill," the soldier said.

Evie gasped as her brother came into view. His pocket had been stitched with his name: JAMES XAVIER O'NEILL. He wore an armband embroidered with the radiant eye-and-lightning-bolt symbol.

"This stuff really gonna help us beat the Germans?" James asked.

"If everything goes as planned tomorrow, you men will be the most powerful force on earth," Marlowe assured him.

"How's about that, huh? Ain't that just bully?" The bloody-nosed soldier said later as he flopped onto his mattress in a long room flanked by rows of neatly made beds. "The most powerful men on earth—the new Americans!"

Luther sat on the bed opposite writing a letter. "What was wrong with us before?"

"Aw, Luther. Don't be a wet blanket," another soldier called from his bed, where he polished his boots. "He's making us special. Don't you wanna be special?"

"Sure. I suppose. But…"

"But what?" the boot polisher said, exasperated.

"What do they want us to do with these new powers?" Luther asked.

The bloody-nosed soldier shrugged. "Fight the Germans! Keep our shores safe from the enemy. Win the war. We'll win *all* the wars!"

"I don't think they're being completely honest with us about what they're doing," Luther said.

"That's Uncle Sam!" A soldier laughed. "Need-to-know only."

"It's just…I've been having odd dreams about this fellow in a tall hat."

"Has he got a gray face and a nose sharp as a beak?" James asked.

"Say, I've seen that fella, too!" another soldier said.

The others quickly agreed.

Luther raked a hand through his dark hair. "The dead, they talk to me now, you know, and some of 'em warned me about that man in the hat. They say, 'We shouldn't let him loose or give him too much power.'"

"What does that mean? Let him loose how?"

"I dunno." Luther drummed his pencil against his thigh. "There's this messenger. A bird. Last night, that messenger told me to be careful. Said it was a trap. And then…then they killed that bird."

The others were listening now, afraid.

"Gee, why you got to say such terrible things, Luther? Why you got to be so spooky?"

"I'm only saying, something about this experiment stinks. They're not being on the level with us. About what's on the other side."

"I can tell you what's on the other side—French girls!" One of the soldiers curved his hands through the air in the shape of a woman's body. The gloom was dispelled by talk of sweethearts left behind, of whether or not European girls were "friendly" and loved American boys. Of glory and right and might.

"Always writing, Luther. What do you write about?" One of the other soldiers ripped Luther's letter from him.

"Give that back!" Luther made a grab for it, but the other soldier was bigger and pushed him back easily.

"'Oh, my darling,'" the soldier read aloud to the others. "'I long to hold you in my arms and wish that we were far from here and safe to love…'"

James snatched the letter away. "Come on, Gilroy. Enough."

"You're always protecting him. Saint O'Neill," the big soldier teased. "Come on, read it to us, why don'tcha? Live a little."

James handed the letter back to Luther. "I know what he writes. I don't have to look." He tapped one finger against his temple and smiled.

"Shit, O'Neill. You'll be the best code breaker in the army. Can you read what everybody's thinking?"

"Not always. But often enough." James winked. "So you fellas might want to be careful." James placed a hand on Luther's shoulder. "Don't let them bother you."

Deep in her trance, Evie smiled, happy to know that the brother she remembered as good and kind had been exactly that. But the memory was shifting. There was a forest of tall pines. A partially frozen lake. A soldiers' camp in a clearing. Four soldiers hunched over a game of cards at a small table. The sergeant gazed into a mirror hung from a branch on a tree as he scraped a razor along his strong jaw. On a shorn stump, an old Victrola turned round and round: "*Pack up your troubles in your old kit bag, and smile, smile, smile!*"

Evie had witnessed this scene many times in her dreams. But this, she knew now, was no dream.

One soldier stared at the Victrola. "Faster," he said, his neck tendons straining as he concentrated. The record picked up speed, making the singer's voice go comically high.

The shaving soldier laughed. "Sounds like a buncha hyenas."

"Now, just a minute! We're not supposed to use our powers yet," one of the soldiers at the table called out as he examined the hand he'd been dealt.

With a sigh, the soldier who'd revved up the record slowed it down again. "Just wanted to dance," he said, breaking into a little soft shoe.

Another soldier lit his cigarette with a flame at the end of his finger. "Handy," he said, and blew it out. "Hey, Luther! What's with the long face? Come join the party!"

Luther stood off to one side, staring into the expanse of forest, his hands in his pockets. "I can't shake the bad feeling."

"C'mon now, Luther. They shot us up with super serum," the shaving man said. He flicked shaving cream from his razor into the bushes, giving them a coating like snow. "We're invincible! We don't have to be afraid—it's the enemy that should be afraid of us!"

The soldier with the fiery fingers leaned back in his chair. "Luther, you honestly think Mr. Marlowe and the United States Army would do anything bad to us? We are the one forty-four!"

"The one forty-four!" the others responded.

"I'm not saying they're doing it on purpose," Luther explained. "I'm saying they don't realize what they're getting themselves into."

"And you do?"

"It's that stuff they put inside me. Gives me a sense for what's going to happen before it happens."

"*Pack up your troubles in your old kit bag, and smile, smile, smile!*" the soft-shoe dancer sang to Luther, and soon, all the men except for James joined in with the teasing.

"Aw, lay off, boys," James tried, but the others only sang harder, finally convulsing into fits of laughter.

Luther exchanged a furtive glance with James, then set off for the trees. Behind him, he heard the sergeant calling, "Aw, Luther! Come on back down after you've finished sulking!"

Luther tromped through the still pines, coming at last to a hilly mound surrounded by sentinel trees. A confectioner's dusting of snow dappled the spongy pine. A moment later, here came James. "Luther…"

Luther's breath came out in smoky bullets. "I'm leaving."

"Be sensible. The experiment's about to begin. You can't leave."

"I can. Through the woods."

"Luther, you'll be court-martialed!"

"I don't think so. Not if my gut is right. Come with me."

James's expression was somber. "I'm not a deserter."

"Better than whatever's gonna happen to us today." Luther took a step closer and wrapped his arms around James's waist.

James tried to pull away. "Not here. What if…?"

Luther silenced his protest with a kiss. "To hell with them. I love you. I want to save us both. Come with me."

James kissed each of Luther's palms and then his lips. "I have to do this. I promised. This is my country."

Luther shoved his hands deep into his trouser pockets and hunched his shoulders. "What if your country is asking you to do something you know is wrong?"

"Then I'll accept the consequences. I signed up, and I'll honor that."

"Do you think your country would fight for you? For us?" Luther scoffed. "After all, you can read people's thoughts now. You know what's inside them."

James angled his face toward the sky, cloudy gray with hints of blue. "You'd be surprised at what people think. It will all be fine. You'll see."

He kissed Luther's forehead, then trekked back into the woods, toward the base, leaving a trail of footprints behind. Luther didn't follow right away. He needed stillness. He needed to think. Along the lake's edge, he looked out at the snow-dusted mountains and tried to shake his growing dread. More than anything, he wanted to believe as James did—that the people in charge of the experiment knew what they were doing and it would all be okay. But Luther had held back what he'd seen that had scared him most:

"Let me into your world," the gray-faced man with the soulless eyes had whispered to Luther with a nearly orgiastic joy. "And I will tear it asunder."

Whispering voices came from the forest.

"Who's there?" Luther said. But he knew already. He could feel the press of the spirits at his back. The whispering grew louder, a clarion bell reverberating inside him:

"...It's a trap, a trap, a trap..."

"...You are not safe from what comes. What comes. What comes..."

"...You must stop this stop this stop this..."

Luther bolted for the camp. As he neared, he could hear the men's laughter. They were at ease. Bored. Passing the time. He had the feeling he had seen this all before: The quartet playing cards. The sergeant shaving. The dancing soldier beside the turning Victrola. *Smile, smile, smile.* His mouth in a half grin, James watched a hawk circling overhead. The air was crisp, the sky gray and calm. Light snow fell. Luther had never been more afraid.

We must stop this. The words wouldn't come. What if he was wrong? What if he screamed the warnings—*the warnings of the dead*—and looked the fool?

"Don't pick up the phone!" Luther said, breathless with fear.

The others regarded him curiously. Three seconds later, the field telephone rang. The sergeant wiped his jaw, pocketed his razor. "Spooky," he said, shaking his head. The sergeant listened, nodding. "Yes. Yes. Ready, sir. Over and out."

Luther took a step backward. *Say something. Say* something.

The sergeant yanked up his suspenders and grabbed his helmet. "Soldiers, this is not a drill. The time is now!"

"The time is now!" the men echoed, abandoning their card game midplay and running for position. "Luther! I said, positions! That's an order!"

Luther turned toward the forest. He would not die for a bad cause.

"Luther!" James called from the circle.

Luther saw his brothers-in-arms holding hands, ready. And then he had a sense of them, skeletal and screaming.

"Soldier! Take your position!" the sergeant ordered.

"James," Luther whispered, but James was no longer looking at him.

Above the Marlowe estate, two streams of blue lightning shot up, piercing the cloudy sky, filling it with tentacles of blue light. The sky moved and groaned like a giant sea beast in pain, and in the next second, the electricity reached down like a staticky blue hand, surrounding the men of the one forty-four. Luther broke into a run, dropping his gun. He was numb with fear. *Don't look back. Just go. Keep running.* But at the top of the hill, his heart reneged. *Deserter.* Luther turned. Down below in the clearing, the men of the one forty-four still held hands. Swirling mist wrapped itself in a deadly caress around their shaking bodies. The men stood fast, but their expressions—wide eyes, open mouths—betrayed their fear.

"Do...you see...that?" the soft-shoe dancer said in a strangled voice. "Dear god!"

"Hold!" the sergeant ordered through his own pain.

A slap of thunder echoed in the woods. The sky ripped open, a terrible birth. Fractured light pierced the men, pouring through their flesh. Luther could see their whole skeletons as if they were X-rays of themselves. And now they were screaming as they floated up toward the mangled sky and whatever lay inside its dark wound.

Luther's horror was deep water; he was drowning in it. He could not move, could scarcely breathe. A pinpoint of silence held the moment in place, and then a blast of white raced across the ground with such force it destroyed the trees and knocked Luther through the air. He smelled burning flesh, felt a pain greater than anything he had ever known, hot as a branding iron.

And then he was unconscious.

For days, Luther dreamed. In his dreams, he saw the funny gray man with the stovepipe hat. "Greetings, Luther Clayton. Deserter. Do you hear your brethren crying?"

Luther did. He heard them screaming: *Help us. Help us. Help us.*

When Luther came to, his head pounded. And his legs were gone below the knees. There were voices in the room. Real voices. Jake Marlowe and a pompous general and a sergeant at arms. Luther saw them through the slits of his heavy eyes.

"Margaret Walker tried to smuggle out documents and expose the operation. We've jailed her for sedition." The general.

"And Miriam?" Marlowe.

"An enemy of the state. We can't allow such power to go loose. We'll be keeping her under lock and key."

"What about Will?"

"He's a broken man. No threat that we can see," the general said. "Mr. Marlowe, what happened to my soldiers? Where is the one forty-four?"

"I don't know. But if I could just re-create the experiment with adjustments—think of the enormous good it could do, all that energy—"

"We'll be shutting down the division, effective immediately."

"No! General, just give me a chance to perfect it—"

"That machine is far too dangerous. We've already lost Rotke Wasserman and the entire regiment to this disaster. We'll send the telegrams to the families with our sympathies. We'll take it from here, Mr. Marlowe."

"Sir, I think he's awake." The sergeant at arms.

They all turned to Luther now.

"Luther? Can you hear me?" Marlowe. He looked a wreck.

Luther nodded. Pain shot through him from his forehead down his spine, but he felt nothing below his waist.

"Did you see what happened to the one forty-four? Do you know where they are?"

"They're with him," Luther croaked.

"Who?"

"The land is old, the land is vast, he has no future, he has no past, his coat is sewn with many woes, he'll bring the dead, the King of Crows."

The general's upper lip curled. "What the devil does that mean?"

"He's gravely injured, General, and shell-shocked. There's no telling."

The general stood at Luther's bedside and patted his arm with confidence. "You'll be right as rain soon enough, soldier. A grateful nation thanks you for your service."

But the screaming did not stop. Luther saw his ghostly friends in every corner of his mind. *Help us!* they begged. Oh, he would go mad!

The Shadow Men came to see him in the dark of night.

"Are we taking him out?" the one asked the other. He straightened a loop of piano wire between his gloved hands.

The other Shadow Man snapped his fingers in front of Luther's face. "He can't say anything. His mind's gone."

"Still."

"We wait for orders," the Shadow Man said. "Needs to look like he died in his sleep."

Reluctantly, the other Shadow Man pocketed his wire. "See you tomorrow, deserter. Sweet dreams."

Just before dawn, Will Fitzgerald stole into the ward and crouched beside Luther's bed. "Luther, can you hear me? It's Will Fitzgerald."

Luther turned his face to Will's. He hadn't shaved in a few days and his eyes were swollen and red. Will whispered, "I'm sorry. I didn't know. I didn't know."

In the dark of night, Will helped Luther to a waiting car. "Ben Arnold?" Will asked the driver.

The driver nodded, and Will deposited Luther and his crutches into the backseat.

"Where'm I taking him, Mr. Fitzgerald?"

"Somewhere he can't be found." Will handed Ben all the money he had.

"Sorry to hear about your fiancée," Ben said. "The machine really do that to her?"

Will's mouth was set in a grim line. "Just make sure you help him disappear."

Ben Arnold set Luther up in a flophouse on the West Side, not far from Times Square. The war ended. An armistice was signed. Bombs exploded on Wall Street. The country raided houses and deported "aliens." Motor cars rumbled through the skyscraper canyons. Ragtime birthed jazz and jazz birthed an age. Women cut their hair and raised their hemlines to dance. The country outlawed liquor; bathtub gin made outlaws. The neon lights of Broadway had never beamed brighter. People placed their faith in stocks; they were rich and getting richer.

On the streets, Luther Clayton begged for food and spare change. The one forty-four still screamed on the battlefield of his mind. The dead whispered to him, told him secrets. A pretty flapper passed by and tucked a dollar into his tin cup. *Her*, the dead whispered. *She's the one.* Her face was familiar. Like James's. She smiled. Her smile, like his.

The screaming got worse. The Shadow Men found him. They'd been watching for some time. They came with their dark suits and false smiles and murdering hands that looked so clean. "We need you to complete one last mission, soldier." They put the gun in his hand. Told him to shoot the girl. "It will stop the screaming. Do this, and everything will be fine."

They lie, the dead warned from their graves. *They have always lied.*

But there were other dead, and they were hungry and mean. The ones who belonged to him. Their voices drowned out the others. "Kill her," they urged. "Kill her so that we might be free!"

Luther raised the gun. Watched Evie's face shift to surprise. His hand shook. The screaming reached a fever pitch. The other Diviner, Sam, stopped Luther from shooting. There were police and a ferry ride to the island and the cell. But the screaming hadn't stopped.

"You failed us!" the hungry dead hissed. "He will punish you!"

But the other dead whispered softly as a mother's lullaby: *Rest. Then speak of what you know. Show them what you have seen. Witness until their comfort yields to questions. Till their eyes cry with truth. Till their ears would hear the voices of tomorrow. Till their hearts, heavy with knowledge, beat in understanding.*

DARK NIGHT OF THE SOUL

When Evie surfaced from her reading with Luther Clayton, her body trembled uncontrollably. Her stomach roiled as if she'd been on rough seas. She'd been under too deep for too long.

"You knew my brother. You..." she said at last between shaking breaths. "You loved him," she said softly.

Luther's face was wet. His pale, chapped lips quivered. "Y-yes. James. They never...should've d-done it."

Evie's throat ached with the bitter truth of what she'd seen. What they'd done. She knew the truth now. She knew, and there was no going back.

Luther looked into her eyes. There was some fire still left in him. "S-save him. Save them. Set them all f-free."

"How? Where are they? Tell me how to find them!"

"They're with him. The K-King of C-Crows," Luther whispered. "Follow the Eye. The Eye keeps it open. Heal...the breach."

"I don't understand what that means, Luther. What is this Eye—how do we find it? How can we close it? Please. Please, can you tell us?" Evie pleaded, but Luther had struggled to hold on to that much. He had retreated into his memories again and was lost. Evie tucked the blanket around him and shut the door.

In the common room, the radio in the corner played an opera program softly as Evie told Memphis, Ling, and Sam everything she'd witnessed with Luther. A steely-eyed Sam sat on the edge of an abandoned wheelchair and pounded his right fist absently against the spokes. "They did that. Will and Sister Walker, Rotke and Jake." He paused. "My mother. They shot those soldiers up with super serum and turned them into an experiment. They might've done that to us at some point."

"Haven't they already done that to us?" Evie said bitterly. She was pacing again, like Will. She didn't care.

Memphis straddled the piano bench, his arms folded across his chest.

"There's something about us and that other world. Don't you feel it? Like we're joined in some way. We're the ones who can talk to the ghosts and the King of Crows. We're the ones who've seen that eye symbol in our sleep."

"Seems like that would make us awfully valuable," Evie said.

"And dangerous, like I said," Sam chimed in. He jerked his head toward the hallway. "Looks like we got company."

Conor Flynn stood in the open doorway, twirling a piece of his hair. "I need to draw," he said, marching to his spot at the table and taking out his paper and the pencil Isaiah had given him.

"If these ghosts are a hive mind being controlled, then who's the puppet master? Somebody has to be whipping them up," Ling said from her spot on the divan.

The scratching of Conor's pencil distracted Evie.

"What are you drawing, Conor?" she asked.

Conor didn't answer. He drew as if he was channeling, his pencil moving with quick strokes. The others crowded around, watching in horror as the picture took shape. On Conor's page, an army of hungry ghosts advanced on a boy in a boater hat just like the one Henry wore.

The lights winked. On. Off. On. Off. As if blinking out a message.

"The Hell Gate?" Sam asked.

Memphis shook his head. "Nobody's blasting in this storm."

"Maybe it's the storm, then," Sam said.

Conor's head snapped up. "They're coming. *Onetwot'reefourfiveseven...*"

Memphis, Sam, and Evie raced to the windows. Dusk had given way to dark very quickly. Lightning arced violently above Ward's Island. A giant hand of blue-gray fog reached over the top of the Hell Gate until they could no longer see the bridge at all.

"You ever seen fog move like that before?" Memphis asked.

"No," Evie whispered.

"Onetwot'reefourfivesevenOnetwot'reefourfiveseven..."

Memphis hurried from window to window, checking to be sure that they were tightly latched. And then he backed away from the view of the fog spreading across the island like an avalanche.

"Henry's outside in that," Ling said.

"One two...One. Two. T'ree...onetwot'reefourfiveseven..."

"We can't go out there now," Sam said.

"And we can't leave him there!" Ling insisted. She swiped Conor's picture and held it up to prove her point.

"What about Isaiah and Theta?" Memphis said. "I should've stayed with him!"

"...Fivesevenonetwot'reefourfivesevenone..."

"All right. We go back to the main building for Isaiah and Theta. And then we get Henry," Sam said.

There was a breath of sudden quiet in the room.

"Why has he stopped counting?" Ling asked.

Conor's eyes were huge and he was breathing in short bursts like a frightened pup. A cacophonous burst squawked from the radio, as if it were moving rapidly through stations in search of a signal. There followed a long hiss, and then, softly at first but growing ever louder, a buzzing like a swarm of flies.

"Turn it off," Evie said.

Sam did but the sound persisted. Shrieks and sobs burst through the buzz as if the history of the asylum itself was trying to make itself heard through the machine. The flickering lights bounced shadows over them all. Through the open door, the Diviners could see bewildered attendants rushing frantic patients into their rooms, soothing them as best they could. "It'll be just a moment; I'm shutting the door."

At a desk, one nurse pressed the bar on the candlestick phone repeatedly. "Hello? Hello! Gee, I can't get anyone to answer. It's gone dead!"

"The doors are sealed shut to the other wards," a male attendant said.

A physician in a tweed suit came out of his office. "Here, now, what's all this? What's happening?"

"Oh, doctor, we don't know!" the terrified nurse said.

Down at the far end of the hall, the faulty lamps began winking out one by one, plunging the passageway into deep shadow. Faint wisps of blue-gray mist pushed in around the window frames and curled along the floor. Darkness crawled up the walls like a fast-growing mold.

"What *is* that?" Ling whispered.

"It's them," Conor said. "The Forgotten. They're here."

The storm still howled over the barrenness of Ward's Island, but Henry didn't care. He set off across the muddy fields toward the wispy lights of the Hell Gate Bridge, peeking out from behind a veil of heavy fog. The wind was an assault and the rain soaked him through. He welcomed both; they matched his mood. He walked fast and without purpose, as if he could outrun his feelings. Feelings were dangerous. Feelings could trick you. They'd tricked his mother. Trapped her. Imprisoned her inside her own head. He just couldn't be in there. It made him think of his mother, like nails across his heart.

"To hell with you!" he yelled into the battering rain. He was glad it was raining because he was crying. "To hell with…you," he said again, but it had lost the bite, and now the goddamn feelings were flooding in along with his memories.

When Henry was a child, he'd adored his mother, Catherine DuBois, above all others. When Catherine was up, she was bright and sparkling, a pretty, talkative woman who would play exhaustive games of hide-and-seek with her son in the family's elegantly decaying mansion on one of the Garden District's finest streets. "I'll find you! You can't hide from me!" And she did find Henry, every time. Because Henry always wanted to be found. On a late spring day, she'd gather wildflowers and arrange them in a vase. "Doesn't that look pretty, Bird?" she'd say, calling Henry by her pet name. "Why do you call me bird, Mama?" Henry asked once. His mother smiled. "Because you remind me of a little songbird, singing to the sky. Besides," she'd said, her smile lessening, "birds are free to go." The best of times with Catherine, though, was when she'd sit with him at the piano, showing Henry how to pull music from the heavens through Chopin, Debussy, Schumann, and ragtime, her fingers making unfettered runs up and down the keys. "That's it, Bird. Open yourself wide up, dahlin'," she'd say in her sweet drawl when he'd take his place at the piano. "Let the music move through you." To Henry, his mother was magical.

But when "the howling dogs" came to visit, his bright, magical mother faded by degrees. "Depressive," the doctor whispered. "A nervous condition," his aunts said. Henry hadn't known what the words meant, but he came to think of it as a harsh winter that would not leave his mother's soul. When the howling dogs arrived, Catherine would sit for hours in the ancestral cemetery, slim fingers working the beads of her rosary, as she stared beseechingly into the weathered faces of stone saints. When the howling dogs curled up inside his mother's mind, dark-eyed and hungry, Henry would watch his mother smiling in that empty way at the endless guests seated around his father's dining table, all the while her hand shaking on her butter knife. When the howling dogs settled in atop the bones of former happiness, Catherine could scarcely rouse herself from her bed. She'd sleep the day away. And when Henry came to visit, sitting gently on the side of the bed, she'd open her tear-swollen eyes. "I'm sorry, Bird," she'd say, and close them again. Once, in the middle of the night, Henry woke to a racket in the kitchen. His mother had taken every piece of silver from the drawers, convinced there was a poison she had to polish clean from their shining surfaces. "Tainted," she'd muttered, scrubbing at the tongs of a fork, the hollow of a spoon. "All tainted."

"Maman, let me help," Henry said, taking the silver from his mother's grip and placing it back in the case.

She'd cupped his cheeks between her shaking hands. Her face was his face, same long nose and delicate mouth. But there was so much pain in hers; her blue-green eyes watered. "They were thieves, you know. We are descended from thieves and vagabonds and murderers. Oh, little bird. You should fly away from here. Far, far away. My bird, my bird, my bird…"

And Henry hated himself because he'd wanted to do just that. He'd wanted to run from his mother's pain, his father's lies and cold silences, and the slow rot of his family's aristocracy. They were sinking, and Henry didn't want to sink down with them. Was it wrong to want to live? His mother's first act of rebellion had been to encourage her son's music, to make sure he had a voice for everything inside him—music to soothe the howling dogs so they couldn't hurt him in the same way they'd hurt her. Her second act of rebellion had been to push him from the sliding, sinking nest.

Fly away, Bird. Fly, fly away…

The day her mind broke, his mother had taken one of those shining knives and crawled into the bath. She'd meant to silence the howling dogs for good. Henry had found her, pale and bleeding. The doctor had come to dress her wounds. Henry's father refused to admit his mother to a sanitarium for fear of gossip. "She needs rest." The doctor agreed, a bond sealed between men. They gave her opium. They looked away. And Henry's mother became the unofficial ghost of their ancestral mansion, floating through the elegant rooms where, if you looked too closely, you saw the tears and worn spots in the papered walls, the soot on the velvet drapes, the fraying along the seams of the antique dining chairs.

This was what Henry ran from. This was what the jokes masked. It wasn't callousness. It was pain and loss so great he could only let it in a little at a time, filtered through the safety of melody and rhythm. It was the way he survived. And to hell with his friends if they didn't understand that. And to hell with anybody who couldn't feel for those people in the asylum, people like his mother, struggling valiantly against their demons. He was tired of keeping everything in for everybody else's sake.

Henry tripped over a rise in the ground. "Oh, I *hate* this place!" He kicked at the muddy mound. God, it felt good. He kicked again, violently, splattering himself with muck and not caring. That was for the howling dogs! And that was for the suffering of his mother! That was for the hurt deep inside! Kick, kick. Kick. Ki—

His stomach realized it first. A carnival-ride swoop of raw, primal instinct that dizzied him with dread. He'd tripped over a new grave. *He was kicking at a new grave*. In his anger, he'd wandered aimlessly through the fog into the potter's fields. All around him were piles of freshly packed earth.

"Okay, Hen. Time to exit stage left," he joked to himself to keep his fear at bay.

Carefully, he stepped across the fresh earthen mounds. They'd been tightly packed by the prisoners' shovels. The rain was still coming down. In the heavy fog, he could just make out the hazy yellow glow of the asylum's dotting of windows. He'd made it halfway through the potter's fields when he felt a slight rumbling, like a train approaching underground. But this was not the city and there was no subway on Ward's Island. Henry took another step, and another. *Don't look, just keep moving.* His pulse throbbed in his ears; he could actually hear it in time with the rain—quick. And scared. Henry felt something brush his ankle. *Don't look, don't look, don't*—

He stood perfectly still and cast a glance to his right and down.

There was dirt on his shoe.

No. Dirt was *falling* onto his shoe, tumbling down from the shifting top of a new grave.

Henry chanced a look around him.

Graves. Everywhere.

And they were beginning to crumble.

❄

"What the hell is that?" Sam whispered.

At the end of the hall, the mist thickened into a dense bank of living fog, shadows among shadows. Vague forms emerged, indistinct from one another: The same pallid skin peeling off in ribbons of rotting flesh. Diseased mouths dripping with oily black drool. Rows of thin, razor-sharp teeth. Their eyes were the gray-white of pond ice and seemed to see nothing. Instead, the ghosts swept their heads left and right, sniffing in the way an animal hunting prey would.

"The Forgotten," Conor whispered urgently.

Inside the rooms, some of the residents seemed to sense the danger. They cried out in warning. With a fearsome screech, the Forgotten pressed up against the doors, looking for a living host.

"Hey!" Ling cried. "Leave them alone!"

The Forgotten turned as one toward the Diviners, growling hungrily.

"Ling," Memphis whispered. "What are you doing?"

"We can't let them get to the patients. We have to do something."

The Forgotten bared their sharp teeth as they sniffed the air. They let loose with another loud shriek.

"You certainly got their attention," Sam whispered. "What now?"

"Run. Hide!" Conor said, and took off fast as a March hare, darting down a staircase to the right.

"Wait! Conor! We can't let him go out there. I won't let something happen to him," Evie said, running after him like a protective sister.

"Dammit, Evie! Stay here. Lock yourselves in. I'll get her," Sam said, and gave chase.

"Isaiah!" Memphis said. Was his little brother all right? Was Theta? "Come on. We can't wait. We gotta get down those stairs before—"

"I! Can't! *Run!*" Ling howled with all the anger she had inside. She'd never said it out loud like that before. But there it was. Ling never asked for help. Help made you vulnerable. But she was scared. She didn't want to be alone with those things. She needed a friend. "Please don't leave me," she said.

"Okay, okay," Memphis promised. The Forgotten were moving closer. If Ling and Memphis stayed in the common room, they were sitting ducks. "Think, Memphis. Think." There was a wheelchair in a corner under a blanket. Memphis ran to it and brought it to Ling.

"I think we gotta try to get out of here while we can," he said.

Ling helped herself into the wheelchair and angled her crutches like sabers. "Ready."

Despite his fear, Memphis managed a smile. "Yes, you are."

He peeked around the corner. They were coming. "Any ideas?"

"Conor said that counting kept them out of his head. I'm guessing at this, but I think there's something about a constant noise that blocks out emotion and keeps them from locking onto whatever's inside your head, like, *Old MacDonald had a farm*," Ling sang, and motioned to Memphis to continue.

"*E-I-E-I-O*," he finished. "Okay. We sing nursery rhymes. You ready?"

"No."

"Me, neither."

"*Old MacDonald had a farm, E-I-E-I-O . . .*" they sang in unison.

The Forgotten were all around them in the fog. As Memphis pushed Ling's wheelchair down the long corridor, he could feel their powerful emotions and stories searching for a host. But the singing was working. It kept the ravenous ghosts at bay.

"*And on that farm he had some ducks*," Ling sang just as Memphis sang, "*pigs*."

"*Ducks*," he corrected quickly as Ling went for "*pigs*."

The confusion was only a few seconds, but it had allowed their fear to spike. The Forgotten sniffed it out.

"Hold on tight, Ling," Memphis said, pushing Ling's chair and running for all he was worth. Behind him, he could hear the terrifying screech of their collective anger. His legs burned but he didn't stop until he'd reached the safety of a large broom closet. He squeezed them both inside and locked the door behind them.

"Quick—count in your head," Memphis urged.

Ling shut her eyes tightly, silently counting to one hundred. The screeching moved farther away. At last, she stopped and let out a shaking breath.

"They gone?" Ling asked, panting.

"I-I don't know. Think so," Memphis answered, sagging against the wall.

"It's always ducks first," Ling said in a tight whisper.

"What?" Memphis whispered back.

"Old MacDonald. It's ducks, then pigs, then cows."

"Maybe in Chinatown. But in Harlem, I learned it pigs first." He put his ear to the door, listening. "I think they've moved on."

"I'm sorry," Ling said quietly. "I shouldn't have asked you to stay. I can't expect you to risk your life for me."

"You'd do the same for me. I know you. Besides, you're the smartest person on this team. We need you."

"Thank you. I think you're pretty smart, too."

"Something I always wondered about, though. How come you never once asked me to heal you?" Memphis asked. "Did you ever think about it?"

Had she thought about it? Just every time she saw Memphis. She imagined herself walking up and down the streets of the Lower East Side as she once did, no buckles digging into her skin, no crutches callusing her palms, no pain. There were times when it was all Ling could do not to beg Memphis to change her back to the way she had been.

But she wasn't the same person she had been. It felt, somehow, as if a healing by Memphis would *un*make who she was now. As if she would lose what she had come to know about herself in the past few months, about her strength and resilience. And if there was to be a cure for her paralysis, then science would find it. Not just for her but for others, too. Maybe she'd even be a part of that.

"I do. But I don't. Do you understand?" Ling said.

Memphis thought about it. "Not really," he said.

It dawned on her that this was the first real, in-depth conversation she and Memphis had ever had. Sometimes it seemed as if he lived a world away, uptown in a place she barely knew, far removed from the narrow streets of

Chinatown. She liked Memphis. There was so much she wanted to ask him, about their powers. About healing. About his life. She hoped they'd survive this terrible night and she'd get the chance.

Memphis risked a look out. The corridor was clear. No ghosts, no fog. "Find the others?" he asked.

Ling nodded. "And it's ducks first," she said definitively.

※

Sam and Evie had run after Conor, who had led them on a chase down into a basement of dark corners and low ceilings.

"You see him?" Sam asked as they peeked around a noisy boiler.

"Huh-uh. And I don't like basements. Nothing good happens in basements. That's where one-toothed murderers always live," Evie whispered. "In basements."

"Well, my mother used to put pickled herring in our basement," Sam said, inching forward.

"See what I mean? If it's not ghosts and one-toothed murderers, it's pickled herring."

"Maybe we should let him take his chances and go back upstairs with the others. Frankly, I'm not so sure I wanna be alone in a basement with Conor Flynn, the priest murderer."

"Just one more minute, please? I'm worried about him," Evie said.

"Okay, Baby Vamp. Okay."

The basement was dank and smelled of the river. Several empty stretchers lined the hallway, and Evie shuddered to think of what could be hiding under those wadded sheets. *Just keep walking*, she told herself. Off to the right was the plunge bath cut into the floor. Water pushed inside and sluiced up the walls in violent spasms. The lights weren't working. The storm had seen to that. There was a washroom, and Evie realized rather suddenly that she had to go.

"Stay right here. I need to iron my shoelaces," Evie said.

"Now?"

"Sam. *I need to go!*"

"Fine. But could you be quick about it? Creepy down here."

"I wasn't planning to write epic poetry," Evie grumbled, and shut the door behind her.

Sam leaned against the cold brick to wait. "Swell. If it ain't ghosts, it's weak bladders."

There was a thud and a crash. Sam's heartbeat quickened. He didn't want to leave his post outside the washroom with Evie inside, but he needed to know what might be down there with them. Cautiously, he crept through the dark basement, blinking to let his eyes adjust. He heard a faint mewling off to his right. Stray cat? No. More like soft crying.

Sam peered around the corner. Conor sat on the floor with his knees drawn to his chest and his arms wrapped around his knees. Sam was light-headed with relief.

"Conor. Hey. We, uh, we were looking for you," Sam said, strolling over and taking a seat next to the boy.

Conor turned his face away, and Sam had the idea the kid would be embarrassed if Sam mentioned the crying, even though he shouldn't be.

"I was wondering if you could tell me more about the lady in your head. About Miriam," Sam said.

Conor sniffled and wiped his nose on his sleeve. "She started talking to me 'bout a month ago. She tol' me how to keep the ghosts and the man in the hat out of my thoughts with my counting. And I can always feel when it's not right and I gotta count. No sixes, though. I can't land on a six. Sixes are bad," Conor whispered.

"Got it. Sixes are bad. This lady say where she might be?" Sam asked.

Conor nodded vigorously. "She says they keep her underground where her powers don't work as good. But they don't know that she's been working on getting stronger. They don't know that. She says if she can get above-ground, she can talk to all the Diviners."

Sam's head was spinning. Could Conor really be talking to his mother? Was it the same Miriam? He didn't want to hope, but he couldn't help it. A lump had formed in his throat.

"You're sad," Conor said.

"No. No, I'm not."

"You're sad and you're lying about it."

"Everybody lies. It's how we get along in this world. I don't talk about sad things," Sam said, irritated, then felt bad for it. "So where is this underground place where Miriam lives?"

"Dunno." Conor fell silent. He tore at his cuticles. They were raw, all of them, as if he picked at them daily. "I ain't seen my own ma in years."

"Oh. What about your pop?"

"Ain't seen him since I was five. No matter. 'Fore he left, he used to beat me wit' whatever was around."

Sam flinched. His old man had a temper, but he'd never once hit Sam. Mostly, his father was stubborn and sure he was right. He liked things to go his way. Who didn't? But Sam remembered other things about him, too, like the time his father had taught him Torah and helped him learn to ride a bicycle. Sam hadn't called or written his father in a year. Now he had the sudden urge to do that. Maybe his old man would bellow at him to give up on his mission to find his mother and Sam would hang up the telephone, angry and disappointed to be right. But maybe not.

"I'm bad. I'm wicked," Conor said, and chewed at his cuticles.

"You're not bad," Sam said, even though Conor had murdered a priest, which seemed like the very definition of *wicked*.

"They want me to be sorry 'bout how I done Father Hanlon, but I ain't. He shouldn'ta tried to take Jimmy for ice cream."

Cold fear trickled through Sam. He was alone with a boy who, Diviner or not, was capable of murder. "Yeah? Why's that?"

"I didn't want him to do to Jimmy what he done to me," he mumbled.

"What did Father Hanlon do to you?"

Conor put his thumb in his mouth, chewing at the damaged skin along his nail bed. He twirled a section of his hair, tugging hard, as if he could make himself come apart and disappear. His voice was thick with unshed tears. "He tol' me nobody would believe me. His word against mine, an' he was a priest. Who'd take the word of a street kid over a priest?"

The full horror of it rose up from Sam's stomach. He struggled to catch his breath. "So, you tried to stop him from hurting anybody else?"

Conor nodded.

"I understand. You're not wicked, kid. Somebody is, but it ain't you."

The washroom door creaked open and slammed.

"Baby Vamp, stealthy you are not," Sam muttered. "Wait here," he said to Conor. Sam ventured back out into the dark, open basement, but he didn't see Evie. There was a tap on his shoulder, and Sam yelped and whirled around to see Evie right behind him. "Don't sneak up on me like that, Sheba," he said, putting a hand to his chest. "You nearly scared me half to death."

"I'm so cold," Evie said.

"Yeah. It's freezing down here."

"Warm me up?" Evie asked, biting her lip on a smile.

Sam raised an eyebrow. "This is a bad time to be pulling my leg, Sheba. We've got ghosts to figure out."

Evie drew closer to Sam. "What if I'm not pulling your leg? What if I've missed you?"

"I've missed you, too," Sam said, confused. "Wait. On the level?"

Evie smiled. "Mm-hmm. But I thought you didn't want to be with me."

"Me not want to be with you?" Sam's eyebrows shot up. "Are you kidding?"

"Does that mean you *do* want to be with me?"

For weeks, he'd tried to put Evie out of his mind and heal. Their pretend romance hadn't been pretend for him at all. But he had his pride, and he wasn't about to let her know just how deeply he'd fallen. And then, when he'd seen her go off with Jericho to the collections room, he'd figured that was it. She liked the giant. The big, beautiful giant.

"Sheba, are you sure?" Sam asked.

Evie pulled his face toward hers with both hands. And then she kissed him. Deeply. The kiss was a surprise, but it only took seconds for it to rip away the scab on Sam's heart, for him to lose himself to it. His brain was fighting to make sense of things: *I'm in an asylum. Being chased by ghosts. Evie is kissing me.* He didn't know which of those seemed the most far-fetched.

Evie took his finger and put it in her warm mouth, sucking on it. It felt incredible. Sam gasped. "Do you like that?" she asked.

"Yeah. Yeah, I do."

"How about this?" She unbuttoned his shirt and moved her mouth across his chest, licking up his neck. He could feel himself hardening.

"Say…um. Where'd you learn to do that? I, uh, I wanna send that person a thank-you note." Sam's eyes fluttered.

"Kiss me," Evie said again.

Sam cursed their timing. "I'd love to. But I left Conor around the cor—"

"Kiss me," Evie said, pushing Sam against the brick wall.

He thought he saw just a hint of blue-gray smoke behind her and felt a chill that doused his passion fast.

"Say, Sheba. You find anything interesting in that washroom?" Sam said, moving slowly toward it.

"Why aren't you kissing us?" Evie said, more insistently. But her voice sounded funny, like several voices speaking at once.

Sam yanked open the door to the washroom. There was a cracked window down at the end. The room was thick with vapory ghosts. Their teeth shone in the dark.

"Definitely not pickled herring," Sam whispered.

Evie's eyes tilted up. She shook as if learning a new dance.

"Oh, no. No, no, no." Sam grabbed Evie. "Come on, Sheba. Fight it."

"We just want a kiss! A kiss to remember us by!" the ghosts inside her shrieked.

"They got inside her!" Conor said, racing toward her with a long hook he'd found.

"Whoa there!" Sam said, holding Conor back just as the ghosts inside Evie slipped out, leaving her dazed and staggering.

"Kiss us, kiss us!" the ghosts demanded.

"Sorry. I only date one at a time," Sam said. He grabbed Evie's hand and pushed Conor through the basement toward the stairs. The ghosts howled with anger.

"This way!" Conor led them into a cramped, unused room with a sweat box.

"How do you know where to go?" Sam panted.

"The lady," Conor said. "Here." He pointed to a window with no bars.

"Beautiful!" Sam snugged it open. "Ladies first."

"Sam?" Evie said, coming around.

"Yeah. You're gonna hate me for this but…" And with that, Sam pushed her out the window. Sam heard her land with an "Oof!" followed by an angry "Saaam!"

"She's okay," Sam said, nodding. "You next."

Conor slid through the window and made the small drop to the ground. Sam followed. He slid down the muddy hill and nearly plummeted into the churning currents of the Hell Gate.

Evie yanked him to safety by the edge of his shirt, ripping it. "Thanks. You owe me a shirt," Sam said.

"You owe me twenty dollars."

҉

Up front in the administration building, an antsy Theta smoked a cigarette and looked out at the rain and fog settling over the island. Memphis and the others had been gone a long time. Shouldn't they be back by now? And where was Henry? It didn't help that Isaiah was sullen and focusing all of his hostility on her.

"You wanna play cards?" she asked, a peace offering.

"No, thanks," Isaiah mumbled as he drew.

"I know you don't like me," Theta said finally.

"Never said that."

"You didn't have to."

Isaiah cast a sidelong glance at Theta and went back to his sketching. "Since you been around, Memphis don't have time to play ball with me or go to the games or nothing. He'd rather be with you."

"Memphis loves you more than anybody."

"No, he don't."

"Yes, he does." Theta took a deep breath. "And anyway, I'm about to be around a lot less."

"How come?"

"I got my reasons."

"Swell. Now Memphis'll blame me."

"No. He won't."

"Yes, he will! When you're a kid, you always get blamed for everything!" Isaiah said.

"You won't get blamed for this," Theta said sadly. She took a drag, let it out. "It really bugs you being treated like a kid."

"And how," Isaiah said on a sigh.

Theta stubbed out her cigarette. "You're right. That's not fair. Come on. Let's go find the others."

Isaiah looked wary. "Yeah?"

"Yeah. Come on. Let's ankle."

Theta wanted this night to be over. Even more than the thought of spending the night in the asylum, she dreaded the conversation with Memphis to come.

It was the lights Theta noticed first as they approached ward A. They were winking on and off. It was disorienting. And very creepy. The doors were shut, but when Theta reached for the knob, they creaked open.

Isaiah stopped short. "I got a bad feeling."

"Like a regular bad feeling, like your stomach hurts...or a *we oughta run* bad feeling?"

Isaiah was scared, but he didn't want her to know it. Hadn't he said he wanted to be treated like a big kid, like the rest of them? If he looked like a coward, they'd probably never let him come along again. He stepped into the corridor.

"Smoky in here," Theta said, coughing. "Somebody musta forgot to open a flue or something." As they made their way down the hall, Theta saw that the doors to the patients' rooms were open, but many of the patients were missing. Others sat on their beds staring out.

"The Forgotten, the Forgotten, we are the Forgotten," they whispered as Theta and Isaiah passed by.

Isaiah was truly frightened now. Even more so when he heard screams and deranged laughter coming from somewhere he couldn't see. There were marks on the clean walls. Bloody handprints. The laughter got stronger.

"Theta," he said.

"Yeah. I see," she said. "I think we better turn back."

They turned around and the doors slammed shut, sealing them inside.

Isaiah's eyes rolled back in his head. His body shook. "We are the Forgotten, forgotten no more," he said in a strangled whisper.

"Isaiah! Oh, please don't do this, please don't," Theta begged.

Someone was coming toward them. A doctor moved carefully down the dim hall, pushing a wheelchair in front of him with a nurse seated there.

His coat rested on the seat, across the nurse's lap, and his shirtsleeves had been rolled to the elbows. The doctor's head swept left and right, looking.

"Doctor!" Theta called. "Can you help me? My friend is sick...."

The doctor's head whipped in their direction. The faulty light blinked on, off, on, off. But it had been enough to see: Blood spattered the good doctor's suit. The nurse's eyes were fixed and a gash marred her pretty throat. The doctor reached under his coat and retrieved the ax hidden there. His gaze drifted ceiling-ward. His lips stretched into a tight smile. His teeth glinted in the blinking light.

"She questioned my authority, the bitch. Can you imagine?" The doctor laughed. It was the laugh Theta had heard earlier, the deranged one.

"Polly Pratchet had a hatchet. Worked it night and day," the doctor said, grunting as he swung the ax. "Polly Pratchet had a hatchet. Now you'd better pray!"

"They got inside him," Isaiah said, coming out of his trance. "He belongs to them."

Theta grabbed Isaiah's hand and ran, searching for a place to hide. Behind them, the doctor's voice splintered as if several of him spoke at once: "We are the Forgotten, forgotten no more."

They came to a stairwell that led down to the second and first floors. Isaiah pulled back on Theta's hand and shook his head. "We shouldn't go down there."

The doctor staggered after them, dragging his ax along the floor behind him, leaving a trail of blood. Theta could just make out the wisps of blue mist coming off him, as if he were made of ice inside.

"We can't go back that way. This is the only way out."

Theta knew not to ignore Isaiah's premonitions. But what choice did they have? She stretched her fingers, as if trying to work heat into them, but no spark would come. Theta peered over the stair railing. The flickering bulb overhead made it hard to see. Down below, it was completely dark. Worse, the staircase wound around; if somebody or something was hiding around a curve, they wouldn't know until it was too late.

"All right. I'll go first. Stay behind me, okay?"

Isaiah nodded, and they stepped into the stairwell, away from the madman with the ax screaming behind them. Theta took a few tentative steps.

Her legs quivered. She feared they'd give way completely. She'd never been so terrified. The scraping of the ax echoed even in the stairwell's gloom. She reached the first landing, between the second and third floors. "Okay. It's safe."

Isaiah stepped down quietly behind her.

"So far so good," she said.

But the passage to the second floor was much darker. Theta could barely make out the steps in the gloom. Anything could be down there. The doctor laughed as he clanged the ax against the door. He was inside the stairwell!

"Same plan," Theta said. "Follow my lead."

Carefully, she ventured to the second floor, feeling for each step, hoping nothing would grab her as she moved down. She reached the second-floor landing without incident. Isaiah caught up to her.

"Just one more," she whispered. Isaiah nodded. "You, uh, don't see anything, do you?"

Isaiah shook his head. "I'm too scared. I can't tell."

Theta crept down into the deeper dark. She was nearing the next landing when she nearly missed a step. On instinct, she gripped the railing. It was freezing. And wet. Her hand came up with something sticky. She dared not move. Her breath came out in white puffs.

"Theta?"

Theta didn't want to take her eyes off whatever might be lurking in the gloom below. Oh, god. Oh, god, she'd led them right down into it!

"Theta!" Isaiah whispered frantically.

Her mind wanted to slip away. Like with Roy. *No, Theta. Stay awake. Stay here. Isaiah. Help Isaiah.* She turned to look up at Isaiah on the landing above her. The fog was behind him, creeping closer. "Theta," he said, terrified. He knew. Of course he knew.

"Isaiah. Isaiah, be very still," she whispered.

Her heart beat out of control. She thought she might faint. She couldn't faint. Not with Isaiah in trouble.

"Come to me. No! Don't turn around."

She stretched out her hand. It was shaking. Why was there no fire?

"That's it. One step at a time," she said.

Isaiah put a foot on the step below. And then another. Theta could tell he wanted to run. Behind him, the fog followed. Theta could make out the ghostly shapes of women wearing ragged dresses from a bygone era. Moth-eaten shawls hung about their shoulders. Rotted bonnets rested atop their pale, skeletal heads. They moved as one, their voices overlapping: *"Child. Child. A child. Child. Give us the child. Our children, all lost! All gone! We need the child, the child, the child…"*

Isaiah was nearly to her. Theta could almost touch him.

The ghosts howled their displeasure. So many teeth! Theta recoiled, and the murky women wrapped their ghostly arms tightly around Isaiah, pulling him in.

"Theta!" Frantic, Isaiah reached for her.

"No!" Theta grabbed Isaiah and tucked him close.

"The child is ours!" the women hissed, racing around behind her.

"No. He's. Not." Theta whirled to face them. Sudden heat flooded her palms as she pushed the ghosts away. They wailed in agony. They could feel pain!

"Come on, Isaiah!" Theta said. She yanked off her coat and wrapped it around her still-hot hand, then looped her arm through Isaiah's, half dragging him down the stairs at record speed. Down in the dark of the stairwell, the ghosts shrieked and shrieked until their echo sounded like the cry of a dying animal.

✳

In the storm, Henry stood perfectly still, watching in horror as pale, glowing fingers pushed up from the broken ground. The ghosts rose one by one, shaking off the dirt of their graves. The stench of death hung over them. The lights of the asylum glinted against the fog. How far was it? How many graves were there between Henry and the way back?

A little girl turned toward Henry. Decades-old grave dirt stained the pinafore of her old-fashioned dress. Her crepey skin was the color of morning ashes and pitted with pockmarks. Her eyes were cold and fathomless. She cocked her head and sniffed at Henry.

"H-hello," Henry whispered. *She's just a kid*, he told his hammering heart.

"Hungry!" the little girl said. A thin stream of black drool dripped across her cracked bottom lip.

"Hungry," the others agreed.

On a terrifying hiss, the little girl opened her eel-shine mouth wide as a snake's. She had a lot of teeth.

"I really hate the t-teeth," Henry said.

The ghosts' feet hovered just above the sopping ground. Their voices swirled in the night air. "We are the Forgotten. You have forgotten us. Forgotten us. Forgotten. We are the Forgotten. We will live inside you and you will not forget us again."

"Wait. Wait!" Henry yelled. "Y-you don't want to hurt me!"

The ghosts stopped their advance. They seemed to have heard him.

Like a dream, Henry thought. *Pretend this is a dream.*

"You don't want to hurt me," he said again, using the same persuasive voice he'd used in his dream walks to stop a nightmare in its tracks. "You don't want to hurt me." He backed carefully toward the asylum.

"We don't want to hurt you," they said.

"That's right." He lifted his foot carefully over a pallid hand working its way up from the earth, stifling a scream as he did. The lights of the asylum were getting closer. Step by step. It was working.

The ghosts began to follow Henry, like terrifying pets.

"You don't want to follow me, either," Henry insisted.

"We are the Forgotten, forgotten no more."

"Stay," Henry said. He felt ridiculous, but the ghosts hovered above the broken graves and did not follow. "Good ghosts," Henry said. "Very good."

He stepped over the last grave, and every bit of his calm evaporated. With a loud yell, he stumble-ran the rest of the way toward the asylum. His screams were so loud he could barely hear the Forgotten screeching after him: "Hungry! Hungry! Hungry!"

He rounded the corner of the asylum, nearly hitting Evie, Sam, and Conor head-on.

"Henry!" Evie said, embracing him. "Oh, you're all right."

"Where's everybody else?" he gasped.

"Don't know," Sam said.

The growling was getting closer.

"No time for a tearful reunion," Henry gasped. "Just keep running!"

※

Theta and Isaiah burst out of the stairwell, and Theta dragged a bench in front of the door, as if that would do anything, but it made her feel better. She unwrapped her ruined coat and dropped it to the floor, and the two of them sagged against the opposite wall, gasping for breath.

"You...okay?" She panted out, and a wide-eyed Isaiah nodded.

The door to the stairwell slammed against the bench. The possessed doctor grunted as he pressed his shoulder against the jammed door, and then he swung the ax through the narrow opening, bringing it down on the bench's back, splintering it.

"Polly Pratchet had a hatchet, worked it night and day!"

"Not you again," Theta said on a ragged breath.

"Theta!" Memphis called from the other end of the hallway. Ling was with him. There were running footsteps and more shouts—"Memphis?" "Ling!" Henry's voice. And Evie's. They were with Sam, and for just a second, Theta was so relieved to see all of her friends that she forgot about the doctor with the ax. The door to the stairwell flew open with superhuman strength, sending the bench skittering across the floor toward Theta and Isaiah.

The doctor lunged at them, ax held high. He brought it down again, and Theta and Isaiah jumped forward, narrowly missing its sharp blade as it sliced into the wall. The doctor laughed as if it were the funniest thing in the world. With a grunt, he freed the ax. "That'll leave a mark. I always wanted to leave a mark. But people were always questioning me. Let's see what sort of mark I can leave on you!"

He came at them, grimly determined, eyes shining but dead. There was no time to think. A scream tore out of Theta's throat as the heat roared through her. Blue-orange flames raced from her fingertips to her shoulders. Her arms were like the brilliant wings of a firebird.

"Stay back," she warned.

"We are the Forgotten," the doctor said in a splintered voice. "We will not be forgotten. He has promised. The child. The child. The child."

He charged for Isaiah.

Theta grabbed hold of the doctor's arm. The ghosts inside screeched as the fire burned through the sleeve to his skin. Theta was transfixed by the spectacle. There was something both brutal and beautiful in it. The doctor stared at his own burning flesh, smiling as it spread up his arm. She could see that he wanted to resist, but he was too mesmerized by the flames overtaking him. And then he fell to his knees, screaming in pain as the Forgotten left his burning body.

"Theta! Watch out!" Sam cried.

The Forgotten rushed her. Startled, she threw out her hands. The ghosts writhed in agony as the flames engulfed them. Horrified, Theta stumbled back. She put her still-burning hand against the wall to steady herself. The flame caught on the drapery and spread quickly. It licked up the walls, bubbling the plaster into scorched blisters.

Like Kansas, she thought. *Oh, god. Just like Kansas!*

But this time, it wasn't just Roy. There were so many people here.

Isaiah jumped up and rang the fire alarm. "Fire! Fire!" he shouted.

The Forgotten were in retreat. They folded into the fog and slipped out around the windows. The sealed doors opened. Choking black smoke filled the hallway.

"Get them out!" Theta yelled.

Attendants and nurses were running in from the other floors, helping to evacuate the patients and doing their best to smother the fire.

"Theta?" Memphis was looking at her strangely.

Flame still scalloped the tips of her fingers.

Now he knew. They all knew.

☀

The fire had been put out. Now the staff were busy seeing to the patients and trying to understand why one of their own had once again committed an act of violence. In the ensuing chaos, Evie and the others had managed to sneak Luther and Conor with them to the administration building, where they were now crowded in the visiting room again.

Theta wrapped a blanket around a shivering Henry as he told the others first about his ghostly encounter in the graveyard and then, when he felt braver, about life with his mother and her illness.

"Gee, that's rough. I didn't know about your ma. I'm sorry, Henry," Sam said, chagrined. "You know what? Take a punch. Right here." Sam tapped his jaw.

Henry held up his elegant, piano-playing fingers. "I'm not chancing my bread and butter on your mug, Sam. It's jake."

"I'm an ass."

"Well. That's true."

"Why you gotta be so agreeable?" Sam said.

"Depressive," Evie said, testing the word on her tongue. "I didn't know there was a name for that feeling. Like there's a rain cloud in your soul." She knew that feeling well. Sometimes she was the life of the party. But other times she was lonely, bleak, and sick with disgust at herself, and certain that the people who said they loved her were only pretending. She called these times the "too muches": too much feeling, like opening a door and seeing, really seeing, into some deep, existential loneliness underlying everything. When the "too muches" arrived, Evie feared that whatever hope lived inside her would drown from the storm of her own aching sadness.

"I suppose I thought no one would understand," Henry said, picking up a small cast-iron bulldog figurine from the desk. He liked the weight of it in his hands, an anchor to keep him from floating away into the ache that gnawed him when he thought of his mother.

Theta caught Memphis staring at her. Quickly, he looked away, and it registered deep in her gut. Maybe he'd be glad to be rid of her now that he knew what lived inside her.

"When were you gonna tell us?" Ling asked Theta.

"Never, if I coulda had my way."

"Golly, Theta. All those times we talked, all those nights at the museum. Didn't you trust us?" Evie asked.

"I knew," Sam said.

"*Sam* knew?" Memphis said, and it was hard to miss the hurt in it.

"I knew, too," Henry said.

"I see," Memphis said, turning away.

"Theta. You knew all about us," Evie said. "Why—"

"Don't you get it? The rest of you got good powers. Memphis heals! Ling and Henry can help people in dreams. Isaiah and Evie can read the future and the past and figure stuff out. Me? All I can do is destroy."

Isaiah sidled up to her. "You saved my life. Twice."

Impulsively, Isaiah threw his arms around Theta, and she returned the hug, grateful for it.

"We can sort this out later. Right now we gotta figure out how to get these ghosts to go away," Sam said. "Who's got ideas?"

No one spoke.

"Don't all jump in at once. Form an orderly line," Sam said.

"Uncle Will said that ghosts used to be human, and that humans want things. The question is: What do these ghosts want?" Evie asked.

"They don't want to be dead," Henry offered. "They won't accept the finality of death."

"'Cause they been forgot," Conor said. "They're angry. That's all they feel all the time. Angry and mean. They want youse to feel it, too."

"So...they're *bullies*," Sam said.

"They're a mob," Memphis said. "How do you stop a mob?"

"With a lot of guns and things that blow other things up?" Sam said.

"Not for long," Evie said. "And anyway, it won't work on ghosts. They're already dead, remember?"

Memphis tapped his finger against his lips and stared out the window at the night. "The Forgotten. The Forgotten," he muttered.

"Uh, Memphis? You going ghost on us?" Sam asked.

Memphis turned away from the window and faced the others. He folded his arms across his chest and nodded, as if he were having a private conversation with himself. "Conor just said the ghosts are angry. That they've been forgotten." A thought was fighting to take shape in Memphis's head. He was thinking of the 135th Street library. All those books, all those stories waiting to be discovered. Stories that needed telling. "Will says that we have to see them ghost by ghost. We need to break up the mob. Draw the ghosts out."

"How do we do that?" Evie asked. "There are hundreds of them!"

"We get them to talk," Memphis said. "We let them know we're listening."

Sam snorted. "Did you see what they did to that doctor with the ax? What they did to the nurses? They don't wanna talk; they wanna invade. Take over. They wanna hurt us."

"I wish we'd had more training with Sister Walker," Ling said. "We don't know what we're doing."

"I don't think they knew what they were doing, either," Theta said, popping her chewing gum.

"Look," Sam said, rubbing the bridge of his nose. "I'm just saying, what do we do if they decide to climb inside any of us and take us for a bad ride? What if, while we're listening to their spooky bedtime stories, the Forgotten get us to act on our worst fears and"—Sam glanced at Evie—"hidden impulses."

"Yeah. How will we know if it's us or a ghost?" Isaiah asked.

"Preferably before we start eating each other's faces," Henry said. "'Oh, pardon me, I thought you were my pal, Ling. But now that you're *trying to eat my face*, I can see I was wrong about that!'"

Ling grimaced. "If I were going to eat a face, it would not be yours."

"I'll have you know my face is *quite* edible," Henry insisted.

"Anybody in this asylum could be infected. Anybody could be somebody other than who they claim to be," Theta said. "You can't be sure that a friend is a friend."

"So what now?" Evie asked.

"Seems like whatever we do, we've got to take the fight to the source. To the potter's fields," Henry said.

Theta ground out her cigarette. "Swell. Every time I think this night can't get worse, it does."

The lights dimmed and winked.

"They're coming back," Conor said. "We better go now."

❋

Henry poked his head out the door. Down by the nurses' station, the lights were out again. Fog seeped around the window cracks and waterfalled over the windowsill. It circled one of the nurses, who burst into hysterical laughter. "Everything dies," she said, pulling out strands of her hair. "Oh, our lives are such folly!"

"Hen? Whaddaya see?" Theta asked. The others were crowded behind him in a clump.

Henry gave them an awkward smile over his shoulder. "It'll be fine. Let's ankle."

Evie took hold of Isaiah's hand. "Just keep walking," she told him.

Henry pushed Luther Clayton's wheelchair. Memphis kept a watch on Conor, who moved with feral quickness. Far behind them, the deadly fog advanced.

"If anything comes at us, Theta, can you keep 'em back?" Ling asked, and Theta knew what she was being asked to do.

"Gee. That happened fast," she said bitterly.

"We need to hurry before this gets any worse," Memphis said, opening the front door. The clammy air stuck to their skins. The disorienting fog was everywhere. Even the bright lights of the city seemed to have been swallowed up. It was as if they'd been cut off from the rest of the world.

"Anything could be waiting in this," Ling warned.

"Stick close," Henry said. "It would be easy for us to lose one another out here."

Sam turned to Conor. "The lady telling you anything?"

Conor shook his head.

"Hurry," Luther said, so suddenly it made them jump. "Grave … graveyard."

They pressed on, keeping alert for anything that might be coming at them in the gloom. Ling wished this were a dream. If it were, she'd be able to speak more easily with the dead. And, if something terrible happened, at least she'd be able to run. The bottom of her crutch met the rise of a grave. The air had grown noticeably colder. The smell of rot returned.

"I think we're close," she said.

The fog rippled as the wraiths took shape—cold eyes, mummified faces, bared teeth, and, underneath it all, the palpable feeling of rage and thwarted need.

Henry took a step forward. Theta yanked him back by his sleeve. "Whaddaya think you're doing?" she whispered.

"This worked last time." He inched forward again, his hands up in a placating gesture. "Y-you don't want to hurt us."

The rotted mouths twisted into cruel smiles. "Oh, but we do," they said as one, and let loose an unholy screech that sent Henry running back to the group.

"It really did work last time," he insisted.

"What do you want?" Evie shouted.

"Want?" The Forgotten cocked their heads.

"You must want something. Isn't that why you came back? We can't help you if we don't know."

"We are the Forgotten. We want everything," the ghosts said again.

"No. You're not forgotten," Memphis said, coming to stand beside Evie and Theta. "Tell us. Tell us who you are. We're listening."

The ghosts blinked as if trying to remember something that they'd thought irretrievably lost.

"Who are *you?*" Memphis pivoted, staring directly at one of the ghosts, though it terrified him to do it. The creature's opalescent eyes showed Memphis's reflection.

"Mi...chael," the ghost answered with considerable effort.

"Michael. You're Michael," Memphis repeated. The ghost's eyes edged the slightest bit toward brown. The outline of a scar appeared across a faint chin.

"Michael Donelly. I died in the gutter, stabbed through, with no one to mourn me."

The mood of the Forgotten shifted, as if it were a person at war with himself.

But then, one by one, they began to speak:

"My name was Josiah Stelter. I had a family, but they didn't look for them, just buried me alone in this cold, hard ground, as if I were no man a'tall but an animal...."

"Thomas Kincaid. I couldn't give up the drink. Died in the inebriate house with my guts bleeding..."

"Old Bess, they calls me—and they calls me to midwife. Consumption put me here, in the refuge. Died there, too. But the babes I delivered, most grew up fine and strong...."

285

"…My crime? 'Twas to be poor…"

"…Worked for that family till my fingers bled and what did it get me? Nuttin' but…"

"…Erased…

"Erased…

"Erased…

"Erased…

"Erased…

"We have been erased, erased, erased…"

The ghosts were becoming much more distinct. A touch of bloom on a cold cheek. Wire spectacles perched at the end of a nose reddened by drink. Faces thinned by constant hunger. Skin bruised or pitted with smallpox scars.

Names filled the night:

"My name was Emily Cousins…"

"…Raphael Munoz…"

"…Anthony Esposito…"

"…Rebecca…"

"…Charlotte…"

"…Big Sal…"

"…They called me Silver Tongue, for I could charm any lady I fancied.…"

"…They called me No-Name, for I was stolen from my people.…"

"…Was was…

"…Was was…

"I am…

"I am…

"We were the Forgotten. Do not let us be forgot."

"We won't," Memphis assured them. "It's okay. You can move on now. You can be at peace."

"You lie!" The accusation came from a man at the end. "He has told us the truth of you! You will lie and lie and lie to keep us from our power!"

The Forgotten began to lose shape again, speaking with one voice: "We will eat you down to the bones. We will suck the magic from your souls and have it for ourselves!"

"What's happening?" Ling asked. "What did we do wrong?"

"It's him," Conor said. "*He's* doing it."

There was a slight wobble in the air, as if the night were made of water. The wraiths shrank back.

"What just happened?" Evie asked.

"Wait! Do you remember the day at the museum when we created an energy field and nearly melted the credenza?" Ling asked.

"Odd time for a trip down spooky memory lane, Ling!" Sam said.

"We need to try to do that again."

"How? We don't know how we did it the first time," Theta said.

"It's that or be eaten by those things in the fog."

"When you put it that way…" Henry said. "What did we do then?"

"Stand together," Ling said.

"The Diviners must stand or all will fall," Evie said, Liberty Anne's words suddenly making sense.

"The time is now. The time is *now*!" Luther cried.

The Diviners quickly joined hands. The steady pounding of the rain gave way to a sinister drone, like the massing of a million flies hovering above a battlefield of screaming wounded.

"Oh, god…" Theta said, shaking her head as if she could shake the sound from her ears.

"Concentrate!" Ling shouted above the din. "Think of…think of sending them back."

"Here goes…" Sam said.

He could feel the others, then, as if they moved with one body, one mind. The air rippled again. It pressed against the Diviners like a storm moving in, till they felt they might be ripped apart. And then the edges of the night peeled back, as if reality were nothing but a dream. The Forgotten screeched. "But he has promised—no!" There was a thunderous boom. And then there was nothing. The fog had cleared. The graveyard was quiet except for the soft, steady patter of rain and wisps of light falling like incandescent ash.

"Everybody okay?" Memphis asked, pulling Isaiah into a tight hug.

"Yes," Evie managed. They'd destroyed the ghosts. They'd saved people. But she couldn't deny that there had been something darkly exciting about the incredible power of that moment. Her skin still hummed. She felt slightly euphoric, as if she'd drunk the perfect amount of champagne.

"They're gone. We got rid of 'em," Sam said.

"But *where* did they go?" Ling asked, mostly to herself.

"Onetwot'reefourfiveseven. Onetwot'reefourfiveseven..." Conor repeated. Except for his mouth, he'd gone as still as a cornered rabbit.

"No. No!" Luther cried out. His head rolling right and left. *"Don't let him in!"*

Evie took Conor by the arms. "Conor? Conor!"

Conor tapped his fingers nervously against Evie's arm in a counting sequence. "It was a test," he said. "He...he set up the Forgotten. He wanted...he wanted to see what you can do. Now he knows. He knows!"

The rain reversed, sucked back up into the night. There was a roar in their ears, as if they stood at the top of a mountain. The sky flashed with strange blue lightning, and in it, they could see the imprint of a great wound-like gash that flared and faded. And then it felt as if they were falling through time, and when they landed at last, they stood in a denuded circle surrounded on all sides by a nightmarish wood where a silent army of the dead waited. A cold moon bled its glow into the thready gray clouds of a starless night sky.

A sudden breath of wind rustled the brittle leaves on the ground. The dead things in the dark whispered with reverence: *"He comes! The King of Crows!"*

A creature emerged from the woods, a sticklike man, with the air of a praying mantis, but the enormous blue-black feathered coat he wore gave him the bearing of a usurper king. On his head was a stovepipe hat that swirled with shadows. Lightning crackled all around him. A Gordian knot of black silk rested at the stiff, rounded collar of his shirt like an undertaker's tie. The center was stuck through with a shining gold pin, a radiant all-seeing eye shedding a lone lightning bolt tear. There was an agelessness to the man. He might've stepped through any door in time. He had skin like a drought, gray and cracking. In some spots, the flesh was almost threadbare, with a diseased shine to it. Faint red veins moved across that flesh, borders shifting constantly. His fingers were long, his nails sharp and yellowed. His eyes were black as a bird's and utterly soulless. To look into them was to feel as if you were standing at the edge of a tall cliff. Vertiginous.

He smiled. "Greetings, Diviners. We meet at last."

THE KING OF CROWS

The night seemed to move with the frantic rhythm of an impaired heart.

Not one of the Diviners could look away from the man in the stovepipe hat. His shiny blue-black coat squawked and fluttered as if fashioned from an endless stream of furious birds pecking for dominance. As he moved toward them, he seemed to grow taller, his shadow falling across more of the land.

"Here you are: The thief. The fire starter. The object reader. The dream walkers. The clairvoyant. And the healer. Do you know who I am?"

"The man in the stovepipe hat," Evie whispered, frightened.

"I prefer the King of Crows," he answered. "After all, why be a man when you can be a king?"

Where the man walked, beetles pushed up from the ground and scuttled toward the cover of mulch. "The moment your country first sinned, I emerged, slick and formless. Born of your restless ambition. Your greed, and hunger. You, who tell yourselves a story of yourselves. Do you imagine you can rid yourselves of me? You have *created* me! I am you, incarnate—a new god for a brave new world. I am written into your history now. I am written into you. And oh! What a nation of glorious dreamers and devourers!"

He opened his coat. In its lining, one could see the soul of the nation: The first ships sailing into Plymouth Bay watched by wary eyes. The longhouses, buffalo hunts, and rain dances. The magnificent trains belching smoke across the miles of prairie. The pages of broken treaties fluttering down over the stolen land where those trains steamed ahead. The battlefields—redcoats and tricornered hats, the Blue and the Gray, West Point lieutenants on horseback charging braves with faces painted in symbols of black and red. There were mountains and rivers begging to be explored, and mighty oceans lapping at the rocky shores of promise. There were fences and guns, forts and reservations. The missions rising in the scrub of California. The clapboard churches springing up like kudzu. The synagogues and temples. A people in need of salvation. There were fields ringing with the call and response of slaves clapping out prayers and songs of survival, defiance felt in every stomp and shout. Dust flecking mail-order brides trussed in trousseau finery seated beside stranger-husbands on a wagon west; those same frontier women, faces creased by sun and hardship, as they worked the farm, fed the hired hands, screamed in childbirth, and sewed their dreams into the squares of quilts and hems of wedding gowns. Oil wells breaking open the earth till it bled. Town squares held together by the ley lines of polite smiles, whispered gossip, and simmering resentments. Cities humming with noise. Birth and death. Song and dance. Industry and invention. Science and magic. Greed and want. Faster and faster it swirled, blurring into a history stitched with bloody thread. It was much too bright to bear, and the Diviners blinked against its terrible light. The creature closed his coat, but what was inside still shimmered around the edges, begging to be let out.

His thin lips stretched into a mirthless smile. "How *insatiable* you are. I feed from your desires. From the violence you cloak in dreams. And now, I, too, am grown insatiable. I would have more. Behold, my Manifest Destiny of the Dead!"

The King of Crows swept his arm wide, a circus barker's invitation. Behind him, restless spirits glowed like a sea of bone. They burned like hunger. Memphis saw Gabe among these dead. Gabe, with his mouth torn away. Gabe, who had once been his friend.

"Memphis..." Isaiah whispered beside him.

"I see, Ice Man."

"But what about you, Diviners? You who bridge worlds." The very air seemed to stutter, and then the King of Crows was in front of Theta. "Theta Knight. The fire starter. Left on a church step. You had a different name then, a name scattered to the winds." He blew on the tips of his yellowed nails. Lightning tripped along his fingertips and died. "Such is the story in this country of scattered names and lost people hunting for the missing pieces of themselves."

Theta felt a fierce yearning deep inside. "You...you know my real name?"

The man smiled. "What would you give to know?"

The King of Crows moved down the line and stopped in front of Sam. "Little thief. Sergei Lubovitch—ah, excuse me. Sam Lloyd. Will you always have to steal what you want? Or perhaps you enjoy going through life invisible, though I suspect you yearn for much more."

The King of Crows grinned his rictus grin. "And what have we here? The dream walkers. How *enchanting*. Tell me, when you escape into dreams each night, do you imagine yourself as little gods? Does it help you escape your loneliness? Your pain? Do you feel less the misfit?" he asked Ling. "Or the unwanted son?" He looked to Henry. He shut his eyes, fingers playing the air. "Yes. I can feel your desires."

The King opened his eyes again, fixing his gaze on Evie. "I have something you might want, object reader."

"I doubt it," Evie challenged, even though she did not feel brave.

The King of Crows cocked his head in two quick jerks. "Not even your brother?"

And before Evie could say another word, the man in the hat rolled his hand with a flourish. Against the thick murk, Evie saw James and the other soldiers as she'd seen them many times in her dreams: playing cards, trading jokes, lacing shoes, unaware of the terror to come. "Sometimes death is a blessing."

"What do you mean by that?" Evie said, feeling newly afraid.

The King of Crows closed the images in his fist and threw them away. "What would you give me to know? What bargain would you be willing to make with me?" The King of Crows opened his arms, palms upturned, bobbing them gently like scales struggling with weight.

He took two elegant strides forward, his long black coattails fluttering behind him, and stopped in front of Isaiah, his smile hardening. "You see much, clairvoyant. Perhaps too much. Tell me, Isaiah Campbell, would you see your own fate writ here inside my coat?" The man in the hat toyed with the feathered edge, letting out just a bit of yellowed shine. "What would you give to change it? Or"—he cast a meaningful glance toward the rest of the Diviners—"to change the fates of others?"

"Stay away from my brother!" Memphis was nearly chest to chest with the King of Crows. He drew in a sharp breath. This close, the strange man was even more terrifying. Flies crawled along the shifting vein work of his mottled skin. His lip curled, revealing a mouthful of thin, pointed teeth. But his eyes...it would be easy for any fella to lose himself in the power of their dark pull. Memphis felt as if he stood with one foot over the edge of a new grave, in danger of falling. Instinctively, he took a step back, blinking till his eyes ran with tears.

"And at last we have *the healer*." The King of Crows said, drawing out the designation. "We have unfinished business, you and I."

From deep in the trees, Viola Campbell emerged, nearly swallowed by the shroud of her feathered dress. Her eyes were large, her face full of grief.

"What would you give me for your mother's freedom?" the King asked.

Viola started. "Don't make a bargain with him, son. I told you, you should never bring back what's gone—"

The King of Crows pointed his clawed hand in Viola Campbell's direction, and her words turned to squawking.

"Memphis," Isaiah whimpered. "Memphis, it's Mama."

"Let her go," Memphis demanded.

The King of Crows sighed and the feathers of his cloak sighed as well. Their fringed spines curved and wriggled as if trying to break free. "Ah, poor mother. Death should offer freedom from life's trials and tribulations. Its…injustices. It should offer rest at long last. Would you not agree, healer?"

Viola struggled in vain to speak. But her voice had been taken by the King's magic.

"I said, leave her be."

"She could rest in peace, you know. But I'll need something from you first." The man held up a long gray index finger. His yellowed fingernail was sharp as a scalpel's point. "A promise. A bargain struck in good faith. In time. In time… For unlike some, I honor my word. This"—he swept his arm wide, gesturing to the ravenous dead—"is not my doing. It is theirs. What they did. Choices have consequences. Tell me: What is most valuable in any world? Where does power lie? In wealth? In titles?"

When no one answered, the King of Crows stuck out his arms. His hands were tightly clenched. "Information," he said, drawing out the word. "What we tell. What we hold back. Truth…" Slowly, he opened his right hand. In it rested a newborn chick, slick with afterbirth. "And secrets…"

He opened the left. A slim green garden snake wound between his spread fingers. "You wish to find the Eye."

"Yes," Evie answered. "Do you know what it is or how we find it?"

"Information," the King of Crows repeated. He closed his fists. The chick and snake disappeared. He hooked his thumbs beneath his lapels and paraded before the Diviners. "Let us play a game to see if you are worthy of my largesse."

"We're not playing anything with you," Sam said.

"The game is already in play, little thief, whether you join in or not. But ask yourself—who has held the truth from you? Not I. You have no idea what they have done. *What they continue to do*. You are in great danger, Diviners."

Once more, he swept his hand against the air, and a picture appeared of two men in gray suits, hats pulled low across their brows. The men drove, and behind them, the roads of America stretched long as shadows. The King of Crows blew out a puff of air and the scene was gone.

"Very well. I shall offer you a small something to show good faith. Tell me, when you"—he fluttered his hand—"*dispatched* my dead just now, did you feel a surge of pure power?"

"Yes," Ling answered. It made her feel a bit dirty to say it. But then Evie said, "You, too?" And one by one, the others nodded.

"Did they not tell you that with each wraith you destroy, your powers grow? Ah, I can see from your faces that they did not." The King of Crows clicked his tongue against his teeth. "So many secrets. Like how the Eye came to be, its terrible purpose, and what it has to do with your brother, object reader."

"Please, oh, please..." Evie started.

The King of Crows pulled at the tattered, smudged lace of his long cuffs. "That is not my story to tell—not without a price. It is yours to find." He looked out over his sea of dead. "You wish to know truth of it, then seek the answers from the dead. Of course, they may not give the information so *willingly*."

"Are you *asking* us to destroy your ghosts?" Theta asked.

The King's thin lips stretched into a semblance of a smile, cruel and mesmerizing. "I ask nothing, fire starter. I tell you nothing. Your choices are yours alone."

He took a few steps back.

"But I have tarried too long. Tonight is for introductions only. We will meet again, most assuredly. In what manner—ah!—that remains to be seen. Aaah, Conor Flynn. Son of the streets. Finder of lost things. *There* you are. You've been trying to hide from me, have you not? Someone has helped you with that."

Conor trembled.

"Let us up the ante in our game. Checkmates and balances and whatnot. I shall take this one with me. As leverage."

The King beckoned and Conor stumbled forward as if compelled until he collapsed into Viola Campbell's motherly arms.

"Shhh, baby," she said, holding him close. "Shhh."

"Let him go! Conor has nothing to do with this! That isn't fair," Evie demanded.

The King of Crows glowered. He spoke through tight teeth. "You speak to me of fairness?" His fingers toyed at his lapels and a bit of history's unbearable shine threatened at the edges. "Fairness. Very well. I shall give you a bargain: Find the answers you seek from the dead, and I shall return him to you. Awake, my children," the King of Crows commanded in a voice that was not loud but demanded full attention. "Rise, my army."

Broken and rotting and hungry, the dead crawled from their graves and gathered behind their leader. Lightning split the clouds.

"As for you, Luther Clayton," the King said. "You were owed to me, and I would have payment for their sins. That is justice."

Luther's head rolled from side to side. "No," he whispered again and again, his voice rising to a scream. "No!"

Evie charged toward Luther. The King of Crows put up a hand, and she felt as if her breath were turning solid in her lungs, weighing her down.

"Would you come for me so soon, object reader? You might save your strength for a battle yet to be." Something awful pulsed in the King's face as his mouth set into a grim line. But just as quickly, he let Evie go. She coughed, pulling the putrid air deep into her aching lungs. "We've only just begun our dance."

The King of Crows smiled at Luther Clayton. "Have your fill, children. For we are the storm. We are come to claim what is ours. I alone will care for you. I alone give you what you require. Feed."

Luther screamed as the dead rushed forward, jagged mouths open. The King of Crows tugged at the brim of his tall hat in the slightest of gestures. "Happy hunting, Diviners."

With that, the Diviners were jolted from the vision. It seemed as if they tumbled through space until they stood once more in the potter's fields. The rain had stopped. Across the river, the city's neon bloomed. Several ferries were arriving at the pier. Firemen and medics hurried toward the asylum with stretchers and hoses. The fog was gone. So was Conor Flynn.

And atop a disturbed grave was what little remained of Luther Clayton.

MISTAKES

It was still dark but edging toward dawn when the Diviners returned to the museum. Evie had called Will from the asylum, telling him only that he and Sister Walker should be waiting for them in the library. The Diviners had answered questions from the police about what had happened to Conor Flynn, who was listed as missing, and to Luther Clayton: *Jesus, how did the poor fella end up...like* that? *Did one of the patients do it? Was it Conor?* Detective Terrence Malloy had arrived at last. The Diviners hadn't seen him since the Pentacle Murders case six months before, when all of this had started. He'd taken one look at Evie and the others and shaken his head. "How come every time I see you folks it's something nobody can explain but something I know is gonna cause me no end of headaches? Go on home," he'd said on a sigh. "I got any questions, I know where to find you. Give my regards to your uncle."

The lights were burning at the Creepy Crawly. As the Diviners descended on the library, an anxious-looking Will and Sister Walker rose to their feet.

"Thank heavens you're back," Will said. "What happened out there? We were very worr—"

Evie marched up to Will and slapped him hard. "How could you? *How could you!*"

"We know everything," Sam said, coming to stand beside her. "What you did during the war to those soldiers. Your experiment? We know the whole story."

Will rubbed at the fresh mark on his face. "Somehow I don't think you do."

"You've been lying to us about everything. Even after we asked you to be honest with us," Ling said. She could barely look at Sister Walker. "I trusted you. I admired you."

"Anything we held back we did in order to protect you," Sister Walker said.

"In order to protect yourselves, you mean," Ling said.

Evie was sobbing now, and it felt as if she were swallowing down the world and its awful sins along with her broken cries. "He was my b-brother. Your *nephew*, Will. And you let him die! No—you got him killed. You got all of them killed!"

"It...it was an accident. I swear it," Will said.

"Oh, why can't anyone just tell the truth?" Evie pleaded.

"Because..." Will started. "Because it's so hard to know what the truth is. It shifts, depending on who's telling it and when."

Evie's finger was a dagger stabbing at the air between them. "No. *That* is a lie you tell yourself so you can sleep at night! You just don't *want* to know that you had anything to do with that horror! Well, thanks to poor Luther, I was *there*. I *saw*! I *know*. You can't take that from me by spinning some new story into butter. I won't let you! And now Luther Clayton is dead! He's dead because of your lies, murdered by those horrible beasts and the King of Crows!"

"What happened to Luther?" Will demanded.

"Those wraiths got to him. The King of Crows unleashed them," Henry explained.

Will's eyes widened. "You met the King of Crows? You *spoke* to him?"

"How did this come about?" Sister Walker wanted to know.

Evie snorted derisively. "A man is dead, but who cares about that?"

Sam shoved his hands in his pockets and slumped against the wall, exhausted. "We made one of those energy fields and destroyed some ghosts—"

"Destroyed them how?" Will asked, wary.

"And then we were in this creepy place full of the hungry dead, in case you wanted to hear the rest of that sentence."

"Yes, we destroyed them," Evie said. "Without your help."

Will raked a hand through his thinning hair. "What is he up to now?" he muttered more to himself than anyone present.

Sister Walker reached for her notebook and a pencil. "What did he say to you?"

"That you couldn't be trusted. That you've been lying to us all along," Sam said. "Guess he was right about that. I'm the con who got conned."

"Please. I need you to remember what you saw and precisely what he said to you. It's vitally important," Sister Walker said.

"We're not telling you anything else, Miss Walker," Memphis said. "Not till you're honest with us. For once."

"You have a right to feel upset, Memphis, but—"

Memphis's voice boomed. "Stop telling me what I have a right to feel and start telling us the truth!"

Sister Walker seemed the slightest bit rattled, but then she collected herself. She stood tall, smoothing a hand down her dress and speaking with a curated calm. "All right, then. Yes. It was us. All of us at the Department of Paranormal—Will, Rotke, Jake, Miriam, and me. *We* opened that door to the world of the dead. We were as naïve as we were ambitious. The King of Crows baited us, and we took that bait without question. We let him into our world with our ignorance. We made a mistake, and now that mistake is back to haunt us with a vengeance."

"We assumed that because the experiment had been a catastrophic failure, that was the end of it, and the opening into that world had been sealed once more," Will continued. "The government shut down the Department of Paranormal. Margaret burned the files so that the experiment could never be repeated. She paid the price for that."

"I was imprisoned until they decided I was no longer a threat," Sister Walker said. "They left me with nothing."

"For years, there was no sign of any activity. We had no reason to suspect that there was anything to fear. And then the signs started: Ghost sightings. Hauntings. A sinister presence lurking in the country. I tried to ignore it. To pretend it was anything other than what it really was. But soon, it became apparent: The door had never fully closed. That energy was leaking into our world. And with it, the King of Crows. He has some game he's playing, but we don't know what it is, and that is the truth. Cornelius tried to warn me about him, but I wouldn't listen. Liberty Anne had told him to be careful. And now I am telling you: The man in the stovepipe hat is cunning and cruel. He is ruthless in his desires, and not to be trusted," Will insisted.

"Are you describing him or yourself?" Evie snapped.

"You are our only hope of getting the answers we need about him if we're to be safe from him and his army. Your powers joined together in purpose can heal that breach at last! We cannot stop our work now. You've seen for yourselves that the storm isn't just coming—it's here. It's here, and we must stop it from getting worse before it's too late!" Sister Walker said.

"See, that's your generation all over—you muck up everything and then expect us to fix your messes," Sam growled.

"I understand your anger. Mistakes were made," Will said.

Evie's eyes flashed. "No! *You. Made. Mistakes.* You were the one who talked about our choices. About evil being what humans bring about. You *made* evil."

"There are choices you make, things you do, that you don't know are wrong when you do them. Only time gives you that perspective. Only history," Will pleaded.

"We made mistakes," Sister Walker said a bit more crisply. "And now we must atone for those mistakes. I'm sorry, but it's going to take all of us to fix it."

Evie's laugh was bitter. "After you murdered my brother? After what you did to our mothers? After you engineered us to be your little army of freaks and kept the truth of it from us? When did we ever get a say in any of it?" Evie shook her head and backed away. She couldn't even look Will in the face. Not after what he'd done to James and the other soldiers. "I hate you for what you've done. I'll hate you till my dying day! I will never, ever have anything to do with you again!"

Evie bolted from the room.

"We didn't know. I swear we didn't know," Will said again as the others filed out.

As if that made any difference.

※

Sam ran after Evie, calling her name. She sank to her knees on the museum's damp yard. Sam scooped her up and held her to him. "Hey, hey, hey, Sheba. I've got you. I've got you. Listen, you and me and the others. We'll see this thing through. All right? C'mon, Baby Vamp. Shake your head if you hear me."

Evie turned her tearstained face to him. Her cheeks were splotchy, her eyes swollen. "I'm so angry, Sam. So, so angry. I want to punch at the world and keep punching, but what good would it do?" She hiccup-cried with rage.

Sam cupped her face gently. "You. Me. All of us. No matter what."

Finally, Evie allowed a small nod, whether of agreement or defeat, Sam couldn't be sure. But it was a start. He helped her to her feet. The others were in the yard now.

"What do we do now?" Henry asked.

"So far, our decisions have been made for us. It's time we started taking back the power," Memphis said.

"We have to get Conor back," Evie said.

"What about the rest of it?" Ling asked. "How do we find out about the Eye?"

"You think the man in the hat was telling us the truth about asking the ghosts for clues?" Henry said.

Evie couldn't rid her head of the image of the dead descending with open mouths on Luther Clayton. "It's all we've got to work with. We hunt those things down. We make them tell us what 'Follow the Eye' means. And we ask about the King of Crows, too—what he wants and how to defeat him. We'll use that knowledge to get Conor back, to find out about my brother, and to close the breach and fix what Will and Sister Walker and Marlowe started once and for all."

"What do we do with the ghosts once they tell us what we need to know?" Ling prompted.

"We obliterate 'em. Every single one," Sam said.

"I don't know," Ling said. Hadn't she spoken with ghosts in her dreams? Hadn't they given her and others advice? Were there "good" ghosts and "bad" ghosts, the new breed Sister Walker and Will had mentioned? What if all the ghosts were connected somehow—and connected to the Diviners as well? "Seems shortsighted. After all, we don't really understand what sort of energy they are or where that energy goes when we—"

"I just want them gone," Evie said firmly.

"And it seems like it makes us stronger. We gotta build up our power if we're gonna go up against what we saw last night," Sam said, and Ling couldn't argue with that.

"What about those Shadow Men?" Henry said. "I've got the feeling they don't want us around at all."

"Those bastards have my mother somewhere. I look forward to kicking in their teeth," Sam said, and spat.

"Memphis, what'll those Shadow Men do to us?" Isaiah said.

"Anybody wants to come after you, Ice Man, they gotta go through me first," Memphis assured him, but Isaiah didn't look comforted.

"We need to make ourselves indispensable. It's harder to disappear people who are seen," Evie said, wiping away her tears. Theta handed her a handkerchief and Evie blew her nose. "I say we announce ourselves as the only choice to eliminate the city's ghost troubles. I'll call Woody, get him on the trolley, and ask people to call in to the *News* with any sightings. We'll have ourselves splashed across the papers every day if we have to."

"Not me," Memphis said. "Papa Charles and Owney Madden can't see what I'm doing, or I'm a dead man myself."

"Gee, I don't know. We say we're chasing ghosts, we'll be the laughing-stock of New York," Theta warned.

"You seen the headlines? People are scared of the ghosts. We take care of 'em, we'll be folk heroes," Sam said.

"I'm not worried about some ghosts scaring people," Ling said. "I'm worried about what people do when they get scared."

Will and Sister Walker watched from the museum's lighted window, gray silhouettes.

"I can't stay with the professor anymore," Sam said, nodding over his shoulder.

"You can bunk with Henry and me," Theta said, and Henry nodded.

"Second question: Where do we meet now that the museum's not an option?" Henry asked.

"The Hotsy Totsy?" Memphis suggested.

Sam winced. "That cover charge is steep. Not that I can't steal it, but that leaves the rest of you."

"It's too hard for me to get there from Chinatown," Ling said.

"We could meet at the Winthrop," Evie suggested.

"White folks can meet at the Winthrop," Memphis said tightly with a glance to Ling, who nodded.

"Swell. We're the only Diviner ghost service in town without a meeting place," Sam said, tugging on the brim of his fisherman's cap.

"We can use the rehearsal room in the building on Twenty-eighth Street where David and I compose. It's noisy, but it's cheap," Henry said.

"This afternoon, we meet up in Tin Pan Alley, at Henry's spot," Evie said.

"Memphis, I'm beat," Isaiah said, stifling a yawn.

"Just a minute, Ice Man."

Memphis trotted after Theta. "Theta," he called, but she didn't stop. Memphis held her arm gently. "*Theta*. Talk to me. Please?"

He slipped his fingers through hers. "Careful," she said, but Memphis held on.

"You're not gonna hurt me. You're not," he insisted.

"Now you know what's inside me."

"Yeah. The girl I love."

"You know what I mean."

"So what? I don't care about that."

"But you will. One day you'll look at me and you won't feel safe."

"No. I won't. I love you. That won't change."

Theta's resolve was falling apart. If she told Memphis the truth about Roy, he'd want to stand up to Roy. And then Roy would hurt Memphis. Maybe more than hurt him. She had to end it decisively. Burn it all down. Make him hate her. That was the only way to keep him from coming back. That was the only way to keep him safe.

Theta drew on every bit of her acting skills. "It ain't that. It's you and me. We live in different worlds."

"Hasn't stopped us yet."

Theta forced a coldness into her voice. "Things have changed. I've got a contract with Vitagraph. I'm going to be a star. I can't risk that on you. Sorry, Poet. We had a good run."

The hurt showed on Memphis's face like a bruise, and Theta wanted to snatch back every word. She was breaking inside. "Theta? What are you saying?"

"I think I've been clear. You and I are over. It's been over for some time. I'm sure you could feel it. I…I just didn't know how to tell you. Honestly, I'm glad it's out now. It's better this way."

Memphis turned his face up toward the sky, nodding slowly. The back of his throat ached with bitterness. He'd opened himself wide. He'd taken her as she was and asked no more. But none of that was enough. None of it was bigger than skin. Whoever said love conquers all was a fool.

"You'll love again," Theta said, as if it were nothing.

"Not like this."

"Memphis! I'm tired!" Isaiah called. He was nearly falling down with exhaustion. Once again, Memphis was caught between worlds—the living and the dead, his brother and his girl, duty and desire. Love. And hate. Above him, the stars were fading behind New York City's perpetual hazy glow.

Maybe he'd been wrong about Theta. Maybe she was a killer after all.

"Memphis?" she said, soft and aching, and for just a minute Memphis wanted to believe that she still loved him. That this was a bad dream. But he was starting to wake up about the world, about real nightmares.

He was still holding her hand, he realized. He dropped it now. "You know what? When I said you could never hurt me, I was wrong."

When Roy would hit her, Theta's mind sometimes allowed her to float away from the pain. But there was no getting away from the pain Theta felt as she watched Memphis walk away and take the protesting, weary Isaiah's hand on their way to the train.

"You copacetic?" Henry was beside her, his arm around her shoulders.

"No."

"Yeah. Me, either."

The Diviners split apart like an atom. The last dregs of the night swallowed the energy and held its unstable breath. History placed its bets.

In the brown sedan parked at the corner, the men in the dark suits kept watch.

Sam walked Evie back to the Winthrop. "I could stay if you want me to," he said.

"I should go to bed," Evie mumbled.

"Oh, sure. Best thing, really. What happened back at the asylum, when you…and me…I mean I know you were possessed. Otherwise, you wouldn't have…you know. And with such…enthusiasm."

Evie blushed. "Right. I-I wasn't in control."

"Yeah. Just…ghosts."

"Ghosts," Evie confirmed.

"Thought so." Sam managed a weak smile. "Well, there's still a little time left in this miserable night, and I know a speakeasy on Fifty-second where the dames are happy to see you at this hour."

"Yes, wouldn't want to disappoint your harem," Evie grumbled.

"You know…" Sam started. He threw up his hands in defeat. "Never mind. Strictly business. Diviners, Incorporated."

"Good night, Sam!" Evie growled.

"Yeah, you, too!"

"Dames. Who needs 'em?" Sam groused on his way up the street, one hand tracing the outline of his lips where her kiss had been.

※

It was Mabel Evie called when she got back. Mabel who came to her side, even though it was very early in the morning. As they lay on Evie's bed, she listened to an emotionally drained Evie spin out the whole fantastical, terrifying story.

"Gee, that's awful," Mabel said. It felt like a stupid thing to say, but it was all she had. She knew her friends in the Secret Six wouldn't understand any of this. Mabel wasn't even sure that she did. She was no Diviner. She didn't see into mysterious realms or talk to ghosts. Sometimes that made her feel removed from the threat because she only heard about it through the others. All she knew was that Evie had called her because, somehow, a thread still connected them. Because Mabel was Evie's best friend, and being a good and reliable friend was pretty heroic when it came down to it.

"I'll help you," Mabel said, squeezing Evie's hand.

"With what?"

"With whatever it is that needs helping. We can't let evil win, no matter what, no matter where. If it's coming for one of us, then it's coming for all of us."

Evie threw her arms around Mabel's waist and kissed her cheek.

"Mabel Rose, you are my North Star," Evie said quietly. "I pos-i-tute-ly don't know what I'd do without you."

"You'd probably be in jail," Mabel answered, but Evie was already sound asleep.

BLIND JUSTICE

Bill Johnson sat up on his cot. The house was quiet and still, no smell of bacon or coffee wafting out of Octavia's kitchen. So, still night, then. He'd been dreaming of a time when his name was Guillaume and he was young and strong and working the cotton fields down south. He'd dreamed of Samson. How he'd loved that old plow horse. At night sometimes, Bill would sneak into the barn and rub Samson's soft nose. Samson would nuzzle Bill's calloused hands. "Ain't got no sugar for you today, old boy," Bill would chuckle. And then he'd put his forehead to Samson's and twine his fingers in the horse's dusty mane. Joined like this, Bill could hear the proud beast's strong heartbeat roaring through his own body, syncing their rhythms, and the two of them would stand just for a minute in perfect harmony. As if they could sense Bill's gentleness, the other animals would draw near. One by one, they'd settle. Sometimes, Bill would climb into the pen, lie down on the soft hay, and fall asleep beside Samson.

That spring, there was a terrible flood. The waters rushed through the camp like an angry fist. The land was a grasping mud as far as anyone could see. The foreman, Mr. Burneside, shouted at everyone to save the crop. That was pure profit washing away out there. Then he saddled up Samson so he could ride out and enforce his order.

Bill knew the horse was no match for all that mud. "Mr. Burneside, sir, I don't believe poor Samson can manage all 'at mud."

"I'll worry about the horse. You worry about my crops, boy, or you'll be off my land."

The rains kept coming. Out in the field, Samson stepped into a hole that couldn't be seen under so much angry water. With a terrible shriek, he fell, throwing Mr. Burneside into the raging flood. Bill ran to Samson, but he could see the horse's leg had snapped clean in two, and when he put his hands on Samson, he could feel the horse's heart galloping wildly with fear and pain. They'd put a bullet in him for sure. But how long before they could do that? How long would the poor animal have to suffer like this? Would the gunshot hurt? Would Samson be frightened?

Bill would not leave his friend to suffer. "Shhh, shhh, boy. It's just your old friend Bill come to see you. Don't worry none. Shhh," he soothed. He put his hands on the horse's mangled leg and sang softly. The connection took. The horse stiffened for a count of two, then stilled as Bill ushered him gently into peaceful death.

When Bill came out of his trance, tears ran down his face, and he was glad for the cover of rain. Mr. Burneside was screaming at him from a prickle berry bush where he'd washed up.

"You damn fool! Get over here and he'p me up!"

Bill's anger was alive and ready to strike. He strode through the flood-water and stood over the foreman, casting a powerful shadow across the ravaged land. "Told you not to take Samson out."

"I'll do what I like with my horse."

"Ain't your horse no more. He's free."

Tiny motes of electricity danced along the tips of Bill's trembling fingers. The inside of his head roared like a storm.

"I said he'p me up!" Mr. Burneside commanded.

Bill didn't move.

"Goddamn it, you gone deaf, boy? I said he'p me up!"

"Yes, sir." Bill grabbed hold of Mr. Burneside's hand, tightening his grip, the electricity flowing between them, and Bill couldn't deny the pleasure he took in seeing the foreman's eyes widen with fear and knowing.

Mr. Burneside's son called out: "Hey! Daddy? Daddy, where you at? Guillaume? Whatchoo doing? Hey! *Hey!*"

Bill had run deep into the trees. Now that his anger had receded like the waters, he was frightened. The men would come for him soon, he knew. Come with their ropes and their brands and their guns and heaven knew what other cruelties. It was another sharecropper, Jed Robbins, who came for him first. "Guillaume, Mrs. Burneside is calling for you. You got to come back."

"And let 'em hang me from that old oak? No, sir."

"Ain't like that. Young Mr. Burneside says he saw you pulling his daddy outta the water. Said you saved his daddy's life. Say if it wadn't for you, his daddy mighta died. Looks like he caught a stroke out there when he fell offa that horse."

Back at the house, Mr. Burneside lay on the cot. His face was slack. His eyes, though, found Bill's. They were full of fear and accusation.

Jed Robbins looked at him funny, too, and Bill wondered if his sin was out for all to see.

"What you looking at?" Bill said.

Jed pointed to Bill's head. "You got a stripe a gray right down the middle of your head. Wadn't there this morning."

Word got around. There was something of a shine to Guillaume "Bill" LeRoi Johnson, something from beyond. Word got all the way to the Department of Paranormal. Some folks came to ask him questions about his gifts, and Bill heard the word *Diviner* for the first time. The Shadow Men came after, and Bill went with them. He let Margaret Walker poke and prod him. Test his powers. Then those Shadow Men asked him to do things he didn't want to do.

"We need you to help your country now, Mr. Johnson," they said.

He'd done it. It was a time of war. What choice did he have? Most of the men he'd killed were bad men, weren't they? Men the world was better off without. That was what Bill told himself. But some of those men looked like Bill. Like maybe their only crime was wanting change. It all took a turn with prisoner number twelve.

"What'd he do?" Bill had asked. He was afraid. Deep in his gut, he could tell this didn't feel right. None of it felt right anymore. His body hurt all the time.

"You don't need to know that, Mr. Johnson," the Shadow Man assured him.

Bill took a step toward the man and faltered. "Yes, sir. Believe I do need to know."

"He's one of those agitators. We caught him and his coconspirators plotting to blow up a mine in a country pertinent to our interests."

The man had been beaten. He didn't seem any more dangerous than Samson. Bill couldn't bring himself to move against the man. "No, sir."

The man in the suit sighed heavily. "Have you ever heard of blind justice, Mr. Johnson?"

Bill nodded. The courthouse back home had a statue of the blindfolded lady. He'd seen it once on a trip to town.

"We are the blind eye of justice. Justice that happens out of sight. We are the sword, swift and sure."

The beaten man at Bill's feet didn't speak English. He looked to Bill with a mix of weariness, fear, and contempt. The man spat at Bill's feet.

"You see?" the man in the suit said, as if that were all the proof needed.

Bill took hold of the beaten man's neck, and then a strange thing happened. It was as if Bill had been transported to a dream. He stood in a patch of land surrounded by a dark wood shrouded in mist. The trees didn't look like any he knew. No Spanish moss or mesquite. These were giants with limbs thick as a working man's arms that spread up and out into a tangled latticework of tinier branches clasped together like a prayerful man's fingers. No leaves grew here that Bill could see. A snake slithered along a branch and plopped to the ground. Deep in the grainy mist, faces appeared—chalk-pale with deeply shadowed, unseeing eyes. Bill wanted to run, but where?

"Guillaume LeRoi Johnson."

At the sound of his voice, Bill whirled around. There was a table and a deck of cards. Seated at the table was a strange creature, a thin gray man whose skin was as mottled as a moth's wings. He wore a magnificent blue-black coat of oil-shine feathers, and on his head was a tall black hat. His long fingers ended in curved, yellowed fingernails caked in dirt, and Bill had a feeling of this man using those fingernails to dig himself out of a grave so deep it led to another world. The man in the hat shuffled a deck of tarot cards, cutting them into neat piles. His hands moved so fast it was like a bird's wings fluttering.

"Guillaume LeRoi Johnson," the man repeated. "Bastard son of rape, grandson of a slave mother and the master of the house. Born of violence and despair. *Diviner.*" And something about the way the man said it, slow and awestruck and menacing, goose-pimpled Bill's skin. "Do you know who I am?"

Bill shook his head.

"I am also a bastard son. Born of this nation's dreams and greed. Its idealism and its ignorance. Its hope and its violence. Would you like to be free of the shackles those men have placed upon you?"

"I surely would, sir. Yes, I would."

The man in the hat smiled. "Make a bargain with me."

Bill made the bargain under the yellow moonlight in that strange, dark forest where skeleton birds cawed toward the starless night. Where the dead watched and waited for you to fall.

When he came to, he was squeezing the broken neck of prisoner number twelve.

And then it was done. Again and again, he performed his duty without question. Men. Women. One as young as thirteen. Another as old as seventy. Each time took more of him with it. He was no longer Guillaume or Bill. He was no man. He was death. After one year, he looked forty. After two years, he barely recognized himself. His body ached like the devil. The skin of his hands was paper-thin and wrinkled. Veins popped up like tree roots. Two of his teeth rotted. Bill dug them out with his fingers and spat the bloody slivers into the sink. He hobbled to the mirror, but the reflection that greeted him was an old man's.

And then his vision darkened and disappeared.

"What's happening to me?" Bill asked. He begged for help. But there was nothing to be done. He was washed up and used. His talents gone for good.

"Thank you for your service to this country, Mr. Johnson. You're free to go," the Shadow Men said.

That was it. No money. No care for his blindness. Not even a medal. They left him on the side of the road like an unwanted dog.

Just like the man in the hat had promised, he was free of the Shadow Men. At a price.

And there was Memphis Campbell, walking around with his friends, not paying a price at all. Out there healing up white gangsters—yes, Bill had heard the rumors—but he wouldn't even spare some for a friend. For one of his own. Every day, Bill swallowed down his bitterness. Now it came burning up inside him. To hell with Memphis Campbell.

While the house slept, Bill treaded carefully down the hall. He'd walked it so many times he could feel it. He was inside the boys' room now—he knew by smell. He could hear Isaiah snoring. Carefully, he lowered his hand, placing it on the boy's arm, hoping Isaiah would not wake. *Easy, Bill. Easy, now*, he said to himself, just like he used to say to Samson all those long years ago. But he couldn't quite draw it out. Something wouldn't let him. He wanted to howl. Rage. Tear something down. "Take," he muttered. "Take, take, take." The connection seized Bill like a pair of strong hands. Bill knew in his gut that wherever this was pulling him was a bad place. A feeling crawled over his skin like biting fire ants. And then a familiar face loomed before him.

"Hello, old friend," the King of Crows said. His dark eyes were bottomless wells of terrors beyond imagining. They were in that forest again. The sick moon bled into the empty black night. When the King spoke, his razor-sharp teeth gleamed. "Do you think you can take what's mine? You, of all people, should know better. Have you forgotten me so soon? I will colonize your soul with fear until, in your despair, you'll think my yoke a boon. So you wish to see, do you? Very well. I shall grant your wish."

Inside that world between worlds, the King of Crows raked his sharp fingernails across Bill's face. Bill fell back as if burned, breaking the spell with Isaiah.

"My eyes!" he gasped. When he blinked, he saw terrible things: A husband slitting his wife's throat. A band of white rangers taking the scalps of Indian children as they tried to run to safety. The hungry dead winking from a cornfield where they feasted on the mutilated carcass of a fly-ridden cow.

"Uncle Bill?" Isaiah said sleepily from his bed. "That you? Whatsa matter?"

Bill hurried from the room, tapping his way back to his own. He sat on the cot breathing heavily. He shut his eyes and the terrible scenes got worse—hangings and lynchings and men blown apart by war. So he stayed awake, fearing each blink until finally, by morning, the spell was done. Nothing permanent, then. Just a reminder of the King's power. Of what he could do.

THE DEAD

The history of the land is a history of blood.

In this history, someone wins and someone loses. There are patriots and enemies. Folk heroes who save the day. Vanquished foes who had it coming.

It's all in the telling.

The conquered have no voice. Ask the thirty-eight Santee Sioux singing the death song with the nooses around their necks, the treaty signed fair and square, then nullified with a snap of the rope. Ask the slave women forced to bear their masters' children, to raise and love them and see them sold. Ask the miners slaughtered by the militia in Ludlow.

Names are erased. The conqueror tells the story. The colonizer writes the history, winning twice: A theft of land. A theft of witness.

Oh, but let's not speak of such things! Look: Here is an eagle whipping above the vast grasslands where the buffalo once thundered bold as gods. (The buffalo are here among the dead. So many buffalo.) There is the Declaration in sepia. (Signed by slave owners. Shhh, hush up about that, now!) See how the sun shines down upon the homesteaders' wagons racing toward a precious claim in the nation's future, the pursuit of happiness pursued without rest, destiny made manifest? (Never mind about those same homesteaders eating the flesh of neighbors. Winters are harsh in this country. Pack a snack.)

The history is a hungry history. Its mouth opens wide to consume. It must be fed. Bring me what you would forget, it cries, and I will swallow it whole and pull out the bones bleached of truth upon which you will hang the myths of yourselves. Feed me your pain and I will give you dreams and denial, a balm in Gilead.

The land remembers everything, though.

It knows the steps of this nation's ballet of violence and forgetting.

The land receives our dead, and the dead sing softly the song of us: blood.

Blood on the plains. In the rivers. On the trees where the ropes swing. Blood on the leaves. Blood under the flowers of Gettysburg, of Antioch. Blood on the auction blocks. Blood of the Lenape, the Cherokee, the Cheyenne. Blood of the Alamo. Blood of the Chinese railroad workers. Blood of the midwives hung for witchcraft, for the crime of being women who bleed. Blood of the immigrants fleeing the hopeless, running toward the open arms of the nation's seductive hope, its greatest export. Blood of the first removed to make way for the cities, the factories, the people and their unbridled dreams: The chugging of the railways. The tapping of the telegram. The humming of industry. Sound burbling along telephone wires. Printing presses whirring with the day's news. And the next day's. And the day after that's. Endless cycles of information. Cities brimming with ambitions used and discarded.

The dead hold what the people throw away. The stories sink the tendrils of their hope and sorrow down into the graves and coil around the dead buried there, deep in its womb.

All passes away, the dead whisper. Except for us.

We, the eternal. Always here. Always listening. Always seeing.

One nation, under the earth. *E Pluribus unum mortuis.*

Oh, how we wish we could reach you! You dreamers and schemers! Oh, you children of optimism! You pioneers! You stars and stripes, forever!

Sometimes, the dreamers wake as if they have heard. They take to the streets. They pick up the plow, the pen, the banner, the promise. They reach out to neighbors. They reach out to strangers. Backs stooped from a hard day's labor, two men, one black, one white, share water from a well. They are thirsty and, in this one moment, thirst and work make them brothers. They drink of shared trust, that all men are created equal. They wipe their brows and smile up at a faithful sun. The young run toward the horizon, proclaiming their optimism to the blue skies: "I am working toward greatness."

The girl told no starts the engine of her brother's abandoned plane: "I am working toward greatness."

The family steps onto the planks of Ellis Island, hearts turned toward Liberty's torch: *"Kaam kar raha hoon."*

The boys draw water from the well and plant their seeds: *"Estoy traba-jando hacia la grandeza."*

During these times, the dead hold their breath. The heart of the land beats with fresh hope. That we will hold these truths to be self-evident, and crown thy good with brotherhood. Sweet land of liberty, of thee I sing.

In our shrouds, we look up and watch you.

You, milking the cow. You, dreaming in the field. You, who look to the stars and proclaim yourselves. You, who fall in love and marry, who birth and plot and strive. You, who blow yourselves apart with war. You, who mourn your losses and curse those same skies. You, who bury your dead. You, who ask, "Am I enough?" You, who pray to leave a mark. You, so full of life. You, capable of such moments of transcendent beauty that it shifts the atoms of history into an ecstatic sigh. You, who erect the monuments so that you'll remember, for a time. You, who will also wither and die.

We marvel at your endless capacity to dream and create and, yes, even to love. To keep inventing yourselves. To ignore history's lessons. To rewrite the story again and again.

We wish you love. And dreams. And hope.

We wish we could keep you from making the same mistakes.

We wish we could extinguish your hate.

We wish we could walk among you just to be close to the living.

Sometimes, we do.

We watch the sun rise and sink, day after day after day, faster and faster, until time is a string moving so swiftly it appears not to move at all.

We, the ancestors.

The ones who came before with the same dreams.

The same false inheritance.

※

The people are afraid now. Too much history rises from the graves.

Ghosts take shape in the cornfields. Behind the factories. Along the rivers. At the creeping edges of the cities and towns. They burn brightly like a secret revealed. The night is illuminated by truth so sharp it scrapes breath from the lungs of those who finally see. The people are anxious for vague reassurances.

But this is the history: blood.

We are the dead.

We are the keepers of the stories.

We hold the history of blood and promises.

We are speaking.

Are you listening?

Will you hear?

PART TWO

GHOSTS IN GOTHAM

The Daily News

EXTRA! GHOSTS IN GOTHAM!

Exclusive to T. S. Woodhouse

The days are numbered for the creepy crawlies allegedly lurking in the city's dark alleys, making a nuisance of themselves in swanky hotels, and spooking the speakeasies. Manhattan is giving up the ghost, thanks to the combined efforts of a dedicated team of Diviners. Led by the Sweetheart Seer herself, comely Evie O'Neill, who only so recently braved the fire out on Ward's Island to save the lives of the poor souls housed there, a fire started, they say, by malevolent spirits from beyond, these Diviners are making the city safe again. Woe unto the things that go bump in the night, for it's hip, hip, boo-ray for this brave ghost-banishing team.

Theta lowered the newspaper and lifted one perfectly arched eyebrow. "Led by comely Evie O'Neill? Oh, brother."

"What are the rest of us, chopped liver?" Sam said.

Evie's eyes were wide and innocent. "Can I help it if Woody put me first?"

"Yes!" everyone said at once.

Evie pretended to be miffed, but she was thrilled that Woody had singled her out and called her comely to boot. Her only objection was that the story had been buried on page six in the "Seen and Overheard" section. Hopefully, that would change, and soon. She'd have to talk to Woody about it. They needed more attention if they were to find ghosts, solve the mystery of the Eye, and get Conor back, too.

"Any calls yet?" Evie asked Mabel.

"A few," Mabel said, passing over her notes. They were gathered in the tiny Tin Pan Alley room where Henry and David composed music. The building was noisy but it was cheap, and Mabel, David, and Alma had promised to come in a few hours each day to answer the telephone they'd installed, which, so far, was not ringing as often as Evie would've liked. That morning, they'd scoured the papers for mentions of ghost sightings, finding one or two worth looking into.

Evie read through Mabel's notes. "Drunk. Not credible. Drunk. Thought I saw a ghost but it might have been my brother in his underwear. Drunk. Are there any naked ghosts and do they touch you in your naughty…" Evie paused, frowning.

"I hung up on that one," Mabel said, blushing.

"We've got a tough road to hoe to get people to believe us," Theta said.

"And to get off page six," Evie grumbled, tossing the useless notes into the wastebasket.

"Just remember to keep Isaiah and me out of the papers," Memphis said.

"I don't need that kind of publicity, either," Theta said. She smiled at Memphis, but he looked away, as if he hadn't seen her at all, and Theta called on her acting skills to make it seem as if she weren't broken inside.

The phone rang and Mabel pressed the receiver to her ear with one hand as she scribbled notes with the other. "And where did you say you saw these ghosts? At your mother-in-law's house? You think she's possessed by an evil spirit? Uh-huh."

Mabel looked to Evie with a *help* expression. Evie grabbed the phone and put on her brightest radio voice, all elocution-shaped vowels. "An evil spirit in your mother-in-law, you say? Well, I'm afraid there's only one cure for it, sir. Yes, you'll need to spend *all* of your time with her. Yes, every *blessed* minute. Constant watching. Ask her to dinner and to be a fourth for your bridge party. That's what these 'evil spirits' demand. Do whatever she asks of you. You don't want to be cursed for life, do you?" Evie held the receiver out. "Huh. He hung up, the chump."

"I can't imagine why," Alma said from the piano where she had been sitting with David, singing along softly to a new tune he was working on. "How many real calls have you gotten today?"

"Five," Evie said.

"Mm-mm-*mm*. And were any of 'em on the level?" Alma asked.

"Not yet. But we will get them!"

"You know, not all the newspapers are so enthusiastic about your ghost-hunting activities," David said, scribbling lyrics on staff paper. "They want to know why Luther Clayton died—and why he was last seen with you when it happened."

Evie sobered. "All the more reason to hunt down ghosts and get the answers we need."

"Any clues from last night's dream walk?" Sam asked.

Henry shook his head. "We couldn't find Conor anywhere."

"Isaiah? Any visions?"

"Sorry," Isaiah said glumly.

"Memphis, Ling, have you found anything at the libraries?" Evie asked.

"I haven't had the opportunity to go," Ling admitted. "My parents need me in the restaurant."

"I managed an hour yesterday." From his knapsack, Memphis pulled out three library books and opened the topmost to a drawing. "There are some slave and native accounts that mention the man in the hat. One from a diary at Jamestown, and another in Salem just before the witch trials. I found a few sightings dating from the American Revolution and the Civil War and Reconstruction," Memphis said, opening the other books to the pages he'd bookmarked with slips of paper. "Seems he's drawn to the energy of unrest, like Dr. Fitzgerald said. And he has many names: The King of Crows. The leader of the dead. The man in the stovepipe hat. The beguiler. He who returns. The bargain master."

"Why so many names?" Theta asked, hoping Memphis would direct the answer to her. But he didn't look at her once.

"I think it's to confuse people. Some of those Diviners talked about him like he's a god. Others say he likes sowing confusion and chaos, that he likes playing games."

"Which is why we're not gonna trust him blindly," Sam said.

"We have to trust him a little if we're going to find this Eye," Ling said.

"The only other curious thing I found was a mention of the man in the hat keeping a messenger, some poor caged spirit who can go back and forth between his world and ours."

"Like Western Union?" Alma asked.

"Telegram from the dead," Henry mused. "Gee, I really hope it's a singing telegram."

"Why does he need a messenger?" Alma asked.

"Don't have the answer to that yet," Memphis answered.

"How come we haven't ever heard any of this before?" Henry asked. "None of this is in our history books."

"Maybe the historians weren't looking in the right places," Memphis said. At Henry's quizzical expression, Memphis added, "I mean, who cares what a bunch of Diviners have to say?"

The phone rang again. "Good morning, Diviners Investigations," Mabel said, her pencil ready.

"I am famished!" Alma announced. "I know a swell joint not far from here. Anybody else hungry?" She looked at Ling.

Ling reached for her crutches. "I'm always hungry."

Alma smiled brightly. "Miss Chan, you are going to eat like a queen today. Do you like pork?"

"I'm half Chinese," Ling said, as if that should settle it.

"I better shove off, too," Memphis said.

Theta came and stood by his side as he put on his coat and wrapped the scarf she'd given him as a Christmas present around his neck. "Hey," Theta said, smiling shyly.

"Hey," Memphis said back without smiling.

"Nice scarf."

Memphis said nothing.

"I saw that Langston Hughes is giving a reading up at City College," Theta tried. "I thought maybe we could go if—"

"I'm busy," Memphis said.

"Memphis…" Theta started.

"Isaiah's waiting. 'Scuse me," Memphis said, brushing past her.

Theta looked to Henry, who came and hugged her. She felt like crying but she couldn't. Not yet. She still had to meet with Roy.

Theta had arranged to have lunch with Roy at a restaurant not too far from the theater. She'd wanted to be in a public place, where he couldn't do anything to her. It had been a few days since his ultimatum, and she still hadn't figured out what to say to Mr. Ziegfeld. She wished she could make it all go away.

When she saw Roy sitting at a table at the back, Theta's stomach clenched. Slowly, she made her way to him. He stood up, pretending to be a gentleman, not for her sake but for everybody watching, Theta knew. Before he could help her into her chair, Theta sat down across the table from him and ordered a coffee, black, no food. She didn't plan to stay long.

"Gee, you look pretty, Betty. Sorry—*Theta*. Can't get used to that," Roy said. "'Course, I woulda picked a different name, something that didn't make you look so highfalutin odd, but you probably didn't give it much thought."

Theta hated how that little slap he'd attached to the compliment got to her. She pulled out her cigarettes. Roy scowled. "Ladies shouldn't smoke."

Theta wanted to smoke, though. Badly. She wanted to blow the smoke in Roy's face. At the thought, her hands warmed. What if the fire sparked here in the restaurant and everybody saw? She put the cigarettes away and dropped her trembling hands to her lap, relieved when they cooled once more.

"You talk to Mr. Ziegfeld yet?" Roy asked.

"I been trying. He's been busy with a new show," Theta lied.

Roy glowered. "That's why you need me as your manager. I'll get him to pay attention," he said, and Theta cringed, imagining Roy acting overly familiar with Mr. Ziegfeld, embarrassing her. "As it happens, I'm making a name for myself here already. I been working for Dutch Schultz. You heard of him?"

"The gangster?"

"Gangster," Roy scoffed. "He's a businessman. A real regular fella! He's taking over some nightclubs up in Harlem. Gonna let me run one."

"Oh. Harlem, huh."

"The coloreds don't know what they're doing. Dutch is gonna set up shop. He just needs those high-hat Negroes like Papa Charles and Madame Sera-something outta the way first. That's where we come in."

"Whaddaya mean?" Theta asked, her heart racing.

"That ain't your business. It's man business. You just keep singing and dancing and get me that meeting with your boss."

"Yeah. Sure, Roy."

"I gotta do some business for Dutch. I'll be in and outta town over the next week or so. And when I get back, you have that meeting set up for me. Okay? I sure would hate for Mr. Ziegfeld to find out some other way that you got a husband, *Betty*," Roy said with a satisfied smile.

Every bit of Theta's fire left her. She was so cold inside. Cold and dead.

❄

That night, the Diviners went out on their first good lead. The owner of a former flophouse near the seaport that was scheduled for demolition called to say that his workers were too spooked to go inside anymore. They had heard strange crashes, thudding footsteps, and a woman's crying, but they could never find the source of those noises. Tools would go missing, and later, they'd find those tools had been arranged neatly on the floor of a room where no one had been. Windows latched at day's end would be wide open the following morning.

The Diviners entered the decaying house with flashlights blazing. It smelled of mold and urine and years of neglect. More than that, there was a great sadness to the house, a palpable storehouse of human misery. They traveled upstairs to the fourth floor, flashlights bouncing off the rotting floorboards.

"Feels cold," Ling said in warning as they approached the last door on the right.

"Yeah," Memphis said, watching his breath come out in a bluish puff.

Condensation freckled the tarnished brass doorknob.

"Ready?" Sam asked.

The others nodded. Sam pushed, and the door opened with a creak. Inside the narrow shell of a room hovered the ghost of a woman with disheveled hair and a dress that might've been in fashion forty years earlier. The dress bowed out around the middle, revealing her to be with child. A noose had been cinched at her neck, the ligature burns still bright along her broken skin. The rope hung down her side like a braid. At her feet was the winking image of a turned-over chair. She regarded the Diviners with a detached curiosity. Her eyes were dark. She had not turned. Yet.

"Have you come to help me rest?" she asked in a scratchy voice like a last dying gasp.

"Yes," Evie managed, swallowing down her fear. "We have. But we must ask you some questions first."

The ghost did not object. She clasped her hands. "I want to rest, but I am hungry, so hungry all the time, like a sickness, and I cannot find rest. It is the Eye. It won't let me rest. I feel it burning in the dark of me."

At the mention of the Eye, a tremor passed through the ghostly woman. Veins of rot climbed up one cheek. She shuddered as if with an acute pain.

"We gotta work fast," Sam said.

"Where is the Eye?" Memphis asked.

The woman regained her composure. She smiled, ecstatic. "Resting in…in a field of…of gold. It shines like…like a promise. It is open! Oh, I would have its promises, for I am hungry!"

"Look," Ling whispered to the others. The woman wavered between states: One minute, she was a lost soul, a shimmering, faded photograph of the human she must've been once. But the next, she had blurred into one of the terrifying dead, sniffing the air with blind hunger, teeth gnashing, eyes going icy.

Already, the Diviners were coming together, ready to tear her atoms apart. "Whatever you're gonna ask, ask it now," Memphis said, positioning himself slightly ahead of Isaiah to protect his brother. "I got a feeling we only have seconds left."

"Where is Conor Flynn?" Evie demanded.

The woman was disintegrating before their eyes. "Would you not even know my name?"

"Where is Conor Flynn?" Evie repeated.

"He is among the dead. Safe for now in the wings of the caged one."

"She's answering in riddles," Isaiah said.

An insect-like whine had arisen. A fly landed on the woman's nose. Another crawled across her lips. "Hungry…"

"Wait! What keeps the Eye open?" Ling said. She squeezed Henry's hand, ready.

But the woman was losing her battle. She bared her newly sharp teeth and answered with the plural voice of the hungry ones: "You do."

With a bloodcurdling screech, she lunged forward, but the Diviners were ready for her. The room appeared to warp and bend inward. The tension created raised the hair on their arms and pulled hard at their back teeth, but then there was a release, followed by a sudden swoop of euphoria, and in the next second, the ghost was nothing but a few remaining sparkles of light.

It didn't take long for reports to spring up of other Diviners joining the ghost-hunting fray. One of them, a psychic in Murray Hill, posed in her fern-laden parlor beside a crystal ball while holding up the supposed ectoplasm of a ghost she claimed to have caught "rummaging through my cupboards like a common criminal!"

"Ectoplasm my foot!" Sam groused. "That's cheesecloth and some wet noodles. Big phony!"

"They're trying to horn in on our act," Henry said, folding up the newspaper. "There are ghost-hunting parties taking place. Well, they're usually too blotto to do much, but it's the principle."

It seemed as if overnight, the Diviner business in town had shifted from "Sees all! Knows all!" to "Protects all!"

Racketeering, the mayor cried, and vowed to put any "Diviners, ghost hunters, or other disreputable types taking advantage of gullible New Yorkers" out of business. To make matters worse, Evie hadn't been able to get Woody to accompany them on a mission ever since the night he'd staked out a supposedly haunted warehouse with them and it turned out to be raccoons in the walls.

"You know how long it took me to live that down in the newsroom, Sheba? Don't answer—I still haven't lived it down. Every day, some joker leaves me a little drawing of a ghost raccoon on my desk. My editor put the kibosh on the whole ghost angle. And anyway, I'm busy trying to hunt down leads on this Project Buffalo story whenever I can," Woody said, lowering his voice.

"You mean when you aren't gambling," Evie complained.

Woody's voice was a shrug. "I can do both."

A few days later, Evie returned to the Winthrop spattered with mud after they'd chased down three ghosts in a moonlit field behind a filling station in Astoria. The expedition had left Evie exhausted and filthy, but also strangely giddy. There was something about the energy boost from exterminating the ghosts that felt good. Powerful. It made her want more.

As Evie approached the front desk, the night manager gave her a once-over before pasting on a smile. "Good evening, Miss O'Neill."

"Good evening, Mr. Williams. I've been meaning to ask: Is it true that the Winthrop does not rent rooms to Negroes?"

Mr. Williams looked surprised. "Why, yes. That is our policy."

"It's a terrible policy. I'd like you to change it."

"Why, Miss O'Neill, the Winthrop's policy is only for the comfort of its patrons."

"Well, gee, I'm a patron, and I'm uncomfortable with your policy," Evie said.

The night manager was very polite. "I'll alert Mr. Stevens to your concern, Miss O'Neill."

"Yes. See that you do." Evie sniffed and twirled her mud-splattered beaded handbag.

"There are two messages for you, Miss O'Neill."

Evie smiled as she read through the first one, a letter from Jericho:

Dear Evie,

I hope this letter finds you well. There's nothing much to report from my letter dated two days ago, except to say that I miss you two days more than I did then.

You really should see the rose garden here. It's beautiful, like you.

Fondly,
Jericho

Evie smiled and tucked the letter into her brassiere until she could add it to the pile of Jericho letters in her underwear drawer. The second note was addressed *Attention: Evangeline O'Neill*. There was only one person who called her Evangeline, and Evie was already angry before she read Will's message.

> Please don't make the same mistakes I did, Evangeline. I waited too long with Cornelius.
>
> Come to me before it's too late. Will.

Come to me. Like a command. Same old imperious Will. Evie tore up the note and tossed the pieces in the wastebasket.

❋

When Evie arrived for her radio show the next evening, Mr. Phillips took her aside. "Evie. I'm not happy about this ghost business."

"Oh, but Mr. Phillips! I'm simply trying to keep the city safe," Evie said, batting her lashes, all innocence. "My intentions are good. Just like Miss Snow's."

"Yes, well," Mr. Phillips grumbled. "Can you try to make the good seem less...unseemly? We don't want to scare off your sponsor, remember."

"Sure, Mr. Phillips," Evie promised. But how did you make a very real threat seem like anything other than the danger it was?

On the air, Sweetheart Seer Evie kept everything light and breezy and entertaining, just like Mr. Phillips had asked. She helped people find missing family trinkets and reassured them that their lost relatives had truly loved them while they were alive. She told them what they wanted to hear, and they were happy for it. "May the good spirits look after you," Evie intoned at the end of the show, blowing kisses to the audience as she exited the radio stage to warm applause. That bit she'd stolen from Sarah Snow. When Evie passed Sarah in the WGI dressing room, "God's foot soldier on the radio" didn't look pleased.

Sarah caught Evie's eyes in the mirror as she pinned a fresh corsage to her dress. "The only spirit who can look after us is the Holy Spirit, Miss O'Neill."

"Yes. But I understand he's very, very busy," Evie said through smiling teeth.

"Do you place yourself on par with the Almighty?"

"No. I'll leave that to you," Evie shot back. It was a misstep to bait Sarah like that, but Evie was tired of Sarah's holier-than-thou routine.

Sarah looked at Evie like a judge from on high. "I do worry about what you and your kind might be unleashing on our nation."

That goes both ways, Evie thought.

The very next morning, Harriet Henderson had a column devoted to Sarah Snow, complete with a staged photograph of Sarah surrounded by adoring children at an orphanage.

"I worry that Diviners play on people's fears. You shout, 'Ghost!' and suddenly, people see ghosts," Sarah was quoted as saying.

Hear, hear, Miss Snow, Harriet Henderson wrote. *Perhaps it's not ghosts who are the trouble but Diviners: For if there truly are restless spirits haunting the streets of New York, causing mischief and meaning us harm, how do we know it wasn't these very Diviners who've brought them to us? Perhaps it isn't ghosts we should be afraid of but Diviners themselves!*

"Told you she doesn't like you," Mabel said, reading over Evie's shoulder.

"It's no time for smugness, Mabesie."

"There's always a little time for smugness," Mabel said, shrugging on her coat. The phone was ringing again.

"Mabesie, could you…?"

Mabel gave a toss of her bobbed hair. "Believe it or not, I do have a life outside this room. Get it yourself."

"Diviners Investigations," Evie said, and scrabbled for a pencil.

※

That night, the Diviners were called first to a small hotel in the Theater District, where the ghost of a general sat at the white-clothed table in the private dining room. His uniform was splashed with blood spilled in some long-ago war.

"Why are the ghosts coming?" Ling asked.

"We come through the breach," the general ghost said so emphatically his bushy sideburns puffed out with his cheeks. "It is unstable, though. Once the Eye is complete, it will be our time."

"What can you tell us about the Eye?" Ling demanded. "Is it a place?"

"It is a great heart of gold humming with industry."

"Is that where Conor is?"

"No. It's where the others are." The general's eyes began to pearl. The rot of the grave bloomed on his lips, eating them down like acid.

"He's starting to turn," Memphis warned. "Get ready."

A long exhale of curling black smoke poured from the general's mouth on a guttural whine of a laugh that stank of death. "He keeps you busy with his questions, doesn't he?"

"What do you mean?" Ling asked. But it was too late. The general stood, drawing his sword from its scabbard. "I charged upon them in the field, and I would charge upon a thousand more, for I am hungry! Your days are numbered. The Eye will see to it. We are coming!"

"Now!" Sam commanded, and they watched as the general was torn from the world for good.

"Anybody else feel kinda...good after that?" Sam asked as they hurried to another ghost sighting, this one out in Green-Wood Cemetery.

"Like for just a minute you've plugged yourself into the sun?" Ling asked.

"Yes," Henry agreed, and the others nodded.

"Memphis? You're awfully quiet over there," Sam said.

Memphis stole a glance at Theta. "Can't a man be alone with his thoughts?"

"Sure. Except you're not alone," Sam said.

Don't lie to yourselves: We're all alone, Memphis wanted to shout back.

"I just want to get this done," he said.

HARVEST SONG

He should've known it was doomed from the start, but Memphis had wanted to believe in miracles again, so he'd let himself fall straight toward the fist coming at his heart. A mangled mess lay behind his ribs now. He could scarcely breathe for the pain. Like he'd been torn from happiness in a trail of blood. The only emotion more powerful than the pain was his rage. His anger was a bullet shot indiscriminately, flying through space, in search of a target.

"Memphis, did you send in your application yet?" Mrs. Andrews had asked him the day before as he tried sneaking out of the library after dropping off his cache of books.

"No, ma'am. I forgot."

"Again? Memphis!" she chided, shaking her head. "You'll miss the deadline."

"I suppose I will." He hadn't meant for it to come out the way it did. Mrs. Andrews raised an eyebrow at him.

"Sorry, Mrs. Andrews," he said, ashamed.

"No harm, Memphis," she said a little crisply but not unkindly. Then she placed a hand on his shoulder, looking up at him with clear eyes. "I don't know what it is, but don't forget to come back to yourself when it's finished. Too much good to go throwing it away."

She stamped a book and handed it to him. *Cane* by Jean Toomer. "I saved it for you," she said.

He tried to give it back with a lackluster "'Fraid I don't have time to read much these days."

Mrs. Andrews pushed it right back at him. "Make time," she commanded.

He thanked her. Downstairs, he watched the Krigwa Players blocking out a scene from a new play. Behind them, Mr. Douglas's powerful scenery soared above the little stage, a story in color and shape. Stories. He cared about those once.

The days numbed him. Around him, Harlem swirled with life: The men laughing on the other side of the Floyd's Barbershop glass. The trolley rattling down 125th Street. The little girl eyeing the sweets while her mother examined a bin of yams for the best ones. A pretty girl waiting for the bus, singing a song Florence Mills made famous. The Benevolent and Protective Order of Elks parading past in their ceremonial aprons. The world felt like a windup toy he wished he could pinch between his fingers and still.

Memphis opened the book Mrs. Andrews had given him. Inside was a poem, "Harvest Song": "*I am a reaper whose muscles set at sundown. All my oats are cradled. But I am too chilled, and too fatigued to bind them. And I hunger.*"

Memphis shut his eyes. Early that morning, the Diviners had answered a call from the caretaker at Green-Wood Cemetery out in Brooklyn who'd seen "a pack of bright, skulking terrors." Terrors did skulk in the dark, and the caretaker was right to be afraid. They'd set off with their flashlights, jumping at every marble angel, every shadow that fell across a headstone. Berenice flitted above Memphis, hopping from tombstone to tombstone, squawking. "Shush, now, Berenice," he'd tutted. But the bird wouldn't be calmed. At one point, the crow tugged at his sleeve, as if urging him back. Memphis heard a sound and followed it to a crypt. There he'd come face-to-face with a wraith in tattered bedclothes hunched over the carcass of a mutilated, half-dead squirrel. The wraith's mouth and jaw were smeared with the twitching animal's blood. Those razor-sharp teeth gnawed at the poor squirrel's tendons and bit through bone with a sickening crunch. The butchered bodies of two birds and a rat lay nearby, as if the thing ate blindly, never getting its fill. It was alone, though, separated from its hunting pack. So was Memphis. This one was beyond questioning and useless to them. Heart beating fast, Memphis backed away, cracking a twig underfoot. The creature's head snapped up. Those white-marble eyes locked on Memphis's and he froze. Nearby, the crow spread its wings as if it could shield Memphis from danger. The wraith let out a pitiful cry. It sounded confused, lost, perhaps lonely for its brethren, if one could call what it ran with any kind of brotherhood.

"Here, now. It's all right," Memphis said. He didn't know why he'd said it. For those few seconds, Memphis had felt a strange connection to that lost, wretched creature trying to sate its longing. Pain did not end at the grave. Had this unfortunate thing once carried a beating heart inside? Had it walked the same streets as Memphis, shared the same dreams? Did it have a story?

The wraith had cocked its head as if trying to understand. Memphis could hear his friends calling his name as they came running. The thing in front of him growled and dropped into a defensive stance. It unhinged its jaw and hissed, showing its pointed, bloodied teeth matted with animal fur and muscle. Memphis had been trying to reason with it. But there was no reasoning with these filthy things. He needed to remember that. Ghosts had been people, Will had once told them. And people showed themselves for what they were eventually. Even people who said they loved you. Memphis understood that now.

"Now!" Sam called. The Diviners stood together, concentrating until their power multiplied. Memphis felt nothing but hatred as the ghost looked up for just a moment, a silent howl of betrayal on its pallid face just before they created the energy field and sent it into oblivion.

Afterward, once the fierce glow of ghost-banishing had faded—"*I fear knowledge of my hunger*"—Theta had put her hand on his arm. "That thing was so close! You copacetic?"

"Fine. I got to get Isaiah home before Octavia wakes up and finds us gone," he said, and left her standing there in the cold of the graveyard.

"Why you mad at Theta?" Isaiah asked as Memphis tucked him in.

"Mind your own business," Memphis said, and Isaiah had rolled over without a word. That was two people he'd hurt in one night. And he called himself a healer. He wasn't anything. He was just existing. Memphis took off his shoes and socks. There were new sores on his ankles. He tried to ignore them and go to sleep.

The next night, in a corner of the Hotsy Totsy, Memphis opened his book and read: "*I am a deaf man who strains to hear the calls of other harvesters whose throats are also dry.*"

He watched the band going to town and the chorines cutting loose. On the dance floor, it was glorious, stomping mayhem. Memphis felt none of it. The music was hollow. The dancing was hollow. The smiles were hollow. He was hollow. A ghost among the living but no one noticed.

He thought again of the thing in the graveyard showing its teeth. And now he wondered—had it been promising to hurt him? Or had it been afraid of him? He didn't know. He didn't know if what they were doing to the ghosts was the right thing. And the doubt was beginning to eat away at him.

He woke in the night, thinking of Theta, remembering every good night they'd ever had. The way the brightness strafed the Palisades as the two of them sat with their arms wrapped around each other, watching the river from the lighthouse. The softness of her lips. The husky cackle of her laugh. The quiet huff of her breath against his neck when she fell asleep with her head on his shoulder. Gone. All gone. He tried to funnel the howl inside him into words. But there were limits to language. Sometimes, he stood among the tall stacks at the 135th Street library staring at the spines of all those books, all those people hungry to tell what they saw, what they felt, what they hoped other people also saw and felt. They wrote it all down so they wouldn't disappear. So *they* wouldn't disappear. A testimony: *I was here.* So many stories. Why did he think his would even matter?

He tucked away his notebook and didn't look at it once.

Papa Charles came for him. Without a word, Memphis followed his boss to the back rooms of the Cotton Club, where Memphis healed up a couple of Owney's thugs. And then he pocketed the money, though he'd long since forgotten what he was saving for. He spent too much money on a fine suit he didn't wear but once. He bought a new leather glove for Isaiah. He stuffed rent money in Octavia's fake sugar jar in the kitchen. At the club, there were drinks for the chorus girls who hugged his neck and told him he was "an angel." When a dancer named Pauline kissed him and placed his hands on her hips, Memphis felt nothing. Hollow. Hollow. *"My throat is dry. I hunger."*

"Sorry," he told Pauline, and she cursed his name on the way out.

At the lighthouse, Memphis stood outside and tossed rocks into the Hudson, watching them sink. He'd known their love was bad odds. But wasn't all love betting against the odds? He was the damned fool who'd gone and believed.

"I fear knowledge of my hunger."

All of these thoughts weighed on Memphis as he walked up and down

Madame Seraphina's block, trying to work up the courage to ring her bell. When at last he did, she opened the basement door and smiled at him. The white turban she wore exposed the round, high-cheeked beauty of her face. The porch light made the apples of her cheeks shine as if polished.

"Come," she said, and went inside.

✺

Seraphina showed Memphis to her formal parlor, which had been painted a deep royal blue that made Memphis think of a sky just past sunset. She settled into the chair opposite his and crossed her long legs. "So. Here we are, you and I."

"I've come about my mother. You said she came to see you before she passed. I want to know why," Memphis explained.

"Your mother was worried."

That didn't seem strange to Memphis. She was a mother. Mothers worried. "What was she worried about?"

"She said she'd made a bad bargain."

"What sort of b—"

"You want information. I want information. You first." Seraphina leaned back and rested her slim forearms on the chair's plush velvet arms. "Four of my runners got shook down yesterday. I had to go to the precinct for them. I heard from other bankers. They are having the same trouble. Cops—and Dutch Schultz. Yet Papa Charles is untouched. How is Papa Charles keeping his business safe?"

If Memphis told Seraphina the truth about his healing, he'd be betraying both Papa and Owney. There was no telling what they might do if they found out he'd shared their secrets. Memphis's stomach tightened. "Papa doesn't tell me everything. I'm just a runner."

"So you say. But I hear the two of you make visits to the Cotton Club late at night—yes, I have eyes on the streets, too. If you're just a runner," she sneered, "then why is Papa Charles taking you to see Owney Madden? What is Owney doing for Papa?"

"He just needed someone to come along," Memphis lied. "For protection."

Madame Seraphina smirked. "Protection is why he has Yannick and Claude."

Memphis tried the power of his charm. "That's all there is to it," he said, tossing off a shy smile. "That's all I know."

Seraphina leaned forward, eyes flashing. "Do. Not. Lie. To. Me. I did not come to this country and rise up from its streets to be dismissed in my own home!" She cupped Memphis's chin in her silk-soft palm. "Cowards ignore women. *Men* listen. If you will not respect me, you can leave. But then you will never know what your *manman* confessed to me."

Papa Charles had told Memphis about the honor among men. Memphis hadn't really thought much about how that honor was built on the idea of keeping women out. On a belief that they should not be trusted. After Theta, Memphis felt that Papa had been right. But Seraphina wasn't going to tell Memphis anything unless he was honest with her, and he needed to know the truth.

"Some of his runners got arrested," Memphis said carefully. "And Papa pays his dues." Everybody had to pay off the police if they wanted to run a business. That was common knowledge uptown. "But these cops are getting paid by Dutch Schultz."

"Everybody knows that," Seraphina said, dismissing Memphis's comment with a wave of her hand. "What is Charles asking you to do for Owney behind closed doors?"

Memphis hated to think about what Papa Charles would do if he found out Memphis had been telling Seraphina his business. "He's having me heal up Owney's men when they get hurt. Owney's still more powerful than Dutch. Papa says if we get Owney on our side, make an alliance, we can keep Dutch from taking over. That Owney will protect us."

For just a moment, Seraphina was so still that Memphis could scarcely hear her breathing. And then a laugh tore out of her, loud and guttural and tommy gun–quick. She slapped her knee. "Oh, Charles, Charles. You old fool."

"It's worked so far."

"So. Far," Seraphina said, drying her eyes. "Papa Charles thinks if he makes nice, these ofay will accept him." She shook her head.

"I'm sure Papa Charles will look out for us," Memphis said, feeling defensive.

Seraphina snorted. "Papa hobnobs with radio stars and the mayor. He thinks they accept him as one of their own, just another businessman. He forgets that in this country, he is a black man first. They will never let him in, not all the way. Owney will ignore his promise. And when Dutch Schultz calls the shots, the white people will back him. What do they care as long as they can dance where they like?" Seraphina lowered her chin and leveled her gaze at Memphis. Her eyes were flecked with gold, like a tiger's. "No one feared the rabbits until they took over the garden. The white gangsters have been occupied with bootlegging. But now they're pushing into *our* numbers game. Bit by bit, they will take all we have built. And they will destroy the Harlem we love."

The news unsettled Memphis. He didn't like healing Owney's men in the first place, and the idea that it might all be for naught made it worse. Still, he had to believe that Papa Charles knew what he was doing.

"I've told you what you wanted to know. Tell me about my mother like you promised."

Seraphina leaned back against her chair again. "Your mother said she had taken bad medicine. She was afraid it had cursed you and your brother. Do you know this?"

Memphis nodded.

"She told me that because of the bad medicine, there were people who would come for you. She had wanted to protect you and your brother from those bad people. And that was when she made her mistake."

"What mistake was that?"

"She called upon a bad spirit from the land of the dead. She made a bargain with the King of Crows."

Memphis's heartbeat quickened till he could hear the rhythm of his blood in his ears like drums. "What kind of bargain?"

"My turn," said Seraphina. "Why do you do this healing?"

"Told you why. Papa said it would help us."

"Papa said, Papa said. You do everything Papa tells you? You make any decisions for yourself?"

"I made the decision to come here," Memphis sniped. "I want to hear about my mother."

"Your mother knew she was dying," Seraphina said after a pause. "And she feared she would not be here to watch over her boys. She was worried about threats here and from beyond—a coming storm. So she went to the graveyard barefoot, and that night, he appeared to her. He told her that he would make sure the bad men could not find you and your brother. He promised that she could watch over you from beyond. For a price."

"What price?"

Seraphina sighed. "This, I don't know. But I do know that crows are powerful. They are messengers of the dead. They can travel between worlds."

"Between worlds..." he whispered. Something was fighting to take shape in Memphis's mind. The room tilted sideways as it came to him. "Berenice?"

Seraphina made a face. "Who is Berenice?"

It was impossible. But the more Memphis thought about it, the more he realized that the bird that had been following him for months had been keeping watch like a guardian. *Like a mother.* Instinctively, he looked to the window. The crow was just outside, waiting. Memphis kept a grip on the chair; it felt as if he could float away so easily.

"Can the curse be undone?" Memphis asked.

"I only know so much. I don't play with bad magic. And he is bad magic," Seraphina said. "You want to know? Ask the ghosts."

Memphis thought again of the thing in the graveyard. Of the spirits they'd annihilated over the past few nights. Guilt twinged in his chest.

"No," Memphis said.

Seraphina pushed air through her teeth and pursed her lips in mild rebuke. "You afraid of spirits? They're with us always."

"I know that better than most," Memphis snapped.

"You do, huh? It's *you* who needs to find your way home, Memphis. Walk with your ancestors. See. Feel. Know. Let me give you some protection at least."

"Your protection didn't work very well for my mother," Memphis said, angry.

"How do you know it didn't? There's all kinds of magic in the world."

"Why do you want to help me?"

Seraphina shrugged. "I like your smile."

She laughed then—a big, powerful guffaw that brought out Memphis's smile against his will.

"You see there? Powerful. There is something of the Oungan in you. I sense it. You shouldn't turn your back on it. Encourage it. Let it grow. Let it be in the world. *And stop being afraid of spirits.* Now. Wait here for me."

Memphis did as he was told. A while later, Seraphina arrived with a small leather bag on a cord. "Here. Keep this with you. A connection to all that has come before, to the *lwas*, to your ancestors, to your birthright in this world. It will protect you."

"How?" Memphis asked, tucking it into a pocket of his coat.

"That, I can't see. But you'll know when the time comes."

Madame Seraphina saw Memphis to the door. "Why you run around with that old blind man?" she asked rather suddenly, catching Memphis off guard.

"Mr. Johnson? He's my auntie's boarder. He's nice enough."

Seraphina said nothing. Memphis felt the need to defend Bill against judgments unsaid. "He's been awfully good to Isaiah. In fact, he's saved Isaiah's life a few times. Every time Isaiah has one of his seizures, it's Mr. Johnson who's been there."

Even as Memphis said it aloud, something stirred in his gut. Something with teeth.

Seraphina's brow furrowed. "There's something left-handed about that man."

"You don't know him like I do," Memphis said. He was feeling defensive now. And worried about what he'd done, telling Papa's secrets to his competition. That was a stupid mistake, and it chilled him.

"Maybe not. Your brother keeps having fits? He should come to me. I will help him."

And suddenly, it all made sense to Memphis. It was a saleswoman's pitch to get them to come back. He felt that he'd been had. He had half a mind to toss the gris gris bag back to Seraphina and tell her to keep her magic. "I look after my brother just fine."

"As you say. But I would be careful around Mr. Guillaume Johnson."

Memphis startled at the name. "What did you call him?"

"Guillaume," Seraphina said innocently. "Guillaume, William, Bill. It's all the same name." Seraphina's eyebrows furrowed. "Now you really do look like you've seen a ghost."

Memphis reeled away from Seraphina's place and down the street, lost in his thoughts. Guillaume. No. It couldn't possibly be the same person! That was ridiculous. Guillaume Johnson, if he were still alive, would be, what? Thirty-seven, thirty-eight, maybe? And he'd sounded like a big, powerful man. Blind Bill Johnson was a broken-down bluesman, stooped, with a lined face and gray hair. He was not a powerful Diviner who could steal the life from things.

"Impossible," Memphis muttered to himself. "Impossible."

Behind him, he heard somebody's sharp whistle. It was answered with another whistle, and another. One by one, Dutch Schultz's men showed themselves from their hiding places. They looked ready for a fight. *Shit*, Memphis thought. He looked over his shoulder. Two more of Dutch's men were on the sidewalk. One of them carried a nasty-looking lead pipe.

Memphis walked faster. The whistling bounced back and forth between the men, a signal, a game. Memphis broke into a run, but by the time he reached the next street, Dutch's men had him cornered. Memphis counted five of them in all, and who knew how many more might be hiding in the shadows?

"Well, if it ain't one of Papa Charles's boys," the man with the lead pipe said. He had a football player's build and a quick meanness about him that Memphis had seen before. The kind that could turn on a dime. Maybe that was how the fella had gotten the burn scar down one side of his face. Memphis knew this one was as dangerous as any hungry ghost.

"We hear Papa Charles has been dealing with Owney Madden, plotting against Dutch. Dutch don't like that. And you're gonna tell us exactly what your boss is up to." The man smacked the pipe against his open palm to get the message across.

"Roy, Boss don't wanna start a war," one of the others said nervously.

"Boss ain't here!" the one named Roy barked. Even his smile was mean. He held up the pipe. "He said to get answers. And that's what I aim to do."

Memphis put out his hands in a peacemaking gesture. "Listen, fellas, I don't want any trouble...."

"That's a shame. Looks like you found it."

Roy reared back for a hit when out of nowhere, the crow dove down and pecked at his face, drawing blood. With a cry, he covered his eyes. The lead pipe clattered to the ground, and Memphis picked it up, swinging it in a circle. Blood ran over the gangster's fingers as the crow kept pecking. The crow leaped to the second man's head, digging into his skin with its pointed claws and beak until he fell to his knees, screaming.

The third man drew his gun, but Memphis knocked it away with the pipe. The crow flitted in front of the fourth man, threatening.

"Shoo! Shoo, you crazy bird!" the fourth man said, backing away.

Memphis didn't wait. He took off running, slowing only when he reached an alley and saw that he was not being followed. He dropped the pipe and sagged against the bricks, panting heavily. A minute later, the crow found him. It settled onto a window ledge and made a soft, whirring sound that was a cross between a gentle coo and a sad cry. Memphis's mind stretched nearly to its breaking point as he tried to make sense of it all:

Messengers of the dead. Move between worlds. Promised she'd watch over you from beyond.

For a price.

"Berenice?" Memphis said, and it felt as if the world had narrowed to just him and the bird blinking at him from the ledge. "No. Can't be."

But then he held out his hand. "Mama?" he whispered.

The bird hopped onto his open palm and nuzzled its head against his skin, leaving small streaks of the gangsters' blood.

"I'm gonna heal you, Mama." He put his hand on the bird and it squawked away with a great ruffling of feathers. The bird moved its beak back and forth, as if shaking its head. "Okay. Okay, Mama. I'm sorry."

The bird hopped back onto Memphis's open hand.

"But I promise you this: I'm going to free you, Mama. I will free you."

But first he was going to free his brother.

"Mama, I need to know—is there something not right about Blind Bill? Is he hurting Isaiah? Tap the ledge twice for yes."

The crow blinked at him. Memphis felt ridiculous talking to a bird. He'd hit a new low. But then, very deliberately, it tapped its beak against the stone—once, twice.

341

THE VOICE OF TOMORROW

Memphis found Blind Bill at home on Octavia's settee listening to a radio program with Isaiah. Just the sight of the old man next to his brother made his stomach turn.

"Need to talk to you, Mr. Johnson," Memphis managed.

"Shhh! I'm trying to hear!" Isaiah said.

"This can't wait. I'll be out front," Memphis said.

A few minutes later, Bill came tapping out onto the sidewalk. "What's eating you?"

"Not here."

Memphis led Bill across Eighth Avenue and into St. Nicholas Park, guiding him to a remote area. The spires of City College poked up above the newly budding trees.

Bill cocked his head, listening. He saw grainy silhouettes of trees. "What we doin' in the park?"

"I know what you've been doing to my brother."

"Don't know what you talking about. Ain't got time for this foolishness," Bill grumbled, turning away on the path.

"I know...*Guillaume*," Memphis said louder. "I found the old records in the museum basement. I know you're Guillaume Johnson, the Diviner who could steal the life from things. And I know you've been using that power on my brother. I know everything!"

Bill stood very still. He could sense Memphis's coiled rage ready to snap. "Then you know what they done to me. What that Walker woman done. How she let those Shadow Men take me away and break me. Tell me: How old I look to you?"

"Don't have time for this—"

"How old?" Bill demanded, striking the path with his cane.

"Sixty. Sixty-five."

"I'm *thirty-seven years old*. They did this to me. Sister Walker and them Shadow Men. It ate me up inside. Took my sight. This is what's left."

Memphis let this sink in for just a moment, then shook his head. "I don't care! You hurt my brother. You're the reason he's been having all those seizures. You're the reason Isaiah gets so sick—'cause you're using whatever power you've got to draw the life out of him." Memphis's anger boiled over. His brother. His little brother! He'd trusted Bill. "There's nobody around in this park right now. Just you and me. I ought to kill you."

"You could. Nobody would blame you. But you don't know what it's like to take another man's life. It changes you. You can't never get yourself back, not the same way."

"If it means keeping Isaiah safe, I'm fine with that."

"I never meant to hurt the boy."

"I don't wanna hear it."

Bill leaned on his cane. "I needed a number, and Isaiah, he had the sight. Dutch's men was coming for me. I...I didn't mean to hurt the boy. But then I could feel your healing power running in his veins, flowing into me, giving me little bits of my sight back. I knew it was coming from you, and I figured I might could heal myself up that way. I was wrong, though."

"You're a monster."

"You think you know everything? You don't know shit, boy! You. Don't. Know. *Shit*," Blind Bill thundered. He took a stuttering breath and wiped away tears with a calloused hand. "I seen things you ain't never seen. I done things, things they made me do, things that ate my soul up—that still eat my soul. If you'd a healed me up like I asked, none of this had to happen! But you couldn't be bothered to help an old blind man, could ya? Too fulla yourself, Mr. High Hat!"

"Shut up!"

"Or maybe you ain't as good as you say."

"Shut *up*!"

"You wanna prove yourself? Put your hands on me." Bill slapped his big, weathered hands hard against his chest. "Come on! Show me what you can do, boy!"

"Don't call me *boy*," Memphis snapped.

"Gimme back my sight or kill me. Huh? Do it. Go on. Put so much juice in me I fall out dead. Or you afraid of that? You 'fraid to really put it to the test? To know what you got deep down inside you? Maybe it ain't so fine. So *good*," Bill said, the word a sneer. "Maybe we ain't all that different."

Blind rage rose up inside Memphis. He'd never wanted to hurt somebody as much as he wanted to hurt Bill Johnson. With a roar, he rushed Bill, taking the big man by surprise as he knocked him down and pressed his palms against Bill's eyes. Bill's shouts joined Memphis's battle cry. Lightning crackled around the two of them. Memphis leaned in with all he had, until his body shook and he blacked out.

When he came to, he was sprawled on his back on the path in St. Nicholas Park. His legs trembled. His hands ached and burned. The skin of his thumbs were blistered where they had touched Bill's eyes. *What happened?*

Nearby, Bill Johnson lay on his side, still as death, his blind man's cane gripped in his left hand.

"Mr. Johnson? Mr. Johnson!" Memphis said.

Bill Johnson's arms and legs twitched once, twice. And then he gulped in a lungful of air like a beached fish. He coughed as he sat straight up. The cane fell from his hand and clattered to the walk as he pressed his hands to his eyes with a great shout. And then, just as suddenly, he was laughing, a great hiccuping of joy. His eyelashes fluttered, like wings trying for flight. "I can see! Oh, sweet Lord, I can see!"

He turned his newborn eyes to Memphis. "You…you healed me," he said in wonder.

"Yeah."

"I thought you was gonna kill me."

An exhausted Memphis sat up gingerly and cradled his knees. "I wanted to. But any fool can do that." He meant it as a slap. So maybe he wasn't over wanting to hurt Bill just yet.

Bill shook his head. "I don't deserve your mercy."

"My mother would say that Jesus forgives. But I ain't Jesus. I better never catch you around my brother again. Get your things outta my aunt's house and go. Understand?"

Bill nodded. "Can I at least say good-bye to the boy?"

"No. I want you gone."

"All right," Bill whispered. Tears still streamed down his cheeks. The night was all lit up like a carnival. The light stung, but his eyes couldn't get enough. There were constellations peeking out beneath the bright haze of the city. Down the path, some lovers had stopped to kiss under the honeyed glow of a street lamp. "Thank you," he said softly. "Won't throw away my second chance."

"I don't care what you do. Just get gone," Memphis spat back. He examined his hands, wincing. But as he watched, the blisters began to fade.

Memphis looked over at Bill Johnson and caught his breath.

"What is it? What's wrong?" Bill said. He'd lived in darkness for fifteen years. Now that he was free, he didn't want his miracle to disappear like a dream.

"Your hair," Memphis said, pointing. "The gray. It's fading."

❋

As promised, Bill gathered his things and left without saying good-bye to Isaiah. Out on the stoop, under the porch light, Bill already seemed years younger. "I know you don't wanna hear from me. But you gotta watch out for them Shadow Men. Don't you let 'em even know about what you and Isaiah can do. Keep yourselves real quiet, understand? You don't want them coming after you or your friends."

"I can look out for Isaiah and me," Memphis said, shutting the door in Bill's face. He slipped into the bedroom he shared with his little brother and took off his shoes.

Isaiah stirred. "Thought I heard Uncle Bill leaving."

"Thought you were asleep," Memphis said, peeling off his socks and garters.

"Did he go?"

"Yes."

"How come?"

Memphis took a breath. "Just had to. That's all."

"Where's he going?"

"Don't know. Don't care. He's not family."

"Is to me," Isaiah said sulkily.

"Well, he's not. I'm your family. Me and Auntie."

"Didn't he like living with us? With me?" Isaiah asked. He rolled over to look at Memphis. His eyes shone with tears.

Memphis's heart ached. His brother had lost so much in his short life. And now Memphis was taking away someone Isaiah had come to love and trust. Well, the world was full of people and things you thought you could trust, and that trust gave you a black eye for it. Just because Mr. Conrad, who ran the five-and-dime, smiled and gave Isaiah a penny candy when they came to shop didn't mean that the same Mr. Conrad would open his door to them if they were in trouble. Just because you loved somebody with your entire soul didn't mean they wouldn't break your heart. And just because somebody loved you didn't mean they'd be able to stop themselves from hurting you to get what they wanted. Day by day and ghost by ghost, it was getting harder for Memphis to hold on to hope and faith in the goodness of people. But he wouldn't take that from Isaiah.

"It's not about you. Just something that had to happen," Memphis said hollowly.

"Like Mama," Isaiah said, and Memphis's heart felt like it would burst.

"Is Mama in heaven? *Is* there a heaven, Memphis?"

Once, Memphis would have answered yes. No question, no doubt. But he was no longer quite so sure. Of anything. Even the idea of a heaven made him a little angry. Why place his faith in some peaceful, distant country when the one they lived in needed so much work right here and now?

Ling believed in the beautiful universe. In the hallelujah glory of atoms transforming, exploding, and becoming something new. Sister Walker had believed in fighting for justice. Henry had his music. Sam, his mission to find his mother. Mabel fought for the rights of workers. Even Evie believed in something, that something being Evie a lot of the time.

Memphis laced his fingers through his brother's smaller, softer ones. "Little man, I believe in this right here. I got you. You got me. We got us."

Isaiah broke into a rapturous, slightly embarrassed grin that warmed Memphis through. That was it, then. Memphis believed in the hope and love shining out from his brother's eyes. That was the greater power he wanted right there. He'd believe in that love; he'd fight for that hope.

Isaiah yawned and rolled to face the wall. "Tell me a story."

Memphis hugged his brother close. "Once upon a time, there were two brothers, and nothing in this world or the next could tear them apart...."

Memphis talked until his brother snored softly. For the first time in ages, truth came down inside Memphis, and he sat with his notebook to try to capture it.

THE VOICE OF TOMORROW

America, America, will you listen to the
    story of you?
You bruised mountains, purpled by majesty.
You shining seas that refuse to see.
You, haunted by ghosts of dreams,
From the many, one; the one, many.
I am in you and of you, America.
You of amber waving grain, shining
Like fool's gold in a plentiful river.
I am the dream coming, yes,
The Voice of Tomorrow
Ringing in freedom's ear.
Do you hear it now?
Calling, calling, all:
Listen, America—
I am the story.
I am you.
I am.

Memphis's pencil rested. He folded up his poem and stuck it in an envelope. On the front, he wrote, *Attention: Mr. W. E. B. DuBois. The Crisis.* And though it was the middle of the night, he mailed it in.

It was almost tomorrow, after all.

The moon smiled down on the bright skyscrapers, full of promise. It shone on the graveyards, where the restless spirits rose up, hungry and full of rage. It hovered above the houses where the ghosts prowled, getting closer to the people. It followed the brown sedan as it prowled the city streets, looking for Diviners.

The phone was ringing in Evie's suite when she entered, and Evie grinned when she heard Jericho's voice on the line.

"Is this the famous Sweetheart Seer?" he said. His voice had deepened. It did things to her stomach.

"Two shows a week. Don't touch that dial," Evie purred.

"I wouldn't dream of it."

Evie lay back on the bed, picturing Jericho's face the way he looked when he was thinking about something and the light caught the edge of his face like a fire. "How is life upstate? I'll bet you sit by the fire with wolf-hounds at your feet now. Tell me the truth: Are you wearing an ascot?"

Jericho laughed. It was a hearty laugh, surprising for Jericho, and it made Evie grin like mad. "No ascot. No wolfhounds. But I'll be sure to ask Marlowe if I can have both. I can see that I have a reputation to uphold."

Evie giggled. Flirting. He was flirting? This was a new Jericho. He sounded happier, and she was glad. Going with Marlowe had obviously been the right thing to do, no matter how much Evie disliked him. She wanted to tell Jericho everything that had been going on since he left, but she wasn't sure if anyone might be listening in. After all, she knew Jericho's letters were read before they were sent. So instead, they talked of spring coming and made jokes. Evie felt lighter than she had in some time. She ached to see him.

"Is everything really okay there?" Jericho said suddenly.

"Yes, fine," Evie said. She didn't want to worry him. "I'll tell you when I see you."

"That would be nice. Seeing you, that is," Jericho said, making Evie's face go warm. "And I hope to have news for you about that antique you were curious about. Nothing to report yet." And then: "I miss you. I wish you were here. It's lonely without you."

I miss you. So simple and honest that it took Evie's breath away. That was the thing about Jericho that made him different: He was not cynical or guarded. He did not play games.

"I miss you, too."

"Be careful, won't you?"

"I will," Evie said. "Give my regards to the wolfhounds."

"I'll name one Evie. It will, naturally, be my favorite."

His favorite. Evie bit her lip to keep the smile from taking over her face.

"What's wrong with you?" Theta asked when she returned to Evie's room with ice. "You look like you swallowed a whole Mary Pickford movie."

"Jericho," Evie said on a sigh.

Theta shook her head, sighing. "Evil. Your romances are like a tennis match—Sam one day, Jericho the next. I can't keep up." Theta settled the ice bucket on the dresser and took out her flask. "Here. Ice. We're making Poor Man's Manhattans."

"What's that?" Evie said, putting out two glasses.

Theta smirked. "You whisper 'vermouth' over the glass, then fill the rest with whiskey."

"Say, I like your Manhattans! But what's the ice for, then?"

"For the headaches we're gonna have later."

"Ah."

Theta raised her glass to Evie's. "Here's mud in your eye."

They each knocked back a generous swig, and Theta welcomed the burn and the booze. She needed its courage. "Say, uh, you remember when you read my bracelet that time?"

"Sure," Evie said, squinting. "You were running. You looked scared."

"Because I *was* scared. I was running from my husband, Roy."

Evie halted her drink at her lips. "Go on."

"He wasn't a good man." Theta told Evie everything then. About Roy's rages and the beatings. About the fire she started that she thought had killed him. About the menacing notes, the terrible shock of seeing Roy again after thinking he was dead, and Roy's threats. By the time the whole story had come out, Theta had nearly finished her drink, and she wasn't sure if it was the hooch or the confession that had made her feel looser.

"He was waiting for me outside the Bennington today."

"Oh, no!"

"He wants things between us to be like they were, and he wants that meeting with Flo. I managed to stall him—told him Flo's all broken up about a sick aunt—but I can't do that forever. At some point, you run outta sick aunts."

Evie slammed her glass down, sloshing whiskey over her wrist. "He can't do that to you! Why, I'll march over there right now and—"

"Nothin' doin', Evil. This is my mess to sort out."

"But you don't have to do it by yourself, Theta. You have friends."

"I know. But you don't get Roy like I do. He's dangerous. You gotta handle him just right. I can't let this blow up."

Evie glanced sidelong at Theta. "Is that why you broke it off with Memphis?"

Theta glugged back a little more of her whiskey. She nodded, miserable. "I didn't want Roy to hurt him. He hates me now—can't say I blame him. But I miss him something awful."

Evie scooted close and put her arm around Theta. "Oh, gee, honey. Did you tell Henry?"

"I don't wanna worry him. He's still getting over Louis. I just needed to tell somebody or I'd go crackers." Theta stared at her hands. They were quiet, no hint of the raging fire coiled inside. "Sometimes I think maybe I would like to burn it all down. Start over. Make different rules for the world."

Evie clinked Theta's glass with hers. "Hear, hear. Well, once we stop supernatural evil from leaking into our realm and taking over."

Theta shook her head. "You can't stop evil. You can only push back as hard as you can. Another?"

"And how!"

They drank until they could blot out the ghosts. But they slept with the lights on.

※

Ling had taken on a dream-walking job from one of her neighbors in Chinatown, Mr. Moy. "I want to propose and I need to make sure this is an auspicious match. I want you to ask my grandmother," he said, handing over his grandmother's delicate ivory fan.

"That will be five dollars," Ling said.

Snorting, Mr. Moy gave her three. "The gossip is that you have failed the last two times. The spirits didn't speak to you. I am willing to take the chance that your luck holds. So, three for now. Two more if you deliver a message from my grandmother."

That night, Ling entered the dream world with apprehension. The gossip was true. She'd not heard a peep from the spirits lately, and she was beginning to feel desperate. This was her gift. This was what she could do that set her apart, and as her muscles had atrophied, she had come to rely on that skill more and more to make her feel important. When she reached a place that she recognized as being a memory of Auntie Moy's—the village in China she had left as a young bride—she called respectfully for the dead woman, her panic rising when her calls went unanswered. Then, suddenly, storm clouds moved in over the village. And along the edges, ancestral spirits shimmered. Their faces were grim. Auntie Moy was among them, and Ling felt great relief. She bowed her head with respect and opened her mouth to speak.

The spirits turned their backs to her, and then they were gone.

Isaiah was drawing when the vision came over him. He found himself standing at the crossroads near the farmhouse he'd seen before. But when he looked to his right, Conor stood in the cornfields, and behind him was a shimmering hole showing that terrible place where the King of Crows lived.

"Isaiah," Conor called.

"I'm here," Isaiah said. The wind whistled in his ears something fierce, and he heard a swarm of wasps screaming inside it. "Where are you?"

"I'm in his world," Conor said. "I could go back and forth. That's why I hadda keep my mind shut. So he couldn't get in. The longer he holds me, the more of my power he can suck up. You gotta find the Eye."

"We're trying. Is...is my mama there?"

Conor looked over at Viola's sleeping form under a quilt of feathers.

"What happens once we find the Eye?" Isaiah asked.

"You hafta destroy it. You gotta heal the breach so he can't come in with the dead. Watch out for her." Conor pointed behind Isaiah.

Isaiah turned and saw the strange girl with the crumpled peach hair ribbon. She was watching him from the sagging porch. In the vast dark woods stretching behind Conor, the night had a thousand of those burning eyes.

"Gotta go," Conor said, and he wrapped his arms around his knees. "Onetwot'reef-f-four…"

And then the vision was gone. When Isaiah looked down, he'd drawn it all. Just like Conor.

THE CARD READER

"I know you don't want me to leave the grounds," Jericho said to Marlowe over a lunch of roast beef and potatoes. "Would you mind if I had a guest? I haven't seen anybody under the age of thirty since I got here."

Marlowe sipped his milk. "Who did you have in mind?"

Jericho concentrated very hard on cutting his beef. "Evie O'Neill," he said, sneaking a surreptitious glance at Marlowe.

Marlowe was silent but frowning, and Jericho feared he had lost already.

Jericho cleared his throat. "I, uh, also wanted to bring Ling Chan. She wants to be a scientist, too. You're her idol. She thinks the world of you!"

"That so?" Marlowe said, warmer.

"Yes, sir."

Marlowe added another lump of sugar to his coffee. He squinted against the sun streaking through the dining room's faultlessly clean windows. "Fair enough. Tell them to come up on Friday, then. I'll send a car to meet their train. They can stay the weekend."

"Really?"

Marlowe's eyes twinkled. "Yes, really. Why not? We'll need to continue with your training, of course."

"Of course. Gee, that's swell. Thank you," Jericho said. He was ecstatic about getting to see Evie again and guilty for the deception.

"Go on, then. Give her a call before you burst out of your skin," Marlowe said, wiping his mouth and leaving his napkin for a silent servant to carry away.

The Winthrop's telephone operator informed Jericho that Evie was not at home. Jericho thought about leaving a message, but he wasn't sure she'd get it. Instead, he tapped out a quick note, posting the letter straightaway. He couldn't wait to show her how strong and muscular he'd become in the short time he'd been at Marlowe's estate. The knowledge that he'd see Evie again soon put Jericho in an excellent mood. He felt fantastic. Never fitter.

Once Marlowe was safely out of the house on exhibition business, Jericho set off to see if he could find the elusive card reader. He missed Evie, and he really wanted to be able to write to her and say, "Victory!" He wanted her to see him as a hero.

For some reason, he was drawn back to the long room on the second floor that had once housed the soldiers. He pushed at the door. It opened with a creak. Inside, soft afternoon sunlight pooled on the worn rug. Jericho passed down the middle aisle created by the beds lined up on either side of the room and let his fingers trail across the iron bedposts. He stood in a patch of sun. It was warm, and his mind drifted. Memories of Sergeant Leonard bubbled up. Jericho recalled the two of them racing around a track, Sergeant Leonard taking the lead, making Jericho catch him. He'd won easily, and a winded Jericho had been frustrated that he couldn't keep up. Sergeant Leonard had patted Jericho's shoulder. "One day, you'll run circles around me, around all of us, kid," he'd said. "Don't patronize me," Jericho had said and taken off running. It wasn't until later, after he'd exhausted himself on the track and come back to find Sergeant Leonard still at the track waiting for him with a glass of water though it was dark, that he realized Sergeant Leonard's sincerity and kindness. A thread of shame tightened around Jericho's heart at the memory. Sergeant Leonard had been a good friend and a good man. If nothing else, he wanted to do well on Marlowe's tests to honor his friend's sacrifice.

Jericho's heightened hearing picked up the sounds of the house: The hiss of the radiator. The gurgle of water in the pipes. The servants talking in another room, the housekeeper giving instructions on the evening service, Ames the butler: "…The book is called *The Passing of the Great Race*, and it's everything to do with how our proud white race is doomed unless we can stop this tide of immigration and mongrelization of America.…"

"Ah, you're all wet, Ames-y." The Irish cook. Mrs. Farrelly. "We're all immigrants here. Unless you're an Indian or you got brought in chains."

"I wouldn't expect you to understand." Ames.

"I understand plenty, you old coot."

Jericho thought he heard a woman crying again. He strained to hear. Yes, there it was! But where? He stood in the center of the room, listening. A strange sensation of cold came over him, and then the room was filled with the hubbub of men talking, and one voice in particular whispering, "Check the closet...."

With a gasp, Jericho whirled around. No one was there, but he'd clearly heard someone speaking. Hadn't he? His heartbeat picked up and with it came a second memory: the moment when Jericho realized that Sergeant Leonard was tipping into madness, that he hadn't beaten the Daedalus program curse after all. He'd found his friend sitting on the floor of the shower, staring at the tile wall.

"You hear that, Jericho?" his friend had said, water spilling over his twitching lips. "Do you hear that?"

"Hear what?" Jericho said. There was only the pounding of the shower.

"That."

Two weeks later, Sergeant Leonard was dead.

"I am not going mad," Jericho said. "It's just the adjustment to the serum."

Jericho approached the closet with great apprehension. When he tugged open the sticking door, a fluttering of moths whooshed out on a spiral of dust. Inside was a curious wooden cabinet. At first glance, he thought it was a sewing machine table. But on the right side were a series of typewriter-styled keys, some switches, and a lightbulb. To the left was some sort of automatic feeder chute. In the center was a sorter, and on top, a printing press with a paper roll attached. The machine was electric; a long plug hung from the back of it like a tail. U.S. DEPARTMENT OF PARANORMAL had been stamped on the side.

The card reader.

SHADOW MEN

The day was crisp and sunny, a last blast of winter before the thaw. Mabel hugged herself to keep warm as she watched the skaters taking the season's last turn around the ice rink in Central Park. The April weather might be unpredictable, but Evie was not. Once again, she was late.

Mabel sighed as at last, here she came, cheerily waving a pair of skates in one hand.

"What took you so long?" Mabel grumbled as Evie plopped onto the bench and removed her shoes.

"I wasn't sure what to wear," Evie confessed. "If I die on the ice, I wanted my last outfit to be memorable."

And that was the thing about Evie—she had a way of making you forget why you were unhappy with her to begin with, replacing it with a longing to be her pal always and forever. Evie shrieked and pawed at Mabel as they wobbled onto the slick ice.

"You'll bring us both down!" Mabel shouted, but they were both laughing.

"Wouldn't that be something? We'd be a tragic flapper ice sculpture in the heart of New York. A landmark, like the Woolworth Building!"

"The Woolworth Building isn't going to break a leg if it falls!" Mabel giggled. "Now I understand why you sat in the café the last time we went skating and never touched the ice. Here."

Mabel linked her arm through Evie's and guided her carefully around the outer edge until they found their stride. Sunlight sparkled in the budding trees. Spring was imminent. Mabel could feel it in the air. The Secret Six would probably call this outing frivolous. Who but the privileged could afford to spend an afternoon ice-skating in the park? But the sun felt so delightfully warm on her face, and Mabel would make use of this time.

"Evie, I need your help," Mabel said, her breath coming out in little puffs.

"What are we doing? Burying a body? Carrying out revenge upon your enemy of a thousand years? I am yours, Pie Face!" Evie thumped her breast and they teetered again.

"No more dramatic gestures, please," Mabel begged. "There's this woman I met, Maria Provenza. Her sister, Anna, disappeared a few months ago. Maria said that Anna could tell fortunes. She was a Diviner. And that these men came and took her away."

Evie slid toward the railing, her arms out to grab hold. "Wh-what sort of men?"

"That's the funny thing: She said they wore dark suits and lapel pins with an eye-and-lightning-bolt symbol."

Evie nearly toppled over. "Shadow Men!"

"That's what I'm thinking, too." Mabel wiped a thin sheen of sweat from her brow before it could drip into her eyes and sting. "But then I started thinking, maybe you could read something of her sister's and tell me what you get. This poor woman. Evie, if you'd seen her…"

"Anything for you, Ma—aaah!" Evie slipped and Mabel righted her. "Besides, I'm terrified of these little boots of death. Please lead me to safety."

❀

Evie took shelter at a table in the Bennington's shabby dining hall while Mabel ran upstairs. When she returned moments later, Evie pushed a cup of tepid cocoa her way. "Same old Bennington. Drink that if you dare."

"No, thanks." Mabel signaled to the waiter, who brought her a coffee. She poured a thick coating of cream into it.

"Since when do you drink coffee?" Evie asked.

"There are lots of things I do now," Mabel said, as if daring Evie to ask more, and Evie couldn't help feeling that she'd missed something vital about Mabel these past few weeks while she was preoccupied with training and ghosts. She felt as if she should've been paying closer attention.

Mabel handed over Anna's disturbing sketch. Evie turned the picture sideways and upside down. "Well, I can tell you one thing—Anna Provenza was no Picasso."

"It didn't make much sense to me, either. Some sort of ship?" Mabel suggested.

"Or a very fat spider."

"But look, there's the eye symbol." Mabel tapped the spot where Anna had drawn it. "Maybe she was onto something."

"Certainly worth a try." Evie let her fingers drift across the sketch, but it was dull beneath her touch. Evie pressed harder, fighting the exhaustion of the past few nights' activities. She caught something, a machinelike sound that reminded her of blood pulsing quickly. She couldn't see where the sound was coming from; she only knew that it produced a feeling of absolute terror.

She broke away.

"Did you see anything?"

"Not really. Just a strange whooshing sound. But it was very frightening. Mabesie, I think we should go see this Maria Provenza right away," Evie said. "And then, afterward, we could go to the Hotsy Totsy."

"Yes to the first, no to the second. I don't have time for nightclubs, Evie. I'm trying to change the world."

"What do you think I'm doing?" Evie challenged.

"It isn't the same thing," Mabel said, and Evie was annoyed.

"Are you not allowed to dance while saving the world, Pie Face? Because that sounds dreadful."

"Why do you always have to make a joke?" Mabel said, exasperated.

Evie sipped her cocoa and Mabel her coffee, and the distance stretched between them.

"Anyway, I can't," Mabel said. "I have a meeting with Arthur."

Evie shook off her irritation and scooted forward, all excitement. "Another mysterious meeting. What are you not telling me, Mabesie? Or will I be forced to read something of his to find out?"

"Don't you dare! And besides, who said you're the only one allowed secrets, Mademoiselle O'Neill-ski?"

"But I don't have secrets from you," Evie said, the hurt seeping out. The coffee. Arthur. Secret meetings. Mabel had changed. And she hadn't bothered to keep Evie informed.

Some part of Mabel was enjoying Evie's discomfort. *Yes*, she wanted to say. *I am so much more than you ever allowed me to be. More than you ever saw.* But there was Evie, her pal, biting her bottom lip as she only did when she was trying not to let people know how vulnerable she was. Mabel softened. It was true that Evie had always been there to hear every one of Mabel's secrets. It was Evie who'd always said that Mabel was the real star in the family, not her mother. Evie who had taken Mabel's side in every argument. And Mabel desperately wanted Evie to know about her other life. What good was having a secret if you couldn't share it?

"All right," she said, taking a deep breath. "I am not supposed to be telling you this, so you have to promise *to take it to your grave*!"

Evie mimed crossing her heart. "And hope to die."

Satisfied, Mabel leaned forward. "I am a member of the Secret Six," she said at last, craning her neck to be sure she wasn't overheard.

Evie looked perplexed. "Is that a dance troupe? Tell me you haven't taken up mime! Because I could certainly understand not wanting anyone to know about that."

"The Secret Six!" Mabel said with more energy. When Evie still looked blank, Mabel groaned. "We're rebels? *Revolutionaries?* Honestly, don't you ever read anything besides the gossip pages? We've been in all the papers!"

As it came to Evie, her teasing smile faded. "Wait a minute. The Secret Six. Didn't they dynamite a factory somewhere? Mabel…aren't they *anarchists?*"

Mabel sat up very straight. "So what if we are? This world needs a bit of shaking up. And anyway, the Six have never hurt anyone—not like the Pinkertons, the capitalists, and the government. *We* fight for the worker."

"Fight for the worker how, though? Mabesie…" Evie paused, unsure of what to say. She didn't want to make Mabel mad. "You're not doing anything foolish, are you?"

Mabel leaned back against the booth. "You have some nerve. What about you? What about your…ghost removal policy."

Evie rolled her eyes. "It's hardly a *policy*."

"That isn't the point."

"We're trying to find Conor *and* keep our country safe, I'll remind you."

"At what cost?" Mabel asked. "I'm not sure that what you're doing is right."

"I see. Are you becoming a champion of ghosts' rights now?" Evie snapped, and immediately regretted it. Mabel went quiet. "I'm sorry, Pie Face. I just don't want you to get hurt!"

Mabel responded with cold fury. "You know who's getting hurt? Workers. Poor people. Immigrants. Every day. It's a rigged game, Evie. The people at the top say they believe in the people at the bottom until those people try to climb up. And then the people at the top step on the hands of the climbing people they claim to believe in and cast them down the ladder."

"I'm sorry for what I said. Truly I am."

"It's fine."

"No, it isn't." Evie chewed softly on her bottom lip. "What about your parents?"

"They don't know," Mabel admitted. "Oh, look, I love Mama and Papa, but they're so old-fashioned! They only let me hand out pamphlets and carry picket signs. I want to be in the fight! I want to get my hands dirty!"

"Mabel Rose for president!" Evie said, punching the air with her index finger. She took Mabel's hands in hers. "You're the best person I know, Mabel Rose. If you vouch for Arthur Brown and the Secret Six, they must be jake."

Mabel blushed. "I'm not the best person."

"You are, so! You're good and kind, and you want to make the world better."

Evie kissed Mabel's cheek, and Mabel rested her forehead against Evie's. It felt good to be close friends again, to trust Evie with her secrets. It had never occurred to Mabel before to ask Evie to read something of Arthur's, but now that the idea was in her head, it wouldn't leave. He *was* awfully secretive. What if he had a sweetheart somewhere? What if Mabel could know more about the wounds of his past and make them better? She was good at fixing broken things, and it would be so easy to know....

"I do have something of Arthur's," Mabel blurted out, hating herself a little for it. "Not that I'm saying you should read it."

Evie smirked. "You're not telling me not to read it, either."

Mabel reached into her pocket and pulled out Arthur's card, the one he'd given her the day they'd met. "I really shouldn't."

Reluctantly, she handed it to Evie, who held it up to her forehead like a soothsayer. "What mysterious mysteries will be revealed *tonight* on...the Sweetheart Seer!"

"Oh, this is a terrible idea! Forget I said anything!" Mabel snatched the card back, tapping her fingers against it on the table.

Miss Addie wandered through and the girls watched her, dribbling salt from the pockets of her dress, mumbling something about "Keep Elijah in his grave."

"Same bad cocoa. Same spooky Adelaide," Evie said. She downed the last of her drink. "Come on. I want to go see this Maria Provenza."

While Mabel was distracted with gathering her belongings, Evie pocketed Arthur's card.

☀

By the time Evie and Mabel arrived on Carmine Street, it was dusk. Street lamps cast a sickly glow down the block.

"This is it," Mabel said, hopping up the steps to Maria's building and knocking at the door. An older man answered. He squinted suspiciously at Evie and Mabel. "There's no booze here. This is not a speakeasy."

"I'm looking for Maria Provenza? She lives in Four-L," Mabel explained, and smiled, hoping it would make them seem like trustworthy souls, but it only made the man scowl harder.

"Those people? They're gone, and good riddance." He spat over the railing.

"What…what do you mean, gone?" Mabel sputtered.

"Deported," the man said slowly.

"For what?" Evie asked.

"Treason, that's what! Galleanists, the whole bunch of 'em. The police found all sorts of anarchist papers—*seditious materials*—up there in that dump they were all packed into. Foreigners. Send 'em all back, I say." He pointed a finger at the girls. "You girls oughta steer clear of that nonsense. Go home to your families."

He disappeared inside, slamming the door in their faces.

"But I was there. That's not true. They had no seditious papers," Mabel said numbly to Evie as they walked arm in arm back up the mostly deserted Carmine Street. "They were people just trying to get by, selling paper roses on the streets. Someone wanted them gone."

"The Shadow Men," Evie said, and Mabel nodded.

Night was coming down hard now. Evie shivered. "Remember when we were just scared of getting pinched by the cops for getting blotto at the Hotsy Totsy?"

"Or being lectured by my mother for sneaking out my window?"

"Mabel, *daahrling*, I did not raise you to behave like a common *hooo-ligan*!" Evie said in her best impression of Mabel's mother. They shared a giggle, but it was short-lived. "Sometimes, I wish we were girls again, safe."

Mabel snorted in contempt. "When has it ever been safe to be a girl?"

The train rumbled over the tracks above Sixth Avenue.

"I have to meet up with Arthur," Mabel said.

"Can't I tag along? I want to meet this mysterious Arthur Brown!"

"Sorry. I can't. Rules. You're not even supposed to know. Remember?"

"Oh, I wouldn't stay. I just want to lay eyes on the revolutionary speci-men." Evie wiggled her eyebrows and giggled.

"I'd better not. He might get upset," Mabel said.

Evie sobered. "Well, that doesn't sound kosher, as your father would say."

Immediately, Mabel got defensive. "You don't know him like I do. He's got his reasons to be careful."

Evie knew Mabel. She knew that telling Mabel not to do something was as good as pushing her toward it. She was stubborn that way—and too much of a romantic. No doubt she'd see Arthur as a wounded boy who needed her love to become a healed man. Sewn into Mabel's goodness was a twin thread of grandiosity: Saving people gave Mabel the feeling that she was special for doing so. It was Mabel's drug, and she was very addicted. Not that Evie cared if that was Mabel's blind spot. After all, everybody had something about them that could be lovely on the one hand and annoying as hell on the other. And anyway, it was clear that there was no arguing it tonight.

Evie threw her hands in the air in defeat. "All right. I can't fight the great reformer Mabel Rose." She kissed Mabel's cheek. "Fare thee well, sweet Pie Face."

Mabel waved good-bye and turned up Bleecker Street.

"Mabesie!" Evie called.

Mabel turned back. Under the glow of the street lamp, she looked like a sweet-faced angel. "Yes?"

"Be careful, please? No, don't you dare make that annoyed face! I adore you. The truth is, I'd be lost without you."

"Yes. You would." Mabel laughed. "I love you, too."

Mabel continued on her way. She did love Evie. And she felt guilty for not inviting her along, especially when Evie had been standing there in the cold. With those wisps of her bobbed hair sticking out crosswise around the sides of her fashionable cloche, she'd looked less like Evie O'Neill, Sweetheart Seer radio star, and more like Evie, her best friend, and Mabel was hit by a pang for the times Evie had just mentioned, when they were writing letters to each other about film stars they swooned over and how delicious milk shakes were.

Yes, it was true that the Six was a secret. But the deeper truth was that as much as she loved Evie, Mabel didn't want to invite her. She didn't want to watch Evie suck up all the attention. This was Mabel's place to shine, and she didn't want to compete with Evie's bright glow.

This business with Maria Provenza had her worried, though. Somebody had planted those papers, Mabel felt sure. Arthur would say you never really knew people, but Mabel's gut told her that she did know that Maria Provenza wasn't an anarchist; she was just a woman worried about her missing sister. And if the Shadow Men really had taken Anna Provenza, then where were they keeping her—and why?

Mabel thought again about Anna's vision and the warning from the Diviner at the camp. They'd both said that danger was coming. That Mabel should be careful. Arthur would say she shouldn't believe in Diviner warnings. Evie would put all her faith in them. And there was Mabel, caught in the middle. Mabel's whole existence was about belief in causes and change. But for once, she didn't know what to believe.

The coffee shop's windows blazed into the night. Arthur sat inside at a table. Mabel stopped to check her breath and fix her hair. In the glass, she thought she saw the reflection of the burly man. She whirled around, searching the shadows across the street, but it was just an ordinary man on his way to wherever he was going, and so she went inside.

☀

Evie knocked at Henry and Theta's door.

"To what do I owe this great honor?" Sam asked, arms folded.

"Oh, clam up, will you? I'm worried about Mabel."

Sam welcomed Evie inside, and she plopped herself down on Theta and Henry's one decent chair.

"Mabel? Mabel's probably the one person you don't need to worry about," Sam said, bringing over two Hires root beers and taking a seat in the smaller, rickety chair. "She's got her head on straight. Why, I'll bet she's downstairs right now making up a box for the poor."

"No, she's not, either. She's out with a boy."

"Well, bully for her!"

"I'm not so sure. This boy might be trouble."

Sam smirked. "You want me to go steal his wallet, tell him he can't have it back until he promises to be a prince to Mabel?"

Evie managed a brief smile. "No. At least, not yet."

"Aww, listen, Sheba. Mabel's a good egg. She wouldn't go for any funny business."

"I hope you're right."

Sam took a swig of his root beer. "But speaking of funny—something funny happened to me today."

Evie scrounged in her purse for her compact and checked her complexion in its small round mirror. "Funny haha or funny strange?"

"I had the feeling I was being followed."

"By whom? Adoring packs of schoolgirls?" When Sam didn't answer, she asked, "*Was* it adoring packs of schoolgirls?"

"You finished?"

"Since I didn't get a laugh, I suppose I am," Evie said, and powdered her nose.

Sam took another swig of his root beer and wiped his hand across his mouth. "I didn't see anybody when I turned around. I just had this . . . hunch. That weird feeling in my gut."

"Who would want to follow you?"

Sam quirked an eyebrow. "You want me to make a list?"

Evie closed her compact with a snap. "No, thanks. I hate to see you have to work so hard. I know what a toll thinking takes on you."

Sam shot her an annoyed look. "Okay. Then how about this: Maybe the people who have my mother. Maybe those creepy Shadow Men."

Now Evie was worried about both Mabel *and* Sam. "Funny you should mention our elusive friends the Shadow Men," Evie said, and she told Sam about the encounter she and Mabel had just had with Maria Provenza's bigoted landlord.

Sam listened with a grave expression. "Something sure stinks, all right."

"Sam, I don't think you should go anywhere by yourself."

His grin was wolfish. "Yeah? You offering to be my bodyguard, Lamb Chop? Gee, that'll be kinda awkward on my dates, won't it?"

Evie rolled her eyes. "Fine. Get pinched by those creepy Shadow Men. See if I care."

"Don't worry about me, Baby Vamp. I'm a street rat. Been looking after myself for a long time," Sam said, finishing his root beer. "Still—it's all the more reason to know what's on those cards, see if we can find other Diviners who might hold more pieces of the puzzle. Have you heard anything from the giant up in Valhalla, yet?"

"Frequently. And once he called me long-distance!" Evie said breezily. *Two can play at this game, Sam.* "But so far, he still hasn't found your card reader."

"Well, maybe you can give him a noodge?"

"A what?"

"A noodge. A little prodding," Sam explained. "I'm getting antsy here."

"Fine. I'll send him an urgent letter." At the door, she wrinkled her nose. "Noodge? Is that a real word?"

"It's Yiddish. Like . . . *Ikh hob dikh lib.*"

Evie narrowed her eyes in suspicion. "What does *that* mean?"

Sam smiled. "Maybe one day I'll tell you."

※

When Evie got back to the Winthrop, she took Arthur's card from her pocket and placed it on the table, debating. She knew she shouldn't read it, but Mabel had been so secretive that it had piqued her curiosity.

"I really shouldn't," Evie said aloud. And then she was frantically pulling off her gloves and pressing Arthur's card between her palms.

A memory of Arthur and Mabel's first meeting flared. He'd rescued her from the police at a rally in Union Square. Their chance meeting was sweet. She saw Mabel's face as Arthur had then, all curly copper hair and big eyes. Evie could feel the kernel of attraction between them. She should stop, she knew. She would stop. As soon as she knew if her best friend was okay. But then the card took a turn. Evie felt fear and danger and deception. She saw Arthur in a cell. A man in a brown hat sat across from him. Evie caught the flash of a badge. Police? No. Bigger than that. "It's your choice, Mr. Brown."

Arthur scoffed. "Choice. Ha."

"Just do what we say. We'll take it from there," the brown-hat man said.

Evie had no idea what that meant. She pressed further, but the card wasn't giving her anything else, and now she was sorry she'd read it. Objects had a voice, and this one was screaming at her. Should she confess to Mabel what she'd done? Mabel would probably never speak to her again. Should she say something to Mabel's parents? Only a snitch would do that, and Evie was no snitch. Besides, Mabel's mother hated Evie.

Evie did know one thing for certain: Arthur Brown was in some sort of trouble. Bad trouble.

"Oh, Mabesie. What have you gotten yourself into?" she whispered.

※

That night, the Diviners atomized a family at an abandoned house in Queens.

The neighbors had called it in—disturbances, rattling, pets gone missing. The old house's dining room still had paper on the walls, a delicate lily-of-the-valley pattern that must have been pretty once, before the dirt and decay set in. The ghostly family—a husband, his wife, and pinafored twin girls who couldn't have been more than seven—sat at the table as if they were merely waiting for their supper. Sam and Memphis had barraged them with questions, but the man and his wife only seemed confused and a little afraid.

"We don't know," the woman said, her voice sounding as if it were coming through a tin can. "We don't know why we're here. It was a carriage accident, you see. A carriage accident."

Memphis could see the line across the husband's abdomen where he'd been crushed. Here and then gone.

"They're lying," Evie said to the others. "They have to know something! It's a trick."

"What if they're not lying?" Ling asked. "Henry?"

"Gee. I don't know," Henry said, glancing from face to face.

"It was a carriage accident," the ghost wife insisted. "I saw the horses sliding sideways. Then we tumbled down the hillside. Gone, all gone in the blink of an eye."

"We should do it quick, before they turn," Sam said.

The father put a hand to his wound. "We were to see my brother in the country."

"Maybe they're not going to turn," Ling said. She couldn't stop looking at the twin girls, who clung to each other. They were frightened. Of her.

"Where is Conor Flynn?" Memphis asked.

"A carriage accident, I tell you," the ghost wife pleaded. "That's all. I don't know why we're here."

"Ready?" Sam prompted.

"Yeah. Okay," Memphis grumbled. He couldn't bring himself to look at the family. He was glad Isaiah wasn't there.

"Why are we here? Why? Why…?" the woman cried as the Diviners came together and blasted them apart.

No one spoke on the long walk back to the train.

A PUNCH IN THE GUT

After a sleepless night, Evie called Mabel and asked to meet her at the Bennington.

"What's the matter?" Mabel said, taking a seat across from Evie at a table under the faulty Victorian chandelier. "You sounded dire on the telephone."

"I have a confession to make," Evie said. She took a steadying breath and readied herself for Mabel's anger. "I read Arthur's card. Wait! I'm sorry. I know that I shouldn't have, but you were so mysterious about him, and I was worried—"

"You had no right!"

"It was wrong of me, I know. But, Mabesie, I was right to be worried. Arthur's not on the level."

Mabel tensed. "What do you mean? Is there another girl?"

"No. Not that I saw."

Mabel went back to being irritated. "Well, what, then?"

"He's in some sort of trouble. I saw him in a police interrogation room. I think he was with an agent of some sort."

"That's ancient history. His brother went to jail. They questioned Arthur, but he was innocent so they let him go. That's probably what you saw."

"No. No, this felt more recent, Mabesie—"

"Evie…please stop."

"This man was trying to get Arthur to do something that felt very wrong and very dangerous."

"I don't want to know—"

"Mabel, Arthur's *lying* to you—"

"I said, I don't want to know!" Mabel thundered, stunning Evie into silence. Mabel's eyes filled with angry tears. "Why do you have to ruin everything?"

"I don't…I didn't mean…"

"I loved Jericho and you had to have him. You, who could have anybody! And now you want to keep me from Arthur."

"No. That isn't true, Mabesie. I only want to keep you from getting hurt."

"Well, you can't!" Mabel wiped at her eyes. "If I want to get hurt, that's my business."

"Mabel," Evie tried. "This isn't you."

Mabel grabbed her purse and stood up. "You haven't known who I am for some time, Evie."

A miserable Evie sat alone, stirring the undrinkable cocoa. What she'd done had been awful; she knew that. But she couldn't unknow what she'd discovered about Arthur Brown, either. And now Mabel hated her for it. Maybe what Evie had seen *had* been from long ago. But Evie couldn't let it alone yet—not with Mabel's happiness in the balance. It was time to have a talk with Arthur Brown.

At Evie's knock, Arthur opened his door wearing only trousers and his undershirt. He was sinewy and handsome in a rugged way. Evie could see why he had swept Mabel off her feet. He folded his arms across his chest and leaned against the doorjamb with a bemused smile that irked Evie immediately.

"I don't remember ordering any Fuller brushes or Bibles," he said. "Shop's downstairs, miss. In case you're lost."

"Arthur Brown?"

Arthur's expression went from smiling to wary. "Who wants to know?"

"I'm Evie O'Neill. Mabel's best friend."

Arthur laughed. "Well, well, well. The Sweetheart Seer herself. To what do I owe this honor?" He threw a glance over his shoulder. "I don't think I have any ghosts hiding in my humble abode, but you're welcome to check."

Evie balled her fists at her sides. He was being contemptuous, but for Mabel's sake, she'd swallow her pride. "This won't take long, Mr. Brown. I wanted to tell you that…that I read something that belonged to you. It was very informative."

Arthur laughed. "Yeah? I don't go for that Diviner hocus-pocus."

"You might if you'd seen what I did. You and a government agent? A man in a brown hat? He had some very interesting things to say to you."

Arthur stopped laughing. His eyes narrowed, and for a minute, Evie felt afraid.

"Oh, yeah? How'd you get something of mine to read, anyway?"

"I-I took it from Mabel's room when she wasn't looking," Evie lied.

"What a fine friend you are."

"The point is, I know you're in trouble with the Bureau of Investigation. I know you're lying about who you are."

"That so? Sorry, Miss O'Neill. Like I said, I don't put much stock in Diviner visions."

He was trying to be offhanded about it, but Evie could tell he was nervous.

"I only wanted to say that if you do anything to hurt my friend, I'll come after you. I swear I will."

Arthur saluted her. "Duly noted. Now, if you'll excuse me, I was in the middle of getting dressed. So long, Miss O'Neill."

Arthur tried to shut the door. Evie stuck her foot inside, blocking it. "Please don't hurt Mabel," she said a little desperately. "She's good. And kind. All she wants is to help people. She's the best person I know."

Arthur stopped looking smug. "I'll look out for her, Miss O'Neill. I promise," he said softly. "You're not the only one who loves her."

MISSING MASS

Alma and Ling sat in the cramped Tin Pan Alley music room waiting for the phone to ring, even though it hadn't for several hours. Ling rested her cheek against her fist, staring at the wall. Alma played the same three notes on the piano. They'd been spending more time together lately, going to the pictures or stopping at the confectionery to share an ice-cream sundae. Ling had come to look forward to their time together. But today she was distracted. She couldn't stop seeing those twins' ghostly faces. How confused they were. How scared. It gnawed at Ling's conscience. *What were they doing?* This hunting and interrogating ghosts hadn't gotten them any definitive answers, just more riddles. The whole quest felt more like an elaborate game designed to keep them busy.

"What are you thinking so hard about over there?" Alma asked Ling at last.

"Atoms."

Alma raised her eyebrows. "Uh-huh."

"We're all collections of atoms. All of us. But what happens to those atoms after we die? Does our matter become a different energy? Is that what ghosts are? And is that energy a soul, or is it only an echo of a human?"

"Uh-*huh*," Alma said.

"Energy can't be created or destroyed, but it can be transformed from one kind of energy to another. And as matter—all those atoms—is converted into energy, some mass goes missing. That's Einstein's theory of relativity, E equals MC squared."

"Oh, sure. *Everybody* knows that."

"What if the Department of Paranormal's experiment during the war produced some incredible new form of energy? If the soldiers were the mass, what happened to them?" Ling mused. Some theory was fighting to take shape, but she wasn't there yet.

"And here I thought you might say, 'I was thinking about you, Alma. What a delightful companion you are.'"

"Sorry. I'm boring you."

Alma swung around on the piano bench to face Ling. "You're not boring me. I just don't understand a lick of it. And I don't want to know about ghosts. I only want them to go back. They frighten me. They don't scare you?"

"They didn't used to," Ling said. She'd drawn comfort from them and their messages. It had made her feel that her ancestors were looking on after death. She liked that. Liked the idea that whatever she was would live on in some fashion. That death was not final. It had given her a sense of a beautiful, ordered universe. But now she'd angered the ghosts. The ancestors weren't speaking to her. And she was beginning to wonder if hunting ghosts was a mistake.

"Let's talk about something else," Ling said. She wasn't good at this.

Alma bit her lip and looked up at Ling through her lashes. "Well. Let's see what happens when our atoms collide." With that, Alma leaned forward boldly and kissed Ling softly on the lips.

Heat spread across Ling's cheeks.

Alma smiled seductively. "I do believe you're blushing, Miss Chan."

"Yes," Ling whispered. "I am."

Alma leaned in for another kiss. Ling pulled back. Alma looked confused.

How to explain that the blush wasn't passion, but embarrassment and discomfort? The truth was that Ling didn't feel what most people seemed to feel. She rarely felt truly aroused beyond the theoretical. The idea of kissing was just that—an idea. Not unwelcome, but it didn't seem to reach into her depths. At least, it hadn't yet. Alma was beautiful and sensual and warm. Ling liked her so much. She was attracted to the idea of Alma, to her spirit and wit. She wanted to be around Alma. But she didn't know if she wanted to pet with Alma, and if she truly didn't want to make love to Alma—fizzy, alive, gorgeous Alma—then it was the proof to Ling's hypothesis that she simply didn't have the sexual drive that most people did.

"Is it me?" Alma asked, straightening her spine.

"No! No," Ling said.

"Is it because I'm a girl?"

Was it? Ling's mother would have a conniption fit if she even suspected.

She'd drag Ling to confession and probably never let her out of the house again. But Ling lived in the scientific world. She'd long since stopped believing what her mother believed. And Ling knew deep down that her attraction was not to boys. Her time with Wai-Mae in the dream world had awakened that part of her. Being around Alma had proven it beyond all doubt. "No. It isn't because we're girls," Ling said shyly.

"Then what is it?"

In her lap, Ling clasped her hands tightly. She didn't like sharing herself. Holding herself in check often felt like her only weapon for navigating the unforgiving, intrusive world. If you told people about yourself, what was to stop them from using those private hurts and joys against you sometime? Once you let people in, you were vulnerable. Nothing frightened Ling more than that—not ghosts with teeth or Shadow Men or the man in the stovepipe hat. But she owed Alma truth, she knew.

"I feel very deeply. Even romantically. But those feelings live inside my heart and my head. I can't translate them to the rest of me." Ling said "the rest of me" quickly and quietly. "I don't know if I want to be touched in that way. I don't know if my love is a physical love."

Alma was disappointed, Ling could tell. She didn't really understand. Few people did. Sex sold everything. It was in every advertisement, song, and Hollywood movie. Who was the freak who didn't want to make love?

"Oh, Lord, Ling." Alma let her breath out in a long exhale.

"I'm sorry," Ling said, ashamed.

"Don't be," Alma said. She snorted, gave a weary smile and a shrug. "*C'est la vie*. I gotta stop falling for these girls who don't fall for me, though."

"I didn't say that!"

"Now I am confused."

"Can we…take it slowly?" Ling asked.

Alma bit her lip again. "I'm in no rush." She tucked Ling's hair behind her ear. "Was that okay?"

Ling smiled. She nodded. "It was nice."

"Do you like to hold hands?"

Ling unfurled one of her very rare smiles. "With the right person, yes."

"And am I…?"

"Yes."

The phone rang. "Diviners Investigations," Ling answered, still holding on to Alma's hand.

"Is that your telephone voice? You sound like you're at a funeral."

Ling rolled her eyes. "What do you want, Evie?"

"Can you come to Theta and Henry's? We're going to try another dream walking."

※

"Tell them what you told us," Memphis said to Isaiah.

Isaiah recounted the vision he'd had of Conor and the cornfields and the strange girl. "I drew this. I think...I think it came straight from Conor. Like he was drawing through me."

"Like channeling," Ling said.

The picture was exactly like the one Evie had seen back at the asylum, the Eye and the floating soldiers. "We want to try to reach Conor through this."

Henry's eyebrows shot up. "Okay. But Conor didn't draw that. Isaiah did."

"I know. It's a gamble. But we're down to gambles at this point."

Henry scooted a chair over, close to Ling. They each held a corner of Isaiah's drawing. Sam set the metronome in motion, and within minutes, they'd slipped into sleep and dreams.

The first thing Henry noticed when he woke inside the dream was the sweet, bright haze of sunshine, like an egg wash spread over the warm day. He could actually feel the sun on his back, lulling him. The second thing he noticed was that Ling was not beside him.

"Ling?" he called.

There was no answer.

Where was she? Where was *he*?

Looking around, he saw that he stood on a leafy street of tidy brick houses and white-picket fences. Black-eyed Susans swayed on their stalks. A horse-and-buggy trotted past. The man at the reins tipped his hat at Henry.

"Mornin'," the man said.

"Mornin'," Henry answered.

A boy in short pants tossed newspapers from a bag slung over his shoulder. One landed near the porch of a pale brick foursquare—the *Zenith Caller*. Zenith, Ohio. That was Evie's hometown. He was inside Evie's dream, then. The door of the house creaked open. Henry went inside. Filmy Irish lace curtains sucked in through the open windows on a breeze. A fan whirred on a table blowing across a bowl of melting ice. Summer. A small, fair-haired woman rocked in a corner, hemming the edges of an American flag, which pooled on the floor in mounds.

The creak of the rocker, the gentle whine of the fan's blades, and the hazy sun were hypnotic. Henry felt as if he could stay in this dream forever. A girl in a ruffled pinafore, her hair done up in a large blue bow, jumped out from behind the wall of the dining room. "Find me!" she said, and ran, and Henry knew beyond a doubt that it was Evie as a child. The same mischievous glint in her blue eyes. The white of her pinafore bled into the sunshine streaking through the tall windows, blurring her as she slipped out the side porch door. Henry ran after. In the kitchen, a much younger Will jotted down notes without looking up. The eye-and-lightning-bolt symbol shimmered on the notebook's cover.

Henry pushed through the side door.

The house had gone now. He was in a forest. Snow dusted the ground. There was a clear lake, a hawk soaring above it. A circle of chairs sat on the pine-needle floor of the clearing. There were boys in uniform, sitting stiff-backed, hands on their knees, waiting—for what, Henry did not know. On a tree stump, a Victrola played an old war song. Through the dense trees, Henry caught sight of Evie wandering through. She was no longer a child but the Evie of today. Henry had a vague, emotional sense of her that stretched back far longer than he'd known her. He knew somehow that she hated licorice and cried when a neighbor boy accidentally ran over a frog with his bicycle.

A tornado of black birds swirled up before Henry; he put up his hands to block their wings, but they were nothing more than figments fading into the air. Panic seized Henry, though he couldn't say why. It was as if he knew that some terrible fate beckoned, as if this was a dream he had lived through countless times before. He was running through the forest. Trying to get away from whatever unseen monster chased him. Trying to get back to the happy memory of the house. Henry's heartbeat quickened—he could hear it in his ears, a walloping rhythm, like the clang and whoosh of a great machine. It hurt to breathe. He'd run in a circle, back to the clearing and the Victrola. Trees fell as if trampled. The clanging grew louder. In the chairs, the boys in uniform had become ghosts with skeletal faces. Fierce light blazed through the falling trees, and within it, like an alien sun, was the eye symbol tearing the sky apart while the soldiers screamed and screamed. Pain. So much pain. As if his body and mind were being stretched beyond all endurance. He no longer knew who he was. He had to remember: *I'm Henry. Henry Dubois IV.* But when he looked down, he saw that a name had been stitched onto the front of his uniform.

JAMES.

XAVIER.

O'NEILL.

Henry's blood pounded in his head as he woke. His body hurt, and he couldn't move.

"Henry? You copacetic?" Evie's face swam into view.

"Yeah. Rough…landing." He felt as if he might vomit. "Where's… where's Ling?"

"I'm here. I couldn't get inside the dream." She didn't sound happy about it.

Henry gagged. He had sweated through his shirt.

"Here. Hold on." Memphis laid hands on Henry's arms, and soon, Henry's sickness began to subside.

"Thanks," he said, gingerly rotating his arms.

"Hen, you sure you're jake? You scared me," Theta said, sitting at his side.

"Yeah. I think so."

"What happened? What did you see?" Evie asked.

Henry took in a few deep breaths. "I wasn't just an observer in somebody else's dream. This time, I was actually inside the dreamer's body. Sort of a kidnapping."

"Has that ever happened to you before?" Memphis asked.

Henry shook his head. It still hurt a little. "I saw terrible things. Worse, I was living them. And I was powerless to stop them. Except that, as I said,

I wasn't me. I was someone else." Henry looked over at Evie. "I'm fairly certain that I was having James's dream."

There was a whine in Evie's ears, as if she were on the verge of fainting. She steadied herself by grabbing the edge of the table. "But you said that Ling wasn't with you."

"Right," Ling said, and Evie could see from the look on her face that it was dawning on her, too.

"And…when you dream walk, you only see the living. So how…?" Evie trailed off, letting Sam say what she couldn't seem to manage.

"How's that? James is dead."

Henry nodded. "I know. And dead men don't dream."

※

How could Henry have experienced James's dream? That was impossible. Unless James was still alive. But he'd been killed during the war. Evie had seen it in Luther's memories. Hadn't she?

"Are you sure?" Evie asked.

"I…I don't know. But I've never walked in a dead person's dream before."

"Suppose it could've been Ling's doing, then?" Memphis suggested.

"But I couldn't get inside the dream with Henry," she answered. *And the dead aren't speaking to me right now.*

Memphis put a hand on Henry's shoulder. "Evie was right beside you. Could you have been picking up on her emotions somehow, living through her memories?"

"I'm telling you: I was in his body, living his dream."

Evie nestled closer to Henry and looped her arm through his. "What do you remember?"

Henry blinked up at the ceiling. "A house—brick foursquare with Irish lace curtains at the windows, a side porch off the kitchen."

"That sounds like our house!"

"Then I was in a forest. I heard this awful hum rushing through me, sort of like the throbbing of a wounded, mechanical heart. I thought it would drive me mad."

"Did you ever see what it was?" Ling asked.

Henry shook his head.

"Does that mean James *isn't* dead?" Theta asked.

Evie would give anything for James to still be alive. To hear him calling, "Where is my sister, brave Artemis?" as he used to do on warm summer evenings when the two of them would run around the garden trying to catch fireflies in mason jars to light the night. After James was killed, Evie had never again tried to catch lightning bugs. They were magical creatures, and she couldn't bear to cage them.

Henry was picking absently at his shirt cuff. He looked unhappy.

"What's the matter, Henry?" Evie asked.

He winced. "Wherever James is, I don't think it's a good place. There was terrible pain and fear. I'm sorry to tell you that."

Evie didn't know if what Henry had experienced was a dream or something far too real, but she couldn't bear the thought of her brother suffering.

"He has to be dead," Sam said. "Evie saw what happened to the one forty-four when she went into Luther's memories. Will and Sister Walker confirmed it. All those soldiers—they're gone."

"Yes. But gone where?" Ling said.

Evie walked all the way back to the Winthrop to try to clear her head. At a newsstand, she bought the late-edition *Daily News*, frowning at a flattering front-page article about Sarah Snow and how she would be giving the opening prayer at Jake Marlowe's Future of America Exhibition, complete with a great quote from Mr. Phillips about Sarah being "WGI's brightest star!"

"I thought I was WGI's brightest star," Evie grumbled. And then, on page seven—*seven!*—was a tiny article by Woody about the Diviners banishing a ghost from a warehouse on the West Side.

"Say, aren't you the Sweetheart Seer?"

Evie looked up to see a smart-set couple, all long pearls and spats, walking a wiry terrier.

She brightened. "That's right!"

"There's a ghost—save me! Save me!" The man burst out laughing.

"That isn't funny," Evie said. It felt like being slapped.

"Come now. It's all a publicity stunt, isn't it? You and your phony friends. Your days are numbered," the man sneered.

"She used to be so delightful on the radio. Now she's just a real wet blanket," the woman agreed as they went on their way.

By the time Evie reached the Winthrop, her misery was a fully fleshed companion. She'd thought that hunting down ghosts and getting rid of them would've made the Diviners the talk of the town, welcome at every nightclub and swank hotel. She'd thought the citizens of New York would be grateful. But more and more, they were laughing at Evie and her friends. The Diviners were becoming a city joke. And they still had no answers about the Eye or Conor.

Evie picked up the phone to call Uncle Will. Then she thought about what Henry had told her, about James being in some sort of terrible place, and she slammed it down again. She was cheered to see that Jericho had mailed her a letter. She sliced it open with a fingernail, hoping she hadn't ruined a perfectly good manicure, and read:

> Dear Evie,
>
> I hope this letter finds you well. Spring is trying to arrive here. I believe I saw a brave daffodil poking its yellow head up from the cold ground today. You would love the estate and all its furnishings. As a matter of fact, I saw an old antique that might interest you, Buffalo Gal. I know how you've been looking for just such a piece for your new home, and I know how you love to take on a Project. Perhaps you can come get a read on it and tell me if it's of value?

```
        Mr. Marlowe invites you and Ling Chan
     to his estate this Friday to stay the
     weekend. He'll send a car to meet your
     train. I'm sure you'd love it here. It's
     very beautiful. Say hello to the others
     for me.

                              Fondly,
                              Jericho
```

Evie fell back on the bed, smiling her first smile of the day. At least one thing was going right. They could finally get those cards read. And Jericho. She would see Jericho.

ALWAYS WATCHING

Theta couldn't sleep. When she shut her eyes, she thought of Memphis. She missed him so much it felt as if she'd been emptied. As if she'd been abandoned on the church steps once more. And soon, she'd have to answer to Roy as well.

Archibald jumped up on the bed and pressed his whiskered face into hers. She kissed his furry head. "What am I gonna do about this mess, pal?" she asked the cat as he purred.

Theta poured Archibald a saucer of milk. There was a knock at her door. Theta tensed: What if it was Roy? What if he'd smooth-talked his way past the doorman like she knew he could do?

Theta opened the door to a distraught Miss Addie.

"I...I can't find it. I can't find my apartment," Miss Addie said, running a trembling hand through her loose gray hair.

"Come on," Theta said, throwing on a robe. "I'll take you back."

It was heartbreaking, Theta thought, the way Miss Addie could be so clear about some things and then her mind would lock up and she'd sit blinking out the window at the day, getting frustrated or angry or silent. Theta had been making a habit of stopping in to see the Proctor sisters each evening. She liked the way they took care of her, liked listening to their tales of days gone by—*A great big steam train...Well, by the time I arrived at Aunt Martha's that pink dress was coated in coal dust*—but the tales that thrilled her the most were their stories of the paranormal. They told her about the charms they'd made—*this one is for strong blood and this is for good sleep*—the babies they had helped midwife back in Virginia, the spells they'd cast: for love, for courage, for safe passage both in life and in death. About the ways of salt and sage, of candles and earth, of clapping and bells.

But what is most important is intention, Miss Addie had cautioned. *You must work always to understand your own heart so that it cannot be used against you. Know yourself here and here*, she'd said, pressing the tip of her gnarled finger just above Theta's heart and then to her forehead.

As they waited now for the elevator, Miss Addie suddenly stiffened. "He's here," she whimpered. "Oh, we must hurry! There's not a moment to waste!"

They rode the elevator to the Bennington's crumbling basement and stepped out into the gloom. Theta jumped as the golden doors closed behind them and the elevator rattled back up. It was very dark. The only light came from the weak glow of street lamps leaking through the high clerestory windows. Theta toggled the light switches but they didn't work.

"I don't think we should be down here, Miss Addie," Theta warned.

"My salt!" Addie said, reaching into her pockets and coming up empty-handed.

Theta pressed the button for the elevator. "It's okay, Miss Addie. Let's go back upstairs and have tea. There's nobody..."

Theta strained, listening. There it was—a shuffling, scraping noise somewhere deep in the basement. *Mice*, she told herself. Because lies were the only defense she had. Even though her heartbeat said otherwise. So did the gooseflesh rising up the center of her back. She'd just detected a smell. Rot. Decay. Death.

Theta pressed the elevator button repeatedly. The elevator sat at the tenth floor as if she hadn't called for it at all. "Miss Addie, let's get out of here. We'll take the stairs."

Miss Addie mumbled incantations under her breath, stopping short as one word whispered out of the darkness like a long-held desire: *"Adelaide..."*

"Wh-what was that?" Theta asked. Her knees buckled slightly. Her mouth was dry as sawdust.

"It's him," Miss Addie said, terrified. "It's *Elijah*."

The basement suddenly seemed enormous and too small at once. The shuffling grew louder until Theta wanted to scream. In the dark, she made out a tall figure, coming closer. The figure stepped into a shaft of street light. Theta gasped. Elijah might have been handsome in life. In death, he was a hideous specter. Maggots crawled from the wounds on his body and fell to the basement floor with a plop. His Confederate uniform was eaten through with rot, the few remaining buttons tarnished. His face was skeletal, half of his cheek eaten away so that Theta could see through to the teeth inside, the black drool dripping from the sides of his cracked, pale lips. *Monster*, she thought.

He spoke: "*You did this to me, Addie. You brought me back....*"

"I didn't mean to," Miss Addie whispered. "I loved you so."

"*You're the reason I have no rest.*"

Miss Addie put a hand to her heart. Theta didn't know if she was more afraid that Miss Addie would die right there or that she'd die and leave Theta all alone with the terrifying Elijah.

"*I have come for you, Adelaide. You are mine, my love. We will be together forever and ever....*"

"No, please. It was a mistake! I don't want it," Miss Addie cried.

Elijah did not like this. His voice became angry: "*Too late, Adelaide. You made the bargain. Now you must honor it. Or have you no honor, Adelaide Keziah Proctor?*"

A disorienting chorus of whispers shot around the basement: "*The old bitch. Bitch. Thinks she has power. Kill the bitch. Suck the power from her veins. She should pay for what she did. Old bitch. Show her no mercy!*"

With a growl, Elijah reached for Miss Addie, and Theta thought of Roy. *Monsters.* Fury rose up inside her. Flame engulfed her arms as she screamed, "Get back!"

Elijah stopped where he was, a grinning menace.

"Get back, you son of a bitch!" Theta growled. It was primal. *She* was primal.

Elijah unhinged his jaw and screamed with demonic force. Miss Addie cried out in terror—*No, please, no!* Fear returned to Theta, dousing her fire. Her hands were small and cold. And she had only one thought left: *Run.*

She grabbed Miss Addie's arm and hurried up the stairs with her until they'd reached the safety of the lobby, where the night doorman and the elevator operator stared at the two panting, terrified women as if they had emerged from hell itself.

Upstairs in the Proctor sisters' living room with its many charms of protection, Theta wrapped Miss Addie in an afghan. Miss Addie sat in her chair staring out the window at the park as Theta told Miss Lillian about everything that had happened in the basement with Elijah.

Miss Lillian poured out three cups of strong, woodsy-smelling tea. Confetti-like leaves floated up to the top of the cup. "Drink your tea, dear."

"I want to know about Elijah."

"When Elijah was killed during the War Between the States, my dear sister was lost to her grief," Miss Lillian said. "She studied every enchantment and spell until she found what she needed: a working to return the dead to life."

"If you don't mind my saying, that sounds like a bad spell."

"She was sixteen," Miss Lillian said gently. "What did she know? Only that she would do anything to have her Elijah back again. That night, for the first time, she met the King of Crows."

Theta sat straight up. "Miss Addie's talked to the King of Crows?"

"Oh, indeed, she has. It's where her troubles started. She bargained with him for Elijah's life. But the King of Crows tricked her, you see. Elijah returned to her, as promised, but not as he had been."

Theta shuddered thinking about the thing she'd seen in the basement coming after Miss Addie.

"What can you tell me about this King of Crows?" Theta pressed. Maybe she could find out something that would help them find Conor or the Eye. "Where does he live?"

Miss Lillian frowned. "Live? No. He must steal from others to live. He's a trickster and seducer. He preys upon your worst instincts, upon your greatest fears and deepest wounds. His treaties are bad promises that feed on the dark of our souls."

Miss Lillian shook her head and tucked the afghan up around her sister's neck. "Once, his influence was limited. Something has loosed the restraints on the energy of the dead and allowed him greater power in this world."

"But why? What does he want here?"

"Oh, my dear." She closed her eyes and exhaled, weary. "He wants everything. Greed is in his very bones. His soul is a great emptiness that can never be filled. Nothing will ever be enough for him. You've seen his monsters, like Elijah—they take from the living, but most of it goes to *him*. He *takes*. That is what he does. It is his only reason to be, his sole enjoyment. He feeds on pain and chaos and trickery. Power is his true aim. He would do anything to hold it, anything to stay and corrupt."

"You're in great danger, I fear. All of you," Miss Addie said quietly, still looking out at the budding branches of Central Park, pale in the rising light. "You and all of your friends. The dead are everywhere. He will keep corrupting them. He will try to corrupt the good spirits to his will." Miss Addie turned to Theta. "But you can help to stop him."

"How?"

"How. How! Your *fire*!"

Theta was taken aback by Miss Addie's sudden burst of anger. "I nearly burned down the psychiatric hospital! People could've died! I don't understand this thing that lives inside me."

"You saved Adelaide tonight with that thing that lives inside you. You mustn't let it best you. You're in charge of it. Not the other way around," Miss Lillian said with a hint of scolding.

"I can't help it. It just…comes on me whenever I'm angry or upset or…" Theta thought of kissing Memphis. *Or full of desire.* "I can't stop it."

Miss Lillian scoffed. "Stop it? Why, that's a fool's errand. Shape it, yes. Stop it? You can't. You mustn't."

"The gift is yours. It has chosen you," Miss Addie insisted.

"What if I hurt somebody with it?"

"Haven't you been hurt?" Miss Lillian asked.

Theta thought of Roy's fists. Mrs. Bowers's cold cruelty. Even the first wound of abandonment. "Yes."

"And here you still are. No. The question is this: Haven't you been hurt enough?"

Miss Addie suddenly sat forward and picked up Theta's teacup, examining the leaves. "You're brokenhearted. I can feel it. No wonder it hurts so. For this is true love," she said sadly.

"The world has always feared what we can do," Miss Lillian said to Theta at the door. "Why do you think they've tried to hang and stone and burn us? You can claim your power or let them take it from you."

"For the last time, I'm not a witch."

Miss Lillian smiled and patted Theta's cheek. "Keep telling yourself that, dear."

Back in her apartment, Theta spread salt over the windowsills and across the threshold as she'd seen Miss Addie do, saying the words of protection she'd heard the old woman say many times. Then she sat on the sofa and cuddled Archibald, who burrowed into her side. "You might wanna steer clear for this, kitty." She kissed his head, then placed him on the floor.

She examined her hands. They were just ordinary hands.

"This is dumb, but here goes," Theta said to the empty room.

What's in my heart? What's in my mind? she asked herself.

Warmth pooled in her palms, getting hotter. She thought about what the Proctor sisters had said. What Sister Walker and Will had said. She thought about her friends and the way it felt when they were together.

What's in my heart? What's in my mind?

For just a moment, her concentration was as clear as a beam. She felt a deep connection to a past she didn't know. One with fire, sun, and sky. The heat spread up her arms and settled deep in her belly until Theta felt as if she could set the world on fire. She liked this feeling. She saw Roy screaming as she burned his face. She liked that feeling, too. And suddenly, the heat was everywhere, an inferno inside her. Her hands were white-hot with so much power that it terrified Theta. As if her joy and rage and lust would consume her.

"No!" she cried.

She stumbled toward the bathtub, feeling as if she were scorching the very ground as she ran. She fumbled with the tap, filling the tub with cold water, and then she tumbled into the bath to soak herself, pajamas and all. Steam rose from the water. Nervously, she looked back to see if her apartment was on fire. Or if she'd left scorched footprints across the floor.

But it was perfectly fine.

OTHER DIMENSIONS

"Ah, there's my golden son now! Say, you look like a million bucks!" A grinning Marlowe called out from the breakfast room as Jericho entered wearing the new clothes Marlowe had bought him: tweed trousers and a pullover sweater that fit him like a glove and made him look like a rich college swell. He'd packed on so much muscle that he'd needed a new wardrobe.

"Think Evie will like it?" Jericho asked, taking a seat at the table where a perfectly sectioned grapefruit sat waiting for him. He dug in with the silver spoon.

Marlowe's smile dipped. "I think any young lady would like it. You should cast your sights higher than Miss O'Neill. After all, you're a prize! Why throw yourself after some Diviner with a less-than-sterling reputation? And now I hear she's cooked up some sort of publicity scheme around ghost hunting," Marlowe said with obvious distaste.

Jericho glowered. "Evie is a swell girl. And I'm not throwing myself."

"Now, now, don't get sore. I'm simply saying you can do better. Why, after this exhibition, when the girls get a gander at you, you'll have your pick. It will be, 'Evie who?'"

Jericho couldn't imagine such a thing. For him, there was one girl, and Evie was it. He was thrilled to receive her reply that she would be up to visit come the weekend, and he wasn't about to let Marlowe derail his good mood. "What will you do with this serum once it's perfected?" Jericho asked, forking waffles onto his plate.

Jake's eyes gleamed as he stirred his coffee. "Why, sell it, of course. What if, simply by taking a New and Improved Marlowe VitaHealth Tonic each day, expectant mothers could grow a nation of healthy, exceptional Americans whom you could count on to make the right-thinking choices? Crime would plummet. Industry would advance. Patriotism would soar." Marlowe leaned back against the cushion of his chair. "We would be the greatest and most powerful nation on the face of the earth."

Jericho swallowed down his bite of waffle. "But isn't that strange and wonderful unpredictability part of humanity? Aren't all of our differences what already make us a great nation?"

Jake leaned forward again, his dark brows furrowed. "Some people just can't be assimilated. Remember the bombings that took place on Wall Street a few years ago? The work of foreigners! What if war came to us again? How could we be sure that the Italian shoemaker or German sausage-maker would be loyal to America?"

Jericho didn't like the direction the conversation was taking. He'd been warming to Marlowe, and this was a cold note. "You still haven't said— what will *I* do at the exhibition?"

"Mostly demonstrations of your superior strength and health. The perfect walking advertisement for the glorious future of Marlowe Industries's newest health advancement. And it'll make me a very rich man to boot."

Jericho laughed. "You're already rich. Why do you need more money?"

"You can never be too rich," Marlowe said with a wink. He paused, then: "I need the money to fund my real passion."

Jericho had assumed the super-powered vitamin tonic—and Jericho's part in it—was Marlowe's real passion. He couldn't help feeling a bit rejected by this new knowledge that he was second. "And what's that?" he asked coolly.

Marlowe smiled like a man with the most delicious secret in the world. "What if I told you that there is another world out there, Jericho? A dimension of untold wonders just waiting to be discovered and claimed?"

"I'd probably say you've read too many H. G. Wells novels."

Marlowe sipped his coffee. "Oh, it's real, all right. I've glimpsed it. I made contact with it once. It spoke to me. But the power coming through was too much for my poor little machine to take. Ever since, I've been working to make improvements in the hope of reestablishing contact. We're awfully close. I can feel it."

Jericho had no idea what Marlowe was talking about. It really did sound like something from a fantasy novel.

"Can you imagine what that would mean, to control such a vast amount of energy? What new creations and wonders might be wrought from it? 'Oh brave new world!' I'd be the new Columbus!" Marlowe pounded the table with his fist. Jericho had never seen him so excited. "Of course, to reach into that dimension requires quite a lot of energy, too. But I did it before and, by golly, I can do it again. *That's* the American spirit!"

"Could I see this machine?" Jericho asked.

"Not yet. When it's ready. For now, it's our little secret," Jake said, grinning, and even though Jericho knew not to trust him, not completely, he couldn't help feeling that he'd been chosen by Jake. And being chosen felt good. Special.

Jericho cleared his throat. "I've, uh, been meaning to ask you, who is that woman I saw here, Anna Provenza?"

A shadow passed over Jake's sunny face. He stirred his coffee even though he'd already stirred it. "Oh. Just someone I'm trying to help. Poor girl."

"What's wrong with her?"

"Mental patient. Hears voices. Thinks she sees the future."

"A Diviner, then."

Marlowe trained his gaze on Jericho. "Do you know what Diviners are? They are a plague upon the nation."

"My friends are Diviners."

"So were some of mine," Jake said, and Jericho could hear the hurt in it. "They're not to be trusted, though. That sort of strangeness, well, it's unnatural. It leads to clannishness—that sort sticks to their own kind. They think they're better than the rest of us. They'll turn on you eventually. Be careful." And then, like the sun parting clouds, Marlowe smiled. "But enough of this. We have work to do."

In the basement laboratory, Marlowe showed Jericho to a long, hinged-top tank with a ladder on the outside. The tank had been filled with water, like a bathtub.

"What is this?" Jericho asked.

"It's called sensory deprivation," Marlowe explained. "You'll be floating inside, completely relaxed, while the vitamin tonic enters your bloodstream. There's a microphone inside. We want to know what you see and hear while you're in that meditative state."

A panicky feeling came over Jericho. Ever since the time he'd spent trapped in Jake's iron lung contraption, Jericho had developed a fear of confined spaces. Just looking at the thing made his heart race. "You want me to climb inside that?"

Marlowe frowned. "Come now. You're not afraid, are you? It's just water."

Yes, Jericho wanted to say. *I am, in fact, afraid of being sealed up in that thing like a watery coffin.* But he didn't want to look like a coward. And besides, he didn't really have a choice.

Marlowe administered the vitamin serum, and Jericho could feel it warming his veins as Marlowe guided him to the tank. He climbed inside. Pure panic overtook him as Marlowe shut the lid, sealing Jericho in darkness.

"It's all right," Marlowe's voice assured him. "Just relax."

Jericho tried, but he hated the isolation. It was like a practice death. To calm himself, he conjured the memory of that Ferris wheel ride with Evie again. He pictured her laughing face, and beyond it the whole of the sky. Soon, he began to lose sense of his borders. It was as if he had no body at all. Time was meaningless. Jericho wasn't sure how long he'd been floating there when he began to hear murmurs, like eavesdropping at a summer picnic from a distance.

"I hear…voices," he said.

"Good! Good." Marlowe. "Can you hear what they're saying?"

"Open…the…door again as before…but this time, you must keep it open."

The murmurs turned into an insect-like hiss that made Jericho's skin crawl.

"Talk to the voices, Jericho. Ask them how I do that."

"Hello," Jericho said. "How do we keep it open?"

The insect drone grew louder. It was as if he were at a summer picnic and a fierce thunderstorm were bearing down. "The souls must be refreshed," Jericho repeated. "He will give further instructions soon. But you must not fail this time…."

That terrible sound made Jericho's heartbeat go wild. Underneath, it sounded as if all the demons of hell were loose. And in his current state, he felt joined to it. Like he was back in his dream watching the sky tear open, exposing the horrors hidden inside.

Calm, Solnyshko, calm, a woman's voice directed. It was the same voice that had warned him not to stay during his first week at the estate.

"Who is that? Who's talking to me?"

"Jericho, do you hear someone?" Marlowe. "Who's in there with you?"

"A woman."

Tell them nothing about me! the woman instructed. *Talk to me only in your head. I can hear your thoughts.*

But why?

You are in danger. You must get away.

What do you mean? Why am I in danger?

The past is a ghost. He is making a terrible mistake. You must stop him.

"Jericho? Are you all right?" Marlowe's voice.

"Yes," Jericho answered. At least, he thought he had. It was hard to tell. His edges were blurring into unreality. He was the water in the tank, and the water was Jericho. He was eternity.

"You mentioned a woman," Marlowe said. "What did she say? Who's in there with you?"

Say nothing, Solnyshko.

"No one. She went away. I mean, all the voices went away."

"Okay," Marlowe said, and Jericho could hear the disappointment in it. "We'll try again tomorrow."

Jericho heard the hinges on the tank creak. Marlowe was letting him out.

Thank you, the woman's voice said.

Who are you? Jericho thought.

He sensed light spilling across his face, smelled the antiseptic room, felt hands reaching in for him.

My name, the voice said, *is Miriam.*

THE NEW JERICHO

The next afternoon, Jericho waited in the foyer, counting down the minutes until Evie arrived. He'd slicked back his hair with pomade and put on his best suit. From the garden, he'd snipped one red rose. The door chimes rang. "I'll get it, Ames!" Jericho called out.

He opened the door and held out the rose. "Welcome."

"Aww, Freddy, you shouldn't have," Sam said, taking the rose and threading it through the buttonhole of his coat. "This is so sudden! I don't know what to say. Oh, okay. You've won me over, you big brute. The answer is yes."

With that, Sam jumped into Jericho's arms.

"Wow. You got even more giant…er. He's a mighty oak of a man! My hero."

Jericho put Sam down with a thud. It wasn't just Sam. Henry had come along, too. "What are you doing here?"

"Golly. Don't tell me I'm not welcome. I put on aftershave and everything. Smell." Sam leaned his jaw toward Jericho. Jericho pushed him back, and Sam reeled for a second before catching his balance. "Holy-moly, that's impressive. What've they been feeding you, Freddy?"

"I didn't know you were coming. I thought it was just Evie and Ling."

"Oh, dear," Henry said.

Evie looked horrified. "Oh no! I could've sworn I told you it was the four of us."

"I brought pastries," Henry said in apology. He held up a box tied with string.

"It's fine. I'm sure it'll be fine," Jericho said. "There are certainly plenty of rooms."

A sheepish Evie moved closer to Jericho. "I'm awfully sorry, Jericho. But Sam wasn't about to miss out on the card reading, and Henry needed some country air and—oh, I hope it's not a terrible bother." She kissed Jericho on the cheek, and Jericho didn't care what he had to tell Marlowe. He was just glad to see his friends—especially Evie.

Sam whistled. "This is some fancy prison they got you in, Freddy. Or do I call you Sir Frederick now?"

"You call me Jericho. For a change," Jericho said.

While the others settled in, and after Jericho had explained apologetically to the less-than-thrilled Ames that there would be extra guests for the weekend, Jericho waited in the ballroom. He stared at the fancy oil painting of Marlowe's dead ancestors, a long line of stern, pale men posed atop horses or beside hunting dogs. They all had the same expression in their eyes: a simple acceptance that they were the masters of their fates and nothing would get in the way to change that.

"Must be nice," Jericho said.

"What must be nice?" Evie said, sweeping into the room like the sun inching across a cold floor.

"Having you here is nice," Jericho said, grinning. "Even if I have to put up with Sam, too."

He crossed the room with the relaxed gait he'd now come to own and stood beside Evie. She smelled good, like rosewater and vanilla. He had a strong urge to kiss her, and he wondered what she would do if he swept her up in his arms and did just that. "I've missed you."

He guided her to the chaise and sat beside her, their knees nearly touching. "Here. A welcome gift." Jericho placed a folded paper figurine in Evie's hand.

"A dog?" Evie asked.

"A wolfhound," Jericho corrected. "Evie, meet Evie."

Evie laughed. "Gee, this is swell!"

"Sorry. I couldn't quite figure out how to give her a proper ascot," Jericho said, and the two of them laughed as if they were drunk. Gently, Jericho brushed a wayward curl out of Evie's eyes, and he saw her catch her breath. Jericho thought that if Nietzsche was right about the eternal recurrence and that one's life repeated, unfolding in the same fashion throughout all time, then he would be glad of living this moment over again, with the sun shining through Marlowe's pretentious stained-glass windows and falling on Evie's upturned cheeks in a wash of color.

"*Amor fati*," he said.

"What's that mean?" Evie said. It wasn't the reflection from the windows, Jericho realized. Her cheeks were really flushed.

"It means love of fate." Impulsively, he wrapped his fingers in hers and pulled her close. He kissed the top of her head, inhaling the scent of her hair. It smelled clean; it smelled hopeful.

"You seem so...different," Evie said, gazing up at him. Her stomach did that twirling thing. What was it about Jericho that attracted her so? She didn't know entirely, and she was tired of trying to explain it to herself. It just *was*. Especially with the way he was looking at her now.

"I *feel* different," Jericho said. "I feel terrific, in fact. This new stuff Marlowe's been giving me has made me much stronger. Less..." *Afraid*, he wanted to say. He was the new Jericho, and the new Jericho wasn't waiting for life to come to him. "Well, I feel really good. It's almost like...like I'm part Diviner now."

"What do you mean?"

"I can hear the maids talking all the way down in the kitchen sometimes. And I can run for miles without tiring. Yesterday I lifted a steel cabinet over my head." Jericho laughed and leaned in to Evie with a conspiratorial grin. "You can see why I needed some companionship."

"And how!" Evie said, laughing, too. She hadn't realized how much she'd needed to get away from New York and gossip and ghosts. And even though she knew they had a mission, seeing Jericho felt like a small respite. She wished she could call Mabel right now—*Mabesie, you'll never guess where I am!*—and then she'd pos-i-tute-ly swear to turn all of Marlowe's fancy ceramic figurines on their heads just to make her happy. But Mabel hadn't spoken to Evie since their fight, and thinking about it would only make her sad. She was determined not to be sad this weekend.

"So this is where the party is. Sorry I missed it," Sam said, barging through the doors. He gave Evie and Jericho a long sideways glance. Then he walked around the room as if studying it.

"Are you casing the joint, Sam?" Evie said, annoyed by his interruption.

"No. I'm having déjà vu." Sam folded his arms and squinted at the meticulous oil paintings of pinch-mouthed men.

"Again?" Henry quipped, coming into the room along with Ling.

"Because you were here before," Evie said. "I remember it from reading your mother's photograph. This is where she brought you when you were little. Right over there—that's where Rotke tested you with the cards."

Sam sat in the Louis XVI chair Evie had pointed out and rested his hands lightly on the arms, as if he could find the memory that way. He shook his head. "I got nothing. It's almost like somebody tried to keep me from remembering."

"There were other children here, too," Evie said.

"Diviner kids?" Henry asked, and Evie nodded.

"So what happened to them?" Ling asked.

"I don't know," Evie answered.

"That's why we've got to read these cards," Sam said. "So we can find them. Jericho, where's this card reader and when can we fire it up?"

"We'll have to wait until tonight," Jericho answered, keeping his voice low. "Marlowe is hosting some sort of gentlemen's club dinner. The whole house will be occupied with that. Nobody will notice us."

Ling stood in the middle of the room grinning one of her rare, unguarded smiles. "I can't believe I'm in Jake Marlowe's house."

Despite everything they now knew had happened during the war, Ling still admired Jake Marlowe. He'd made terrible mistakes, she knew, and he didn't seem to love Diviners very much, but he was also a top-notch mind. Some people couldn't separate the man from the work, but Ling could. With luck, maybe he'd see something in her, too. Maybe she would change his mind about Diviners. "He's contributed so much—all those inventions and medical advances. And all of it has happened so fast, just since the end of the war."

Jericho hadn't thought about it, but Ling was right. By all accounts, Marlowe had been struggling before then. He'd been a failure in many regards. But in the past nine years, he'd had one triumph after another. His stock had soared. He was an American hero.

"And I hear he may find a cure for paralysis," Ling said.

"Yes. He's working on that and much more. He's very close," Jericho said. If the experiments Marlowe was running on Jericho could somehow help Ling in the future, that alone would be worth it.

A truck marked MARLOWE INDUSTRIES ambled up the long driveway and parked outside.

"What's that?" Ling asked.

"Uranium delivery from the mine. They come every week," Jericho explained. "There's a lead-lined pool in a shed where he stores it."

"I was too embarrassed to ask before, but what *is* uranium?" Evie asked.

"Uranium is a radioactive element capable of producing tremendous energy and heat," Ling explained. "When you mine uranium ore, you get radium."

Henry snapped his fingers. "Say, maybe he's using it to make himself one of those water jars, a fancy new Revigorator. Aren't they lined with radium and all that jazz?"

Ling made a face. "Nobody should drink radioactive water."

"Radiation is supposed to be good for you! That's what all the advertisements say. Even Al Jolson wears Radio-X radium neck pads to keep his vocal cords relaxed!"

"That's not what the ghost of Mrs. Leong told me. She said it would make our bones crumble and our jaws rot off," Ling said.

"Ugh," Evie said. "I'm rather attached to my jaw."

Henry sang, "*Oh, the jawbone's connected to the—*"

"It all goes back to atoms," Ling said, talking over him.

"That's what my Sunday school teacher said," Evie said.

"*Atoms.* Not *Adam.* Everything is made up of atoms. You. Me. This chair."

"You know, I felt a real kinship with this chair," Sam quipped.

Ling's glare was penetrating.

Sam whistled and put up his hands. "Sorry."

Satisfied, Ling continued: "Most atoms are stable. But that's not true with radioactive substances. Their atoms are unstable. When they disintegrate, they give off energy. Uranium by itself isn't all that valuable. It's the radium it produces that everybody wants. So what does Jake Marlowe know about uranium that the rest of us don't?" *And why is the uranium being delivered here to his estate?* she thought.

Jake Marlowe's footsteps, sure and even, announced him before he entered. He was a handsome man, slender and well dressed, with a head full of dark hair parted neatly on the side and slicked back from his chiseled face. But more than his movie-star looks, it was his charisma that shone through—Jake Marlowe had "It."

"How do you do? I'm Jake Marlowe," he said, as if he needed any introduction. "Welcome to Hopeful Harbor."

"Ling Chan. I'm looking forward to your Future of America Exhibition, sir," Ling said, trying to hold back her excitement. "I still have your IOU." She pulled the crinkled paper from her purse and showed it to Marlowe, who squinted at it.

"Wonderful! Well, I'll have to make good on that promise." Marlowe smiled, and Ling felt as if he'd granted her fondest wish.

"Henry DuBois. The Fourth," Henry felt compelled to add.

"Sam Lloyd. The Only," Sam said.

"Thanks awfully for having us, Mr. Marlowe," Evie said with exaggerated politeness. She did not like Jake Marlowe, but for this weekend, she would try to think of him only as the man who had saved Jericho's life.

"Miss O'Neill," Marlowe said, his smile faltering for just a second before he launched it again, like a trustworthy vessel. "I'm awfully sorry I won't be able to join all of you for dinner this evening. I'm afraid I have a prior engagement. But if there's anything I can do to make your stay more hospitable, do let me know." And with that, he was gone.

Henry elbowed Ling. "You'll be giddy for at least a week, won't you?"

And Ling was so happy that she didn't even roll her eyes at Henry.

"I'd better go make sure everything's okay," Jericho announced. He sidled up to Evie, whispering low: "Invent an excuse and meet me in the rose garden."

Evie waited exactly thirty seconds, then gave an exaggerated yawn and announced that she needed a nap. She slipped outside, finding Jericho among Marlowe's neatly trimmed hedges. He looked so handsome standing there in a spot of sun that it quite took her breath away.

"Let's go for a walk," Jericho said.

When they were a distance from the estate, Jericho detoured to a gazebo covered by trailing ivy. The flowers had just started to bloom. They smelled wonderful.

"Golly, I can't get over how much you've changed," she said. When had he gotten so incredibly handsome?

"I feel different. Before I was just existing, in a way. I always felt so apart from everyone else because...well, you know. I never seemed to know what I wanted."

"And now? I mean, have you, um, do you know what you want?"

"Yes," Jericho said, staring down at her with those clear blue eyes that seemed to see everything.

She swallowed the lump caught in her throat. Evie rarely got nervous around boys. But that was just it—Jericho had never been a boy. Quickly, she changed the subject. "And, um, what about Marlowe? Have you found anything about what he knows of Project Buffalo?"

Jericho flinched. "Is that all you care about—Project Buffalo?"

"Well, no. Of course not."

He took another step toward her and stroked the back of his hand across her cheek. "You are so beautiful."

Evie knew she was not beautiful. She was, if anything, cute. But Jericho thought she was beautiful. No one had ever said those words to her and meant it so completely. It took her breath away. On impulse, she kissed him. When she pulled back, he was staring at her with an intensity that made her blush down to her toes. She could feel the heat coming off him. She wanted him to kiss her so badly that she thought she might die.

He leaned down and whispered low and deep in her ear, "Come with me."

He took hold of her hand and she followed gladly.

They sneaked upstairs to Jericho's room. Jericho shut the door and locked it. It was just the two of them.

"Well," Evie said. "Here we are."

"You asked me if I knew what I wanted," Jericho said. "Being here, discovering myself, I've learned that I want to be with you. I don't want to waste another minute."

"You don't?"

"No."

In three long strides, Jericho crossed the distance between them and wrapped his muscular arms around Evie, pulling her to him. And then they were kissing, their bodies pressed tightly together. This was not the sweet kiss of October. This was pure, unchecked passion. Evie hadn't been able to let herself fall fully for Jericho because Mabel liked him and Evie would die before she'd hurt Mabel. And then there were her confusing feelings for Sam. But now that was all in the past. There was nothing to stop her from being with Jericho.

Still kissing her, he lifted her up and deposited her gently on the bed.

Then he crawled toward her, lowering his body to hers. Evie pressed her lips against Jericho's. He snaked a hand up inside her dress, caressing her thigh. Evie's mother had always told her that no decent girl would pet like this. *Maybe I'm not a decent girl*, Evie thought, because she very much wanted Jericho to keep doing what he was doing to her. She liked kissing him, she found. His mouth was warm, and when he stroked a hand across her breast, it made her shiver all over.

He buried his head in her neck and murmured, "I love you, Evie."

It should have made her happy. But for some reason, it made her sad instead. As if she knew she would only disappoint him eventually. "You don't even know me. Not really."

Jericho raised his head. His face was flushed, and the way he looked at her now, with real desire, made her feel dizzy in the best possible way. She wanted to live in this moment right here forever. Her emotions bounced around like the Metaphysickometer's needle, from desire to doubt and back again. She wondered if that was normal.

"But I want to know you. I want to know everything," he promised between kisses. "I've missed you so much."

Evie smiled. "How much?"

"Let me show you," he said, with such assurance it made her feel a little drunk. She loved how much he wanted her.

He unbuttoned the front of her dress and moved his mouth along her collarbone and down the center of her chest. He cupped one of her small breasts, and Evie thought she might explode. He was just guiding her hand down, to the front of him, when there was a loud knock at the door.

Evie sat up quickly, knocking Jericho in the nose.

"Sorry, sorry!" she whispered as he covered his injured nose with both hands.

His eyes were watering from the hit. But he was laughing quietly through the pain. "It's okay. You can kiss it and make it better later," he whispered.

"Dinner is served, Mr. Jones," Ames called from the other side of the door.

"I'll be right there, Ames!"

"Very good, sir."

"I'd better go and freshen up," Evie said, and kissed him again. It had been thrilling and maybe a little scary feeling his body between her thighs, his hardness pressed against her. She liked that she could do that to him just as much as she liked what he did to her, the way his kisses made her tremble.

"You look fresh enough to me. You couldn't possibly get any fresher," Jericho insisted.

"Sorry, pal. Bank's closed."

Evie pushed Jericho back. He groaned and flopped against the bank of floofy pillows.

Evie smoothed down her dress. She hoped she looked presentable. "See you at dinner."

Jericho moved a pillow over his crotch. "Eventually," he said, grinning.

Evie sneaked out, closing the door quietly behind her. When she turned around, she yelped in surprise. Sam was a few feet away, leaning against the wall, his arms folded across his chest.

"You startled me," she said.

Sam wasn't his usual good-time, smirking self. In fact, he looked as if someone had run over his dog. "What is it about that guy?"

"I don't know what you mean," Evie said, a flush working its way up her neck.

"Come on, Evie. Don't con a con man."

Evie was both embarrassed that he'd caught her and furious that he was judging her.

"What do you care? You're out with a different chorus girl every night. The papers say so!"

"The papers say a lot of things. Is it because he's a brooder, a real Heathcliff?"

"He isn't a *brooder*. He's just a very deep thinker. He's…philosophical. Some girls happen to find that charming."

"Yeah, real swoon-worthy. Frankly, I never understood why girls go for that. It's like the fella's announcing he's a miserable time, but I swear, that's like honey for some dames. *Misery* honey."

Evie's eyes flashed. "Maybe you're the one who's miserable. You're certainly conceited."

"At least I know how to make a girl laugh."

"And pull her hair out."

"You know, some girls like that hair-pulling," Sam said.

He was being deliberately provocative. Evie got up in his face. "Then remind me to shave my head bald."

"Wait! Just answer me this: Does he make you happy?"

"If you must know, he makes me feel like I'm the only girl in the room."

"That's not the same thing."

Why was he doing this to her? "Are you one of those fellas who only likes a girl if another fella wants her? Maybe you should ask yourself that question. Now, if you'll excuse me, I need to dress for dinner," she said, moving past him.

Sam reached out and held her hand softly. "Evie..."

For just a minute, she was reminded of their fake romance. Except that the expression on his face seemed very real. Was it real? Was anything with Sam real? No. Sam-n-Evie, the romance, had had its chance. It hadn't worked. This was just Sam being his usual pot-stirring self. And once he had a girl wrapped around his finger, he lost interest. She knew too well from experience.

She let go of his hand. "I don't want to be late for dinner."

Sam leaned his head back against the wall, thumping it gently. "Swell job, Lloyd. You schmuck."

※

After a delicious private dinner that featured more silverware than anybody knew what to do with, they retired to the library, where they played cards and waited until they could steal into the room with the punch card reader. They listened to the hubbub of servants taking coats and men welcoming one another, of Marlowe ordering "our best port," even though Sam had the idea that these were the very people who'd voted for Prohibition, then turned around and decided the rules didn't apply to them. The men's voices went fuzzy with distance as they retreated to another part of the house, and then it was silent. The grandfather clock in the foyer struck half past nine.

"Can we go now, Freddy?" Sam cajoled.

"Yes," Jericho said, leaving his cards on the table. "And don't call me Freddy."

Jericho led his friends toward the former soldiers' room. "Quickly," he said, ushering them inside and shutting the door.

"Don't see me," Sam said, waving his hands over it. "That should keep anybody's eyes from glancing this way for the next five minutes or so."

Just above them, they could hear vague noises from Marlowe's club meeting: The crack of a billiards game. Muffled laughter. Low talking. They were safe for now.

"So this is where my brother was before…" Evie said, giving the room a once-over. She longed to touch everything in the hope that some trace of James lingered here.

"It's this way," Jericho said gently, and led them toward the back. He opened the closet door. Sam whistled.

"So that's it, huh?" he said, stroking a hand across the tabulating machine. "I'll say this for Marlowe, this is a beauty. The one at Macy's wasn't like this. Say, Jericho, gimme a hand with this thing, will ya?"

Jericho dragged the machine from the closet as if it weighed no more than a sack of potatoes.

"I coulda done that," Sam said.

Henry patted him sympathetically on the back. Ling shook her head.

Sam plugged in the machine. He pushed a button and it hummed to life.

"Here goes nothing," he said, and fed the first card into the intake slot. A series of slim metal fingers bobbed up and down as they attempted to type out a report. The machine wheezed and shuddered.

"What's wrong with it?" Henry asked. "It sounds like an angry cow."

Smoke poured from the agitating card reader.

"No, no, no!" Sam tried to intervene and got a shock. He hissed and shook out his fingers.

"Stop it before it catches fire!"

Ling hooked her crutch around the cord and yanked it free from the outlet. With a last stuttering sigh, the machine spat out the severely mangled card and went dead.

Ling examined a few of the other cards. "Maybe they're too old and dirty. Probably the machine is, too."

"What do we do now?" Henry asked.

"Nothing, that's what," Sam said, sinking down onto one of the beds. "We can't read these cards, we can't find any other Diviners. We can't know about ourselves and what they did to us. And I can't use that information to find my mother." Sam buried his head in his hands. "Could you…not look at me right now? Thanks."

Evie had never seen Sam like this. He was usually the one finding a way forward. It was a little scary to see him at such a loss. She reached for the mangled card.

Sam glanced up. "What are you doing?"

"I'm going to try to read it," Evie answered, sitting beside Sam on the bed.

"You already told us you can't read it," Ling said.

"I couldn't before. I still might not be able to do it. But *we* might. We already know that together we can strengthen one another's energy and skills. With all of us working together, I might be able to break through."

"You'll be sick," Sam warned.

"So I'll be sick," Evie said.

"Are you sure, doll?" Sam asked.

"Just hand over those cards and gather 'round," Evie said.

Henry, Ling, Sam, and Evie huddled together on the bed while Jericho stood nearby.

"I wish this didn't involve so much touching," Ling grumbled.

"Concentrate, please," Evie said.

The card was cold, like before. It hadn't been held in many years. Evie wondered if people were like that, too—if something in them died when they were denied affection for too long. A memory bubbled up: Evie was a child desperate for her mother's attention. But her mother was busy with housework. Evie threw her arms around her mother's waist. "I'll keep you here in my cage!" she'd giggled. Her exhausted mother had a schedule to keep. Irritated, she'd pushed Evie away. "Evangeline, you wear me out!"

A great wave of loneliness surged inside Evie at this sudden memory. That was the trouble with object reading—she was open and unguarded. All the feelings could come flooding in, and none of her usual defenses— booze, parties, flirting, sarcasm—would keep them out.

She heard Jericho's deep, sure voice: "Are you okay, Evie?"

"Fine," she whispered. *Begone, loneliness. I've no time for you.*

Evie could feel the card's barriers giving way and she leaned into it. *Come on, show me who you are....* Its history began to come alive. First, there was the secretary who'd punched in the code. She was nursing a grudge against her sister for some small slight. Next, the messenger boy running the card to a new location. He wore short pants and suspenders and loved baseball. The warmth of his affection for the game spread through Evie. Every person who'd handled the card left behind emotions until the cards seemed as human as humans themselves. It made her think about the tubes and wires inside Jericho. The longer they were there, the more they became fused to his flesh, threaded to his organs until it was impossible to know what was man and what was machine. Humans infected all they touched.

Numbers and letters blinked fast behind her eyes, dizzying.

"We're here with you. You can do this." Henry's voice in her head. Ling and Henry's dream walker energy began to relax her, as if she were drifting off into a deep sleep. She needed to find the person who could read the code.

"Sam," Evie whispered. "Can you help me see better?"

Sam's hand was on her shoulder. She could feel him. And then, all at once, she broke through layers of old memories to Rotke Wasserman. Rotke knew what was on the cards!

> Subject #9. Diego Perez. Mother: Maria
> Perez. Race: Negro (Dominican). Address:
> 155 W. 62nd St., New York, New York.
> Vitamin injections weekly. March 4,
> 1914. Age 5. Vivid dreams. Still wets
> bed. No abilities. September 22, 1915.
> Age 6. Levitated two pencils. Five
> seconds. October 5, 1915. Levitated
> coffee cup. Ten seconds. December 12,
> 1915. Levitated coffee cup. Twenty
> seconds. December 29, 1915. Headaches.

```
Nosebleeds. Aural hallucinations.
Sleeps for long stretches. Mother
worried. Radiation therapy
recommended, JM.
```

JM. JM… Jake Marlowe. Had to be.

Something flashed at the bottom of the card, but Evie's mind couldn't quite make sense of it. And then the card went dark.

"Hand me another one, please," Evie said. It was coming faster now. She pawed through the remaining cards as if she were the machine itself. Small details poked through:

```
Subject #28. Michael Murphy. Mother:
Eileen Murphy. Race: Irish.

Subject #67. Anna Schmidt. Mother: Hanna
Schmidt. Race: German.

Subject #101. Israel Miller. Mother:
Esther Miller. Race: Jew.
```

Evie raced through, searching for information: *Vitamin injections. Vitamin injections. Vitamin injections. Disrupts radio signals. Hears spirit voices. Dream walks. Astral projection. ESP. Created ball of light in my presence. Telepathy.* What she was seeing on these cards was astonishing. She wanted to know more but there was no time to linger. Already, she was pressing her body's limits. Something was nagging at her, though. It was that line at the bottom of the first card. It had been added later, she could tell. And it had been added to the other cards as well.

"Evie. Not too long, okay?" Henry said. "Be careful."

"Just one more," Evie answered.

```
Subject #144: Sarah Beth Olson.
Mother: Ada Olson. Address: Route 144,
```

Bountiful, Nebraska. June 1, 1915.
Hears spirit voices. Some prophecy. May
5, 1916. Mother reports that subject
speaks to an imaginary friend, the
man in the stovepipe hat. Mother is
frightened by this. Girl has frequent
seizures. Do not recommend proceeding.

The man in the hat! This girl had spoken with him. But why did they recommend not proceeding? There was no note added at the bottom of this card. There was a flash, and Evie glimpsed Miriam Lubovitch Lloyd. She had the same dark brows and amber-flecked eyes as Sam. Miriam did not look happy as she spoke to Rotke. "They are only children. We must protect them. I do not trust those men. I know Jake does not like me, a Jew."

"But I'm a Jew, and he wants to marry me," Rotke answered.

"There is an emptiness in his soul," Miriam said. "He wants to use me to keep the Eye open. But I refuse. I refuse!"

"Evie? Her nose is bleeding." Jericho's voice.

"We should stop." Sam.

"No. Just one more minute…"

What had been coded at the bottom of the cards? She had to know. The memory was close. She could feel it. She barely tasted the tang of her blood coursing over her lips and into her mouth. There it was! A final coded note on the card just as she'd felt on all the others: *January 25, 1920. Subject deceased.*

❈

"Head back," Jericho scolded, pinching the bridge of Evie's nose. "You don't want to start bleeding again."

"They're dead. They're all dead," Evie said in a nasal voice.

"What killed them?" Henry asked.

"What if the vitamin tonic that made us also makes us sick over time?" Ling posed.

Evie looked to Jericho. "Can you ask Marlowe?"

"Every time I've tried to talk to him about Project Buffalo, he's refused."

"We could always go back to your uncle and Sister Walker and ask them," Sam said.

"No! I will not have anything to do with them. They can't be trusted," Evie said. Her head swam. She had pushed too far and now she felt awful. "Subject number one forty-four is still alive, though. At least, there's no note on her card. Sarah Beth Olson. Bountiful, Nebraska. Oh. Oh, no. Ugh. I think I'm gonna be sick."

Sam noted the look of disappointment on Jericho's face and tried to hide his smile.

"I'll help you to your room, doll," Sam said, jumping up before Jericho could. It was petty on his part.

He didn't regret it.

LITTLE FOX

Back in his room, Sam rummaged through every drawer. He didn't really expect to find anything related to Project Buffalo, but now that he was here where the project had taken place, where his mother had worked and, according to the official reports, died, he wanted to know everything. There was nothing in the drawers, of course. Just some stationery and rich-people tchotchkes. "A letter opener shaped like a peacock?" Sam shoved it back into a drawer and shook his head.

After Evie had upchucked and before she'd fallen sleep, she'd confessed to Sam what the card had shown her about his mother. "Something about protecting children and Jake not liking her. And Sam, Sam, she...she said he wanted her to keep the Eye open, but she wouldn't...." Evie burbled, half out of it.

"What? What about the Eye?" But Evie was already asleep.

Sam remembered his mother as loving but firm. She was direct and opinionated. He could imagine somebody like Jake Marlowe not liking that very much, and he wished he could've watched his mother square off against that big-shot goy. He wondered if he would ever see his mother again, if he would ever hear her calling him "Little Fox" in her native Russian. He wondered what he would say to her if he did now that he knew she had been part of Project Buffalo during the war. He couldn't escape the truth: The mother he loved had been as complicit as Will and all the others.

"Ma?" he said to the empty room. "Ma, it's me, Sergei. I'm here."

Silence. He hadn't expected a response, of course. Just because her memory lingered didn't mean anything. But his heart sank a little anyway.

He thought about his father back home and found that he missed him. He thought about Jericho, about how, standing next to him, Sam had felt small and dark and foreign, with his streetwise accent, gritted up by the South Side of Chicago and the Lower East Side of New York's immigrant melting pot. Sam looked hard at one of the gold-framed photographs on the wall. In it, a dozen blue-eyed, tux-clad men sat at a table looking unbothered and smug, as if they expected that the world would bend to them. After all, the world usually did. Sam felt that whatever he'd managed to grab for himself could be taken away at any moment. That was why he held on so tightly. He wondered if he would ever feel like he could let go or if he'd always feel as if he had to fight for his place.

"Jesus, Sergei," he said, reprimanding himself with a roll of his eyes. "Leave the philosophy to the giant. You're becoming a real flat tire. How's about we find something to steal?"

Sam sneaked out of his room and moved silently down the hall. The night had worked on him, reminding him that he was not on top. He was spoiling for a fight. He slipped a silver ashtray into his pocket. That had to be worth some money. There were probably plenty of things in this house that nobody would miss.

Sam sneaked down the winding staircase, peering through its braided, wrought-iron balusters to make sure it was safe. Light seeped out around the half-open door of Marlowe's private study, where his club meeting was taking place. From where he stood in the shadows, Sam could smell the cigar smoke. Close but out of reach. Outside. Always on the outside. Sam burned with a desire to be on the inside for once. He wished he could hear what those stuffed shirts were talking about.

Wait a minute, he thought. *I can.*

It was a risk. He wasn't sure how much time he'd have. But Sam loved risks. He was a gambler, through and through. He grinned. "Why the hell not?"

"Don't see me," he said, cloaking himself. *Hey, Jericho*, he thought with a snort. *I can do something you can't do, pal.* And then he let himself into the room.

Wealthy men in tuxedos sat in cushy club chairs playing backgammon and chess. Brandy snifters dotted the tables. The heavy cigar smoke tickled Sam's nose and throat, and he had to work not to cough or sneeze. Walking among the powerful men undetected, Sam got a thrill. *Oh, brother*, he thought. *How much would I love to move stuff around?*

Over by the roaring fireplace, Marlowe raised his glass. "To the Founders Club. Long may they reign."

"Hear, hear!" the men in cushy chairs said, raising their glasses.

The Founders Club! Sam's head buzzed—this wasn't just any club meeting. These were the fellas who had financed Project Buffalo. Sam hoped his invisibility act would last a little longer.

"How is our pet project coming along for the exhibition, Jake?" a beefy man with a red nose growled around the cigar in his mouth.

"Oh, fine, fine. Jericho's making excellent progress. Tomorrow we'll give him the full dose."

"Imagine it: a class of perfect, pure Americans—done right this time," a thin man with sloped shoulders said as he moved a chess piece across the board, and Sam didn't know what that meant. And what were they doing to Jericho?

He moved farther into the room, standing so close to the men he could practically move the chess pieces himself. It gave him a sick thrill. He was tempting fate. He didn't care. He liked knowing he could move among them and they'd never know it. They didn't control everything.

"And have you heard any more from your mysterious friend beyond?" a mustachioed, bald man asked as he sipped his brandy.

The great Jake Marlowe looked upset. "No."

"Honestly, Jake, when *will* you stop trying?"

"Never! I'm no quitter," Jake said.

"You're going to run out of Diviners soon."

"Not if I can make more of them again."

The men laughed. "Well, don't use tainted stock this time. That was your trouble—experimenting on lesser stock."

"At least if something went wrong with the formula, we didn't have to care," the beefy man laughed.

"Yes. Shame about how it all turned out," another man said, as if they were talking about a failed garden instead of human beings. "Dr. Simpson was making progress with sterilization at the asylum before that unfortunate fire. He'll need a new surgery now. The Supreme Court will say yea to *Buck versus Bell*—I'm sure of it. Then the state will be able to sterilize the unfit without interference."

Sam could feel his anger rising. He wanted to throw over the chessboard and watch the pieces scatter. He wished Theta were here to burn the room down. He wanted to watch it go up in flames.

"But can you imagine the threat if those little Diviners had been allowed to come into their full power? The war certainly showed us what had to be done," the cigar-smoking man said. "Oh, I've discarded, Charles."

Sam wanted to stay and find out more, but his skin tingled and itched, a warning. Any minute now, he'd be visible. One of the chess players shifted in his seat, looking behind him.

"What is it, John?" his chess partner asked.

"I had the strangest feeling there was someone behind me, watching us. The brandy, I expect. I should call it a night."

"Or you should have more brandy!"

Time to go. Quickly, Sam darted out of the room and tiptoed down the hall a safe distance. From the dark of a sitting nook, where Sam had stopped to scratch his itchy skin against the molding, he could still hear the men laughing. Sam was sick with anger: Their mothers had been chosen and experimented upon because they'd been considered expendable.

The war certainly showed us what had to be done. The cigar-smoking man's comment haunted Sam. What had the schmuck meant by that? Every time it seemed they got a piece of the Project Buffalo puzzle, they found the puzzle itself was much bigger than they had ever imagined.

Sam stole into the hallway, hoping he could make it back to his room undetected. As he passed the empty soldiers' room, he was seized by a strange feeling, something from so deep in memory it felt nearly like bone or breath. He took a step into the room. A tiny voice whispered: *"Little Fox! Is it you?"*

"Mama?" Sam called. He was answered only by the scratch of trees against the window and the boastful talk drifting out from Marlowe's party.

But he could swear that for just a moment he had felt the unmistakable presence of his mother.

THE ÜBERMENSCH

The next day at afternoon tea, Jake Marlowe swept into the dining room. "I'm afraid Jericho is needed for some tests. But we'll return him to you soon enough," he announced.

"Can't it wait?" Jericho asked. He wanted to be with Evie, not spend the rest of the day down in the basement laboratory like some rat in a cage.

"No. I'm afraid it can't," Marlowe said, and then he was gone again.

"Guess you better do what Dad says," Sam gloated.

Evie kicked at him under the table, but Henry got there first.

Once Jericho was gone, Sam told Henry and Ling about his night with the Founders Club.

"You could've been in real trouble if they'd caught you," Ling said.

Sam smirked and hooked his thumbs under his suspenders. "Me? I'm too good to get caught. But you shoulda heard these chumps talking about Project Buffalo. They *wanted* to experiment on people like us, so-called mutts. People they thought couldn't fight back. Because to them, we weren't 'real Americans.' If something went wrong, they didn't care."

"This is why I never leave the city. Bad things happen in country houses. Just look at all of literature," Henry said. "Uh-oh. Ling is wearing her serious face."

"I always wear my serious face," Ling said. "I was just wondering something. You grew up rich, Henry. How did your mother get included in this experiment?"

"We were well off, not rich."

"Why do rich people always pretend they're not rich?" Ling said.

"I know that Mama had three miscarriages before me, and my father saw it as her personal failure to produce," Henry said, nearly spitting out the last word. "It only worsened her depression. She saw plenty of doctors. Now that I remember, I overheard Flossie telling a friend that my father had taken Mama to New York to see a 'special doctor.' It's possible that's how she made it into the program. If so, between my overbearing father and her delicate mental state, she would've been in no condition to refuse. You still have your serious face on, Ling."

Ling nodded. "That's because I have a serious question: What do you do with a little army of very powerful Diviner 'mutts' if you don't like or trust those people to start with?"

Down in the lab, Marlowe rolled up his sleeves and readied a syringe of serum. This formula was different—thicker and a midnight blue. "What's that?" Jericho asked.

"I've made some modifications. We're going to really give it to you today, Jericho. No half measures. Let's see what we get with the full serum," Marlowe crowed as the nurse and a doctor readied the room.

"Have you tried this on anybody else?" Jericho asked. He tried not to show how frightened he was as the nurse tied tubing around his biceps and swabbed alcohol across the hollow of his arm.

"No. You're the first." Marlowe squeezed the top of Jericho's shoulder. "You should be proud."

But all Jericho wanted to do was to yell stop. *I don't want this; please don't do this.*

The nurse frowned as she took his pulse. "My goodness, his heart's beating very fast."

"We should get started. Not make him wait any longer," Marlowe said. *Stop talking over me. I'm right here*, Jericho thought.

Marlowe plunged the syringe into Jericho's vein. The new serum wasn't cold like the other stuff. It was warm. Uncomfortably so. It whirred through his veins like an invasion of bees skittering toward his heart. Everything around Jericho seemed a threat, as if the world were closing in, ready to take and take from him, reducing him to his most primitive emotions. Panic fluttered against his chest, beating to be let out. He moaned, muscles spasming. His fingers balled into fists, then spread out again, as if reaching for help.

"Easy, Jericho!" Marlowe's voice.

And then, all at once, the scratching inside his veins gave way. The fear was gone. In its place was a feeling of sheer, unstoppable power. Take from him? From *him*? The Übermensch? A mocking laugh burbled up from deep inside Jericho. Well, he'd protect what was his—he'd hit first and hit hard! He wanted to win. No, he wanted to *conquer*. It was exciting and primal, this feeling. Jericho was reduced to his senses, and his senses were acute. He could hear a gull sipping water from the lake half a mile away. Could smell the antiseptic harsh and prickly in his nose. Could see every paintbrush stroke on the laboratory walls. He was the sweep of history and the arrow arcing toward an unseen future. His blood raced as if he were running through heavy trees, a kingly beast prowling its fiefdom, ready to pounce at anyone who dared challenge his authority.

Jericho inhaled deeply. His lungs seemed infinite. Evie. He'd caught the scent of her.

The restraints ripped in half as he broke through them. He could sense the nurse's terror, vaguely heard Marlowe's shouts as he pushed off from the table. But Evie was his only, all-encompassing thought. Carts crashed as Jericho pushed them out of the way. Glass tubes shattered on the floor. A doctor stood between Jericho and the elevator. Jericho thought about snapping his neck like a twig.

"Leave him alone!" Marlowe cautioned the others. "Let him go."

Jericho spied the elevator key. *Take*, he thought. He shoved the key into the elevator and rode it up to Marlowe's decorative library. The colors in the room were vividly bright to him. He was shirtless, but the cool air didn't bother him. His body had never been more awake. The elevator was ascending. Arguing, panicked voices inside. Time to go. He was hunting. Hunting for Evie. He drew in another lungful of air.

She was in the rose garden.

Jericho threw open the door, the iron hinges bending slightly as he did, and then he bounded across Marlowe's manicured lawn. Evie drew him, narrowed the world until she *was* the world. He saw her at the bottom of the long green slope, sitting in the gazebo, reading a book, surrounded by an explosion of flowering dogwood. She looked up. Smiled. He leaped a tall hedge with no trouble and strode toward her as if commanding an army. Her smile disappeared.

"Jericho?" she said.

He could hear her heartbeat quickening in alarm. But his blood was powerful. It spoke to him: *I am the Übermensch, a god among men. The world belongs to me.*

He wanted her.

"The time is now," he said, and threw her over his shoulder, heading quickly to the woods on legs made even stronger by the serum coursing through him. Frightened and confused, she struggled against him. He held her tighter. They'd reached the clearing. He lay her down on the soft bed of pine needles, pinning her hands to the ground with his.

"Jericho! What are you doing?" Her voice was high-pitched. Terrified.

Some part of Jericho fought up from the depths. *No*, it said. *What are you doing? Wrong. Not like this.*

"Jericho! Please!"

He wanted her. Hadn't she come to him last night? Hadn't she kissed him and let him put his hands on her body? She wanted him. That was the only answer. He wanted her and he would have her. Like a hero. Like a conqueror. Conquerors did not ask. They took. He crushed his lips against hers. When she turned her face away, he forced it back and kissed her harder. She tried to shove him off. His hands pushed hers back against the grass, holding them down. He was on top of her. The victor. *To the victor go the spoils. No. No. Not like this.*

She fought. It infuriated and excited him. Her knee tried to come up and jab him in a sensitive spot. But he was bigger. Stronger. He ripped at her dress and she screamed. She slipped a hand free and slapped him hard. He liked it.

The report of a gun echoed in the forest. Jericho jolted as the tranquilizer dart pierced the back of his right thigh. He whirled around, angry. Ames held the gun. Jericho leaped up and lunged for it. Ames fired. Another dart caught Jericho in the side. Already, he could feel the drug entering his system, tripping along the veins and wires alike. *Fight or flight. Hail, hail, the conquering hero.* He staggered toward Marlowe. The third shot buckled Jericho's knees, but he kept going. He had only one thought: *Win. Win at all costs.*

"Dammit, man, fire!" Marlowe instructed. Another dart and Jericho was now crawling, scraping up fistfuls of dirt in an effort to advance. "The world…belongs…to…" And then he was motionless, the scent of Evie's perfume still inside him like a dream he needed to own.

Just before he lost consciousness, the serum began its retreat from his system, leaving him cold and confused, like an animal that had chased its prey and now stared up from the depths of a pit trap into which it'd fallen. He saw Evie's horrified, tearstained face as Henry threw his coat over her and led her away.

"I'm sorry. So sorry," he whispered, and blacked out.

※

In a gilded bathroom styled like an Egyptian palace, Sam sat on the marble floor beside Evie and held a cold washrag to her bruised lips. "When that son of a bitch wakes up, I'm gonna punch his lights out."

"No, you're not. That won't solve anything."

"It might."

"It won't. And I'm perfectly all right."

"Bushwa, you are! You're still shaking," Sam said. "Excuse my language."

"Whatever Marlowe's putting into Jericho made him do that," Evie said.

"Yeah? Or maybe that's just an excuse. Maybe that serum is just meeting up with what's already inside Jericho to begin with. You ever think about that?" Sam folded the rag over, finding a cool spot and applying it to Evie's forehead.

She winced as it hit a raw spot. "Ow!"

"Sorry."

Evie took the washrag from him and held it to her face. "Really, Sam. I'm okay."

Sam leaned back against the giant tub carved with rosettes. "This place gives me the creeps. It feels all wrong." Sam gave Evie a long, searching look. "On the level—you jake?"

Evie could feel tears wanting to come, but she was determined not to let them. Jericho had attacked her. He wasn't a stranger. He was her friend. But this morning, it felt as if she'd never really known him at all. "No. But going to bed seems like my best plan tonight," she said.

"You want me to stay?"

"I doubt there'll be trouble tonight. All those tranquilizers in his blood."

"I don't know. The giant's pretty strong. I heard Marlowe say he'd be back to normal by morning. Whatever that means."

"I'll be okay." She struggled to her feet, reached into the bathtub, and pulled up a baseball bat. "Found this in a closet. I'm keeping it close."

Sam rinsed out Evie's washrag and laid it on the side of the sink.

"Lock your door?" he said on the way out.

"Oh, yes. And a chair under the doorknob."

On the walk back to his room, Sam detoured through the moonlight-dappled ballroom. He felt that strong presence again. It seemed to be coming up from the earth itself. He thought he heard his name being called very faintly.

"Mama?" he said to the still room once more, but there was no answer.

※

After Evie had locked her door and shoved a chair under the knob, she crawled into bed and pulled the covers up to her chin. Many times Evie had fantasized about petting with Jericho. In her fantasy, she imagined surrendering to a dominating Jericho. She'd liked it as a fantasy. There was something wild and hedonistic about the idea of allowing herself to be taken over by a big, strong, handsome man, as if she had no say in the matter and so no responsibility for making love with him: *Why, it just happened! What could I do? I was helpless!* But in reality, it hadn't been that way. It had been confusing and utterly frightening to have no say and no control, like a rag doll wielded by a careless child. It was like not being a person at all.

Now that she thought about it, what Jericho had done to her, well, wasn't that what Marlowe was doing to Jericho? Taking away his control? Making him an experiment, an object that Marlowe didn't even take the time to read? Did Marlowe even see Jericho as a person anymore? Had he ever?

What if Sam was right, though, and there was some part of Jericho that really was that brute in the woods? What if it couldn't be blamed completely on the serum? That thought made Evie's stomach hurt. Tomorrow was their last day at Hopeful Harbor. Marlowe said Jericho would be back to normal in the morning. What if he didn't remember what he'd done and he was sitting there at breakfast tomorrow morning as if nothing had happened? What would she say?

She wouldn't go to breakfast.

No, that was a terrible plan. If there was anything Evie was unsuccessful at, it was avoiding breakfast. Most likely, Jericho would still be asleep tomorrow morning, she told herself. But just in case, she'd take the baseball bat with her.

She punched her pillow and waited impatiently for sleep. When it came, it was violent. Evie dreamed of the soldiers. Their faces, pale and ghostly, were carved in shadow, their eyes as prominent as a dying fish's. There was a sound like a howling wind full of bees, and under that, a galloping, clanging heartbeat keeping time. The men shouted to her across a great distance, their voices sailing past in a fast whine like bullets:

Help usEye Stop stopHelpStop O
Godhim stopfree usss
HELP. US.

The soldiers' screaming mouths opened unnaturally wide, as if the screaming had distorted their very bones. As if they were coming apart and there were no words for the agony. Conor Flynn appeared. His eyes were haunted. "Can you hear it? The Eye is close. You gotta find it. You gotta stop him. I can't keep hiding from him forever," he said.

When Evie woke the next morning, a note had been shoved under her door.

I am so sorry. Can we please talk? Jericho.

Just reading the note upset Evie. But she didn't want to leave with only yesterday stretched between them. She needed answers.

Jericho was hunched over his untouched plate of eggs and flapjacks when Evie walked in, baseball bat in hand. He saw her and stood, like a gentleman would. Evie startled and raised her weapon. "I'm no Babe Ruth, but I have a decent swing."

"You won't need it. I promise," Jericho said. "Ames is in the kitchen, right there."

Evie flicked her eyes toward the swinging door behind Jericho with the inset porthole window. Through it, she could see Ames and the kitchen staff hard at work. "From what I saw yesterday, Ames would be no protection."

"His gun would."

"Let's talk," she said. Jericho took his seat again, and Evie sat at the opposite end, keeping the long dining table between them. She did not drop the bat.

"I'm sorry. I'm...I'm horrified," Jericho said, staring down at his plate. He still seemed a bit dazed, and Evie wasn't sure if it was the tranquilizer darts or the guilt or both. Her earlier resolve retreated some. She hated that she felt frightened of Jericho and angry at Jericho and sorry for him and angry that she felt she should have sympathy for him when she was the one who got hurt. And still, underneath it all lurked that twisted, awful physical attraction to him. Never had she been more confused.

"Jericho, what's in that serum Marlowe's giving you?"

"I don't know. He won't tell me."

"It seems dangerous."

"It's keeping me alive right now," Jericho said, glancing up at Evie for just a second, then having to look away again. The shame he felt was like a trapped animal scratching inside him.

"Maybe it's not," Evie said. "Maybe that serum is making you sick and dependent. What if you stopped taking it? You could come back to the city with us. Right now. Today."

Jericho's head shot up. "Go back...with you?"

"On the train," she said, and the implication was clear: with us but not *with me*.

Jericho shook his head. "I can't. I made a promise." He sneaked another look at Evie. There was a bruise on her neck. The shame was overwhelming. "I wouldn't blame you for hating me. But if you could see it in your heart to give me a second chance..."

The way he was looking at her now, like the Jericho she had known and loved, the studious boy with all the books who had talked soothingly to her on the roof of the Bennington when she had been at her most vulnerable, the one who fed the pigeons, who burned with ambition just like she did, who understood the darkness that roamed her own soul—did that Jericho deserve another chance? Was she being unfair? Had what he'd done to her been brought about solely because of Marlowe's serum, or was Sam right and the serum had only brought out something that already lived deep inside Jericho?

Yes, he was beautiful. Yes, her body still yearned for his touch, she hated to admit. And she'd seen tremendous good in Jericho. But now that she let herself see more clearly, there was something else in there as well. A deep, dark struggle whose ending she couldn't read, something that both intrigued and frightened her.

"I don't hate you, Jericho. But I'm all balled up right now. What happened yesterday…well, I need time to think," Evie said.

Jericho nodded. "It's more than I deserve."

Evie shut her eyes and let out a long breath. "Don't do that."

"Do what?"

She blinked her eyes open. "Don't say things that make me feel sorry for you."

Sam and the others arrived. Their suitcases were packed and waiting in the foyer. Jericho could feel everything slipping away from him. He'd always said that a man was defined by his choices. He didn't want to only be defined by what he'd done yesterday.

"Before you go, there's something I want to show you," he said.

"She's not going anywhere with you, pal. Not without the rest of us," Sam said.

"I can speak for myself, Sam," Evie said. She looked into Jericho's face for an uncomfortable moment. "What is it?"

"I need you to follow me into the woods. All of you," Jericho said.

Sam picked up the bat. Evie pushed his hand down. "I think we should trust him on this."

Sam hoisted the bat onto his shoulder. "You know what helps with trust? A baseball bat."

☀

Henry had appropriated the old wheelchair in the abandoned soldiers' quarters, which he used now to carry Ling into the forest over pine needles that stuck to the rickety wheels like stiff brown hair. Up ahead, Evie and Sam trailed after Jericho as he led them deeper into the forest.

"I've seen this picture," Henry said in a low voice. "Where the trusting victims traipse off into the woods. It doesn't end well."

"I can hear you," Jericho said from several feet away.

"Superhuman hearing," Evie reminded him.

They came to the charred clearing. "This is where I've seen the soldiers," Jericho said.

"It's...it's just like my dream. Just like what I saw with Luther." Evie ran to a moss-covered tree stump. "This is where the Victrola plays. This is where it happened. Where my brother..." She swallowed hard.

"It feels like a graveyard," Ling said. A flock of birds circled into the sky, crying.

"There are things I need to tell you. Things I've held back because I... I thought I was being disloyal to Marlowe. One night, I saw two men in dark gray suits dragging a young woman upstairs—"

"Shadow Men?" Sam asked.

"I think so, but I can't be sure," Jericho said.

"What are Shadow Men doing at Marlowe's estate?" Ling asked.

"The men said that she was a mental patient that Marlowe was trying to help. But she sounded perfectly sane to me—sane and terrified. When I asked Marlowe about it later, he said she was a Diviner."

"Have you seen her since then?" Henry asked.

"No. Not a peep. She wanted me to know her name, though. She kept screaming it at me: Anna Provenza."

"Anna Provenza!" Evie exclaimed. "Mabel spoke to her sister, Maria. Her family was deported as anarchists. Mabel swears it's not true, though. She said Anna disappeared and the family had been looking for her ever since." Evie wished she could talk to Mabel. About everything.

"Why would you deport a family but keep one sister you claim is a mental patient? That doesn't make any sense at all," Henry said.

"Maybe he really is trying to help her," Ling said. She didn't want to think bad things about Jake Marlowe.

"So, what does Marlowe want with Anna Provenza?" Sam said.

"There's more," Jericho said. He flicked his eyes to Sam.

"What?" Sam challenged, and for a minute, Jericho wanted to hold back. *It is our choices that define us*, he reminded himself.

"Marlowe did an experiment with me. Something called sensory deprivation. I felt as if I were not in my body but floating in some other dimension, some porous realm between worlds. I heard voices. Terrible voices."

Evie frowned. "Where were they coming from?".

"I don't know. Marlowe wanted me to talk to them, though, and tell him what they were saying. The voices told me that the door must be opened as before and that the souls must be refreshed."

"What does that mean?" Evie asked.

"I honestly don't know. But there was another voice that broke through and told me to keep quiet. That those voices couldn't be trusted. I honestly didn't know what was happening—whether I'd just imagined it or not." Jericho looked at Sam again. "The woman had a Russian accent. She told me her name was Miriam."

"Just like Conor!" Evie said. "Sam..."

"You...you talked to my mother?" For all the reasons Sam had disliked Jericho, this one hurt the most. Why would she speak to these other fellas—to Jericho, of all people—and not to her own son? "What did she say? Did she tell you where she was?"

"No. But she said I was in danger. That he was making a mistake."

"What if—" Ling stopped short.

"What if what?" Henry said.

"What if she was talking to you from the land of the dead?"

"No!" Sam said, pointing a finger at them. "She is not dead! Conor heard her, too."

"That's no guarantee," Ling said.

"How do we even know it's your mother, Sam? What if it's just one more trick from the King of Crows?" Evie said.

A reedy horn blasted faintly in the distance.

"Our car," Ling said. "They'll be looking for us."

Evie gave the clearing one last backward glance, hoping for some signal from James, but it was just a dead place inside the woods. "I don't like that you're here with him," Evie said to Jericho on the walk back to the estate. "It's not too late to come with us."

"I don't think I should just now," Jericho said, and let the why remain unspoken. "I'll stay here and keep looking for clues. See if I can find out anything more about Anna Provenza. It's the least I can do. Somehow, I'll get up to that solarium and poke around."

Back at the estate, Marlowe's fancy Rolls-Royce was packed and ready to transport the Diviners to the train station. "Well. We'll see you at the exhibition, I suppose," Evie said, looking uncomfortable.

"Sure. At the exhibition," Jericho echoed.

He ached to hold her. He would probably never hold her again.

Evie watched Ames shutting the lid of the trunk over their cases. She didn't know what to think. She'd cared deeply for Jericho; still did, really. Like her, he was deeply flawed. His open admission of his faults and foibles was a relief compared with the sanctimonious, sure-of-themselves people she'd known in Zenith, Ohio. The ones who'd turn up their noses at messy girls like Evie, then slink off and commit their sins in the dark. But was it enough? Where did you draw the line? Evie's heart ached as she shook Jericho's hand and climbed into the backseat. She had never been less sure of the lines between right and wrong, between desire and destruction in her life.

"So long, Jericho," she said.

"So long, Evie," he echoed.

Good-bye, Jericho thought. Because this *was* good-bye. Even if she didn't say it outright. He hated Marlowe for what he'd done. And he hated knowing that a beast lurked somewhere inside his own soul. *I'm sorry*, he wanted to shout to the heavens. *I'm sorry, I'm sorry, I'm sorry.*

"Don't take any wooden nickels," he said. It was what Sergeant Leonard always said. For all Jericho knew, it was the last thing he'd probably ever say to Evie, and it was the dumbest.

As the car curved down the long driveway, Evie glanced back at the turreted estate. Jericho was still standing there with the sun glinting off his shoulders until it seemed that he was the sun itself.

NO REAL HARM

Jericho found Marlowe in his pristine study. "How was your visit with your friends?" Marlowe asked.

"Evie will probably never want anything to do with me again after what happened yesterday."

"No real harm came to her," Marlowe scoffed.

Jericho reeled. "No real harm? I attacked her!" Jericho wanted to punch Marlowe. "What's in that serum you gave me? I want to know. I *deserve* to know."

"I told you, vitamins."

"What else?"

"It's a highly calibrated secret formula patented by Marlowe Industries."

"*What else?*" Jericho demanded.

Jake Marlowe's eyes went flinty. "You really want to know?"

"Yes, for the hundredth time—yes!"

"Diviners' blood."

The room went sideways. Jericho thought back to Will's letters to Cornelius. Samples. All those samples. "You said you don't believe in Diviners," Jericho said. It was all he could think of in the moment. His mind simply wouldn't work.

"Not their mumbo jumbo, no. But I can't deny that the energy they produce is of enormous value. They are extraordinary in their way. Connected to that other world, you see. The trouble is…" Marlowe looked pained. "Frankly, some of these Diviners are of less noble stock."

"How do you mean?"

"Coloreds. Jews. Catholics. Degenerates. They're not real Americans."

Jericho couldn't believe what he was hearing. The minute he let his guard down with Marlowe and started to feel sympathy for him, the real Jake Marlowe came bubbling up like tainted water from a rusted fountain.

"But I've figured out a way around that, see. I take their blood, strip out what I need, and irradiate the formula to purify it."

"You're putting irradiated formula inside me?"

Marlowe chuckled. "Jericho, radiation is the safest thing in the world. Why, it's good for you! Makes the blood strong! I drink Marlowe Industries radium water, myself."

For weeks, Jericho had been operating at peak performance. He'd reveled in it. But now he could scarcely think. "What happens to the Diviners? How do you find them?"

"Now, see here, it's all on the up and up," Marlowe said, sounding like an exasperated parent. "These Diviners are volunteers who sign up through Fitter Families for Future Firesides at state fairs and whatnot."

"And do you explain to them what you're doing?"

"All research is protected. You know that. They volunteer because they want to do what's right for their country!"

"Like that woman I saw? Anna Provenza?"

Marlowe's expression darkened. "Anna is different."

"She's not a mental patient, is she?"

"She's an anarchist. She had a choice—go to prison and see her family deported or come here as a volunteer and contribute something meaningful to the future of the country. I'd say that's a pretty fair trade. More than fair, in fact."

"Her family's been deported anyway."

Marlowe looked surprised but recovered. "I had nothing to do with that."

Jericho felt as if he had been thrown into the deprivation tank, all his edges blurring again. "What happened to her?" he demanded.

"Anna? She's perfectly safe."

"Let me see her."

"I'm afraid I can't do that. By order of the United States government. She is still a criminal."

Some terrible realization was fighting to take shape in Jericho's enhanced mind. "You need them," he said as the thought occurred. "You need them to keep that door open, don't you? Because they're connected to that world!"

Marlowe's expression told the truth of it.

"Now, Jericho, don't be hasty—"

"I'll find her, then." Jericho pushed away from the table.

Marlowe leaped to his feet, following. "Jericho! Where are you going? Jericho! Come back here!"

Jericho stormed toward the library, only to see the men in suits coming toward him with a syringe. "Now, Mr. Jones. You don't wanna do this."

"Don't hurt him!" Marlowe shouted. "I need him."

The men darted forward, and Jericho took off at a clip for the forest.

You can't catch me, he thought. *I am faster and stronger and bulletproof. You made me that way, you bastard.* He'd never run so fast in his life. The trees flew by like painted splotches. When he'd reached the charred clearing, he stopped. Had they followed? They would. He should go now. Run for the train station. No. They'd be watching the train stations. Anna Provenza was still trapped somewhere inside Marlowe's estate. Jericho had to go back for her. The two of them could leave together. But how would he find her? The estate was enormous and he had no idea where they'd kept her. And the minute Jericho stepped foot inside the mansion, those Shadow Men would have him down in the lab for more of Marlowe's experiments.

From where he stood, Jericho could see the castle-like roofline of Hopeful Harbor. Such a pretentious architectural detail, and so like Marlowe, fancying himself a king, a ruler. But wait—the roof. The roof! Jericho could get in that way. He was pretty sure he had the strength to climb up the tower and get onto the roof. It was high time Jericho found out what Marlowe was keeping in that locked solarium anyway. Maybe it was Anna.

He ran back, creeping from tree to tree. He wished he had Sam's ability to go invisible. The Shadow Men walked toward the servants' entrance.

"He'll be back. He can't go far," one of them said.

And Jericho held his breath until they were inside.

Then he darted for the back of the estate.

As he'd predicted, climbing up the side of the tower was no trouble for him now, thanks to his incredible strength. He landed on the roof with the softness of a cat and crept the few feet toward the solarium, which ran nearly the length of the roof. Drapes had been drawn across its massive windows, making it impossible to see in. Jericho would have to go in blind. He tried the door. It was unlocked. Of course—who would lock a door on the roof? Carefully, he parted the drape and peered in, relieved when he saw that no one was there. Silently, he slipped inside.

It appeared to be another laboratory, but unlike the one in the basement, this one seemed to be dedicated solely to the strange golden machine taking up the center of the room. Metal legs secured the contraption to the floor, and its huge, rounded belly hummed with a fierce energy. A pair of tall poles flanked either side. Staticky threads of blue lightning shot back and forth between those poles. Two chairs, heavy with restraints, had been placed next to each pole. Wired metal helmets rested in the seats. An antenna was connected to the machine's top with a crank to allow it to be raised to the sky, and when Jericho looked up, he saw a movable panel in the roof. On one side of the machine was a sort of teletype contraption rigged to a roll of paper, as if it were waiting for a long telegram. There was a hinged door in the center. Etched into the door was a symbol Jericho knew well.

"The Eye," he murmured, touching it briefly. He was woozy with a rush of thought: This was what Evie was looking for! It wasn't a place or a person; it was a machine. It had to be the machine Marlowe had spoken of, the one he hoped could reach into another dimension. Directly below the Eye symbol was a mysterious, pulsing blue orb. Jericho stepped closer to get a better look and slipped. He swiped his fingers across the bottom of his shoe, and they came back wet and red.

Blood.

The solarium's floor rumbled—the elevator on its way up. Quickly, Jericho wiped the bottom of his shoe clean on his sleeve. He looked around frantically for a place to hide and darted behind a folding dressing screen. The elevator door opened. A Shadow Man, tall and lean, dragged a frightened, exhausted Anna Provenza forward. The other, stockier Shadow Man escorted an older woman with dark hair and dark eyes. She wore thick shackles on her wrists and ankles, and she didn't seem frightened so much as resigned and aloof, as if her mind were miles away.

"I am sorry, child," the older woman said, and Jericho recognized her voice immediately as the one that had calmed him in the deprivation tank. One look at her face and he knew: This was Miriam Lubovitch Lloyd, Sam's missing mother. The moment he thought of her name, Miriam stopped cold.

"What's the matter now, Miriam?" the stocky Shadow Man said, irritated.

"Nothing," she said, and let herself be led forward. But her energy was like a current Jericho could feel between them. She turned her head slightly in the direction of the dressing screen, and then Jericho heard her voice inside his head. *Do not move. Stay and see. This is truth. I am sorry.*

As the men in suits strapped Miriam into one chair and Anna into another, Marlowe arrived, looking very annoyed as he whipped off his suit jacket and rolled up his sleeves. "Did you find him?" he asked the Shadow Men.

"No. But we will," the tall Shadow Man said. "I've alerted all agents. They'll watch the train stations and the roads. He won't get far."

Marlowe pointed his finger very close to the man's nose. "You'd better find him before the exhibition."

The Shadow Man didn't flinch. "You don't tell us what to do, Mr. Marlowe. We outrank you."

A scowling Marlowe left the Shadow Man behind and came to Miriam's side. "Hello, Miriam," he said.

She spat in his face. He wiped the offense away with his pocket square.

"We have to charge the machine, Miriam. You're the only one we've found who can balance the energy from the Diviners and the other side and keep the breach open. You know that."

"You don't know what you do. What you awaken."

"Yes, yes, I've heard that all before." He patted the machine's golden belly. "This beauty has brought forth some of my greatest innovations. It's a miracle."

"This machine is a devil. It is open to the other side. To *him*. You know what powers its terrible heart."

Marlowe glared at Miriam. "When we conduct the experiment again and establish a stable connection, we won't need to use Diviners to charge the Eye anymore. We'll have all the energy we need. Endless resources! Abundance! We just need an answer from the other side about how to proceed."

"This, you cannot do! He tricks you. That is what he does. Don't you see? *You* serve *him*."

The tall Shadow Man smirked. "Whatever this entity is, this man in the hat, the United States government is very interested in acquiring him. He could be the greatest weapon on earth."

"You will kill us all," Miriam said.

"Hook her up so she'll shut up," the other Shadow Man said. "Crazy Russian Diviner."

"Now, now. There's no call for that," Marlowe chastised, and the man quieted.

From his hiding place, Jericho watched Marlowe settle the metal helmet onto Miriam's head. The other, he placed on Anna. He donned heavy rubber gloves and extracted a yellowish rock from a canister marked URANIUM, which he tucked inside the machine.

"Don't," Miriam begged. "The soldiers' souls are trapped inside the Eye. It is torture for them. And for the Diviners you use."

Jericho knew Miriam was saying this for him, so that he would know.

"There's no one trapped inside, Miriam. I've told you this before," Marlowe tutted.

"Not true. The soldiers power your machine. Our sin powers it," she said, and she sounded close to crying.

"I don't know why you torture yourself so, Miriam," Marlowe said with a sigh.

Marlowe slid a large pair of goggles over his eyes. He faced the machine, flipping switches and turning gears. The hum grew louder. A flickering halo formed above Miriam and Anna and shot down, encasing them in a cone of multi-ringed light. The machine glowed brightly with some new burst of energy. In the room, the lights brightened. The radio blurted on so loudly Jericho had to cover his ears. Only the machine's teletype remained silent. Marlowe watched it closely.

"Anything?" the tall Shadow Man asked.

"No," Marlowe answered, clearly disappointed. "No message."

He cranked up the dials. Anna fought against her restraints. Her body shook. "I hear them! They cry. Blood and pain. It gives him power! You must not...you must set them free!"

She cried out with visions beyond comprehension. What she saw was burning her up from the inside. Blood poured from her nostrils. Smoke rose from her skin where red burns appeared. But Marlowe and the men kept their eyes on the ticker tape, not caring what was happening to the Diviner in the chair.

Jericho had to stop this insanity. He would rush them. Knock them out. Then he would free Anna and Miriam. The Shadow Men might get off a few shots first, but he had to try. But before he could move, Miriam cried out:

"No! Go now! Do not look back! Warn them! Tell the truth of it!"

Jericho knew the warning was meant for him.

"What's she saying?" one of the Shadow Men sniped, moving quickly to Miriam's side.

Anna Provenza was screaming now with the power of the terrible visions breaking her apart. Jericho willed himself not to scream, too.

"Can you calm her down, Miriam? I can't think!" Marlowe growled, eyes on the teletype.

While the men were distracted, Jericho slipped out the door again, Anna's screams still ringing in his ears. He leaped from the roof and vomited into one of Marlowe's rosebushes. Then he took off toward the woods, running faster than he ever had before, disappearing deep into the cover of forest. He had to get back to the city and warn the others. But the Shadow Men would be looking for him. He'd need to avoid the train stations and main roads. He'd have to make it back on foot, through the countryside. And he'd have to hope that there was enough serum in his bloodstream to keep him alive.

SOLID CITIZENS

Branchville, New Jersey
Spring Fair

In the Fitter Families for Future Firesides tent, the white-capped nurses cleaned up the last of the day's syringes and cotton swabbing while the doctor made his report. It was nearly suppertime, and the doctor was eager to return to his comfortable home, where his wife was cooking him a steak. So he frowned as two men in dark suits pushed aside the tent's flaps and sauntered inside. They looked out of place here but didn't walk like it. Instead, they carried an ease of ownership, as if the world would bend to them with just a finger.

"I'm afraid the eugenics tent is closed until tomorrow, gentlemen," the doctor said.

The men stepped in front of the good doctor's desk, blocking out the day's dying light.

"We're associates of Mr. Madison's. I'm Mr. Jefferson. This is Mr. Adams."

Mr. Adams pressed his fingers to his hat brim but did not tip it.

"Oh," the doctor said, straightening his tie. "I thought I was supposed to give the files to that Madison fellow."

"We're all citizens, united in our cause." Mr. Jefferson smiled a pebbly smile. "Did anyone of interest pass through today?"

"Ay-yup. Found one from Cape May who might be the real deal. He told us he can disturb radio signals. Watches don't work on him, either. In fact," the doctor chuckled, "he stopped *my* watch! It was the darnedest thing you ever saw, wasn't it, Muriel?"

The nurse smiled and continued cleaning.

"I'm sure it was a hoot," Mr. Jefferson said. "Did he make mention of our friend?"

The doctor nodded. "He's had dreams of a man in a tall hat, just like you said. I can't say I understood a word of it. But here's his file."

"Is he on our list?" Mr. Jefferson asked his partner, keeping his eyes on the page of information—name, age, home address, psychological profile. People were so trusting. They gave over their privacy quite easily in exchange for a brass trinket that told them they were special.

Mr. Adams peered over Jefferson's shoulder. "Yep. Subject number thirty-four."

The doctor edged in closer and lowered his voice. "Say, uh, what's all this about, anyway, man to man?"

Mr. Jefferson shut the file and handed it off to Mr. Adams. "It's a matter of national security. We believe these so-called *Diviners* are dangerous. They're inclined toward criminality, anarchy, and other degenerate behavior. A fault in the bloodline, you see."

"Oh, I do! I *certainly* do. That's just science," the doctor said confidently, pointing to the eugenics board inside the tent. "When my daughter, Sally Ann, wanted to marry her fella, I told her, 'Now, Sally Ann, you better let me do a blood test on him first, make sure he's the right sort.'"

"I'm sure you can appreciate how serious it might be if this radical *sort*, with their strange powers, were allied with our enemies or foreign powers in any way. The fundamental values of our nation would be at risk."

The doctor waved his finger in the air. "By gum, I knew it! I knew something wasn't right about those people!"

"Some men can see through the veil," Mr. Jefferson said. His smile did not reach his eyes. "The United States thanks you for your efforts in helping to identify these dangerous people and appreciates your silence in the matter."

"You can count on me, Mr. Jefferson—I'm a solid citizen. Happy to help in any way."

Mr. Jefferson patted the man's arm. "You already have, doctor."

Mr. Adams fired up the brown sedan. "Anybody found Marlowe's lab rat yet?"

"No. But we will. Madison is on it. Odds are good he'll make his way back to his friends."

"Why can't we round 'em up?"

"In time, in time."

"Where to?" Mr. Jefferson asked, pulling onto the road.

Mr. Jefferson twisted the piano wire around his gloved fingers. "Cape May, of course. And then I believe it's high time we paid a visit to Sam Lloyd."

A GOOD TIME

Herbie Allen, the creep, had followed Theta out of rehearsal and was droning on about a "peppy" new tune he'd written: "I don't mean to brag, but folks who've heard it have said it's the best doggone tune they've *ever* heard and that it's going to make me a *millionaire*!"

"That a fact?" Theta said without interest.

"That's what they say." Herbie winked and put his hand on Theta's back.

Roy came roaring out of nowhere. He grabbed Herbie by the lapels and shoved him hard against the brick wall. "Whaddaya think you're doin' with my gal?"

"Gee, I-I didn't mean anything by it. No harm, old boy," a terrified Herbie said, and even though he was a creep, Theta didn't want this.

Roy sneered. "Call me old boy again and see what it gets ya."

"Roy. Roy, please," Theta begged.

Roy let go of Herbie, who scurried into the crowds on Forty-second Street without even a backward glance to see if Theta was all right.

"Roy. I work here," Theta pleaded.

"Yeah," Roy said, brushing down his sleeves and righting his jacket. "And I wanna know when I get to meet the big cheese, Ziegfeld. We made a deal."

"And I'm working on it."

"Now."

"He's not even here, Roy. That's what I was tryin' to tell ya. He's got a show in New Haven. He'll be back in a few days, and I promise I'll get you in first thing," Theta said, heart hammering.

Roy turned soft, his big brown eyes like a doe's. "I miss ya, Betty Sue. Miss you like a goddamn ache in my guts."

It was how he used to pull her back to him after a beating. He'd cry and say he was sorry and that he'd never do it again. Then he'd tell her how beautiful she was, how he couldn't live without her, and Theta would give in. Worse, she'd think it was her fault somehow. A piece of that old wiring sparked inside Theta for a minute: *Look how much he loves me*. But she wasn't that girl anymore. She'd had a life outside of Roy, her own life, with friends and the Follies—and Memphis. If it hadn't been for Memphis and how good he was to her, she might think what Roy was giving her really was love. She knew better now.

"I'm gonna take you out like a queen. You like that, huh? I got money. Show you a good time. Steak. Dancing. The works! I want everybody to see us together. Want everybody to know you're my girl." There on the street in front of everyone, he kissed her. And she remembered that Roy didn't love; he claimed.

Embarrassed, Theta pulled away. "Okay, Roy. Sure. Sounds good."

"I'll pick you up at eight," Roy said, squaring his fedora on his head.

"Tonight?"

"Tonight," Roy said.

※

That night, Roy picked Theta up for their date in a fancy new Studebaker.

"A loaner from Dutch," Roy crowed. "This is just the beginning."

He pinned a corsage to her dress and kissed her, and Theta nearly vomited.

"Where we going?" she asked.

"The Hotsy Totsy!"

Theta felt faint. "Oh. You sure you wanna go there?"

"Whaddaya mean? I hear it's the place to be! Dutch has his eye on it. He wants a report from me."

"Dutch wants to take over the Hotsy Totsy? But doesn't Papa Charles run that club?" Theta said, worried.

"Not for long." Roy gave her a sidelong glance. "Say, how do you know Papa Charles?"

"Oh. I just…I heard. He's real popular up there. Gets written up in the papers."

"You get up to Harlem a lot?"

"Here and there."

"Here and there," Roy sneered. He stared at her. "Why do I got the idea there's something you ain't on the level about, Theta? You wouldn't lie to me, would ya? You know I don't like lies."

"I know, Roy. It's swell you taking me out like this." Theta forced herself to smile. She didn't want to rile him up. But silently, she prayed: *Please, please don't let us run into Memphis.*

When they arrived at the Hotsy Totsy, Theta was a mess. All it would take was one slip from the people she knew there, and Roy would know the truth about Memphis. She'd worn two pairs of gloves in case her hands got the idea to act up, but around Roy, she was usually too frightened to make even a spark. The waiter placed a new table right up front for them, close to the action, and for once, Theta wished she could fade into the background. When she saw Alma coming toward her, all smiles, Theta froze.

"Say, Theta! Don't you look a picture," Alma cooed. "Memphis is 'round back. I could—"

Theta cut her off. "Alma! I don't believe you've met my husband. Roy Stoughton."

"Your ... husband?"

Theta nodded. She hoped Alma could read the warning in her eyes.

"Pleased to meet you, Mr. Stoughton," Alma said coolly, extending her hand.

"Can you get us a drink, honey? We're thirsty here," Roy barked.

"I'll send a waiter." Alma shot Theta a withering glance, and Theta wished she could crawl under the table and never come back.

And then, in the wings, she saw Memphis. Just the sight of him, leaning against the wall, his notebook under his arm, made Theta's heart beat faster. They were supposed to get married and move to Hollywood. Now they were worlds apart. Memphis hated her. And she had been blackmailed into being with Roy. It was like being stuck in a living nightmare that not even Henry and Ling could free her from.

"Seems like you been up here a lot. Enough to make friends," Roy said.

"You know how it is. Show business. The dancers all know each other," Theta said, hoping he'd buy the fib.

One of Dutch Schultz's men took a seat at their table. He bent low and whispered in Roy's ear. "Boss needs you to help with a problem. He thinks he knows who's doing the healing for the competition. Fella who works for Papa Charles. His name is Memphis Campbell. He wants you to take care of him."

"When?"

"Tonight."

Theta listened in terror. She had to keep Roy here. She had to warn Memphis. "I gotta powder my nose. 'Scuse me, gentlemen."

On shaking legs, Theta pushed through the crowd. But when she got backstage, Memphis wasn't there. She went back into the club. Their table was empty.

"No, no," she said.

Alma was just coming offstage. "Alma! You seen Memphis?"

Alma appraised her coolly. "Who wants to know, *Mrs. Stoughton?*"

"It's too long a story to tell now, but I ain't happy about being Mrs. Stoughton, believe me. And I think Memphis is in trouble. Big trouble. My husband works for Dutch."

Alma's eyes widened. "He's been going out back to write sometimes."

"Thanks!" Theta said, and ran out of the club. When she got to the alley behind the club, she put a hand to her mouth. Roy and two of Dutch's men surrounded Memphis. Three against one.

"We shoulda taken you out when we had the chance. You gonna start healing for us, Diviner. Or we're gonna end you right now," Roy was saying. "And if some crazy bird comes around, we'll shoot it, too."

"Roy! Don't!" Theta screamed. She ran and put herself between Roy and Memphis.

"Theta?" Memphis said. He already had a bloody lip and a swollen cheek. "What're you doing? Get out of here."

Roy looked from Theta to Memphis, the realization taking root. "I'll be damned. I mighta known. Mighta known you was lying this whole time."

Dutch's men cackled with glee. "Aww, Roy. You got yourself a situation."

Roy's eyes were murderous. "Get over here, Betty."

Floating. Up to the ceiling. Not here. Theta couldn't float away this time. Not with Memphis in danger.

Theta shook her head. "No."

"I said, get over here!" Roy yanked Theta by the hair, dragging her away from Memphis.

"Leave her alone!" Memphis said, grabbing hold of Roy by his jacket sleeve.

"I'll kill you right here," Roy said. He took a swing, catching Memphis just above the ear. Memphis winced. His ear still ringing, he fell back and dropped into a boxer's stance.

The fire bristled inside Theta, aching to come out. She worked to get her glove off.

"I don't think so, Betty." Roy wrenched her arms behind her back, and the fire retreated again as Theta cried out in pain. "Come at me again and I'll break her arms."

Memphis put up his hands. "Okay. Okay. Don't hurt her."

"This who you been whoring around with, Betty?"

"I . . ."

"Huh?" Roy gave Theta's arms a sharp pull. Her eyes filled with tears.

"I love . . ."

"What?"

"I love him! I love . . . him."

"Theta?" Memphis said softly.

"I was trying to protect you," she said.

Roy shoved Theta back. He pushed up his sleeves on his march toward Memphis. "I'm gonna beat you to a pulp. Then it's your turn, Betty."

"Leave 'em be," Bill Johnson thundered, coming into the alley. Memphis almost didn't recognize him at first. He looked to be a man easily ten years younger, with a full beard and very little gray left in his hair.

"You gonna take on all of us?" Roy challenged.

"Won't need to." Bill took a step forward. He was a big man, and his shadow fell across the men like a giant's. "Said: Let 'em go."

"Or what?"

Bill reached down and grabbed Theta's corsage, which had fallen to the street. He squeezed, and the flowers browned and wilted. He tossed the corsage away.

"Let 'em go," Bill said again.

Roy backed away. "Come on, Betty Sue. We're leaving. *Now!*"

"She's not going anywhere with you," Memphis said. He stepped between Roy and Theta, but Theta slipped around and stood next to Memphis, side by side.

Roy's carefully polished hair had gotten mussed up. His collar was sprung, and Theta knew he'd be really sore about that tuxedo. He tugged down his vest and pointed a finger at Theta and Memphis. "You'll pay for this. Mark my words. Fucking circus freaks! They oughta lock you all up. They oughta put you in the chair and watch you fry!"

"Come on, Roy. She ain't worth it," Dutch's man said. He patted Roy's back and guided him toward the waiting car.

In the alley, Theta rubbed the ache from her injured arms and wiped her nose on the back of her glove.

"I'm sorry for everything I said to you after that night at the asylum. For pushing you away. I didn't want him to know about you and Isaiah. I was afraid he'd hurt you. I know what kinda man he is, and I couldn't let that happen. That's why I broke it off with you, Poet. That's the only reason. I had to make you hate me. I knew you'd come after me. I knew you'd try to make it right."

Memphis kissed Theta. He wrapped his arms around her and it was like coming home after a hard day in the cold. "I'm sorry. I'm sorry," she kept saying into his chest.

"Shhh, shhh," Memphis said.

"Well. Glad you're all right," Bill said, and started away.

"Mr. Johnson!" Memphis called.

Bill stopped and turned to him. "Bill."

"Bill. Thank you."

Bill nodded. "Least I could do. Got some sins to work off."

Memphis and Theta were kissing again, blind to everything around them.

"Come on," Memphis said.

Memphis broke into the lighthouse, and he and Theta lay on the blanket they'd kept there for months. Theta had never tasted a kiss so sweet as the ones she shared now with Memphis. Suddenly, she pulled away. "What if I hurt you?"

Memphis grinned. "It's a nice way to go."

"I'm serious, Poet."

"You won't. I don't think you can." He held up his hands. "Healer."

Memphis kissed Theta, and she kissed him back. His hands pressed against her back just where she wanted them. And the only warmth she felt was the pull of her desire for him. They lay on the floor of the lighthouse. The lighthouse's shining orb gentled its beam across the sleeping river. As Memphis moved on top of her, Theta kept her eyes on his beautiful face, lost in shadow, then bathed in light, his joy so bright to see. She felt a new fire this time, one that raced through her body with pleasure.

She rested her spine against the soft skin of Memphis's chest. He draped an arm across her, and the two of them lay pressed together like spoons in a cozy drawer.

"Roy will come for us, you know. He won't stop," Theta said quietly.

Memphis kissed the tender spot beneath her ear. "We'll fight back."

And Theta let herself be lulled by the idea that maybe, just maybe, they could win.

THE SECRET SIX

In the back of a borrowed dairy truck, Mabel shivered under a blanket and stared up at the moon. It was fat and beautiful, but that didn't help them much tonight, when the Secret Six needed to stay hidden. Arthur cut the truck's headlights and parked near the river. The Secret Six scrambled out and gathered behind the shelter of an eastern hemlock. In the distance, Mabel could see the miners' tents like a dotting of flowers in the field. Arthur climbed up the tree to scout with his binoculars.

"The militiamen are off getting drunk on cheap moonshine just like the miners said they usually do about this time of night." He climbed back down and brushed the needles from his peacoat. "We have to act before they get back. There are only two guards right now, both positioned by the front gate. Gloria, you'll draw them out to the field so we can sneak in."

"Got it," Gloria said, rolling her stockings down below her knees like a true flapper.

"Once you do, Mabel and I will set the bomb at the mine while Luis and Aron set the explosives by the company store. That explosion should draw their attention and give us cover to run straight back to the truck," Arthur said, handing everyone gray fishermen's sweaters and wool caps to help them blend into the night. Behind the tree was an old Dodge they'd hidden the day before. Arthur lifted the hood and tampered with some wires. "That oughta do the trick," he said, closing the hood and wiping his hands. "You ready, Gloria?"

"And how," she said, sliding into the driver's side. The men pushed the car out of the trees and onto the slope of the road. The engine chugged to life, sounding like a sick cow. Gloria stuck her hand out the window in a quick little wave.

"Let's go," Arthur said, leading the others the long way around, away from the tent city where the patrolling guards were. The sudden bark of a dog made Mabel jump.

"You jake?" Arthur whispered.

Mabel tried to make sense of all the feelings whirring inside her. One part of her was terrified. The other part felt electric, ready to burn. They were going to *blow up the mine*. She was breaking the law. That was wrong. But so was Jake Marlowe's treatment of his workers. Those militiamen shooting up the camp and frightening the miners, that was wrong, and nobody was doing anything about it. So maybe what they were doing was right? It was all topsy-turvy.

"Mabel?" Arthur placed a hand gently on her arm.

Mabel looked out at the campfires of the tent city, and she reminded herself that this was what they were fighting for.

"I'm jake," she said, and hunkered down behind a tall rise of dirt to keep watch through her binoculars. Gloria drove the hobbled car through the field in an erratic line, making a terrible racket.

The guards jumped to their feet and hoisted their guns. "Hey, now! This is private property!"

Mabel held her breath. If Gloria didn't pull off this part, they were done for. The guards might even shoot her. The car shuddered to a stop and Gloria stepped out, wringing her hands. Her voice drifted across the field: "Oh, can you help me, please? I don't know what's the matter with this thing! Papa will be so unhappy with me if I've ruined another auto!"

"Oh, please, please," Mabel whispered. Her heart hammered away.

The guards exchanged looks and put down their rifles. "Well, let's see what the trouble is, little lady," one said, and opened the hood.

"Gee, *thank* you!" Gloria said flirtatiously.

Mabel felt a pang of jealousy. Of course Gloria had been chosen for this part of the mission: They'd needed someone pretty.

"It's time," Arthur said.

They yanked their gray wool caps over their ears and scrambled down the dirt cliff and onto the tracks, darting between the stilled mine cars, ducking under the quiet conveyor belt. In the dark, the mine appeared monstrous, a shadowy giant in repose.

"Let's go," Arthur said, and then the two of them scurried across the dusty train ties and slipped into the devil's mouth.

"Here. Give me your hand." Arthur reached back and took hold of

Mabel's fingers, guiding her into the pitch dark. They didn't dare shine a light yet for fear of attracting attention. The air was dense with dust. Mabel could feel it scratching at her lungs with each breath, and she could barely stand to imagine what it must be like nearly two hundred feet below. It was all she could do not to run screaming out the way she'd come.

"Okay. Now we can use that lamp," Arthur whispered.

From under her sweater, Mabel brought out the flashlight, shining it on Arthur's gloves as he handled the explosive, packing in dynamite, scrap metal, and powder. He worked quickly, and Mabel tried not to think about how deftly he moved, like an experienced bomb maker. Once his work was done, Arthur tucked the detonator under his arm and backed away from the mine shaft, threading out the fuse line as he did. "Be my eyes, will you, Mabel?" he said.

Mabel cut the flashlight and swiveled her head, eyes searching for possible trouble. The wind carried the sound of the car's engine starting up once more. "Oh, listen! Purrs just like a sweet kitten," Gloria said. She honked the horn—their signal—and laughed. "Oops! Silly me!"

"Gloria's leaving. We'd better hurry," Mabel said.

As they crept back into the cover of the woods, off Marlowe's property, Mabel stopped.

"What's the matter?" Arthur asked, doubling back.

A rush of panic flooded Mabel. She wanted to lie down and shut her eyes like a child playing hide-and-seek. She was taking her first steps as her own person, away from Evie and Jericho and her parents. She wasn't at all sure of herself. Not one bit.

"Arthur, tell me what we're doing is right."

Arthur wrapped his arms around her, holding her to his chest. It felt so good, so right next to him. She decided to let that be her answer.

"Ready?" Arthur asked.

Mabel nodded.

"Duck," he said, and pushed in the detonator.

For two seconds, it seemed to Mabel that the entire world had stopped to hold its breath. Then a great fireball exploded from the mine's mouth. The mine collapsed in on itself. Choking black smoke poured out. It was mesmerizing and terrifying. Everything was burning. Even from a safe distance, Mabel's cheeks felt singed and her eyes stung. A few seconds later, the company store exploded, too, sending shrapnel flying in all directions.

"Come on!" Arthur said, and Mabel followed, running full out.

By the time Arthur and Mabel made it back to the hiding spot near the river, Mabel had to bend over to catch her breath. Behind them, the night was on fire. Jake Marlowe's mine lay in ruins.

"You made it," Gloria said, coming out from behind a tree.

"Yeah," Arthur gasped.

"Where are Aron and Luis?"

"They'll be here," Arthur insisted. "Come on. Let's get this covered."

The three of them piled boughs on top of the Dodge.

"You were terrific out there," Mabel said to Gloria when she'd caught her breath again.

"Thanks, Mabel. For a second, I thought I was a goner," Gloria admitted. "Isn't this exciting?" Impulsively, she kissed Mabel's cheek, and Mabel felt like they were two girlfriends with a delicious secret. It was so much more important than being friends with Evie and Theta. Mabel and Gloria were part of a movement, a cause. Evie? Evie was chasing ghosts and selling soap. For the first time in her life, Mabel felt special and necessary. This was not her mother's moment or Evie's or anybody else's; it belonged to Mabel.

"I am working toward greatness," she whispered to herself.

Gloria stripped off her dress and struggled into her shapeless farmer's wife dress and apron, pulling an unfashionable flowered hat over her bobbed hair. A ball of knitting completed the domestic picture. Arthur stepped into a pair of baggy coveralls and darkened his hair with coal dust.

"How do we look?" Arthur asked. "Like a couple of dairy farmers?"

"I don't know a lot of dairy farmers, but I'd say yes," Mabel said.

Shyly, Mabel removed her sweater and cap, and Arthur wrapped all of their old clothes around a rock and sank them in the river. He climbed into the driver's side; Gloria, the passenger side. Mabel clambered onto the truck's long bed, clinking past the crates of milk bottles they'd planted to back up their story. Then they waited for Aron and Luis. Over the percolator hum of the truck's motor, Mabel could hear the distant shouting. An eerie orange glow lit up the sky. Smoke poured through the trees like a St. Walpurgis Night festival. Already, the fire was burning toward the road.

They could even feel some of the heat where they were. Mabel raised the binoculars. Guards were running about. Some of the militiamen had joined them. They grabbed buckets of sand and water for the fire. Even some of the striking workers had joined in to help. Still there was no sign of Aron and Luis. Where were they? Mabel thought she'd scream from nerves.

"It's been five minutes. We should go," Gloria cautioned from the front seat.

"We can't just leave them!" Mabel cried.

"That was the plan. We all agreed. They knew the risks," Gloria said.

"Just one more minute," Mabel pleaded.

Chewing the inside of his cheek, Arthur looked from Gloria to Mabel and back out at the eerie backlit trees.

"*Arthur...!*" Gloria warned.

"Just another minute," he said.

"It's too hot. They might close the road!" Gloria said. "We'll get caught if we d—"

The *slap-slap-slap* of three quick rifle shots pierced the night, making Mabel jump.

"What was that?" Gloria whispered.

Two more shots rang out. With shaking hands, Mabel raised the binoculars. She could see the militiamen running for their trucks.

"Mabel?" Arthur.

"They're getting into their trucks." Her heart felt as if it would burst from fear. "They're on the move."

"That's it. We can't wait another second," Arthur said.

Mabel held on tightly as Arthur shifted the truck onto the old dirt road. She wanted to cry, but she was too frightened for tears. She kept the binoculars pressed against her eyes, searching for any sign of Luis and Aron.

"Come on, come on," she whispered prayerfully.

Gloria leaned out her window, angling her face toward the back. "Mabel! What are you doing? Lie down under the tarp this instant!"

"I haven't given up yet," Mabel said.

"You're going to get us arrested—or killed!"

Shapes darted between the dark trees. For all Mabel knew, it could be militiamen coming for them. Her heart beat so fast it felt as if it would burst.

She squinted hard against the plumes of irritating smoke blowing toward them, and then she was smacking her palm against the side of Arthur's door. Aron and Luis were racing after the moving truck.

"There they are! I see them!" she cried.

Arthur jerked to a stop, keeping the motor running, and Mabel crawled to the back and helped haul her exhausted friends onto the truck bed. Aron and Luis sprawled onto their backs, gasping for breath.

"Thanks for...waiting," Luis managed between fits of coughing.

"It was Mabel who spotted you," Arthur said over the motor's hum.

"Ah, Mabel Rose, you are true to your name and just as sweet," Luis said on scant breath.

Aron grinned. "We did it! Those bastards won't be making money off scab labor anymore."

"We're not safe yet," Arthur warned. "Stay quiet and hidden."

Mabel pulled the tarp over the back of the truck, and the three of them crouched down behind the stacked milk crates. Mabel cracked open one of the bottles and handed it to the boys, who swigged generously and coughed just as heartily. The truck jostled down the rutted road—just a dairy farmer and his wife making the morning rounds. But soon they slowed to a stop.

"Why are we stopping?" Luis whispered.

Mabel peeked out from under the tarp and her heart sank. "Pinkertons. Blocking the road," she whispered.

"We're done for," Aron said.

"Shhh. Have faith," Luis said.

Mabel lifted the tarp ever so slightly and saw an agent approach the driver's window. Arthur snugged his cap down lower over his newly darkened hair. There was coal dust on his shoulder. She hoped the agent couldn't see it.

"Morning. My wife and I saw the fire," Arthur said, making his voice calm and country. "What's the trouble?"

The agent looked at Arthur for a long time. Mabel was sure her pounding blood could be heard from under the tarp. If they were discovered, they'd go to prison for certain. But there was always the chance the agents might just shoot them there and then, and be done with it.

"Anarchists just blew up the mine," the agent answered at last.

Arthur shook his head in disapproval. "That a fact? Well, I'll be."

"It isn't safe anywhere nowadays," Gloria said.

"No, ma'am. It sure isn't."

Let us go, let us go, let us go, Mabel prayed silently.

"Mind if I check the back of your wagon, there?" the agent said.

Mabel pressed a hand to her mouth to keep the scream in. Beside her, she saw Luis's lips moving in silent prayer. Aron trembled, his eyes tightly shut.

"Not at all," Arthur said. "Just getting a jump on the morning run. Got a long drive ahead. Taking the cream all the way to Camden today. Care to wet your whistle? Got a bottle right here. Finest milk in New Jersey, if I do say so myself."

"Don't mind if I do," the agent said. He took the bottle from Arthur and swigged half of it down. His rifle gleamed in the fire-tinged night. "That *is* awfully fine cream."

The agent peered at the tarp again. He took a step forward. Mabel held her breath as he sipped from the bottle. But then he stepped back, smiling. "Well, I'll let you get on your way, then. You folks be careful, though. Don't pick up any strangers out here. We got orders to shoot to kill."

"Will do. Thank you, sir," Arthur said.

The truck lurched forward, and Mabel didn't let out her breath till she could see the agents and the fire receding into the night.

EVERYTHING WAS DIFFERENT NOW

By the time the Secret Six had made it back to Manhattan, it was nearly four in the morning. After they'd ditched the truck on the West Side, the adrenaline loss left everyone limp and sleepy. Arthur promised to see Mabel back to Evie's hotel, where she'd told her mother she was staying for the night.

"Come up for a second first?" he said as they stood outside the bookshop.

While he searched for his key, Mabel leaned her head back to take in the full scope of the night sky. Were those the same stars and moon she'd seen before they'd blown up the mine? Everything felt different now. *She* was different. When they entered Arthur's flat, it also seemed different with just the two of them in it, the street light shining through the window and pooling onto the floor. It was both threatening and exciting. Mabel was nervous. She let her fingers trail over the back of a chair. The sensation made her dizzy.

Arthur lowered the blinds and Mabel's heartbeat quickened. In the slashes of light, she could see the outline of his firm body, the sinewy muscles cut like a navy yard brawler's.

"Why do you do that?" she asked.

"What?"

"Raise and lower the blinds so much."

"I don't know. I like the street light at night, I guess. It's comforting. I know I'm a little old for that, but…" He shrugged, sheepish. One minute, Arthur was streetwise and bold, full of swagger. The next, he was boyish and sweet. Right now the way he was looking at her was anything but boyish.

"I-I should probably go home," Mabel said, though she didn't want to leave.

Arthur closed the distance between them. "Didn't you tell your parents you were staying the night with Evie?"

Mabel swallowed hard. "Yes."

He took hold of Mabel's hand and laced his fingers through hers. Mabel could scarcely breathe. Arthur cocked his head. "Is...is there another fella?"

Another fella. It was funny to Mabel now to think that she had ever wanted Jericho. Cool, detached Jericho. They were chalk and cheese. Arthur was a fire and, at twenty, a man. It was only just now dawning on Mabel that she had found someone to match her passion.

"No. Not anymore," she answered.

"I like you so much, Mabel Rose. Do you...?" He left it unfinished.

"Yes."

Arthur drew Mabel into his arms and kissed her.

The only other kiss Mabel had known was with Jericho. Even then, she'd suspected he had done it more out of curiosity and politeness than real desire. Now that she was being kissed properly, she knew the difference. Arthur held her tightly. The stubble of his chin scratched her cheek, not unpleasantly. She had the fleeting thought that she'd need to cover it with powder later—maybe Theta would have some? But then she was lost to that fire again.

Arthur broke away, and Mabel wanted him back.

"Stay?" Arthur pushed back the curtain. His bed lay behind it.

For just a second, Mabel wished she could call and ask Evie what she should do. But Mabel had been breaking the old rules tonight. She was a new girl. No, a new woman. She needed to make her own decisions. She was shy about showing her body. Slim flappers with sun-golden tans were the fashion. Mabel's body was curvaceous and soft, pale and a little freckled. What if Arthur didn't like the way she looked and felt? He moved behind her and unbuttoned her dress, letting it slip to the floor. He kissed tenderly from her right shoulder up her neck to her ear. Mabel moaned as his hands came around front and cupped her full breasts under her chemise. And then her chemise was on the floor. She curled into herself, seated at the edge of the bed.

"I want to look at you," Arthur said. His voice was husky. It made Mabel's stomach flutter, made her head dizzy.

She turned to face him, keeping her arms protectively crossed over her chest like a shield. Arthur was naked. Mabel gasped. She'd never seen a naked man before, and she'd certainly never seen an aroused naked man.

The moonlight shone on Arthur's tight muscles, making them seem carved of marble. There was a dusting of hair that led from his navel down to the part that both fascinated and terrified her. She was doing this, then. *They* were doing this. This was real.

"I want to see you. All of you," Arthur said gently. He ran the back of his hand down one of Mabel's crossed arms. Mabel lowered them, exposing herself, blushing as Arthur took in all of her. Arthur leaned forward and kissed her sweetly on the lips. Then he laid her back on the bed and kissed her breasts, moving farther and farther down. Instinctively, she clamped her legs shut.

"No?" Arthur whispered, coming back up to face her. He swept her hair back from her forehead and looked into her eyes.

"Yes, but…"

"But what?"

"I'm…I don't know what to do."

Arthur kissed her. "I do," he whispered.

Slowly, she opened her legs. Mabel had felt many wonderful things: the first snow landing on her upturned face. The warm summer sun shining down on her toes in the Coney Island sand. But when Arthur touched her between her legs with his warm, sure fingers, she was certain it was the most exquisite feeling she had ever had in her life. He kept at it, building heat there until she thought she might burst from ecstasy. Warmth shot from her belly up to her head, and she cried out and flung her arms around Arthur's neck. He smiled and reached into his nightstand drawer and brought out a small package.

"A raincoat," Arthur said, taking out the rubber and putting it on. Mabel looked away, embarrassed. It seemed silly to be embarrassed by this considering what he'd just done to her, what they were about to do, but somehow watching this act made everything seem all too real.

"I love you, Mabel Rose," Arthur said, and then he was inside her. At first, there was a little pain. But then, as they moved together, it went away. Mabel felt warm and free. Her mind whirred:

He said he loves me.

I am now a woman.

My mother would kill me if she knew. My father would kill him.

Will they be able to read it in my face? Will everybody?

I got there before Evie did—I was finally first.

Everything is different now.

Arthur cried out and went very still. For a second, Mabel was afraid she'd hurt him. He collapsed and rolled to the side of her, breathing heavily. Grinning. He was grinning from ear to ear. *I did that*, Mabel thought. *I made him smile like that.*

"Come here, you," Arthur growled, and drew Mabel into his arms. "Mabel Rose. My beautiful Mabel Rose." They lay like that for some time until they fell asleep.

❀

Only a few blocks away, Henry and David sat beside each other at the piano and finished up a song they'd been working on well into the night.

"*And with each kiss such bliss is mine, you see. For he's the boy whose heart beats sweet for me.…*" Henry sang. He looked shyly at David. "They'll make us change that line, you know."

"Yeah. I know. But I wanted to hear you sing it to me just once."

"I'll sing it to you anytime," Henry said.

"That true?" David asked, keeping his eyes on the piano keys. And Henry could feel the real question lurking underneath: Do you *really* care about me? Or are you still in love with a ghost?

After Louis, Henry had held back some part of himself. He was afraid of being hurt again. There'd been so much loss that sometimes, Henry worried that he would always walk through life with a thin glaze over the cracks in his heart. But sitting there on the piano bench, looking at David's sensual profile, listening to him play with the melody they'd written together, it was almost as if he could hear Louis whispering to him: *You got a lot to live for,* cher. *You can run from it or you can fight for it.*

When Henry didn't answer, David turned to face him, puzzled. "What?"

"This," Henry said, and kissed David deeply.

David put two fingers to Henry's lips. He bent his forehead to Henry's. "Don't toy with me. I can't."

"I'm not playing. I swear it," Henry said.

451

This time, David kissed him so passionately they fell off the piano bench.

"Ow!" David said, rubbing his arm.

"Sorry. I'll stop—"

"Shut up and kiss me."

Then they were tearing at each other's clothes, fumbling with buttons on their way to the couch. David kissed down Henry's bare chest, listening to his gasps of pleasure. And then Henry wrestled David onto his back; his hands snaked into David's thick curls as he pressed his mouth to David's, their tongues dancing, bodies pressed together.

"I could sing you another verse," Henry said, stopping to lean his cheek on his palm.

David grabbed Henry down on top of him. "Don't. You. Dare," he growled, and slid his hands into Henry's trousers until Henry's jokes were gone; he could think of nothing but what he and David were about— tongues and lips and fingers—and how incredible it felt to choose happiness, to let yourself be so completely alive. To let go of your ghosts.

❄

Sam couldn't sleep. The radiators blasted at full heat. He'd cracked a window to let in some cool night air, but it was his thoughts that kept him up as much as the temperature. He'd been thinking of Evie. Why couldn't he just let go?

Sam didn't open up to many people. But there was something about Evie that drew him out and made him vulnerable. Sam had been up in an aeroplane with Barnstormin' Belle. He'd flown on the trapeze and walked a wire with the circus. Most people thought that was bravery. But nothing was braver than letting somebody really know you, warts and all. Nothing was braver than trying to love and be loved. He shut his eyes and imagined Evie in his arms. And then his hand was reaching under the blanket as he fumbled with his pajama bottoms. It was Evie he thought about while he touched himself. Evie he wanted so much it was almost a physical ache. Evie he saw as the pressure built. Sam groaned and arched as the exquisite rush zoomed through him. He was sweating and flushed.

"Jesus," he said, panting.

Jesus didn't answer.

❈

Ling had gone to bed clutching Alma's hair ribbon. When she awoke inside the dream, she was at a dance marathon. Under a glittery cardboard half-moon that dangled from a string, couples with numbers on their backs moved around the edges of the wooden floor—all except for Alma. She danced alone in the center, a ballet of one. Ling watched her pirouette and high-step in awe. She moved closer and closer until she was standing in the center, too, while Alma danced around Ling. It made Ling dizzy, so she closed her eyes, feeling Alma's presence, like atoms swirling, becoming something new. She shivered all over; her skin tingled. Ling tilted her head back, grinning, leaning into the energy Alma created. It was almost like being caressed by the dream itself. And when Ling opened her eyes, the moon threw off sparkling prisms of light as it twirled on its string high above her.

❈

Mabel woke just after six. Beside her, Arthur slept peacefully, his lips—the lips that had been all over her just hours ago—parted just slightly. He was so beautiful. Mabel ached between her legs, but she wanted to do it all again. It had been the most incredible night of her life. But the longer she lay in Arthur's bed, listening to his gentle breathing, the more a panic-limned doubt began to seep in: *We blew up Jake Marlowe's mine!* Last night, as she'd watched it all burn, she'd thought, *You won't be making money off the backs of poor people anymore.* It had felt righteous. It had felt like justice.

But now, in the early morning's cold light, she wondered: *Had* they done right? No one had been hurt. The Marlowe mine and the company store, the symbols of all that was wrong with management, had been destroyed. Still. They'd made change with bombs. With that one act, Mabel had turned her back on everything her parents had taught her.

Mabel needed to talk to someone or she'd go mad. She slipped out of bed and crept down the stairs. Mr. Jenkins kept a telephone behind the counter near the cash register. She dialed the number she knew by heart and waited as the operator put her through.

"Mmm'lo," Evie mumbled on the other end. "Wrong party..."

"Evie? Evie, don't hang up! It's Mabel."

"Mabel..." Evie slurred, half-asleep still. "Wh-What time's it?"

"Very late. Or very early. Depending."

On the other end, Evie was fighting to stay alert. Mabel could hear it. "Oh, I've missed you so much. You a'right, Mabesie?"

Mabesie. With one word, Mabel was pierced. She wanted to tell Evie everything—about the raid. The dynamite. How exciting it had been. How Arthur Brown had looked with the fire behind him—a terrible angel, a beautiful monster. About what they had done in his bed. What she wanted was to hear Evie tutting that Mabel worried too much and to go to sleep; everything would look better in the morning. She wanted to hear of Evie's trivial troubles: A dull party. A runner in her favorite stockings. Sarah Snow. But their lives were worlds apart now. Mabel and the Six were fighting for real change; Evie and the others chased down ghosts. Mabel had never even seen a ghost. She'd taken Evie's word for it that ghosts existed. But maybe it was time to stop taking Evie's word for things. Maybe if you didn't believe in ghosts, you didn't see them.

Mabel had called Evie out of habit, she now realized, like trying to suck your thumb when you were long past its comfort and feeling foolish for it.

"I'm fine," Mabel said. "I'm with friends."

"What friends?" Evie sounded hurt.

Mabel ignored her. "I just wanted..." *To say I miss you. To pretend that we could be best friends the way we used to be.* "I just wanted to see how you were getting along."

"At six thirty in the AM?" Evie mumbled sleepily.

"Sorry. Go back to bed."

"Wait!" Evie said. "Mabesie, I miss you. I'm sorry 'bout what I did."

Mabel blinked up at the ceiling. It was leaking. She moved the garbage pail into place with her foot.

"Say, let's make a plan, mm-kay? A won'erful, won'erful plan," Evie murmured.

Mabel blinked faster. "Sure. We'll do that. Go back to bed."

"Okay, then." Evie yawned. "Tomorrow. We'll talk tomorrow."

"It is tomorrow," Mabel said, and hung up.

Mabel crept back into Arthur's flat. Dawn was struggling to be born.

"Mabel?" Arthur called. "Where'd ya go?"

"Nowhere," Mabel said. He was so handsome and rumpled.

Arthur reached out to her with one hand. He folded down the covers. "Come back to bed. I'll warm you up."

You've made your bed, now you'll have to lie in it, Mabel's grandmother had said to Mabel's mother once upon a time. Mabel had made her choice. There was no going back.

She slipped between the sheets and into Arthur's arms.

Everything was different now.

※

In the early dawn, Jake Marlowe's mine still smoldered. The wisps of gray smoke joined the mist dancing along the tops of the blue hills. The day's first light shadowed the canvas tents where, inside, the miners and their families slept and dreamed. On the edge of the camp, the militiamen gathered. They passed the guns down the line, hand over hand until all were armed.

The foreman pulled back the chamber on his rifle.

"Let 'em have it."

FIGHT FIRE WITH FIRE

"I hate to say good-bye," Mabel said as she leaned against the doorway of Arthur's garret. She wanted nothing more than to lead him back to bed and spend the day in his arms. But she'd been gone too long as it was.

"That makes two of us," Arthur said, kissing her deeply. "See you tonight?"

Mabel nodded. *Tonight and tomorrow and forever,* she wanted to say.

Arthur stood at the window, looking down. Mabel waved up at him and he waved back as she went on her way. Across the street, the man in the brown fedora stood under the street lamp, staring up. He tucked his newspaper under his arm and turned up Bleecker Street. Arthur slipped out of the bookshop and followed the man, keeping a safe distance all the way to Bedford Street, where the man knocked at number eighty-six: Chumley's. Arthur waited a few minutes, then went in. The brown-hatted man was already at a table in the back, a drink in hand.

Arthur took a seat next to him and ordered a Coca-Cola.

"You're late," the man growled without looking over.

"I couldn't get away."

The man snorted. "I'll bet. You responsible for that business at Marlowe's mine?"

"You told me to gain their trust. To encourage them."

"Well, you certainly did that." The man took out a pack of Wrigley's gum. He offered it to Arthur, who shook his head. "And what about Mabel Rose?"

Arthur's jaw tightened. "What about her?"

"She's the enemy. Or have you forgotten?"

Arthur sipped his soda. "You don't know her. She's a good egg."

"She's the daughter of muckraking socialists. She cavorts with Diviners and anarchists. I'd say that's far from innocent. The Bureau wants her taken down, too. We get her, we get her parents. We get her parents, we get a whole load of socialists in jail."

"That wasn't part of my deal."

"Your deal was whatever we say your deal is," the man said. "You avoided prison, Arthur. If you want to keep on avoiding prison, you'll feed us the information we need until we round up every Red in this town. We still have your brother, you know. We could execute him at any time. We could take you back in. Blowing up Marlowe's mine wasn't in the plans."

"I had to make a decision. Nobody got hurt!"

"Keep it down." The man waited until the people around them had gone back to their booze. "I know you, you little agitator. You *wanted* to blow up that mine. And I suppose Miss Rose was part of that little excursion."

"No. She didn't know anything about it."

"You lying to me, Arthur?"

Arthur stared the G-man down. "I'm telling you: She's innocent."

The man socked Arthur, bloodying his lip. People looked on, shocked. And then they looked away again.

"The Bureau wants an arrest. Mr. Hoover wants to purge this country of radical scum. Your job was to deliver the Secret Six, nice and neat."

Arthur wiped his lip with his knuckles. "You already have my brother!"

"And now we want the rest. Minus you, of course. By the way, you might be interested in this. It'll be in tomorrow's paper. Don't disappoint us, Mr. Brown." The man grabbed his brown hat, squaring it over his ears, and left the newspaper on the table.

Arthur read the front page. Then he went into the bathroom to throw up.

☀

Arthur wandered to Washington Square Park, where he sat for hours, watching the cars drive under the arch, the newspaper still tucked under his arm. By the time he returned to his apartment, the Secret Six were there waiting for him.

"There you are!" Gloria said. "We were about to send out a search party."

"Arthur, what is it?" Mabel asked, concerned. "And what happened to your lip?"

He swiped a mug from the sink, filled it with cold water from the tap and swallowed it all down. Then he dropped into a chair and buried his face in his hands, squeezing his fingers in his hair.

"Arthur?" Mabel said, softer this time.

He swiped a hand down over his face. "Early this morning, the militia boys went after the miners with guns. The women and children took cover in the holes they'd dug inside the tents." Arthur paused. He was fighting for every word. Mabel felt as if he were speaking to her from very far away, as if she were in a dream and her one mission was to keep whatever he said next from coming out. "It was chaos in the camp. And then the lanterns caught on one of the tents. The wind was strong."

"No," Gloria whispered, burying her face in her hands. "No, no, no, no."

"The women and children were trapped in the tents. The tents were on fire. The children…" Arthur stumbled on the word. "The children screamed. And the men just kept shooting."

"Those sons of bitches," Aron said, sniffing back tears. Mabel had never seen Aron cry.

"Hearst is already putting the blame on the miners. Saying they started it," Arthur said, throwing down the newspaper. Gloria scooped it up and read aloud, "'Anarchists to Blame for Fiery Fiasco. Striking Workers Blow Up Mine and Set Fire to Camp.' Those liars!"

"What do you expect? Marlowe can have the story written any way he likes," Aron said.

"Twelve dead kids and they're blaming the striking workers. And the Secret Six," Arthur said. "Mr. Hoover has vowed to put more muscle behind finding us. I don't think we should meet here anymore. They might be watching."

The night before seemed incredibly far away to Mabel now. She tried to remember the feel of Arthur's arms around her as they lay in his bed under the creaking attic roof. Everything had seemed so right; now nothing did.

"We told them to trust us," Luis said. "We said they would be safe. That Marlowe would cave. What do we do now?"

In the high white shine of the street lamp leaking through the garret windows, Arthur's eyes were the bright blue of the day before. "We make Marlowe pay."

By the time they'd finished talking, it was nearly dawn. The milk wagons jangled up Bleecker Street. In the distance, the elevated Sixth Avenue train rattled around a curve. The newspapers would be hitting the streets in bundles any minute.

"Luis, you know where to get what we need."

"Yeah. I know a fella. Doesn't ask too many questions. He's sympathetic to the cause."

"Are we decided, then?" Arthur said.

"Yes." Gloria held out her hand.

"Yes," Aron and Luis said, adding theirs on top.

Arthur turned to Mabel.

"You're talking about assassination. About murder," she said, looking down at her hands. They seemed small and useless to her just now.

"Like they murdered all those children," Gloria shot back.

"Fine. Leave her out of it. We'll do it without her," Aron said.

"No," Arthur said. "It's all of us or it's none of us. Mabel?"

Mabel thought of her parents, fighting for justice their whole lives. She thought of their small victories, eked out by pennies. They'd always said that there was no room for violence. It was an inviolable rule. In her mind, Mabel saw her father at his typewriter, diligently reporting on some new struggle or cause. She saw her mother standing up to her own family, turning her back on an easy life of wealth in order to marry a penniless Jewish socialist. They were principled, her parents. They'd be horrified to know where she was, who she had become, what she was thinking of doing. But she was not part of their generation. She had come to see that their ways were antiquated. What had their methods gotten anyone? Not enough. Twelve dead children, burned to bones, lying on a field in New Jersey because of one man's greed. Her parents were wrong. There were no rules anymore. You had to fight fire with fire.

Mabel joined hands with the others.

THE EXCEPTIONAL AMERICAN

In the days before the opening of Jake Marlowe's Future of America Exhibition, New York had the feel of a giant carnival. The days were warmer. The rains that started the month had now given way to late-April sunshine. Beauty parlors were packed with girls having fresh marcel waves put into their hair. Store windows advertised SMART SUITS AND HATS FOR THE MAN WITHOUT LIMIT, THE MAN LOOKING TOWARD THE FUTURE OF AMERICA! The mood was optimistic. No one gave a damn about ghosts. It was as if overnight, everyone had agreed that what had come before was nothing but a bad dream best forgotten.

"All anybody wants to talk about is this exhibit," Woody explained to Evie over pie at the Automat when she'd begged him to write another story about the Diviners. "Sorry, Sheba. But that's the truth of it. I couldn't get you an inch of column space. The ghost craze is over. Diviners are on their way out, like yesterday's dance sensation."

"But it isn't a craze!" Evie insisted. "There is real evil at work, Woody."

He shrugged. "Not when Jake Marlowe makes folks feel good about being American, like they can't lose."

The phone had stopped ringing at Diviners Investigations. Evie had taken to scouring the papers for any mention of a sighting. "Just like Will," she chided herself. The only ghosts they'd hunted down, near a slip in the seaport, had taunted them openly. "Do you think you can stop this? You'll never best him." And just before they annihilated the wraith, sending its atoms who-knew-where, it had fixed them with a stare: "This is the history: blood." When the exhilaration of the kill had fled them, they collapsed, skin crawling, stomachs aching as if they might retch. They were exhausted. And no closer to finding Conor.

Evie had heard nothing from Jericho since the awful weekend at Hopeful Harbor. She supposed that was as it should be—she needed time to sort through her messy, conflicting feelings. But she was sad to have lost their friendship. Mabel wasn't returning her calls, either. "Sorry, I'm just awfully busy," Mabel had said the one time Evie had managed to catch her at home. She'd sounded strange, though—evasive. And Evie wondered if their friendship would ever recover.

❋

With only two days to go before the exhibition's opening, WGI was hosting a celebration for Jake Marlowe at a swanky hotel near the New York Stock Exchange and broadcasting it on air live. Will Rogers would perform. So would W. C. Fields, Fanny Brice, and rising star Theta Knight. And there would be an interview with Sarah Snow and Evie O'Neill—the Divine and the Diviner.

At the sound of applause, Theta elbowed Evie. "Here comes your competition." She nodded toward Sarah Snow, who was gliding through the ballroom in her signature white—a long satin dress for the occasion and a fresh white corsage nestled against ropes and ropes of pearls, which Evie was sure had not been provided by Jesus. Sarah waved, and then she joined Jake Marlowe, gazing up at him with beaming adoration.

"She's laying it on a bit thick, isn't she?" Evie grumbled.

Theta adjusted Evie's rhinestone headband atop her freshly styled bob. "Listen, kid, you got one mission: Get out there and sparkle for WGI so that old buzzard, Mr. Phillips, and everybody else in here thinks you're the cat's pajamas. You're gonna have to watch that tongue of yours. Can you manage it for one night?"

Evie pasted on a big smile. She batted her lashes like a deranged ingenue. "Look at me! Aren't I just the dahhhlingest? I only talk about the weathahhhh and the goodness of people's heahhhts."

Theta smirked. "Get it all out now, Evil, before you step up to that microphone."

Evie scowled. "There isn't even any hooch!"

Theta gave Evie a gentle push toward the room. "Go be charming."

The hotel's ballroom swirled with Important People: congressmen, the mayor, radio and motion picture stars. Everyone had turned out for Jake Marlowe's big gala. The theme was "The Exceptional American." Everything had been draped in red, white, and blue crepe. Wearing an angelic expression, Sarah Snow moved from table to table, shaking hands with the fawning wives of men who were also working the room, doing whatever took them to the top. The joint smelled of perfume, steak, cigar smoke, desperation, and ambition. Evie wanted to be as far from Sarah as she could get. She headed for the other side of the room.

Passing through the ballroom, she caught snippets of conversation:

"...I hear Miss Snow received two thousand fan letters last week...."

"...Two thousand? Why, I heard it was five...."

Envy burned up Evie's throat. Her pasted-on smile drooped.

"...I like Marlowe. He speaks his mind...."

"...He oughta run for president. After all, I hear the Democrats are putting up Al Smith again, and he's a Catholic...don't wanna answer to the pope...."

"...Like this Mussolini fella. Now he's really taken Italy by the reins and instilled genuine national pride. Seems like we need a little of that over here...."

"Hear, hear! America first."

Someone tapped Evie on the shoulder. She turned and found herself face-to-face with T. S. Woodhouse.

"I need to talk to you, Sheba," he said.

"Can't it wait? I—"

Woody opened his tuxedo jacket, showing her his flask.

"Lead the way, Mr. Woodhouse," Evie said.

In the hustle and bustle of the hotel kitchen, Evie knocked back several belts of strong whiskey, coughing heartily. Her lungs were on fire. "Whoo!"

"My bootlegger is a good man," Woody said.

"What did you want to talk about?" Evie asked when she found her voice again.

"Remember that matter you asked me to look into?"

"Jumping into the river in concrete overshoes?" Evie teased.

Woody smirked in appreciation. "That was good whiskey. Don't make me sorry I shared it. I meant Project Buffalo. Take a look at this."

He slid over the day's newspaper. Evie unfolded it and glanced at the page.

"You wanted me to know that there's a sale at Gimbels?"

Woody tapped the article above the ad. Evie's brow creased as she read. It was a small police blotter paragraph about a man who'd been found dead in the East River. Evie gasped when she came to the dead man's name. "Bob Bateman!"

"Strangled with a wire."

"Just like Sam's informant, Ben Arnold."

Woody nodded grimly. "I found an interesting connection between your Bob Bateman and Sam's Ben Arnold. You ever hear of these Better Baby contests?"

"There's no such thing as a better baby. They're all monsters in pinafores who scream and spit up on your best dress."

"You're gonna make a fine mother someday."

Evie took another swig of whiskey. "You were saying?"

"They were contests offered by Fitter Families for Future Firesides."

"Those tents they have at state fairs? Jericho and I saw one of them upstate in Brethren. They're eugenics programs, aren't they?" Evie said, holding back on what she knew. She wasn't ready to let Woody in on that yet. "Some nonsense about breeding superior people, as if we were sheep."

"Some people are sheep," Woody said. "Anyway, they were supposed to help women have some idea how to make their babies healthier. Guidelines. But they were also an anti-immigration campaign. Some folks don't like the idea of America being a melting pot. The slogan was 'a better baby means a better country.' Turns out Bob Bateman and Ben Arnold worked for Fitter Families. Now, here's where it gets interesting."

Woody paused for effect.

"Woody, if you turn this into an Agatha Christie novel, I'll…" Evie grabbed a saltshaker from the counter. "I'll bludgeon you with this."

Woody cast a dubious glance at the tiny silver shaker. Evie put it down with a flounce. "Well, I'd have to hit you a lot. But I'm up to the task, I assure you."

"The same folks helping to fund Fitter Families also gave money to the U.S. Department of Paranormal. An outfit comprised of the most powerful men in America—Rockefeller, Carnegie, Harriman. It's called—"

"The Founders Club!"

Woody frowned. "You stole my big finish."

"I know about them. They were at Marlowe's estate when we were there. A secret club meeting."

Woody jotted down a note. "I've been sniffing around these Fitter Family tents here and there. They're not just giving folks tests to see if they've got a bogus goodly heritage so those same folks can go home with a medal to show off. They're asking people if they've got any special psychic talents and whatnot."

Evie's brows furrowed as she remembered the pamphlet she'd seen at the asylum. "Why are they looking for Diviners?"

"Dunno. But I heard a rumor that when they do find one of those special types, sometimes those people go missing later." Woody shook his head. "Something's rotten about this whole story, kid."

"I suppose you think we're making it all up," Evie said, steeling for a fight.

"On the contrary. I think we're onto something big."

The kitchen doors swung open, and with them came the sound of Sarah Snow singing a hymn with her band, the Christian Crusaders. Woody frowned. "Sarah Snow's getting mighty popular."

"Sarah Snow, Sarah Snow," Evie griped, and took another drink. "Honestly, if I never hear that name again…"

"She's got a pulpit on the radio."

"I'm on the radio, too, you know!"

"I'm just saying: Reading Aunt Polly's brooch to find a lost key to a safe-deposit box isn't the same as somebody telling folks that God doesn't like Diviners and thinks they're dangerous. I've seen how that tide can turn. Watch your back, Sheba."

Evie knocked back more booze. "I can handle myself just fine."

Woody's brows creased into a V. "Don't you have to give an interview tonight, Sheba?"

"I can handle my hooch just fine, too."

The whiskey had softened the edges of Evie's nerves, which was a good thing because Sarah was already onstage by the microphones, and the sound boys were gesturing wildly to Evie. Sarah might've gone for white, but Evie had gone for gold, like a star, and her mouth was painted a perfect Cupid's bow red. She smiled as she flounced toward the stage, then remembered she was supposed to be "good" and straightened her spine like a politician's wife. *See? Look how very lovable and demure I am! Don't you like me now?* Some of the Blue Noses still looked at her with disapproval. As much as Evie wanted to pretend that their judgments didn't matter, they crawled under her skin and made her nervous.

"Stand here, sweetheart," the engineer said, leading Evie to her spot. He sniffed, smelling the whiskey on her breath, and Evie wished she'd gobbled a peppermint candy. Everybody was here. And Mr. Phillips was watching. Beside Evie, Sarah was the picture of serenity. Evie sought out Theta at the back of the room. Theta nodded, and that calmed Evie some.

"Why, look who's here! It's none other than two of WGI's greatest ladies of the airwaves, Miss Sarah Snow and Miss Evie O'Neill, the Divine—and the Diviner!"

The audience laughed good-naturedly. The reporters started in easily enough with lots of softball questions about how excited Evie and Sarah were to attend the exhibition ("Oh, very!"), their favorite nightclubs (Evie: "The Hotsy Totsy and the Twenty-one Club." Sarah: "My nightclub is the church, and Jesus never charges a cover."), and what they liked best about being on the radio (Evie: "My wonderful fans!" Sarah: "My faithful listeners.").

The familiar killing gleam showed in Woody's eyes. "Miss Snow, you're a real supporter of Prohibition. What've you got against a good time?"

Evie suppressed a giggle. She could kiss Woody.

Sarah chuckled. "I believe you don't need spirits if you've got the Holy Spirit, Mr. Woodhouse," Sarah said in her comforting midwestern accent, her vowels as flat and familiar as prairie grass. No one had made *her* take elocution lessons, Evie noted.

"Didn't Jesus turn water into wine?" Evie said. "Why, he was the original bootlegger!"

Some of the reporters chuckled, but at many of the tables, there were pinched faces. Evie's mouth went dry.

"What do *you* make of all these supposed ghost sightings in our city?" Harriet Henderson. *The old snake.*

The slightest crease appeared in Sarah's normally serene brow. "I can't help but wonder if these terrifying apparitions are signs from the Lord that we should return to old-fashioned values. And turn away from Diviners."

Sarah pointedly ignored Evie and looked toward those tables of overly powdered rich women and the reporters furiously jotting down her words. "It's all very *entertaining* to read secrets in a handkerchief or ring, I suppose. But dancing in nightclubs won't fill the bowls of the hungry. Telling fortunes above a tea shop won't help the man who's out of work or worried about losing the family farm. There's only one power I believe in, only one true Diviner, and that is Jesus Christ Almighty."

"Sounds like you're taking a page from Jake Marlowe, Miss Snow. He's not including Diviners in his Future of America Exhibition. He says they're un-American." Harriet cast a furtive glance Evie's way.

I've been set up, Evie realized.

"I'm afraid I must agree with Mr. Marlowe," Sarah said with a gentle shake of her head. "These are frightening times. Americans are frightened of threats from without and within. I can't help but wonder: What if any of these so-called Diviners were anarchists? What if their loyalties were not to America first? Why, with their special powers, they could be very dangerous, indeed."

"Say, I hadn't thought about that," one reporter muttered, taking down notes.

Evie knew this jaded lot; most of them had a secret flask and a betting form in each pocket. They weren't usually the sort to fall for this, but not one of the reporters pushed back.

Sarah beamed. "But here's our Mr. Marlowe now! I'm sure you'd much rather hear his thoughts than mine. Jake, join us, won't you?"

Sarah beckoned Marlowe, and the crowd erupted with cries of "Speech! Speech!" Evie could feel the night slipping away from her. The crowd sang "For He's a Jolly Good Fellow" until an abashed Jake Marlowe took the stage. Sarah laid her hand on his arm and gazed up at him with adoration again, and Evie wondered if she practiced that expression in her mirror each night as she slathered on her cold cream.

"I didn't know you went in for that old-time religion, Mr. Marlowe," a reporter said.

"Well, I didn't realize just how pretty some of God's missionaries were," Jake said, and Sarah pretended to be embarrassed, but Evie knew she loved it. The audience loved it, too.

"When's the wedding?" someone shouted to much laughter. Sarah and Jake were giving them quite a show.

"Like Miss Snow, I care very much about this country," Jake said, turning serious again.

"I care about our country, too!" Evie said feebly. She put extra polish on the silver-tongued vowels she'd been practicing an hour each day, but the whiskey was catching up to her. Her words weren't as crisp as she'd like. "Diviners help all sorts of people. Why, just last week, a little girl came to me with the collar of her dog. Poor little thing was all brokenhearted. I got a read off the collar, and within the hour, she'd found little Fifi."

"Our lady of lost pets," a reporter joked just loud enough to be picked up by the microphone. This got a roar of laughter from everyone, and Evie's cheeks burned. She also wished her head weren't quite so fuzzy. Woody's booze had been much stronger than her usual. She shouldn't have drunk it so quickly on an empty stomach. It had hit her hard and fast.

"My brother died serving this country," Evie blurted out, and immediately regretted it.

There was a glint in Marlowe's eye.

"Say, weren't you and Miss O'Neill's uncle once best friends?" a reporter asked.

It was the first time that Jake Marlowe's smile faltered. "Once," Jake said meaningfully. "But we're very different fellas. He has an obsession with our history, with our ghosts." Jake Marlowe shook his head. "We're a country of the future. We're not haunted by anything."

"But, Mr. Marlowe, they say that those who don't heed the lessons of the past are doomed to repeat them."

"Not if they're Americans!" Marlowe said, the microphone echoing his words into the crowd in split-second waves that met with thunderous applause. "But these Diviners, well, what if they could know secrets about us they shouldn't? I think that's a real threat. I'm afraid I find the entire idea of Diviners unseemly. And Un-American."

Evie couldn't hold herself in any longer. "I hear the Ku Klux Klan feels the same way. So you're in fine company, Mr. Marlowe!"

There were gasps in the crowd.

"Uh-oh. Trolley's off the tracks," Theta whispered to Woody at the back of the room.

Onstage, Marlowe's eyes glittered with something hard. Seeing his expression was like hearing a shot half a second before seeing the gun. "Is that so? From what I hear, your brother wasn't a war hero but a deserter."

"That's a lie and you know it!" Evie slurred.

"What did she say?"

"She called Jake Marlowe a liar!"

"The nerve!"

"Terrible girl."

Terrible girl. Evie might as well have been back in Ohio, listening to the small-minded gossips. That nasty smallness was everywhere, it seemed. The whiskey had been a mistake. It had made her dizzy. It had also made her bold.

"You know what happened to my brother," Evie said through clenched teeth. "It was you. You and the Founders Club and those terrible Shadow Men and—and Project Buffalo!"

"Dammit," Woody muttered under his breath.

Jake smirked. "My, even the United States Army was in on this supposed conspiracy? It seems I'm in excellent company."

The room roared with laughter. At her.

What could Evie say? That they had a telegram proving James's death? That was a lie. She was telling the truth, even if she had absolutely no proof of it. It was her word against his, and he would win.

"James was no deserter," was all she could say. Her face was hot.

"I would have liked to have spared your poor parents the truth, but very well, Miss O'Neill. You've pushed me to this: Your brother, James O'Neill, was a deserter. He was shot and killed trying to desert his post by a *real* war hero, Luther Clayton. And now Luther Clayton is dead. Why, if I were as conspiracy-minded as you are, Miss O'Neill, I might suspect that a Diviner with a radio show paid a poor, shell-shocked veteran to stage a shooting just to keep her in the public eye. And then I might wonder why that poor soldier died after that same Diviner visited him."

Evie was reeling. "That isn't true and you know it!" She grabbed for the microphone and stumbled, nearly tumbling off the stage, until Sarah righted her. She sniffed, frowning at Evie.

"Why, Miss O'Neill," Sarah said in a whisper she had to know would be picked up by the live microphone. "Have you been drinking?"

The audience was booing Evie openly now. "Get her off the stage!"

Mr. Phillips was motioning for Sarah to sing. "Ladies and gentlemen, at this celebration of our great nation, won't you join me in a favorite hymn?"

As Evie left the stage, some of the men at the expensive tables still booed her while their wives looked at her with contempt. And Evie realized that Sam had been right—no matter how much she tried to make herself fit, eventually, the real, smart-mouthed Evie would come bursting out of the confining party cake with all of her opinions and wounds on display.

Onstage, the Crusaders played Sarah's signature hymn while she sang along in her sweet soprano: "*Onward Christian soldiers, marching as to war, with the cross of Jesus, going on before…*"

One by one, the people at the tables took up the song. They sang as one voice. Inside, Evie was crumbling. Tears coursed down her cheeks. Theta wasn't singing. And neither was Woody. He offered Evie his handkerchief. "Tide's turning, Sheba," he said soberly.

As the song drew to its close, a man burst into the room, his eyes wild. His shouts couldn't be heard above the din in the room, though.

"*What? What's he saying?*" the guests repeated to one another until the man's desperate cries could at last be heard.

"Ghosts!" he screeched. "Ghosts in the streets!"

WE WILL BE HEARD

An ominous fog bank spread across the far end of Wall Street, rolling slowly forward. From inside it came the steady thrum of marching feet and the clanging of chains—a phantom army on the move.

"What is that?" Woody asked from the steps below, his notebook open and his hand shaking.

"That thing people told us not to worry about," Evie replied.

"Ghosts!" The murmur passed through the crowd, not yet hysteria.

"Stay here. I'm going to call in the troops," Theta said, squeezing through the crush of curious swells and back into the hotel.

The dark, billowing cloud advanced another block, then stopped. For several long minutes, the ghosts, shrouded in gloom, kept their distance. An electric stillness filled the air, a storm held under a bell jar, just waiting to be unleashed. The crowd burbled with nervous excitement and growing dread: "What are they doing?" "I don't know." "Will they hurt us?" "Where are the police?"

Theta raced back to Evie's side, breathless. "I called Henry and Sam. They're grabbing everybody and coming down here."

"How long?"

Theta gave a New Yorker's shrug.

Sirens rang out, followed by the shriek of whistles as the police arrived. They pushed back the people and set up barricades, as if that could stop what waited in the fog.

"Ling! Over here!" Theta called, spying Alma helping Ling navigate through the gawkers lined up ten deep on the sidewalks. News had spread fast.

"I got here as quickly as I could. Mr. Leong will be upset when he doesn't get his tea," Ling said. "What is happening?"

Evie pointed to the end of the street.

"Are the others...?"

"On their way," Theta confirmed. And not two minutes later, a taxi swerved to the curb, and out jumped Henry and Sam.

"'Scuse us, 'scuse us. Would ya move outta the way, pal?" Sam barked as he and Henry pushed through the crowd to join their friends.

"Where's Memphis and Isaiah?" Theta asked.

"Uptown," Henry explained, and Sam groaned. There was no telling when they'd show up. It was a long way through New York City's infamous traffic.

More whistles sounded as the police fanned out along the barricades and aimed their guns at the menacing fog.

"Fire!" the captain called, and the streets echoed with tight pops of gunfire.

"Hold!" the captain shouted.

The streets smelled of smoke. The fog was still there, unchanged.

"Did we get them?" a policeman asked.

As one, the ghosts screeched. The sound, terrifying, echoed through the canyons of Lower Manhattan. And then they marched forward, terrifying the crowd of onlookers, who screamed and pushed. Some of the guests tried to run back to the hotel, sending others tumbling on the steps. It was chaos.

"We'll be trampled!" Theta said, trying to help Ling to a safer place. But there was no safer place. The six of them stood in the middle of the street as the police fell back.

"They're panicking," Ling said.

"Probably because there's a ghost army headed straight for us," Sam answered.

A man in a tuxedo pointed to the Diviners. "Do something!" he shouted, and soon others picked up the call. "Yes, do something!"

"Everybody's watching us," Henry said.

"Might be a good time to show 'em what we can do," Sam said. "To show 'em we're the real McCoy."

"Not without Memphis and Isaiah!" Theta said.

"Theta! Theta!" Memphis was running toward them, with Isaiah gasping at his heels. "What's happening?"

Theta nodded toward the murky ghost army headed their way.

"How many you think?" Sam asked.

"Twenty, twenty-five," Ling said.

Henry shook his head. "We've never tried to take out that many before."

On the steps of the hotel, people screamed. "Do something! Save us!"

The ghosts were getting closer. Figures emerged in the murk, taking clearer shape.

"Slaves," Memphis said. "The ghosts of slaves."

The Diviners came together. Electricity sparked off the sides of the buildings and climbed up the front of the Stock Exchange. The people gaped in awe. *"Did you see that? What is that? What are they?"*

"Get ready. It's gonna take a lot of energy to blast 'em," Sam called.

Memphis stared at the iron shackles around the ghosts' feet and necks. Something shifted inside him. "I…I don't know if this is right," he said to the others.

"But, Memphis, everybody's watching us!" Isaiah said.

"Doesn't matter if it's wrong," Memphis said. He took a step forward, heart beating fast as he addressed the ghosts. "You need to leave these people alone," he tried. "Go back now. Go back to your graves."

The ghosts spoke as one: "And if we refuse, Healer?"

"You…you know who I am?" Memphis asked.

"We know much."

"Memphis…" Theta warned.

"Get rid of them! Destroy them!" the people shouted. Their voices were a frenzy. A bloodlust.

"Then we'll have to send you back ourselves," Memphis said to the ghosts.

"Would you send us back without knowing our story? We will speak. We will be heard," the ghosts whispered in one groaning voice. "We know this street. We built it. There was the auction block where we were bought and sold. Where our children were torn from us. If we were to cry for ourselves, there would be no land, only an ocean of salt. And when we rebelled, they murdered us. They left our heads to rot upon sticks along Wall Street for all to see."

The ghosts surged forward quickly and reached their hands into Memphis's chest. He felt the cold spreading as their molecules were joined. His limbs shook like downed wires in a storm.

"Memphis!" Theta screamed, but Memphis was already under, dragged into the world of the dead.

"See," the ghosts whispered, and their voices swirled inside him. "Feel. Know."

The ship pitched violently on the rough seas. The dark was all-consuming. It smelled of sick, of vomit and urine and defecation. Above all, it smelled of fear. Memphis could feel the presence of so many others. More chained men beside him, above him, below. One long human chain of misery. Cracked, desperate voices prayed to the gods, begging first for freedom, then for death. Iron shackles chafed Memphis's wrists and ankles.

The rolling green of farmland and tobacco fields. Men in powdered wigs shot rifles at birds. In the distance, the big house—domed, scrubbed, white—loomed like a predator.

"Release!" the gentleman of the house called.

The birds flew up. The shots rang out. Bloodied feathers fell from the sky and pierced the ground. The slave gathered the dead and dying birds, some still twitching, in a bag. In his study lit by precious tallow candles, the gentleman kept his ledgers. Columns that weighed souls like grains of rice. The slave stood at the ready. At his master's commands, he could only nod, his tongue having been cut out.

"We hold these truths to be self-evident…"

The auction block loomed, a gateway to misery. The frightened, half-dead and chained, blinking in the light of a new world.

"That all men are created equal…"

A family scattered to the winds like seeds whose blooms were a resilience borne of grief. The chains. The iron masks. The teeth torn from mouths. The dogs set loose.

"That they are endowed by their creator with certain unalienable rights."

The crack of the whip.

"That among these are life, liberty, and the pursuit of happiness."

"Stop!" Memphis screamed.

When Memphis came to, he fell to his knees, crying in the middle of Wall Street. His blood itched beneath his skin like a rash he could never fully scratch. He had seen. He had felt. He knew. When he looked up into the faces of the ghosts, he remembered the wraith in the graveyard and the family at the table and his mother's tearstained face lit by the jaundiced moonlight in the land of the dead.

"Tell our story. Do not forget us," the ghosts whispered.

The people on the steps had grown impatient in their fear: "Why don't you do something about this?" "Yeah! Make 'em go away!" "Kill them!" "Get rid of them!"

Memphis stood.

"Memphis, come on," Sam urged. He reached for Memphis and Memphis shrugged him off.

"No."

He turned to face the people cowering on the steps of the hotel. "No. These are our ghosts. They're here. We're gonna have to learn to live with them."

"What's he saying?" "He's gone anarchist on us!" "I knew we couldn't trust those Diviners!"

"They just want us to listen," Memphis said to the others. "We've been trying to get rid of them instead of listening to what they need to say to us. Your uncle was right about that, Evie: We have to see them ghost by ghost."

The people gathered in front of the hotel were still terrified, though. Terrified people were a threat. Ling had been right about that, Memphis knew.

"Look upon your sins," the ghosts cried.

"What's your name?" Memphis asked the ghost in front.

"My name?" The ghost turned his head toward the night sky as if it might be written there. "My name is Lost. For I was stolen. What is stolen, haunts."

"They're going to riot soon," Ling said, casting a wary glance at the people on the steps and the police reloading.

"I need you to trust me on something," Memphis said.

"Okay, pal," Sam said. "You're scaring me, but okay."

"We're with you." Evie and Henry and Ling nodded. Theta took his hand.

"We will tell your story. You will not be forgotten. I wish you a peaceful rest," Memphis said to the ghosts. He placed his hands against the chest of the leader. As they were joined, he saw birds against blue skies. He heard the laughter of children. And for just a moment, he saw his mother in her feathered cape lying under a stripped tree in that blighted land of shadow and yellow moonlight with Conor Flynn nestled close under her wing. She sat up, smiling through tears.

"Yes," she said. "Yes. I believe in you, my son."

Memphis let go.

"Healer," the man whose name was Lost said. "He builds the new Eye from the ashes of the old. It will keep the door between worlds from closing ever again. It will allow the King of Crows to stay here forever. To sow chaos and division. Hate and terror. Until your dreams lay in tatters and you no longer recognize yourselves. You must not allow this to happen."

The ghosts walked through the Diviners, fading bit by bit, until they were a part of the city itself.

"They're gone," Evie said.

But the people on the steps looked at the Diviners as if they were a threat.

"Dangerous," somebody said.

"Oughta lock 'em up."

Sarah Snow came forward, her arms raised. "Let us pray, brothers and sisters. Pray for the soul of our nation! To be rid of those who would tear it asunder! Heavenly Father…"

The people bowed their heads.

"You thought telling the people the truth would make a difference." Ling shook her head. "Now they just hate us for telling them the truth. People want to be safe, not free."

"What now?" Evie asked.

But Memphis had his head angled toward the sky. "We're listening," he said. "We're listening."

A SPIT IN THE EYE

Sam had seen Evie back to the Winthrop. And after the shock of the night's confrontation with the ghosts had worn off, Evie told him about the rest of the terrible evening, from Woody's revelations to Jake's lies and her own humiliating downfall. "Gotta hand it to you, Lamb Chop. When you go for something, you go all in," he said, feeding her more aspirin and water.

"If Jake Marlowe wants to attack me, I'll take it. But James did everything they asked of him and more. He was a hero, and now Jake's calling him a coward and a deserter. I hate Jake Marlowe. I hate him so much."

"I'm not arguing with you, Baby Vamp. He won this round."

"He's rich. He'll win all the rounds," Evie said. "Sam, Project Buffalo happened, but we have no proof. And now those Shadow Men are going around killing people who *could* prove it. And somewhere out there is the King of Crows playing games. It feels as if nothing matters. Truth, honor, trying to do what's right. None of it matters."

"That's awfully cynical."

"I feel cynical."

"There's still stuff to believe in. Still good."

"Yeah? Like what?"

"Well, for one, we're still fighting. We haven't given up."

"What else?" Evie challenged.

"For another, Memphis and Theta are back together. We did something spectacular tonight, something that felt…right. And Mabel Rose is out there working for the people."

Evie nodded. "What else? Keep telling me the good things."

Sam could feel a head of steam building inside him. But he didn't know if he'd be brave enough to let it out. "There's a Douglas Fairbanks picture at the Strand. A swashbuckler. You love those."

Evie closed one eye. "You're telling me not to lose hope because there are pirate pictures?"

"I'm trying here, Baby Vamp. When you're facing evil, a good pirate picture doesn't hurt."

Evie's mouth twitched into a bit of a smile, but she fought it. She liked hearing Sam's list, and she didn't want him to stop. "What else?"

"Nah. I've told you already."

"Oh, please. Just one more."

Sam cocked his head. "Just one more, huh?"

"Yeah. But make it a really good one."

"A good one."

"Yes."

"Okay."

Sam's heart thudded against his ribs. He was dizzy.

"Then how about this."

And with that, he leaned forward and kissed her. Evie put a hand to her lips and stared at Sam.

"Um. You might say something here. Or slap me. Hoping it's not that, though," Sam joked, and swallowed hard.

"How do I know that's real?" Evie said after she'd caught her breath.

"Let me prove it." Sam kissed her again, longer this time.

And for the first time that night, Evie did feel loved. Sam wasn't telling her to act more like a "good girl." He didn't want her to be anybody but who she was. Why had she tortured herself by not letting him in?

"I'm still not convinced," Evie said. Her head buzzed. "You…you might have to make your case more strongly."

Sam's grin was wolfish, but inside he was balloons and champagne, a full goddamn birthday party. "Sure thing, Lamb Chop."

Evie put a finger to Sam's lips and frowned. "I believe I have made my feelings about that name plain."

Sam licked up the length of her finger, drawing a gasp from her. "What can I say? I'm a naughty boy."

"How naughty?"

"Would you like to find out?"

Evie knew she should come back with a quip, but everything felt too real right now. She needed to be real with someone. "I would. But I'm afraid of what I'll find out. I just need something that doesn't feel like a lie."

"Okay." Sam swallowed hard, took a deep breath. "Then here it is: All the times I say, 'Don't see me'? With you, I wish I had an opposite power: See me. See me, Evie. See all of me. There's a fella who loves you right here. I'm not perfect. I'm a handful. But you know what? So are you. There. Not sugarcoating it."

"But . . . what if I love you and you go away?" Evie said, almost a whisper.

"Sheba, *I'm sitting across from you right now.* Don't you see that I'm not going anywhere?"

And she knew he was being honest. There was such fear in the world. But love was everywhere if you looked. It was the best thing about humans. That they could stare into the abyss and still open up their hearts. A spit in the eye to fear.

Evie laced her fingers with Sam's and rubbed her thumb gently across the delicate fretwork of veins at his wrist, the pulse of her thumb against the pulse beneath his skin, faintly felt but sure and constant. Later, she wouldn't be able to say who had kissed whom first. It didn't matter. It only mattered that they *were* kissing. They lay side by side on the peach satin quilt of her bed, bodies smashed together, Evie's top leg wedged between Sam's so that she could feel the heat of him pressed against her, making her dizzy from this new rush of desire.

Sam pulled away suddenly.

"Wha-what's the matter?" Evie panted. She wanted him back. Wanted nothing but to be doing what they had been doing. Ached for it.

He took her face in his hands and stared into her eyes, narrowing his own. "You're not possessed by ghosts this time, are you?"

Evie wrenched her head free from Sam's palms. "Sam, honestly!"

He grinned. "Just checking."

Evie kissed her way up the salty sweetness of his throat, to his ear, which she nibbled very softly, then whispered, "I am the Forgotten, forgotten no more."

"Holy moly!" Sam jumped and Evie fell back against the pillow in a fit of laughter.

"Oh, Sam, your face!"

"Not amusing, Sheba," Sam chided, but he was laughing, too.

Evie's giggles subsided, and now she caught her breath. He was beautiful to her. She reached her hand toward him, and if she lived for a hundred years more, she would never forget his expression, as if he had been lost in a dark wood for a very long time and she had just opened the door to him, light spilling out to let him know he was home at last.

"Where were we?" Sam asked, crawling back to her.

"We were right…" Evie kissed Sam. "About." And again. "Here."

"Here?" Sam pressed his lips to hers, warm and sure.

"Mm-hmm."

Sam scooped Evie up into his arms, and she wrapped hers around him, the two of them threaded together like a knot that would not easily be undone. It all moved rather furiously then. Sam unfastened the buttons of Evie's dress, and it slid to the floor in a sparkling pile. Evie lifted Sam's undershirt over his head and kissed the scar near his collarbone.

"Aerialist accident in the big tent," Sam explained.

"Mmm. Tell me later."

His trousers hit the floor along with his socks. Her slip was off. Sam fumbled with the hooks of her garter.

"I thought you were a ladies' man," Evie joked, taking over and rolling off her stockings. She was nervous.

"I'm not a hosiery salesman, though," Sam shot back. He sounded a little nervous, too. Evie removed her brassiere. Sam tugged off his boxers. Evie's pulse drummed in her head. She'd petted—every girl had, even the ones who pretended they hadn't. But this was a lot more than petting. She'd never seen a naked fella up close before, much less one she desperately wanted, even if she didn't know what to do next. She and Sam slipped under the covers. And then, suddenly, the whole night was too much. She was afraid. It was silly, wasn't it? She'd been ruined by Jake Marlowe and Sarah Snow. They'd faced a street full of ghosts, and she was afraid of this, this joining of bodies, this step toward love? Her cynicism was leaving her. She was opening herself up to something more. It was somehow the scariest thing in the whole world.

"Could we…could we just lie next to each other?" Evie said, eyes brimming with tears. "Just for a little while?"

"You're killing me, Sheba."

"Please? I'm sorry. I'm sorry."

Sam lifted her chin. "Hey. Don't be sorry. It's okay."

With that, he flipped onto his back and stared at the ceiling with great concentration.

"What are you doing?" Evie asked.

"Thinking of the least sexual thing I can imagine. Ghost *bubbes*. They're making ghost borscht and talking about their bowel troubles. Jeepers. I might never make love again. This is traumatic."

Evie burst out laughing. Then: "Sam. I changed my mind."

Sam turned to her. "About...?"

"You know." She reached under the covers and touched him, biting her lip at the surprise of what she felt.

Sam gasped. "You sure?" His voice was soft and a little breathy.

Evie nodded.

Sam wet his thumb with his mouth and slipped his hand between her legs, touching her gently there.

"You're sure-sure?" Sam murmured again, and sucked along her clavicle.

She felt as if she were an electrical wire thrumming with life.

"Sh-shut up and k-kiss me, Sam."

That night, as she lay wrapped in Sam's arms, Evie dreamed of stars falling through the sky, streaking tails of smoke until the sky was starless. The King of Crows raked his fingers across the dark until it bled. He licked the blood from his fingers with a forked tongue. "People will believe anything, you know. You only need them to be frightened enough."

480

THE SHADOW SELF

Theta had crept home in the early morning hours and slept for a while. When she left for rehearsal, she found that Memphis had left a letter for her. Excitedly, she tore it open and read:

Dearest Theta,
Eighth letter of the Greek alphabet, Symbol of Eternity, My Creole Princess,
    Today I saw your face in every crowd. In the shopgirl's furrowed brow, the tilt of a mother's head toward her curious son paused on the threshold of some new mischief, in the raised arm of a businessman hailing the bus before it leaves the curb, in the bow and sweep of the workers' backs as they balance atop the steel beams of the new Olympus. None was stranger to me, for every motion, every expression, every gesture seemed limned with the light of the Eternal Sympathy that connects us one to the other, the cosmic string of the universe that pulls from me to you. Outside my window, the blood of the city coursed along in a steady rhythm of trolleys and motorcars—"How-you-do?" and "Move it along!"—the percussive rumble of the Manhattan Possible, the angel's-wing whisper of six million dreams taking flight. But there was only one heartbeat for me.

Theta, Theta, Theta. I heard it beneath the hum of Broadway's bright lights. I heard it in the steady flow of the mighty Hudson, that wondrous river. I heard it in the clickety-clack of the elevated train and in the swift stepping of feet across congested thoroughfares, in the whistle of the traffic officer, the call-and-response of the shoeshine boys—those park-side preachers plying their trade, washing the feet of angels unaware. I heard it in a young girl's laugh and in the sigh of a descended Nubian Queen leaning from her window on St. Nicholas Avenue as she surveyed her kingdom of fire escapes and chimney smoke and washing on the line, her grasp one day within reach. I heard it, too, echoing from the halls of Ellis Island, where so many hopes press together they make of their discordant notes a new song whose melody is both celebration and lament, an echo and a prelude. And still the heartbeat calls to me: Theta. Theta. Theta.

"Among the men and women, the multitude, / I perceive one picking me out by secret and divine signs," the great poet Mr. Whitman wrote.

I can't say what the future holds. That is my brother's gift, not mine. I only know my heart has picked yours from the multitude, a secret sign, a small piece of the Divine, and it will not let go.

Forever,
Memphis

"You all right, Miss Knight?" The Bennington's doorman looked concerned. "You're crying."

"Yeah. I do that sometimes," she said, smiling.

But when Theta arrived at the New Amsterdam Theatre, her good mood vanished. She could tell something wasn't right. Wally barely made eye contact, and he patted his stomach like he did when he was nervous. "Oh, uh, hiya, Theta. Flo wants to see you in his office right away."

At first, Theta was afraid it was about what had happened at Jake Marlowe's party. The newspapers had reported on the disturbance, though many recanted, saying they couldn't be absolutely sure they'd seen ghosts—they'd just heard other people talking about it. The police refused to comment, reassuring the public that they should go about their business and enjoy the exhibition when it opened. But Harriet Henderson's column reported that there had, indeed, been a threat, and that the Diviners had refused to do anything about it. And if it hadn't been for Sarah Snow and the power of prayer, she hated to think what could've happened to the good citizens of New York City.

"Miss Knight. Take a seat, please," Mr. Ziegfeld said as Theta let herself into his office and perched on the edge of a chair. He was looking at her like she was a kid who'd done something disappointing. "I received a call from Harriet Henderson today. Seems there's a story she's sitting on."

Theta steeled herself to respond about the ghosts and her part in it.

"About a certain Follies girl who has a secret Negro lover up in Harlem?" Mr. Ziegfeld finished. "Is this true?"

Theta tried to swallow and found she could not. Her heartbeat thrummed in her ears. She hadn't expected this at all. There was no point in lying, she knew.

"Yes," Theta said, small as a mouse.

And now Mr. Ziegfeld looked at her with far more than just disappointment.

"Harriet was going to run with the story, but as a personal favor to me, Mr. Hearst agreed to kill it in exchange for exclusive access to you from now on."

Harriet would own her.

"How…how'd they…" Theta's mouth was so dry she couldn't swallow. "Find out?"

"An anonymous source. But the source claimed to have more secrets to bring to light. Many more. You can never see this fellow again. Is that understood, Miss Knight?"

Theta's head swam. Everything she'd tried to keep secret—her power, her past, her lover—was all being dragged into the light. There was nowhere to hide.

"Kitty had an affair with a married fella and came through okay. And Mae West got arrested for her show 'cause somebody said it was obscene. She's a bigger star than ever."

"There are scandals and there are scandals, Miss Knight. But some stories can't be rewritten. You being involved with a Negro is one of those stories. Why, it's against the law in most states in this country!"

"You ever think those laws might be wrong?" Theta said. She was queasy with fear.

Flo's stare was flinty. "I heard your screen test at Vitagraph went very well. If this gets out, do you think the Vitagraph boys will make a picture with you? I'm looking out for you."

Everything out of Flo's mouth was a threat dressed in the polite finery of protection and fatherly concern. It couldn't hide how awful it was.

"And I don't want you living with Henry anymore, either. Everybody knows he's not your brother, and even though he's obviously no ladies' man..." Flo said with distaste. "He's still a fella. You'll move into Miss Sheridan's Women's Dormitory, where the rules about gentlemen callers are properly enforced. And no more cavorting with that Sweetheart Seer and those unseemly Diviners. You will have nothing further to do with Diviners as long as you are in my show."

"Anything else?" Theta said, and there was no disguising her disdain.

Flo's eyes flashed. "Yes, there is—is it true you're married?"

And suddenly, it all made sense. Roy. Roy had done this to her. Hadn't he vowed revenge?

"I can see from your expression that it's true. That solves our troubles. We'll arrange for an exclusive with Harriet about your sudden wedding. How happy you are. The public can't get enough of love stories. That'll throw any vultures off the scent of scandal."

"This ain't a love story," Theta mumbled. Roy. She'd never be free of him. Her hands grew hot. "I-I need some air. I think I'm gonna be sick."

"Miss Knight!" Mr. Ziegfeld said crisply. "This is my show. I have a reputation to protect, and that includes your reputation. Without me, you'll be nothing. Ask yourself whether you want to be a star or a nothing. I'll expect your answer by tomorrow at the latest. I hope you'll make the smart choice."

On the way out, Theta tried to ignore the stares and whispers coming her way. She wanted to put her hands on the walls and watch the place burn down with everybody inside. Just thinking that frightened Theta. She really did feel sick now. Looking back, it seemed like her life had been a series of traps and snares. And every time she got free, somebody else tried to tie her up again.

There was a note waiting for her when she got home, and this time it wasn't from Memphis. It was wrapped up with an insulting picture of an actor in blackface. *Told you I'd get even, Betty*, it read.

Theta sat at her kitchen table staring dumbly at the note for some time, until she heard Henry whistling as he came through the door.

"What's the matter, *cher*?"

Theta took a shuddering breath, trying to draw it deeply into her lungs, but she couldn't. "He said he'd get me, and he did. I thought I could outrun him. I was wrong. Flo knows. About me and Memphis. It was Roy. He told Harriet Henderson and she called Flo."

"Did he can you?"

"No. But if I don't break it off with Memphis and move into a nunnery where he can watch me, he will. I'll lose his 'protection.' Harriet'll run with her story. I'll be finished. And who knows what'll happen to Memphis then?"

"Aww, Theta." Henry pulled her into a hug, and if Theta hadn't been completely numb, she would've broken down in the kindness of his arms.

"If I say yes, Hen, he'll own me. Everybody always wants to own me. If I don't say yes, I'll lose everything." The room's edges kept blurring. Theta's eyes stung.

Henry kissed the top of her head. "Not everything. You still got Memphis. And me. You've got all of us. You got your family."

And Roy. She could picture him at home in his room, smug and mean, ready for the next fight. That was the trouble with men like Roy. They just kept coming.

Unless you stopped them.

Theta pressed away from Henry. Her body didn't quite feel like hers, like when Roy used to hit her and she'd slip away to the ceiling, as if it were all happening to somebody else. She put on her coat.

"Theta? Where are you going, darlin'?"

"To end it. To end Roy."

"Theta? Darlin'. That's not the answer." Henry laced his fingers through hers, and she barely felt it. "Let's talk it over. I'll put on some shoes and change my shirt, and we'll go down to the Automat and have some lemon meringue pie, and we'll figure out this whole mess. Okay, *cher*?"

"Sure," Theta said. She floated in her skin. Nothing felt real.

Henry's voice drifted out from the bedroom, where he was getting dressed. He was telling her some story about Sam and Evie. It was just blather. He was trying to cheer her up. She wasn't really listening. She picked up the day's newspaper. In her hands, the edges blackened and curled up. And then she slipped out the door.

The street lights blurred into halos as the elevated train rumbled into the station. Theta rested her head against the window and watched the city fly by. He'd done it to her again. Not with his actual fists this time, but it was a punch all the same. Theta had spent so much energy trying to convince herself that she could never be anything like Roy. That there was not the same violence in her soul.

She could. There was.

What was it Dr. Jung had called it? The shadow self. Right now Shadow Theta enjoyed the heat pooling in her palms. Shadow Theta wanted Roy to know her power. She wanted to see the fear in his eyes.

Theta exited the train. She walked the crowded, dirty sidewalks of the Bowery, ignoring the men calling after her. Theta was barely aware of her body. She pressed against a wooden post and didn't care as it warped and browned under her touch. Sweat dripped down the valley between her shoulder blades. Her internal temperature soared. She dropped her coat in the street. She didn't need it. Her mind whirred:

"Where's my supper, Betty Sue? You need reminding that I don't like ham?"

The village burning. The men shooting. People bleeding into snow like trampled petals. Her frantic mother trying to run. The basket left on the church steps.

Abandoned. Alone.

"Why can't you fix yourself up a little?"

Mrs. Bowers pushing Theta onto the stage. "You get out there and make them love you."

Or I won't love you.

"You think you can win against me, Betty Sue? You'll never win against me!"

Theta stood on the street outside Roy's building, looking up. Third floor, third window, just above the fire escape. A light was on. He was home. Good. Theta went inside. Her palms were sweating. She pounded hard at Roy's door and watched the black flower of her fist-print bloom on the wood.

"'S open."

Roy lay in bed, muscled arms behind his head, the triumphant king in repose. She saw the bottle and smelled the booze. For a moment, the old fear returned. Memories of the way he could make her feel so small, so unsure, so worthless. The heat in her palms receded.

"Betty. Well, well, well. Not so high and mighty now, are ya?" he smirked.

Theta shut the door behind her, turning the lock.

"Roy." Her voice was strange in her ears. Dark. Hard. She didn't mind. It suited her. Had she ever really listened to herself before? Had she never heard that part of her coming through?

Roy mouth twisted into a cruel smile. "I told you not to double-cross me."

"Yeah. You did at that."

"I knew you'd come crawling back."

A flicker of heat returned to her fingers.

"Do I look like I'm crawling?"

"I got you where I want you now, Theta. You don't play ball, Theta Knight is over. The Follies? Vitagraph? Gone."

The bodies in the snow. The men with guns. Her home, burning, burning.

"Who's the winner now, Betty?"

"You are," Theta said hollowly. "It's always rats like you."

Roy glared. "Watch your mouth."

"It's always rats like you," Theta said louder. "Unless somebody stops 'em."

"Yeah?"

"Yeah."

"Don't make me hafta hurt you, Betty."

"My name's not Betty."

"Betty. Sue," Roy spat back.

Theta laughed. She didn't know why, but she couldn't stop.

Roy, unsure, laughed, too. "You think this is funny?"

"Yeah, I do," Theta said.

Roy's smile hardened. "I'll show you funny."

With surprising quickness, he leaped up and grabbed a handful of her hair, squeezing her close to him. Theta struggled against his hold, but he had her good. He tugged hard. Electric pain shot from her scalp down her neck. Tears sprang to her eyes. It had been two years, long enough for this pain to be a shock.

The Roys of the world coming more and more.

Theta screamed as the heat roared through her, bright and hot and full of vengeance. The scream was not one of fear—it was an announcement. A warning before the charge. Roy fell back onto the floor, gasping. The fire burned brightly inside Theta; she glowed like an avenging angel. He put up a hand to block the bright heat. He was afraid, just as she had been all those times before.

"Wh-what are you?"

"Justice," Theta said.

"Please," Roy begged. "Please don't."

"Please don't what?"

"Please don't hurt me."

How many times had she pleaded with him using those same words? And every time, he'd hurt her anyway. Until she'd learned not to make a sound.

"I want you to hurt, Roy. I want to see you suffer. Like you made me suffer. I want to hear you beg me to stop, you son of a bitch."

Smoke rose from her coal-hot palms. When she pressed it to his cheek, it would hurt. It would mark him forever. She wanted that. Wanted him to wear her brand for the rest of his life. After all, she'd been wearing his on her soul all this time.

Roy was on his knees, begging. Theta took a step closer, and he shouted for help. Like she'd cried for help once upon a time, and no help came. She was done with that now. She reached for him. The door splintered open. And then she heard Memphis: "Theta! Theta, don't do this. Please." It was so hard to keep her mind on his words. The fire wanted out.

"Theta. We're here. We're all here." Evie's voice.

Vaguely, she was aware of them. There was Henry, looking more worried than she'd ever seen him. Evie, Sam, and Ling were beside him. Memphis took a step forward.

"You should stay back," Theta said.

"See, I can't seem to do that," Memphis said.

He took another step forward.

"I could hurt you."

"No, you won't. You're not Roy."

Theta had started to cry. "I want to hurt him. I want to kill him."

"I know that feeling," Memphis said. "I got no right to ask you to let him go, but I'm asking anyway. For your sake, not his."

"Get this crazy bitch offa me!" Roy screeched.

Theta turned to him, palm out. Her body was aflame. She got close enough for him to shrink back from her heat. *Know what's in your heart*, she heard Miss Addie telling her. "Settle," she whispered to herself, and, as if it had always known she was in charge, the heat abated. Theta shivered from the sudden loss. But not for long, because her friends had her in a hug like a shield. Roy jumped and ran for the door. On his way out, he pointed a finger at Theta and her friends. "This ain't over. I'll get you for this!"

Theta and Memphis were locked in each other's arms. Memphis rubbed her back and Theta buried her face in his shoulder. Then she lifted her head and smiled at him. They kissed while the others looked away.

"I, uh, don't think we're needed anymore," Henry said. They started down the steps.

"Hey! Where you going?" Theta called after. "I'm starving!"

Ling grinned. "Lucky for you I know a good restaurant."

They gathered around a table in the back of the Tea House and demolished plate after plate of Mr. Chan's best dishes.

With a satisfied groan, Sam leaned back against his chair, his hands on his protruding gut. "Ling. How would your mother feel about a Jewish son-in-law?"

Theta sat next to Memphis and watched Mr. and Mrs. Chan laughing about some private joke. They were a mixed couple, and they were happy. No one seemed to be bothering them. But they were also here in the few blocks of Chinatown. What happened when they crossed Canal Street into the rest of the city? What happened when they went out into the rest of the country?

Memphis passed Theta a bowl of rice. Their fingertips touched and she smiled.

Evie raised her cup of tea. "To Theta."

"To Theta," the others echoed.

"What's the matter?" Ling asked, because Theta was crying.

"This is the first family dinner I ever had," she said.

"The first of many," Evie promised.

"You did it," Memphis said. "You stood up to Roy. He can't hurt you anymore."

Theta nodded. She had won this round. But Roy would be back. She knew him too well.

On the way back to the Bennington, Theta stopped the taxi outside the theater on Forty-second Street, taking a long look at it. She scribbled something on the back of a sheet of paper torn from Memphis's notebook, addressed it to Mr. Ziegfeld, and shoved it under the theater's closed doors. The note read: *Dear Flo, Thanks for everything. I quit. Theta Knight.*

THIS LIFE WAS GOOD

Papa Charles sat at his polished mahogany desk in his office at the Hotsy Totsy with his ledger books in front of him. Around him were the trappings of the successful life he'd made for himself since arriving in New York at the age of sixteen with nothing more than his wits and his dreams: A photograph of Papa Charles in his Elks Club sash, shaking hands with Harlem's elite, another of him with Harlem's winning basketball team, the Harlem Rens. An antique globe nestled in its wooden cradle. The cigar smoldering in a marble ashtray—a gift from a famous bandleader who'd played the club. The last of the Hotsy Totsy's revelers had stumbled out at six or seven, just as the sun made its entrance. It was eight now, and except for his bodyguard Claude on the other side of the door, Papa Charles was alone. It was good. This life was good.

Dutch Schultz and the white bootleggers were a problem, though. Seraphina had been right about that. He should have made a stand well before now. He'd thought that using Memphis's talents would appease Owney Madden and forge an alliance. But those men only cared about money and power. They were loyal to a code of violence, nothing more. When the hour was decent, Papa Charles would go to Seraphina. That only left one other thing to make right.

Papa Charles pulled out the letter of recommendation for City College that Regina Andrews had asked him to write for Memphis. He signed his name, sealed it up in an envelope, and left it for the day's mail.

There was a knock at the door.

Had Claude forgotten something?

"What is it?" Papa Charles called.

The door opened, and two white men in charcoal-gray suits entered so quietly they might as well have been shadows. They shut the door behind them, and even this was noiseless. Where was Claude?

"Charles King?" the smaller man said.

"Who wants to know?"

The man smirked and pulled on a pair of black gloves. "I'm Mr. Adams. This is my associate, Mr. Jefferson. And you are Charles King, Papa Charles to people in the know. Businessman. Banker. Investor. Owner of several nightclubs, pool halls, and various other establishments."

Papa Charles put on the genial face he used to great effect with policemen looking for illegal booze and drunken customers spoiling for a fight. "Well, well. You seem to know my résumé pretty well. What can I do for you gentlemen?"

There were two of them. One was a warning. Two were a problem.

"You fellas with Dutch? Is that what this is about?"

"No," the smaller man said. He gave the globe a spin, letting the tip of his finger hover close to the twirling surface.

"Well, then. We open again this evening 'round eight o'clock. Got an outfit outta St. Louis playing, the Bee's Knees. They're real good. Some say the bandleader's the next Duke Ellington. Come back then."

"Where's the healer?" the other man, the bigger one—Jefferson?—said.

"Who?" Papa Charles said.

"The healer. Memphis Campbell. And his brother, Isaiah. Where are they?"

Papa Charles realized he had misread the moment. This was bigger than Dutch or Owney. And far more dangerous. His fingers fumbled under the desk for the gun taped there. The smaller man was on him in a blink, the piano wire wrapped tightly around Papa Charles's neck above his starched collar. The most important banker in Harlem kicked and clawed, but there were two, and they worked in perfect sync like well-trained musicians trading riffs. The big man pinned Papa Charles's arms to the chair. The smaller man yanked up on the wire. And the last thing Papa Charles saw before the sharp edge of the wire slit his throat and the life drained from him was his opulent office in the basement of an empire he'd built with nothing more than his wits and his will in a country that told him he could.

In a country that could take it all back.

Mr. Adams let Papa Charles's lifeless body drop back against his velvet chair. He removed Papa's pocket square and used it to wipe down the piano wire. "Burn everything," he said. "We've got old friends to visit."

Mr. Jefferson splashed the room with kerosene. It splattered down Papa

Charles's bloodstained bespoke shirt, over the beautiful desk, and across the envelope addressed to City College. Mr. Jefferson trailed the kerosene over Claude's lifeless body and down the hallway beneath the Hotsy Totsy as he and his partner backed toward the alley door.

Mr. Jefferson lit a match, watched the flame dance down till it nipped his fingers.

With a smile, he tossed it in.

※

Theta slept snuggled next to Memphis, and for the first time in ages, she had no nightmares. There was only one curious dream. In it, a Cherokee woman, part of a long line of Cherokee trudging, exhausted, across a winter trail, turned to Theta. "It's just beginning," the woman said.

BLUE SKIES SMILING AT ME

Evie was still asleep as Sam got up and dressed. It was coming on eight. He hadn't slept like that—deeply, soundly—in a very long time. There had been a dream, and in the dream, the sun shone down on streets slick with morning dew so that they shone like gold. Sam had walked those streets, and in the dream, he was happy. Toward the dream's end, the wind had kicked up, hinting at a storm at Sam's back, but he'd awakened to see real sun leaking through the drawn drapes.

He was happy. He was happy.

He wanted to wake Evie and kiss her again and again, tasting happiness on her mouth as if he could get drunk from it. But she looked so peaceful with her hair fanned out on the pillow that he couldn't bring himself to do it. Instead, he scribbled a quick note—*gotta run an important errand. I'll be back by ten.* He wrote *I love you*, then scribbled it out. Too soon? Too soon. Instead, he addressed the note to "Lamb Chop."

She'd be so annoyed.

Grinning, he grabbed his fisherman's cap and coat. "I love you," he whispered quietly. *"Ikh hob dikh lib."* He kissed Evie's head. She rustled in her sleep, turning away. "Fine. I see how it is. I just wasted my best Yiddish on you," Sam joked to himself.

He loved her. Was in love with her. Had always loved her. And it seemed that she loved him, too. It was funny how the world could change on a dime like that. One minute, you were some poor chump pining after a girl you thought didn't feel the same way about you, and the next, you were lying together, arms entwined, chest to chest, so close you could feel her heartbeat under her soft skin. You were looking into her eyes and seeing your whole future written there.

There was a lot to fight. The future battle was daunting. But right now, this moment, was a time for hope, too. For fresh starts. For forgiveness.

Sam said hello to everyone on the street. He laughed. What was happening to him? What was happening to "Don't See Me" Sam Lloyd, the lone wolf, the *I look after myself* bad boy? It was funny how their odd little family of friends had changed him. Made him feel safe. Theta, Memphis, Henry, Jericho, Mabel, Ling, Isaiah, and especially Evie. They'd been there for him. Opened the parts of him he was afraid would be closed off forever. Why had he wasted so much time bottling up his feelings? What did that ever get anybody but dumb fights?

He had friends. He had a home in them.

And Evie was home, too.

The sky had bloomed into endless fields of blue. Not a cloud to be seen. He was walking faster now, that sudden flowering of hope pushing him on. He'd tell Evie everything. Let her know that he loved her. Let her know how much he loved her.

The glory of that sky, the hopeful fluttering in his heart, this was all. And so he hadn't noticed the two men in the dark suits, following him so stealthily that they might as well have been moving shadows.

"Sergei Lubovitch?"

At the mention of his real name, Sam whirled around, his eyes widening. He put up a hand just as Mr. Jefferson embraced Sam like a long-lost cousin and jabbed a palmed syringe into Sam's thigh. "Too late. Don't move," he whispered. "Wouldn't want to hit an artery."

Sam collapsed in Mr. Jefferson's arms. He heard a woman asking, "Gee, is he all right?"

"Help," Sam croaked. He was going numb. His mouth barely worked.

"My cousin is sick. We're taking him to the doctor," Mr. Adams lied. He and Mr. Jefferson dragged Sam toward the brown sedan.

Sam's eyes sought the eyes of people on the streets. *Help me. Can't you see this isn't right?* But the people liked the answer the men in the dark suits had supplied; it absolved them of any responsibility, and they moved on with their busy lives. Only one person seemed alarmed—a kid shining shoes. He looked from Sam to the men and back again, suspicious.

"He don't seem okay, mister," the kid said. "Say, ain't that Sam Lloyd?"

Yes! Yes, it's me, Sam thought.

Mr. Adams tossed the kid a quarter. "Cousin Bob'll be fine. You didn't see anything."

Sam gave the kid a last desperate glance: *Trust what you see.* "Tell Evie," he tried to say, but he wasn't sure if he'd said anything. He needed to warn Evie and the others. They were all in danger. Sam's legs had stopped working. He felt cold and his eyelids were heavy. The men in the dark suits laid Sam across the backseat of the sedan. Sleep was coming and he couldn't stop it.

The last thing Sam saw before he lost consciousness was the sweet blue of the sky.

THE FUTURE OF AMERICA

The day came up temperate and dry with a silky morning haze that would easily burn off by noon. Sarah Snow woke with a feeling of loss and foreboding. Her sleep had been haunted by awful dreams of her parents. In her dreams, the ochre dust of Northern China whipped up and coated their mangled bodies like dirty shrouds. They called to her: "Come. Come with us." In the next moment, she saw Robert lying in the grave. Parasites crawled out of his mouth and eyes. His whispered warning floated on the wind: "Sarah, do not go."

Sarah had been trained to look for God's signs. Was this a sign?

The first time God spoke to Sarah Snow, she was thirteen and her parents were dead, though she didn't know it yet. Her family had been living in China as missionaries, spreading the gospel. It was Sarah who saw what her parents did not: Hungry bellies made for easy converts. None of it was real faith. The smug naiveté of her parents embarrassed Sarah. It hardened her heart to God and miracles. She spoke the words and smiled insipidly when looked at closely, which was rarely. But she did not believe. They could not pry that from her; it was her one rebellion.

It was Robert who changed everything. Robert Thaddeus Carter was fifteen to Sarah's thirteen, the son of Pentecostal missionaries who received the Holy Spirit in tongues and mystical visions. He had a reputation as a blessed boy, a healer. Spiritual gifts, they called it, and Robert was the most gifted of all.

"I've glimpsed heaven, dear Sarah," he told her once as they pulled water from a well. His voice shook with a joy she had never known. "It's a beautiful place with shining palaces of pure gold. Oh, Sarah, it's real, it's all real."

The two of them would spend time discussing the Bible, Sarah as a way to get close to Robert, Robert because he believed without doubt. She adored him.

A kala-azar epidemic took Robert. Pale and sweating, he lay on a pallet, his hands and feet grayed with disease. His parents believed him possessed by demons. "We must show the Devil that we are stronger than he is," Reverend Carter said. For three days, they prayed over Robert as he shook, delirious with fever and prophecy. On the fourth day, they buried him in the hard earth and marked his dusty grave with a simple cross. Sarah felt as if her heart had been buried as well. She read the Bible. She said her prayers. She ministered with her parents. But inside, she was hollow.

On the day her parents died, Sarah had been tidying up the schoolroom when she stiffened as if a warm desert wind passed through her, head to toe. Tears sprang to her eyes, though she couldn't say why. She felt strangely full and content. It was Robert's voice she heard, a whisper on the wind: "Sarah, be not afraid, for I am with thee...." For the space of a breath, she swore she saw him shining in the doorway like a floury thumbprint left on a clean table. She blinked, and the sensation was gone as quickly as it had come over her. "Come back," she begged quietly. "Oh, please. Come back!" She heard her name called again, this time loud and anguished. Sarah's earlier contentment was replaced by dread. A convert raced across the plain, waving his hand. There'd been a motoring accident. Her parents' car had lost control in the mountains and struck a tree. They'd been killed instantly.

A steamer carried the orphaned Sarah Snow back to America, where a well-meaning (if not particularly affectionate) Methodist couple took her in. At seventeen, she married and settled into life in a small town. But her ambition was greater than being a housewife in a backwater town. And when her young husband died rather suddenly, too, Sarah found she was more relieved than grieved.

A touring car took her across the nation. Every time Sarah placed her hands on the shoulders of a broken man or woman asking for God's grace, she hoped for a repeat of that moment she'd experienced in the schoolroom the day her parents died. The day she thought she saw Robert Carter come back from the dead. A moment when she felt connected to something larger. When it didn't come, Sarah lost faith a second time. She lost faith in the wonders of the world. In magical boys like Robert T. Carter. Maybe Robert had been sent to tempt her, like Satan tempting Christ in the desert. By making her think she could be so much more. He'd tempted her with the idea that she might be special. Anointed by God. Why else show her such wonders in another human being only to deny her those same wonders?

And then came the Diviners. People like Evie O'Neill and her friends were a cheap imitation of Christ's glory, a pox on the nation, one that needed curing. And Sarah understood now that the Almighty had been training her all along, patiently waiting for her to ascend to his call. She would answer it with fire, as his soldier.

Yes, God had been waiting for her. That must have been the message of her dream. She would not disappoint him. Why, today was the start of everything! Hundreds of thousands would come to the exhibition. They would hear her, hear the Word. Besides, Jake Marlowe had chosen her personally. Sarah had been lonely, and Jake had been so kind. Together, the two of them would be unstoppable. She was being silly, letting a dream get to her. Snake oil salesmen. That was what Diviners were. What match were they against the hand of the Almighty?

By the time she pinned the fresh orchid to her Crusaders cape, Sarah had pushed aside her misgivings. Jake had sent a driver for her.

Mrs. Jake Marlowe. Yes, that was a fine name.

Sarah stepped out into the glorious spring day. It smelled of roses. It smelled of success.

☀

From his room high atop the Astor Hotel, Jake Marlowe scowled at his watch. "Where the devil is he?"

"We've looked everywhere, Mr. Marlowe," the man said apologetically.

"He's six-foot-four and the size of Adonis. You're telling me he can hide that easily?"

"Sorry, sir."

"Fine!" Marlowe grumbled, straightening his collar. "We'll have to head to the fairgrounds without him. But don't stop looking."

☀

In her hotel room, Evie paced, stopping only when she realized she was acting just like Will. Where was Sam? He'd promised to be there by ten, and it was now nearly ten thirty.

She was furious with him. And worried. Once upon a time, Sam might've run off, chasing after some lead by himself, leaving her in the lurch. But he'd never do that to her now, not this morning, not after what they'd shared last night. That had been very real. She knew it. She felt it deep down.

But what if something had happened to him?

There was a knock at the door, and Evie ran to it, relieved.

"Finally! You'd better have a good excuse, Sam—oh."

It wasn't Sam at the door but a kid. His fingernails and shirt were stained with shoe polish. "Miss O'Neill?"

The boy looked scared, Evie noticed. "Yes. That's me."

"Lefty Cunningham. I come about a friend of yours, Sam Lloyd." The boy reached behind him and brought out Sam's hat. "He's in some trouble, Miss. Bad trouble."

Lefty told Evie about the men who'd come and taken Sam away in the brown sedan. By the time he'd finished, Evie was more frightened than ever. She gave Lefty a dollar and asked him to keep what he knew quiet for his own protection.

Sam's hat sat in her hands. She could feel it wanting to whisper its messages to her.

"Show me where you are, Sam," she said, and pressed into its secrets for all she was worth.

※

Mabel examined Anna Provenza's drawings. What was it Maria had said? That Mabel would help people. Not guns. Not violence. Her stomach hurt. What would her parents say when they found out? All her life, her parents had advocated for change without violence. *I trust you to make the right choices, shayna.*

She sank to the floor and pressed her palms against the sides of her head.

Arthur and the Six were going to kill Jake Marlowe. And if she knew about it and did nothing, she had blood on her hands. Jake Marlowe was the emblem of everything Mabel and her parents fought against. He was an arrogant genius whose wealth had protected him from life's pain and unfairness, a man whose ignorance made him careless with other people. He was ruthless and self-centered and callous. He still didn't deserve to die.

Mabel had always trusted she would do the right thing. It was her greatest vanity, her belief in her own goodness. She was as blindly arrogant as Marlowe.

"What have I become?"

There was still time to fix it. Mabel grabbed her coat and raced toward the door.

"Mabel! Where are you going?" her father called.

"To fix something, Papa," Mabel said. "I love you."

She kissed him quickly on the cheek and ran down the stairs, taking them two at a time.

She just hoped she wasn't too late.

※

By noon, thousands waited outside the gates, and more streamed across the flat land. Cars were parked wherever they could find a spot. As they waited, the people were full of good cheer. They basked in the day's warmth and stunning beauty—*"Have there ever been such blue skies? Why, that Marlowe can even arrange fine weather!"* At last, the gates were opened and the people poured in, pushing toward the many wonders wrought by Jake Marlowe. The fairgrounds were awash in music. On a bandstand to the left, a sign proclaimed, THE DONNER FAMILY—a mother and father and their three daughters, singing old-fashioned, gospel-tinged American folk songs. A little farther on, the Goodrich Zippers, a banjo ensemble, performed an athletic jazz tune: *"Everything's JAKE—now-a-daaaays!"* Children ate popcorn from red-striped paper cones or chased after adventurous balloons they'd accidentally let slip. Isaiah gawped, wide-eyed, at everything. His smile was so big Memphis and Theta couldn't help smiling, too.

"Memphis! Can we have popcorn?" Isaiah asked.

"'Course we can," Memphis answered.

"You want popcorn, Theta?" Isaiah asked.

"I never say no to popcorn."

"Looks like quite a line. Go on with Theta. I'll find you," Memphis said, peeling off.

"Where should we go first?" Isaiah asked.

They were passing by a Fitter Families for Future Firesides tent. A nurse with a clipboard called to passersby, "Do you have a goodly heritage? Come and find out! You there! Wouldn't you like a shiny medal, hmmm?"

Isaiah's eyes lit up. "I surely would!"

The nurse's smile wavered. She'd clearly been angling to get a young, fair-haired couple inside, not Isaiah.

Theta glared at the nurse. "C'mon, Isaiah. Looks dull in there."

"But I want a medal," Isaiah said.

"He wants a medal," Theta said to the nurse. She put a hand on her hip and stared the woman down.

The nurse nodded tightly, resigned. "Very well, then."

It was warm inside. Several desks lined each side of the tent. White-capped nurses bustled about with medical forms while a doctor peeked his head out of a curtained area in the back that had clearly been set up for physical examinations.

"Wait here. We'll be right with you," the nurse said.

Theta took a seat beside a family of four. The mother bounced a baby gently on her knee.

"Can I look around, Theta?" Isaiah asked.

"Sure. Just be careful."

A moment later, a nurse handed Theta a form.

"Oh, it's not for me," Theta said.

"It won't take a minute. What is your name?"

"Theta. Theta Knight."

The nurse's head shot up. "Say, aren't you with the Follies?

"Was," Theta said sadly.

"Why, I remember now—you're friends with Evie O'Neill and those Diviners. Oh, I'm sure Dr. Simpson would like to talk to you personally. He's in the back. Now, you wait right here. I won't be a moment."

The nurse walked briskly toward the curtained-off area. At the desk next to her, Theta overheard a nurse interviewing a girl about Theta's age.

"And have you ever experienced any unusual gifts, like premonitions or feeling awake inside a dream?"

"Gee, sometimes I know when the telephone's about to ring."

The nurse smiled. "And have you ever seen in your mind or dreams a vision of a man in a tall hat?"

The question made Theta's stomach tighten. At the back of the tent, the nurse was speaking with a bespectacled doctor and nodding toward Theta. Theta's fingers began to tingle, a warning. They needed to leave. *Now*.

But where was Isaiah?

✶

In the middle of the long tent was a roped-off area with a big sign with a picture of Uncle Sam. The sign read, AMERICAN EUGENICS SOCIETY: THE SCIENCE OF HUMAN BETTERMENT. Underneath, there were all sorts of exhibits. One drew Isaiah's attention. It was a board called INHERITANCE OF COLOR, and it had a bunch of dead mice pinned to it by their tails. There were formulas, like in math: PURE WHITE + PURE WHITE = PURE WHITE. Apparently, the worst thing was mixing white and black or normal with abnormal. Then you got what the board called "tainted." It said that tainted was very bad. Tainted and abnormal were what the eugenics people wanted to breed out. People who were feebleminded or prom-i-scuous, whatever that meant, or who were like Conor Flynn. People who had fits, like Isaiah had.

Isaiah began to sweat.

That was why they were passing laws to keep white and black from mixing, the board explained, why they wanted to ster-i-lize "tainted" people. Isaiah didn't know what *sterilize* meant, but it didn't sound good.

The exhibits said America needed to fix this problem. They called fixing it "selection." "Selected" and "pure" people were the goal of eugenics. "Selected" people made civilization. "Tainted" people ruined it. The board said that if people were careful about breeding for their pigs and cows, why wouldn't they be careful about breeding in Americans?

Isaiah thought of Memphis in love with Theta and Theta in love with Memphis, and he understood for the first time just how dangerous their love was for them. Even though they were supposed to be free, they weren't.

His stomach hurt all of a sudden like he'd eaten too much candy, and he wished he could throw it up. Isaiah glanced furtively at all the people in the tent: white mothers, white fathers, white nurses, white doctors. When they looked his way, he saw the hare-quick downturn of their mouths before they corrected it. He felt it before he saw it. The way you could smell rain before the first drop hit your skin. He shoved his own deep, dark brown hands into his pockets, as if by hiding some part of his body, he could hide all of himself.

In the next second, he felt Theta's hands on his shoulders, turning him away from the exhibit. He could sense her feelings. She was angry and sad, but she was also scared. Really scared.

"Hey, Isaiah, let's get outta here. These people are all chumps."

Isaiah was angry and hurt. These people were mean. They would never give him one of those pretty medals. He'd just have to give himself one, then. Isaiah swiped a brass medal and shoved it into his pocket. He tightened his fingers around the edges, and the future jolted through Isaiah like a fast fever. His body shook with horrors. Camps and barbed wire and golden stars on striped pajamas, bones and shoes and teeth. He didn't know where this future was, how long from now, only that it was more horror than he could imagine. Foam bubbled up at the corners of his mouth.

"Isaiah!" Theta shouted. "Isaiah!"

☀

As Henry and Ling approached the ticket booth, he smiled at her.

"What?" Ling asked, suspicious.

"Miss Chan, why, I do believe you are the belle of this ball."

Ling made a face. "Why would I want to be a bell?"

"It's an expression. You look beautiful."

"I do not," Ling said, blushing.

"I'm sorry. I meant to say, who is that hideous beast in drag?"

"Now you're just trying to annoy me."

They'd reached the ticket booth. Ling handed over Marlowe's hand-written IOU. It was creased from constant handling.

"What is this?" the ticket taker said, scoffing at the flimsy paper.

"It's from Jake Marlowe himself. He signed it. See?" Ling said.

The ticket man shook his head. "Not to me, it's not. Tickets are two dollars and fifty cents. Each."

Ling's mouth hung open. "But...but that's a fortune!"

"There must be some mistake, sir. Miss Chan was promised a ticket," Henry said.

Behind them, the others in line grew restless: *"Get out of line!" "Step aside—let the paying customers through!" "What's the trouble? Oh, just someone wanting to come in for free." "Oh, look! There's Mr. Marlowe!"*

On the other side of the gates, a determined-looking Jake Marlowe cut a striking figure walking through the crowd, shaking people's hands, welcoming them to his great vision of the future.

"Just a minute!" Henry said, and raced toward the gates. "Mr. Marlowe! Mr. Marlowe!" he called. "Mr. Marlowe!"

Jake Marlowe peered through the golden bars at Henry, his smile faltering. "Mr. Marlowe, it's me, Henry DuBois? I'm here with Ling—Miss Chan. Sir, they won't honor your IOU. They say we need a ticket."

Marlowe stood for a second more, then walked away, glad-handing his way through the crowd.

There were few feelings that Ling hated more than shame, and now her face burned with it.

"Told you," the ticket man said. "Everybody needs a ticket. Two dollars and fifty cents. Each. Next!"

"I shall write to the mayor!" Henry said to the gawkers and gossipers. "Let's go. Heads high," he murmured low into Ling's ear, and they retreated to a bench a safe distance from the colorful swirl of the exhibition. Ling's eyes were blurred with angry tears as she stared across the bustling fairground at the pavilions and booths on the other side of Marlowe's gates, and at the white-domed Hall of the Future, where the glories of science would thrill other people. Where it was all happening. Without her. She'd given Marlowe the benefit of the doubt. She'd defended him to Mabel and the others, and he had looked right at her and denied her. Shamed her.

Henry handed over his handkerchief. "I'm sorry."

Ling blew her nose. "I knew. That's the awful part. I knew. I just didn't want to believe it."

"To hell with Marlowe. I'll buy you a ticket. Why, I'll buy you four tickets, and you can go four days in a row and stick your tongue out at that pompous fool every time!"

Ling snorted through her tears. "You don't have enough money for one ticket, much less four."

"That's true. But it felt like the time for gallant speechifying. I rose to the moment rather well, I think."

Ling was overcome by her love for Henry, jokes and all. It was funny how that could happen, how something strong and good could rise up from under the pain. Henry was her friend. She wished she could say something, *I love you* or *You are the best friend I've ever had; I hope I'm a good friend to you, too.* She hoped he could feel all that was unsaid between them. Somehow, she thought he would.

Ling handed back Henry's handkerchief. "Thank you."

Henry grimaced and held the snotty cloth by a corner before tucking it into his pocket. "Don't mention it."

The two of them watched the streams of people entering the gates of the fairgrounds. The children waved little American flags.

"We'll come back tomorrow," Henry said. "I'll get a little money from David and Theta, enough to buy you a ticket. They'll let you in."

Ling stood up, balancing her weight on her crutches. "No."

"No?"

"I don't want in anymore. Not to that club. We'll make our own exhibitions."

She gave Jake Marlowe's sprawling vision of America's future a last backward glance.

"To hell with Marlowe," she said.

※

Mabel threaded through the crowds at the exhibition, her heart beating wildly. Jake Marlowe would take the stage at the Grand Pavilion at one o'clock. It was now twelve forty-five. She had to move fast. She tried to remember what she'd seen when Arthur had shown them the blueprints. The Hall of Wonders was in the center of the fairgrounds. Inside was a custodians' room. That was where Arthur was supposed to go to pick up the rifle Gloria would bring hidden inside a baby carriage. Aron would help put the rifle together. Luis would toss a tear gas grenade to provide cover for Arthur's escape. Mabel's job had been to buy the bullets and provide an alibi, if it came to that. Her stomach hurt anew at the thought of what she'd done. Almost done—there was still time.

It was Gloria she spied first, standing off to the side in the Hall of Wonders with the baby carriage, just another spectator. Mabel marched up to Gloria and grabbed her shoulder.

Gloria's smile was a second too late. Her eyes showed panic. "Golly, Mabel! This is a surprise. What are you doing here?"

"I won't let you assassinate Marlowe," Mabel said.

"Keep your voice down," Gloria hissed. "Do you want to draw the attention of every cop in this place?"

"Maybe I do."

Gloria narrowed her eyes. "I knew you couldn't be trusted. And anyway, you're too late. The plan's in motion."

"I'll go straight to Mr. Marlowe. I won't let Arthur shoot him."

"Shoot him?" Gloria let out a small laugh. "Still the Girl Scout. Do you think we're just taking out Marlowe?"

"Aren't you?"

"He'll be onstage with Mr. Rockefeller and the mayor. We can take them all out. We'll send a message they can't ignore—that they don't own us. This is a new American revolution!"

Gloria's words fought to make sense inside Mabel's brain. "I don't understand."

"You don't need a gun when you can use a bomb."

Mabel felt dizzy and hot. "But…the Grand Pavilion will be full of people," Mabel said, and her voice sounded like it belonged to someone in another room. "Innocent people."

"No one's innocent," Gloria said.

"I have to talk to Arthur."

"It was Arthur's idea, you little fool!"

"I won't let you do this."

Mabel turned to go. Gloria pulled her close. Mabel felt the gun in her side.

"Move," Gloria said. "Now."

Gloria forced Mabel into the custodians' room. Aron and Luis were there. Seeing Mabel, they jumped up from their seats.

"What's she doing here?" Aron asked.

"She came to stop us."

"Please. Please don't do this," Mabel pleaded.

Aron crossed his arms. He seemed nervous. "No one listens to reason. They only pay attention to force. It's the only way."

"There's no such thing as the only way. You're not advocating for reform. You're promoting nihilism. There are *children* out there!" Mabel pleaded.

"*They* kill children all the time. How many children did they kill in the tents? How many do they let die in poverty every day? Whose children matter?" Aron said.

"*Listen* to yourselves!" Mabel shouted. "Do you want to be known as murderers?"

"Quiet!" Gloria said. "When Marlowe takes the stage, the bomb will go off. Keep talking and we'll shoot you here and now."

Mabel had watched her mother give speeches and wished that she could be like her—beautiful and charismatic, a force of nature. But she wasn't her mother. She was only herself. Her one weapon was her fierce belief that ordinary people could come together and make a better world. "Please," she said, choking on the word through tears. "I'm only asking you to listen to me for one minute. If you do this, you're saying that we don't believe in our own people! That we have no faith they'll do what's right."

"Maybe the people are terrible," Gloria said.

"Not all of them. Not even most of them. I won't believe that. I won't." Mabel took a shuddering breath and pressed a steadying hand to her stomach. "What you're doing isn't change. Not the kind that matters. It's anarchy. It's terror. I don't know everything, but I know that this—bombs and guns and threats—won't make for a better world. Just a more frightened and angry one."

Mabel looked at all of their faces. They were her friends. They might shoot her for an idea.

"Arthur's under the stage," Luis said.

Aron grabbed his arm. "What are you doing?"

Luis shook off Aron's hand and opened the door. "Go now. While you still can."

"Now, wait just a minute!" Gloria gripped Mabel's sleeve.

In a flash, Mabel slipped free, leaving Gloria holding her empty coat.

Mabel ran quickly through the fairgrounds, weaving her way through the crowds eating popcorn and hot dogs, past the people who'd stopped to admire the architectural splendor of a fountain spraying into the clean, crisp air. They had no idea of the danger they were in. It was up to Mabel to save them.

It was up to *her*.

The weight of the realization paralyzed Mabel for a moment. She leaned against the side of a booth housing a prototype of a giant robot that thrilled its human audience by assembling a radio piece by piece. "That's right, folks—the future will be fully automated! Robots doing human work!" the inventor crowed.

The robot answered in its mechanical voice, "I have seen the future."

What should she do? Should she go to the police? Would they even believe her? The city had a lot invested in the exhibition going well. No one would want to cause a panic over the wild accusations of some girl, a socialist, no less. They'd think she was only trying to cause trouble, to gain attention.

Still. She had to try. Mabel stood in the middle of the footpath, ignoring the grumbling from the irritated people navigating around her as she whirled around, eyes searching for a blue uniform. She spotted two cops by the Wonders of Electricity pavilion and set off at a clip, then slowed. What if the police *did* believe her? Then she'd be turning in her friends. And Arthur. She'd betray Arthur. Every member of the Secret Six would go to prison, Mabel included. She imagined her parents' bereaved faces. How horrified and hurt they'd be. Aron and Luis could be deported. And Arthur could be sentenced to death. A vision of Arthur being strapped into the electric chair brought Mabel to a stop just a few feet shy of the two police officers.

One of them gave her a funny look. "You all right, Miss?"

"Yes," Mabel said, breathing heavily. "I . . . I just got turned around is all."

"Easy to do. It's a big place! What are you looking for?"

"The Grand Pavilion." Her voice was so small.

The officer pointed behind her. "Boy, you did get turned around. It's that way, Miss. But you'd better hurry. I hear Miss Snow is about to start."

Mabel nodded her thanks and turned away.

Her father had always said that persuasion trumped force. *Give people the benefit of the doubt*, shayna. *Appeal to the good inside them. Show them you will work with them. Offer hope in place of hate.* Hope and reason gave people a chance to think for themselves, to be a part of the solution. Yes. Hope. She'd go to Arthur and reason with him. She'd get him to see that they were all poised on the razor's edge of becoming everything they'd been fighting against. There was another, better way. There always was. Yes. Hope. Yes.

Mabel slipped into the Grand Pavilion. On the broad wooden stage, the Christian Crusaders played a noisy march. The bang of the drum, sharp as a gun, startled Mabel and she jumped. Everywhere she looked there were children. Whole families waving small flags on sticks. A mother bent to wipe the mouth of her little boy. Oh, god. *Faster, Mabel!* She pushed her way to the back and the door that led down to the housings. A policeman stopped her. "You can't go that way, Miss. It's not open to the public."

"Oh," Mabel said, trying not to cry. "I've lost my brother. I have to find him. He . . . he went this way."

And then Mabel did cry. The overwhelming fear. The betrayal. There was no stopping her tears.

The policeman softened. "Aww, now, Miss. Go on, then. But don't tell anybody I let you back there."

"Thank you. Oh, thank you," Mabel cried.

Hope. Persuasion. Appealing to the good. It had worked in this moment. She hoped the policeman's faith was not misplaced. She had to stop Arthur from making a terrible mistake.

Quickly, Mabel slipped down the stairs. As she came around the corner, she stopped short at the sight of four Pinkerton agents huddled together, smoking. One of them was Brown Hat, the man who'd been following them the past several weeks. Mabel hid in the shadows beneath the stairs and waited.

"You think he's on the level?" one of the Pinkertons asked.

Brown Hat hooked his thumbs underneath his jacket lapels. "That gutter rat? I wouldn't trust Arthur Brown farther than I could spit."

"He's been your informant for a while, though. If not for him, we wouldn't've been able to catch those anarchists downtown. We arrested that bookstore owner, Jenkins, today."

Arthur?

Arthur was a stool pigeon?

Mabel's knees buckled, and she grabbed hold of the stair railing for support.

Brown Hat tossed his cigarette to the ground and wiggled it dead with the toe of his shoe. "And then he blew up Marlowe's mine. That wasn't part of the plan. He was supposed to deliver the Secret Six to us, but he didn't show up for our meeting last night. Once a traitor, always a traitor. I'm betting he's here somewhere. We're gonna turn this place out looking for him."

Mabel pressed herself against the wall as the agents' feet thundered past her head and up the staircase. It was all lies. She'd loved him. She'd thought...

Bile scratched up her throat, and she gagged against its hot truth. She didn't know whether to run back to the others and tell them they were walking into a trap or chase after the man in the brown hat and demand to know everything. If she did, he'd arrest her on the spot.

No. There was only one person who had the answers she needed.

Mabel made her way to the basement. Her tears had dried. Her earlier panic had become an icy numbness thick in her chest. She found the small room directly under the stage and quietly let herself inside. Arthur had his back to her. He was crouched over the bomb at his feet.

"Arthur," she said coldly.

He leaped up, eyes wide. "Mabel! What are you doing here?"

"I know all about it. About you."

"What do you mean?"

"I know that you're a double agent working with the Pinkertons. You're a *spy* for them. All this time, you've been lying to us. To me." Mabel's voice broke on the word. The tears were coming. She sniffed them back. "You didn't want to help workers. You wanted to bring down the movement."

Arthur's expression went slack for a moment, but he didn't deny it.

Mabel had half been waiting for him to tell her how wrong she was, but she could see now that she was right, and she both hated and respected Arthur for not lying to her just now.

"They were going to execute my brother. They let me out of jail and told me they'd commute his sentence if I worked for them. But that was before what happened at the mine. Those children burned to death in their tents. Women shot by machine guns. It was before I fell in love with you. You changed me, Mabel. I had been half-dead, but you made me believe in the cause again. You made me want to be a good man."

A bitter "ha" escaped from deep in Mabel's throat. "I'm supposed to believe that?"

"You don't have to, but it's the truth, Mabel, I swear."

"Your word doesn't mean anything," Mabel shot back. "I suppose indicting the Roses' daughter as a member of the Secret Six was supposed to be the feather in your cap."

"They were going to use you to blackmail your parents into cooperating. But I told them you were innocent!"

Tears blurred Mabel's vision. "Gloria's right—I'm such a fool."

"Mabel, I promise you, I love you. I want to marry you."

Arthur moved toward Mabel. She pushed him away hard even as she wanted to hold him. "Don't."

"How can I prove I love you?"

"If you truly love me, you'll destroy that bomb."

Arthur looked down at his creation. One switch, Mabel knew, and it would tick down to destruction. "He's a bad man. The whole system's rigged and rotten, Mabel. We need to send a message."

"Not this way." Mabel stood firm. "I'm not leaving, Arthur. If you set that bomb, you'll kill me, too."

"Mabel. Please."

"Once, you saved me. In Union Square, remember? Pulled me into an alley and into your world. Now I'm saving you."

Arthur teared up. He wiped his eyes with the back of his hand. "It's not a good world, Mabel."

"Yes, it is. It just needs a lot of help." Mabel was crying, too. "We can do that, you and me. I still have hope, Arthur. I can't give up on the world just yet."

Arthur looked at Mabel. He was tearing up again, and Mabel fought the urge to comfort him. He swiped an arm across his eyes. "Sometimes it feels like…" There was a catch in his voice. "Like the world has given up on me."

"I haven't given up on you," Mabel said.

Tears slid down Arthur's face as he reached out and gently stroked Mabel's soft cheek.

"Okay," he said.

"Okay?"

"Okay." Arthur knelt before the bomb. He lifted his face to Mabel's. His eyes were red. "For you, Mabel Rose."

Footsteps pounded toward them. Arthur leaped up. Mabel moved to his side. The four Pinkerton agents entered the room, guns drawn. Brown Hat was at the front. "Make a single move and I'll shoot you where you stand! This is the only warning you get."

"Put your hands up, Mabel," Arthur said gently.

"Well, if it isn't Mabel Rose. And what do we have here? A bomb. Looks like you delivered after all, gutter rat."

"Mabel has nothing to do with this!" Arthur said.

"It isn't what you think. He was just about to destroy it," Mabel explained.

Brown Hat smirked. "Sure he was."

"Please. If you could just listen for a minute…" Mabel took a step forward.

"Mabel, don't!" Arthur shouted.

It happened very fast. The first bullet grazed Mabel's right arm; the second found its home in her belly, exiting through her back, severing her spinal column. Mabel felt a searing heat, followed by cold, and then she felt nothing as she fell to the ground.

✳

In the Grand Pavilion, the radio men made sure the wires were secured and tested the microphones.

"Just get right up on it, Miss Snow," one of them said.

But Sarah Snow knew exactly what to do. She'd waited a lifetime for this moment. As she took the stage, she smiled at the vast sea of tiny, waving American flags and wished that her parents could see her standing here. A lump rose in her throat. She couldn't afford to tear up now. After all, Jake Marlowe needed her. He'd asked her to take charge, and take charge she would.

Sarah raised her arms. "Brothers and sisters, citizens, welcome. What a glorious day the Lord has made!"

The tiny flags agitated like electric current.

"Here, in this great city in this great nation of opportunity, the American dream is alive and well. Jake Marlowe is bringing us the future. And, oh, what a glorious future it is, indeed! Do you feel that? Do you feel that future inside you? Do you feel it in your hearts, brothers and sisters?"

The flags answered affirmative.

Sarah Snow. Chosen. Anointed for greatness by the Almighty.

"Let us raise a hymn of praise to America."

The Christian Crusaders took up their instruments once more.

Sarah stepped up to the microphone and let her voice rise: "*My country, 'tis of thee, sweet land of liberty, of thee I sing….*"

※

"Mabel!" Arthur called, desperate. "Mabel!"

"Arthur?" Mabel croaked out. She couldn't move her legs.

"Help her!" Arthur growled.

"Stay where you are, Mr. Brown!" Brown Hat commanded as he moved closer. "Where are the others?"

Arthur said nothing.

"I'll let her die," Brown Hat said.

"They'll be leaving the fair right about now," Arthur said.

"Weston, Cooper!" Brown Hat called to two of the other agents. "Go find them. Make the arrest. Agent Lynch, stay with me."

It was just Brown Hat and the other agent left now. From where she lay, Mabel could hear Sarah's pretty soprano coming through the microphone, filling the Grand Pavilion above them.

"They're st-starting," Mabel murmured, and coughed.

"Please. She's hurt," Arthur pleaded.

Brown Hat's expression didn't change. "I don't care."

Arthur fell on the other agent with furious blows. Brown Hat answered with a bullet to Arthur's thigh. Arthur cried out. The wound bled profusely. It had managed to hit in a very bad place, he knew. Above him, the band played on. This wasn't the way it was supposed to happen. He had a knack for screwing up. Perhaps there was still a chance to correct that, to make one lasting contribution. Arthur Brown left a slug trail of blood behind him as he crawled toward the bomb.

Brown Hat kicked him in the face. Arthur fell back, and the agent brought his shoe down on Arthur's outstretched hand, pinning him there.

"You idiot," Arthur said through teeth clenched against pain. "I was trying to disarm it!"

Brown Hat nodded. "I know."

Without another word, Brown Hat turned and shot the younger agent, who jerked like a marionette and dropped to the ground, dead. The man in the brown hat stepped calmly around Arthur and the dead agent and placed the still-ticking bomb high into an alcove underneath the stage, out of Arthur's reach.

"So long, gutter rat," he said, shutting and locking the door on his way out.

✺

"Memphis!" Theta shouted. "Help!"

"Isaiah? Isaiah!" Memphis gathered his shaking brother in his arms, and they carried him to the grass. People were staring. "Isaiah?"

Isaiah's eyes had rolled back in their sockets. "Fire," he cried. "Fire!"

"Hey, now, boy, you can't be yelling fire in a public place," a man scolded, and Memphis wanted to hit him.

"My brother's sick!" Memphis growled.

"Then get him outta here," the man shot back.

"What's the matter?" a policeman asked.

"That little boy's calling fire."

"Memphis, we better go," Theta said.

"I said, my brother's sick!" Memphis yelled. He wanted to punch somebody and he wanted to cry, and he didn't know which he wanted more.

"All right," the policeman said kindly. "Let me help you get him outside."

Isaiah's eyes snapped open. He sat up. "Bomb. Bomb. There. They're here. Warning us." Isaiah pointed to the charred field. The tents and bodies were gone, but the ground still bore witness to the massacre. "Do you see them?"

Dead children lined up across the field.

"Do you see them? They're telling us to go," Isaiah said. "Now."

"Say, now, what's all this about a bomb?" the policeman asked.

"My brother, he's special. A Diviner," Memphis explained.

"Bomb! Bomb!" Isaiah screamed.

"Say, now, what's he going on about?" The officer blew his whistle. "You stay right there!"

Across the grass, two men in dark suits were making their way from the Fitter Families tent toward Memphis, Theta, and Isaiah. Theta saw them approaching.

"Grab Isaiah and run," Theta said.

"What? Why—"

"Just do it, Poet."

Memphis scooped Isaiah up in his arms and staggered as quickly as he could toward the gates and out into the flat Queens field streaming with curious people making their way toward Jake Marlowe's utopia. Several policemen had their nightsticks out, but it was the Shadow Men Theta feared.

Theta let the heat come. And then she blasted a strip of grass at her feet. A small fire blazed across the entrance to the exhibition. Already, the policemen ran for buckets of water. They'd have it out in no time. But it would be enough to get away, she hoped.

"It was that girl—that Diviner," someone shouted behind her as she ran. "She did it!"

※

The song soared to the rafters inside the Grand Pavilion.

"Sweet land of liberty."

It bubbled forth from the lips of the people and echoed through the radio playing on a table inside the Fitter Families tent under a poster touting the qualities of the perfect citizen.

"Of thee I sing."

Its muffled but familiar strains drifted down into the depths of the small room below the stage, where, with his last bit of strength, Arthur Brown dragged himself on his elbows toward Mabel, leaving behind a trail of blood.

"Arthur?" Mabel called softly.

"I'm here," Arthur managed through teeth gritted in pain.

"It got so cold."

"Yeah." The bullet in Arthur's thigh burned. His trousers leg was soaked red.

"Did…" Mabel wheezed. "Did we stop it?"

Arthur glanced in the direction of the still-ticking bomb. He moved his face closer to Mabel's.

"Yeah. We did," he answered, taking her hand in his.

"And do…do you really…?"

"Really what?"

"Love me?"

Mabel's sight blurred until above her, she thought she saw a great gathering of doves. Their scalloped wings fluttered like the fans in Theta's Follies show, the one she'd seen with Evie the night they'd sneaked out. Had that been so long ago? Seemed like ages. Evie. She'd call Evie and tell her that everything was okay. She'd tell her all of it now. You shared the truth with your friends. Yes, she would call Evie.

Mabel's smile quivered, an echo of the birds' wings. To her ears, their cooing was like the tick of a steady clock. The iciness in her stomach spread. Her breathing slowed. She coughed. Blood spattered across her pale lips. It was hard to speak.

"People are…" Mabel wheezed. "Mostly good, you…" Wheeze. "Know? Mostly." She tried to take a breath. It was hard. Like breathing through layers of gauze. Where were her parents? She loved them so. "Mostly. I believe that with…" A bloody cough tore through Mabel's lungs. "…With all my…all my heart."

The doves became a giant cloud. The cloud was all Mabel could see,

517

stretching everywhere at once. It reached down, wrapping her in its embrace. And there was singing somewhere. Sarah Snow's faraway voice.

"From ev-er-ry-y mountainside, le-eh-t free...dom..."

"Listen," Mabel croaked. She had so little air left. "The doves. They've stopped ticking."

"Rrrii—"

AFTER

After, when people talked of the explosion, they would all remember the blue, blue sky. It was such a glorious, cloudless blue that the billowing black smoke appeared like the pencil scratches of an angry child. They would say that the smoke could be seen from the windows of office buildings near Grand Central by busy people momentarily paused in their work. It could be seen by curious ferry captains hauling twists of rope onto wobbling boat backs, and by tired governesses pushing prams along the East River promenade near the sparkling apartments of Beekman Place. It was impossible to imagine that such harm could ever come under the promise of such a blue sky.

The city stalled, weighted by its grief. It rained. For two days, the sky soaked the ground in its tears. By the time they went to bury Mabel Rose in a private cemetery outside the city, the graveyard was a sopping mess. There was a rabbi who gave a prayer and a poet who gave his, an offering of words, because words were needed even if they seemed as flimsy as a paper aeroplane thrown into a bruising wind. Mrs. Rose sobbed into her handkerchief. Mr. Rose kept an arm around his wife's shoulders. His face had been hollowed of anything but pain. The Roses' friends had helped to pay for the funeral. Not one dime came from Mabel's wealthy grandparents. They were not in attendance.

Evie, Henry, Ling, and Memphis had pooled their money to buy a carnation wreath, a patchwork of color, for the grave. Evie had asked that Mabel be buried with one of Evie's rhinestone headbands that Mabel quite liked. "So she won't be lonely. You'll have all our memories with you always, Mabesie." Isaiah had offered his baseball, too. "Just because," he'd said with no other explanation, for what more was there to say? The gravediggers lowered Mabel into the ground. One by one, her friends stepped up and tossed their handfuls of dirt onto the simple pine coffin, listening as each heartbreaking clump hit with finality. The gravediggers set their shovels to work, tamping down the wet earth. There was no headstone yet, not for another year, so Evie marked the grave with a rock. She stared at the dirt on her fingers. Grief squeezed her tightly in its grip.

"Oh, Mabel, Mabel," she cried. "How can you be gone? It isn't possible!"

Theta put her arm around Evie's shoulders. She was crying, too, but trying to hide it. Somebody had to be strong. And it was Evie's turn to cry.

"I should've stopped her. I should've done something," Evie sobbed into Theta's shoulder.

"Shhh," Theta murmured. "It wasn't your fault. Mabel made her own choices."

"She was the best person I ever knew other than James. She was so good," Evie said, half-choked on her tears.

"Sometimes," Ling said from under her umbrella.

Evie's head was up, teeth bared. "What is that supposed to mean?"

"I mean that she was complicated. Everybody is," Ling said quietly. "Don't erase her like that. She deserves better."

"I don't think she can hear that right now," Henry whispered in Ling's ear.

Ling stared at the new grave. "Then when can she?"

There were new ghosts in the streets. Hollow-eyed. Questioning. *Why?* The mayor declared a citywide day of mourning for the victims of the bombing and a public memorial for Sarah Snow. In death, Sarah had become even more popular. Her beatific face shone down from billboards in Times Square: OUR HEARTS ARE WITH OUR FALLEN ANGEL, SARAH SNOW. High school girls who once worshipped Hollywood motion picture stars now wore corsages and black armbands to show their grief over their lost radio evangelist. As Sarah's funeral procession passed down a crowded Fifth Avenue—six white horses drawing a white coffin under a giant spray of white roses—the girls pressed themselves against the barricades, sobbing.

"We will find and punish the people responsible for this tragedy," the mayor promised. It was echoed by the lawmakers and citizens.

In a city jail, Aron and Gloria awaited trial for the bombing. Luis had been shot dead at the fairgrounds with his hands still up in surrender. Gloria's wealthy parents had found her a good lawyer. In the press, the lawyer insisted that Gloria had been brainwashed by the anarchists, that she knew nothing of the bombing. The newspapers were sympathetic. They ran a picture of Gloria in a simple dress, hands folded almost prayerfully in her lap: CONNECTICUT COED CONNED BY CROOKS.

Alliteration.

On the tenth floor of WGI, in Mr. Phillips's smartly appointed corner office with the big windows dotted with rain, Evie sat on the other side of her boss's desk, her hands fidgeting in her lap, her heavy heart still capable of racing. This, she knew, was not a happy meeting, though she hadn't any idea of why Mr. Phillips wanted to speak with her.

"Evie." Mr. Phillips's voice caught on her name and he cleared his throat. "There will be some changes to WGI's programming. We are requiring a new loyalty oath from all of our radio stars."

"Loyalty oath?" For the first time, Evie noticed the one-page contract on Mr. Phillips's desk.

"Yes. It's fairly standard. Nothing to worry about. It simply states that you are a loyal citizen of the United States. And that you disavow anything *un*-American."

"But what does that mean?" Evie said, genuinely perplexed. "Who decides what's un-American?"

"Now, now, as I said, it's nothing to worry about. Just a formality. You're simply stating that you are not a radical or an agitator or, ah, *friends* with any suspected radicals. That you would report any such radicals to the proper authorities."

Evie read through the page. She looked up at Mr. Phillips. "You want me to say Mabel was a terrible person. To say that I didn't know her and she wasn't my friend. You want me to disavow Memphis and Ling and Sam."

Mr. Phillips looked suddenly old to Evie. As if he'd gone to bed but woken in the morning more exhausted by sleep. "If you want to have a show at WGI, you'll need to sign, Evie."

Evie could lose her show. She imagined the busybodies back home in Ohio, the ones who thought she'd never amount to anything, being proven right in their minds. How they'd cluck their tongues over it and nod smugly. *Told you that one was a bad apple.*

In a daze, Evie left her seat. She wandered to the tall windows and looked out at the gray smoke wafting past jagged skyscraper roofs, and at the spring rain dotting the shiny glass windows. The view from up high had always thrilled her. Next, she cast her gaze down to the pavement below and the ant-like people racing about, unseeing.

"Evie?" Mr. Phillips called. He was waiting. He didn't like to wait, she knew.

Evie walked back to the big desk and took hold of the pen. It was heavier than it looked. She rolled it between her fingers.

"You see, Mr. Phillips, the truth of it is, I am so very American." She slapped the pen down on the onerous paper and slid them both toward her boss. "And that is precisely why I can't—no, why I refuse to sign this."

"If you don't sign, I'll have no choice but to fire you."

"My dear Mr. Phillips," Evie said sweetly. "You can't fire me. I quit."

Evie was now one of those anonymous ants on the street. She tried to put her gloves on the wrong hands, gave up, and shoved them in her pocketbook. It wouldn't close. So many objects. Why did she have all these *things* in her handbag? She took the gloves out again, tucking them under her armpit.

A panhandler stuck out his empty hat. "Help, Miss?"

Evie looked into her pocketbook. First, she gave him everything in her coin purse, which came to two dollars and twenty-seven cents. Next, she put in her gold compact, a gift from a store owner who'd wanted a mention on the radio. Evie pulled out her sterling silver flask. It was the first item she'd bought for herself with her money from the radio show. Evie unscrewed the tiny top and took a solid swig. She held it over the open hat, then brought it back.

"Oh, applesauce." She took one last swig for good measure. And then she dropped the flask into the man's hat.

"God bless you, Miss!" the man called.

"That would be nice," Evie said over her shoulder. "But I won't hold my breath."

The weather turned warmer.

Blue skies returned. But they were not the same blue. The sky was paler, harder. In the city, it was becoming dangerous for Diviners. A psychic in Greenwich Village, dragged from his storefront shop by a mob, lay in a hospital with three broken ribs. "That's for Sarah Snow!" his attackers had shouted as they kicked the confused, crying man. Blame was the balm for the city's fear and grief. It was the finger-pointing to the other—*You! You did this! It's your fault!*

※

Evie sat at Theta's tiny kitchen table. Her feet ached. She'd walked for miles before finally ending up at the Bennington. Theta poured them two glasses of milk and stirred in some Ovaltine.

"What are you going to do now, Evil?" Theta asked, putting one glass in front of Evie.

Evie swallowed down half. It was thick and chocolaty and good. "I'm going to find Sam. Those Shadow Men took him. I know it. And I'm going to follow every clue until I hunt him down and get him back."

"You tell your uncle and Sister Walker what you're up to?"

"They killed my brother. I'm not telling them anything ever again."

Theta nodded, sipped her milk. "What about Jericho? You heard anything from him?"

Evie shook her head. Her bones ached. She could barely keep her eyes open.

Theta stood up. "Okay. That's it. I'm putting you to bed."

"I'm not tired," Evie said on a yawn.

"Yeah, yeah, tell it to Sweeney. Come on. Upsy-daisy."

Theta helped Evie from the chair, plopped her into bed, and pulled up the blanket. "Tomorrow we're going after Sam."

Evie looked up into Theta's lovely brown eyes. "We?"

"That's what I said, isn't it? Hold on. You got a hair in your mouth. *Yech.*" Theta smoothed back Evie's hair from her face. Then she turned off the lamp. "Scoot over, Evil. I'm coming in."

Evie wiggled her back to the wall, and Theta lay down beside her in the dark. Evie's heart had taken a beating. Now it swelled with gratitude. "You don't have to go with me, you know."

Theta rolled over, facing Evie, their noses nearly touching. "Evil?"

"Yes?"

"I love you. Now, shut up and go to sleep."

Evie dreamed of a humming machine and of the Eye shining out from

523

it. Everywhere, the Eye, like a golden sun shedding its tears of light. And then the Eye was on the forehead of the King of Crows. His skin absorbed it, covering it with gray scales and tufts of spiny feathers. When Evie looked closer, his body was a map of lines, ever-changing. Set into his long face were two black eyes flat as jeweler's velvet so that every longing was reflected back as a jewel, a thing to covet. His thin lips stretched into a mustard-gas grin.

"Are you coming for me? Do you fancy yourselves heroes? How glorious! Now the real fun begins. Soon I will take all you love and watch you burn. Sweet dreams, Object Reader."

The man in the hat pressed his thumb of forgetting against Evie's forehead, and she felt herself fall.

BAD LUCK

With Isaiah at his side, Bill Johnson stacked boxes in the back room of Floyd's Barbershop. It felt good to use his hands. To work. His eyes watered from all the light, but Bill couldn't get enough of it. Ever since Memphis had healed Bill, it had been the talk of Harlem, in the pool halls and store-front churches, in the Elks Club meeting rooms and at stoop-side chats among neighbors. The day after the healing, when Bill Johnson had walked into Floyd's Barbershop looking ten years younger, the men had gathered around. Some had touched his face, and Bill didn't care that his face was wet with his own tears while they did.

"It's a miracle. It's a gall-danged miracle," Floyd had exclaimed. "What can I do you for, Mr. Johnson?"

"Well, sir, I reckon I could use a good shave," Bill had said.

"Miracle," Floyd had said again, snapping the apron around Bill's neck.

Even now, in the other room, where the men took up with talk of base-ball and then the terrible fire that had taken Papa Charles and the Hotsy Totsy, Bill knew they'd get around to the topic soon enough: miracles. Miracles could happen. The papers were full of ghosts and hate and tragedy. But on the streets, change was in the air. The people still danced toward hope. Even Octavia had come around after she'd heard what Memphis had done for Bill. The night before, she'd cooked a whole chicken and put Memphis's plate down first with the choicest cut. After the blessing, she'd watched him eat that chicken, her gap-toothed smile peeking out from behind her lips like sun pushing apart rain clouds. It was a pretty smile, and Bill was grate-ful to see it at last. He felt like he couldn't get enough of that smile.

Memphis had regarded his aunt warily. "What is it?" he'd said, mid-chew.

"You look like your mama just now," Octavia had said. "Like she's right there in your face."

And Bill had felt it in a powerful rush, like the flapping of mighty ancestor wings inside his soul: *Take flight with us, Brother Bill.*

The bell tinkled above the barbershop door and the men in the other room went quiet. Bill's shoulders tensed. Years as a blind man had taught him to read silences well. This was not a welcome silence.

"Afternoon, gentlemen."

It had been many years, but Bill knew that voice well. He could never forget it. Bill's hands shook from a very old fear. He peered around the corner. Gray suits and hats. They might be older, but there was no mistaking them. Adams. Jefferson. The Shadow Men had found him at last.

Bill's heart liked to jump from his chest as he heard Floyd, polite but not friendly: "Afternoon, gentlemen. What can I do for you?"

"We're looking for a young man, Memphis Campbell? Do you know him?"

No. Not there for him. For the brothers!

"Whatcha want with Memphis?" Floyd asked.

"We believe that Mr. Campbell is a traitor. He's one of those anarchist Diviners."

Floyd laughed. "Memphis? Naw. Boy's a poet. He's all heart."

"He's also a traitor to the nation. Anybody harboring him as a fugitive of the law will face prison time as well."

The mood in the shop sobered. Bill could sense the fear from where he stood. And he hoped Floyd wouldn't let that fear push him into doing anything stupid before Bill could get in there.

"What're they saying about Memphis?" Isaiah asked.

Bill crouched down, whispering urgently. "Son, do as I say now. You hear me? I want you to slip out back here, climb over the fence. Run to your aunt Octavia's house and tell Memphis I said to hide till I can get there. Don't open the door to nobody. You understand?"

Isaiah started to speak, and Bill put a finger to his lips. "Understand?"

Isaiah nodded. Bill pried open the back door. "Go on."

Bill slipped on his blind man's glasses and grabbed his cane, tapping his way out into the sitting room. He hoped and prayed nobody would be fool enough to comment on it. And then he hoped and prayed that the Shadow Men wouldn't recognize him. It had been many years, and even with the healing Memphis had put on him that had peeled back the years, Bill had a certain weariness to his face now and probably always would.

"Bill!" Floyd called as he sharpened his razor on the strop. "These gentlemen looking for Memphis. Said he's in some kind of trouble with the law."

"That a fact?" Bill said.

"You know where he is?" the smaller Shadow Man asked. Adams. The scent of pistachios hung over him. It made Bill's knees tremble, remembering.

Bill didn't dare turn around. He kept his eyes on the floor. "I heard that fool got hisself mixed up in a gambling debt and had to run off to some cousins down 'round Virginia. Floyd, you 'member his cousin, Francois Mackandal, live up in the hills?" Bill said, coding his words behind a smile. "Yes, sir. Just two days ago they left. Old Francois got a farm down there, if I heard right. Oughta make a man of him. Yes, sir. Don't imagine he'll be back before summer," Bill added quickly. "Bad luck."

"Yes. Bad luck," Mr. Adams said. "We heard he's got an aunt who lives here, though. A Miss Octavia Joseph. You know where she lives?"

Behind his dark glasses, Bill watched Adams in the mirror. Bill remembered those tiny teeth and the smell of pistachios. The things those men did to him. The things they made him do. Even now, it twisted his guts. The tips of his fingers remembered, too. They called to him, wanting revenge.

"No, sir. 'Fraid I don't," Bill said, and tapped his way out the door, his heart beating with each rap of the cane. He managed two slow blocks, till he was sure they weren't behind him. And then he broke into a run, heading straight for Octavia's house.

✸

When Octavia opened her door, Bill Johnson was standing there, looking like the Devil himself was after him. "Miss Octavia. I got to come in. Please!"

"What's the matter?" Memphis said, coming into Octavia's pin-straight parlor.

"Shadow Men know 'bout you. They're at the barbershop right now, asking where you live. We got to get outta town."

"I'm not running. Let 'em come," Memphis said.

Bill took hold of Memphis's arm. "What about Isaiah?" he said quietly. "You know what they done to me. What you think they gonna do to your brother? Make a stand later. Now we run."

"What on earth you talking about?" Octavia said, wiping her hands on her apron.

Octavia was a good woman, the sort of woman Bill wished he could marry. He would spare her this pain if he could. "The men who killed Papa Charles, they know what Memphis and Isaiah can do. They want 'em for it. They're on their way."

Octavia put a hand to her mouth. Bill took her in his arms, held her. "I got to get them out of town. Before it's too late."

"Memphis. Isaiah. Pack your things," Octavia said.

Quickly, Memphis and Isaiah stuffed a rucksack with only what was necessary. Isaiah was sad to leave behind his leather catcher's mitt, but he packed some drawing paper, a pencil, and a small photograph of his mama and daddy back in happier days. Memphis added his notebook and pencil. He paused at the copy of *Leaves of Grass* that Theta had given him. He wanted to call her, to tell her he was leaving, but it would have to wait. He shoved the book into his rucksack, too.

Octavia wrapped some corn bread in wax paper and added it to their bounty. Octavia cradled Isaiah's cheeks between her palms. "When you're out on the road, don't you talk to a soul unless they talk to you first. Keep your head low till you're around your own. The less people know about you, the better."

"Yes, ma'am."

She kissed his forehead. He threw his arms around her waist, and she sniffled back her tears. "You listen to Uncle Bill and your brother, now. Do what they say. And don't forget to pray."

Isaiah nodded against the softness of her belly.

"Come on, Ice Man." Memphis took his brother's hand.

"Take care of my boys, Mr. Johnson," Octavia said, wiping her eyes.

"Like they was my own," Bill promised.

"Memphis John." Octavia worried her hands for a minute, and then she pulled Memphis into a tight hug. Aunt Octavia was a solid, strong woman. But Memphis could feel her fear. When she released him, her face was resolute. "Go on, now."

"They'll come here," Bill warned.

Octavia snorted. "Good luck to 'em, then."

Memphis checked to make sure that all was clear, and then the three of them were stealing down the street, eyes searching every corner, every shadow.

※

Octavia Louise Joseph, born in Haiti to a teacher and a nurse, brought to America when she was a baby. Octavia, who'd taken her first steps on the sidewalks of Baltimore, made her way to New York City, taught school, who'd buried a sister and raised her sister's kids. That Octavia called on all of her strength as she sat on the sofa with her Bible.

"Jesus, help me now," she whispered.

Across the street, a brown sedan slowed. Two men in gray suits got out. Octavia put a calming hand on her stomach to soothe the butterflies inside.

"You will not get mine," she said quietly, and waited for the enemy at her door.

※

Will stood on the sidewalk outside the museum. A wash of bloodred paint had been tossed across its limestone facade. The sign had been defaced as well. Just one bold red word: *Murderers*.

Will let himself in. Glass crunched under his shoes. A rock lay in the spray of shards. The stained-glass window had a jagged hole in it now. Will picked up the rock, feeling its banal weight in his hand. He didn't bother turning on the lights. He slipped into the library, left the rock on a table, stacked kindling and newspaper—SARAH SNOW: OUR FALLEN ANGEL—in the cold mouth of the enormous fireplace, and fanned the spark till it caught. It was too warm for a fire, but he lit one nonetheless. The flames cast shadows up the walls and across the ceiling's mural of the Founding Fathers signing the Declaration of Independence, a host of angels and demons looking on.

There were ghosts in the room: Rotke, Mabel, Cornelius, James. Will couldn't see or talk to them. He had no talent for that. But he could feel them nonetheless. Their presence was a steady weight on his heart, as if all their hands pressed against his chest at once.

Remember us.

Remorse and fear nearly overtook him, and so he was grateful when Margaret Walker came into the library and put the mug of steaming coffee beside him.

"Well, that's it, then. The tax office won't hear our appeal now. The museum is officially done for," Will said, his voice a hollow echo in the nearly empty library. It made him unbearably sad to think of Cornelius's strange home for the supernatural being bulldozed to make way for some modern apartment building with no memory of what had stood there before.

Margaret eyed the rock. "Another one."

"Yes. It's going to get ugly, isn't it?"

Sister Walker let out a grunted *hmph* as she poked the dying embers. "You say that like someone who's never had to see how ugly things really are."

"Yes," Will said. "Yes. What do we do?"

Will's question was rhetorical, but Sister Walker had little time for the rhetorical. "Do you understand now? Are you beginning to see?"

"I am."

Sister Walker gave the ashy kindling one last good poke and it sparked into flame. She hung the poker on its hook and wiped her hands clean. She turned to Will.

"Good. Now we fight."

Someone was pounding at the museum's front door.

"Did you lock it?" Sister Walker asked warily.

Will nodded. The pounding got louder. Will palmed the rock and the two of them moved quickly down the hall. Will threw open the front door, surprised to see Memphis there with Isaiah and a tall man Will had never seen before.

"Professor. They're after us. I need to come in," Memphis pleaded.

"Memphis? Are you all right?" Sister Walker stopped in her tracks at the sight of Bill Johnson. She put a hand to her mouth as her eyes widened. "It's you."

"Afternoon, Miss Walker," Bill said, removing his hat. "Been a long time."

"Guillaume. I thought you were dead."

"In a manner of speaking, I was. Lost in the wilderness, you might say.

But I'm coming back, yes, I am coming back. Those Shadow Men, though, they looking for us. I got to get Memphis and Isaiah away from here."

"We can keep you safe," Sister Walker said.

"Like you kept me safe before?" Bill challenged. He shook his head. "Ain't taking orders from nobody no more. I'm the only one knows what those Shadow Men can do. How many of 'em there are, how they think. I'm taking these boys to safety. While I can."

"I have a car. I can drive you," Will said.

"They'll be watching the roads—and watching you, sir. Both of you. Memphis here had an idea."

Memphis nodded toward the collections room. "The tunnel. The old Underground Railroad passage. We can get out that way."

"Memphis, that hasn't been used in decades. There's no telling what shape it's in or if it still has an opening somewhere. You could end up trapped down there," Will said.

Isaiah looked frightened. Memphis thought about what it would be like to walk for maybe miles underground, only to reach a dead end. What if they got lost? What if there was a cave-in? But what choice did they have?

"Professor, right now those men are in Harlem asking after Isaiah and me. How long before they find us? My face is known," Memphis explained. He shook his head. "No. Has to be this way. We're leaving. Through the tunnels."

He hoped he was making the right decision.

Will nodded. "All right. You'll need provisions. Wait here," he said, heading toward the kitchen.

"Where else would I go?" Memphis whispered. He could hear Will rummaging in the kitchen. Sister Walker was staring at Bill Johnson, at the smatterings of gray in his black hair, the lines on his face, Memphis realized. He was no longer the young man she had known once upon a time. She spied the mark upon his hand.

"Shadow Men gimme that. A brand to make me theirs." He appraised Margaret coolly. "What 'bout you? You got yourself a mark from your thirty pieces of silver? Or your hands still smooth and clean?"

"I tried to stop them," Sister Walker protested.

"Not hard enough," Bill said.

Sister Walker narrowed her eyes. Her voice was a low warning. "Don't you dare preach to me, Mr. Johnson. I spent time rotting in a prison cell for my act of resistance."

"So I heard," Bill answered. "What's done is done. I done wrong, too. We carry our sins forward, Miss Walker. What matters now is doing right by these boys. Time to step to, Margaret Walker."

And Sister Walker remembered Lavinia Cooper. The light shining into the room where she lay in Frederick Douglass Memorial Hospital. *Before the Devil breaks you.* Well, let the Devil try. Margaret Walker was up for the fight. "Who do you think has been getting these boys ready for the battles ahead, old man?"

Bill's lips tipped into a smile. "Ain't old no more. Plenty a kick left in me."

Will charged into the collections room with a gas lantern and a burlap sack. "There's some apples, cheese, bread. Canteen of water."

"Thank you," Memphis said. It wasn't much, but it was something. It would see them through a few days if they were careful. Memphis would give his ration to Isaiah if it came to it. He thought of Theta again; she'd have no idea where he'd gone. "Professor, can you tell Theta that I'll get in touch just as soon as it's safe?"

Will nodded. He kicked back the carpet and yanked up the iron ring on the secret entrance to the cellar. A plume of dust circled up. Memphis's heart began to beat faster.

"Do you know where the tunnel lets out, where it ends?" he asked, peering down into the dark hole.

"Cornelius never said. I'm afraid you'll be traveling blind," Will cautioned.

Bill snorted and swung his legs over the edge. "Been doing that most of my life."

He lowered himself down the rickety steps, dropping to the basement's floor with a rustling of the dirt. Isaiah and Memphis followed. Will handed down the sack of provisions, which Memphis passed to Bill, and the lantern, which Memphis kept. He looked over at his brother's wide eyes. He needed to keep Isaiah safe. That was everything.

But where was it safe?

"May the spirits guide you," Will said from above, and closed the door.

Memphis let his eyes adjust to the dark. The air was close. It smelled of earth and dust. Of the past and the future.

"What do we do now, Memphis?" Isaiah asked.

Memphis took a deep breath. He lifted the lantern. Its glow fell across the murals that had been painted on the road to freedom and shone what light it could into the long uncertainty ahead.

"One foot in front of the other," Memphis said. "We keep walking."

✺

After Will had covered up the passage again, he marched into the library and up to the second floor. From his hollowed-out copy of *The Declaration of Independence*, he retrieved the files he'd kept on Project Buffalo. Most of it was there. Enough of it to be damning at least.

"I'm taking this to T. S. Woodhouse," he announced to Sister Walker. "I'm telling him everything and letting him print every word. We have to stop this madness."

"You think anyone will believe us?"

"We have to try."

"There more files in here?"

Will nodded. "Upstairs. Tucked into *The Federalist Papers*."

Margaret smirked. "You do like your gallows humor, Will."

Margaret went upstairs, disappearing into the stacks, not wasting any time. It was so like her, and Will realized how much he admired Margaret. How much he needed her. She had been a true friend. She made him braver, always had. An overwhelming feeling of gratitude and love bubbled up inside him.

The front door opened and closed so softly that it might not be heard by a visitor. But Will knew the sounds of the museum as if it were part of his own body. He was alert. Ready.

"Afternoon, William," Mr. Adams said as he and Mr. Jefferson entered the library. Mr. Adams touched fingers to the brim of his hat without removing it. "It's been a long time."

"Not long enough," Will shot back.

Adams snickered. "And here it was I thought Margaret Walker was the spitfire. Speaking of, where is the troublesome Miss Walker?"

"Do you think Margaret Walker is foolish enough to stick around here?" Will said loudly on a laugh, hoping that his voice carried up to the stacks. *Oh, stay hidden, Margaret!*

"Sorry this isn't a social call, William. We're here on business. Now. Where are the files? We know you must have them. And where are Memphis and Isaiah Campbell?"

"Too bad you don't have a Diviner to help you find the things you've lost," Will said.

Jefferson backhanded him for it. It shouldn't have been surprising, but it rattled Will nonetheless. Upstairs, he saw Margaret's frightened face peek out from behind the stacks. Will wiped the blood from his split lip. He wished he had a cigarette.

"Now, now. Don't be impertinent, William," Mr. Adams said. "We'll find them, with or without your cooperation. But with your help is a far better scenario—at least, where your health is concerned."

Will nodded and walked slowly to the mammoth fireplace. "Cornelius Rathbone had this carved especially for the library. It actually has a name. It's called the Fires of Knowledge. Did you know that?"

"Touching." Adams had pulled a round of thin piano wire from his pocket. He wound the ends around each of his middle fingers.

Will reached down and palmed a handful of old ash from the fireplace's unkempt hearth. It was gritty and stained his fingers gray. Around him, he could feel the ghosts of Cornelius and Liberty Anne. "'It is a far, far better thing that I do, than I have ever done,'" Will said.

"That from Cornelius Rathbone, too?" Jefferson sneered.

"It's from a book. Dickens. *A Tale of Two Cities*."

"I don't get it."

"No. I don't expect that you do."

Adams tensed the wire between his fingers. "Where are the files and the Campbell brothers, William? I won't ask a third time."

"They're long gone," Will lied. "Your days are numbered."

Adams grinned. "Not like yours."

The agent took a step forward. Will tossed the handful of ash into the man's eyes. Adams howled in rage and pain. In the space of the three seconds it took for William Fitzgerald to bolt across the library's Persian rug toward the half-open doors, the futility of his situation welled up inside him in a way that nearly resembled hope in its giddy freedom. He was alive as he had not been in some time. All his nerve endings burned with life, as if discharging their last impulses. His mind whirred with memory. He thought of the first time he saw Evie in this room, like a ray of rogue sun forcing itself through the gloom, as he lectured to schoolboys about America's supernatural past. He thought of studious, quiet Jericho sitting at the table with his books and cocksure Sam creeping around, always looking for an angle to work. He thought of Memphis Campbell's poetic, shining soul and Isaiah Campbell's unbridled optimism and of their frightened, determined faces as he'd lowered the cellar door, and he hoped they were well on their way. He thought of dear, funny Henry and brilliant, straightforward Ling and resilient Theta with her hidden strength—all of them refusing to be pressed under by the world's thumb. He thought of James and Luther and the wrong he had done them, and he prayed he would know their forgiveness yet. He thought of Margaret, his friend and occasional enemy, but mostly friend, and he hoped fervently that she had heard his warning and had hidden herself. She would be needed in the days to come.

At last, he thought of Rotke's beaming face in the cold winter sun, her laughter whipping along the wind: *Oh, Will, that's you all over!*

Rotke, his love.

Behind him, Adams, blinded by the ash, hissed in pain. Jefferson, recovered from his momentary shock, was in pursuit. Will tipped over the chair behind him, impeding the bigger agent's progress. Up ahead, the stuffed bear's dead eyes stared, unseeing, as Jefferson caught Will by the ankle, bringing him down hard, knocking the air from his lungs. Will could not speak or move. He could only lie on his back, looking up, at Jefferson's furious face as he landed a blow to Will's jaw, shattering it, then up again at Adams behind Jefferson, tightening the piano wire between his gloved fingers, and finally, up at the painted ceiling where men inked ideals into parchment, a root worker held aloft her mandrake, a host of angels and demons fought on the prairie lands of a new world, and around the mural's edges, Diviners looked on, watching, waiting and wary and ready.

He hoped, he hoped.

"Any last words?" Adams snarled.

Blood filled Will's mouth. *"Vive la résistance."*

In the stacks, Sister Walker clutched the secret files tightly to her chest and listened to the last dying gasp and gurgle of her friend Will Fitzgerald. Tears stung her eyes. A scream clawed at her throat.

"That's been a long time coming." Adams.

"What do we do with him? Torch the place?" Jefferson played with the matchbook in his hand. His eyes gleamed.

Adams shook his head. "Leave him. Let him be found. Someone should pay for this murder, don't you think?" Adams tsk-tsked. "Those Diviners. They can't be trusted, you know. Enemies of the state. Perhaps it's time we let the nation know just how dangerous they are."

THE TIME IS NOW

The Shadow Man entered the cell like a ghost. "Good evening, Miriam."

From her chair, Miriam Lubovitch Lloyd registered the man's odious presence and continued reading her book without comment.

"Whatcha reading?" At Miriam's silence, the Shadow Man angled his head sideways. "*A Geological History of the United States.*" He righted himself, chuckling. "Well. You certainly know how to have fun."

"Why are you here? Is not mealtime. You come to torture me more?"

The Shadow Man frowned. "*Persuade.* We persuade, Miriam. I've come to let you know that, thanks to you, our agents are bringing in one of our lost chicks. Your Sergei is coming home, Miriam."

Miriam's split-second joy was doused by anger. "You don't know the fire you play with. Theirs is not power you can manipulate. It is grown too big for your control. I can feel it."

"Anything and anyone can be manipulated. Isn't that right, Miriam?" The Shadow Man's gloved hand rested on her shoulder. "Besides, we're not accustomed to losing. We'll get them in line. *We* are not afraid of a bunch of uncontrolled, misfit kids."

Miriam shrugged off his touch. "Aren't you?"

The Shadow Man sighed like a weary parent. "Miriam—we're on the same side. You help us, and we'll see to it that you're reunited with your son."

"What will you do to him first?"

"Just a few tests, that's all. I'm sure he's a patriot who'd like to do his duty."

Miriam narrowed her eyes. "Patriot," she sneered.

"Everybody wants freedom. No one wants to pay for it. Or to think about who has to do the ugly work to secure that freedom," he said quietly.

Miriam put her book on the table and stood. She was considerably smaller than the man, but on instinct, he took a step back. "You promised me something if I help you. So. I did. I help you. I cannot help Anna anymore," Miriam said, and watched the Shadow Man grow uncomfortable. "I want to walk. Outside. In fresh air."

"Now, Miriam. That wouldn't be wise of us, would it? Keeping you underground keeps a lid on that Diviner power of yours. I still remember when you managed to get that poor secretary to give you a postcard. And then you had her mail it for you, convinced her it was *her* idea all along." He tutted.

Miriam kept her eyes trained on the wall. "Could I at least go to the solarium to see the trees?"

They chained her, of course. Iron to contain her gifts. Shackled, she shuffled across the observation deck's slate floor. Slate was good. Natural. Grounding. She curled her toes against its ancient power. It was a good antidote to the iron. The sun was just setting. The solarium's tall windows looked out on acres of orange-painted trees, centuries old, and the snow-dusted mountains beyond. There was great power in them, too. But the men didn't need to know that. Underground, it was much harder for her gifts to travel.

But not here.

The chains on her mind were loosening. The men had made the mistake of giving her a reason to live. They'd made the mistake of going after her son.

Miriam smiled at the scenery. "Pretty."

"Don't get any ideas," the Shadow Man said.

In answer, Miriam presented her shackled hands. The Shadow Man smirked. Miriam turned back to the fading sun. Her smile disappeared. The experiments performed on her during the war had yielded interesting results. When the Shadow Man had asked for locations of Diviners, he hadn't said they had to be living. Miriam appealed to them now, to the dead. *Help me.*

The slate, the trees, the mountains beyond, and the dead: Their combined power thrummed softly inside her. And then, something like a great switchboard lit up in her mind. Like that infernal radio that played through the floor grate, she was transmitting, sending out a mental SOS in the hope it would reach some Diviner out there.

In the dark of the Underground Railroad tunnel, Bill and Memphis slept. Isaiah woke, trembling with visions. His hand reached for the charcoal in his pocket. "Yes. Yes, I see you," he said softly as he drew what he saw on a patch of flat earthen wall.

In her sleep, Theta stood on the edge of that forest. An eagle soared overhead. A brave emerged from a redwood hollow. But Theta couldn't understand what he said. "West," Ling said, suddenly beside her. "He's saying, 'Go west.'"

"Did you feel that?" Henry asked David. They lay together in Henry's single bed, their bodies still slick with sweat.

"What?" David said, still half dreaming.

Henry sat up, rubbing sleep from his eyes. The room was still. "Like somebody calling for help."

Under a moon waxing toward full, roustabouts hammered posts into spring-soft ground and raised the tents for the next day's show. Full-bellied and exhausted, the animals gentled onto their hay and went to sleep. In a bright red-and-white-striped circus wagon warmed by the glow of a lantern, the Great Zarilda, Seer of Fortunes, shuffled her tarot deck and laid down her cards, frowning.

Johnny the Wolf Boy brought her a cup of tea. He scratched at the dark, downy hair along his neck. "What is it, Zarilda?"

The Great Zarilda turned over another card. Three of Swords. Betrayal, lies, turmoil. "I believe our old friend Sam Lloyd is in terrible danger."

In a pale yellow bedroom on a farm in the Heartland, the girl shook violently.

"Jim, get the strap!" her mother cried, and the girl's father wedged the thin belt between her molars seconds before the edges of her teeth bit hard into the soft leather, adding to the constellation of puncture wounds already there. After a moment, the trembling subsided. The girl lay still.

"Just lie back easy now, Sarah Beth," the girl's father said.

The farmer closed the door. In the small kitchen, his wife went back to scrubbing out the cast-iron pot. On the table, the Sears, Roebuck catalog lay open to a page of shiny new Singer sewing machines they couldn't afford. The farmer lit the lantern. "Gonna see to the cows," he said, not expecting an answer.

In the soft evening light, the farmer looked out at the long, flat line of the horizon, broken only by a lone telephone pole in the distance, the future edging closer. He surveyed the yellowing acres of failing corn, the gnarled hickory tree, the pigs rooting for scraps in a pen bordered by a rotting split-rail fence, and the sagging porch of the old house that had been built by his grandfather's hands as a legacy to his children. Promising black soil had gone to scrub and dust in places now that the farmer and his wife had been forced to let the hired hands go. And anyway, most of them were wary of Sarah Beth, who stared into space and babbled about strange visions that frightened the farmer and his wife.

Sometimes those visions came true.

That scared them more.

From his pocket, the farmer took out the sheriff's notice: foreclosure on the family farm at 144 Benedict Road, Bountiful, Nebraska. Without some miracle, the little that was left would all be lost. And where would they go then? How would they care for Sarah Beth?

"The land is old, the land is vast, he has no future, he has no past, his coat is sewn with many woes, he'll bring the dead, the King of Crows."

The farmer startled. A moment ago, his daughter had been lying on her bed, eyes closed. Now she was a few feet away.

"Sarah Beth. What are you doing out here?"

The girl had that icy stare. The one her mother feared might belong to demons.

"They're coming."

"Who's coming, honey? Aunt Evelyn and Uncle Roscoe are over to Omaha this week."

The girl rocked back and forth. "The Diviners."

Sudden anger rose in the farmer. "Sarah Beth. Go on back to your mama now. Hey-oh! Ada!"

"Storm's coming. And with it come the dead," the girl said, urinating into the parched earth.

The farmer was a good man, but even good men have a breaking point. "Ada! Ada! Doggone it, come out here and get Sarah Beth *right now*!"

Dutifully, the farmer's wife bustled out, wiping her hands on her apron. "Mercy me, only had my back turned for a minute. Come on back in the house now, Sarah Beth, 'fore you catch your death."

"The King of Crows is coming for the Diviners," the girl repeated, smiling. "Ghosts on the road! Ghosts on the road! Ghosts on the road!"

She shrieked, and a plume of black birds raced up to meet night's descent.

✻

Adelaide Keziah Proctor lay quietly in her bed. Through the open window, she smelled honeysuckle. She was sure of it. Summer. Summer would come soon. She was tired, though, and so she shut her eyes and dozed.

In her mind, she rode swiftly through Virginia grasslands on the back of a white horse. She enjoyed the feel of the wind on her face as they raced up a hill. At the top, Addie could see quite far—into the green-gold valley and to the hunched backs of the blue-gray mountains just beyond. The fields below bloomed with every color of wildflower imaginable. The air was perfumed with their sweetness. Addie patted the horse's neck and took in a breath. Her heart beat fast from the ride and she needed rest.

Down in the valley, she could see a little clapboard church. She spurred the horse toward it. Inside the church's steepled tower, a bell tolled loudly. The church doors swung open. Six men in black coats carried out a coffin. Their sharp-toed shoes disturbed the dust on the road like beaks biting into earth. The silk veils of their black top hats fluttered behind them in the breeze. The wind had grown fierce. Heavy clouds moved in, a storm approaching. Addie slipped off her horse and led him toward the church for shelter. Just till the storm passed.

It was very dark inside the church, and the horse arched its head and refused to go any farther, so Addie left it and continued alone. Her foot caught under something unseen and she went flying, landing with a thud. Her hands met with dirt. She had tripped over a long, thick vine. She heard slow, measured footsteps drawing near and saw a pair of those sharp shoes. They'd been polished to a shine as high as new pennies placed atop a corpse's eyelids.

Addie looked up. The King of Crows towered over her, smiling his mirthless grin. "Did you think you could best me, Witch?"

His voice echoed in the forest. The crows answered in squawking chorus.

Addie struggled to her feet. The fall from the horse had winded her—she could barely catch her breath. Her heart beat out a warning. She tried to turn back, but the way was no longer clear. She stood now in a dark forest thick with slithering brambles. Along the branches of the bitter-frost trees, a murder of crows fluttered like blue-black leaves in a breeze. The dead rustled in the spaces in between, and above, the sky was a vast and starless night. This was his place. The land of the dead.

Far behind her, Addie saw a rectangle of daylight narrowing to nothing as the pallbearers sealed the church doors.

"A debt must be paid." The King of Crows held a daisy in the scarred palm of his gray hand.

Adelaide Proctor's heart thumped like a herd of wild mustangs.

"Good-bye, Adelaide Keziah Proctor." The King of Crows closed his fingers one by one over the daisy. And then he squeezed.

Blood and petals slipped through his shaking fingers.

Addie shut her eyes and clutched at her chest, gasping in pain.

The crows screamed and screamed.

When Addie opened her eyes again, she saw the coffin lid sliding over her face. She pressed frantic hands against her wooden prison.

"No!" she cried.

The hammers were already at work; Addie could hear them pounding in the nails that sealed her inside. Clumps of dirt splattered against the top of the pine box like heavy rain. In her mind, she could see bloodied daisy petals falling slowly over her new grave.

As her heart slowed, Adelaide Proctor took in a shuddering breath. But it was not enough for a scream.

※

Whispers coiled about the graveyards. Sins bubbled up from the dirt and confessed over tombstones in a chorus of regret:

"...I once killed a man for spite...."

"...Butchered the women and children as they ran from their teepees and took the land for our own..."

"...All that good love thrown away, oh, what a fool I was..."

"...No, no, please, she said, but I did it anyway...."

"...I'm sorry. I'm sorry. I'm sorry...."

But some sins were boasted still:

"...It was mine—*mine!*—and I'd have it no matter what...."

"...So we gave 'em the blankets. What's one less Indian in the world...?"

"...'Twas Mercy Good turned the milk sour. And thou shalt not suffer a witch to live...."

The confessions swirled around the tall, dark hat of the King of Crows. He smiled. "Yes. Oh, yes," he murmured, as if listening to sweet chamber music. "More. Give me more."

Strings of hot blue energy crackled along the tips of his fingertips. He bared his teeth. "I hunger."

The dead brought forth a young doe they'd found. It had been separated from its mother. They fell upon it, feasting, and then the King of Crows sucked the power from the dead.

He scowled. "Not. Enough."

In the cold of the graveyard, Conor Flynn shivered in his filthy nightclothes. The King of Crows fixed his soulless gaze on the young Diviner. "What is it to see the world? To see beyond death and destruction into the heart of humanity? Tell me my future, young Conor Flynn, and if it pleases me, I might spare you."

Conor wished the lady were in his head now. But she could not reach him where he was. All around, the dead waited. Conor could feel their hunger. Their need. It all came from the man in the hat. His very presence sowed discontent. Oh, yes, Conor could feel it now, the way the man joined to the dissatisfaction and petty old hurts the spirits had carried with them to the grave. Human. Human till the end and beyond. The man made them believe they should not end but have more. Made them crave it: *We would have everything! It is our due! Oh, this world is not enough, not enough, not enough!*

Conor had a bad feeling in his gut, like on the day Father Hanlon asked Jimmy if he wanted to go for ice cream. There were terrible things in the world, and nobody seemed to care. But Conor did, despite everything. He'd saved Jimmy, hadn't he? He heard that a nice family adopted him, and now Jimmy lived in a house with a mom and a dad and a dog named Teddy. Conor's legs shook as he tried to imagine it: Jimmy on the front porch of that nice house, his fingers in Teddy's fur while the dog licked at his face and made him laugh. A good life. The lady, Miriam, had told Conor something once as he lay on his cot in the asylum, rocking himself to sleep. Just before he'd drifted off, she'd spoken to him like a mother. "Whoever saves a life, it is as if he has saved an entire world," she'd told him. That had stuck with Conor. The idea that anybody, even a kid like him, could make a difference.

Conor slipped into his vision. He could hear the souls of those poor soldiers crying out to him to be set free at last. He wished he could save them, but they were beyond his reach. He waited, and the voices quieted. The vision took hold. The sun was the color of an old dog's pus-smeared eye. Conor stood at a crossroads under that dodgy sun. Two possible futures stretched out before him. He could not say which path would win. But he feared for his friends.

"What do you see? I would know," the King of Crows demanded.

If Conor told, his friends would be in even greater danger. He would tell the man just enough to appease his appetite.

"There's a girl," Conor said. "She's a seer, too. Sarah Beth."

"And what of our Diviner friends, hmm?"

"Didn't see nothing," Conor lied, tapping his fingers one, two, three against his skinny thighs, again and again.

The King of Crows's dead stare bored into Conor's until he nearly fell down weeping. "I ask for more and you give me nothing," he said. The man in the hat rested his dirt-caked fingers around Conor's slim neck. Beetles crawled from the demon's pointed sleeves and scuttled up his arms till he seemed sewn from them. "I'm bored with you," he said. "I would have new thrills. More. More, more, more."

Conor looked to the woman in the black-feather cape. Her eyes held the grief of the whole world. Those eyes more than anything made Conor afraid.

"Shut your eyes, baby," the lady said, and he'd never heard a sadder voice in all his brief life.

The King of Crows released Conor, pushing him toward the hordes of hungry dead. "Do as thou wilt!"

The dead began to advance.

Conor trembled. "Onetwot'reefourfiveseven. Onetwot'reefourfiveseven. Mother Mary, full of grace... No! No! *No!*"

Conor's last desperate cry was ripped from his throat as the dead fell upon him with their greedy hunger. Viola Campbell could not stop it, but she would not look away. She screamed, and her screams sounded like frightened birds.

"Feed me!" the King of Crows demanded as Conor's screeches dwindled to gurgling and then nothing. Dutifully, the dead approached and opened their terrible mouths. Lightning crackled around the man in the hat. His head tipped back as he sucked up the energy from his army of dead. He licked his lips. The scar-like veins pulsed with new blood. His eyes shone, cold and dead as black diamonds.

"Yes. Yes. The time is now," the King moaned, and laughed up to the starless sky.

Viola Campbell buried her eyes in her hands. "Oh, my son, my son. Would God I had died for thee..." she said, and hung her head and cried.

☀

The glow of the electric lamps backlit Jake Marlowe as he sat in his bedroom, cradling his bruised head in his hands. Several days' beard growth darkened his cheeks. The secretaries had been fielding calls every day from the newspaper boys who wanted Jake's comments for the morning hot sheets. They had been informed that Mr. Marlowe wasn't speaking.

Jake poured out more of his family's one-hundred-year-old Scotch from the old cellar. He didn't usually drink, but he'd been at it for several days now. Time blurred. He stank. He didn't care. On the table was the model for Marlowe's utopian American exhibition. "Here's to the future," Marlowe said, and poured his Scotch over the whole thing.

Down the hall, fast footsteps rang out.

"Mr. Marlowe! Mr. Marlowe!" One of the scientists. He rattled the locked doorknob.

"I've told you, I don't want to be disturbed," Marlowe said flatly. Everything he'd built lay in tatters. He didn't think he could take another blow.

"Mr. Marlowe! Please, may I come in?"

Reluctantly, Marlowe left his chair. He staggered to the door and unlocked it, leaving it open as he moved back to his chair and sat with a plop. "What is it?"

The excited man stopped to catch his ragged breath. "The machine, sir. It's switched on. It's *receiving*."

Marlowe was suddenly alert. "Is there any word from him? Any new message?"

The young man nodded.

"What does it say?" Marlowe asked.

"'I am ready. The time is now.'"

Author's Note

Before the Devil Breaks You is a work of fiction, and, as such, the reckless author has taken certain liberties to keep the story moving. What liberties, you might ask, being a curious sort? For one, the interior of the Manhattan State Hospital for the Insane (sic) of this book is a fictional amalgam constructed from various New York State Kirkbride-model asylums of the time. (The Kirkbride plan was quite popular then.) This allowed me to shape-shift the interior to suit my needs. However, the Manhattan State Hospital *did* have a bowling alley, which was possibly my favorite detail, and if I could've worked in a ghost bowling scene . . . well, let's just say it wasn't for lack of trying. There are liberties and then there are liberties.

Mental illness/health is a topic near and dear to my heart. In reading reports from mental health workers of the 1920s, it was clear that they wanted the best for the people in their care. Efforts were taken to use art and music as therapy (the detail about the visiting opera singer is true!), restraints were mostly forbidden, and the hospital made frequent appeals to the state for more trained staff and funding. This stands in stark contrast to the horrors of the institution written about in journalist Nellie Bly's 1887 expose, *Ten Days in a Mad-House*, when the asylum had been located on Blackwell's Island (since renamed Roosevelt Island) and abuse was rampant. Nellie's reporting brought about sweeping reform. Truth can do that.

The boys' refuge where Conor would have spent time was also notorious for being punitive, if not downright abusive. Prisoners from the local penitentiary were also frequently used as unpaid labor on the grounds. And there are still thousands of unknown dead buried on Ward's and Hart's Islands, the marginalized victimized even in death.

While some aspects of this story are fictionalized, many are rooted firmly in historical record and fact, and yes, there are facts, they are not "alternative," and they come with receipts. The KKK was alive and flourishing in the 1920s. So were Jim Crow laws and immigration bans and quotas. The Supreme Court decision handed down in *Buck v. Bell* (May 1927) allowed states to sterilize inmates of public institutions without their consent due to "hereditary defects" that included epilepsy, "feeblemindedness," "moral degeneracy," and mental illness, but which was often employed against the uneducated, the poor, people of color, and overwhelmingly for women rather than (white) men. This was an outgrowth of the American eugenics movement—racist pseudoscience that went on to influence public policy, segregation, anti-miscegenation and anti-immigration laws, and, arguably, the American mind-set for decades to come.

Jake Marlowe's Hopeful Harbor was partially influenced by the Eugenics Record Office at Cold Spring Harbor Laboratory on Long Island, New York, which was at its height in the 1920s. Very wealthy Americans such as the Harrimans, Carnegies, and Rockefellers supported the eugenics-based institution and its promulgation of bigotry and racism disguised as science. (Real science, on the other hand, is awesome and the reason we have NASA and the polio vaccine.) But by giving eugenics the imprimatur of both medical science and law, including a law passed by the highest court in the land, America further sanctioned racism.

As I write this, we are in an especially divisive era in American politics. There are questions about who holds power, who abuses it, who profits from it, and at what cost to our democracy. It is a time of questions about what makes us American, of shifting identities, inclusion and exclusion, protest, civil and human rights, the strength of our compassion versus the weakness of our fears, and the seductive lure of a mythic "great" past that never was versus the need for the consciousness and responsibility necessary if we are truly to live up to the rich promise of "We the People."

We are a country built by immigrants, dreams, daring, and opportunity.

We are a country built by the horrors of slavery and genocide, the injustice of racism and exclusion. These realities exist side by side. It is our past and our present. The future is unwritten.

This is a book about ghosts.

For we live in a haunted house.

Acknowledgments

I always think there should be an extra ten pages in these books to truly thank everyone who has been so helpful. But then you wouldn't be able to lift it. There are loads of good people who have helped to make this book a reality over the past two years, but my memory is faulty, and this list is, I fear, woefully inadequate. If I have unwittingly forgotten anyone, apologies and dinner on me. (Hopefully, that's interpreted as "I pick up the check" and not "Please throw your pasta at me.") A fruit basket of thanks to the following:

Unflappable rock star editor Alvina Ling, who can tell you that a scene that you spent three weeks carefully constructing stops the story cold and needs to die a quick death—and makes you love her all the more for it. Bethany Strout, whose further editing was as thoughtful and incisive as she is. The awesome, indefatigable Nikki Garcia and Kheryn Callender, who kept the wheels turning and the lights on. Talented designer Karina Granda for the beautiful new covers. Superhero Copyeditor Christine Ma and Superhero Proofreader JoAnna Kremer, for their exacting, thorough work. I imagine them going through that sentence saying, "Libba, you don't need both exacting *and* thorough." You live with me always now, my friends. The hardworking editorial, marketing, publicity, art, production, sales, and school & library departments of LBYR and the great team of Megan Tingley, Lisa Moraleda, Victoria Stapleton, Jenny Choy, Heather Fain, Jen Graham, Ruiko Tokunaga, Jane Lee, and Allegra Green, to name but a few. I am so happy to be in your company and in your Company.

Research goddess Lisa Gold, who can find reams of information on the most obscure topics lickety-split. Suspect she might be a unicorn. Invaluable assistant Tricia Ready, arranger of research trips, finder of additional research, securer of permissions and a hundred other Necessary Things. Possible skilled secret agent. My favorite not-so-secret agent-agent, Barry Goldblatt, brave and honest and true, for everything, always and forever.

Beloved writer pals Justin Weinberger, David Levithan, Dan Poblocki, Justine Larbalestier, Danielle Paige, Erin Morgenstern, and Zoraida Cordova for the company and moral support. The brilliant Holly Black, Sarah Rees Brennan, and Cindy Pon, for that late-night plot problem–solving convo at the North Texas Teen Book Festival. Your brains should be left to science! (After you're finished with them, of course.) The Tuesday night writing group: Aaron Zimmerman,

Emmy Laybourne, Nova Ren Suma, Kim Liggett, Michelle Hodkin, Emma Bailey, Bonnie Pipkin, Sarah Porter, Susanna Scrobsdorff, and Julia Morris.

Fierce love and thanks to the sisters of my heart: Laurie Allee, Eleanor Boschert-Ambrosio, Pam Carden, Brenda Cowan, Gayle Forman, Emily Jenkins, Kim Liggett, Susanna Schrobsdorff, and Nova Ren Suma for every damn thing and then some.

The awesome Preeti Chhibber and Bhairavi Nadgonde for the Hindi translation, Robert Schamhart and Gayle Forman for the Dutch, and everyone on Twitter who gamely tried to help me translate Latin. (Those four years in the Junior Classical League didn't take, apparently.) The winning translation was, I believe, from the ever-helpful Lee Jackson, author of shivery Victorian mysteries you might enjoy.

If you ever find yourself in need of a golf cart history tour of Ward's and Randall's Islands, I highly recommend the lovely and delightful team of Eric Peterson and Anne Wilson of the Randall's Island Park Alliance. Thank you, Eric and Anne, for your time, knowledge, patience, and excellent driving. Thanks, also, to Judith Berdy, president of the Roosevelt Island Historical Society, for allowing me to invade her home and paw through her many binders full of history. And thanks to psychoanalyst and professor Richard Sacks, MA, LP, and Cheryl Levine, LCSW, coordinator, Brookdale University Hospital Medical Center, for so generously sharing their psychiatric knowledge. Continued appreciation for the staffs at the MTA Archives, the New York Public Library, the Museum of the City of New York, the New-York Historical Society, and the Museum of Chinese in America. Those notes never stop giving.

The Listening Library crew at Penguin Random House for their amazing work: Dan Zitt, Katie Punia, Rebecca Waugh, and Rachel Walker, audiobook director David Rapchik, and the unbelievably talented audiobook narrator, January LaVoy. Shout-out to the wonderful crew at Gotham Group, especially my film agent, Eddie Gamarra. And to Tiger Beat (Daniel Ehrenhaft, Barnabas Miller, and Natalie Standiford) for the brain-melting rock 'n' roll breaks. PDKO, y'all. Also: The wonderful staffs at Think Coffee, Building on Bond, Southside Coffee, and especially Roots Cafe.

Last but not least, thanks to my son, Josh Goldblatt, who has become quite a fine storyteller himself.

Anyone I may have forgotten, I humbly apologize and want you to know that it's only the fault of my wonky brain and is no reflection on your ultra fabulousness. Come claim your dinner credit anytime.